AQUA TERRA IGNIS AER

ZODIAC ACADEMY
CURSED FATES

CAROLINE
PECKHAM

SUSANNE
VALENTI

Place
Terra House
r Hall
Mars Laboratory
King's Hollow
The Howling Meadow
The Wailing Wood
The Orb
Earth Observatory
Venus Library
ercury
ambers
Aer House
Air Cove
Fire Arena

WELCOME TO ZODIAC ACADEMY

Note to all students: Vampire bites, loss of limbs or getting lost in The Wailing Wood will not count as a valid excuse for being late to class.

DARCY

CHAPTER ONE

This isn't it.
I won't let him go.
I'll follow him beyond the veil.
I'll climb into the stars and drag his soul back out of them if I have to.
This. Is. Not. It.

The twisting maelstrom of snow swirled around me and a shadow caught my gaze amongst it. I let my Phoenix fire fall still, dropping my head to search the thick fog of white before me. A figure had moved in the mist, I was almost sure. Or maybe I was just so desperate for It to be true.

"Hello?!" I cried, running forward, stumbling over rocks and snow as I sped blindly into the blizzard.

The sound of footsteps crunched toward me and my pulse thumped wildly out of rhythm.

"Help!" I screamed.

I rammed into someone and stumbled back, their hand latching around my wrist before I lost my footing.

My heart splintered as my eyes fell on him. Because surely the stars were trying to destroy me tonight. Of all the Fae to answer my call, why did it have to be *him*? His long, dark hair was flecked with snow, his brow taut with worry as he took in my bloodstained clothes.

"Seth," I rasped, then tugged on his hand because what choice did I have? "I need your help," I growled determinedly.

He nodded in alarm and followed without question as I dragged him as fast as I humanely could towards the cave. I tore inside, barely able to draw breath as I saw Orion on the ground, looking so pale, so absent. Blood pooled around him, the puddle so wide we had to run through it to reach him.

"Orion," Seth breathed then yanked his hand free of mine. "What the fuck happened?"

My lungs compressed as I turned to him, searching his face for any sign of compassion. But it was too dark to see his expression clearly and in the depths of my soul, I knew it was possible that he wouldn't care. But that wasn't going to stop me.

"Don't ask questions - help him!" I demanded.

I shoved him toward Orion with all the strength I had as more tears blurred my vision.

Seth dropped to his knees and ripped Orion's shirt open, resting his hands on his chest and casting healing magic. "Shit. Darcy…I think he's dead."

"He's not fucking dead until I say he is!" I shouted so loud that my voice rang around the cave and echoed back to us. I fell down beside Seth, giving him a pleading look. "You're at least going to try, aren't you?" My voice cracked because I didn't know. Seth had hurt me so deeply, hated me so fiercely. He'd never cared for Orion, but was he really heartless enough not to help?

"Aren't you?!" I snapped, shaking him.

"I'll give him everything I have," Seth promised as the green healing light spread further from his hands. A ragged breath left me and another sob ripped free of my chest.

I clutched onto Seth's arm, too terrified to touch Orion and feel how cold he might be, how still. My tears rolled onto Seth's jacket as sheer panic reached into my heart. He wasn't moving. Wasn't responding at all.

"Please," I begged, turning my head toward the cave roof and imploring the stars to listen. "Don't take him from me. I'll give you anything you want. *Anything*."

I felt Seth's eyes on me, but when I looked down he was focusing on Orion again.

Seth clenched his jaw, magic pouring from him as his brow creased with concentration. "Come on you asshole, wake up and tell me you hate me."

I unknotted my sweater from Orion's waist with shaking fingers, terrified to look at the stab wound, but I had to see. I had to know.

Blood oozed from the wound and I clamped my hands over it with a wail of grief. "Why isn't it working?"

I fell forward, my ear resting against Orion's chest as I desperately listened for his heartbeat. "Please don't leave me."

I couldn't hear anything over the sound of my own thrashing pulse and I quickly pulled away, dragging Seth's hands back onto him.

"Keep trying," I commanded and he rested his hand directly onto the wound, letting Orion's blood coat his skin as magic flowed from him in waves. The green light pulsed in time with my heavy breaths as Seth poured more and more of his magic into healing him. The wound started to close, but it was so slow, the skin knitting back together at the edges, but not nearly enough.

"Power share with me," Seth said through his teeth, his muscles bunching with exertion.

I turned away, hurriedly letting a line of Phoenix fire roll from my hand and burn in a twisting coil behind me, warming my back and slowly trickling some more magic into my veins. Then I laid two bloody hands over Seth's, shutting my eyes in concentration. I didn't have much to give yet, but any drop I had was his. There was just one problem: I had to let down my barriers to power share with my mortal enemy.

"Do it," Seth growled and I squeezed my eyes tighter, trying to force the barrier down even though it felt like a wall of iron at the edges of my skin.

"I can't," I gasped.

"You can," Seth growled. "Do it for him."

I pictured Orion, focusing solely on him and how easily I could let his magic flow into my veins. We'd done it instinctively plenty of times. It was as simple as breathing.

My barriers fell and we both inhaled sharply as my magic clashed with Seth's, winding around it and twisting into something truly powerful. The green light grew brighter as I gave Seth every scrap of power in my veins. His magic felt lighter than I'd expected, not cold and dark and cruel. It was like a warm embrace, soothing, calming, like the man it belonged to really wanted to get me through this ordeal.

The wound healed so slowly it was painful to watch, and Orion never stirred. I could hardly bear to look at his face, the blood around his mouth, the stillness of his features.

I won't let you go. I promised I'd do anything in my power to keep us together and I'll do it, goddammit. I will do it.

Seth's magic began to slow and he cursed under his breath, tugging more forcefully on my power, but I was starting to hollow out. I wasn't replenishing fast enough and I had little left to give. I could feel Seth's magic waning too and the panic that invoked in me was insufferable.

"No," I begged of him, of the world. "We can do this."

"Darcy…"

"*Don't*," I snarled, refusing to meet Seth's eye. "Keep going."

He nodded, but the green light was fading and the wound wasn't nearly healed enough.

I refused to accept the reality that was closing in on me on all sides. The world was becoming so small, I didn't know how I'd ever fit in it without him. I'd be crushed by the loss of him.

"I'm almost out," Seth said heavily, like he really cared. And fuck, I needed him to care. I needed him to scrape out the magic from every crevice of his body and pour it into Orion in the hopes that it would be enough to save him. The fire behind me wasn't restoring my magic fast enough; I was channelling it into Seth as quickly as I was gaining it. And if Seth ran out, I knew we'd fail. *I'd* fail. I'd break our promise. I could feel it burning within me, but it was shrinking like a flame about to go out.

My hope stuttered and panic reached into me, demanding I accept the truth. That he was really gone. That my world was going to be absent of him for the rest of my life. And that thought was enough to tear my heart in two, never to be repaired.

We hadn't had enough time. And he was too young to die here, broken and cold in some cave. Fate was bloodthirsty and callous, taking him like this when all he'd wanted was to save his sister. It broke me in a way I didn't think I'd ever heal from.

Seth pulled one hand back, wrapping it around my shoulders. I tried to shake him off, but he wouldn't let go. His grip tightened and he nuzzled into my hair.

The ground shuddered beneath me and my tear-soaked lips parted as I looked to the cave entrance. A huge shape moved out in the snowstorm, disappearing a second later.

"Darius," Seth gasped.

Hope tore through me like a blazing ray of light. "Darius!" I screamed, the desperation in my voice clear.

He came charging in, pulling up a pair of sweatpants. His gaze swept over us, taking in our hands on Orion's stomach then moving to his best friend's face with a look of utter horror.

"Help us!" I begged and he knelt down on my other side, laying his hands over mine.

"Drop your barriers," he commanded both of us and for some reason, it was easier with him. The strength of the two Heirs tugged on my magic and I forced my mind onto the Phoenix fire at my back, drawing on its power and feeding, feeding, feeding it to them.

The green healing light flared once more as Darius's power joined what remained of ours. The rush of his magic was burning hot, flaring through my veins like pure starlight. The healing energy grew stronger and stronger and my chest physically hurt as every ounce of magic was dragged from my veins, forced to do the Heirs' bidding.

I couldn't see the wound beneath the green light and had to squint against it as I lost sight of Orion behind it.

"Fuck," Darius grunted, slumping forward as he gave everything he had.

"Don't give up," I pleaded.

"Not for the world," he swore.

A groan sounded and my whole chest nearly burst with relief. "He's *alive*," I gasped, the light dimming so I could see him beyond it.

"Holy shit, it worked," Seth rasped and the three of us removed our hands at once.

I inhaled sharply. The wound was gone, nothing but a red scar lining his skin amongst the blood

My gaze flicked to Orion's face and his eyes snapped open a second before he lunged at Seth. He knocked him over backwards with a snarl, ripping into his throat with his fangs.

"Lance!" I screamed, leaping forward as relief and terror tangled inside me.

Seth was shouting in rage as Orion savagely drank from him, blood spilling over his clothes as he tore his throat open.

"I haven't got any magic left – stop him!" Seth yelled, shoving his shoulders.

Orion pinned him down, gripping his hair and violently wrenching Seth's head sideways to gain more access.

"Fuck!" Darius grabbed Orion by the shoulders, but he was like an animal, ripping into Seth's flesh until he started gargling on his own blood.

"Stop!" I begged, fear clawing at my heart as I realised he was going to kill him. I grabbed hold of Orion too, tugging back with all my might. With a roar of effort, Darius tore Orion off of him and bared his own throat.

"Bite me," Darius demanded. "Take what you need."

Orion sank his fangs into Darius with a desperate hunger, clinging to his arms and nearly knocking him off of his feet. Darius clutched onto him, pressing his face into his hair as he held him. "I can't believe I almost lost you after..." he trailed off, pulling him even closer and the sight sent warmth into my frozen limbs.

I stood trembling, balling my hands up to stop myself from interfering. He needed to feed. He was drained beyond belief and disturbing him now was clearly dangerous. But hell, I wanted to go to him. I needed to wrap my arms around him and feel the heavenly pounding of his heart.

Seth swore between his teeth as he clutched his neck, blood rushing down to stain his shirt.

"Darius," I warned and his gaze fell to Seth who looked on the verge of passing out.

"Alright Lance," he said gently, clutching him with a heavy sigh. "That's enough."

Orion pulled back a step, his gaze whipping to me. He was a beast coated in blood, his gaze consumed by shadows. Then the darkness receded and his eyes were full of love and apologies and fear. His eyes suddenly fell closed and he stumbled backwards unconscious. Darius caught him before he crashed to the ground, lowering him to lay down with a look of concern.

I gasped, rushing forward and kneeling by his side.

"It's blood loss," Darius explained in a hollow tone. "He'll need time to recover."

"Yeah, I'm starting to understand how that feels," Seth wheezed as Darius dropped to his side and pressed a hand to his neck to heal him. "Thank fuck you didn't run out of magic during that or he'd have killed me."

I pressed my hand to Orion's cheek, feeling the warmth of him and sagging forward as my heart started to settle. He was going to be okay. We had time stretching out before us, years and years and years. And I was going to cherish every damn one of them. I wasn't going to let a second go by without coveting each moment we had together.

My relief washed through me, but a darker emotion was chasing it away as my thoughts started to click together. Rage bit at my heart and I rounded on Darius with a snarl, standing up to face him. My Phoenix fire flickered behind him, casting his face in shadow.

"Where were you?!" I snarled, shoving him in the chest as he pulled Seth to his feet. "We needed you. *He* needed you."

"I…" Darius shook his head. "Something happened."

"Not good enough," I hissed, throwing my palms into his chest again and he made no move to fight me off. "You knew how much this meant to him!" I threw a punch at his jaw, then clawed at him in my fury. How could he have abandoned him tonight of all nights? If he'd been here, we would have had enough magic left to face Clara. None of this would have happened.

"I know," Darius said weakly and something in his posture looked so defeated that I sensed something awful really had happened to keep him from coming. "How did this happen?"

I glanced at Seth, swallowing thickly as I realised I couldn't talk about this in front of him.

Seth folded his arms, his body bloody and his eyes shadowed. "If you think I'm gonna walk out of here without an explanation, you're really fucking deluded." He looked to Darius. "Are you keeping secrets from me with a teacher and a fucking Vega?"

I could have sworn Darius flinched at the word *Vega*. "You know I practise dark magic with Lance," he said, his voice kind of empty as he looked to me. "Go ahead. You can speak in front of him, I trust him." He walked past me, dropping down beside Orion and lifting him into his arms.

"Well I happen not to trust him," I said bitterly, moving after Darius to brush my hand over Orion's forehead and check he was still okay.

"Clara came back," I told Darius as evenly as I could without falling into a pit of anger. Of hate. I'd helped bring her back, I'd had a hand in almost losing Orion. But if Darius had been here…if Tory had. Where was she? "Clara did this to Orion. She seemed lost to the shadows."

"Hang on, Clara Orion, as in his sister?" Seth balked, moving to my side as we walked out of the cave. Darius clutched Orion to his chest, staring at him like he had a thousand words to say to his friend.

"It's a long story," I said wearily.

"Yeah and I'm waiting to hear it," Seth said sharply.

"Not now." I looked to him and he frowned, reaching out as if to touch me then thinking better of it.

"Alright," he grunted. "Are you…okay?"

"I'll be okay when he's okay," I said, turning to look at Orion again. Snowflakes collected in his hair and those that landed on his cheeks melted with the heat of his flesh. The sight soothed every screaming nerve ending inside me.

Darius glanced over at me with a frown, something twisting in his gaze. I realised my mistake, pressing my lips together as he surveyed me in the dark. I could barely see any more of him than his shadowed silhouette, but I could feel his scrutiny. I couldn't hide my feelings for Orion, not right now, not when I was still rattled to my core. So I remained quiet, and I was thankful when Darius did too.

"Seth," Darius growled, stopping as the snow fluttered down over us. "You need to go. We'll talk about this later."

"You're sure you don't need any help?" Seth asked, looking to me then Orion like he gave a damn. And I guessed he must have or he wouldn't have still been standing there. I was too exhausted to know what to do with that thought. Seth Capella had saved his life. He'd done all he could, come to my aid when I needed help. And that was confronting in so many ways, I couldn't handle it right now.

"No. I'll take him home," Darius said firmly.

Seth nodded, frowning before heading away down the beach, the storm swallowing him in seconds.

"Where's Tory?" I asked, wondering if his absence had anything to do with hers too.

"Dunno," he grunted, placing Orion down on the ground and shedding his sweatpants. "Are you coming with us or going back to your House?"

"I'm coming," I said without a second's hesitation.

"I can take it from-"

"I said, I'm coming," I snarled and Phoenix fire flashed at the edges of my eyes.

He nodded mutely, turning away from me and leaping forward, his enormous Dragon form tearing out of his body and landing in front of me.

He gently scooped Orion into one of his taloned feet, his reptilian eyes fixing on me. I could have sworn they were less gold than usual, ringed with darkness.

I shed my coat and pulled my shirt off, revealing my halter-neck sports bra beneath it. I let my Phoenix wings free and a fiery blaze spread out either side of me as they extended. I picked up Darius's sweatpants to take with me, figuring he'd probably appreciate them at the other end of this flight. My stomach soared as I launched myself into the sky, following the golden dragon tail which was twisting away from me into the battering snow storm.

I urged fire into my veins to chase away the freezing air and raced beneath Darius, soaring through the thick clouds. I pressed my hands to Orion, letting the fire in my blood seep into him too. Nothing felt as good as the heat of his skin against mine. He'd come so close to death, my mind was still in shock knowing he was still here with me now.

We sailed through the maelstrom, racing across campus and it wasn't long before we landed in the woods close to Asteroid Place.

Darius placed Orion on the ground a moment before he shifted and I withdrew my wings, plunging us into darkness. I tossed Darius his sweatpants and when he had them on, he lifted Orion into his arms again and moved toward the gate. I kept close to him, wondering what the hell would happen if a professor found us here like this, covered in blood with an unconscious teacher, sneaking into their private residence.

I took Orion's hand as we reached the gate, pressing his palm to it to unlock it with his magical signature. We crept forward past the pool, heading down the alley between Orion and Washer's chalets. I touched his hand to the door again and Darius arranged him over one shoulder so he could hold his own hand against it too.

"He's got a bunch of magical locks on this door," he muttered in explanation, his brows pulling together in concentration.

A moment later, the door swung inwards and we hurried inside.

I shut it behind us and breathed a sigh of relief as warmth swept over me, following Darius through to Orion's bedroom where he laid him on the bed.

I immediately crawled onto it, moving to his side and taking his hand. Darius stood watching us, just a shadow in the dark, but I couldn't conceal my feelings for Orion. They were too raw, my heart too exposed.

"You care about him," he stated, his voice horribly empty.

"Yes," I said powerfully, defiantly. Because he was Orion's friend and I didn't care if he knew right now. He had to accept it one day anyway, because I was never going to stop loving him.

"And he cares about you?" His voice still had that strangely hollow quality to it I didn't understand.

I wasn't going to answer for Orion, so I just stayed quiet. But maybe that was answer enough. "Where were you tonight, Darius?" I asked, my tone sharp. "What was more important than helping your friend?"

"I have to go replenish my magic so I can heal him some more," he said, completely ignoring my question. "I'll be back in a few hours." He headed to the window, pushing it open and jumping out of it without another word.

I scowled after him in fury, unable to believe he wouldn't even give me an explanation for abandoning Orion tonight. I moved to shut the window then hurried to the bathroom, fetching towels before getting a jug of hot water from the kitchen.

I couldn't stand to see Orion looking half dead, covered in blood. So I sat beside him, washing it away as best I could, trying to erase the pain that had nearly split me in two. But I had a feeling that some part of this night would always be with me, scarred on the inside of my chest. I'd almost lost him to the shadows, to his sister. And now Seth was entangled in this too. He wouldn't let it lie, he'd want an explanation.

I set a fire burning behind me, twisting and dancing in the air as it worked to restore my magic. I'd never felt so powerless as I had when Clara had hurt him. And it terrified me that her shadows could suppress my Order like that, taking charge of the shadows in me and keeping my Phoenix subdued.

I tried to chase away the awful fears as I tugged the remains of Orion's shirt off and washed away the stains on his arms, his stomach, his mouth. His breathing was soft but his brow was pinched like he was entangled in a nightmare. So when I was done, I curled up beside him, resting my head on his chest and humming a nameless tune, just something to let him know that I was here. And I wasn't going anywhere, even if every star in the sky decided to fall down and burn the world tonight.

CALEB

CHAPTER TWO

It was almost three in the morning and I was exhausted from a night of partying, but for some reason I just couldn't settle myself enough to try and sleep. Every time I dozed off, it almost felt like something was prodding me awake again, like the damn stars didn't want to let me settle.

My brain was working on overdrive and my power was running low enough to be distracting. What I really wanted was Tory Vega, and every time I tried to turn my mind away from that idea, it just spun right back around to her like her name was being whispered in my ear or something. But if I just woke her up in the middle of the night, I was fairly sure she'd put me in the dog house for a week. Not that I was even sure things were back on with us anyway. She hadn't outright rejected the idea at Christmas, but she'd hardly put a date in her diary either. She had said to ask again in the new year though and technically it *was* the new year…

I groaned, knocking my head back against my pillow then tugged my Atlas closer. One message couldn't hurt and if I was really lucky, it might just pay off.

Caleb:

I can't sleep and all I keep doing is thinking of you alone in your bed… want

some company? ;)

I eyed the message for a long moment, waiting to see if the red ticks would illuminate to let me know she was awake and had read it. A smirk captured my lips as the red ticks popped up.

Tory:

Come over.

Tory:

But don't ask any questions.

Questions about what? I almost wrote out that response before realising that that was a question. I was dancing a thin line with Tory's temper most of the time without her handing out warnings, so I wasn't going to risk pissing her off and losing my shot at a night in her bed. I could cope with a no questions rule.

I jumped out of bed, pulled on a pair of sweatpants and a hoodie before kicking on my sneakers and heading out of my room with nothing but my Atlas and keys.

I shot out of Terra House using my Vampire speed and sprinted across campus, passing The Orb and the other school buildings before tearing south towards Ignis House.

A blaze of fire lit the sky high above and I looked up just in time to see a huge Dragon silhouetted as it passed over the moon. Darius was out late. I briefly wondered what was keeping him up, but my focus was more targeted on the girl waiting for me.

I threw a handful of fire at the symbol above the door to Ignis House and shot in as it opened, racing up the stairs, through the common room and up again until I was right outside Tory's door.

I pushed a hand into my blonde curls to tame them a little after my run and knocked on her door.

She pulled it open a moment later, catching the front of my hoodie and dragging me inside as she pushed up onto her tiptoes to kiss me. The lights were off, but the cool light of the moon shining off the snow outside gave me just enough to see her by.

She was wearing baggy sweatpants and an oversized sweatshirt and her hair was tied in a messy knot on top of her head. But Tory Vega could wear a potato sack and still look like a fucking goddess. My dick was hard before I'd even knocked on her door and as she pushed her tongue into my mouth a groan of longing escaped me.

I caught her waist and lifted her up, her legs hooking around my hips as she ground against my hard-on and she released a moan which had me practically exploding already.

I sat her on the edge of her desk and pulled back as I tugged on the hem of her sweatshirt, breaking our kiss as I yanked it over her head.

She wasn't wearing anything beneath it and my heart beat a little faster as I took in the full swell of her breasts, dropping my mouth to capture her left nipple instantly.

She moaned again, leaning back to give me more access as I dragged my teeth over the pebbled flesh, my hand palming her other breast as I teased that nipple too.

Tory reached between us and unzipped my hoodie, pushing it back off of my shoulders in a firm demand. I stood upright as I shrugged it off of me and she dropped her gaze to my chest as she trailed her hands across my flesh.

My blood was pumping hot and fast, urging me to take more from her. My fangs snapped free as the bloodlust rose but I held back, wanting to take pleasure from her body before savouring her blood.

I caught her chin, tipping her head back so that I could look at her. I longed to see the desire in her eyes and taste her full lips against mine again.

Tory resisted my demand for a moment before looking up at me, her long eyelashes sweeping up until she met my eye.

Two black rings surrounded her irises and I jerked back on instinct, my hand falling from her chin and my lips parted in shock as I just stared at her.

"What the fuck Tory?" I breathed. "You're Star Crossed. How...*who?*"

"I told you no questions," she growled, reaching for me again. "I just want to forget about it."

"Are you insane?" I demanded, shaking my head as I tried to process this, to understand it on any level. Who the hell would say no to their destiny like that? Who would be insane enough to turn their back on their one true love. "What have you done? Who did this to you? I-"

"It's done, Caleb," she snapped and for a moment it looked like the black rings around her irises grew and flared until her whole eyes seemed black with shadows. "I can't go back and change it and I don't want to talk about it."

She took a shuddering breath and closed her eyes as her fingers curled around the edge of the desk she sat on.

I stepped closer, my chest aching with the need to do something about this, to change the stars, fix her fate, any number of impossible things that could alleviate some of the pain I could see consuming her.

I took her hand in mine, her fingers burning hot as her fire magic blazed beneath her skin, making me call on my own power to avoid getting burned. She opened her eyes and that darkness I'd imagined was gone, only the two black rings left there now but somehow that was worse.

"But, Tory..." I was just staring at her, my mind wheeling as I tried to come to terms with the fact that some other asshole had been selected by the stars to be hers. Her perfect match. One true love... Except he'd said no. Or she had. And I just couldn't understand it. I'd seen her earlier and she hadn't had the black rings in her eyes then, so this must have only just happened.

"Make me forget, Caleb," Tory breathed, her voice cracking with the plea.

I could feel the pain coming from her now, the desperation. She was breaking, broken...someone had done this to her. Someone had chosen to do this to her and I just couldn't understand it. If the stars had chosen her for me,

I'd have grabbed hold of her in a heartbeat and never let go.

I was staring into her big, green eyes, the black rings surrounding them taking every inch of my attention. It didn't make sense, I couldn't understand it...nobody chose to be Star Crossed. If the stars gave you the chance to pick your Elysian Mate you did it. No question. No matter what. Hell, if I found myself standing opposite that fucking hat boy I'd say yes.

"I'm so sorry, Tory," I whispered. My flesh was burning with desire for her and it felt like the stars themselves had guided me here, driving me towards her to help heal her of this pain.

"I don't want you to be sorry," she replied, her gaze hardening. "I just want to forget."

The fire in her eyes was enough to snap me back into action. There wasn't anything I could do to fix what had happened to her, but I sure as hell could do what she'd asked.

I kissed her again and she pulled me closer, her hands gripping my hair and tugging just enough to let me know she didn't want me to go easy on her.

She bit my lip and I growled as my grip on her hips tightened, my fingers pushing against the material of her sweatpants. I fisted my hands around her waistband and tugged on them, forcing her to raise her hips so that I could pull them off of her.

I dropped to my knees as I tugged them over her ankles and stayed there, pushing her legs apart as I moved forward to devour her.

I hooked her left knee over my shoulder and ran my mouth up the inside of her thigh as she gripped the edge of the desk, her head tipping back as her breathing grew heavier, more demanding.

As I made it to the centre of her, I pressed forward hungrily, running my tongue over her, my skin tingling as she moaned in encouragement, her hips bucking against me.

I gripped her thighs, pushing them wider as I continued to feast on her, the sound of her pleasure making me so hard I had to fight against the urge to take her already.

I shifted my hand and pushed two fingers inside her, her moans filling the room as I bent her body to my desire.

I could feel her tightening around me and I groaned as I sucked harder, driving my fingers in once more as she fell apart. I devoured her pleasure, riding her through it until she sagged back on the desk.

My dick was throbbing with need and I stood up, pushing my pants off and kicking them aside with my sneakers.

Tory's pupils were wide with desire and she slipped off of the desk, kissing me hard, demanding more. She wasn't some fragile thing needing reassurance, she wanted me to take her body hostage and make her forget the asshole who had said no to her. And I wasn't going to disappoint.

I caught her waist between my hands and turned her so her back was to me before pushing her up against the wall.

She gasped as I pressed against her, every inch of my desire driving against her ass and letting her know just how much I wanted her.

She moaned a little, turning her head to the side and reaching over her shoulder so that she could pull me around to kiss her again.

In my excitement, my fangs scraped over her bottom lip and her blood spilled across my tongue. A growl escaped me as my Order form pushed its way to the surface and I couldn't help but suck her lip into my mouth, taking a trickle of her blood and power into me as I did.

Tory gasped as I knocked her legs apart and I gripped the base of my dick before guiding it up and into her. She moaned hungrily as I pushed in slowly, savouring the feeling of how tight she was around me and letting her adjust to the position I held her in, pinned against the wall.

"More," she breathed and I growled again, giving her what she wanted with a sharp thrust of my hips.

She moaned each time I drove myself into her and I gripped her ass in my hands, my fingers biting into her flesh as I pounded into her harder and harder.

"Fuck," Tory groaned. "Harder."

I gave her what she wanted, my mouth finding her neck as I kissed her and slammed into her faster, harder, giving her everything, a desperate ache filling me as I tried to hold off a little longer.

"Bite me," she begged and I looked at her in surprise as she tipped her head aside, baring her throat to me. We'd never done that during sex before and as much as my instincts made me crave it, I knew she didn't really enjoy being bitten so I hadn't ever asked it of her.

"Really?" I asked, because I was half a second away from doing it and I wasn't sure I'd ever wanted to bite someone more.

"Yes," she gasped as I slammed into her again. "Do it!"

I gave up on trying to hold back and my teeth pierced her skin as I fucked her even harder, the pressure building in me so fiercely that I knew I could only hold it back a second longer.

Tory cried out as I forced another orgasm from her body and the taste of her blood rolling over my tongue made me explode inside her a second later.

I was pinning her against the wall so hard that the tremors of her flesh were rocking through my body. I drank deeply from her as her blood and power filled me in a way that had my heart racing.

I could hear her pulse pounding an exhilarated rhythm and I was pretty sure that she would collapse if I let her go.

The bloodlust had me firmly in its grip and I swallowed more and more, ecstasy filling me as I savoured the combination of her body and power.

I forced my fangs out of her flesh with some difficulty and drew back, pulling her down onto the bed as we caught our breath.

Some of her hair had fallen out of the messy knot she'd tied it in and I pushed it out of her face as I looked at her.

She offered me half a smile, but it didn't reach her eyes. The pain of what had happened to her was creeping back in already and I was struck with the desire to kill the asshole who'd said no to her.

"Tell me who he is," I growled. "I'll destroy him for doing this to you."

Tory frowned at me for a moment, reaching up to run her fingers along my jaw.

"He wasn't the one who said no," she said slowly.

I opened my mouth to reply, but my Atlas started ringing at the same moment. Tory's eyes slipped from my face to my hoodie which was on the floor by the door, my Atlas still in the pocket.

"You should answer that," she breathed.

I wanted to object, but it was the middle of the night now. No one would call me at this time unless it was important. I reached out to heal the bite on Tory's neck before I got up. Blood was staining her pillow and had run down her chest to her nipple. I leaned forward and licked the line of it off and she watched me with hooded eyes.

The call rang out then started again instantly.

I forced myself to leave her in the bed and dug around in my hoody until I located my Atlas just before the call rang out again.

I raised an eyebrow as I realised I'd received thirteen messages as well as the calls. I'd obviously been too distracted with Tory to even hear them coming in.

Before I could read any of them, it started ringing again and I spotted Seth's name on the ID before I answered it.

"Hey, man. What's going-"

"Cal...*fuck* we don't know what to do. He won't say anything...this is bad. Just get to King's Hollow now. We need you," Seth sounded completely panicked, but the call cut off before I could reply. A lump of ice formed in my chest. Something was wrong. Really fucking wrong.

I grabbed my sweatpants and pulled them on, looking up at Tory guiltily.

"I'm sorry," I said. "I wouldn't go if it wasn't urgent. But something's happened. I don't know what, but-"

"It's fine," she said, not even seeming surprised. "Just go."

"I'll come back if I can," I promised her, not wanting to leave her like this but not really having any other choice.

"I'm sorry, Caleb," she said, her voice cracking. She was chewing on her bottom lip and tears slid from her eyes.

"Why?" I asked, frowning as I moved towards her again but she shook her head and I knocked against an air shield before I could get close. "What's wrong?" I asked in confusion.

"I shouldn't have told you to come over," she said, her breath hitching as she fought against the tears. "It was selfish, stupid. I don't know what I was thinking, for a moment I forgot that you're his...I'm sorry."

"Why would you be sorry?" I asked with a frown, trying to push against the shield as Tory scrubbed the tears from her cheeks but more just fell to replace them.

My Atlas started ringing again and I glanced down at Max's name before frowning at Tory with a sinking feeling in my chest. The stars would have been pushing her towards her mate before tonight and there was only one other Fae that I knew who she'd been drawn towards like that. If I hadn't been so caught up thinking with my dick then I might have connected the dots sooner. Why the fuck *hadn't* I connected them sooner? It was so obvious, so fucking obvious. My heart pounded against my ribs hard enough to hurt and there was a faint ringing in my ears as I fought against the desire to voice my fears. Because if I was right then what we'd just done...

Tory looked at me for a long moment and I couldn't help but stare at the dark rings in her eyes. I was seriously hoping that my hunch was wrong but as my Atlas started ringing again, I got the strongest sense that I wasn't.

I swallowed against a thick lump in my throat and took a step back.

She still hadn't answered my question, but I found that I didn't want her to.

"You should go to your friends," she said, raising her chin in an attempt to hide just how much she was hurting.

"I don't want to just leave you here like this..."

"I told you, I shouldn't have let you come. I was just trying to forget, but it was wrong, especially with you... I really am sorry, but I just want you to go now."

"Are you sure you're alright?" I asked slowly, unsure if I should really leave her while she looked so fucking broken.

"I'm a big girl, Caleb. And I have to own my choices so you shouldn't feel any pity for me," she said, pulling the blankets up to cover her as she sat back against the pillows. But I didn't get the impression she was really going to sleep.

"Okay. I'll see you later then." I hesitated for a moment but she didn't say anything to stop me so I kicked on my sneakers, grabbed my sweatshirt and headed out into the corridor.

My Atlas had stopped ringing so I sped out of Ignis House with my Vampire speed and raced straight through The Wailing Wood to King's Hollow.

I skidded to a halt at the base of the enormous tree and took a deep breath as I psyched myself up to go inside. I chewed on the inside of my cheek then blew the breath out again. If I'd fucked up, I had to just own it. I had to deal with it.

I pushed the door open and stepped inside but before I could set foot on the stairs, Max appeared at the bottom of them. I felt his silencing bubble crash over me half a second before his fist collided with my jaw. Pain flared through me and I staggered back a step from the force of the blow.

"What the fuck, Cal?" he roared, closing in on me and crowding me back against the wall as he seemed to be fighting the temptation to hit me again. "Where the hell have you been?"

"What was that for?" I cursed, my fangs snapping out as tension coiled through my body from the attack and I snarled at him, squaring my shoulders.

"I could smell the fucking lust on you from half a mile away," Max

23

growled. "You've been with Tory Vega, haven't you?"

I swallowed a thick lump in my throat because there was only one reason why that would be making him this angry and the thought of it made me sick.

"It was Darius?" I asked in a hollow voice, the fight going out of me in a heartbeat. I deserved anything he wanted to throw at me.

"Of course it was! Who the fuck else would it have been?" Max bellowed and his anger crashed into me as his emotions danced on the air as his Siren gifts flared.

I had to work at reinforcing my mental shield to stop myself from succumbing to the potency of his rage and I knocked my head back against the wall behind me, groaning as I took on the full implications of what he was saying.

"I'm sorry, man," I breathed. "I just…I don't even know how I ended up going over there tonight. I was drunk out of my skull when I went to bed but then I just woke up, stone cold sober and thinking about her…more like obsessing over her really. And I couldn't settle at all until I acted on it-"

"It was the stars," Max growled suddenly, dropping down to sit on the bottom step and pushing his hands through his hair. "They're already working to force them apart…"

I frowned as the rage in the air fizzled out and slipped into despair which licked keenly against my mental walls. Max's heart was breaking for Darius and the chasm of grief opening up in my chest told me plainly enough that mine was too.

I thought about the way I'd been drawn towards Tory tonight, how I hadn't been able to resist the urge to go to her and how devastated she'd seemed when she apologised to me for letting me come over. She'd been pushed at me too. The stars were already playing their games in payment for her choice.

"*Fuck,*" I breathed, dropping down beside Max. "What do we do?"

"This is my fault," he groaned. "I could feel the pull between Darius and Tory. He even tried to ask me for help with it and I…I just shut him down. I pushed him to keep on working against her. If I'd just listened to him, made myself consider the bond I could feel between them properly then maybe I could have given him better advice."

"I just slept with the girl he was destined to love and *you're* blaming yourself?" I asked incredulously.

"I could feel it, Cal," Max insisted. "I just didn't want to. I'm the only one who could have seen this coming. I'm the one who should have realised that the pull he felt towards her was more than just lust and infatuation. If I'd just spent the time listening to him when he tried to talk to me-"

"This isn't on you, Max," I growled, wrapping my arm around him and pulling him close. He drew me into an embrace so tight it was bruising and I could feel his agony trickling into me as his skin was pressed to mine and the contact enhanced the power of his gifts.

"It's not on you, either," he replied roughly. "The fucking stars…a *Vega*. Shit, who could have come up with something so fucked up? It's like they wanted this to happen to him. I'm starting to think he's fucking cursed. He's had to deal with so much shit in his life and then he's finally offered something good and pure and light and it has to be with the one person he could never offer the world to."

"We should go to him," I said, though my gut twisted uncomfortably with the feeling that I'd betrayed him.

"Don't tell him where you've been," Max breathed and I stilled at that suggestion. I'd never lied to one of the other Heirs like that.

"I have to," I replied, shaking my head as we both stood and started up the stairs. "He deserves more from me than lies."

"I've never felt emotions like the despair he's feeling right now," Max breathed. "I don't know what he might do if he finds out."

"He can do what he likes to me," I replied darkly. "I deserve it."

Max frowned like he wasn't sure if he agreed with that. "It's the stars that deserve it."

"They might have pushed me at her, but I'm my own man. I'm responsible for my actions."

"I don't know about that," Max muttered before dropping his silencing bubble.

We headed up the stairs and the tightness grew in my chest as we made it to the door at the top. Max clapped a hand to my shoulder, pushing a sense of calm at me to soothe my anxiety but for once I didn't let his power influence me. I had to own this. No excuses.

Darius was sitting in the large, wing backed chair beside the fire, his gaze distant as he looked into the flames but as Max closed the door behind us, he looked our way. I inhaled sharply as I spotted the ring of black circling his irises. The difference in Tory's eyes had been confronting, but I'd seen Darius practically every day for most of my life and despite the fact that his eyes had been dark before this, the change in them was profound.

Seth was pacing back and forth behind him, soft whimpers escaping him as his Wolf instincts clearly pushed him to comfort Darius. Though I was guessing his comfort hadn't been welcomed when he'd tried.

Max moved to take a seat on the couch while I lingered by the door.

I shot forward and pulled Darius into my arms before he could stop me. "I'm so sorry, man," I breathed, holding him tightly as he just sat there and let me.

The heat of his skin was almost burning but his posture was slack, like he didn't even give a shit about anything anymore.

I didn't let go and eventually he released a long breath. "You smell like her," he muttered.

I flinched back like he'd punched me, glancing at Max for a moment but he only frowned.

"I'm sorry," I said, my voice cracking with how much I meant that.

"I didn't know, I didn't mean to… Not that I'm excusing it. I should have realised when I saw her eyes, I just-"

Darius looked at me for a long moment, his jaw grinding and I waited for him to unleash his rage on me. Which was really the least I deserved.

"She chose not to be mine so it's not like I get any say in what she does now, is it?" he said eventually, dropping back into his chair and looking away from me towards the fire once more.

Seth released a low howl and I ran a hand over the back of my head, feeling about ten times worse than I would have if he'd just punched me.

"We can fix this," Seth said, looking between me and Max encouragingly. "There's gotta be some way to get the stars to change their minds, right?"

"Don't you listen in class?" Max growled.

"Everyone knows you only get one shot at it," I added in a low voice like that would make my words mean less somehow.

"We're the most powerful Fae in Solaria!" Seth snapped. "The stars will listen if we tell them to!"

Darius got up and walked across the room to the chest where he kept his gold. He pulled out a bunch of rings and pushed them onto his fingers one by one then threw a handful of gold chains over his head to rest against his bare chest.

He lifted the huge chest into his arms with a grunt of effort and tipped the rest of its contents all over his chair before sitting down amidst the heaped gold coins and jewellery.

"I need to focus on Lance. Not impossible ideas about defying the stars," Darius said and I frowned in confusion.

"What's wrong with Lance?" I asked.

"I found him half dead in a cave in Aer Cove," Seth muttered. "It was some dark magic gone wrong. It took everything me, Darius and Darcy had to keep him alive. And I'm still not convinced he'll stay that way."

Darius growled darkly at that suggestion and Seth promptly stopped talking.

"What the hell happened tonight, Darius?" Max asked softly, leaning forward in his chair and pressing his Siren power out around the room to try and comfort him.

Darius dropped his gaze to the rings on his fingers and shook his head. "I can't talk about it. When Lance is better, he might be able to explain but my…" He trailed off, not even able to finish that sentence thanks to the Dark Coercion his father had used on him.

"For fuck's sake," Max growled, his jaw clenching with rage over the situation.

"And what about Tory?" Seth asked, moving closer to Darius then backing off again like he was at war with his instincts over what to do for him. "Why did she say no?"

"Why do you think?" Darius snapped, glaring at Seth with enough venom to make him growl back before he could stop himself. We were all

Alphas and direct confrontation between us never ended well for anyone.

I shot between the two of them, laying a hand on Seth's arm to sooth him before Darius flipped. Seth forced the tension from his limbs and looked away, dispersing the atmosphere between them before it could escalate.

"He's just trying to understand," I said in a low voice.

Darius's eyes flared with his temper for another moment as he looked at me, but then the fight went out of him again.

"She didn't exactly give me a full list," he said bitterly. "But I would imagine it includes the time I almost drowned her, when I burned her clothes off in front of my entire House, when I shoved her in the mud and called her a whore, when I took part in that whole Halloween fiasco where we tried to destroy her reputation and a thousand other things besides."

"It's because they lived too long in the mortal world," I said, hunting for an answer even though there wasn't one. "She just didn't understand. She didn't realise how final this decision would be. She can't have. She told me she was drawn to you at the Eclipse, if she'd just had a chance to act on those feelings with you then she wouldn't have-"

"We did act on them," Darius snapped. "After I caught her when she destroyed my bike and again at the palace at Christmas. Sex clearly wasn't enough to change her opinion of me."

My eyebrows rose at that admission because I'd had no goddamn idea about that.

"But if you were sleeping with her then she must have gotten to know you more?" Max asked with a frown. "Surely she saw beyond all the power claiming shit and-"

"Sorry to burst your bubble, princess, but it wasn't some declaration of love. It was the two of us giving in to the heat that burns between us when it flared too hot to resist. But she made it clear enough that that was all it was to her."

"And what about what it meant to you?" Seth asked.

"After everything I'd done to her it didn't really seem like my place to expect any more than she was willing to offer, so I didn't push it." Darius leaned back in his chair and rested his head against it. "Obviously now I wish I'd dealt with it differently...I just didn't realise we were running out of time..."

Max's face scrunched with pain as he caught a hit of Darius's emotions and Seth released another mournful howl to the ceiling.

"This isn't right," I growled even though I knew it wouldn't change anything.

"It's what I deserve," Darius said, his tone hollow once more. Darkness seemed to shift across his eyes for a moment but before I could look more closely, he closed them. "I don't want to talk about it anymore."

"Okay," I agreed because I couldn't think of a single thing to say that might be of any use anyway.

"Let me help you sleep," Max offered, getting to his feet and walking towards Darius with his hand extended.

"I don't deserve to escape this feeling," Darius muttered. "Besides, I have to go home as soon as I've recovered my magic. I have to face my father, he'll want to decide how the press deals with this and…there are other things going on at home which I'll need to check on."

"I won't take your pain if you don't want me to. I'll just make you sleep," Max swore. "Just for a few hours before you have to face Lionel."

Darius hesitated a moment longer then reached out to take Max's hand.

I could feel Max's power pushing me towards sleep too and Seth yawned widely beside me.

I caught his arm and guided him out of the room before we fell under Max's spell and we headed to the bedroom I'd claimed for my own here in the Hollow.

The room was big with white sheets on the bed and all kinds of my crap strewn about the place from Pitball medals to textbooks. There was a long window along the far wall with a view looking out over the snow covered trees.

"What do we do?" Seth asked with a soft whimper as I closed the door behind us.

"I don't know," I admitted as I dropped down onto the edge of the bed, gazing out at the view.

Seth sat beside me, nuzzling against my shoulder affectionately.

"I really fucked up tonight," I breathed, thinking back on the moment I'd seen the black rings around Tory's eyes. I should have realised who it had been right away. But it was like my thoughts hadn't been in order and all I'd wanted was to lose myself in her.

"You didn't know," Seth murmured, taking my hand and squeezing it. "The stars are going to use anything and anyone they can to keep them apart now. You were just the first of many things they'll use to drive the wedge between them…"

"It's not right."

"I know. But what can we do?"

"Something. Anything. I don't even know what yet. But I'm going to make up for this," I swore. "I'm going to find some way to fix it."

ORION

CHAPTER THREE

I woke from a darkness so thick, it had bled into every part of me and held me captive. The world was a haze and I couldn't piece together which parts of my nightmares had been real and which had been imaginary. A heaviness weighed on my heart and a prickle in my right arm made my hand twitch. But I couldn't piece together what that feeling was, even though it was achingly familiar.

A warm body pressed me down and I reached for her, knowing her by scent alone. But there was another scent in the room, tainting everything about this moment of waking up with her which should have been so perfect. Blood.

What happened? Where the hell am I?

Slowly, it came back together, the memories stirring in my mind in a thick pool of oil. We'd brought Clara back, and then...

I shuddered and Darcy groaned softly in her sleep.

Clara...my own sister, she'd driven the draining dagger into me and drank too much of my blood. I remembered Blue gazing down at me, each of her tears making me ache. The words *I love you* had fallen from her lips and sounded like the sweetest song in the world. Then darkness, nothing but darkness.

My head throbbed, but my chest hummed contentedly with the fuel of magic and I recalled being awake in that cave, drinking from Darius and-

"Fuck!" I bolted upright and everything tilted. *Seth.*

Darcy sprang to her knees in alarm, staring at me in shock. "Are you alright?" She reached for my hand and I realised she was shaking.

"Blue," I groaned, grabbing her and pulling her against me, needing her like I needed air to breathe.

She wound her legs around me, burying her face in my neck and clutching onto me like the world would stop turning if she didn't. She released a sob that wracked through her whole body and the pain in it hurt me too.

"It's okay," I hushed her.

"Lance, you have no idea-"

I silenced her with a kiss, seeking out her mouth and tugging her so close it felt like our hearts were about to collide through our flesh. I let my magical barriers down and she gasped, our power merging and dancing together like they'd missed each other.

"What happened?" I asked heavily as she drew away, unsure if I wanted to know. "How did I get back here?"

"Darius," she said, resting her forehead to mine. I held on tight to her waist, not letting her get any more space between us than that.

"He turned up at last then did he?" I snarled, my fangs extending in anger. My thoughts were still a fog and the shock of what had happened was too much to process. But my rage over Darius letting me down was as keen as it had been before.

"He said something happened." She shook her head, clearly not knowing any more than that.

"And Tory?"

"I don't know. I left my Atlas back at the cave. Yours is broken." She pointed to the device on my nightstand, a huge crack splintered up the centre of it.

I lifted a hand up and curled a lock of her hair around it which was coated with blood.

"Come on," I said gently, meaning to scoop her into my arms and carry her to the bathroom, but my strength failed me. "Fuck," I hissed as a tremor wracked my body. I was dizzy with blood loss and I blinked away a haze of darkness curtaining my eyes.

"Here, it's alright." She guided me out of bed and I growled, hating to appear weak in front of her.

There was so much we needed to say, but both of us were dirty and bloody and I couldn't bear to see her looking like that a second longer so I let her gather up some clothes and lead me through the house to the bathroom on the other side of the lounge. I didn't want to let myself think about Clara just yet, because I was fairly sure my heart was going to break when I did.

We headed straight into the large shower unit and my vision faltered for a second as I turned the water on. I gazed down at her bloodied clothes and flesh and my heart crushed in my chest. I turned her around, washing the blood out of her hair, pulling her clothes off as I made sure I got every last bloody mark. I found bruises all along her spine and choked back the razor sharp lump in my throat as I healed them away.

This is my fault. I was the one who asked her to be there last night. I should have realised it wasn't safe. That Clara might not be herself.

The water swirled around us, turning red by our feet, taking the evidence of tonight with it, but taking none of the lasting hurt inside me. The scar across my stomach would likely never go completely, but I brushed a line of healing magic over it anyway, helping it fade a little more.

Darcy turned to me when she was clean, stripped bare and her eyes full of pain and relief, the two emotions so raw they ate at my heart. She tugged my clothes free and washed away the lasting imprint of blood on my skin until there was nothing but a sea of unspoken words hanging between us and the water.

Something told me she didn't want to voice them, and I certainly wasn't ready to face the impact of this night. So I pressed her back against the wall and laid kisses on her to chase away the horrors in her eyes. She ran her hands over me like she wanted to be sure I was real and I let her explore every inch of my skin before I lost myself in her body. The only words to pass our lips were I love yous and they were the only ones I cared for right now.

We stayed joined until the world weighed a little less and I could finally think straight again. Then we headed from the shower and I put on a pair of sweatpants and Darcy pulled on one of my T-shirts.

I glanced toward the window as we exited the bathroom, finding the sky beginning to pale, snow still tumbling against the pane. Something told me when the sun rose today, the world would be a much darker place.

I led Darcy back to my room and caught the sound of movement just before we stepped through the door. Darius stood by the window, his arms folded and his body draped in gold from chains to rings and a thick bracelet.

He glanced between us, realisation in his eyes and I gritted my jaw. Fury sliced me apart and I didn't even care that he was seeing us together because *fuck him.*

"Where were you?" I snapped and he bowed his head.

"We need to talk alone," he said. "Gwen, you need to go and talk to your sister."

"Why? Is she okay? What have you done to her?" Darcy demanded and I frowned at Darius, trying to figure out what was going on.

There was something different about him, but I couldn't work out what it was apart from the general air of defeat about him. It hit me that something serious had happened as I felt the weight of it in my chest. The Guardian bond burned a little hotter, demanding I help him and I resented it forcefully because where had he been when *I* needed *him*?

"I haven't done anything," Darius said, avoiding her gaze. "She did it to us."

"What is that supposed to mean?" Darcy snarled, hurrying to the window.

"You can't go out in this storm like that," I said in alarm, stepping forward.

She glanced back at me as Phoenix fire swirled in her gaze. "I'll be just fine." She looked to Darius. "If you've hurt her, I'll kill you."

Darius nodded like he didn't even hear her and my heart crushed as she threw me a look of goodbye.

"You'll be okay?" she asked and I nodded firmly.

"Yes. Go," I urged, though the last thing I wanted was to be parted from her right now. But it was clear Darius needed me. Even if I did want to rip his head off in that moment. The bond didn't give me much choice.

Darcy slipped out the window and Darius shoved it shut behind her, tugging the curtains across sharply.

I turned to face him and he strode to the nightstand, switching the lamp on and beckoning me closer.

"What's going on?" I asked in a low tone, moving toward him, half wanting to punch him for not showing up tonight, but the look in his eyes was staying my hand. And as I got closer, I realised it wasn't just the look in his eyes. There was a fucking black ring around them.

"*No*," I gasped, grabbing hold of his shoulders as I moved right up close to be sure, my gaze flicking between each of his irises as I begged the stars that this wasn't true.

"We had our Divine Moment," Darius said flatly, like he didn't have enough energy to say it with any emotion.

"Who?" I breathed, but I knew who. He didn't have to say her name, but he gave it to me anyway.

"Tory," he sighed, the first time I'd ever heard him call her anything other than Roxy. "She fucking said no, Lance." He fell against me and I wrapped my arms around him, gripping him tightly as the world seemed to fall apart all over again. Last night had changed everything. I'd thought almost dying had been bad, but this...

"Fuck...Darius." I gripped him closer, the bond between us practically wailing as his pain suddenly washed into me more keenly. I clenched my jaw against it, gripping the back of his head as I did the only thing I could do and stood there until he found enough strength to move.

"It's over," he rasped. "It's all fucking over."

I shook my head like I could offer something in denial, but no words came. My best friend was Star Crossed. And no one in the history of the world had ever been able to go against the stars once that decision had been made. But it was such a rare choice anyway...there was only one famous case I could distinctly remember where a woman had refused her Elysian Mate after he'd been responsible for killing her father. But that choice made some sort of sense, Tory's didn't. Darius might have hurt her, but didn't she understand the weight of this kind of Star Bond? It would overcome anything, *everything*. Darius would have spent the rest of his life making up for all he'd done to her, he would have watched over her more fiercely than the moon did the Earth. He'd have given her the world.

Had she even realised the immensity of what she'd given up? Had she really been so stubborn that she would choose a life without love in it? Doomed to pine for Darius for the rest of her days and never have him. The stars would make it their mission to keep them apart now. Nothing would go their way even if she regretted the decision. It was impossible. It was downright cruel.

To herself. To him.

Darius pushed me back onto the bed and fell down beside me, winding his arms tighter around my waist. Our bond flared like it never had before, because there was nothing I could do to help him. This was beyond my control. But I was still forced to act, to do something to make this right even though there was nothing I could offer.

Thankfully, having him this close started to ease the ache and the bond hummed with need as it drew us closer until my hand was knotted in his hair. It took everything I had not to fucking kiss him, or drag him into the shower and soothe him like I had Darcy. It was totally messed up.

Fuck you Lionel. Fuck you right up the fucking ass for all you've done.

"Don't say it'll be alright," Darius growled.

"I won't," I sighed.

"I'm sorry I wasn't there for you," he said. "By the stars, you could have died." His rough jaw grazed against mine and I groaned, trying to draw back enough before this bond took too much control of me.

"It's alright, I didn't."

"It's not alright. Fucking hell, Lance. Could this night get any worse?"

"Doubt it," I muttered. His flesh was scalding hot against mine, but I didn't let him go even when smoke coiled out of his mouth. He needed me this close and I'd burn for him if I had to.

"Sorry," he said, shutting his eyes as he tried to rein in his Dragon. "It just hurts so fucking much. What the hell am I gonna do now?"

I shook my head, wishing I had an answer, but I came up empty. We fell quiet and he rested his forehead to my shoulder as he tried to deal with this awful fucking thing that had happened to him. And tomorrow, everyone would know. The whole academy would see the rings in their eyes. It would change the way people behaved around them. Elysian Mates wasn't something any Fae took lightly.

"What happened with Clara?" Darius asked, his voice heavy like he was afraid to ask. "She was the one who stabbed you?"

I nodded as pain ripped into my chest. "She's gone...I don't know where. I don't know if it was even her, I'm doubting everything." My heart started to splinter. I still didn't want to face this, but I knew Darius needed something else to focus on. So the bond pushed the words out even though I wasn't ready to voice them. "Maybe it wasn't her at all, just a phantom in the shadows."

"She was real enough to hurt you," he growled. "Shit, what if..." He trailed off and I leaned back to get a better look at his expression.

"What?" I pressed.

"Well, she was bonded to my father the same way you are to me. If that bond still exists, maybe...fuck, maybe she's gone to him."

My throat thickened at that idea. It was an awful fucking thought. That she still held some allegiance to Darius's father in her heart. But if the shadows really had consumed what had remained of my sister, it made sense that she would be drawn toward that dark path.

"Let's hope not," I breathed, wondering what I'd do now. I needed to find her, but if she had been willing to kill me, I didn't know if there was anything to find. Maybe she was just a husk filled with darkness. Maybe her face was just a memory and her words had just been sweet lies to make us do her bidding.

I thought of the way she'd hurt Tory in the shadows and cursed myself for being so reckless. For taking Blue that close to her. It was a miracle she'd spared her…

My heart finally came apart, wrenching open the wound which had almost mended during the time I'd thought I could save my sister. The loss which had broken me full bodily and now had come back to haunt me in the flesh.

"Drink from me," Darius demanded, but I shook my head. "Please, it's the least I can do." He tilted his head to one side, fisting his hand in my hair as he dragged me nearer. My nose brushed his neck and the pounding of his pulse called to me like a Siren's song.

"I don't want to cause you more pain," I said through my teeth, trying to pull back despite the hunger carving out my insides.

"You won't." He forced me closer and I succumbed to the urge, slicing my fangs into his throat and tasting the intoxicating heat of his blood.

I groaned, holding him still as I swallowed mouthfuls of his power. The bond sharpened, but I focused on Blue, forcing all treacherous thoughts from my head about Darius. I would never break our trust for the sake of Lionel's twisted magic.

I finally found the strength to pull away and dropped down onto my back, putting some distance between us. Darius rolled onto his back beside me too and we stared up at the ceiling in silence.

"When I saw you in that cave, I thought…" Darius cleared his throat. "I thought I was about to lose you, too." He took my hand and I automatically linked my fingers with his. "I'd be lost without you. I'm so sorry for everything. For what my father did, for Clara."

I swallowed the jagged lump tearing at my throat, squeezing his hand. "I'm sorry too, Darius."

He released a heavy breath and I figured now was the time to say everything. Because my scrape with death had put a lot of things into perspective for me.

"I'm in love with Darcy Vega," I stated, not looking at him. "And she loves me too."

"I know," Darius answered in a low voice. "I knew the second I saw her in that cave crying over you, and I knew the moment I saw you walking into this room with her."

I couldn't gauge how he felt about that, his jaw locked and his eyes still set on the ceiling. My heart pounded as I waited to see if he'd say anything more.

"I tried to tell you the day you and Tory hooked up, but then…" I frowned, my gut twisting at how we'd argued over the Vegas. How stupid that seemed now.

"You thought I'd hate you for it because of what I said about them," he guessed in a broken tone.

I didn't answer, because there was still that possibility. Even after what had happened to him, I didn't know how it might change his view on them. Maybe he'd hate them more. But whether he did or not, I was done pretending. And I'd deal with whatever way Darius decided to react to it. For Blue.

Silence stretched between us and Darius released my hand. My heart squeezed as I waited for him to shout and lose his mind as he sat up and stared down at me. "Don't ever let go of her, Lance. You fucking fight for her until your last breath, you hear me?"

I moved to sit and knocked my forehead against his with a huge sigh of relief. "Thank you."

He clapped me on the shoulder. "You got any more deep dark secrets you wanna share, brother? It's almost dawn and we might as well start tomorrow without a single lie between us."

"Just one," I said with a frown pinching my brow. "Seth found out about us at the Halloween party. He's been threatening to tell Nova, making Darcy do whatever he likes to torment her."

A dangerous growl slid from Darius's throat. "He won't bother you anymore."

I bowed my head as relief rushed through me and loosened the knot around my heart. But with a glimmer of hope for me and Blue, came a lifetime of misery for my friend and her sister.

"Darius," I said seriously, fixing him in my gaze. "I vow on everything I am, if there's a way to change your fate, I'll find it."

His mouth twitched, but I could see my words gave him no hope at all. So I drew him back into my arms and held him until the birds sang the dawn in and the sun dragged its way into the sky like it weighed a thousand tons.

XAVIER

CHAPTER FOUR

I *was flying free over the clouds, soaring, twisting, racing under the shining sun. Then something dark clawed its way across my vision and the clouds were consumed by a heavy shadow.*

A whinny escaped me and I winced as the shadows drew near, coiling around me until I couldn't see.

I jolted awake and shivered as the cold air in my room enveloped me. I tugged my covers higher under my chin with a sigh. My parents' blood ran hot with their Order forms and Father refused to give me the courtesy of heating. When he was away on business trips, I could make sure the house was warmer, but unfortunately he was home.

New Year's Eve had been about as fun as watching a Pitball game without the balls. My parents had attended a gala in Tucana while I was left here to quietly watch the seconds tick down to another year in hell. The only good thing had come in the form of a text from Sofia. I took my phone from under my pillow to read it again, a smile tugging up one corner of my mouth.

Sofia:

Happy New Year, Phillip! I hope all of your dreams come true x

I hope they do too. Because one of them is meeting you.

It was light beyond my window and the clock on my nightstand said it was early morning. I didn't bother to set an alarm most days, what was there to get up for?

Mother had gotten me a new Xbox for Christmas, so at least I could escape from this room in one way. But I was so done with playing games. Since I'd shifted into my Order form at the Vega palace and played with everyone in the snow, I longed to go beyond the manor grounds. I wanted to run and fly and soar through the clouds. It wasn't *fair*.

I slid out of bed, moving to the window and drawing the curtains back. Snow blanketed the world, the grey sky still releasing puffy white flakes which swirled lazily towards the ground.

A dark figure caught my eye far across the snow covered lawn and I stilled. I squinted to try and see better, but they were cloaked, standing on the edge of the frozen lake in the distance.

I glanced over my shoulder, figuring I should alert Father, but when I looked back, they were gone. My heart lurched in my chest as I hunted for them. A path had been carved into the snow all the way up to the house, several floors below me.

A shudder gripped my spine.

Something wasn't right.

"Father!" I called.

A bloody hand slammed against the window and I gasped in alarm, jumping backwards as my heart pounded unevenly. A girl clawed her way up onto my window ledge, her body wrapped in a living shadow which swirled around her like a cloak. Her hood floated back to unveil her face and I met eyes of purest darkness. Her mouth and jaw were smeared with blood and a cruel smile rested on her lips. *Vampire.*

"Father!" I ran for the door and the sound of the window opening reached me.

A blur of darkness rushed past me and the girl caught my arm, twisting me around and throwing me against the door with incredible strength. Her eyes lit with a manic gleam as she pressed herself against me. She was shorter than me, but that didn't mean much in Solaria when I hadn't even been Awakened.

"Xavier!" Her cheeks split into a grin and she threw her arms around my neck, hugging me tight. "You've grown so tall, I thought you were your brother."

"Who are you?" I demanded, reaching for the door handle behind me with shaking fingers. I didn't want to be scared, but holy shit this woman looked like a monster fresh out of Resident Evil.

"I'm the princess," she announced, lowering her head to press her ear to my chest. "And you're the king's son," she breathed. "There's so much power in you, can you feel them?"

"Feel what?" I asked nervously. I had my hand wrapped around the door handle, but it opened inwards dammit.

"The shadows," she purred and the cloak around her moved in response, shifting in an invisible breeze. She walked two fingers up my chest and darkness swirled around the tips, pulling on something deep inside me. As she walked them up to my neck, the shadows within me followed like a magnet, drawing me into their sweet embrace.

I forgot my panic as the darkness purred inside me, following the girl's fingers all the way up to where she stopped at my temple. They curled around my vision and power thrummed through me with every pulse of my heart.

"There," she breathed. "You don't have to hide them. They want to be let out."

"Who are you?" I asked again. "What's your name?"

"Don't you remember me, silly?" She stepped back, cocking her head to one side. She wiped at the blood around her mouth and my gaze scraped over her features. My lips parted as I suddenly recognised her pixie nose and the freckles smattering her cheeks. But it was impossible. Darius had told me what had happened to Lance's sister. How could she be here now?

"Clara?" I gasped and she nodded keenly, looking on the verge of tears.

"You remember me!" She rushed back into my arms and I realised I should have taken the opportunity to run, but the shadows were keeping me calm.

She clung to me with the force of her Order form and I choked out a breath as she started sobbing. "Oh Xavier, he's gone. Gone, gone, *gone*."

"Who's gone?" I croaked.

"My baby brother," she sniffed, pulling herself together again in an instant. She stood back to wipe her tears then sighed. "He had to die, he's not been a good brother at all."

"Wait, you mean *Lance*?" I demanded, my panic resurfacing, clawing its way out of the shadows which were slithering around my heart.

She nodded with a pout, then reached past me to the door handle. "Blood for blood for blood." She shrugged, pushing me aside so hard I nearly fell over as she wrenched the door open. "Take me to him. Where is my king?"

I felt her tugging on the shadows in me and I moved into the corridor to follow her, taking in a slow breath. The shadows were feeding on my grief, and it seemed as if I was standing on the edge of an abyss waiting to fall.

Lance is gone. She killed him.

"Xavier!" Clara said firmly. "Take me to your father." A tendril of shadow coiled out from her, wrapping around my waist and drawing me to her side.

"What happened to you?" I asked, my voice too strained.

The shadows were promising me relief from this pain, but I resisted them as hard as I could, not wanting to lose myself to them too deeply. I focused on Darius, letting my love for him anchor me to who I was. My heart tugged at the thought of my brother losing his best friend and the grief cut me a little sharper.

"I was lost in the darkness." Clara turned to me as we walked down the corridor in the direction of my father's office.

Tears swum in her eyes and for a moment she resembled the girl I'd known growing up. I'd played with her in the gardens with Lance and Darius, we'd made camps in the woods and swum together in the lake. She was so familiar and yet there was something so unfamiliar about her too. Like the shadows had claimed a piece of her for themselves, and that part of her was a violent stranger.

If she'd really hurt her brother…killed him…then this wasn't the girl I knew and loved.

We made it to my father's office and fear twisted inside me at the thought of disturbing him here. Even for something as world-altering as this. It was an instinctual reaction. Because disturbing him at work meant meeting the fury of his fists. Period. But I didn't think it would this time.

I knocked on the door and Clara grabbed the handle.

"Wait-" I gasped a second before she threw it open.

My father looked up from his desk with a sneer, but it dropped away the second he saw Clara, his expression shifting into alarm.

"My king!" She rushed forward, leaping over his desk and landing in his lap.

My mouth fell open as Father reared up, slamming her down onto his desk by the throat with a roar. His other hand was raised, full of flames and his eyes glinted green with his Order form. "Who the fuck do you think you are?!"

Clara was smiling like he wasn't hurting her, clinging to his arm as if they were sharing a loving embrace. "It's me," she rasped. "Clara. Your Guardian."

Shadows twisted around his arm, forcing him to release her and his face shifted into recognition. He jerked his arm away like she'd burned him then rolled up his right sleeve so hard he ripped it. I spotted a brand there of the Cancer star sign and Clara lifted her own arm, showing a matching one with my Father's star sign, Aries.

I backed up into the door with a frown pulling at my brow. Clara had been Guardian bonded to my father? Since when?

"By the stars," Father breathed, taking in the shadows surrounding the girl laying on his desk.

She reached for him with her bloody hands and he tugged her to her feet, seeming to have forgotten I was here. He reached out to brush a lock of hair from her face then pinched her chin hard to study her features. "You've been in the shadows all this time?"

She nodded, looking up at him beneath her lashes. "I felt you always, suffering because I couldn't reach you. Didn't you feel me too?"

Father pressed a finger to the mark on his arm. "No. But I feel you now."

He looked at her almost tenderly and I clenched my jaw, unsure what I was witnessing here. I knew Darius and Lance had felt a strange connection between one another because of the bond, but I didn't know exactly what that was like. At the thought of Lance, the shadows rose again, filling my chest and drinking away my pain.

"She killed Lance," I forced the words out and my father stiffened, his eyes snapping to me.

"What?" he snarled ferociously and Clara backed up.

"My brother didn't come and save me," Clara said defensively. "He *abandoned* me."

Lionel snatched her wrist in his grip, baring his teeth. "Tell me this isn't true!"

She winced from his firm hold and the shadows wrapped around his arm, forcing him off of her. My father swallowed hard, his eyes flickering with concern as he eyed her. She was insanely powerful. A threat. And I could see his mind working out what to do about that.

"I needed blood," Clara hissed, pure darkness pouring from her. She jabbed a finger to Father's chest and a snarl rumbled through his throat. "Don't you *dare* reprimand me. You may be my king, but I'm the Shadow Princess!"

Holy shit.

My father schooled his expression, reaching out to take her hand. "Forgive me, Princess," he said in a soft purr and my jaw almost hit the floor. I'd never heard him speak nicely to anyone. Politely maybe, but *nicely*? No freaking chance.

"You must want to bathe?" he suggested. "I can have some new clothes brought to you, would you like that?"

"Yes," Clara said keenly. "That's just what I need after the day I've had."

Lionel steered her toward the door, his gaze falling on me again as he approached. "Call your brother," he muttered. "Find out everything he knows about this."

I nodded, trying to calm my racing heart as he guided her down the hall and she started humming to herself, caressing his arm as they walked.

"I will always protect you," she sang to him.

The further she moved from me, the more I got the shadows under my control. I willed them away and the moment they sank deeper into the recesses of my body, the grief tumbled down on me. I leaned against the doorway to steady myself, my chest crushing at the thought of Lance's death. He had been more than a good friend to me and my brother, he was *family*.

I forced myself to move, heading back to my room and shutting the door. I took a shaky breath and walked to my bed, grabbing my phone and calling Darius. I had to call him three times before he answered and when he did, it was with a grunt.

"Darius?" I gasped. "What's happened? Is Lance really dead?"

"What?" Darius growled. "Who told you that?"

My mouth opened and closed for a second because I knew this was going to sound insane. "Clara Orion is here," I whispered like the walls were leaning in to listen.

"Fuck, I feared she'd go to Father," he hissed.

"What the hell is going on?" I begged.

"She almost killed Lance when he brought her back from the Shadow Realm," Darius explained.

"Almost?" I clung to that ray of hope with all my heart.

"He's okay," Darius said, a heaviness to his tone. "But it was a close call."

"By the stars, Darius, what the hell is happening?"

He started explaining about how they'd planned to bring her back, how Clara had formed some connection with the Vega twins when Father had sent them into the shadows. My mind whirled as I tried to process this insanity.

"Xavier...that's not all that happened last night," Darius said thickly and something about his tone made my blood chill.

"There's more?" I asked, dreading what he was going to say.

He sighed heavily. "Roxy Vega and I had our Divine Moment."

I froze, clutching the phone tight to my ear as hope blossomed inside me. This was a ray of sunshine in miles and miles of darkness. It was a sliver of happiness my brother could claim for his own. No one could refute it, not even Father.

"She refused to be my mate," Darius forced out and my heart shattered into a thousand jagged shards. "We're Star Crossed."

"No," I demanded, damn right refused it. This wasn't right.

"Yes," Darius said quietly and I could practically hear his heart breaking.

"There's got to be some way-"

"There's no way," he said bluntly.

"*Darius.*"

"Xavier...I'm going to come home soon. We can talk then."

"Of course," I choked out. "I'm so sorry Darius."

The line went dead and I dropped down to the floor, hugging my knees to my chest. The shadows were close, gnawing at the edges of my emotions, begging I let them take away the hurt. But I'd lived my entire life under a roof where who I was had been rejected and beaten down. I knew how to protect the real me from my father. And if I could keep it from him, keeping it from the shadows was easy. It was just a shame being me right now hurt like hell.

DARIUS

CHAPTER FIVE

I lowered my Atlas into my lap as I perched on the edge of Lance's bed, my brother's heartache ringing in my ears. And that wasn't even the end of it. I'd face the same questions, the same despair, the same pity from each and every person I encountered from now until they all knew. At that point I guessed the pity would just fade, but it would never truly leave. *Poor Darius Acrux, he hungered for power so much that it destroyed the only good thing he was ever offered.*

I blew out a deep breath and turned to look at Lance. His brow was creased in pain as he slept and I could only imagine he was reliving the horrors of last night. Of him finally getting his sister back from the shadows only to have her turn on him, try to kill him…

Anger burned through me at the thought of that. I might not have had a lot left for myself in this miserable world, but I had him. And I refused to let this stand. Even if fixing it cost me him too.

I got to my feet, dropped my sweatpants and folded them around my Atlas as I stepped across the room and slipped out of the window.

I circled his house and headed to his back yard where I'd have room to shift.

"Well, hello big boy!" Washer cooed and I looked around to find him peering out of his window in the bungalow next to Orion's with his eyebrows waggling. He was butt fucking naked with his dick pressed to the glass, but as I currently had my own junk on show I was guessing I couldn't say shit about that.

"I needed to see my Guardian," I growled at him, looking back over my shoulder as I glared at him, refusing to turn and give him a full show.

"Naughty, naughty," he chided, waggling a finger at me as he shook his hips and the glass squeaked as his dick rubbed across it. "Good thing I can't taste any lust on you or I'd have to tell tales."

I grunted and looked away from him as I dropped my sweatpants and Atlas to the ground. *Fucking pervert.*

"In fact…all I'm getting from you is the strongest sense of…*despair*…"

I ground my teeth and slammed my mental shields down tight.

"I suggest you keep out of my fucking head if you want to keep your job, you sun baked, pruny ball bag," I snarled as I looked around to glare at him again.

"My boy!" Washer gasped, his focus fixing on my eyes and horror filling his gaze. My heart leapt and sank and crumbled into something far less substantial than dust. "Your eyes! You-"

I shifted fast, fire tearing through my limbs as my bones expanded and my skin stretched to accommodate my Dragon form. Four clawed feet slammed into the ground and the growl that erupted from me was enough to shut him the fuck up.

I snatched my sweatpants and Atlas between my teeth and took off flying as fast as I could.

Running away from my problems had never helped me much before, but I didn't need to deal with that bullshit. What had happened between me and Roxy, that was…ours. It didn't matter that it was fucked up and raw and bleeding, it was still ours. We'd been marked by it inside and out and no matter how much I might have wished it had gone differently, that didn't change it.

I raced through the sky, fire erupting from my jaws as I tried to burn out some of the agony in me but it only flared more fiercely.

I soared to Ignis House, shifting at the last second as I shot towards my open window and ran several steps forward in my Fae form before coming to a halt in the centre of my room. My sweatpants and Atlas tumbled across the carpet at my feet and I dragged in a breath as I tried to calm the rage in me. The hurt.

My gaze caught on my bed and I couldn't help but remember what it had felt like to hold Roxy in my arms all night. How had I been so blind? I'd felt it. I'd felt that pull towards her from the moment I first set my eyes on her when she'd walked into The Orb after her Awakening. It should have clicked together for me right then. She'd been standing beside her twin sister, the two of them like mirror images and yet my entire focus had been on her. I'd hungered for her from that first second, I'd studied her in every quiet moment since. She probably had no idea how many times I'd sat watching her across The Orb or in our Elemental lessons. How every time she walked into a room my skin had prickled and burned with this need to go to her. And like a fucking idiot I'd channelled all of those cravings and desires into exactly what my father had wanted me to do. Hurting her, attacking her, trying to destroy her. Everything in me had driven me at her for love, but I'd let his poison twist it into hate. For what?

Power.

What was the point in power if I was alone with it? It wouldn't keep me warm at night. It wouldn't give me a damn thing that I actually wanted. My whole life I'd felt alone in so many ways. And so had she. But instead of coming together, we'd just pushed ourselves apart until-

I expelled a harsh breath and turned my mind from Roxy Vega and everything she might have been.

There was no point in torturing myself over it. No doubt the stars would see to that thoroughly enough without me needing to dwell on it myself.

And I may not have had anything to live for myself anymore. But that was okay. There were other things I could dedicate myself to now. Like making sure Clara Orion went back to the hell she'd just crawled out of and never returned.

The shadows licked keenly beneath my skin and I embraced them as they curled between my fingers, twisting up and around my arms and kissing my flesh as they burned through the pain in my heart and let me focus. They understood the true call of power. And that thirst I'd always had for it was easy enough to latch onto as I let them feast on the darkness in me.

Sometimes I feared I was too like my father. In moments like this, I relished that corruption in me.

The shadows built beneath my skin until my heart stopped racing. It didn't stop aching, not entirely; I doubted there were enough shadows in the entire Shadow Realm to smother that pain, but it was enough for me to focus.

I crossed the room and pulled a pair of jeans and a black wifebeater from my drawer, dressing quickly and kicking on a pair of boots too.

The chest at the foot of my bed stood open and I moved to it, pushing my hands into the mounds of gold coins and jewels and enjoying the flickering pulse of my magic replenishing as I sought out the darkness hiding with the gems.

It only took a moment to lock onto that feeling of raw energy which accompanied my draining dagger and I pulled it from the centre of the treasure with a sigh of ecstasy as the dark magic called to me.

I worked to conceal the blade with my magic, lashing it to my hip and pouring every drop of talent I had into hiding it from sight. I placed illusions over it and concealment spells to make anyone who looked towards it look away again. Once I was sure it was well hidden, I moved to grab a pouch of stardust from my top drawer and took a calming breath.

It was more than a little tempting to coat myself in golden jewellery again. After letting Lance feed from me and only spending a few hours replenishing I was running low once more, but I should have enough for what I needed to do. It wasn't going to be pretty. It would be quick, brutal and necessary. Clara Orion wasn't the girl she'd once been. I was surer of that than I was of anything right now. She never would have tried to kill Lance before this. Whoever that was wearing her skin now, it wasn't her. They'd dragged some kind of monster back out of the Shadow Realm and I'd happily risk my life to remove her from my father's clutches.

I just hoped Lance would be able to forgive me for it once it was done.

I drew in a deep breath and threw the stardust over my head, thinking of home. Not that the Acrux Manor had ever felt much like home to me. But it was the place where I'd grown up, so despite the cloud of dread and fear which clung to its imposing walls, I guessed it really was home.

My room at Zodiac Academy twisted out of existence and the stars glimmered all around me as they swept me away. For a moment I could have sworn I heard them whispering, mocking, plotting, but then my boots sank into the snow at the foot of the drive of Acrux Manor and they fizzled out of sight again. I guessed I wouldn't be surprised if they were plotting against me now. They'd offered me up the greatest gift they could present and I'd sabotaged it so thoroughly that Roxy had turned it down. I supposed I was cursed instead.

I turned my gaze upon the house where all my nightmares lived and strode up the long drive with my jaw set.

The security guards spotted me and offered respectful nods as I headed up to the enormous entryway with the door big enough to admit a Dragon.

No doubt they'd already sent a message to inform Jenkins of my arrival and just as I reached the smaller door set into the Dragon-sized monstrosity, he pulled it open.

"Master Darius," he purred, head bowed low. "What an unexpected pleasure."

"I need to speak with Father," I said, not bothering with small talk.

Jenkins was my father's man through and through, he'd earned me a beating more than once as I grew up, always ratting me out if I did even the slightest thing out of line. And he knew exactly what he was condemning me to with his tales too. He'd seen my mother patch me up plenty of times. Never said a word, just pursed his lips and cleaned the blood off of the hardwood floors like I'd offended him by bleeding on them. There was definitely no love lost between me and the family butler, though he continued to simper and bow at my feet as if he worshipped the ground I walked on.

"Of course. Would you like to make yourself comfortable in the smoking parlour and I'll see when he can accommodate yo-" Jenkins looked up from his bow and met my gaze as he spoke, his mouth falling open in shock as he took in the black rings surrounding my irises.

Before I had to endure the inevitable question, Xavier appeared at the top of the sweeping staircase before me, his hand gripping the golden bannister so tightly that his knuckles shone white through the skin.

"I didn't want to believe it," he breathed, his features painted in heartbreak which cut right through me.

I opened my mouth, but nothing left my lips and a moment later he'd made it to the foot of the stairs and thrown his arms around me as a choked sob escaped him. His embrace was bruising and for a moment all I could do was close my eyes and accept the small comfort of being held in my brother's arms.

"I don't understand," he whispered as he pulled back to look up at me. Though he didn't have to tilt his head as much as he used to. Despite Father's neglect, Xavier was growing into a man and even though he didn't have a Dragon lurking beneath his flesh, there was still a strength in his gaze which spoke of his resilience. You didn't survive in this household without growing a thick skin and learning how to channel pain into strength. "Why would she say no? She loved you, I could see it in her eyes, I could feel it between you, I-"

"Enough," I growled as my heart throbbed and splintered. "Whatever you think you saw, it wasn't that. She might have been drawn to me, but she saw me clearly enough. She locked eyes with the demon lurking within my soul and knew she'd be better off away from me than bound to it."

"Darius!" Xavier gasped. "Don't say that! You can't seriously believe that she's better off not-"

"To what do we owe this unexpected visit?" Father's cold voice tore us apart and Xavier released me as he leapt aside. Softness wasn't tolerated in this household. Our own mother had stopped embracing us a long time ago, and overt displays of affection between the two of us would result in punishment later.

I drew in a breath as I turned to look up the stairs. Jenkins was gone, he'd clearly scuttled off to tell my father that I was here and Mother had shown up too.

I refused to hesitate and lifted my chin as I looked up at the two of them as they paused at the top of the stairs. I looked straight into my mother's eyes and a strangled scream escaped her as she took in the black rings surrounding mine.

She lurched off of the top step and ran to me as my eyebrows rose in surprise.

"How did this happen?!" she cried as she reached me, her hands clasping my face as she forced my gaze down to hers and tears swam in her deep brown eyes.

My mother was a beautiful woman, but it had been a long time since I'd seen anything even bordering on true emotion from her. She was like a pretty doll who walked and talked and hung from father's arm while batting her eyelashes at the people he wanted to impress. I'd heard a rumour once that he sometimes leant her out to his friends to secure political deals, letting them have a night with her in exchange for support to his agenda in the Council. I hadn't wanted to believe it but there was a cold, cynical part of me which was almost certain it was true. And it was impossible for me to tell how she felt about that. Or if she felt anything at all about anything most of the time.

But right now, she was looking at me like her heart was breaking. Like this thing that had happened to me might as well have happened to her.

"Who was it?" Father asked and my gaze whipped to him as his eyes lit with a thirst for the answer. His heart clearly wasn't breaking. In fact, I doubted he had one at all.

I let the shadows loose beneath my skin as I used them to drown out some of my pain, working to hide it from him as I moved away from Mother to answer him.

"Roxanya Vega," I growled, her name sticking to my tongue like a pill too bitter to swallow.

Father's lips tugged into a cruel smirk, his eyes glittering with triumph which I failed to understand.

"So she can take orders well after all," he purred.

"What does that mean?" I demanded, my hand curling into a fist as my Dragon shifted beneath my skin and I moved up the stairs towards him.

"Only that I saw the way you looked at her at Christmas," he replied with a shrug. "And I warned her that the two of you were not a good match. Seems like she agreed with me on that."

"Did you Coerce her to do this to me?" I asked in a low tone as an ugly truth shifted in his gaze and my heart leapt at that possibility. It wouldn't change what had happened, but if I knew she hadn't truly wanted to say no to me, that was *something*…although as I considered that, I knew I didn't really believe it. She'd spoken plainly enough when she tore my heart from my chest. She'd known exactly what she was choosing and why. And I knew it too. I'd earned this fate from her. I'd failed too many times to even dream of anything else.

"Don't be absurd," Father replied. "Why on earth would I want my own son to be so unhappy? Besides, how could I have possibly guessed that you'd be mated to a *Vega?*" His sneer made me want to punch him and my fist tightened, but I restrained myself. I wasn't ready to face my father yet. And there was something else I'd come here to do.

"I know that Clara came to you," I said, changing the subject before I snapped. "After Lance fought to return her from the Shadow Realm and she tried to fucking kill him."

Father arched a brow like he could see where I was going with this and he clearly had no intention of following along.

"Yes. I owe him a debt of thanks. My Guardian has been returned to me safe and sound." The excitement in his cold eyes was impossible to miss and the shadows beneath my flesh stirred hungrily with the desire to tear him apart.

"He almost *died*," I snarled. "She's clearly unhinged and-"

A door banged open in the corridor behind him and I looked up just as a blur of motion shot towards me.

"Darius!" Clara squealed, shooting at me with such speed that I could barely brace for impact before she collided with me.

I was knocked back against the bannister as she wrapped her arms and legs around me and the thin robe she was wearing fell open to reveal her naked body.

The shadows within me roared and flared to life beneath my flesh at her touch. For a moment, I was blinded by them as my knees buckled and I slumped down to the steps beneath her as she straddled me.

She pushed her hands into my hair as I gasped for breath and she tilted my gaze up to meet hers.

The girl I'd once loved like a sister looked down at me but her features had sharpened, her pale skin was almost translucent and tinted black veins pulsed beneath her flesh.

"Look how big you got," Clara gasped, her voice almost childlike but with an edge of darkness which warned me that she wasn't the same girl anymore at all. "So big and strong, like your daddy." Her hands roamed over my chest, my arms, igniting a swell of darkness from the shadows within me everywhere she touched.

I was immobilised by them, my limbs locked as I stared at her. She wriggled on my lap and I frowned as I looked down at her naked body with my skin crawling. There were marks on her pale flesh almost like tattoos, but they writhed and danced on her skin, moving from place to place like living shadows.

"What's the matter, Darius?" she breathed, leaning so close that her breath washed over my lips and the taste of soot and chalk coated my tongue. "Is your heart bleeding for Roxanya?"

She painted a cross on my chest above my heart with a finger, her nail biting into the skin through my wifebeater and causing blood to flow.

"Give in to the shadows and you'll forget her," she whispered. "And then we can destroy her together if you like…"

Her lips brushed mine and a deep growl resounded through my chest as Dragon fire poured through my limbs and burned through the shadows which she was driving beneath my skin.

This creature had tried to kill Lance, she was dark and twisted and bound to my father. The only thing she could cause by being here was further pain. And I refused to let that happen.

She pressed her lips down on mine more firmly and I snatched the draining dagger from my hip before driving it straight at her gut.

Her fingers caught my wrist at the final second, her grip impossibly strong as she stopped my attack and the shadows rose up so thickly that I couldn't see anything but her amidst the darkness. Her fangs snapped out and she lunged at me, but I'd already thrown my other hand up between us.

Fire slammed into her with the force of an explosion and she was knocked off of me, tumbling down the stairs as the shadows rose up all around her.

Father shouted at me to stop, but he didn't intervene as he remained at the top of the stairs watching our fight. Mother and Xavier had run for safety in the corridor beyond the entrance hall, but I only had eyes for the monster who'd tried to kill my friend. Rage consumed me like an inferno, feasting on my grief and giving me an outlet for it as my muscles bunched and my magic burned beneath my skin.

I dropped the dagger and let out a roar of rage as I lunged after her, shooting spears of ice and an inferno of fire at her with every drop of power

I had.

Clara screamed in agony and for a moment I thought I'd succeeded in ending her but before I could press my advantage, the shadows reared out from her and snaked their way around my limbs.

I was thrown backwards, slamming into the wall with a cry of pain as the shadows coiled around me, forcing their way inside me, choking, drowning suffocating. They tore into the agony of my heart and spilled the sharpness of the pain I harboured through me in a never ending torrent which cleaved my soul from my flesh.

I couldn't hear anything, see anything, do anything other than feel the agony of all my failures, the hopelessness of all I'd ever dreamed for and knew I'd never claim.

It was eating me from the inside out, consuming and devouring everything good in me and drawing every hateful, brutal piece of me to the surface of my skin as agony thundered through my limbs.

"That's enough, Clara," Father's voice cut through the fog of shadows and suddenly they withdrew. "I've only got one Heir now after all."

The world came back into focus and I found myself panting at the foot of the stairs on my back with Clara standing over me, a cloak of shadows now hiding her nudity.

"That wasn't very nice, Darius," she pouted. "I'm the Shadow Princess and you're a prince. We should be happy together."

"Fuck you," I panted. "You tried to kill Lance."

"I'm sorry," she said, not sounding sorry in the least. "But he was a bad, bad brother. Daddy told me we need him though, so I won't hurt him again."

"Daddy? Your father's been dead a long time, Clara," I grunted, wondering if she'd lost all sense of reality as I tried to reach for my magic but it was all gone. I was entirely tapped out and stuck at her mercy.

"Silly, I don't mean the man who sired me." She giggled and I frowned as Father's footsteps approached and he stood over me too.

"Clara has that little nickname for me," Father said mildly like that wasn't weird as fuck.

Clara turned to look at him with adoration swimming in her gaze, tiptoeing up to press a kiss to his lips as her hand trailed down over his waistband and cupped his junk. The look my father gave her said he didn't mind that at all and I fought the urge to vomit in my mouth.

"Your wife is right there," I snarled, glancing behind him to where my mother and Xavier stood watching us like they didn't know what the fuck was going on.

Father only shrugged. "The bond between a Guardian and their Ward transcends any other commitments. You should know that well from your relationship with Lance. Catalina is open to the needs of my bond with Clara being fulfilled."

Mother didn't respond to that, her concerned gaze fixed on me like the only thing she cared about in all of this was making sure I was alright.

I was sure my repulsion was scrawled across my face, but they didn't seem to care. Clara was young enough to be his daughter - if she was even truly Clara anymore. I certainly didn't see the girl I used to know shining back out of her eyes.

"Just say you're sorry, Darius, and we can be friends again," Clara demanded with a pout.

"Fuck you."

"*Say it,*" Father snapped and a ring of Dark Coercion laced his tone so thickly that I had no choice but to obey.

"Sorry." The word left my lips, but the contempt with which it was delivered was clear for everyone to hear.

Clara didn't seem to care about that though, and she used her shadows to force me back to my feet before making my spine bend until she could place her cold lips against mine again.

"All is forgiven," she breathed as she pulled back, placing my dagger back into my hand casually, like she had no fear at all of me using it on her again. "And tell Lance I forgive him now too. Daddy says I have to."

"Good." Father took her hand and drew her away from me as he headed down the corridor to the smoking parlour and we all trailed along in his wake.

I hooked the dagger through my belt as anger and defeat twisted through my gut, falling back into line like always. But one day soon, I was determined to buck this trend.

Xavier gave me a wide eyed expression to convey his concern, but I shrugged it off. The physical pain in my body was nothing to the gut wrenching ache in my heart anyway.

I hesitated a moment as I spotted Lance and Clara's mother, Stella, sitting in a chair by the fire, but no one else commented so I guessed she'd been here a while already. She didn't seem too worked up by her daughter's reappearance either. In fact, as Clara strutted in with her fingers laced through my father's, she looked decidedly put out. I guessed if he really was going to start fucking Clara that would be awkward for his old side piece as her mother.

"Aren't you going to greet your aunt, Darius?" Stella cooed and I moved forward to place a kiss on her sharp cheekbone before taking a seat by the fire.

Father sat opposite me and Clara instantly climbed into his lap. Stella clucked her tongue like she didn't approve and I wondered if they were going to discuss this new development or if Father just planned on trading her in for the younger model and leaving it at that.

Mother and Xavier crossed the threshold, but Father fixed them with a glare and sent a gust of wind to push them back out of the room before knocking the door shut for good measure. He threw a silencing bubble over us and I waited to see where this was going.

"You interrupted our discussions, Darius, but I suppose it makes sense for you to join us," he said darkly. "*But you may not repeat any of these plans after you leave this room.*" The Dark Coercion swept under my skin and bound me to his words like a chain tightening around my neck.

"What plans?" I asked. I may not have been able to repeat them, but I could sure as hell work against them if I could figure out how.

"With the shadows firmly in our grasp and Clara returned to me, I believe that I am closing in on my goal of securing enough power to claim the throne for myself. Now that I can control the Fifth Element, I have a clear advantage over the Vegas and-"

"They have the shadows too," Clara pointed out casually and my heart dropped as she revealed the secret we'd been guarding like it was nothing at all.

I gritted my teeth as I forced myself not to react in any way outwardly, but inside my pulse was hammering and fear was closing in on me. Roxy might not have wanted to be mine, but that didn't change how I felt about her. It didn't mean I'd be letting anything happen to her.

"What?" Father demanded, leaping from his seat and damn near knocking Clara on her ass as he dropped her. She managed to recover and flitted back and forth before the fire as he paced.

"Are you sure?" Stella demanded of her daughter.

"Yes, Mom. Quite sure. I almost got Tory to join me in the dark through them a little while ago and I tasted them on Darcy too. The shadows never lie to me," Clara said with a childish smile.

I didn't know what she meant about drawing Roxy to her, but I didn't like it. I knew she'd been tempted by the shadows and I'd been checking up on her as often as I could to try and help her, but that hadn't been easy before she'd chosen to be Star Crossed with me. What hope would I have of helping her with them now? If anything, this curse on us would only drive her closer to them.

Silence fell and my heart pounded as I took in the darkness in my father's gaze. This was it, the final straw. Between their Phoenix Order being revealed and now their hold on the shadows too, it was impossible for him to deny that they were more powerful than him.

And that could only mean one thing. He'd want to kill them.

"They're not even close to mastering their magic," I said quickly. "And they have no way to learn about the shadows, so-"

"Are you seriously trying to shield your whore from me after she ripped your heart out and tossed it to the wind?" Father sneered. He hadn't even asked which one of us had refused the bond. He just knew. He knew and he wanted to twist the knife.

"I just think that trying to kill the Vega Heirs would be incredibly risky. If anyone ever figured out-"

"The Vegas are a problem which I will solve without your help, *boy.* You've made it clear that your judgement has been impaired by them. But don't worry, once you have time to adjust to the curse Roxanya has placed on you, I'm sure you'll feel less inclined to shield her from anything. And once you're ready to impart some revenge on her, I'll be waiting to help. In the meantime, I think we should focus on my more immediate competition. It's time I made progress towards claiming the throne for myself. My grasp upon the shadows is improving. I need to prepare to rise above the other Celestial Councillors."

My heart pounded at the thought of that. I'd known it was coming, but I'd hoped we had more time. And with the Dark Coercion he'd placed on me, I couldn't even warn the other Heirs that he was coming for their parents.

"When?" I breathed, wondering how long I had to derail these plans, how long I had to figure out how to challenge him myself and remove him from his position as the Fire Councillor and take his place.

"Soon." Father growled, refusing to give me more than that despite the binds he'd placed on me. "In the meantime, you need to get back to school and keep an eye on those girls for me. Make sure they're kept beneath your heel a while longer yet. I'll inform the press about your little...*incident.*" His gaze scrutinised the black rings in my eyes for a moment before he shrugged. "I'll tell them that you were the one to refuse. That you put your responsibilities as Heir before the selfish desires of fate. And for good measure, I think we'll bring your wedding forward too."

"What?" I gasped. "You can't- I *can't* get married until I graduate, it's the law. I've got two and half years left at Zodiac before-"

"Fine," he snapped like the law was nothing more than an irritation to him. And I guessed technically it was because he only needed to get the other Councillors to vote with him to have it changed. "We'll make it two days after your graduation then. But I think it's prudent you spend more time with you fiancé in public. I'll set up a photoshoot for the weekend...and I'll get the beauticians to do some work on her too...and make sure they photoshop the pictures...maybe we'll have the shoot at night so there's plenty of shadow..."

I just stared at him with my lips parted as he continued to prattle on about getting the kingdom excited for my marriage to fucking Mildred Canopus just hours after Roxy Vega had torn my heart in two and set my soul alight for good measure. My fucking hideous second cousin with a personality even more repugnant than her face. But he didn't care. He didn't give one shit about that. It was all just a game to him, and I was just a piece on the chessboard. He needed nice little Dragon grand babies to carry on the Acrux name, and who gave a shit if I'd never even be able to get my dick hard enough to make them with her? He'd probably just have her inseminated once he figured that out anyway. That's what he'd done to his Storm Dragon pet when he wouldn't fuck my Aunt Juniper to get her pregnant. And now she had three boys running around her ankles, waiting to see if they'd turn into Storm Dragons too when their Orders Emerged.

Because that was what my father did. He got his way. In everything. No matter what it cost other people. He didn't care that he made Dante Oscura father children he'd never see with a woman who wasn't his wife, he just wanted Storm Dragons with the Acrux name attached. And he certainly didn't care about tethering me to a life of misery so long as I produced the right kind of Heirs too.

Fuck my life.

Eventually, Father grew bored of my silence and miserable expression and told me to fuck off, though he used slightly politer words. We had guests after all. I needed to get back to the academy to make sure Lance was alright anyway. And I guessed I had to face everyone too. No doubt the entire place would be whispering about me and Roxy for the rest of term and I couldn't say I was looking forward to that.

But what other choice did I have? I'd offered her the world, but I'd waited too long to do it. So now I just had to face the consequences of that and live with the fact that this was all my fault. And there wasn't a thing I could do to change it.

TORY

CHAPTER SIX

"**T**ory!" Darcy's voice found me where I was hiding in sleep.
I groaned as I rolled over, tugging a pillow over my head as an incessant thumping started up at my door.

"What's going on, Tor? Let me in!"

I shifted towards wakefulness, but my body recoiled like I was afraid of what I'd find there. My thoughts were fuzzy with sleep, but there was an ache in my body which resounded right down to my hollow soul. I couldn't remember why. I didn't want to remember.

The sound of the door bursting open assaulted me and I recoiled further into my bed as everything came crashing back in on me. The blizzard, the broken promises to Darcy and Orion, the look in Darius's eyes when-

"What the hell is going on?" Darcy demanded. "And where the fuck were you last night? We needed you, Tor! *I* needed you." Her voice hitched on that last sentence and I shoved the blankets off of me as my heart throbbed painfully.

Darcy had thrown her hands over her face to try and stop her tears and I instantly jumped up and wrapped my arms around her, tugging her close.

"I'm sorry, Darcy," I breathed, my soul aching as I felt her pain. I'd let her down last night. She'd been waiting for us in that cave with Orion when-

"What happened?" I asked, fearing that I might not want to know.

"We got Clara back, no thanks to you and Darius," she said, trying to wrench out of my arms but I wouldn't let go. "It took *everything* we had to create the bridge. And then…then…"

"What?" I breathed, sensing the desperation in her voice as a sliver of fear raced through me.

"Then she turned on us. On *him*. She stabbed him with the draining dagger and drank so much of his blood that he barely had a drop left. He almost *died* without the two of you there to help us!"

Darcy ripped herself out of my arms and my lips parted on a thousand empty apologies. But what could I say? I'd done what she said. I'd let her down when she'd needed me more than ever. I couldn't even get that right. She deserved so much more from me than broken promises and meaningless apologies.

Darcy strode away from me towards the foot of my bed, her fists clenching as she tried to restrain some of the emotions warring within her and I dropped my gaze to the carpet by my feet.

"How did you save him?" I asked because she said he'd almost died and I could only imagine that she wouldn't be here now, wasting her time on me unless he was alright.

Darcy barked a merciless laugh. "*Seth.* He heard me screaming for help and proved that he has some kind of soul rattling around in the depths of his depravity. And then Darius finally showed up to help with the rest. Even with all three of us, it was a close call."

"Darius came to help you?" I breathed, my heart throbbing painfully as I spoke his name.

"Better late than never," Darcy muttered bitterly.

I nodded, looking down at my toes where they were curling against the carpet. I'd painted my toenails pink for some reason at some point before all of this and I couldn't tear my eyes away from the colour. It was so light and happy and innocent. Like baby pink. It didn't suit me at all. Why had I chosen such a cheery colour?

"You're not even going to explain yourself?" Darcy demanded, whirling back towards me, but I didn't lift my gaze to her. I didn't want her to see my eyes. I didn't want to give her this excuse like it was okay that I'd let her down just because the stars had a shitty sense of timing.

"I'm so sorry," I said, my breath catching in my chest as I curled my fingers so tightly that my nails cut into my palms. "But sorry doesn't feel like enough. It doesn't make it okay. It doesn't excuse me letting you down like that…"

"So why did you?!" Darcy screamed, making me flinch. I wasn't sure she'd ever yelled at me like that before.

I shook my head, my heart throbbing painfully as I remembered where I'd been last night. The way I'd been getting ready to go and meet everyone down at Aer Cove, but I suddenly found myself late. How I'd felt this urgent tug in my chest, demanding I walk straight out of my room then leading me away from my sister and Orion and the magic I'd promised to play a part in and drawing me down a path I couldn't turn from. My bare feet pressing into the snow because I hadn't even grabbed any shoes, let alone a coat. I'd felt like a puppet on a string, dancing to a tune I didn't know and yet I hadn't been afraid. I'd been hopeful. At least I had been until my brain had caught up with my heart.

"Tell me, Tory!" Darcy demanded, striding towards me and shoving me as her rage and heartache fuelled her actions.

I stumbled back a step towards my bed and she shoved me again when I still failed to offer her an answer.

"What could possibly have been so urgent that you would let us down like that?" The third time she pushed me, my legs knocked against my bed and I fell back on my ass.

I let out a heavy breath and raised my gaze to meet hers.

Darcy sucked in a horrified breath, recoiling as she raised a trembling finger to point at me. "What the hell has happened to your eyes?"

I chewed on my bottom lip, knowing I had to tell her. That she had to hear it from me even if it tore me apart to say it.

"Last night, I...I don't really know how to explain it but, while I was waiting to meet you, something happened. It was like time just slipped away from me and then all of a sudden the stars were calling me to them. I didn't choose to go, they just took me and when I followed the path they'd laid out, I came to a clearing in the snow and..."

"And what?" Darcy breathed, dropping into the space beside me and taking my hand in hers. Blood smeared against her fingers from the crescent shaped wounds on my palms, but she didn't comment on it.

I swallowed a thick lump in my throat. "Darius was waiting for me," I murmured.

My heart lurched, but I forced myself to go on. I'd stood across that clearing from him and he'd looked at me like everything somehow made sense to him. My heart had pounded for him and I'd wanted to dive straight into his arms and never let go. But I'd held myself back, knowing in my soul that that wasn't right. That it wasn't how I'd felt about him the last time I'd seen him. Yes I'd wanted him, ached for him, desired him, but I'd also hated him, feared him, despised him. There was something in the magic of that place which had wanted me to forget all of that, but I knew my own heart. I *knew* it and I wasn't going to have it governed by anyone but me.

"I don't understand," Darcy said slowly. "You mean he'd lured you there somehow, or-"

"No. The stars brought him too. Our constellations appeared in the sky overhead and we were locked in this little bubble of solitude that no one and nothing in the world could shatter. It was ours. He called it destiny."

"What destiny?" she whispered, her grip on my fingers tightening like she already knew. Which she must have. We'd learned about this in class. We'd talked about it with Gabriel. She'd seen my eyes. She just didn't want to believe it any more than I did.

"Apparently the stars chose him for me," I said. "And me for him. And they wanted us to choose it too..."

"He's your Elysian Mate?" Darcy whispered.

"I always did have terrible taste in men," I muttered. "The stars obviously pick badly for me too."

"Did he do this to you? Did he say no to-"

"It was me," I said, shaking my head. "He wanted it. Wanted me. Wanted to own me and keep me and have this hold on me for the rest of my life."

"I don't think that's how it works, Tory. He would have loved you, he would have-"

"Love?" I scoffed. "Who has ever loved me? Look at all the things he's done to me. That isn't love. It's hate."

"But maybe he could have changed. He isn't always so bad. He looked after you before when you needed him, you fought together against the Nymphs. Hell, you even slept with him twice. Why would you deny yourself the chance to-"

"Because it wasn't a chance, Darcy," I said bitterly. "It was forever. All or nothing. Saying yes meant letting him own me. It meant I'd have to love him no matter what he did to me. What if he was just as cruel to me in love as he'd been in hate?"

"You think you might have been stuck in a life where he'd continue to hurt you?" Darcy asked, shaking her head like it was so obvious that wouldn't have been the case.

"Yes...no...maybe. The point is I don't know. How could I agree to forever with someone who had treated me like that? He never even tried to make up for any of it before last night. He never felt a drop of remorse for it until he realised he'd been doing all of those things to the girl who fate had chosen for him."

"But Tory you've *still* got forever with him," Darcy said desperately, her eyes swimming with tears for me. "Instead of forever with him loving you, you've got forever pining for him. Don't you remember what Professor Zenith told us about Elysian Mates? You only get one. And if you don't choose them, you'll never love or be loved by any other..."

"What difference does that make?" I muttered. "No one's ever loved me anyway, Darcy."

"Don't be ridiculous!" she snapped, shaking my arm like she wanted me to realise what I'd done. But I already had realised. And it was too late to change it even if I wanted to.

"It wasn't like I had long to decide," I said, releasing a slow breath. "All I know is that I was suddenly standing there being asked to choose a man who's hurt me time after time. Who tried to drown me and tormented me and... It doesn't even matter now."

"It does," Darcy insisted.

"Why didn't he just apologise *before* then?" I asked, tears burning the backs of my eyes. "If I'd known that he felt bad for it, that he even gave the littlest bit of a shit about everything he'd done to me then maybe I could have made another choice."

"He never said anything to you when you hooked up with him?" Darcy asked softly.

"Nothing about that. He told me he's obsessed with me and that he wants to lay claim to me, but that's not love. It's infatuation at best. Like I was some challenge he wanted to conquer or a prize to win. Why should I have to agree to that?" The bite in my voice was bitter and harsh and entirely forced and I knew that she could tell. But it was all I had. Because if I gave in to the pain of this heartache then I had no idea how dark it might be within it.

"Maybe you should talk to him," Darcy suggested weakly because she knew it wouldn't make any difference just as well as I did. The decision had been made. There was no going back. Talking with him wouldn't change it.

"I don't imagine he wants to talk to me," I said, turning away from her to look out at the cloud filled sky.

"I saw him at Lance's place, he seemed...I don't think he's doing so well..."

A raw slice of pain cut into me at that knowledge. I hadn't wanted to hurt him. I'd just wanted to be free. Free of fate or destiny or the stars. Free to choose my own life and live it how I wanted, not how I was told to.

"It's got to be worth *trying* to talk to him..." Darcy pushed.

"He won't want to talk to me," I insisted.

"I'm sure he can understand why you made the choice you did. And perhaps if you talk then you could try and figure out a way to-"

"It's worse than that," I muttered, the reality of what I'd done last night burning through me. "Caleb messaged me after it had happened and I... I don't even know why, but I was just hurting so much and I wanted to try and forget about it. To try and prove that I could feel something for someone else and the stars couldn't rob me of that..."

"Oh, Tory..." Darcy breathed and I could tell she was disappointed in me. Hell, I was disappointed in myself. I'd literally fallen back on the same old habits I'd always used to distract myself from my problems. And to make it worse, Caleb was one of Darius's closest friends. I hadn't planned it, I hadn't meant to do it, but I'd been drowning when he messaged me, burning up in pain and heartache and I'd just felt so alone. It had been selfish and stupid and it had only really made me feel worse, like I was betraying Darius somehow despite the fact that I'd never been his in the first place. Was that how it would be for the rest of my life? Any time I was with anyone else I'd be thinking of him, feeling like I was in the wrong just because I'd wanted to choose my own fate?

"Maybe I'm the one who doesn't deserve happiness," I said. "Maybe Darius deserves better than *me*."

"Of course he doesn't," Darcy growled. "He had every opportunity to change the way he treated you. He had every chance to apologise if he felt as strongly about you as he claimed to. I understand why you made the decision you did."

"But you don't agree with it?"

Silence stretched between us and Darcy drew me into her arms. I buried my face against her shoulder and the tears slid free of my hold on them as I gave in again.

My aching heart felt a little less frayed as I held her, though in no way healed.

"It's not that I don't agree," she whispered. "It's just...I can't bear the idea that you're cursed now. That you'll never have love because of this. Because of *him.*"

"Well, he wanted to break me. So I guess he got his wish."

Darcy shook her head, but she couldn't really deny it. This pain which had carved its way into my heart when I'd refused him was only growing sharper. I didn't expect it to heal any time soon. In fact, I didn't expect it to heal at all.

I'd wanted to choose my own fate and this was what I'd decided on. So I was just going to have to live with it.

Darcy pulled me into the bed with her and we curled up beneath the covers together like we used to when we were little kids. She didn't ask me anything else about it because there wasn't anything more that I could say. And I just tried to take what comfort I could from the only love I'd ever know.

I emerged from the shower with dripping wet hair and a dripping wet mood. I couldn't help it. This ache in me wasn't going away and thinking of anything other than Darius Acrux was proving to be damn near impossible.

Darcy was sitting on my bed and she looked up from her Atlas as I walked into the middle of the room with a towel wrapped around me.

"Orion?" I guessed as her Atlas pinged and the corner of her mouth curled up with that secret kind of smile which said she was lighting up from the inside out.

"I just feel like I have to keep checking he's okay and he's teasing me about it," she said, lowering her Atlas like she was going to put it away.

"Don't do that," I said, waving at the thing. "My choice with Darius has nothing to do with you and Orion. I don't want you to ever feel like you have to hide your happiness from me."

"I don't think that," she replied, but the tension around her eyes betrayed the truth and I sighed.

We'd been hiding out in my room all day. Darcy snuck out to find snacks at lunch time and she'd been keeping an eye on FaeBook too. Clearly no one had seen Darius yet either as there'd been no stories emerging about us, but they'd come. I couldn't hide in here forever. And I wouldn't.

Today, all of the students who went home for Christmas had returned to the academy in time for classes to resume tomorrow and there was a start of term dinner being held in The Orb.

Geraldine had been texting us all day, double checking what time we were arriving and what we were going to be wearing as if it was a damn royal occasion. I'd been letting Darcy handle the replies. In all honesty, I hadn't dared touch my own Atlas. I couldn't face the idea of finding a message from Darius there. Or worse, not finding one.

"Geraldine has suggested we wear pink," Darcy said mildly and I forced myself to snort a laugh.

Beneath the flow of water in the shower, I'd let the shadows have me. They'd swept me up and stolen my pain and I'd coated my skin in a layer of darkness before I'd banished them again. Every time I did it, it got easier. And it felt a little better too. I knew their call was addictive, but I was too focused on our end goal to care. I needed to master them. I needed to be able to wield them better than anyone else. Better than Orion or Darius and especially better than Lionel. He had the Shadow Princess with him now and we still didn't know what that meant. But I was sure it couldn't be a good thing for us. And I had to admit that escaping my pain and sinking into the shadows for a while was a welcome relief even if it came with risks.

"Fine. Let's wear pink," I agreed.

"I told her we'd go with red. I've already been eyeing up that cute skirt in your closet and I think you should wear this dress."

I looked over at her as she presented the dress to me. I'd bought it before Halloween with vague thoughts of a devil costume coming together before my Pegasus master plan occurred to me. It was short and low cut and kinda screamed I-wanna-get-laid which I definitely didn't need to do again anytime soon.

"You don't think it's a bit much for dinner at The Orb?" I asked.

"Look, Tor, I don't wanna freak you out or anything but you know that people aren't just going to accept the fact that you and Darius are Star Crossed now like it's nothing. There's going to be questions and pointing and photos which will most definitely get leaked to the press and if you don't wanna look like the girl who just had her heart crushed, then…"

I sighed, accepting the dress and smiling at Darcy as she moved forward to do my hair and makeup for me. I never would have asked for the TLC, but she knew when I needed it most and a twin pamper session was clearly in order right now for both of us. Orion might have turned out to be okay, but she'd still had one hell of a fright and I knew it was killing her that she couldn't be with him now. I was half tempted to claim the fucking throne just so that I could change the law about student teacher relationships and set them free.

We took our time getting ready and Darcy didn't even mention the fact that I was clearly stalling as I slowly applied eyeliner to my newly black-ringed eyes. The makeup made my Star Crossed mark stand out even more which was why I'd decided to do it. I needed to rip the band aid off, head out there with my resting bitch face firmly in place and let the nosey motherfuckers at this academy say whatever the fuck they wanted about it right away. Then it could become yesterday's news and I could move the hell on with my life. Easy. Or not so much, but I was going to front it out like a trooper come hell or high water.

When I finally gave in to the inevitable and stood to leave, Darcy caught my hands in hers and stopped me.

"What do you want me to tell people about this?" she asked, her gaze skipping between my eyes uncertainly as she took in the difference.

I was finding the change to my eyes to be one of the hardest parts in this. Not because of any dumb vanity reasons, but because now Darcy wasn't my identical twin anymore. I mean, sure, our hair had been different for ages and we wore pretty different clothes half the time, but that was all superficial. A quick dye job and a set of matching outfits and no one would have ever been able to tell the difference between us...until now.

"Nothing," I said, shaking my head so that the loose curls she'd given me danced across my spine. "Tell them nothing. They can figure it the fuck out for themselves. I'll give our friends a basic explanation and that's it. I don't give a shit what anyone else thinks anyway."

Darcy's eyes watered like her heart was breaking for me and I lifted my chin as I fought off the urge to fall weeping into her arms. I was the one who'd chosen this. I didn't get to cry and pout about it like I was so hard done by. I'd always lived with the consequences of my actions before and I didn't intend to stop now.

I gave her a tight smile then reached out to grab my Atlas. I couldn't leave this room without checking to see if he'd messaged me. I just couldn't.

The first thing that popped up on the screen was my horoscope from this morning and I sighed as I tapped on it.

Good morning, Gemini.

The stars have spoken about your day!

Today marks the start of a new chapter in your life where you will learn to tread the path less wandered. It's time to face the consequences of your actions and find out if you can survive the fallout or not. You may come to blows with a Leo today, but take heart, if you travel the road of least resistance then you can avoid a collision altogether. However, the stars are feeling vexed with you and you may find your luck on a downward spiral for some time to come.

"Brilliant," I muttered, flipping my Atlas around to show Darcy and she scanned it quickly.

"Well, it says you can avoid coming to blows with a Leo so it sounds like you don't have to argue with him at least."

"Yeah, if I travel the road of least resistance which I'd guess means avoiding him altogether. And that sounds great, aside from the fact that I live in the same building as him, attend classes with him, eat my meals in the same place as him and have a political future surrounding that fucking throne which will clearly tangle me up with him for the rest of my life. Not to mention our cosy little shadow lessons." I sighed, turning back to my Atlas so that Darcy didn't have to dignify that pouty rant with a response, but her hand landed on my arm all the same and she gave me a little squeeze.

There were several messages from Geraldine and Sofia, a few mentions in newspaper articles which I didn't read beyond the headlines (there were very mixed accounts of the Nymph attack at the palace over Christmas and depending on what you read, we'd either saved the day or come really damn close to causing everyone's deaths. The only thing all the papers could agree on was us being Phoenixes and we'd had more than a few requests for interviews and photoshoots about that). Nothing from Darius. But what did I expect anyway?

I sighed again, wondering if I was going to make a habit out of making pathetic little noises like that, and locked my Atlas before painting on a smile for Darcy. She was wearing a tight red skirt and a cute black top with roses printed on it. She didn't look like her whole world had almost fallen apart last night and I hoped I didn't either.

"Let's go," I said, kicking my stilettos on and heading for the door.

Darcy moved to my side as I hesitated with my fingers on the door handle, but what was I going to do, hide in my room forever? No. That just wasn't me. When I'd gotten out of the hospital after my ex, Zane, had left me to drown in his car, I'd headed on over to his house, cut the crotch out of all of his pants, piled all his favourite things in his front yard, doused it in lighter fluid and set the whole thing blazing the moment he'd shown up. The asshole had the cheek to call me a crazy whore as he dove in to rescue his shit and I just flipped him off and went right on back to my old routine of walking past his house every day on my way to school. I never let it show that I had nightmares about that crash and spent weeks waking up screaming as I dreamed of drowning. Never chose a different route to take to school despite the way my heart raced and palms grew slick every time I passed by his house. Never said a word to him again no matter how many times he'd tried to get my attention. Because fuck him, fuck letting him have my pain. Fuck letting him make me walk a different way and fuck talking to him when he never once even attempted to apologise and never even showed up at the hospital to check I wasn't dead.

So I'd had plenty of practice at facing down my demons. I had an excellent poker face. And I refused to let a single person see me bleed for Darius Acrux.

We headed out of my room and passed through Ignis house without meeting anyone. We were late and apparently the start of term dinner was a big deal. My Atlas and Darcy's were both blowing up with messages from the Ass Club asking how long we'd be and I left it to her to reply.

As we drew closer to The Orb, the sound of music and excited voices raised in laughter reached us and my pulse started pounding. I licked my blood red lips, glad to have a thick layer of war paint to hide behind as we closed in on what I could only think of as one of the circles of hell.

I guess it would be naïve to hope that no one will notice.

Darcy's fingers brushed mine but she didn't take my hand, knowing I needed to face this alone.

I offered her a tight smile to let her know I appreciated the gesture and she nodded in return.

Just as we reached the door to The Orb, it swung open and my breath caught in my throat as we came face to face with Max and Seth.

None of us said anything, but their eyes locked on mine like they'd been hoping not to see the black rings there.

I bit my tongue, waiting to see what they'd say to me and bracing myself for the harshness of their words, but they didn't come.

Max's face pinched as he looked at me and I knew that he was feeling my pain with his gifts. I didn't even have the energy to try and block him out.

Seth whimpered softly, reaching out to brush his fingers down my arm in a comforting gesture and I was so shocked by it that I didn't even flinch away.

An achingly long moment passed between the four of us then Max stepped aside, holding the door wide so that we could head in.

"Thank you," I breathed as we stepped around them and I wasn't even sure if my thanks were for the door or the lack of assholiness they'd offered me.

I hesitated as we moved into the crowded space of The Orb which had been decorated like a winter wonderland complete with icicles hanging all over the ceiling and frost coating every surface.

Before the door swung shut behind me, I caught a few of Seth's words. "Do you think he's going to show up?"

"I have no fucking idea," Max growled in a low tone and the door closed between us before I could hear anymore. But even that had my heart pounding. It sounded like Darius wasn't here. Which was a good thing. Or was it? I didn't even know anymore.

Darcy led the way through the crowd to the Ass Club and I tried not to feel like I was walking to my execution as I followed her.

People moved aside for us, some calling out greetings but none of them looked closely enough to notice my eyes until I passed Marguerite.

"What the-" She snatched my arm and whirled me around so she could look at me in her sparkly silver dress. Her red hair fell all around her pretty face and she didn't even look hateful, just shocked.

I pulled my arm out of her grasp and dove back into the sea of bodies before she could ask the question, but the whispers started up behind me as I went and the news began to spread.

"Come hither my queens!" Geraldine's voice rose above the crowd and I spotted her raised up over everyone as she stood on a chair and waved enthusiastically.

She was dressed in a puffy pink skirt and a blue crop top which barely managed to contain her huge breasts.

"We have gathered a delectable feast of the most glorious food! You must pop a cheesy ball in your mouth and give it a jolly good suck. And don't forget to dip your dunkers in the creamy-"

Geraldine fell silent as her gaze zeroed in on my eyes, her lips popping open. She raised a trembling finger and started to shake her head in a hopeless kind of denial.

Everyone surrounding us noticed her behaviour and one by one their gazes fell on me too.

Gasps and curses passed around and I could feel so many sets of eyes on me that a blush began to prickle its way beneath my cheeks.

Sofia and Diego were staring and Angelica began to cry. Milton's eyes had stretched so wide that I was worried they might fall out of his head. It seemed like they were all about to talk at once but before they could, Geraldine released a noise which could only be described as a pterodactyl shriek.

If anyone in the room hadn't been looking at us, they were now and some helpful little douche canoe even cut the music.

There's something quite intimidating about a room filled with two thousand people falling silent so that they can try and get a look at you. I was seriously tempted to bolt. And I was wondering why I'd thought it would be best to do it this way. Darcy had suggested getting our friends to come to my room so that I could tell them before the whole campus found out. But I'd wanted to do it like this. All at once. Over and done with. Rip the band aid off. It was starting to seem like I was a fucking idiot to think that though.

"Oh, my lady!" Geraldine cried as words returned to her after her prehistoric outburst. "What in the name of the stars, by the light of the great and bulbous moon and long hard night has happened? Great gargoyles, galloping Griffins, ghastly goulash and gargantuan gazelles! For the sake of Lady Petunia and all that's wrong in the world, how in Solaria did such a travesty occur?"

Geraldine burst into tears, sobbing so loudly that I couldn't even have responded if I'd wanted to.

I exhaled slowly and dropped into a chair, pulling a plate of pizza closer to me and taking a bite. It tasted kind of like cardboard.

A clamour of noise burst out all around me and one question in particular kept ringing in my ears. *Who? Who? Who?*

Darcy took the seat beside me and Sofia moved to my left, winding an arm around me. Diego's hand landed on my shoulder and as I looked up at him in surprise, I found Milton there too. All of my friends closed in around me as Geraldine continued to sob so loudly that her voice echoed off of the walls.

"Oh sweet torture, oh purest hell, how could fate be so cruel?!" Geraldine cried.

"Attention students!" I was saved by the sound of Principal Nova's voice as she called everyone to order and after a few more shouts to get their attention, the students all returned to their seats and turned to look at her.

Geraldine kept sobbing so I tossed a silencing bubble up around her and Angelica as they held each other and tried to come to terms with what had happened to me. It was sweet in a completely over-the-top-Geraldine kind of way and I loved her for it, but it just wasn't me. Sure, I'd cry about this but not here, not where everyone could see me bleed. I refused to. But I did kinda envy her for her freedom. She was so unashamedly herself at all times.

"Due to the ongoing Nymph situation, it is my duty to inform you of new and tighter safety measures which will be put into place at the academy over the coming weeks," Principal Nova called and I turned to look at her across the sea of students.

There were still way too many eyes on me, but I ignored them. Let them look. They'd get bored eventually. My pain would lose their interest. My choice would become just another thing about me that people judged me for and then forgot. I just had to weather the storm until that happened.

"We are tightening the security measures around campus. There will be magical shields going up which will mean no flying Orders will be able to pass on or off of campus without being detected. We have over a hundred new security personnel starting up patrols around the outer wall. Due to this, we no longer feel the need to enforce a curfew within the grounds, but we urge you not to go off campus unless necessary for your own safety. We are also going to start teaching Elemental Combat to all of you, not just the older students and your timetables will be adjusted to include these classes," Nova said. "In addition, all after school clubs will be supervised by an extra member of staff. Professor Prestos has agreed to assist with the swim meets at Aqua Lake, Professor Washer is going to join Professor Orion at Pitball and Cheerleading practice-"

A groan went up amongst the cheerleaders as Washer smiled widely from his position at the front of the room.

Well that's just great. As if cheerleading needed to be any more painful.

Darcy suddenly straightened in her chair and I followed her gaze as Orion strode into the room. No one would have known he came really damn close to death last night. Outwardly he looked exactly like always but as his gaze met mine, my heart twisted sharply with guilt. We should have been there to help him. I couldn't bear to think about what would have happened to Darcy if she'd lost him.

Nova was still talking about the extra security measures, but all of a sudden every drop of oxygen seemed to be sucked from the room as Darius stepped in behind Orion.

His gaze moved straight to me and my heart stilled as I took in the dark rings around his deep brown irises which seemed to stand out so clearly despite the expanse of space between us.

My grip on Darcy's hand tightened as my ears began to ring and a well of pain opened up inside me. I couldn't breathe, couldn't think and absolutely couldn't tear my eyes away from the sight of him standing there looking so broken.

He didn't move. It almost seemed like he was rooted to the spot.

My heart was pounding so hard it hurt and the backs of my eyes began to burn.

"No!" Marguerite shrieked suddenly, interrupting Nova's speech as she leapt to her feet and pointed at Darius. "Not you! Not you and *her!* You can't have been destined for that whore!"

A ringing silence followed her words for all of three seconds as everyone stared between me and Darius in disbelief and suddenly everyone was talking at once, completely ignoring Nova as she called out to get their attention back and they all demanded answers which I refused to give.

My vision blurred as the backs of my eyes burned more fiercely and I ripped my hand out of Darcy's grasp, shoved out of my seat, knocking it over and pushed through my friends.

"Tory, wait!" Darcy called but I just shook my head.

"I just need to be alone," I choked out as I turned and tried to run, but the wall of bodies surrounding it made it impossible for me to escape. "Move!" I demanded but they didn't and I couldn't breathe. I had to get out of there, I had to escape this room, these people, *him.*

I threw my hands up before me and blasted an escape route into existence with a gust of air before racing for the doors.

No one recovered fast enough to stop me and I sped out the exit before throwing a layer of vines over it to seal it shut behind me and give me time to escape.

I ran across the courtyard towards the Lunar Leisure building and skirted the silver walls of it until I made it into the shadows on the far side.

My heart crashed and tore apart against my ribs as I leaned back against the cold wall and tears ran down my cheeks as I wrapped my arms around myself and tried not to fall to pieces.

This was my choice. *Mine.* It shouldn't have hurt this much to follow my heart. And that was what I'd thought I was doing. But if that was the case then why did it feel like I was being torn to bits from the inside out?

"I'm not usually good with crying," Orion's voice came to me and I quickly scrubbed the heels of my hands over my eyes as I tried to force the tears away. "Don't stop on my account though. You did a good job of running away, but it's a little harder to outpace a Vampire than the others." He looked me up and down for a long moment like he wasn't really sure what else to say. "I came to see if you were alright, but you're obviously not-"

I threw myself at him and wrapped my arms around his neck, squeezing him tightly just to make sure he was really standing before me.

"I'm so sorry, Lance," I breathed. "I should have been there to help you last night, you could have died, I could have cost you-"

"We both know that you couldn't have resisted the call of the stars no matter where you needed to be. Besides, I'm not dead," he replied, trying to shrug it off as his arms slowly closed around me, but we both knew there was so much more to this than that. So much pain. He'd gotten his sister back only to find out she was a monster, that the shadows had corrupted her beyond recognition. I couldn't even imagine the agony of that.

"I'm still sorry," I murmured, forcing myself to release him as I stepped back.

"Do you want to talk about Dari-"

"No," I breathed. "I can't...I just, need to move on with my life."

Orion gave me a pitying look which said he didn't believe for one second that I'd be able to do that.

"He understands your decision," he said softly. "Even though he hates it. He knows why you felt you had to..."

"You're a good friend, Lance," I said, wiping the tears from my cheeks. "But it doesn't matter what either of us think about it now, does it? The stars gave us our chance and that's the end of it."

The look he gave me said he wished he could do something to change that, but he knew as well as I did that he couldn't.

"I just don't want you to think he's his Father," Orion said in a defeated tone like he knew that there was no point to this conversation.

"I don't," I replied honestly because I did understand that much about Darius. He wasn't the monster who'd created him, but he had more than enough darkness in him anyway and I'd borne the brunt of that too often.

Orion looked like he wanted to say more, but he just released a sigh which spoke of defeat. "Do you want me to run you back to your House?" he asked as the sound of students partying in The Orb slowly grew again.

"Yes please," I said, offering him a real smile. Escaping was about the only thing I wanted to do right now.

By tomorrow, everyone would be over the shock and I'd walk amongst them with my head held high and my lips sealed. No one else needed to know the details of what had happened between me and Darius. The fact that we were Star Crossed was enough.

"Hop on then," he turned his back to me and I jumped up onto it with the hint of a laugh. Who'd have thought my Cardinal Magic Professor would be giving me piggy back rides around campus when I first started out at this school?

Orion shot away with his Vampire speed and before I knew it, we'd stopped outside Ignis House and I was sliding back down to the ground.

"I'll tell Blue where you went," he said, taking a step back, but I reached out and caught his wrist to stop him before he could shoot away again.

"Thanks."

"You know, I owe you an apology too," he said and I hesitated without releasing him.

"What for?" I asked, my brow pinching.

"When you first came here I assumed the two of you would be weak girls, incapable of rising up to claim the position you'd been born for. I thought you'd be all sorts of things and no matter which of them were true, I didn't once consider the idea that you might actually be capable of claiming your birth right. Or that you might deserve it. And I was wrong about that."

My lips parted in surprise, but I couldn't find any words to give him in response.

"And for what it's worth…Darius is starting to see that too. He might not be ready to admit it, but he can see your potential. And I know it's destroying him to think of all the things he did to you in an attempt to keep you beneath his heel. Even if he believed he was justified in doing it at the time."

Silence hung between us for a long moment and I smiled sadly.

"I can see why Darcy loves you," I said eventually and Orion's eyebrows rose in surprise.

"Are we the sappy declarations kind of friends now?" he asked in a tone that suggested he found the idea of that about as horrifying as I did.

"Well, you're still an asshole, but you're a good man too." Magic spilled from my fingertips where I still held his arm and Orion looked at me in confusion as I conjured tiny brown vines into existence, plaiting and braiding them together until they formed a ring around his wrist.

"What's this?" he asked, raising his hand to inspect it and I had to say I'd done a damn good job too.

"I promised you a friendship bracelet," I teased. "We can get together for a slumber party another time though."

He snorted a laugh at me as he backed up. "I'll treasure it always. Goodnight, Tory."

"Goodnight."

He shot away from me and I was left alone, but somehow that didn't seem so lonely anymore.

DARCY

CHAPTER SEVEN

The first day back in the new semester set my stomach swirling with butterflies. So much had changed. And yet school still continued like nothing had happened. But Tory's dark fate was written in the stars, Orion's sister had banded together with our enemies and the shadows that lived in my veins felt like nothing in comparison to the ones growing on the horizon.

With each passing day, it felt like we were waiting for something terrible to happen. For Lionel to make a move for the throne, or for Clara to come back to finish what she'd started. Nearly losing Orion had made me feel fragile, weak. But we'd been impossibly lucky. And now I knew this time needed to be spent getting stronger. More prepared. Because if Clara or any of Darius's nightmare family showed up again, I was going to be ready to make sure they never hurt anyone I loved ever again.

I headed out of my room dressed in my uniform, taking a deep breath as I tried to settle the unease that had taken root in me. The shadows were more hungry these days, always trying to lure me into a pit of darkness and sweet promises. But somehow, I found it even easier to pull away from them now. When they tugged at me, all I could see was Orion's blood. All I could feel was that hollow, terrible fear of thinking he was gone. They reminded me of Clara, of the worst night of my life. And I'd never let them have me.

I took out my Atlas, reading my horoscope as I walked along the corridor towards the stairs. I was going to pay serious attention to them from now on. If the stars had any warning about my day, I was going to find it and try to heed it. But sometimes they were so cryptic, it was almost like they were designed to make sense only after they'd come to fruition.

Good morning Gemini.

The stars have spoken about your day!

You may feel the world is hanging over you right now. A great task presents itself which you feel far too small to conquer alone. But take courage, for so long as those around you are in balance, you won't have to be. With the moon in your chart, you may feel more emotional at the moment. But take comfort in her lulling presence. It is a time for reflection, focus and preparation for the coming days.

"Morning, babe."

I looked up from my Atlas with a frown, spotting Seth in the stairwell leaning against the wall. He looked like a cruel god with his dark hair and muscular frame, his angular features perfectly arranged into a cool indifference. *Was he freaking waiting for me?*

I slowed to a halt in front of him despite the fact that ninety nine percent of me wanted to keep walking. I still hated him. But there was something slipping through my veins now which I couldn't ignore. Gratitude.

If it hadn't been for him, Orion would be dead. It was as simple as that. And as twisted and as screwed up as that was, it was still the truth. The hardest part about that, was I had to accept that he wasn't bad to the bone. He had a fragment of good in him which I would never be able to ignore because of what he'd done.

"What are you doing here?" I narrowed my eyes and he moved forward, dropping his arm over my shoulders and steering me down the stairs.

I tried to shrug him off, but he held on tight and I ground my jaw as his muscles locked me in place. I didn't see the point in starting a fight for the sake of getting rid of him. And maybe I was a *tiny* bit interested in what he had to say.

"I thought we could have a little chat." He waved his hand so a silencing bubble expanded around us and I shot him a glare.

"What do you want?" I pressed, my tone sharpening. I may have been grateful to him, but I still didn't trust a single hair on his head.

"So suspicious," he taunted. "Maybe I just want to talk about the weather. Or how your roots need doing." He glanced down at my hair and I scowled, trying to shrug him off again. He laughed darkly. "Or maybe I wanna talk about what you and your boyfriend were doing down in that cave on New Year's Eve."

"That's none of your business," I said, my heart thumping harder in my chest.

"Yeah, see...that shit's not gonna fly with me, babe. I'm owed an explanation." He gave me a razor sharp look, proving that he was just as much of a dick as always. "I know you were doing dark magic. But what I don't know is how Orion ended up skewered. Because it sure looked like someone did the stabbing."

I anxiously thumbed my mother's ring on my finger which I'd found at the Palace of Souls. "Why don't you ask Darius? He's your bestie, isn't he?" I asked and his scowl deepened at my words. If Darius wasn't being open about it, then that was up to him. But it sure as shit wasn't going to come from me.

"I'm asking *you* about it," he growled.

"He slipped on a wet rock and fell onto his draining dagger," I said flatly.

Seth wheeled me around, throwing me back against the wall with a snarl. Students scattered around us, squealing in fright. I clenched my jaw, glaring at Seth as magic trickled into my blood. I wasn't scared, I was mad. The kind of mad that made my veins scorch. Part of me wanted to burn him into a pile of ash and never have to deal with his bullshit again. But I didn't think murdering an Heir was going to solve my problems. Even if it would feel freaking amazing.

He pressed his hands either side of me on the wall, caging me in as his upper lip peeled back on a wolfish snarl. "Don't lie to me, Vega. I'm *owed* the truth."

I kicked off of the wall, getting right into his face as anger flashed hotter inside me, but it was starting to tangle with something else. Something softer I wanted to ignore. "That's your trouble isn't it, Seth? You can't do a good deed unless you get something in return for it. Just because you saved him, doesn't mean either of us are going to tell you anything about that night."

He slammed his palm against the wall in frustration. "You ungrateful little-"

My rage gave way to that treacherous piece of my heart and I lurched forward in a moment of madness, wrapping my arms around him and hugging him tight. The earthy scent of him ran under my nose and the heat of his hard body reminded me he wasn't just some coldblooded being.

"I am grateful. I am *so* fucking grateful." Tears seared my eyes and I wondered if the moon was to blame for me being so emotional or if it was just the fact that my relationship with Seth had become so messy that I didn't have words for what I felt towards him anymore. There was a bitter kind of hate that lived in me, digging deeper and deeper. But now there was a warmth toward him too which was just as resilient. Because I could never, *ever* repay him for giving Orion the magic he needed to survive.

I stepped back and Seth stared at me with wide eyes, his features suddenly boyish instead of harsh and distant.

"But you can't really think one good deed, even if it was the best deed you could possibly commit, could make me trust you for even a single second," I said breathlessly, my lungs working too hard.

My dislike of Seth had been so clear cut, I hated that it was foggy now. I hated that I'd hugged him. Hated that I had to feel anything toward him but anger. He was the guy who'd cut off my hair, the guy who held me and Orion hostage to his demands, who'd mocked and humiliated me. I was never going to forget that.

A frown worked its way into his forehead and he slowly nodded. He disbanded the silencing bubble, stepping back to let me pass and I kept my eyes locked on his as I moved down onto a lower step.

"Don't ask me about this again," I said firmly and his lips pursed in that entitled rich boy way that said he despised being denied anything.

I turned away and kept walking, taking a calming breath as I headed down the stairs.

"I still own you!" Seth called after me, his voice ringing around the stairwell. I didn't answer, despite my chest compressing and my jaw tightening.

We'll see about that when Darius Acrux has a word with you, asshole.

After breakfast, I headed to my first Cardinal Magic class of the semester. Tory hadn't shown up to eat and my heart niggled with worry for her as I arrived at Jupiter Hall, making my way through the huge white atrium and upstairs to the classroom.

Students were filing inside and I headed in with Diego and Sofia, dropping into our usual seats.

"I hope Tory's okay," Sofia said sadly, glancing over at me. "I knocked for her this morning but she didn't answer."

"She'll be alright," I said automatically.

Tory was the strongest person I knew. But deep down, I knew she was breaking. This was one enemy she couldn't fight, punch or insult. It was a quiet thing that was going to live with her forever, the knowledge that she could never find love would chip away at her always. I couldn't imagine what she was going through right now, but I was gonna be there for her no matter what.

At ten past nine, Tory arrived with a give-no-shits expression, her hair flowing around her in perfect waves and her eyes thick with eyeliner like she actually wanted to draw attention to the dark rings that circled her irises.

A hushed silence fell over the room and I chewed on my tongue, wanting to slap everyone for treating her like she was some ghost floating around the place.

She dropped into her seat, taking out her Atlas and tossing it on the desk with a clatter.

"Hey," I said lightly.

The last thing in the world Tory would want was people acting like she was made of glass. Which was why she was acting like she was made of freaking platinum. She was gonna front this out with the strongest wall she could possibly build. But inside, I knew she was hurting.

I took out the pastry I'd saved for her at breakfast, planting it on her desk. She glanced over at me with a smirk. "You're a life saver, Darcy." She snatched it up, taking a bite and leaning back in her seat with a moan of enjoyment, ignoring the stares she was getting from around the room.

I glanced at the door, my heart beating faster as I expected Orion to arrive at any moment. I didn't know why I was so on edge. Maybe because every time I'd seen him since New Year's Eve, I'd been reminded that he was still breathing. And all the while I couldn't see him, my heart started to get tricked into thinking something terrible had happened again. Or that I'd imagined him being saved at all and was living in some false, pretty illusion.

Tyler Corbin took out a large bag of Order Snaps and started working his way through the chewy sweets (which came in multicoloured versions of different Orders) as he tapped excitedly on his Atlas.

The door flew open and Orion strolled into the room like he was on time and the rest of the world was early. My mouth dried up as he made it to the front of the class, planting a coffee mug down on his desk and casually thumbing through a pile of papers. Then he looked up and his gaze slammed into mine. I released a breath that had been trapped in my lungs and a smile hooked up the corner of my mouth. His eyes danced with light for a moment and I swear I could have swum in that light forever.

Alive. Safe. Same old Orion.

He snapped around with a bolt of Vampire speed, a pen in his grip as he wrote on the board.

YOU ALL HAVE DIRTY LITTLE SECRETS.

A few people chuckled nervously as he turned back to face the class, his eyes fixing on Tyler as he continued to look at his Atlas and toss Order Snaps into his mouth intermittently. Orion shot toward him in a blur, snatching the sweets and throwing them at the wall so they exploded everywhere. He grabbed Tyler's Atlas in the next breath, tossing it onto his own desk before folding his arms and glaring down his nose at him.

"Do not eat in my classroom!" Orion barked, his harsh tone sending an injection of adrenaline into my veins.

Tyler gaped at him, swivelling in his seat to point at Tory who was still munching on her pastry. "But Tory Vega's eating!" he complained.

"I don't care if Tory Vega is starting her own bakery back there and using Polaris as a rolling pin, I'm talking to *you*, Corbin," Orion snapped and I suppressed a laugh, sharing a look with Tory as she smirked.

"That's so unfair," Tyler complained.

"Fair is a concept," Orion said with a shrug.

"But you're a Libra!" Tyler said in exasperation. "You're all about fairness."

"Wrong. Ten points from Terra. Libras are about justice. And I decide what that means to me. And if I say that Tory Vega can have a bake sale and employ her sister as a cupcake stand, then I will be the first in line for the grand opening. But *you*, Corbin. Do not have that right. So clean up your mess and see me in detention on Thursday."

Tyler pursed his lips, rising from his seat and marching towards the sweets scattered all over the floor, starting to pick them up and muttering about favouritism.

"My favourite students are the ones who don't piss me the fuck off," Orion snapped.

"And the ones who suck his cock best," Kylie whispered from behind me with a giggle and a gust of air rushed over me as Orion shot up to her desk.

I twisted around with my lips parting as I found Orion had hefted Kylie's whole chair up onto her desk and was holding the front two legs as he tipped it backwards. She screamed wildly, throwing out her hands to cast air magic and sending people's notebooks scattering everywhere as she failed to get a hold of her powers.

"If you ever insinuate anything like that in my classroom again, you won't just be in detention for the rest of the month – which you are by the way – you will be packing your fucking bags." He let go of the chair legs and she wailed as the whole thing toppled backwards over the desk. I gasped as she crashed toward the ground, catching herself with air magic a second before her head impacted with the floor.

Orion sped back to the front of the classroom, casually adjusting his tie and taking a sip of his coffee like he hadn't just almost mortally wounded a student.

"Right," he said like there'd been no interruption at all. "Today you'll be learning a concealment spell. Can anyone tell me the three types of magic which can be effective in concealing an object?"

Sofia raised her hand along with a few other students and Orion pointed her out. "Miss Cygnus?"

Sofia cleared her throat. "Illusion, confounding and influence."

"Good, ten points to Ignis," Orion said, tapping the board to bring up a list of examples.

Concealment Spells

Illusion – *magical hiding places*

Confounding – *causing any Fae who approach the concealed item to become confused and forget why they were there or what they were looking for*

Influence – *causing a physical or psychological response to coming close to the concealed object*

"Confounding and influence are more advanced magic, so today you'll be learning a simple illusion. Can anyone give an example of illusion concealment?" Orion asked.

Diego's hand raised and he pointed him out. "A hidden pocket?" he guessed.

"Correct," Orion confirmed. "Other examples might be a hidden door or floor space, or an object can even be hidden in plain view and caused to blend with its surroundings. Illusion magic works like a mask. If you make it to your senior year, these masks can be used for other more advanced magic. Such as concealing your face to look like another Fae." He raised a hand to his face, running his palm across it so a faint blue light trickled over his skin. A moment later his face appeared as Tyler Corbin's. Everyone started laughing, but by the time Tyler looked around from where he was kneeling on the floor, Orion disbanded the illusion and gave him a stern expression instead. "You will also be taught to protect your identities. Most Fae can effectively put an anti-mimicry spell on their appearance. However, powerful Fae can break past these barriers, so it is not totally effective. That is something you will be taught in time."

I frowned at Tory, not liking the idea that someone could just take our identity whenever they liked right now. So long as they were capable of the magic. And our list of powerful enemies was growing every day. I was gonna have to start an excel spreadsheet soon.

Orion smirked as concerned chatter broke out. "Bars, clubs, banks and any other private institutes have anti-mimicry technology installed at the doors, so don't worry about your precious identities," he said, pushing his hands into his pockets. "Not that anyone would bother to impersonate most of you," he muttered under his breath. "Can anyone give an example of a confounding concealment spell?"

"Making someone, um, need the toilet sir?" a girl in the front row offered.

"Yes, a spectacular case of getting the shits can draw a Fae away from your concealed object nicely," Orion said with a grin and everyone chuckled. "But it takes powerful magic to effect a Fae's body like that. Especially when you're not present to cast it."

Orion moved to his desk, picking up a mason jar full of gold coins. He started moving through the classroom and throwing them out to everyone, making them try to catch so coins went flying everywhere.

"Pitball Keeper!" he barked at me before throwing one my way and my heart juddered as I lurched out of my seat and caught it at the last second. He smirked, his eyes glittering with satisfaction. "We may have a shot at beating Aurora Academy in the next game after all."

I grinned, dropping into my seat as he tossed one to Tory. She wasn't even paying attention and it bounced off of her desk so hard, it pinged right into Diego and hit him in the eye. Which was pretty weird considering he was adjacent to her, so I had a sneaking feeling Orion had used his air magic to send it in his direction.

"Hijo de puta," Diego hissed, cupping his eye.

"Language, Polaris. Five points from Aer," Orion snapped at him and I pursed my lips. He could be such a dick sometimes.

When everyone had a coin, Orion headed to the front of the class, placing his own coin down on the desk.

"Illusion is all about subtly," he explained, tapping the wood beside the coin. "You need to study the area you're going to copy and make sure the mask you create around the object is seamless. Poor concealment spells can be noticed a mile off if someone is looking for whatever you've hidden." He glanced around at us all. "And I'm sure at least one of you have items you'd rather keep out of sight. I for one, don't take any pleasure in turning out freshmen rooms. You can only imagine the amount of fucking Order porn and weird and wonderful sex toys I've had the displeasure of discovering. If you get this spell right, you'll have a shot at hiding them. Of course, I am unfortunately very apt at discovering concealment spells so unless you can disguise your magical signature too, you're most likely fucked."

"I wonder how many sparkly Pegasus horn vibrators Caleb Altair has hidden around his room," Tyler mused as he dropped back into his seat with a full bag of sweets and laughter exploded around the classroom.

I glanced at Tory with a smirk, but she didn't even have it in her to smile. And that just broke my heart to pieces.

Orion pressed his tongue into his cheek, leaning back against his desk and clasping the edge of it. "Well, I've only found the one, but Mr Altair's skill could mean every lamp, candle and potted plant in his room are concealing glittering dicks. Not that I'm judging."

More laughter carried around the room and Tyler bobbed in his seat excitedly. "He probably has one concealed in his butt at all times!"

"Another ten points from Terra," Orion barked at him and the class fell completely quiet.

Orion was seriously playing Jekyll and Hide today and the smile dancing around his lips said he was enjoying the hell out of it. Asshole that he was, I couldn't help but love him for being a teensy bit psycho. His idea of fun came with a sadistic little twist. And I was hot for it.

Tyler sank lower in his seat with a huff, but didn't say another word.

Orion pressed his fingers to the coin on his desk. "Bring pure energy to your fingertips and envision the surface you're trying to conceal it within. The clearer the image you imagine, the easier the magic will be to mould. Once you have it in your grasp, a simple hand movement like this-" He ran his fingers over the coin and it instantly vanished. "Will do the trick. If it helps, the movement is similar to that of turning a page of a book. Gentle, with little effort required. If your movements are too harsh, well…"

As if on cue, Diego's table cracked right down the middle as he attempted the spell and Orion pointed it out. "*That* can happen. And if you're more powerful than Polaris – and let's face it, most of the world are – then you can cause a lot more damage than he has. Begin."

Diego growled under his breath as chatter broke out around the room and everyone attempted the spell.

Orion moved up to stand in front of Diego, clasping his hands behind his back. "Again," he demanded and Diego took a breath, looking a little sweaty under the intensity of Orion's glare as he raised his hand above the coin. He did a subtle sweep over it and the coin turned as black as pitch.

Orion's mouth twisted down at the corners. "Focus on the surface." He tapped the desk.

"I'm trying," Diego said firmly. "But all I'm seeing is your loco black eyes staring at me, sir."

Orion rolled said eyes and sidestepped to stand in front of me instead. "Put Polaris to shame, Blue," he encouraged and I held my fingers above my coin.

"He has a point, sir, you're pretty distracting standing there like the Grim Reaper," I said lightly.

He placed his hands on my desk, leaning over me with his fangs on show. "What if you need to conceal a murder weapon with the cops two seconds away, hm? What if you don't do it right because of the stress?"

"Are you teaching me to get away with murder, sir?" I teased and he chuckled in a low tone.

"I'm teaching you to cast magic under pressure," he said, pinning me in those endlessly dark eyes of his. My stomach dipped and heat trickled down my spine. *Yah. Officially distracted.*

I dropped my gaze to the coin and focused on the table surface around it. Blocking Orion out wasn't easy, but I just about managed it before I lifted my hand and gently brushed my fingers over the coin in the way he'd taught us. The coin changed colour to blend with the table, but it was still visible. I pursed my lips, glancing up at Orion for pointers and he reached out to take my hand. The frenzied energy that passed between us made my pulse skip as he guided my fingers over the coin.

"You have to believe it isn't there with all your heart," he whispered, his voice making the hairs rise along my arms.

I swallowed thickly, dropping my gaze to the coin as I released the magic from my fingertips again with him guiding my hand. The moment I imagined the table without a coin on it, holding that picture vividly in my mind, it vanished, as simple as that.

I glanced over to find Tory mimicking us with a taut expression and she managed it too.

Orion glanced between us with a smirk, then lowered his tone. "The Heirs are given more advanced tasks in my classes. If you two ever want to challenge yourselves, you only have to ask." He shot away to help Jillian as her table rocketed up to the ceiling and smashed to pieces.

Tory's eyes brightened for a moment as she looked to me and my heart lifted at the sight.

"We should do that," she said. "We have to play catch up. Hard."

I nodded in agreement. "Definitely. And one day we'll zoom on past them and leave them in our dust trails."

Her mouth pulled up a little at the corner, but she didn't really smile. And I couldn't bear it. If there was anything I could have done to fix what had happened between her and Darius, I would do it no question. The worst thing of all, was that she'd chosen this. Preferred it to the alternative. But were the stars really so cruel that she should be punished for the rest of her life because she hadn't chosen to mate with a guy who'd hurt her in unspeakable ways?

I curled my hands into fists on the table, not knowing what to do with all the rage and hurt that lived in me on her behalf. The shadows clawed their way up under my skin, trying to feed on that pain, take it away. But they couldn't have it. It was mine to bear, and I wasn't going to let them pacify me.

By the time class ended, Diego had gotten the spell right and Orion had taught me and Tory how to hide our magical signatures on our concealments too. It was like withdrawing the energy around the spell we'd just laid, siphoning it away until there was as little as possible used for the concealment, leaving no clues that an object was there at all. I was excited to use it for real, and kinda annoyed I hadn't known how to do this before now to conceal the Aquarius Moonstone from Seth. He might never have figured out I'd given him fleas. But in all fairness, it felt pretty good that he knew I'd struck that blow against him. After all the shit he'd put me through, a little isolation from his pack and constant itchy balls had definitely been due.

The bell rang and we all started heading for the door.

"I need to discuss your Order gifts paper with you, Blue," Orion's voice cut through the air and I fought a grin as I held back.

"I'll save you a seat in Tarot," Tory said with a knowing look and I squeezed her arm in thanks before slipping away toward Orion's desk. Someone tugged on my sleeve and I glanced back to see Diego there with a pale expression.

"Um, Darcy, can I talk to you?"

"Not right now, Polaris," Orion snapped, waving a hand so a gust of air crashed into Diego and sent him flying out the door with the last of the students. The door slammed shut and I glared at Orion, planting a hand on my hip.

"That was rude," I said sternly. He flicked a hand to cast a silencing bubble then shot toward me, taking my breath right out of my lungs as he threw me back onto Tyler's desk and pressed his tongue between my lips.

"I am rude," he growled into my mouth.

I moaned, tangling my hands in his hair as the heat of his flesh brought my body to life. I forgot everything, the world just a hazy grey blur around us as I clung to this man who made every part of me sing. My heart felt like it was trying to claw its way out of my chest to get closer to him, but I knew this had to stop. It was the middle of a school day and though I knew he could hear anyone approaching, my pulse still pounded with adrenaline.

"Lance, if we get caught..." I said breathlessly as he forced my thighs wider around his hips.

"We won't," he growled, knotting his fingers in my shirt.

He kissed me again, pulling buttons free and sliding his hand into my bra, a growl of desire leaving him as he found my nipple pebbled and aching for him. I gasped as he pinched my sensitive flesh, his other hand sailing beneath my skirt and brushing up the centre of my panties.

"Ah," I gasped, his thumb skating over that perfect spot between my thighs.

We were so hungry for each other, everything about our movements was frantic and pawing. He tilted my head to the side, his mouth trailing across my neck as he hunted for a vein, his desire for my blood as keen as his desire for me.

A knock came at the door and he groaned, pressing his forehead to my shoulder in frustration.

He flicked his fingers to disband the silencing bubble and shouted, "I'm busy! Come back later."

"It's just...it's quite important," Diego's voice sounded beyond the door.

"I said not now!" Orion barked, but I pressed a hand to his chest, shaking my head.

"He said it's important," I whispered and Orion pulled his hand out of my shirt, his brows stitching together as he raked his knuckles across my cheek.

"*You're* important," he growled, his thumb pressing down between my thighs the same moment he clamped a hand over my mouth.

"*Lance*," I begged against his palm, though my thighs widened, betraying that plea to stop.

The knocking came again and Orion's head snapped towards the door with murder in his eyes.

"It's about...about your sister, sir," Diego hissed and my heart lurched.

I caught Orion's wrist, tugging his hand free from my skirt and pushing him back. I was flustered and hot all over, but this wasn't something that could wait.

I quickly did up the buttons of my shirt and Orion checked me over before shooting to his desk and dropping into the seat behind it. He rearranged his pants and I fought a smirk before moving to stand before the desk, then he casually whipped a hand at the door to wrench it open.

"In," he demanded of Diego, flipping his fingers to slam the door behind him.

Diego tugged at one side of his black beanie hat as he moved toward us, anxiety flickering through his eyes.

Orion cast another silencing bubble and cocked an eyebrow at Diego. "Well?"

Diego glanced between us, knotting his fingers together. "Well...you know how I told you about how mi abuela made this hat?" He pointed to it.

"How could I forget?" Orion asked dryly, leaning back in his seat with a suspicious expression.

Diego cleared his throat and I gave him an encouraging look. "It's connected to the souls of my family. We can use it to show each other things..."

like our memories."

"That's crazy," I breathed. "So you can see your parents' thoughts?"

"Si." He nodded. "But only what we choose to share with each other though. Once it's shared, it's accessible to everyone connected through mi abuela's red de almas. Her web of souls."

"You're circling the point like a fucking braindead vulture, Polaris. Get to it," Orion snapped.

Diego's throat bobbed and I stepped closer to him, laying my hand on his arm. "It's okay," I said. "What is it?"

"My family are helping the Acruxes." He glanced at Orion nervously.

Orion wet his lips, sitting forward in his chair. "I'm listening."

"They went to visit them last night and I felt them add a memory to the web. When I looked, I saw…I saw…" He started sweating, pulling off his hat and dabbing at his forehead with it.

Orion slammed his hand down on the desk impatiently and Diego flinched.

"I saw la Princesa de las Sombras," he breathed, looking to Orion. "The Shadow Princess. Your sister."

My gut knotted and I clutched Diego's arm tighter. "What was she doing?"

"I can show you," he said. "I want to help."

"You'd go against your own family?" Orion asked in a deadly tone. "Why?"

Diego wrung his hat between his fingers. "It's hard to explain."

"Then try," Orion growled.

I chewed on my lip, waiting for Diego to speak, unsure if I trusted him or not. My heart told me he really wanted to help. But how could I know for sure?

Diego cleared his throat, his cheeks reddening as he turned his gaze to the floor. "The honest truth is that I've never known a home before I came to Zodiac Academy. I've been a disappointment to everyone in my life. My family think I'm useless. And I thought that too for a while…but I can help with this. I can be useful. But not to them, to my friends." He looked to me with a faint smile pulling at his lips that made my heart tug. "To people who have accepted me as I am, who never asked me to be anything but me."

I gave him a reassuring smile, saddened that he felt that way about his family. But I was sure he was telling the truth. Something bone deep told me that.

"Well excuse me if I don't pull out the tissue box and start playing the tiniest violin in the world, Polaris, but I'm gonna need more than a fucking sob story to be convinced." Orion rose from his seat, apparently boner free as he strode around the desk and stared down at Diego with his eyes narrowed.

"Give him a chance to prove it," I said, lifting my chin. "I believe him."

Orion's gaze slid to me and his jaw ticked as he mulled over my words. "I'm not going to take any stupid risks."

"There's no risk," Diego promised. "I can show you the memories through the shadows. That's all. They could never tell you saw them."

Orion ran his tongue over his teeth, moving closer to Diego in an intimidating stance. "If you try to fuck me over, kid, I'll break every bone in your body. And if you try to fuck over the Vegas, I'll rip out said broken bones one by one, put them in a blender and feed them to you through a straw. I know some nasty fucking spells that will make sure you stay alive through the entire thing. Mark. My. Words."

My lips popped open and hell, I was shamefully turned on by him in that moment.

Diego straightened his spine and balled his fists. "I swear I won't." He held out his hand. "I'll swear it on the stars if that makes you feel better."

Orion's eyes slid down to Diego's hand extended between them then he clucked his tongue, turning and striding back to his desk. He opened his drawers one at a time, rummaging through them for something before finally producing a beautiful blue Lapis Lazuli crystal.

"I'll go one better," he said, deadly calm. "You will make a star promise with me and Blue. Then you will do it with Darius and Tory when you see them too. If you break the promise, we'll feel it. And the stars will curse you for the rest of your miserable days. Which will be a sum total of one, during which the bone-breaking-smoothie fest will commence."

I would have laughed if he hadn't looked so damn serious. I really did think my crazy Professor boyfriend would have made Diego drink his own bones in the world's most messed up milkshake.

"I'll do whatever you need to gain your trust." Diego continued to hold out his hand, but it was definitely shaking a little as Orion grabbed it and pressed the crystal to his inner palm and it started to glow. He scored lines across it and I shifted closer to watch as he painted Diego's star sign constellation of Aquarius onto his skin in a mark that glimmered like the crystal. Then he marked the Libra constellation on his own palm and took hold of Diego's hand in what looked like a bruising grip. "You will swear not to breathe a word of what we discuss together, never share a memory or a thought about your time with me, the Vegas or Darius Acrux unless we agree to."

"I swear it." Magic flashed between their palms and Orion dropped his hand, seeming satisfied as he moved forward to take mine. He lifted it, pressing the crystal to my palm and drawing the Gemini constellation across it with gentle strokes. I glanced up at him under my lashes, seeing the worry in his expression and wishing I could soothe it away. I knew how he felt. He was afraid. Afraid of the world falling away from beneath our feet at any moment. And I was scared of the same thing.

Amongst all of the darkness hanging over us, he was a solid beacon of light I could focus on. Him and Tory were the only things that mattered. I had to protect them, keep them close. But we couldn't just hide, or run. We had to stand and fight. And if Diego could help us do that, then this was a chance we had to take.

Diego moved forward, taking my hand and Orion directed me to repeat the words he'd spoken before. When Diego agreed, a cool, powerful magic flooded into my veins. I felt the weight of the deal slipping around my heart, sitting there with the other one I'd made with Orion. When we'd promised to always do whatever it took to stay together.

"Show us then," Orion demanded, looking to Diego with a tight jaw. "Let's see this memory."

Diego's hand was still holding mine and he reached out to take Orion's.

Orion looked like he wanted to hold hands with Diego about as much as he wanted to throw himself from the nearest window and dash his head to pieces on the cobblestones below, but he reached out and did it anyway.

"We have to connect through the shadows," Diego explained. "Reach out to me with them."

I took in a slow breath then let my eyes fall closed as I concentrated. The shadows were waiting, ready, coiled like a snake in my chest looking for prey. They slithered toward Diego without much encouragement and I felt the lull of them surrounding me.

My pulse sounded slow and steady in my ears, the thump thump thump of it the only thing I could hear as I started to drift into the abyss.

Diego and Orion's presence shimmered in my periphery and I felt Diego tugging us into the dark, leading us deep, deep, deep down into the belly of the shadows.

My grip on the Fae world was slipping away as I became weightless, floating in a sea of nothing. It should have been frightening, but the shadows wound through me, keeping my mind calm and my pulse beating out that ever-steady tune.

Thump, thump, thump.

A light expanded before us and suddenly I was gazing at what looked like a cloud, suspended before us in the dark. It was white and yet seemed denser than a normal cloud, like I could dip my fingers into and find a foamy texture awaiting me.

Flickers of light danced through it and with each flash, I saw faces, landscapes, moments. I saw Diego as a young boy standing on a hill in the dark, his eyes wide and his cheeks flecked with red paint. Then it flashed away and I saw him holding his acceptance letter to Zodiac Academy, his face bright with enthusiasm. I felt the atmosphere twist and writhe and suddenly a memory grew brighter amongst them all, drawn to the surface of the cloud and filling the entirety of it, then more and more until it slipped into my mind and played as if I was seeing it through my own eyes.

I was in Lionel Acrux's home, watching as Clara stood up on the dining table. Lionel sat at the far end while his vile followers huddled around it, marvelling at Clara as she wielded the shadows like they were extensions of her limbs. Her body was cloaked in darkness and she filled the entire vaulted ceiling with shadow, casting them all in gloomy tones. Lionel gazed up at it with a sinister kind of victory in his eyes. Like he'd won this war already.

My gut tightened into a ball of rage as I stared at the girl who'd hurt Orion. I knew she was his blood, but I saw nothing but a monster lurking behind her eyes. And if this hadn't been a memory, I would have tried to tear her apart with my Phoenix fire, destroy her for ever laying a hand on her brother.

"Clara Orion will guide us in the way of the shadows," Lionel announced. "She has suffered in darkness for us all and now we owe her our gratitude." He stood from the table, raising a blade before ripping his sleeve back and slicing open his arm.

I gasped in time with the body I was experiencing this memory through as Lionel spilled his blood into a crystal glass, holding it out to Clara with a dark smile.

Clara rushed forward to take it, dropping to her knees before him on the table and swallowing every last drop from the glass.

"You will honour her as I do," Lionel said, an edge to his tone and everyone around the table hurried to offer her blood too. "Our Shadow Princess!"

The memory faded away before she dove on more glasses of blood and I found myself yanked from the darkness, blinking sharply as I took in the room around me. My eyes locked with Orion's as we released Diego's hands and my heart pounded wildly out of rhythm.

Orion's brow was crinkled and he looked pale, broken, his heart shattered. I wanted to rush forward and wrap my arms around him, promising it would be okay. That we'd figure out what to do about his sister. But with Diego there, I could do nothing but stare and feel all the hurt exuding from him like a wave crashing against my soul.

"I can show you everything," Diego breathed. "Everything there is to show."

"Thank you, Diego," I said earnestly, moving forward to hug him. With him, we had a line to Lionel. He was our very own shadow spy, a chance to get ahead of our enemies.

DARIUS

CHAPTER EIGHT

I sat on the tiny beach of Draco Island out in the sea, looking back towards the coast where I could just make out the rocky cliffs that made up Air Cove with my mind sifting over and over the same things time and again.

Roxy. Lance covered in blood. Roxy. Clara strengthening my father's hold on the shadows. Roxy. Father plotting to take down the Celestial Council and binding me in silence with dark magic. Roxy. Mother's face when her perfect façade shattered for the first time in forever. Roxy. Xavier's pain locked up in that hell. Roxy. The shadows calling me closer. And Roxy.

I blew out a long breath as I looked up at the rising moon. Over the years, I'd gotten stupidly good at telling the time by the position of the sun and moon in the sky so that I didn't lose track when I went out flying, and I had about half an hour before I was due to meet the others at Air Cove for our shadow lesson.

But there was something I needed to do before then. I'd been putting it off because I'd basically been avoiding everyone including the other Heirs, but there was an issue that needed sorting.

I pushed myself to my feet and started running along the sand, leaping forward and shifting in the same motion. I transitioned perfectly, my Dragon bursting from my flesh in a flash of golden scales and fire bursting from my jaws as my claws skimmed across the tips of the waves.

I beat my wings hard and took off towards the sky, eyeing the stars with contempt and sending a torrent of fire blazing toward them. Not that they cared. I didn't know if I'd been born cursed or if they'd just found such amusement in my pain so often that they grew to enjoy the taste of it. Either way, the heavens had offered me more than my share of bad luck.

I turned away from them, not wanting to see their mocking glimmer as

I beat a path back towards campus. I flew straight through the detection spells, not giving a shit that Nova would have logged me coming and going from campus. A Dragon needed miles of free sky to fly and circling campus just wasn't going to cut it for me. Especially not at the moment when I needed the comfort of my Order form more than ever. I'd been flying more than sleeping most nights and I had no intention of restricting that any time soon.

The cliffs soon appeared ahead of me and I raced towards them, circling a few times to slow myself down before landing close to Aer Tower and shifting back into my Fae form. I dissolved the concealment spell I'd placed on my stuff which I'd left in a patch of grass on the clifftop and dragged on my black sweatpants and sneakers before picking up my Atlas and sending Seth a message to come and meet me out here. I threw a silencing bubble up over the area so that I could keep our conversation private when he arrived.

I looked down at the tattoos which snaked over the right side of my chest, the initials of the people I cared for most in this world woven into the pattern of flames which washed over my shoulder from the mouth of the Dragon on my back. My thumb skimmed over the X, L, M and C before finally coming to rest on the S where I pressed down hard enough to feel a flicker of pain.

My blood was running hot with my fire magic and I was dancing a thin line with rage most days anyway, so I didn't exactly mind having an excuse to vent some of it.

"Hey, man, what's up?" Seth called as he appeared, jogging around the tower as he moved towards me. "We've been worried about you...do you wanna come hang out at the Hollow?"

I'd been avoiding the other Heirs outside of classes all week and I hadn't exactly had much to say when I did see them. I knew they wanted to help me, but between Max cringing every time he got near me like the merest hint of my emotions caused him physical pain, Seth whimpering and trying to nuzzle me all the damn time and Caleb...fucking Caleb with his fucking face and his fucking blonde hair and his fucking fangs which he got way too close to my girl way too often, not to mention what he did with the rest of his fucking body and-

Not my girl.

Never my girl.

My jaw ticked and I strode towards Seth as he gave me a pitying look like he could read my fucking mind.

"We have a problem," I growled, my hands curling into fists.

"How can I help?" Seth asked, pushing his long hair away from his face. His gaze flicked down to my fists and he straightened his spine as he seemed to realise this was a problem between me and him.

"Have you been fucking with Lance and Gwendalina Vega?" I asked darkly.

Seth licked his bottom lip, his gaze shifting over me like he was wondering how much I knew and how much shit he could feed me.

"It's just a bit of fun, dude. We all agreed to fuck with the Vegas and-"

I snarled as I lunged at him and Seth tried to duck aside as I swung a fist straight for his face.

My knuckles slammed into an air shield at the last second and he growled at me as thick vines sprung out of the ground at my feet, snaring my legs and anchoring me in place.

Seth pointed right in my face as he stayed just out of reach and I glared at him. "I'll give you a free pass for that because you got your heart ripped out, but if you try to come at me again we're going to have a serious-"

Fire flared from my flesh and destroyed the vines in less than a heartbeat and I was on him a second later.

I coated my knuckles in ice and slammed them against the air shield he'd thrown around himself with every ounce of strength I possessed.

The ground shook and quaked beneath me as Seth growled like the Wolf he was. "Why do you care if I torture Darcy Vega?" he snarled. "That was what we all agreed to do when we found out they were coming back here!"

I roared at him as I threw all of my magic into the ice surrounding my fist and his shield shattered as my fist collided with it again.

I slammed into him instantly, catching him around the throat and throwing him back against the stone wall of Aer Tower with a Dragon's growl that rocked right through my body.

Seth's fists pounded into my ribs and for a moment I just bathed in the pain he delivered me as I kept my grip on his throat and pinned him in place. It was a twisted kind of relief to feel something other than fucking heartache. I was almost tempted to release him and let him beat the shit out of me just to escape into agony of a different kind for a while.

"Lance is off limits," I snarled. "Which means the girl he loves is off limits too."

"Fuck you. You don't just get to make the rules!" Seth shouted, punching me so hard that a crack sounded in my ribs.

His palm opened but before he could use his magic to throw me off, I directed my own ice over his hands, binding them to the wall behind him and immobilising his magic in the act.

I bared my teeth at him, squeezing his throat even tighter for a second just so that he knew I held his life in my fist. Just so he could see exactly which one of us had come out on top here.

His eyes flashed dangerously, but not in fear. More like betrayal.

"You'd pick a fucking Vega over your own brother?" he hissed, not even bothering to struggle against me anymore as he shot me a poisonous look. "Who the fuck are you right now, Darius?"

I sucked in a breath and loosened my hold.

"I'm not picking anyone over anyone," I said in a low voice as the shadows flickered beneath my skin, whispering bloodlust in my ears and stoking the pit of rage in me. "But did you ever stop to consider the curse my father put on Lance when he bound his life to mine?"

Seth's gaze dipped to my forearm where the Libra brand stood out red amongst the tattoos I'd gotten of all the other star signs.

"Seems like there are worse things than being bound to one of the most powerful men in Solaria," Seth hissed dismissively.

I growled again, heat flaring beneath my skin and making him wince as I burned him before getting it back under control.

"He had a *life* before this. He had things he wanted, things he'd earned. He should be living his fucking dreams out playing in the Solarian Pitball League right now. Not stuck here *teaching*. His mother is a fucking psychopath, his sister disappeared years ago and he hasn't been able to make a single decision for his own happiness since the moment my father linked him to me. But somehow, in amongst all of that shit, he found a girl to love. But you, selfish motherfucker that you are, want to rip that away from him too?" I was shouting in his face and I didn't even give a shit. I was sick of my father treating my life like it was nothing more than something he could toy with and I wasn't going to let Seth do that to Lance.

Absolute power corrupts absolutely. It was one of those phrases people tossed around, but didn't give much thought to. But there was real truth in that. Power was the root of all my problems. Every fucking one of them. And I wasn't going to watch the people around me abusing theirs anymore.

"Fine," Seth growled, sagging back against the wall as the fight went out of him. "I was never going to tell anyone about them anyway. I just liked fucking with them, that's all."

I looked into his brown eyes for a long moment, seeing nothing but honesty in his gaze and I huffed in frustration before withdrawing my grip from his throat and taking a step back. I let the ice melt away from his hands too but he remained where he was, watching me like he didn't know what the fuck I'd do next. And I didn't even know the answer to that so I couldn't help him.

"Why?" I asked. "Why do you care so much about him being with her?" Because Seth might have been a ruthless asshole, but fucking with other people's relationships wasn't his usual style and something about it wasn't adding up to me.

"I don't," he snapped, but I fixed him in my gaze and waited. Seth never had been good at keeping his feelings locked down from me and the other Heirs, and after a few moments pinned in my gaze he cracked. "Fine. Maybe I do care. Maybe I don't like seeing her with him, laughing and *smiling* and batting her eyelashes at him like he's the best fucking person she's ever met and his cock is so fucking big that she just can't get enough of it. And-"

"You sound jealous," I growled, as I glared at him. "Is that what this is? Have you fallen for her or something?"

"No," Seth snapped, but it wasn't the least bit convincing. "Not... not really." He let out a low breath and knocked his head back against the wall to Aer Tower, touching his fingers to his neck as he healed away the bruises and burns I'd placed on his flesh. "It's just…you know what it's like for Werewolves and our mates. The Alpha in me demands I meet an equal. Someone who can match my power and unless I can find that, I'm never gonna be able to find that true bond with anyone. And I've met a lot of fucking Wolf girls and guys, even Alphas in their own rights, but none of them are strong enough to contend with me. And sometimes…I just get sick of all the pack orgies and want someone who I can just call *mine*."

"Darcy Vega isn't a Werewolf," I huffed, folding my arms over my bare chest and feeling the sharp sting of pain from my broken ribs with a surge of twisted satisfaction.

"No, I know. But she's strong. Besides, it's not like that for me. Yeah, most Capellas are Werewolves, but we aren't exactly an endangered species. My mom doesn't give a shit about me sticking to my Order type when I find my mate. She just wants it to be someone powerful enough to match me so that our children are strong. But that's just it – no one can match me. The four of us are unrivalled in our power so there's no fucking chance of me finding anyone that I might be able to form a true mate bond with like that, and the thought of taking a mate who's less than me is just so fucking depressing. But then the Vegas came along and, well…Darcy liked me, you know? Before I cut her hair off anyway. She kissed me. She wanted me too, at least in that moment."

"So you just got it in your head that you'd take a Vega for your mate and there wouldn't be any issues with that?" I asked incredulously. He'd clearly lost his fucking mind. He knew as well as I did that he couldn't marry a Vega without jeopardising the whole Council. His children would end up stronger than the rest of ours and it would unbalance everything. There was no way his mother or anyone else would allow that shit, and he knew it just as well as I knew it. I'd certainly given the idea enough thought when I'd been obsessing over Roxy. Besides, it didn't look like he loved Darcy Vega from where I was standing. More like he was throwing a fit because he couldn't just snap his fingers and claim her like he could with most things in life.

"I don't fucking know," he sighed. "All I know, is that if I hadn't been such a dick to her in the beginning then maybe things would be different now. Maybe the two of us…" he trailed off as he looked into my eyes and my jaw ticked with barely suppressed rage yet again.

"Yeah, I get that. I've had one or two thoughts like that myself," I snarled bitterly. "About the Vega who really was destined to be mine. Until she stepped beneath the stars with me and told me she'd rather suffer alone and in misery for the rest of her life than be bound to me in any way."

I shoved away from Seth as he whimpered behind me and pushed my hands into my dark hair as I fought against the pull of the shadows as they licked keenly beneath my flesh, aching for a taste of the darkness which had taken root in my hollow soul.

"Sorry, man," Seth breathed behind me, reaching out to grip my shoulder and pressing healing magic into my body to fix my busted ribs. I wished he hadn't done it. The pain had been a welcome distraction. "I didn't mean to compare it to you and Tory. That's not what I meant…"

"It's fine," I growled, looking out over the dark sea. It wasn't, but nothing was so there was no point in bitching about it.

"Please come and hang out with us at the Hollow tonight. We miss you, we need you. The three of us don't know how to help you, but-"

"I'll think about it," I said dismissively and we both knew I wouldn't be showing up. "I've got somewhere else to be first. Just stay the fuck away from Lance and Gwen."

"Okay. But come later. *Please.*"

I strode away from him, causing his hand to fall from my shoulder and I didn't look back as I kept walking. Was I going to see them in the Hollow tonight? Doubtful. They wanted to fix my problems, but there was no fix for them. Roxy had made her choice and that wasn't me. Father had forced me to betray them and bound my tongue with dark magic so that I couldn't even warn them. When I sat amongst my friends I just felt like a traitor and a liar, burning up with all the things I couldn't say and shouldn't feel. It wasn't their fault, but I couldn't change it either. It just sucked. Like pretty much everything else in my life.

A low howl followed me as I left Seth behind and my heart twisted guiltily. I didn't want to shut the other Heirs out. But I didn't know how to let them in either.

I checked the time on my Atlas as I headed down the stairway carved into the side of the cliff which led to the beach below and sighed as I realised I was early. But it wasn't like I had anything else to do anyway.

My skin prickled as I started walking along the beach towards the cave where we held our shadow lessons. I tried not to think too much about the fact that I was going to be spending a few hours in Roxy's company for the first time since she'd thoroughly destroyed me. I'd hardly even seen her since that night and we certainly hadn't spoken. She was clearly avoiding me and I hadn't made any attempt to get close to her either despite the fact that I lay awake at night wishing I could. The closest I came was heading down to stand outside her door when everyone else was sleeping and checking that she wasn't falling into the temptation of the shadows. Unfortunately, she clearly had been using them and I'd already had to press my magic out towards her more than once to pull her back. But she never seemed to realise it was me. Never thought to check beyond her door for whatever she'd latched onto to pull herself out of the shadows. And I was glad. Because if she figured out it was me, she might demand I stop doing it. And there was no way I could just abandon her to the lure of the shadows alone.

There were a thousand things I ached to say to her, but what was the point? It was too late.

I was so caught up in my own personal pity party that I didn't even realise I wasn't the only one to turn up early until I rounded the corner before the cave and almost walked straight into Roxy where she was sitting crossed legged on the ground.

My heart leapt and my mouth dried out as I stared at her, but she had her eyes closed and didn't even seem to have noticed me at all.

"Sorry," I muttered, meaning for disturbing her but kind of meaning for all the rest of the shit between us too.

Her eyes snapped open and for a fleeting moment, her entire pupils were painted black with shadows before she managed to force them away.

"What the fuck are you doing?" I demanded, the bite in my tone coming out more forcefully than I'd intended as my heart leapt with fear for her. But fuck it, she shouldn't be playing around with the fucking shadows on her own and she knew it.

"Practicing," she said icily, pushing to her feet and glaring at me just like she had before the first time I'd kissed her. That memory cut me open and left me bleeding, but she either didn't notice or didn't care. Probably both.

"You shouldn't be practicing this shit without someone else to watch your back," I said, taking a step towards her as my gaze scraped over her face but before I could get anywhere near her, I hit a solid air shield and fell still. I hadn't even seen her cast it which meant she'd gotten a lot faster than she used to be.

"I can watch my own back," she replied, her eyes guarded as she watched me press my hand against her shield. I didn't try to break it. I just laid my palm against it, feeling the gentle caress of her magic against my skin and trying not to take offence to the fact that she thought she needed to protect herself from me with it. "I'll have to get used to that now anyway."

"What does that mean?" I asked.

"I'm always going to be alone now, aren't I? Forever." Her green eyes circled in black flashed and for the briefest moment I saw the pain that word cost her as it passed her lips before she locked it back down again.

"I'm sorry," I breathed, my gaze falling from hers as the guilt over what I'd cost us pressed down on me. She was wearing her running gear, a black pair of leggings and a bright blue sports bra which left enough of her flesh on show to make me ache.

The air shield beneath my palm fell away and I found myself standing hardly more than a foot away from her as she looked up at me, the air crackling between us.

Thunder rumbled overhead and I frowned as I glanced up at the sky which had been clear just moments ago and yet was somehow filled with clouds now.

"Darius…" Roxy said, her tone suddenly softer and I dropped my gaze back to her instantly, forgetting the clouds and anything else in favour of hearing her speak. "I need to know if you meant it. What you said to me when the stars called us together. If you really did regret the things-"

Lightning slammed into the sand a few meters away from us and Roxy screamed as she jumped back. I stumbled aside and nearly fell on my ass as my heart leapt in fright but before I could recover, ice cold sleet fell from the heavens in a torrent.

I threw heat up over my body, moving closer to Roxy to shield her too as I burned the sleet away, protecting us from the downpour. I pulled my draining dagger from my pocket, quickly scoring the marks into the rocks which would open the cave for us.

Lightning slammed into the sand again as we stumbled inside and I caught Roxy's hand as I dragged her away from the storm.

Heat spread along my flesh from the small point of contact and my heart pounded with the force of a hurricane as I looked down at her.

She didn't snatch her hand away, but the pain in her eyes was sharp enough to cut me open as she looked up at me.

The cave floor suddenly started to tremble beneath our feet and I cursed as I looked around at the space and rocks began to fall from the roof to pelt us.

Roxy threw an air shield over our heads to protect us from them but the tremors only grew more intense, the storm outside howling with fury.

"What the hell is going on?" Roxy gasped, her grip on my fingers tightening as the ground bucked hard enough to make us stumble and she fought to exert her earth magic over it too.

It was like the weather and the fucking ground itself had come together to attack us or something, the intensity of the thunder and the earthquake growing with every passing second.

I looked down at Roxy again and my heart twisted as a horrible thought occurred to me. I released my grip on her hand and backed up a few steps.

The tremors instantly lessened, the thunder losing volume too.

I backed up even more and rocks stopped falling from the cave roof as my gaze stayed locked on her. The black rings in her eyes taunted me like they were created just to hurt me every time I looked at them.

"Oh," she breathed as she realised what was happening too. "The stars don't want us close to each other now?"

"Well, at least you don't have to worry about me hurting you again," I said bitterly as the reality of that crashed over me. I couldn't even be near her without the stars punishing us and the thought of having to keep my distance from her forevermore only poured salt onto the wounds of knowing I could never have her. I strode towards the cave exit. "Because I can't get within ten feet."

Before I could step out into the dwindling storm, Lance appeared in front of me with Gwen and that weird hat kid.

"Where are you going?" Lance asked me in confusion and I paused as the tremors in the cave fell still and the rain stopped pouring from the sky.

"I *was* leaving," I said, glancing back at Roxy who was standing with her arms folded and a pout on her full lips which said she was pissed at me, but that was nothing new. "The stars made that storm to push us apart..." I glanced up at the sky as the clouds slowly cleared, wondering what the fuck that meant. "I guess...they just don't want us being alone together."

Lance's gaze darkened as he looked between me and Roxy, but he held back on anything he might have wanted to say as he cut a glance towards the hat kid.

"We'll make sure you're not alone down here again then," Lance said with a heaviness to his tone which said he kinda hated that. And shit, I kinda hated it too. I'd known the stars would work against us, and Max had already been trying to convince me that Caleb had been pushed towards Roxy when they'd hooked up the other night but this…the world physically pushing us apart if we tried to be alone together. What the fuck was that about?

I closed my eyes for a moment, forcing my attention to fix on the reason for us coming here and expelling a breath before opening them again.

"What are you doing here?" I asked the hat kid. Danny? David? Something like that. All I really knew about him was that he'd been a bit too eager to help Roxy get wasted that night in The Orb and had put his fucking hands on her in front of me at the Halloween party too. Suffice to say, I didn't like him. Not one fucking bit.

"Polaris here has come to offer us some assistance," Lance said and the tightness in his jaw said he didn't like the kid either.

"Is that so?" I asked, levelling him with a dark stare which made Gwen shift closer to him, curling a hand around his bicep like she thought she could protect him from me if I decided to do something.

"He's got access to the memories of his family members who are working with your family. He can give us inside knowledge which might tip this thing in our favour when the time comes," Lance explained.

My gaze flipped back to the kid as he tugged on his hat nervously. I knew all about that creepy bit of knitwear and I had zero desire to spend any time with his soul grandma or whoever the fuck was knitted up inside it.

"That doesn't mean he needs to stay for anything else we're doing here," I said, holding his eye until he looked down at his boots.

"Agreed," Lance said. "I just want him to make a star promise with you and Tory so we can be sure he doesn't betray us."

"I swear I just want to help," Dennis said as he looked at me. It was definitely D something.

"Fine," I agreed, I wanted him gone as much as anything else. I couldn't get that image of him dancing with Roxy at Halloween out of my head and to make it worse, I knew that whole thing had only happened because of me anyway. I could have stopped Max from giving her that potion but I hadn't. I let my desire for power and my father's wishes infect my actions again and again.

Lance took a Lapis Lazuli crystal from his pocket and proceeded to get both me and Roxy to make the bond with Denzel. I might have crushed his hand in mine when I did it, but it was hard to say for sure as the whole time my gaze was fixed on the girl I couldn't have.

Once Darren had fucked off, we got on with our shadow lesson and I proceeded to watch every move that Roxy made while she made every effort *not* to look at me.

But when it came to her turn to dip into the shadows, I wasn't the only one staring at her. She practically snatched Lance's draining dagger from him and cut her palm open without a moment of hesitation before letting the shadows pour forth and coat her skin. Within the blink of an eye, she'd covered every inch of her flesh in them and her eyes turned as black as pitch.

"You've been practicing," Lance said in a dark voice as Roxy drew a ball of shadow to sit in her palm. "I thought we agreed you wouldn't do that?"

"I don't think I would have agreed to that," Roxy replied, her voice drawing a shiver down my spine as it was laced with the power of the Fifth Element.

"Fine," Lance growled. "If you're so determined to push yourself with them then let's see if you have as much control as you think you do. You can try to face me with them."

"Is that a good idea?" Gwen asked, her eyes wheeling between her sister and Lance. "What if one of you gets hurt? The last injury you got from doing dark magic wasn't exactly easy to heal-"

"She has a point," I said, frowning at my friend and moving to take his place. "You're still not fully recovered. Let her face me instead."

Roxy's gaze fell on me at last with that suggestion, but the shadows swimming in her eyes made it impossible to tell what she was thinking.

Lance hesitated like he wasn't sure that was the best idea, but he didn't stop me as I moved to stand before her.

"I don't want you to attack him," Lance said. "Just restrain him. If you've got as much control as you think you do then it should be easy enough to do that without causing any pain."

Roxy didn't reply but as she fixed her gaze on me, the barest hint of a smile played around her lips and a lump caught in my throat. Of course she'd be happy enough to have the excuse to strike at me. I was the root of that ache in her eyes.

The shadows rose up all around her and I used my own draining dagger to cut into my palm too, so that I could channel the dark energy into defending against her attack more easily.

A rush of ecstasy tumbled beneath my skin and I inhaled deeply as the shadows ran to me.

Everything seemed to pale and fade as I welcomed their power, only the darkest of my emotions remaining sharp enough to feel fully.

My jaw tightened as I looked at Roxy, the anger which I'd been trying not to feel burning a trail beneath my flesh. She'd chosen this path for us. She'd stolen our shot at happiness.

Before I could force those feelings under control, Roxy threw a net of shadows towards me.

Darkness curtained my vision as I fought to steal control of the shadows she'd sent at me, bending them to my will so that instead of trapping me within them, they moved to coat my flesh and add to my own power.

It took more effort than I expected but with a grunt of determination, the shadows fell to my command.

But Roxy wasn't done there, she sent a second net at me followed by a third and a fourth, the shadows dancing around her wildly so that her long hair billowed around her shoulders with their power.

I took control of the second net but sweat was beading on my brow and as the third hit me, I staggered back a step. Roxy's shadows coiled around me with a cold determination, pressing me back until I hit the rock wall behind me and binding my limbs together as she immobilised me. I fought to bring them under my control for another few moments, but I refused to fight back against her.

The call of the shadows was too strong, the desires of them too deadly. I wouldn't unleash dark magic on her no matter what she did to me.

"*Enough*," Lance barked as Roxy advanced, her gaze flickering with the darkness of the shadows. She looked deadly, beautiful and entirely consumed by the power she was wielding.

For a moment, I didn't think she was going to stop coming at me but as Gwen called her name, she fell still.

It took her several more seconds to draw the shadows back, but the flickering darkness around her finally withdrew and the shadows pinning me in place dispersed too.

"Be honest, how hard was it for you to pull them back then?" Lance asked as he fixed her in his gaze, his brow furrowing with concern.

"Harder after I used them to restrain him, but I still managed it," she said, looking away from me again. I didn't miss the way she avoided saying my name and I tried not to let that burn.

"Only with Darcy to anchor you," he replied gruffly. "I think we should call it for tonight. But I'm warning you not to keep playing with the shadows."

"Aye aye, captain," Roxy replied sarcastically before turning and walking for the exit.

It felt like the air in the cave contracted as she left and the dull ache in my chest sharpened as I was filled with the urge to chase after her, but I didn't move an inch.

Darcy exchanged a concerned look with Lance. "I should make sure she's okay. I'll talk to her and make sure she's not pushing it too far with the shadows."

"They feed on grief and pain," Lance growled, shooting me an apologetic look for half a second. "She'll be more susceptible to their call now than ever before."

"Don't worry, she's tough. She'll be okay." Gwen glanced at me too and the accusation in her eyes cut into me. She blamed me for her sister's unhappiness and I couldn't exactly deny that.

Lance clasped her fingers for a moment and she tiptoed up to press a kiss to his lips, flushing pink as she cut me another look before heading for the exit.

"I dealt with Seth," I called after her before she stepped outside. "He won't bother either of you anymore."

Tension seemed to fall from her body in a wave and she offered me a wide smile which was so full of relief that I could practically taste it on the air. "Thank you, Darius," she breathed before turning and hurrying out after Roxy.

Lance turned to me, running a hand over his short beard as he scanned my features. "Before the storm tried to force you apart, did you manage to talk to her at all?"

"About what?" I asked, forcing myself to stay and hear him out despite the desire to walk out creeping through my limbs.

"About...*fuck*, Darius, about *everything.*"

"No. What's the point?"

"Seriously? You're just going to stick with self-pity and moping? I thought you had more fight in you than that," he growled.

"Fight for what? I can't change this fate. And I wasn't going for mopey, I was going for acceptance." I shrugged, although now that he pointed it out, I was acting kinda like a little bitch.

"I've told you I'm not just going to accept this bullshit version of destiny for you," Lance growled, stepping right up into my personal space and giving me a shove which instantly set the Alpha in me snarling. "So it's time you stopped acting like you accept it too."

"What the fuck else am I supposed to do? Even *if* you managed to find some way around this, which I don't believe for a second that you can, she still hates me, she still had a whole list of perfectly valid reasons to deny me. So what difference would it make?"

"None," he snapped. "None at all unless you prove to her that you're more than just a monster carved in your father's image."

"Maybe that's exactly what I am. It's not like I can deny doing any of the things she hates me for."

"So that's it? You give up? You're going to just spend your life pining after her, marry Mildred, fall into line with your father's plans and be a good little Heir?"

"Fuck you." I shoved past him and walked towards the exit but before I could leave, I slammed into a solid wall of air.

"No, Darius. Fuck *you!* Fuck all the bullshit you spouted to me over the years about fighting back against your father, about working to change his legacy and being a better man than him. Fuck the lies you told about using your time to rule with the other Heirs to make Solaria a greater kingdom, and fuck you for being too much of a coward to just tell Tory Vega how you felt about her before it was too goddamn late!"

I whirled back around, fire bursting to life around my fists before I threw it at him with a cry of rage. The shadows leapt up beneath my skin, but I ignored them in favour of fire. I didn't want the numbness of the Fifth Element, I wanted to burn.

The fireball slammed into Lance's shield and washed over it in a tide of crimson flames before stuttering out and leaving me aching for more.

"Better," Lance said, a hungry smile lighting his features. "Now put that desire to fight to good use. And use it to fix this shit between you and Tory."

104

"How the hell am I supposed to do that?" I demanded. "You've seen the way she looks at me. She hates me."

"Hate dances a fine line with love more often than not. Fix it, Darius. Then if I really can find a way to give you another chance at fate, you'll both be ready to make a different choice." He strode towards me, shoving me aside as I reeled from his words.

By the time I turned to shout after him, he was gone. And I was left alone in the dark with nothing but my own demons to keep me company.

TORY

CHAPTER NINE

Two weeks was a long time in some ways and a short time in others. Apparently it was long enough for most people to stop actively staring at my eyes and their fancy new black rings. Most people, not all. But it was a start. It was also long enough for Geraldine to be able to talk to me without spontaneously bursting into tears every five minutes. We had it down to about fifteen now.

It was long enough for people to stop whispering and start just rudely asking for details instead.

It was long enough for me to stop crying myself to sleep, though I still woke up with tears on my cheeks.

And apparently it was long enough for Darius to schedule an interview and photoshoot with the press too.

I sat in The Orb eating my breakfast on my own thanks to my run taking longer than usual and me missing the Ass Club gathering. My gaze slid over the two glossy photographs which started off the piece titled, *Darius Acrux on duty, sacrifice and his one true love.* One was a close up shot of Darius smouldering at the camera, shirt off, tattoos on show and two dark, black rings circling his deep brown irises. He looked hot as fuck which was its own special kind of torture.

The second photograph was of him wearing a spotless suit, standing behind a huge chair which was basically a throne, his arm tossed over the back of it as he looked down at the girl who sat in it. Mildred Canopus, his fiancé, wearing a flowing white gown, her left hand raised coyly to cover her mouth with a massive motherfucker of an engagement ring sparkling on her ring finger. Her mean little eyes looked bigger and brighter than when I'd seen her in the flesh, her moustache hidden beneath her hand, her skin flawless with makeup and maybe some editing and her frizzy brown hair perfectly styled around her.

My heart pounded as I scrolled down to read the article, knowing that I should just shut my Atlas off and pretend I'd never even seen it. But I couldn't. I just couldn't make myself turn back now even though I knew this was going to hurt. It was like I'd been forged in punishment and pain and I just couldn't get enough of it no matter how much it damaged me.

Celestial Heir Darius Acrux gives his first interview since choosing Solaria over fate and telling Roxanya Vega that he would never be hers.

In this candid interview, we talk heartache and love with the Heir who gave up his Elysian Mate because he knew it was the best thing for our kingdom and he explains how he's managed to defy the stars and find love with his fiancé Mildred Canopus, despite what the heavens had planned. Their wedding has been moved forward to just two days after their graduation and all of Solaria can't wait for the wondrous day.

"Of course I felt a pull towards Roxanya, but I knew in my heart that she'd never make a suitable wife for a Celestial Councillor. She's brash and uneducated, selfish and not suited to ruling at my side any more than she would be to claiming the throne. And I couldn't take the heartache of watching her with so many other men all the time either. I'm a one woman man and I want to give my entire heart, body and soul to one woman alone. And that woman is Mildred."

Of course, it has been well documented that Roxanya Vega's sex addiction had already led her to sleep her way through every single male in her freshman class through seduction and blackmail and it is rumoured she's begun on the women-

A hand slammed down over my Atlas and I flinched as I looked up to find Darius himself standing over me.

"I didn't say a single one of those words," he growled, his eyes burning with a raw kind of anger. "I've already sent my legal team after that reporter and I'm having that article taken down and a retraction printed."

My throat thickened as I looked up at him, feeling eyes on us from all around The Orb.

"Did you really bring your wedding forward?" I asked, hating how softly my words came out and hating even more that I'd really asked that question.

Darius's jaw ticked and his gaze burned with an intensity that seared the flesh from my bones and left me weak and aching for him.

"Father brought the date forward," he admitted and that shouldn't have hurt, but it did.

I tugged my Atlas back out of his grip and stood up suddenly, forcing him to straighten before me and standing so close to him that my chest brushed against his.

The stars didn't seem to mind that with so many people around to witness us, but in that moment I wished they'd tear us away from each other.

"But you're still going ahead with it?" I asked in a low voice that only he could hear. "You'll turn up and walk down the aisle and-"

"Are you seeing Caleb again?" he growled and that froze me in my tracks.

The bell rang to signal the start of the first class of the day and the other students all began to file out of the huge space within the golden dome as I just stood staring up at him.

"No," I breathed eventually. "That night, I was stupid and selfish and heartbroken. I-"

"We don't get a say in whether or not we get to be together anymore," Darius said darkly and the tension in his posture made me ache. I wanted to reach for him, comfort him, do something to ease the weight I could see laying on his shoulders, but I didn't know what I could do. And another part of me didn't want to comfort him anyway; the vengeful, spiteful part of me revelled in his pain and screamed that he deserved it, but in the wake of my own heartache, sometimes it was hard to cling to that idea.

"I know," I said and I knew I shouldn't have asked him about Mildred, but she was just such a fucking asshole. The idea of him with her, Lord and Lady Acrux in their fancy fucking house with their hoard of Dragon babies each with their own fluffy little moustaches just like hers just made me want to… *gah.*

"So, if Caleb makes you happy…" He didn't finish that sentence and it looked like it cost him physical pain to let it pass his lips. He locked his jaw and his fingers curled into a fist.

"Why are you saying that to me?" I demanded.

"Because…" Darius blew out a breath and took me captive in his gaze. "Maybe I don't want to live with the fact that you'll never be happy now because of this."

"You want me to be happy?"

A faint hissing noise started up and I looked around in surprise as a wet drip fell onto my cheek. The icicles decorating the ceiling of The Orb started rattling as more drips fell from them and a faint tremor rumbled through the ground at my feet.

The rest of the students had left and the stars were already working against us even as I waited for that single answer from him.

Before I could get it, Darius turned and strode away from me, leaving me to stare at the way his blazer strained over his broad shoulders as he left the room and the icicles stopped rattling.

I frowned as I considered what he'd just suggested. Did I want to try and claim something with Caleb now? In all honesty, the idea hadn't really occurred to me. Ever since the night we'd spent together after I'd been Star Crossed, I'd barely even seen him, much less thought about him. And it wasn't like we'd ever been more than a casual thing anyway. Yeah I liked him and he made me laugh, but everything with him just seemed kind of vacant when I compared it to the things I'd felt with Darius. If I spent time pining for anyone, it was all aimed at him. Which was the point of this fucking curse, wasn't it?

I glanced down at my Atlas in my hands and frowned at the picture of him and Mildred before switching it off.

I was better off not thinking about him marrying her anyway.

Elemental Combat lessons didn't fit in our regular timetable so they'd decided to give us the lessons three times a week in the evenings after dinner instead of during the day, and I found that I didn't mind that at all. The lessons were so physically and magically demanding that once they were over I was pretty exhausted, so after I spent another hour or two studying I crashed out and actually slept. Which was pretty hard for me at the moment.

Sometimes when I lay in bed at night and the shadows twisted between my fingers, I liked to imagine what my teachers at my old high schools would think of me now. I'd never really applied myself to my studies the way me and Darcy had been this term, and the thought of me staying up past midnight studying night after night would have been unthinkable to me back then. But I'd grown this appetite for knowledge and learning which could rival Darcy's in the last few weeks. Okay, so I wasn't all that interested in history or other academic subjects, but my thirst for magical knowledge was unquenchable. We'd been having additional lessons and assignments with almost all of our teachers and Orion and Gabriel had gone out of their way to spend hours with us to improve our skills. And we really were improving. We were topping all of our classes and were starting to learn magic which was more advanced than a lot of our classmates.

But it still wasn't enough. Because I was done with playing catch up to the Heirs. And I refused to slow down until we not only matched their skill, but surpassed it.

I walked beside Darcy as we headed up to The Howling Meadow where the lessons were held. We were wearing leggings and sports bras, our hair tied back and looking very twinny in our matching outfits. I kinda loved it.

"I heard a rumour today that Marguerite has manticrabs," Darcy said to me in a low voice as we spotted the girl in question up ahead. She was laughing and tossing her red hair, trying to catch the attention of the Heirs who were holding court in the middle of the meadow, lazing on the group of boulders that sat there and showing off with flashy magic like always. Darius wasn't really joining in, but he was standing with them and my gaze automatically hooked on his exposed biceps and the ink that covered them for a moment before I forced myself to look away.

"It wouldn't surprise me," I replied. "Considering she's the one who calls me a whore all the time, I've heard that she's currently sleeping with half the Pitball sub team."

"So is Kylie apparently in a bid to make Seth jealous. Let's hope they both catch manticrabs from the same guy then have a big fight right before your cheer off with their cheerleading squad," Darcy joked.

"Don't remind me," I groaned.

My squad and I had actually been making some pretty good progress on our routine and I couldn't even really claim to hate it anymore. But since Washer had started attending our practice sessions, a whole new level of horror had been added to them. Did we need a teeny weeny bit of help with our stretches? No, no we did not, *blegh*.

As if my mind had conjured the very man I'd been thinking about, Washer stepped out of the crowd and came to a halt before us.

"Well, if it isn't my favourite twins," he purred.

As this class wasn't held near water, he thankfully didn't have any excuse to be wearing a speedo so instead we were gifted a look at his clothes. But as these lessons were after hours, he always dressed down for them. Today he was wearing the tightest pair of leather pants I'd ever seen accompanied by a tiger print button down which seemed to have a lot of Lycra in it judging by the way it stretched around his torso, though of course he'd left half the buttons undone to reveal plenty of sun baked chest.

I exchanged a glance with Darcy as we were forced to fall still and see what he had to say and as expected, his gaze zeroed in on me.

"How are you feeling today, my little Star Crossed lamb?"

"Fine," I ground out, but the pouty look he gave me said he smelled bullshit.

I threw more magic into my mental shields, but ever since I'd made the decision not to be bound to Darius, the maelstrom of emotions warring inside me had become increasingly hard to fully shield from nosy Sirens. I could burn out their invasion with my Phoenix fire, but I couldn't keep that up all the time.

"I've been speaking to Principal Nova about giving you some one on one sessions in private to help you work through this little speed bump," he pressed, inching closer with his hand raised like he thought he might touch me.

I stepped back to make sure there was no chance of that and levelled a glare at him. "No thanks. I don't need anyone poking around in my head."

"Well, sweet cheeks, that's not necessarily up to you. If someone as powerful as yourself is having trouble coping with their emotions it might lead to magical or even Order outbursts, and if we have reason to believe you're *unstable* then it's the school's duty to insist you have counselling sessions with a qualified member of staff. We just want to help." He opened his arms wide like he thought he might tempt me in for a hug and I didn't make any effort to conceal the disgust I was feeling.

"My sister is not unstable," Darcy snarled, shifting forward like she intended to shield me from him.

"If you think for one second that I'll be having cosy little sessions with Professor Perv, in some little locked room somewhere then you seriously need to drag your head out of your ass and-"

"Tory is having one on one sessions with me already," Gabriel's voice came from behind me and I whipped around to find him standing there, shirt off, tattoos on show and glorious black wings slowly tucking in against his back as if he'd just landed. "I had a vision about this very meeting and arranged it with Nova myself this morning."

"Oh," Washer said, placing his hands on his hips like he'd just had his favourite toy stolen from him. Or maybe I was more of a snack than a toy. I was willing to bet that all of this emotional angst was really tasty for a Siren and I was probably looking pretty irresistible right about now. "Are you sure you're the right man for the job, though, Gabe?"

"Don't call me Gabe," Gabriel snapped.

"It's just that I am a little better suited to dealing with affairs of the heart. As a Siren, I can get right down *deep* inside of Miss Vega and really wriggle around beneath her skin as we hunt down every little one of her issues. I'm not afraid to thrust right into the dark nooks and crannies inside of her and really work hard at wringing all of this stress from her lithe young body. We can work through all the naughty things that big bad Dragon has done to her and go over every little detail, until-"

"Phoenix fire burns right through Siren bullshit," I said, slapping a sweet as pie smile on my face as if I wasn't insulting him. "So you won't be getting anywhere near my nooks and crannies."

A shiver ran down my spine at the grossness of that statement and Gabriel snorted a laugh as Washer sighed in defeat.

"Well, if you ever need someone *qualified* to root around inside of you then you know where I am. Even if you don't want to offer up your emotions, I can always just pleasure you instead," Washer offered with a look on his face like a kicked puppy.

"What the fuck is that supposed to mean?" I demanded and in answer, Washer pushed a wave of happy emotions over us which washed against my mental defences and slid back off of them again.

"See? I can make you feel happy," he said with an innocent shrug.

"Ew," Darcy remarked, not even trying to hide her revulsion.

Washer sighed in defeat and headed off through the crowd with his leather pants creaking.

"How the hell does he get away with that shit?" Darcy growled as we watched him go.

"He's fucking Principal Nova and as gross as it is, Sirens really are good in bed – they can enhance lust and pleasure so much with their gifts that Fae get addicted to screwing them," Gabriel explained with a faint look of horror on his face.

"Gross, dude," I commented. "You're gonna make me hurl my dinner up right here and now."

Gabriel snorted a laugh before heading away into the crowd as he called out for attention.

The entire student body was attending these classes and after the first few lessons, the teachers running it had decided to divide us up based on skill and power levels. We'd been placed in the second highest level group with a bunch of Seniors, Geraldine and a few other high powered students from the other years. The Heirs of course had an entire group of their own.

"Today we are changing up the groups!" Orion's voice boomed over the crowd and I turned to spot him standing on the far side of the crowd.

Darcy's eyes glimmered in that way they did whenever she saw him and I bit down on a smirk as I looked at her. She really was hopelessly lovestruck.

"We've assessed everyone's skills and reassigned all of the groups, some of you have impressed us and are moving up, some of you are making us question whether or not you're even Fae enough to be at Zodiac Academy at all and will be moving down. A golden number just appeared above your head, so go and join the group you belong to now!"

A sea of glimmering numbers magically appeared floating above everyone in the crowd and I looked up at Darcy's just as she looked at mine.

"Yes!" Darcy squealed, slapping me a high five as we spotted the glimmering number ones. "I can't wait to kick some Heir ass."

"Sounds good to me," I agreed with a grin that felt kinda fake on my face, but I couldn't help it.

Did I want to go over there and learn how to smash the Heirs' faces into the mud in a fight? Hell yes! Did I want to spend even more lessons stuck in a small group with Darius Acrux? The most disturbing thing about the answer to that question was that it wasn't just a straight no. Because this stupid curse made me yearn for him and pine for him and despite the pain it caused me to spend time around him, that twisted little piece of me hungered for that sweet kiss of agony too.

"Holy guacamole, my ladies! We have all progressed as one!" Geraldine cried excitedly as she shoved through the crowd like a bulldozer, a glimmering number one above her head too.

She swept us into a celebratory hug and I laughed as she crushed me in her strong embrace.

The three of us made our way through the crowd towards the Heirs who were still lounging around the huge boulder in the centre of the meadow.

"Well, well, well, if it isn't the Vegas and their personal bodyguard,"

Seth purred as he looked down at us from his position sitting on top of the rock. "Do you think you're really ready to try and play with the big boys?"

"Big boys?" Geraldine asked in surprise. "I didn't know any big boys were joining our group! Do point them out, Master Wolf, and I'll be sure to give them a jolly good welcome."

I bit my lip on a smile as my gaze shifted over Caleb who was perched on a slightly lower rock, a sad kind of tension in his posture as he met my eye. Max's entire focus had fallen on Geraldine and he moved to stand upright as he looked at her. I honestly had to wonder what exactly she'd done to him in the sack to have won the kind of obsession he was aiming her way because despite the fact that she constantly ignored his attention, he still seemed determined to win it. Maybe her Lady Petunia was a magic vag, designed to lure Siren dick in and then never release it from her spell.

"I think you know what a big boy I am, Grus," Max purred, kicking off of the boulder as he approached her. "And I'm always happy to remind you, if you like?"

Geraldine tossed her chestnut hair and laughed heartily. "I'd sooner tangle my garden with a new weed if it's all the same to you, honey badger."

"Honey badger?" Max asked with a frown. "What the fuck is that supposed to mean?"

"Oh you know," Geraldine said, flicking her fingers at him dismissively as he stood over her with his muscles flexing beneath his wifebeater and his eyes flashing. "You're sweet like honey with the way you chase around after me and you taste great at first. But no one wants to drown in honey - it's far too sticky and a jolly old bastard of a beast to wash off."

"And the badger part?" Seth asked eagerly before Max could reply.

"Because he's a bothersome badger of course," Geraldine said, rolling her eyes like that was obvious and I suddenly found myself laughing along with the Heirs about something.

Well, Seth howled anyway and Caleb sniggered while Max ground his jaw with irritation and Darius...I hadn't looked at Darius yet, but my treacherous eyes were swivelling his way all the same.

He was leaning against the side of the boulder, shirt off now for some frustratingly distracting reason, arms folded, a dark and brooding look on his way too perfect face. I resisted looking at him properly for as long as I could then finally let my eyes raise to meet his when I couldn't take it anymore. He was looking at me. Of course he was looking at me. His gaze burned me whenever we were in the same place. I didn't know if he was a glutton for punishment or if he just couldn't help it but whatever the reason, if we were within view of each other, I could guarantee his eyes would be on me. And I'd be battling to keep mine off of him.

"How much longer are you going to keep fighting this, Grus?" Max asked irritably.

"Whatever do you mean?"

"I *mean,*" Max stepped closer to her and reached out to brush her hair back over her shoulder. "That I can feel exactly how much you like me whenever you let that shield of yours slip, but I just can't figure out what it is that's holding you back."

Silence fell between all of us and Geraldine raised her chin and set her jaw as she fixed her gaze on Max.

"You may find it hard to believe, but a true lady won't just roll over and accept a merciless cad for a suitor just because he manages to water her lawn satisfactorily. I am more than attuned to your personal moral standards and I have no desire to lower myself to them. So call it what you will, foolhardiness, stubbornness or just a pure and true desire to tangle my web with a real gentleman but when it comes down to it, Maxy boy, you have been measured and you have been found wanting. Now please refrain from touching me with your slippery flippers and let us return to our lesson."

Geraldine turned away from him to listen as Orion began directing the class. I exchanged a glance with Darcy as Max pushed his tongue into his cheek before turning away from her too.

"Well," Caleb said in a low voice. "That was awkward as fuck."

I snorted a laugh and he caught my eye with a smirk toying around his mouth. I suddenly remembered what Darius had said to me about him and I looked away again quickly, wondering when my life had first headed down this complicated path and if there had ever been a point at which I could have changed it.

As the class all paired off in their respective groups and moved to find some space around the field to conduct their fights, we found ourselves left in the centre of the masses within a huge ring of space.

"How about it, Darcy?" Seth challenged before the rest of us could suggest anything. "You wanna try and kick my ass for making your life hell?"

"Hell yes," Darcy growled, her gaze narrowing as she looked up at Seth and he laughed as he hopped down from the boulder, using his air magic to slow his descent.

"No Order gifts," Orion said casually as he wandered past. "We don't need a deep fried Heir on our hands."

"No chance of that," Seth growled irritably, clearly not liking the suggestion that Darcy could overpower him with Phoenix fire that easily.

I glanced between the other Heirs, wondering which of them I was going to have to fight, but Darius spoke before I could challenge anyone. "Why don't we take turns to fight today while we get a feel for how each other's skills are progressing? We can watch this round."

"Okay," I said simply, turning my attention to watch Seth and Darcy as they faced off in the space before us. I was more than happy to witness his ass kicking anyway.

"If you want me to go easy on you, babe, you just have to ask nicely," Seth taunted. "Just get down on your knees and say please in your sweetest voice and-"

Darcy shot a blast of water at him so fast that he didn't even have time to shield before it smacked him in the face and knocked him on his ass.

I smirked as she barked a laugh and vines shot from the ground to entangle Seth as he scrambled to get up. We'd been practicing damn hard in class and out of it, using each other as opponents and getting Geraldine to heal the fatigue from our limbs once we were done so that we could complete the rest of our studies too.

Darcy advanced with a savage grin on her face as her vines tightened around Seth but he managed to rip a hand free, stealing command of the vines and making the ground quake beneath her feet as he snarled with determination.

Darcy threw another blast of water at him but it slammed into an air shield and washed over it, splashing us as we watched. I took a step back to avoid it and flinched as I bumped into someone.

I turned, finding Darius behind me and quickly stepped away again as my skin burned from the contact.

He didn't say anything but now that I knew he was behind me, my skin prickled with goosebumps and my breaths became shallow.

Seth regained his feet, clenching his teeth in concentration as Darcy slammed water into his shield and he fought to maintain it. But with a flick of his other hand, he sent a huge vine spinning up from the ground at her feet.

Darcy cried out as the vine sent her flying, throwing fire at it as she tried to burn it away from her, but Seth was too fast. More and more vines shot at her from every direction, slamming into her and winding their way around her body tightly before immobilising her hands too.

She fell back to the ground tangled in them with a grunt of frustration and Seth howled his victory to the sky as she panted beneath them.

"Do you yield, babe?" he asked, moving to stand over her and I clenched my teeth in irritation. But that was okay. We knew we couldn't match the Heirs yet. The point was that we would be able to soon. And with our power we'd be able to crush them for good measure.

"Yeah," Darcy sighed. "I yield."

The vines fell away and he offered her a hand as she got to her feet.

"Good," Orion barked as he passed us again. "Darius against Tory next."

I glanced at Darius as my gut did a kind of weird flip flopping somersault, but his gaze was locked on Orion.

"No," he growled. "I'm not fighting her."

"You are unless you want a week of detention with me," Orion growled right back, stopping to glare at him.

"I said *no*," Darius repeated, his arms folded in a clear refusal.

I looked between them as Orion geared up to go full asshole and I sighed dramatically.

"What's the matter, Darius? Afraid I'll kick your ass and make you look like a little bitch in front of everyone?" I taunted, turning to look up into his black-ringed eyes.

His gaze slid over me slowly and heat followed the path of his eyes over every inch of my flesh that they caressed.

"Hardly."

"Then what's the problem?" I demanded.

He hesitated for a long moment then shrugged. "I don't want to hurt you."

My lips parted at that declaration and the sincerity of those words echoed deep down into me with a truth I couldn't deny.

For a long moment we just looked at each other before I remembered we had an audience and I quickly rolled my eyes. "You're so cocky for an asshole who's afraid to even face me. Just come and fight me – we both know you want to really."

His eyes narrowed at that assessment and he still refused to move. "No."

"Well...*I'm* going to fight. So if you don't want me to make a fool of you, you probably want to fight back."

Orion chuckled darkly behind me and Darius's muscles flexed as he held his ground.

"Come on, Dragon boy," I taunted and I suddenly realised that I'd actually missed his usual challenges and teasing comments. I wanted him to bite back at me, needed him to stand up to my shit and call me out on my crap.

"No."

"Fuck me, are you really going to make me beg?" I pouted as I looked up at him and the barest hint of a smile tugged at the corner of his lips.

"You can certainly give it a try."

Not likely. But my lips pulled up as I came up with another plan.

I reached out and caught his hand, tugging it so that he was forced to unfold his arms and he frowned at me in confusion as an electric kind of heat passed between us.

The sky darkened overhead and I was willing to bet the stars wouldn't put up with us actually touching each other for long even while we had company but that was okay, I wasn't planning on just holding onto his hand.

The moment his guard dropped, I raised my other hand and slammed my palm into his solid chest. He was seriously strong and I was sure I wouldn't have moved him a damn inch but for the force of a tornado crashing from my palm.

A laugh tore from my throat as Darius's eyes widened in surprise and he was thrown back, but I hadn't accounted for the fact that he was still holding my other hand.

I screamed as his grip tightened on me and the two of us were sent flying by my magic, slamming into the grassy hill in a heap as adrenaline thundered through my limbs.

We rolled across the grass and I ended up on top of him, quickly pressing my advantage as I called on the earth beneath him to hold him down.

The grass bloomed and flourished all around us, wrapping its way around his limbs as I fought to tie him down, but he wielded fire to burn it away as quickly as it grew.

With all of my focus on trying to force the grass to hold him, he should have been able to throw me off easily and I braced in anticipation of his attack, but it didn't come.

"Are you still going easy on me, Darius?" I growled as I looked down at him from my position straddling him.

"I told you, I'm not going to hurt you again, Roxy," he replied as he continued to burn my earth magic away as fast as I could conjure it.

"Don't pretend you don't want to," I pushed. "You must hate me for saying no."

Darius growled, but he still didn't attack me. "I don't hate you."

"More fool you then." I tried to push off of him but he caught my thighs, holding me in place with a dangerous snarl as the clouds continued to darken overhead.

I narrowed my eyes at him and switched my attack to water, forming a bubble of it all around him and closing it in over his head so that he was forced to shove me off of him to remove it.

I rolled aside, coating my arms in fire as he directed the water from his face with his own magic and scrambled up too, shaking his head and sending droplets flying from his black hair.

I threw the flames in my arms at him and he quickly used his own magic to gutter them out. I shot more fire at him, then water, air, earth, and he neutralised each and every one of my attacks without once striking back.

The longer it went on, the more infuriated I got, fighting harder and harder to break through his defences with everything I had, but I couldn't even crack them.

Darius's eyes lit with a hungry kind of thrill the longer it went on and no matter how sneaky I tried to be with my attacks or even when I threw brute force behind them, I still couldn't find a way through.

Heat licked down my spine and I found myself wanting to punch his stupid, smug face every single time he burned through my attacks with a blaze of fire or stopped them with a shield of ice. My heart was pounding, my skin tingling and I hated to admit it, but I was getting way too many flashbacks of the way his flesh had felt against mine the few times we'd given in to this heat between us.

"Enough!" Orion called eventually and I dropped my hands to my knees as I panted with exertion. "Fifty points to Ignis for an impenetrable defence, Darius. Minus fifty for not attacking your opponent when you had the opportunity. And you can have one point for determination, Miss Vega."

I flipped him off and his eyes lit with amusement as he called an end to the class and the rest of the students started to disperse.

A shadow fell over me and I looked up as Darius approached.

"You know, one day, I'll be able to get past your defences," I warned him as I stood upright and looked right into his eyes. "And then you'll have to decide if you want to fight back before I kick your ass or just take your beating like a good little bitch."

"Maybe I'll take the beating," he said in a low growl as he moved so close to me that our chests were almost touching. A cold wind whipped around us savagely, tossing my hair about and I realised that almost everyone else had gone. The stars were about to force us apart if we didn't separate willingly. "After all, I clearly deserve it."

"I didn't think you were capable of admitting when you were in the wrong," I breathed.

"Neither did I. But if you want to keep punishing me by straddling me in the dirt, I'm not going to complain about it."

Blood rushed to my cheeks at the heat in his words and I licked my lips before I could stop myself, the pure masculine scent of him wrapping around me like a drug.

"Don't go getting your hopes up, next time it'll be my boot grinding you into the dirt," I warned.

"I look forward to it."

The wind picked up violently and a scream from somewhere above made me look around just in time to leap aside as a Griffin fell from the sky and crashed into the ground right where we'd just been standing.

My lips popped open in shock as he shifted back into his Fae form and started screaming.

"Help meee! I think I've broken my ass bone!" he shrieked and I backed up as Geraldine charged forward to help him.

"I shall assist you, my friend!" she cried. "Allow me to check the area for ruptures."

The guy screamed again as she grabbed him by the hips and pointed his ass in the air before slapping her hand to it as she worked to heal him.

"Holy shit," I breathed, caught between laughter and guilt as I backed up again and the wind continued to gust around us. I was pretty sure that me and Darius were responsible for the stars creating this maelstrom and laughing definitely would have meant I was a dick.

But as the guy gave in to Geraldine's ministrations of his ass and Max started cussing her out for groping him, I couldn't help it. A laugh tore from my lips and I had to clap my hand over them to try and hide it. *I'm definitely a dick.*

The wind continued to howl, causing my hair to billow around me and several of the students at the far side of the field shrieked and started running for cover.

I took a few more steps away and flinched as Darius caught my hand, but before I could question what he was doing, he pressed a small, black box into my palm.

"Sorry it's late," he said in a rough voice before turning and walking away from me down the hill.

I watched him leave as the wind finally dropped, my gaze lingering on the Phoenix and Dragon tattoos which dominated his back and the strangest ache building in me to call out for him not to go.

The commotion died down as Geraldine finished healing the Griffin and he declared his unfaltering loyalty to the Ass Club before hurrying away from Max's rage with his junk cupped in his hands and his bare ass wiggling as he ran.

Geraldine called Max a cantankerous crustacean and demanded he leave too before heading over to join me with Darcy at her heels.

I stood looking down at the box, wondering what the hell it could be as they closed in to look at it too and the wind finally fell still.

"Don't keep me in suspense, my lady! If I have to wait another moment in wondering, I'm going to fall down dead as a doorknob with tension tearing my poor nerves to shreds!" Geraldine gasped.

I scoffed lightly, my grip tightening on the little box as I was caught between the urge to open it and the urge to throw it away. *Gah.*

"You don't have to open it if you don't want to," Darcy said, using her twin senses to figure out exactly what I was thinking.

But not opening it was worse than opening it. Because then I'd be thinking about the damn thing, wondering about it. And I didn't need any new reasons to spend my time obsessing over Darius Acrux.

With a huff of frustration, I pulled the lid off of the box, a small tingle of magic rushing over my fingers which I recognised as Darius's.

"Oh, he spelled it only to open for you," Geraldine sighed, fanning her eyes.

"I swear, Geraldine, if you start crying again, I'm going to toss this in the trash," I warned her.

She buttoned her lip and I looked down at the white card which lay on the top of the box, hooking it out and reading the short note in Darius's curling handwriting.

In this one instance, I may have been full of shit.

We both know you won.

I hope you enjoy your prize

Lot J, top floor, in the parking lot.

Beneath it was a layer of silver tissue paper and my heart pounded to an unfamiliar rhythm as I slowly teased it open, my fingers tingling once more with the touch of Darius's magic.

I pulled it apart and found a black bike key nestled in the paper, a silver Yamaharpie logo standing out on it and making my breath catch.

"Holy shit," I breathed. "Is he for real?"

"He bought you a bike?" Darcy gasped.

"I can't believe he's actually admitting I beat him at something," I said slowly. That just seemed so *un*Darius.

"How romantic!" Geraldine gushed.

"It doesn't change anything," I muttered as I ran my thumb over the key. But if I was really being honest with myself, maybe it did. Just a little.

DARCY

CHAPTER TEN

I lay on top of Orion, a curtain of blue hair surrounding us as I grinned down at him. We rarely slept apart these days. I knew it was reckless, we both did. But since he'd come so close to death and the world felt like it was going to tip on its axis at any moment, neither of us wanted to waste a second apart. Staying at his place was probably insanity, but as he was the only one with a double bed, I always preferred coming here. Not that we were currently making any use of the extra space; I was making Orion into my very own mattress. But instead of springs it had abs.

It must have been past midnight by now, but I didn't feel tired. I felt wide awake, wanting to drink in his company like the sweetest cocktail in the world. My body was still humming with the after effects of him claiming me. I felt his kisses branded on my skin like dripping hot wax, his touches like invisible tattoos.

I will never take a single moment with him for granted ever again.

"Are you worried about Clara?" I asked gently. I knew it was eating him up inside that he couldn't go to Lionel's house and do something about his sister.

Darius's father had banned him from going there, saying that she needed time to 'adjust'. But what that really meant was that even Lionel couldn't control her. From what Darius had said about his visit home, Clara was volatile, violent and entirely unpredictable. Which had been confirmed by the memories Orion had demanded Diego show him of her whenever possible. Even if they didn't help us with anything, Lance was just desperate to find a change in her that I feared wasn't coming. And every time we spoke about it there was this raw pain in his eyes which just cut my heart to ribbons.

His gaze slid from my face and his expression became dark. "Honestly

I'm fucking terrified for her, Blue. I know she attacked me, I know she's not herself. But it's the shadows, it's not her." He clutched my arm and his eyes flicked up again, hunting my gaze. "You believe that too, don't you?"

I knew he needed me to be on side with this. But after seeing Clara driving that blade into him, tearing into his throat with her fangs and draining the blood from his body, I couldn't feel anything but bitterness towards her. Hate. She was a monster. Nothing remotely Fae lived in that body from what I'd seen. But Orion needed me to try, so I could offer him the smallest shred of hope I had.

"I don't know," I said truthfully and his muscles rippled beneath me. I cupped his cheek so he couldn't turn away, my heart pounding a frantic beat in my chest. "But if it is the shadows making her like this, then I'll help in whatever way I can to free her from them."

His throat bobbed with emotion as he nodded. "If I could just go to her..."

"And what would you do if you could? What if she attacked you again?" I demanded, my heart thrashing like a caged animal at the thought of him going near her. I was quietly glad Lionel had stopped him from visiting, because the idea of him walking into that house with that creature who'd nearly killed him made me want to scream until my lungs burst.

"Darius and I are discussing ways to drive the shadows from her body," he said, his jaw pulsing like he was aggravated that he didn't have a simple solution to helping her. "I'll find a way. I will," he added like he was trying to convince himself as much as me.

I brushed the hair from his forehead, nodding my agreement. "If there's a way to save her, I know you'll find it and you'll do it. But please don't take any stupid risks. I can't lose you, Lance. You have no idea how awful it was seeing you there, bleeding, hurting, *dying-*"

He kissed me, gripping the back of my neck to keep me close and my heart found a steadier rhythm once more.

"I'm not going anywhere," he murmured against my lips. "We made a deal with the stars, remember?"

I nodded, drowning in the feeling of him holding me against him. "I'm sorry it had to be Seth who saved you," I said with a hiccough of laughter.

A low growl rumbled through his chest. "I'm surprised he didn't finish the job if I'm honest."

I thought on that, releasing a small sigh. "I guess he's not such a big bad wolf after all."

"Yeah, total plot twist; he saved little red riding hood when he found her bleeding out instead of eating her."

"You're more like big bearded riding hood," I pointed out and he barked a laugh.

"Damn, I must have forgotten to wear my hood during that last ride." He spanked my ass and I gasped in surprise before leaning back to tickle him in retaliation.

He laughed and the sound lit me up from the inside as he caught my wrists and pinned them against his chest. "Bad girl."

I smirked, casting ice magic around my hands, colder and colder, while Orion played chicken. "I don't lose at games like this," he said with a wicked grin. "Remember the Fairy Fair?"

My mouth pulled up at the corner as I recalled him getting electrocuted in the circus tent to apologise to me. I bit down on my lip, knowing exactly how I could get past his defences as I drew a little blood.

He growled, releasing me in an instant and rearing up to suck it from my lip. I laughed as he kissed and sucked it away then I pressed my hands to his shoulders to force him back down onto the mattress.

"I won," I sang and he smirked, his eyes becoming hooded.

"I'm okay with you being my weakness, Blue. Because that means my weakness is a badass, hot as fuck Phoenix with enough fire in her veins to rival the sun. So come at me stars, I'm invincible!" He pointed at the ceiling and I laughed, tucking myself against his chest again and wondering if I was ever going to get this smile off my face.

"Don't goad the stars." I jabbed him in the shoulder. "They'll take it as a challenge."

He chuckled, miming zipping his lips and we lay in the quiet for a while with nothing but our heartbeats breaching the silence.

His fingers threaded between mine and his thumb ran over my mother's ring on my finger.

"Is it weird that I'm wearing it?" I breathed. "Sometimes I worry she wasn't a good person."

He tucked a lock of hair behind my ear with a deep frown etched into his brow. "I don't know about good, Blue, but I know she would have done anything to protect you."

"Do you think she loved me?" I whispered, not sure if I was really expecting an answer from him or just wondering the thought aloud to the universe. Had there ever been a reality where I was a daughter loved by her mother? Did she cradle me against her chest and pray I'd never come to harm? Had she truly cared what kind of girl I'd grow up to be? And would she be proud of the one I was?

Orion trailed his thumb along my jaw, down my neck and across my collar bone, his gaze following the path he took. "How could she not love you?"

Tears burned the backs of my eyes, but I smiled through them, leaning down to touch my lips to his. Because that was the sweetest answer he could have given me.

"Do you miss the mortal world?" he asked as I rested my head on his chest, his voice rough and delicious.

His fingers curved around my shoulder blades, sending a deep shiver rippling through me. Sometimes I wondered if I was addicted to his flesh. He was ecstasy embodied, a drug that left my mind in a fog of bliss. It was weird to think I'd spent so much of my life without him. Now, a future apart seemed impossible. Unbearable.

"Not really," I said thoughtfully. "I never felt at home there, I always felt like somewhere else was calling my name. I just didn't know where to look for it."

"I guess it found you in the end," he said with a smirk in his voice. "Or to be more precise, *I* found you."

"How long were you stalking us exactly?" I asked, lifting my head and narrowing my eyes playfully.

He chuckled, lowering his hand to my ass and squeezing. "I wasn't stalking, I was watching."

"Same thing," I pointed out.

"I just had to make sure you were who we thought you were."

"And how did you know which Vega twin was which once you did?" I mused.

"Magical signatures," he said in that professor tone that got me all hot. "The elite are registered at birth. I had a special device so I could get a reading on you."

"Hmm, what kind of special device?" I grinned, rocking my hips against him and drawing a groan from his lips. My hunger for him was insatiable. Every time I thought I'd had enough, I found myself starving for him all over again.

"It's a long, hard device that lives between my legs. And it likes you a lot," he played along and the dimple in his right cheek appeared, making me lean forward to lick it. He laughed, gripping my hips and grinding me against him with a growl of desire.

Chiming bells sounded somewhere in the room and Orion jolted, rolling me off of him and grabbing his phone from the nightstand. I frowned as he answered, the tension in his muscles making me worry.

"Francesca?" Orion answered and I pursed my lips. *Why does he have a personal ringtone for* Fran*? And why is she calling so freaking late?* "Where?...Okay. Yeah, I'll be there within thirty minutes."

He hung up, stepping out of bed and striding to his closet to grab some clothes and start dressing.

I sat up with my brows pulling together, trying to ignore the warring tug of jealousy in my chest. "What's going on?"

He pulled on a pair of jeans, buckling them up as he moved toward me, leaning down and pressing a kiss to my forehead. My freaking *forehead*. "I'll be back before dawn."

I narrowed my eyes as I followed him out of bed and he turned away to pull on a shirt.

I dragged on my underwear and planted my hands on my hips. "Explain," I demanded. "Because it sounded like you just answered a phonecall to your ex-girlfriend in the middle of the night and now you're running off to see her at the click of her fingers."

Orion turned to me with a frown gripping his features. "Blue…"

"What?" I raised my brows, waiting, my heart thrashing uncomfortably. I didn't like this feeling. I knew we were unbreakable. But I wasn't going to let this go without a solid explanation all the same.

He sighed, reaching down to pick up my jeans and shirt from the floor. He held them out to me with his eyes darkening. "When I tell you, you'll insist on coming. And I'm gonna skip the argument and just say, stay fucking close and follow my orders."

"What the hell are you talking about?" I asked as he moved forward, dragging my dark green shirt over my head. I pushed my arms into the sleeves then snatched my jeans from his hand, not wanting to be dressed like a toddler.

Orion rubbed at the thick stubble lining his jaw. "Me and Darius have been working with Francesca for years to keep the Nymph population under control."

"What do you mean?" The knot in my gut loosened at seeing the truth in his eyes, but my heart started to pound for a whole different reason.

"Francesca has eyes all over the kingdom watching out for Nymphs. There's usually an FIB task force who handle them, but in the past couple of years their numbers have been getting out of control. So she employs us and a bunch of other under-the-board operatives to deal with them. It's completely fucking illegal of course, but Francesca cares more about keeping civilians safe than putting her job on the line. And me and Darius volunteered because, well, we're damn good at it."

"You and Darius…you kill Nymphs?" I breathed, the fact making a whole lot of sense. Like the time I'd seen him talking to Fran at a bar in Tucana, discussing killing somebody. It had been about this. I smacked Orion's chest with a scowl. "Why am I just hearing about this now?"

His lips tipped into a slanted smile, his eyes flashing like he liked when I hit him. "We haven't been on a run in ages, and like I said, it's illegal as fuck. I wasn't gonna incriminate you if the FIB ever came knocking."

I folded my arms, my gaze sharpening on him. "What else don't I know about you?"

He laughed, moving forward and cupping my cheek. "I'm nothing but an open book now, I promise. This is my last secret."

"Why don't I believe you?" I whispered and he stamped his mouth firmly to mine.

"You will," he promised and I tasted that promise on my lips. "I'll give you the play by play of my entire life when we get back if that's what you want, but we've gotta go." He snatched my hand, tugging me toward his closet and a smile pulled at my mouth for the fact that he didn't even have to ask if I wanted to come. Of course I damn well did. I could use my Phoenix fire to destroy Nymphs and it felt good knowing I could be of some use.

Orion took a large wooden box from the shelf at the top of his closet, lifting it down and placing it on the bed. He flipped open the lid and my eyes widened at the sight of the long, silver blade nestled inside. I recognised it instantly; he'd used it when the Nymphs had attacked at the Pitball stadium.

My lips parted as he took it out, swinging it in his grip with impossible ease. "This is a Sun Steel blade," he explained. "Very fucking rare. The FIB use them to fight Nymphs and Francesca hooked me up with one." He grabbed a scabbard from the box and tethered it around his waist.

Of course she did. Fran is so freaking generous.

I made a mental note that his ex had gifted him a fancy ass sword and all I'd given him for his birthday was a bunch of handwritten I.O.Us. Not that I'd had time to prepare for it considering I hadn't known it was his birthday, but still. I wasn't exactly winning the best gift of the year award. No, Fran had secured that alright.

"Your fire will be even more effective," Orion added, a gleam in his eyes like he was excited for this. I kind of was too.

He swung the sword around for a second with incredible skill, admiring it before tucking it into the scabbard. *Dammit Fran, why do you have to be cool?*

"Why aren't you telling me to stay behind?" I asked curiously.

"Do you want to?" He tucked a lock of hair behind my ear and I shook my head immediately.

A dark smile tugged at his mouth. "I'm not telling you to stay because firstly, you're a fucking force to be reckoned with, beautiful. And secondly..." He stepped closer, taking my hand and firmly kissing the back of it. "We make a fucking excellent team, I'd be doing us a disservice to leave you behind."

"You sure know how to talk your way out of trouble, Professor." I cocked a brow and he smirked at my expression.

"I know how to lick my way out of it too, Miss Vega." He grinned suggestively and I laughed as he tugged me out of the door. I grabbed my grey duffle coat from the lounge and Orion shrugged on his leather jacket before leading me to the back door.

We slipped out into the night and I lifted a hand, casting a silencing bubble around us as he led the way towards the fence ringing Asteroid Place. We used air magic to jump over it then started jogging through the trees in Earth Territory.

"How are we going to get off campus without being noticed?" I asked as I ran beside him.

Thanks to Physical Enhancement classes and the brutal Pitball practise sessions, my fitness had improved tenfold. I was even starting to get muscle definition and I couldn't say I missed my spaghetti arms.

"I helped put the wards in place around Campus," he said. "I left a gap in them for me and Darius."

"Is that safe?" I frowned. "What if someone gets in?"

"They'd never find it," he said confidently. "I've put all kinds of concealment spells over it to keep others away. But once I show you it, you'll be able to use it too. Not that you should ever go off campus without me." He threw me a sharp look and I arched an eyebrow.

"So I can be bad so long as I'm being bad with you?" I teased.

"Exactly." He grinned, lunging toward me and throwing me over his shoulder. I swallowed a scream of surprise as he shot away with his Vampire speed and the world became a blur.

We soon reached a dark corner of the outer fence where he placed me down, a little dizzy as I gazed at the iron bars stretching up high above us.

"Here." Orion took my hand, trailing it along the bars and planting it on one which was marked ever-so-subtly with a symbol of the sun. The second my fingers touched it, the bar vanished and Orion guided me through the gap into the bushes on the other side. I glanced back at the seemingly solid bars in surprise then my heart leapt as a man in a black hoodie strode through them behind us.

Darius's eyes immediately slid to me and he halted in his tracks. "What's with the Vega?" he growled and I clenched my jaw.

He was Orion's closest friend and I had a lot to be grateful to him for since he'd helped save Orion, but I also had a lot to hate him for too. Why did the Heirs have to be screwing with my moral compass so much lately?

"Blue's going to help," Orion said firmly, moving forward to clap Darius on the shoulder. "Problem?"

Darius frowned then shook his head. "Whatever, so long as she doesn't cause any trouble."

"*She* has a name," I said airily. "And *she* would appreciate if you didn't speak about her in the third person."

"Alright, Gwen, calm down," Darius taunted and a growl rumbled in the back of my throat.

"It's Darcy," I corrected. "I won't respond to Gwen. So if a Nymph starts sucking the magic right out of your ass, then you might wanna use the right name when you're calling for help."

Darius raised his eyebrows, a surprised laugh escaping him as he looked to Orion. "Gwen's got fire in her belly tonight."

"Stop with the third person crap. And don't call me Gwen," I demanded and Orion shoved Darius in the arm, making him knock into me.

"Call her Darcy, dipshit, or I'll start calling you Demelza," he growled and Darius shrugged. "Come on let's move."

Darius took a pouch of stardust from his pocket, eyeing me through his dark-ringed eyes. The sight made my heart pinch, so I looked away. I didn't know if I pitied him or was glad he was paying the price for hurting my sister. But it killed me that she was being punished too.

"Ready?" Darius asked and Orion caught my hand, pulling me closer and keeping his fingers latched onto me like he was worried Darius was going to leave me behind. I wouldn't have put it past him either.

We nodded and he tossed the glittering stardust into the air.

I was yanked into a sea of stars and my breath got sucked away as we tore through the endless galaxy, using its power to ride through the space between atoms and land at our destination.

My feet hit solid ground and I stumbled, feeling Orion's grip tighten on me. My face bumped into a hard shoulder all the same and I looked up to find Darius steadying me too.

The scent of smoke hung around him like a cloud and I could see the Dragon peering out from behind his eyes, a flash of gold burning through the dark.

"Thanks," I muttered, stepping back, taking in the dark hill we were standing on, the moon hidden behind a sea of clouds.

Darius shrugged, glancing away. "If you prepare to land on unsteady ground you'll always land smoothly."

Heat flushed into my cheeks and I shook my head. "I've always been clumsy."

"Fae can train themselves out of anything," Darius said firmly and I wondered if that was true. I couldn't imagine ever being anywhere near graceful. My fifth foster mother, Mrs Cockleford, had taken us to an art gallery once when I was nine. I'd knocked over a sculpture of a Bengal tiger and caused thousands of dollars in damage to the artist. Tory had determinedly said that wasn't why she sent us back to the foster home a week later. But I knew it was. I swear the less clumsy I tried to be, the more destruction I caused. I'd broken more bones and had more visits to the emergency room in my life than anyone I knew. Probably didn't help that I'd been the type of kid who liked climbing trees, playing in streams and running everywhere barefoot. But I hadn't been the type who liked being told not to do those things either.

"I happen to like that about you," Orion commented. "It means I'll always be able to catch you."

"You're a Vampire, you'll always be able to catch me anyway," I laughed.

"Not when you fly away from me," he growled.

"Do you think I'm so clumsy that I'll hit a rainbow and fall out of the sky?" I taunted and he chuckled.

"Where's Francesca?" Darius questioned, turning toward the dark woodland that stretched away to our right. I followed his gaze and spotted a huge old gothic house standing amongst the tall trees. There were no lights on in the building and something about it sent a prickling sensation up my spine.

"What are Nymphs doing all the way out here?" Orion muttered.

"Fuck knows," Darius growled. "But I'm hungering for a kill."

A flash of light caught my attention to my right and I whirled toward it in time with the others just as Fran stepped out of the trees. She wore a black jumpsuit that clung to her curvy figure, her hazel hair was pulled up into a high ponytail and her eyes were narrowed at me.

"What's with the spare?" she demanded, jogging up to us then slowing as she realised who I was. "By the stars, did you bring a fucking Vega, Lance?" She turned to him, and I swear, if I got third-personed one more time tonight I was going to lose it.

"I can help," I spoke before he could. "I killed a bunch of the Nymphs

130

at the Palace of Souls."

"I heard," Fran said coolly. "But you're still just a freshman who's going to be a liability. This isn't child's play."

"Firstly, I'm almost nineteen, and secondly, I'm well aware it's not child's play. I was aware when I battled for my life and the lives of my friends at the palace. I was aware when I fought at Lance's side when the academy was attacked. I was also aware when I turned a bunch of Nymphs to dust because they can't stand the power of my Phoenix fire. So just to be clear, I'm aware."

Orion fought a smirk, glancing at Fran as she clucked her tongue in annoyance. "Well this is on your head, Lance."

"Noted." He saluted her and she rolled her eyes.

"What's the intel?" Darius asked, looking seriously impatient to start killing Nymphs.

Fran stood up straighter, looking more professional. "Some kids were playing in the abandoned house down there. Their parents said they showed up at home screaming, saying they saw a Nymph. I wouldn't have taken it seriously only we've had a few sightings out this way the past week. It's probably nothing, but I thought we could check this one out together just to be sure."

"Why would Nymphs be here?" Orion asked with a frown. "There's hardly any Fae to feed on. That's not their usual style."

"Beats me." Fran shrugged. "There's a town not too far from here, maybe there's a few picking off anyone who strays into the woods. But this far out? Doesn't seem likely to me. We'll probably be back in our beds within an hour."

"Well there's only one way to find out," Darius said. "Come on."

He took off into the trees sloping down toward the gothic building and I followed with Orion and Fran. The trees were thick and the path we followed was so overgrown that I couldn't imagine anyone had used it for years.

Orion lit a dim Faelight to guide the way forward, the amber glow just enough to ignite the path. Fran moved behind him so I was forced to the back and I had the feeling that was intentional.

The hoot of an owl made my heart tick faster and I gathered magic in my palms to steel my nerves.

I am a Solarian Princess with a bucketload of power in my veins. The Nymphs should be afraid. Definitely not the other way around. Definitely definitely.

The trees opened up at the base of the hill and we emerged before the huge manor house which looked long abandoned. Moss was climbing the dark brick walls and the ancient door was hanging off its hinges, blowing in the wind and making a creaking noise that sent a chill into my blood. Most of the windows were smashed and the inside was thick with shadow.

"What is this place?" I whispered, feeling Darius casting a silencing bubble around us.

"The only information linked to it is that it belonged to someone called Kreevan Dire," Fran answered and Orion turned sharply toward her, his brow creasing.

"Dire?" he questioned, his jaw tight.

"Yeah, have you heard of him?" she asked curiously and I glanced over at Darius as he strode up to one of the windows and peered inside.

"He was an old friend of my dad's," Orion murmured as he took the sword from his hip, his taut expression making me certain there was more he wasn't saying. Which meant he was keeping it from Fran. Which also meant he kept secrets from her. Which made me even more curious about what it was he was hiding.

We strode toward the house and Fran took hold of Orion's arm. "Let's do a sweep and head in around back." She directed me toward Darius. "You two check out the front rooms. If you find anything, Darius, use the usual signal."

"I'll stay with Darcy," Orion said immediately.

"Don't be ridiculous, Lance, it's just a sweep. Besides, she said she's *aware*, remember?" Fran insisted, tugging him on and I had half a mind to yank her ponytail for that sarcastic comment.

"It's fine," I promised Orion, not wanting Fran to think I was some scared little mouse who needed to hold her teacher's hand on this mission. But I knew Orion wasn't going to leave me that easily, so I looked into his eyes and ignored the beautiful Fae clinging to his arm. "I'll be with Darius."

He clenched his jaw then turned to his friend. "She doesn't leave your sight."

"Got it," Darius agreed, then heaved himself through a window and dropped inside, beckoning me after him.

Fran led Orion towards the other end of the house and he glanced back over his shoulder at me with a frown. I gave him a thumbs up and he scowled, apparently not comforted by that. But if he thought I was so capable then he really shouldn't have expected to babysit me through this.

I walked up to the window, taking hold of the ledge and hauling myself up into the house. Darius held out a hand to help me, but I ignored it, landing on the floor beside him a second later, brushing the muck from my hands onto my jeans. I didn't know if he was being nice or if he thought I was incapable, but I was sure as shit gonna prove him wrong if it was the latter.

The room smelled musty and old furniture was rotting around the space. Pictures hung at awkward angles on the walls, layered with dust which concealed whatever was in their frames. To say it was creepy was the understatement of the decade.

"Stay close," Darius murmured, tightening his silencing bubble around us and casting a low Faelight above us. I brought magic to my fingertips as he led the way out of the room, every footstep we took making the floorboards creak, sounding achingly loud in my ears. Despite the silencing bubble, it still made my breath quicken and my heart pitter-patter.

We moved into an old hallway where a wooden staircase led up to another level, but headed past it, moving strategically through the front rooms and checking they were clear.

We arrived in a large kitchen and a vile smell hit the back of my throat. An old refrigerator stood open and mould clung to everything inside it. It must have been years and years old, yet the scent was still pungent enough to make me gag.

"What the hell happened here?" I hissed.

"Looks like whoever lived here upped and left in a hurry," Darius murmured.

"Or died in a hurry," I said thickly, covering my mouth.

"Yeah, or that," he grunted, glancing around the room then ushering me back the way we'd come. "Nothing here."

"There's a door there." I pointed behind him. It was just beyond the fridge and had no handle, but there'd been a door just like it in one of my foster homes that led to a hidden games room.

Darius frowned, moving to the wooden door which blended with the panels, but it was clear there was a slight gap around the edges. He rapped his knuckles on the wood and the hollow noise that came in response made him look to me in surprise. "Well aren't you an observant little shrew."

"Less of the shrew," I said, pursing my lips.

"Can't call you Gwen, can't call you shrew..." he muttered under his breath as he pushed the door to see if it would open.

It didn't give and I fought a smile as I closed in behind him. But I wasn't going to offer him the satisfaction of seeing it.

Darius placed his fingers against the wood and a flicker of light pulsed across it. A lock clicked and my heart lurched as he beckoned me closer before opening it.

I took a steadying breath, ready to cast magic at any second as he pushed it open. A line of dust cascaded over him and the hinges protested as the door swung wide. An even more disgusting scent slammed into me and I wrinkled my nose, my eyes burning. Death hung everywhere. I didn't even have to see the body to know it was there. But as I moved into the room with Darius, I saw it.

The dead guy was hunched over a desk, his skeletal frame still wearing tattered, moth-eaten clothes. His bony fingers rested on a piece of paper and curiosity got the better of me as I raised a hand to my face and cast a bubble of air around my mouth and nose to keep out the smell. Cringing at the eyeless sockets of the dead Fae, I tugged the piece of paper from under his hand, sending his thumb bone cracking off and tumbling onto the floor. *Oh shit.*

A humming filled my ears and I gasped as the familiar tingle of Astrum's magic called to me in the air. It made no sense at all to feel it here, but I knew it was true down to the depths of my bones. There was a Tarot card close by and as my gaze raked down the dead body, I spotted it clutched in his other hand. Darius was already turning to the door, clearly done with this room and

I snatched it fast before tucking it into my back pocket.

I glanced over my shoulder at Darius just as a clattering noise sounded somewhere beneath our feet.

"The cellar," Darius hissed, turning and racing from the room. I darted after him, folding the page and stuffing it into my pocket as I took chase, my heart hammering like mad.

A creepy noise had come from the cellar so that was where we were headed. Great. Perfect. Not at all an issue.

We made it to the dark hallway and Darius ran toward the door under the stairs. It stood ajar and my heart stumbled as he pushed it open. I kept close to him, my arm rubbing his as we stepped into the space, his Faelight just illuminating the top of the shadowy stairs that descended underground.

A bang came from somewhere down there and my heart jolted. *Shit shit shit.*

"It's probably just an animal," Darius whispered despite not having to in his silencing bubble. "But we need to be ready."

I raised my hands and gave him a nod of solidarity. He started descending the stairs and I stayed as close as his shadow, taking slow breaths to try and calm my rampant heartbeat. Another bang made my chest constrict and as we reached the bottom of the stairs. Darius extinguished his light, plunging us into total darkness.

His hand curled around mine, pulling me tight to the side of his body. "Here," he breathed then his fingers brushed over my eyelids and magic tingled across them. When I reopened my eyes, I could see the way ahead. It wasn't like daylight, more like the shadows lifting just enough to see where I was going.

Darius moved forward through a stone archway and I followed him into a huge cellar piled high with boxes and lined with rusted shelves. There was a scent of damp in the air and the cold was biting.

We moved into the labyrinth of decaying rubbish; there were piles and piles of mouldy newspapers, metal tools filled the shelves and all kinds of useless objects were stacked everywhere.

A clang rang in my ears and my heart thundered against my ribcage. *Something is in here with us.*

We rounded the end of an aisle of shelving and I held my breath as my gaze landed on the man kneeling on the floor at the far end of the room, a mountain of stuff surrounding him. He was shirtless and frenzied, digging through boxes and throwing handfuls of garbage aside. Whenever he found anything metal, he looked closely at it then threw it onto the floor with a clang that echoed through my skull. His lank hair was long and sticking to his sweaty skin. He started grunting, panting, seeming desperate as he upended more boxes and ripped the contents apart. It was clear he was looking for something, but what?

Darius raised his hands and my throat tightened as flames flickered at his fingertips.

"What are you doing?" I hissed. The guy might have been crazy, but that didn't mean we should attack him.

"Nymph," he growled, the hate in his voice clear.

"How can you tell?" I breathed as the man threw a box of screwdrivers against the wall and they clattered everywhere.

"I can't," he growled, then stepped forward and sent a blast of fire through the air.

I gasped as it ringed around the man, taking root in an old mattress and flaring angrily at his legs. The guy shrieked in horror, his eyes finding us in the dark as he wheeled around and my heart rocketed into my throat. There was something so unFae about him, something that proved he was nothing but a creature of darkness.

"Fae!" he spat, then his skin ripped apart, giving way to a huge monster fresh out of my last nightmare. His huge, tree like body towered up towards the cellar roof and his dark red eyes gleamed with bloodlust.

Darius raised his hands higher and the fire roared around the Nymph, licking his bark-like skin and drawing a shriek of pain from him. A rattle started up in his body and I knew we only had seconds before it started weakening our magic.

I lifted my hands too, bringing Phoenix fire to my palms, heat blazing under my skin like an inferno. It exploded from my body in a torrent of red and blue flames, twisting around the Nymph and tearing through it until it turned to a pile of ash. The cloud of embers it left behind swirled through the air and all fell dark once more as mine and Darius's fire extinguished.

I took a heavy breath, my eyes finding Darius's in the dark. I opened my mouth to speak, but a horrible splintering noise sounded like a whip in my ears. We looked up in unison and I spotted the huge, spiderweb crack tearing up the centre of the ceiling. I gasped, my lungs labouring as the entire floor above came crashing down. I saw my death as a ton of rubble tumbled toward us and I threw up my hands on instinct, casting an air shield around us in a dome and forcing as much magic into it as possible. A bathtub slammed into the top of it, bouncing off and smashing to pieces amongst the rest of the bathroom suite as it continued to crash over us. A pipe burst and water cascaded down in a torrential flow, my heart juddering as the carnage piled up around us.

A flash of movement caught my eye and I spotted Orion in the doorway to what once had been the bathroom high above us. His eyes were frantic with fear but the second he spotted us down below, encased in the solid dome of air, his shoulders sagged.

"Just so you know, Plan B was me turning into a Dragon and taking the brunt of that," Darius pointed out and I turned to him with a relieved smile.

"And yet here you are, Fae sized and safe."

He cracked a grin, but it didn't meet his eyes and that made my heart twist.

I looked back up at Orion just as a shadow fell over him and I screamed,

"Look out!" but my voice only rang around Darius's silencing bubble. Orion spun around anyway and dove out of sight with his sword raised.

My lungs compressed with fear and I forced air magic beneath us, elevating us up to the next floor. Our feet hit the mouldy carpet in the doorway and I released the air shield as we both ran forward, fighting to get ahead.

Orion was nowhere in sight, but I could hear the thump and shouts of a fight somewhere close by. A thwack sounded against the wall of the room down the hall and we ran straight toward it in desperation, passing the mildewed wallpaper as we tore into the bedroom.

Orion was pinned to the wall by a Nymph, its probes angled toward his chest as he stabbed and stabbed and stabbed at its gut. The creature stumbled backwards with a screech and I released a line of Phoenix fire with a yell of defiance, cleaving it in half before it fell to dust.

A ragged breath left me as I ran to check that Orion was alright and his arms closed around me for half second. Fear soaked into my veins as I pictured him lying on the ground in that cave again, blood pooling out around him.

No no no, god no.

"We've gotta move," he growled. "This place is overrun."

"What are they all doing here?" Darius shook his head just before a blood curdling scream pitched through the air, the noise carrying from downstairs.

"Fuck!" Orion gasped and he shot ahead of us while Darius and I raced for the door, tearing along the hallway and down the narrow staircase.

Francesca was on the floor before us, the Nymph's foot pressing down on her ribs as it reached for her, the rattling, sucking sound it emitted stealing her magic away. I felt my own power subdued and growled as I raised my hands to fight. But Orion was already there, throwing his blade so it wheeled end over and end through the air before slamming right through the creature's skull. The Nymph exploded into a cascade of ash and Orion sped forward, catching the blade out of the air before it hit the ground.

He dropped down to kneel beside Fran, resting a hand to her side and working on her wounds.

"There's more outside," she groaned before she was fully healed.

"I'll deal with them," Darius growled, pulling off his clothes as he raced for the nearest window.

I jogged after him, my heart in my throat as he dove from the window ledge and burst into his enormous golden Dragon form with a deafening roar that shook the entire building.

Six Nymphs were tearing into the trees in Fae form and I frowned at the sight of the bags they were carrying, all fit to bursting with items they must have taken from the house. What the hell did they want from some rotting old mansion?

Darius's Dragon fire lit up the night, cutting a path through the trees as he followed them. Shrieks of agony said he's gotten at least one, but there was no way he'd be able to catch them all beneath the canopy.

I turned to find Fran back on her feet, clutching onto Orion's arm as she thanked him. She was giving him the kind of doe eyes that made me want to slap the look off her face. But I didn't think I'd have a decent enough explanation to get away with that.

"They had bags," I said. "They've taken something from the house."

Orion scrubbed his knuckles across his jaw, his brow creased with thought.

"We need to check they're all gone," Francesca said, straightening her spine as she took back control of the situation.

"If they haven't run from that Dragon out there, I'm sure they're about to," I said.

"We must check all the same," Fran said firmly and I nodded, moving across the hall and sticking my head in the nearest room.

A creepy display of dolls stared back at me from a shelf beyond the bed, but no Nymph. Not that that could have been any more disturbing right now.

"All clear," I announced, finding Orion right behind me as I turned back.

His eyes raked down me like he was checking me over and I gave him a half smile as we headed through the rest of the house together, making sure there were no more Nymphs.

"There's a dead body in a room off of the kitchen," Fran said as she reappeared in the hall. She sighed like that caused her a headache. "I'll have to get a Cadaver Disposal Crew out here to incinerate the bones. I'm not sure what power level Dire was, but even low level Fae bodies need to be dealt with. I just need a good alibi for being out here."

"What do you mean, dealt with?" I asked with a frown.

Orion answered before she could. "Fae magic remains in its owner's bones after they die. It can be wielded illegally by those who use dark magic."

My throat tightened at his words and I nodded, recalling how he'd told me him and his dad used to dig up graves to get hold of such things. And from the look on his face, I guessed Frannykins didn't know about that little pastime or any other of his dark magic dealings. He turned to her as she ran her hand anxiously over her hair.

"We'll deal with it. Darius can destroy the bones," Orion said firmly. "It'll save you the bother."

"Are you sure?" Fran asked hopefully, looking at him like he was her knight in shining armour. And with the blade in his hand, I guessed he could pass. But he wasn't her knight. He was *mine*.

"Yeah, it's not a problem," Orion said, leading the way out the front door onto the overgrown lawn.

Darius flew overhead and the air ruffled my hair as he shifted before diving through a window upstairs.

"Thanks, Lance," Fran said, moving forward to embrace him, her boobs firmly pressed against his chest. "See you soon, yeah? Maybe we can have a proper catch up at your place?" She grinned in a way that made my blood heat and a growl built at the base of my throat as she pressed a kiss to his cheek. Then she tossed a handful of stardust in the air and was gone before he could reply, disappearing into the ether.

"Are you growling, Blue?" Orion taunted and I tossed my hair over my shoulder, schooling my expression.

"Of course not."

He shot toward me in a blur, gripping my waist and grinning down at me. "Sounded like you were. In fact, I think you were about to go full Fae on Francesca." His smile widened like that turned him on and I couldn't help it when my own smile pulled at my mouth.

"Sorry to break up the world's most messed up parents' evening, but we need to talk about those Nymphs," Darius said as he appeared fully dressed in the entranceway, folding his arms as me and Orion broke apart.

"They were acting weird alright," Orion said in a dark tone.

"What did they take?" I breathed.

"Fuck knows," Darius said. "But it can't be good. This feels all kinds of wrong to me."

A beat of silence passed and Orion frowned as he released a breath then pointed at the house. "I told Francesca we'd deal with the body."

Darius raised a brow, a smirk pulling at his mouth. "Good thinking."

I followed them back into the house, glancing between the two of them with their cryptic expressions.

I waited outside the stinking kitchen while they headed into the room with the dead body to burn it and pulled the Tarot card I'd found from my pocket with excitement fluttering through me. I created a Faelight, letting it hover above me so I could see it. The image was of The Tower, the grey walls rising up high from a dark forest below. From my studies, I knew the meaning of this could signify the end of a friendship or abandonment. I turned it over to read the curling silver lettering on the back of it, adrenaline sweeping through my veins.

A fallen star, an empty grave, an eternal vow.

Seek he who broke it.

My heart juddered as I read it a couple more times, having no idea what it was referring to as I pushed it back into my pocket. I'd discuss it with Orion later. Maybe he'd have some clue of what it meant. Next, I took out the piece of paper I'd found with the body, my eyes scanning down the words.

To whoever finds this note, these words are my last.

There's nothing left of my estate to give, the gold is gone, my bank account rests empty. May whatever I have return to dust, left to rot along with me.

I have but a single piece of unfinished business left in my wake…

Of all the dark possessions I ever owned, there was one which still binds me with the greatest of regrets. I hid it well, for as long as I could, but shadows surround it like they are called by its wicked power.

And though I tried to destroy it to remove this artefact from the world which defies nature herself, its power was too great.

In the end, I failed the only good deed I ever set my mind to.

So that's why I have sent it to a Fae who I know will keep it safe, bound in cloth, in a final act of hope before it fell into the wrong hands.

Forgive me for my weakness, stars, but I could not stay in this world any longer. The darkness has claimed pieces of my soul for many years, it is time to put my demons to rest. And to whomever should find this, may the stars shine brightly on your fate. But heed this warning. If you have come here to sift through my worldly possessions in pursuit of this detestable object, I die in the hope that your quest will end here.

No one should own this power.

Not me.

Not even you.

Kraveen Dire

I looked up with a tremor running through me as Orion and Darius returned to the hall, spotting a large pack slung over Darius's shoulder. My brows pulled together as I pointed at it.

"You've put that dead body in that bag, haven't you?" I deadpanned.

Darius and Orion exchanged a mirthful look then shrugged.

"Waste not, want not," Orion said lightly.

"Don't worry, Darcy, I was gentle about it," Darius said with a dark smile. "I dried him out like beef jerky then folded him up like origami, didn't I Lance?"

"He did, it was very tasteful actually," Orion mused and the two of them sniggered.

I shook my head at them, trying to stop the smile that was fighting its way onto my lips. "Should I expect a lesson in bone magic soon then?"

"I reckon Lance has been giving you plenty of *bone* lessons already, hasn't he?" Darius quipped and a laugh tumbled from my throat. It was pretty weird to be standing here in this creepy ass house laughing, with him of all people.

"Yes and this night has interrupted those lessons spectacularly so let's get the fuck home," Orion said, moving forward to take my hand.

Home. That sounded like a real place at last. Not one that just lived in my dreams and fantasies. I really had a place I belonged. And he belonged right there with me.

"Wait, look." I handed Orion the note, figuring I could share this much with Darius. But I still didn't trust him enough to share the card with him. "What do you think it means?" I asked as he finished reading and passed it to Darius.

"I think it means…whatever the Nymphs came here to find, was already gone," Orion said, a flicker of shadows in his eyes.

"That's good at least," I breathed, a shudder winding its way into my flesh. "Because whatever Kraveen was hiding, it doesn't sound good."

"No," Orion agreed. "Not good at all."

"Who was he?" I asked. "You said he knew your father?"

Orion nodded, a grave look pulling at his features. "I don't know much about him. It was a long time ago, but he used to visit my home occasionally. He was a trader of magical objects, but his speciality was the black market. My father bought countless items from him."

"Do you think he's the friend Kraveen mentions in his note?" Darius asked thoughtfully and I wondered if that was who Astrum was referring to in his card too.

"Maybe." Orion shrugged. "I don't know how close they were on a personal level, but they often discussed business together whenever he visited."

"So whatever the Nymphs are looking for…maybe your dad had it," I guessed, feeling like we were onto something important.

"If my father had it, no doubt my wretched mother now has it. Either that or it's still amongst his things in the basement." Orion's brows pulled together. "But until we know what it is, that's not much use to us. I'm not exactly welcome at home these days. Although, I can get in if needs be."

"We can't go searching for some mystery object blindly," Darius commented. "What if we capture a Nymph and torture the information out of them?"

My nose wrinkled as I looked to him. It wasn't that I liked the Nymphs any more than the next Fae, but torturing one sounded pretty dark.

"Not a bad idea," Orion agreed, his gaze hooking on my neck for a moment. It took me a second longer to realise he was hungry and I casually shifted my hair over my shoulder in an offering.

He licked his lips before darting forward, grabbing my waist and sinking his fangs into my throat. The pinch of pain was followed by the wave of his venom that immobilised my magic and I rested my hand on the back of his head as he took what he needed.

When he stepped back, gently running his thumb across my neck to heal the wound, Darius looked between us with his jaw tight. We'd done it so many times by now, it was as normal as breathing. Orion kissed me gently in thanks and a smile lit my face that seemed to burn right through the dark surrounding us.

"You two are…well, fuck the law for saying you can't be together," Darius said, folding his arms.

My heart squeezed at his words and I saw so much pain in his eyes that I strode forward and wrapped my arms around him. It wasn't that I'd forgiven him, or even that I was remotely convinced he was good enough for my sister. But maybe he could have been. Maybe if they'd made better choices, followed their hearts instead of their pride.

"Fuck the stars too, Darius," I breathed and his muscles tightened around me as he held me close. "Fuck every shining, gleaming one of them."

XAVIER

CHAPTER ELEVEN

Lately, I found myself staring out of the window or at the walls, my mind working over everything that had happened recently. Playing video games to escape reality didn't appeal so much anymore. Maybe it was because reality was too loud these days, screaming in my ears and forcing me to pay attention. Or maybe it was because I realised how much of my life I'd been checked out for. And that sucked ass.

I always felt like I was waiting for something to happen. Like I was passing time until the inevitable moment where my cage door was opened and I found myself walking into freedom. But maybe that was just something I'd convinced myself of to make life more bearable. Because the reality was, Father was never going to let me go. Not now he knew my Order could bring shame on the entire family. And I didn't know whether I was more frightened of being caged and hidden for the rest of my life or of the unexpected 'accident' I was going to one day have that led to my sudden, oh-so-fucking-tragic death.

I'd turned eighteen in December and if Father didn't enrol me in an academy this year then he was going to have some explaining to do. And once questions started being asked, it would be harder for him to keep my secret. So with each passing day, I grew more fearful. Because right now, I had no power in my veins, no press taking an interest in my life and was in the perfect position to disappear. So maybe it wasn't a matter of *if* Father was gonna kill me anymore, but *when*.

I skipped breakfast in favour of staying in my room, anxiously trying to come up with a plan. If I could only get Mother out of here. If we could run... find somewhere safe to go. But the one time she'd attempted to help me, Stella had caught her. And now Father would be expecting it. He'd have put more measures in place, more security on the grounds. This house was my prison and I didn't want to die here. Not before I'd actually *lived*.

My phone pinged and my heart beat harder as I fished it off of the nightstand and dropped onto my bed. My skin started to shimmer and glitter as I found a message waiting for me from Sofia. I didn't even try to suppress my Order as it hummed through my veins and sang a lulling tune to my heart. I needed to bask in it for just a moment, to take comfort in it. The need to shift was like an itch that grew to a burn. Every day became harder and harder. Sometimes I locked myself in the bathroom after a shower and shifted into my Pegasus form for a few minutes, gazing at my lilac reflection in the mirror and wondering what it would be like to fly.

I did it even more often since that day at the Palace of Souls with the Vegas, Lance and the Heirs. I coveted that day. I'd replayed it a thousand times in my head. Dreamed about it, relived each second. It made me feel defiant. And feeling defiant made it seem like I was taking action even if I wasn't. But every extra minute I spent after my shower, staring at the shining silver horn that adorned my head, my chin lifted a little higher. And my soul burned a little brighter. I was a Pegasus. A big ass stallion of a Pegasus. And I was proud to be one.

Sofia:

I once flew through a thunderstorm and got hit by lightning.

I once got bitten by a Nemean Lion and nearly bled to death.
I have never gotten a grade lower than an A since I've been at Zodiac.

We'd been playing two truths and a lie for a couple of days and I was starting to run out of fun truths to give her. My life wasn't exactly colourful. I'd done a sum total of zero adventurous things. Not because I didn't want to, but because I'd never had the opportunity. I would totally fly through a thunderstorm given the opportunity. I'd try and ride a Nemean Lion shifter too for a laugh. But for that, I'd have to know people. And I didn't need a calculator to count how many people I knew outside of my family these days.

After my Order had Emerged, Father had pulled me out of high school and given me a new phone, cutting me off from all my old friends. Not that I'd had a whole load of genuine people in my life back then. Half my class had sucked up to me because I was an Acrux and the other half had resented me for the same reason. Finding a real connection in this world was hard enough as it was when everyone was power hungry and looking for a way to ascend. When you were born into it, other Fae could smell it on you like freshly drawn blood. And it didn't take long for the hyenas to circle.

I smirked as I picked out her lie. I'd gathered that she was smart and I dug that. But I had a feeling I knew the answer. And I reckoned she was badass enough to have lived through the other two.

Philip:

I bet Lance Orion doesn't give straight As to anyone.

Sofia:

Very true! But he also doesn't give grades full stop. It's pass or fail with him.

How do you know he's a hardass anyway?

Philip:

He's a family friend.

I hit send before I realised what I'd done. Shit. I wasn't supposed to give out information like that. I was supposed to be Philip, not fucking Xavier. I tapped out another quick reply, my heart pounding out of rhythm. If I let this secret out and Sofia told other Fae, I was going to be in serious trouble. And I didn't think a beating from my father would suffice this time.

Philip:

And when I say friend, I mean my cousin dated him for like a month once.

I rubbed my eyes, knowing that lie just didn't cut it. Hopefully Sofia wouldn't put two and two together. Darius had been the one to ask for help after all. And she wasn't an idiot.

I despised lying to her. And I didn't think she'd ever tell a soul about who I was, but I couldn't risk it.

Sofia:

Cool. Well, you were right...I don't get straight As. And that Nemean Lion

bite hurt like a bitch – possibly more than the lightning ;)

I grinned stupidly at the screen, reading her message a couple of times before wondering how to continue with the game. There was only one truth on my mind at that moment. *I'm so into you and the thing I hate most about my life right now is that I'll never get to meet you.*

I tossed my phone down onto the bed with a sigh, figuring I'd come up with something more light-hearted to reply later. Right then, it felt like I was going to bleed into my next message and I didn't want my misery to touch Sofia. She was too sweet, too pure to be tainted by the darkness living in my life. No, I wanted to keep that behind firmly locked and sealed doors. She was my light, shining as brightly as all the stars put together. And I was never going to let that light dim.

A wild shriek caught my ear downstairs and I frowned at the far-off sound of Clara as she started shouting.

Curiosity got the better of me and I slipped off of my bed, heading out of my room and hurrying downstairs. Her voice carried from the dining hall and I moved toward it with my heart pounding like mad. Whenever Clara got worked up, I always worried how far off the handle she was gonna fly. Knowing she'd almost killed her own brother set me on edge around her, even more so than the fact that she was a freaking shadow bitch. If she was capable of hurting Lance, that made her capable of anything.

"No! No! No!" Clara cried and I peered through the crack in the door where it stood ajar. I didn't wanna get involved in whatever the hell was going on in there. Especially because Clara gave me the creeps. But I'd promised Darius I'd give him any information I could if it seemed important. And something about this screamed important.

Clara was moving around the long wooden table, eyeing an array of objects laid across it. Daggers, gauntlets, chalices, even a huge, gleaming sword with gems inlaid into the hilt. Every time she picked one up, she tossed it across the room, shouting, "No!"

I caught sight of Father at the head of the table, his lips pressed into a thin line as he surveyed her.

Movement caught my eye and the Polarises stepped into view. Drusilla, Miguel and Alejandro.

Drusilla was a thin woman with short, tightly curling black hair and pale features; her husband was equally slim, his eyes gaunt and he had the air of someone with little to no backbone, always jumping into line at his wife's every word. Drusilla's brother Alejandro was the tallest of them all, his eyes cruel and his lips pinched beneath his thin moustache.

They'd been attending dinners with us for months and something about them set me on edge. Maybe it had to do with the weird ass knitwear they never took off. Drusilla always had on a pair of yellow woollen gloves, Miguel wore that ugly effing orange sweater like it was his favourite thing in the world and Alejandro's red woollen scarf was a total contradiction to his bland appearance.

Or maybe it was the way Drusilla had an arctic presence about her or the way her husband's eyes seemed to hold no light in them at all. When he sat still, he could almost pass for a corpse. He was currently flinching every time Clara shouted *no* and Drusilla's chin lifted higher and higher like she was bursting to say something. Alejandro's fingers flexed intermittently and he was the only one who didn't look afraid.

"It's not here," Clara finally announced, slumping down dramatically in a chair like she was exhausted.

"We will make sure the search efforts are doubled," Drusilla said firmly.

"We will find it," Alejandro growled with conviction.

"You have been saying that for quite some time now," my father said in a dangerous tone. "I have entertained this fantasy, but my patience is wearing thin."

Drusilla bowed her head while Miguel quaked beside her. "Apologies, Lord Acrux. But I assure you, if you give us more time-"

Clara banged her hand against the table and my heart jolted. "Our king doesn't have time to waste. He's waiting on you before he acts."

"I understand," Drusilla said, nodding. "As I said, I can only apologise and promise to try harder."

"I assure you I will get this charade under control, my lord," Alejandro promised, cutting a sharp look at his sister.

"Or we can give up this fanciful affair and I can make my move tomorrow without its help," Father said sharply and I swallowed the lump rising in my throat, wondering how long I could get away with standing here before I was discovered.

"Oh, but my king!" Clara's voice suddenly changed to innocently sweet. She rose from her seat, placing her palm on his chest and running it down his shirt. "I *feel* that it's out there. The shadows are seeking it too. You must hold out."

Father's gaze shifted to her and something akin to softness entered his gaze. Something I was sure I'd never seen angled at me or my brother. He lifted a hand, gripping her chin in what looked like a tight hold. "I can wait a little longer for such a gift, I suppose."

She smiled like a cat, brushing her fingers up his arm and licking her lips. "It'll be worthwhile, Daddy. I promise."

I shuddered at that nickname.

Father looked to the Polarises. "You're dismissed. Don't just double your efforts, triple them. I want some tangible evidence of its existence within a week."

"Yes, my lord," Drusilla muttered and I didn't waste another second, darting away from the room and taking cover in the kitchen.

I moved to the refrigerator, grabbing some orange juice and filling a glass. I could barely bring myself to drink it as I stood there thinking over what I'd heard and I shot a message to Darius to let him know what I'd seen.

Whatever they were after had to be trouble. And I was determined to find out what it was. Because I might not have been able to leave the house, but I could start my own quiet rebellion. And I was in the perfect position to gather intel. Ghost Recon style.

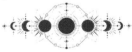

I stood shirtless in front of the mirrored wall that ran along one full side of the state of the art gym in the eastern wing. It was rarely used since Darius had moved out. Mother preferred to swim endless laps of the pool and Father was away so often that he rarely had need of the equipment here.

I worked out like my life depended on it these days. I knew I couldn't rival Father without magic. But getting fit was one way to counter the feeling of helplessness he'd cornered me into. Besides, I was getting a good grip on the shadows so I had that going in my favour I guessed. Clara had taken over from her mother's lessons and though I despised spending time in her company, I had to admit she'd helped me to wield them seriously quickly. Every day it became easier to draw them to the surface of my skin and let them loose. I may not have had access to my Elemental magic yet, but I wasn't entirely unable to defend myself anymore...

I eyed the muscles beginning to show beneath my flesh, running my thumb across my chest and inspecting the ways I'd changed. It wasn't just the weights that had affected my body either. This past year, I'd grown taller, my shoulders broadening, my features losing their boyish softness. I wasn't like Darius with his Dragon bulk; my frame was built of lean muscle. I was made for speed and surefootedness. That suited me fine, because the only thing I'd ever dreamed of was running from this life. And one day soon, I hoped to get that chance. But chances weren't made by the stars alone. I needed to make my own opportunities, so I had to start finding cracks in my prison's walls.

I grabbed my shirt and headed out of the gym, jogging upstairs towards the bathroom on the landing. I moved quietly and knew it was because Father was still home. I was holding out for his next business trip, wishing it could come today. Whenever he was here, the entire house felt like it was holding its breath. I hated that I lived on edge, every slam of a door making me flinch, every pounding of heavy footfalls making my throat tighten and my muscles coil in anticipation of a beating.

I showered fast and was soon heading down for lunch dressed in a pair of slacks and a grey shirt. I preferred grabbing a quick bite myself rather than asking Jenkins to bring me anything. He always ordered the chef to put pickles in everything he made for me despite the amount of times I told him I hated them. I didn't know if the forgetful crap he pulled was faked or not, but I had a feeling it was. He'd never forget the order when it came to Father's lunch. He'd lose his head for it.

I grabbed a couple of slices of bread with the intention of making a grilled cheese when my mother entered the room in a maroon, long sleeved dress that clung to her figure.

"We're having lunch as a family today, Xavier," she said in an airy voice. "Go sit down in the dining room." She wafted me toward the door, but I held back, noticing the tension in her posture.

"What's going on?" I asked, my brows pulling together.

"Your father wants to talk to you about something," she said with a hollow smile and my heart rate flipped into top gear.

"About what?" I asked, concern sliding into my veins. Father didn't talk to me about anything. Not unless he had guests and was forced to make polite chit-chat in front of them.

"Go sit down," she insisted, turning away from me and I swear her shoulders shuddered as I headed past her. I glanced back and she was gliding after me like the vacant spirit she always was.

I headed into the dining room, finding the long table set for four. Me and Mother took seats opposite one another in the centre of the table and I picked up the glass of water that had already been poured for me, draining it in one long go. My foot tapped anxiously under the table as silence stretched between us. I never knew what to say to my mom. Her answers were always so shallow, surface level. If I asked her if her heart was still beating she'd probably smile and nod. She might even casually cut a vein open to prove it. But she'd never tell me anything *real*.

A bang came from somewhere in the room above us and we both glanced up at the same time. The bang came again then over and over and Clara's voice carried to us, making my heart shrivel into a prune. "Yes, Daddy– yes yes *yes*!"

My jaw fell slack and heat burned at the base of my skull as I looked down to find my mother staring glassily beyond my head.

Father started cursing and the chandelier above us tinkled as tremors ran through it.

Anger flashed through me, sharper than I'd ever known it. My mother was sitting right fucking here. He knew we were waiting in the room below. He didn't even have the decency to cast a silencing bubble.

I was on my feet before I knew what I was even planning to do about the rage building in my chest and Mother's eyes refocused, cutting into me. "Sit down, Xavier," she insisted and I clenched my jaw, feeling like I was about to burst a blood vessel as I stood there.

"Oh my Dragon king – ah!" Clara screamed and I squeezed my eyes shut, dropping hard back into my seat.

"How can you let him disrespect you like that?!" I demanded.

I never shouted at Mother, but this was too much. The blank look on her face said she didn't care, but how could this not wind its way into her chest and squeeze the life from her? Maybe she'd been broken so long, she didn't even feel anymore. Most of the time, I reckoned she just tuned out of life. But I wished she wouldn't. I wished I had one damn person under this roof to share my pain with. The worst thing of all, was that I knew if I never got out of here, if Father kept me locked up forever, I was going to end up like that. Mindless, numb. And I couldn't stand it.

Clara moaned like she was in the throes of the best orgasm of her life and I fixed my gaze on my dinner plate, my ears surely about to bleed. Father groaned as he finished too and I found my hand curling around the knife beside my plate. There was either a twisted cruelty in this or he didn't care who was listening. I didn't know which was worse.

A few minutes later, the two of them stepped into the room and my neck prickled at the sensation of them behind me.

Father dropped into his seat at the head of the table with a sigh, swiping up his glass of water and taking a long swig. Clara giggled as she dropped into the seat to his right, combing her fingers through her light brown hair to tame the wild strands sticking out the back of it. She was dressed in a pale pink shift dress I recognised as my mother's and that was just an insult all of its own.

Jenkins appeared with a trolley on cue as if he'd been waiting in the shadows for his master to appear. He laid out our meals while I stared at Father, the muscles in my jaw working hard as I ground my teeth.

"I told Clara to help herself to your things," Lionel said offhandedly. "You don't mind do you, my sweet?"

Mother looked to Clara with a hardness in her eyes for a moment, then she nodded simply, fixing on a polite smile. "Of course not."

"Thank you, Aunt Catalina," Clara said in a sugary voice and that was it. The nail in the coffin. I'd had *enough*.

I slammed my fist down on the table and Father's ice cold stare rammed into me. But I wasn't going to just sit here and allow this to happen.

"How dare you insult my mother like that," I snapped. "She's your *wife*."

An achingly long beat of silence passed and I couldn't break Father's gaze as a murderous glint entered them.

"How *dare* I?" he echoed in a deadly tone that coaxed the hairs to life on the back of my neck. "And what exactly are you referring to, son?" His tone held a hint of a challenge in it, like he wanted to see how far I'd go to stand up to him for the first time in my life. And if I was going to do it, I was going to damn well see it through. Even if it did terrify me to my core.

I rose from my seat, wanting the advantage of height on him if nothing else. I pointed at Clara who's eyes widened in innocence as a snarl built in my throat. "She's twenty years younger than you. She played with me as a kid. She was practically my sister. How can you screw her like it's okay? Like any of this is fucking okay!" I grabbed my plate, launching it across the room so it smashed against the wall.

The sound rang in my ears and my father swatted a finger at me, sending a ferocious blast of air against my chest. I was thrown into the closed doors, my spine impacting with the wood and sending a crack splintering across them before I hit the ground. Father's footfalls pounded towards me and my mother released a murmured noise which could have been fear.

Father reached down to grab me, but I wasn't going to bow down that easily. Not today.

I'd had it with his bullshit.

I threw up my hands and the shadows exploded from me, forcing my father back a step before he raised his hands in a counter attack. The shadows pouring from my body suddenly stuttered out and I saw Clara in my periphery, her hand raised towards me as she locked my power deep down in my chest.

Panic snaked into my body just as Father snatched the back of my collar, hauling me out of the room and Clara laughed wildly as she followed us.

"I'll give you a good reason to bite your tongue, boy," he snarled, marching me across the hallway as I struggled to get free.

He shoved his way into the library and threw me to the ground with a gust of air magic behind the blow. I hit the hardwood floor with an oomph, slamming into the closest shelf of books and sending a bunch of them tumbling down over me.

I scrambled upright, my heart thumping madly in my ears. I'd been kept in check for so long that I hungered to fight back with the force of a starving beast. I wanted to tear him apart for everything he'd done. To Darius, to Mother, to me. He was a plague on this world and I despised every drop of his blood that ran in my veins.

"I hate you!" I roared, throwing my fist at him.

He was so caught by surprise that he forgot to shield and my knuckles cracked against his jaw, sending him stumbling backwards.

Clara stared at us with wide eyes, bobbing up and down on her heels and my heart thrashed as I waited for the axe to fall.

"Now you're in big trouble," she breathed with a wicked grin and I braced to fight as Father's upper lip peeled back.

"So you finally grew a spine at last," he sneered. "But it doesn't make you any more of a man. And it definitely doesn't make you more of an Acrux," he hissed, his eyes travelling down me like I was a piece of dirt on his shoe. "You'll always just be the embarrassment this family has to hide. Or maybe I'll save us the bother and bury you so deep that even the worms won't find you."

"Do it then!" I snapped, my breaths coming frantically.

I may have lost my mind, but I didn't care. I was done hiding in the shadows and tip-toeing around this house, waiting for the day my father had had enough of me. I was exhausted with it. No matter how frightening he was.

I clenched my teeth, raising my fists despite knowing I wouldn't be able to land a hit on him again. But I wasn't going to fall down to my knees like some coward.

"You want me gone, so get it over with," I demanded, my heart tearing down the centre. It hurt that he hated me. Despised me. I wished with all my heart that I didn't care. But his hatred made me ache. Because *why?* What had I ever done to deserve it? "I've never done a thing to you except exist," I spat, my eyes burning as I held back all the pain churning inside me. I'd stopped trying to win his love a long time ago, but some part of me would never truly heal from the hurt of being nothing but a burden to my own father. "So do it," I pressed as he continued to assess me with a cold, empty glare. "Stop me from existing and make your little problem go away."

He came at me fast, flicking a hand to bind my limbs with air magic and fear invaded me like poison. His first punch brought me to the floor, breaking ribs on impact. I wheezed as pain ricocheted through my limbs as he started kicking.

Clara was cheering and clapping with every blow he struck. I squeezed my eyes shut and tried to latch onto something good. There were so few moments in my life that had been truly sweet, but there were a few I'd revisited a thousand times. Playing with my brother in the lake on the grounds, laughing with him and Lance as we caught Faeflies out in the woods, the snowball fight with my friends. Real, actual people who knew me, *liked* me.

"Worthless – waste – of – my – fucking - *time*," Father grunted with every kick and the pain began to blind me.

It ate into my shattered bones and gnawed its way along my veins. I didn't give him the satisfaction of screaming, but my pain was no doubt written into my expression, spelled out in my blood. Maybe he fed on it. Maybe he needed me alive to keep feeding his demons and thriving on my fear. Maybe he'd never end this suffering. Because monsters need prey to feast on, and without me he'd starve.

He was suddenly in my face, kneeling over me and gripping my shirt in his fists. "You ever talk back to me like that again and you really will be counting down to your last breaths, do you hear me?" He shook me before I forced myself to nod, hearing his words through a heavy ringing in my ears. Blood speckled his shiny shoes from my broken nose and he snatched out a handkerchief, wiping them off with a tut before rising above me. "You have a guest arriving in twenty minutes, be presentable. This is your last chance, Xavier. Make an effort with him or I won't be merciful again." He turned away, marching from the room and leaving me with Clara.

I curled in on myself, allowing myself a groan of pain as fire seemed to claw its way beneath my skin. Merciful? How could he think anything he did was merciful? He was cruelty embodied. A heathen with no soul.

The sound of sobs filled my ears and Clara suddenly screamed, dropping down before me and cradling me in her arms and I gasped in agony. Healing magic swept from her body into mine as she rested her face in the crook of my neck, her tears washing over my skin.

"No no no no," she murmured, hugging me tight and I couldn't manage to move to push her away. "I'm so sorry, so so sorry, Xavier."

Her power took root in my body, taking away the pain and healing every fracture and bruise along the way. Clara laid kisses on my cheeks and I grunted as I reached out to press her back. She gazed down at me with a broken look in the depths of her eyes, tears running down her face and making her look almost human.

"You're okay," she whispered. "I'll protect you."

I reached out, my throat tight as I brushed hair away from her face, a thought entering my mind that the real Clara might still be behind all of this darkness that had invaded her. But then she dropped me on the floor and stood up, clapping her hands together.

"Silly boy, don't say naughty things to Daddy again." She gave me a stern look then started singing as she pranced out of the room.

I pushed myself to my feet, wiping the blood from my face with the back of my hand. I was shaken but not deterred. I wasn't going to crawl back into my shell and hide from him. Not anymore. Not again.

I headed out of the room and found my mother standing beyond the dining hall, her eyes shining as she stared at me. Her throat bobbed then she pointed to the stairs. "Go and wash your face and change your shirt before Mr

Gravebone gets here."

"Who's that?" I asked, glancing down at my blood splattered shirt. *Sounds like the head of some wanted gang in Red Dead Redemption. Not exactly comforting.*

"Just go," she insisted, turning away from me and I headed upstairs with a knot in my gut. I hated that Clara had healed me and not my mom. As pathetic as it was, the only time I felt like my mother really cared for me was when she came to tend to my wounds after Father had laid into me.

I changed my shirt and washed my face and by the time I returned downstairs, I was ready to face whoever this guy was. But what I wasn't ready for, was my father waiting for me at the bottom of the stairs. He placed a hand on my shoulder, steering me down the hall to the left and my heart ticked harder, a sense of unease washing through me. Something felt wrong. And my instincts said I should bolt, run for my star-damned life.

"You will do as Mr Gravebone says," Father spoke my ear, his voice a deadly whisper. "Anything he says. I expect you to make progress with him within a month. If not, well, I hope you understand that life can get far more uncomfortable in this house, son."

I swallowed the rising lump in my throat, keeping my lips sealed as he guided me into a lounge at the far end of the hall. A fire stood crackling to one side of the long room and two armchairs sat either side of it. A man rose from one, his pale grey eyes dragging down me. His white hair was swept back over his head and every angle of his face looked as sharp as a razor. A blood red robe hung around him, held in place at his throat with a golden clasp that pictured a perfect sunflower.

Father guided me to the other seat and pushed me down into it, his hand remaining on my shoulder as he stood beside me. "You understand my wishes, Gravebone?" he growled and the man inclined his head.

"I do, my lord. And you can rest assured that not a word of this will be breathed beyond these four walls," he replied in a voice that was softly spoken and creepy as shit.

"Good. You'll be paid at the end of each session. And if I don't see results soon, I'll ensure that the rest of your clientele are aware you're a fraud."

"I'm no fraud," he said, lifting his chin. "I will not let you down."

Father nodded curtly and vacated the room, leaving me with Sir Creeps-Me-Out and the feeling of ants stirring under my skin.

Gravebone reached into his robes and took out a large golden pendulum, moving toward me as he let it dangle from his long fingers. "You know why you're here, I trust?"

"No," I said, sitting back in my chair and fixing him in my sights. "Who are you?"

"I'm an Order Conversion Therapist."

"And what's that supposed to mean?" I gritted out through my teeth, though I could have taken a wild guess.

"Your father has entrusted your secret to me. And I understand the shame you must feel at Emerging as such a low level Order amongst the most powerful family of Dragons in Solaria. I'm here to help."

My tongue was leaden, my pulse was too quick. The word *help* had sounded an awful lot like *harm*.

I said nothing, not wanting to share any of my thoughts about that subject with this guy. Since I'd emerged as a Pegasus, I'd expected to be ashamed of my Order. But it turned out, that wasn't what I felt at all. Sure, I'd been horrified. Afraid. But only because I knew what my father would think of it. Not because I cared about being a Dragon. I'd always dreamed of flying with my brother. I'd gotten the gift of wings, they just weren't scaly and golden like his. They were soft, feathery and lilac. And I was okay with that. I just wished everyone else in the world could be.

Gravebone licked his thin lips, lifting the pendulum before my eyes. "I want you to watch the pendulum's movements while we talk." He started swinging it and I kept my gaze on his face instead of obeying.

"What are you expecting to get out of this?" I asked, the temperature rising in my veins.

"We're going to change which Order you identify with, young Xavier," he said with a bright glint in his gaze.

It seemed like a noose was tightening around my neck and my father was the executioner about to drop the floor from under my feet. I couldn't refuse to go along with this. He'd make my life unbearable. And if I was ever going to get a chance to escape with Mother, I had to buy myself this time to work out a plan.

The heat of the fire washed over me. I was too hot and this guy was too close to me. I could smell incense and tobacco on him and I didn't like the way he was looking at me. Like I was his new pet project.

I shifted in my seat, letting my eyes drop to the stupid pendulum. "What now?"

"How did you feel when you first Emerged?" he asked.

I ran my tongue across my teeth, thinking over the best way to play this. "I was scared," I admitted the truth. "I felt like I didn't have a place in my family anymore." Another truth.

Up until the day Father had found out what I was, he'd treated me with indifference. And it had never in all my years occurred to me that that had been a blessing. Now, I took the brunt of his hate. His fists hammered into my flesh as he poured every drop of resentment and disappointment he had into me because of my Order. And when he told me that life could get worse than this, I wasn't stupid enough not to believe it. "I still don't."

"Orders are a family in themselves," Gravebone said, nodding in understanding and yet his eyes were distant like he didn't have any real sympathy for me. "Right now, you no doubt crave the company of other Pegasuses, do you not?"

I nodded, my eyes still swinging in time with the Pendulum. A heaviness was creeping into my limbs and the more I fought it, the more it took hold of me.

"But you're not one of them, young Xavier," he breathed and his voice seemed further away.

Sleep was taking root in my bones and I found my thoughts harder to grasp. "Not one of them," my mouth moved with the words, though I didn't remember agreeing with them.

"Pegasuses are lowborn creatures unworthy of laying claim to Acrux blood," Gravebone said with more fervour, the disgust in his voice clear. "You are not one of them."

"I'm not one of them," I said again and my voice cracked on the words as I tried to hold them back.

My eyes were closed, but images were starting to swim in my vision. A proud family of Dragons stood on a hill above me and below was a herd of Pegasus, whinnying and nuzzling each other. My heart called to them in a way I couldn't bear to ignore. I moved towards them instinctively and pain crashed through my skull so intensely that I screamed.

"Choose your true family," Gravebone's voice reached me in the dark. "You're not a Pegasus."

"I'm not a Pegasus," I panted as the pain subsided and my thoughts muddled together, making me unsure of myself for a moment. "I'm not one of them."

TORY

CHAPTER TWELVE

I'd always hated getting up early but recently, sleeping in just hadn't felt all that relaxing. In fact, laying in my bed with the shadows coiling around me and my fractured heart bleeding all over the crisp white sheets had become pretty unbearable. Which had led me to start a new routine. One which I was actually okay with. After a night spent tossing and turning and fighting off the shadows (or dipping into them for a while, which happened more often than not these days) I got out of bed, threw on my running gear, and just ran.

There was a beautiful simplicity in that. And something about getting out into the cold, crisp morning air and seeing the academy as it was waking up helped me to centre myself.

So as I jogged down the stairs in Ignis house and pushed the door open, I drew in a deep breath of winter air and let it push the shadows back away from the corners of my mind with a smile. It was six in the morning – a time I had never been familiar with before now, but a time I was starting to like. At least a little.

I started up a quick stretch routine and flinched as I suddenly spotted Darius leaning against the wall to the side of the door. He was wearing sweatpants and a thin hoody with the sleeves cut off, his muscular arms drawing my gaze for a long moment as his dark eyes swept over me too.

He didn't say anything and neither did I. But as I took off up the path for my run, he started running too.

I took my usual route through Fire Territory, circling around towards Water on the main path and his footsteps stayed behind me as he followed. Not too close. Not enough to anger the stars. And there were enough other people up exercising or heading to the library or giving their Order Forms a stretch that we weren't really alone. But something about him following me made my heart pound for a whole other reason than the run.

I upped my pace as my route took me through the rock pools which made up the Shimmering Springs, my cheeks flushing a little as I remembered how hot the passion between us had burned when we'd come together in this place. Maybe I should have realised then that the way I'd felt about him was something more than just lust and hatred tangling together. But even if I had, I guessed it wouldn't have changed anything. Though a guilty part of me did wonder if things would have been different if I hadn't pushed him away from me here. If I hadn't lied and told him it meant nothing to me…

I continued my run all the way out and around campus, passing through every Territory while Darius's footsteps hounded me the whole way. My skin prickled, my blood heated and I couldn't help but wonder what he was thinking, even though I never turned to acknowledge him at all.

I finally ran down the path through The Wailing Wood back towards The Orb with Dua Lipa's Physical pounding in my ears and my pulse thrumming to a heady tune. A flock of Harpies were circling above the enormous golden dome, replenishing their magic with the sunrise and I couldn't help but ache to go flying myself.

I upped my speed as I ran straight for the doors to the huge building and dropped forward with my hands on my knees as I took a moment to catch my breath.

When I looked up, I found Darius there, his hoody off and tattoos shining faintly on his sweat slicked skin as the hint of a smile played around his mouth. I may or may not have pushed myself really damn hard so that he had to work to keep up with me. And he was panting at least as hard as I was so that was something.

The door was thrown open as a herd of Pegasuses burst through it, giggling together about going for a fly in the clouds. Darius caught it before it could swing shut and held it for me so that I could head inside first. I gave him a tentative smile before slipping in and grabbing myself some toast and a bowl of fruit to have for breakfast.

I headed over to a table in the corner to drop my food off before turning back to get my coffee, but Darius appeared again before I could take a step.

My heart leapt as he placed a steaming mug of coffee down on my table, standing close enough for me to catch the mixture of smoke, cedar and sweat on his skin. I was momentarily transported back to the throne room with his hands all over me and my lips pressed to his and by the time I'd blinked the lust away, he was gone.

I watched in confusion as he grabbed a coffee and a breakfast burrito to go then headed straight out of The Orb without looking back again.

I blew out a breath as the excited energy which danced along my flesh finally began to settle and used water magic to clean the sweat from my skin before sitting back in my chair to eat.

Well, that was…weird.

I was so lost in thoughts of peculiar Dragon shifters that I didn't notice

Caleb approaching until he'd dropped down into the chair opposite me.

"Good morning, sweetheart," he said with an easy smile as he tossed an arm over the back of the chair and dominated my space. But not in a threatening way, more like his aura was just so big that he couldn't help it. All of the Heirs were like that more often than not and I found that I didn't really mind it so much these days.

"You're talking to me now then?" I asked casually, but inside I was cringing.

I took a bite out of my toast to distract myself from the warring feelings taking hold of me.

"Mmm, well I was never *not* talking to you. I was just trying to be considerate of Darius's feelings," he said, leaning forward to steal a slice of my toast and I scowled at him. I mean, seriously, don't come between a girl and her breakfast. "But then he said something to me last night which made me reconsider."

"Oh yeah?" I asked.

"Yeah…he, uh, suggested in a roundabout way that he accepted the two of us hooking up. As in, he doesn't blame us, or even the stars for it."

"And how do you feel about that?" I asked as a prickle raced down the back of my neck.

Darius had said that I should continue hooking up with Caleb if it made me feel happy, but that was just it. It didn't. I liked Caleb and he was one hell of a lay but after we'd been together that night, all I could think about was Darius. And even though the two of us weren't together, had never been together, I'd felt guilty for falling back into Caleb's arms.

"Well, if I'm being totally honest, I think it's a sack of shit. Darius hated us being together from the very first time we hooked up. And I guess I just wasn't paying enough attention to realise that it went beyond some stupid rivalry thing or jealousy over me bagging the hottest girl on campus before he could. He's not exactly easy to read at the best of times… Anyway, I'm getting off point."

"And what is your point?" I asked as I finished my slice of toast and picked up my bowl of fruit.

"That I fucked up. *We* fucked up. You were never meant for me, sweetheart." He gave me one of his winning smiles, but the tightness around his eyes said he wasn't as relaxed about that as he was claiming to be.

I sighed, swallowing a strawberry before I replied. "No. I was meant for a man who tormented and worked to destroy me instead. Fate just seems to like shitting on me."

"I'm not saying I regret it," Caleb said slowly. "At least not most of it. You and me, we just click, we have fun and laugh a lot together, you're hot as fuck, I'm even hotter-"

I snorted a laugh at that, rolling my eyes at him.

"Is there a point to this?" I asked.

"I just wanted to clear the air." He shrugged innocently. "Would you believe it if I said I miss you?"

"I haven't gone anywhere," I pointed out.

Caleb's eyes skimmed between mine for a long moment as he surveyed the dark rings in them. "I guess not."

"I really am sorry," I blurted, sensing he was about to leave again. "I know I said it that night, but...I was in such a dark place after me and Darius were Star Crossed. And I like you too, Caleb, we do have fun and if I'm honest I've always kind of used sex to escape from the shittiest things in my life. It doesn't excuse it and I swear I didn't do it on purpose. I guess I've just separated you from the other Heirs in my head for a while now because you're not a complete and utter asswipe-"

"Thanks?" Caleb raised an eyebrow at me, but I carried on before he could stop me.

"I only mean...it wasn't intentional. To put you in that position with your friend. I was drowning when you messaged me. I just needed something to help bury the pain of it and-"

"Don't worry about it, sweetheart," Caleb said with a sigh. "You were in a shitty place and you needed someone to pull you back from the brink. Besides, you and Darius never really got off of the starting block, did you? The fucking stars have a lot to answer for there. I know there's a lot of shit that's mysterious about Elysian Mates, but some people can go years knowing each other before they get called beneath the stars. Forcing the two of you to answer to fate after a few months filled with pretty spectacular reasons for you to say no was cruel."

"Maybe the stars always wanted this to happen." I shrugged like that didn't burn me up inside and Caleb pushed himself to his feet, reaching out to cup my jaw and make me look up at him.

"Yeah? Well maybe the stars can get fucked then," he said fiercely, his navy eyes burning. "They might be able to put rings in your eyes, but they don't get to force you to be miserable."

"Don't they?"

"*No.* So take a deep breath and suck it up, sweetheart. Because the girl who came back swinging at us after she nearly drowned in that pool doesn't let anyone tell her what to do. Not even destiny."

"So, what do you expect me to do? Look up at the stars and yell *fuck you* while flipping them off and burning their bullshit to the ground?" I joked, although my blood tingled with the idea of that, because it was exactly what I wanted to do. I'd never been the kind of girl to let anyone tell me my own mind. I'd never been the kind to bow down to destiny or any shit like that. I made my own fate. And I had no desire to spend the rest of my life pining for Darius Acrux.

"Yeah. That's exactly what I expect." Caleb offered me a real smile and I couldn't help but return it. I had to admit, that sounded pretty fucking good to me.

I soared through the clouds above the sea beyond the academy with the wind causing burning embers to trail from my wings as I beat a path across the sky trying to catch Gabriel. Darcy had cut her flight short to steal a few hours with a certain Cardinal Magic Professor and I was just glad that she was finding it easier to do now that Seth had backed off.

All in all, the Heirs were actually being…not nice exactly but certainly less repugnant. And I wasn't sure if I liked it. I mean, sure I didn't want them to be heinous assholes all the damn time, but I also didn't want them to stop just because I was supposed to be Darius's destiny or anything like that. I wanted them to stop because they didn't want to be assholes anymore. Or better yet because they *weren't* assholes anymore.

"I saw a vision of you asking me about that tarot card Darcy found," Gabriel called as he circled back around towards me and offered me the smug grin he saved up for whenever he used one of his visions to preempt the future.

"It's a possibility," I agreed, calling over the wind as I looked at the water far below us.

"Well I might have an answer for you if you ask," he teased.

I rolled my eyes at him and turned back towards campus. "How about this then – we race back to Neptune Tower and if you get there first I'll ask. But if I get there first, you'll give me a summary of how this conversation is going to go without making me jump through hoops?"

"Bad choice, Tor, Harpies are much faster than Phoenixes," Gabriel taunted and I didn't miss the way he'd just decided to start calling me by Darcy's nickname for me, but I also kinda liked it.

"Only just," I scoffed. "Besides…I don't have to worry about that wind."

"What wind?"

I raised a hand and blasted a wall of air at him hard enough to send him tumbling away through the clouds and his laughter chased me as I shot away, flying towards campus as fast as I physically could.

My flaming wings beat furiously and Phoenix fire sprung to life all over my body a moment later. I had to fight to stop it from consuming my clothes and I lost a little speed as I concentrated.

Gabriel shouted something which sounded like *dirty cheat* a moment before a torrent of water crashed over me. It sizzled out of existence against the heat of my flames and I was engulfed in steam which blinded me for a moment as Gabriel's laughter tore past.

I commanded the air around me to clear the steam and beat my wings harder as I gave chase, the tower looming ahead of us as we raced across campus.

Gabriel was right about Harpies being faster…*just*. But it didn't mean

I was going to give in. As he dove towards the tower roof, I threw all of my power into my air magic, creating a powerful updraft beneath him and sending him catapulting up into the clouds again.

His curses met with my laughter as I shot towards the roof, landing lightly before dropping to sit on the russet tiles with my legs dangling over the edge.

I withdrew the flames from my skin, but kept my wings free as I waited for him to arrive.

Gabriel dove from the clouds at the speed of a comet before landing beside me and dropping down with a huff of frustration.

"You fight dirty for a princess," he growled.

"I'm pretty sure being a princess in Solaria requires it," I pointed out.

"You may have a point."

"That's what it takes to be Fae, right? You have to be ruthless, determined, savage, heartless-"

"Not always," he replied in a low voice.

"Often enough."

We sat in silence as the truth of that weighed down on our shoulders and Gabriel's arm pressed against mine. There was something about him that just put me at ease. I had serious trust issues at the best of times and I really never made friends easily. In fact, most of the time I had to assume that people only really wanted to hang out with me as an extension of Darcy unless they wanted something from me. But it wasn't like that with Gabriel. I felt a genuine connection with him that had nothing to do with any of that and everything to do with the two of us.

He nudged me playfully and I nudged him back. The second time he did it, he shoved me so hard, I fell off the roof.

I screamed as I began to plummet and his hand snatched mine as I grabbed the edge of the roof and beat my wings, scrambling back up.

"Dickwad," I panted as I sat down beside him again with my heart racing and he laughed.

"I don't like losing," he said with a shrug like that made it okay for him to push me off a roof.

"Asshat," I muttered but I was smirking too.

He was the kind of friend who would stand up to my bullshit, bristle in response to my resting bitch face, call me out on my own crap, push me off a roof when I cheated him and have my back to the brutal, bitter end. Ride or die. In short, the best kind of friend there was. Which considering the short time I'd known him seemed insane, but I just knew it was the case.

I thought back to the lesson we'd had on star bonds and had to wonder if he was my Nebula Ally. The kind of friend the stars chose especially for me because I needed him. Although the stars were on my shit list so I wasn't going to be offering them any gratitude even if that was true. But I was tempted to ask if he felt it too or if I was just being a weird little stalker claiming to be his BFF.

"Yes, I believe so too," he said with that knowing smirk.

"Stop answering questions I haven't asked yet. It's weird." I kinda loved it though.

"Pfft. What's the point in wasting time waiting for you to ask when I already know what you're going to say? Besides, if I really am your Nebula Ally then you must like it really because I do it all the damn time and if it annoyed the fuck out of you then you wouldn't be able to stand me." I rolled my eyes, but didn't deny it. "Besides, this isn't my first rodeo. I've got more than a few Nebula Allies so I know how to spot the signs. Me, you and Darcy are like a little dream team just waiting to happen. Besties for life."

I didn't miss his mocking tone, but I liked it anyway. "Well, it's time the stars gave me something good for once," I said. "Rather than just fucking me over all the damn time."

Silence hung between us as we kicked our legs above the ten floor drop and Gabriel sighed. "I owe you the conversation about the new tarot card Darcy found, but I can't offer you any insight into it right now. The only thing I could glean from the stars is that it relates to something immeasurably important, but they refused to give me any more than that to go on. So instead, I'm going to say something to you which you won't like. And you're going to throw a fit and storm off and then be even more pissed at me because I predicted it and you said you wouldn't throw a fit but you still did."

"What?" I asked with a frown. I was in a seriously good mood. It was a beautiful day, I'd made progress with my Tarot and Potions studies and I'd mastered an advanced concealment spell that Orion had had us working on for over a week. My team's cheer routine was looking fucking killer in practice and I'd only pouted over Darius like five times today. Hell, I hadn't even touched the shadows all afternoon. I was as peachy as a nectarine and couldn't see any sign of that changing. "I'm not going to throw a fit, Gabriel. Hell, I don't even know *how* to throw a fit. I'm as chill as they come."

"That's a load of bull and we both know it. Anyway, I'm not going to apologise because you need to hear this. I've *seen* it. Plus I'm going home for the weekend after you storm off and you'll be begrudgingly apologising to me on Monday morning in Tarot class… Oh, scrap that, you might still be pissed and give me the scowly face all day actually. There are a few factors that will determine how long it takes you to realise I was right. It just depends on how pigheaded you are and with your track record…"

"Stop being cryptic and just give it to me straight," I demanded.

"Fine. But don't punch me… In fact-" Gabriel shifted until there was a good meter of space between us and I raised an eyebrow at him. "You're going to try and punch me and if anyone sees us, you'll end up in trouble with Nova for attacking a teacher. I can't be fucked with the effort involved with fixing that headache. Nice right hook by the way."

"Gabriel, just spit it out," I demanded.

"Okay." He sighed, levelling me with a dark stare which was quite a deviation from our lighthearted back and forth. "You just claimed that the stars fucked you over, but do you really believe that?" he asked, pinning me in his gaze. There was something so familiar about his eyes, something that drew me in and made me want to trust him. Made me feel safe.

"Of course I believe that. They selected an Elysian Mate for me who had never shown me anything but cruelty and violence. They didn't even give me the opportunity to choose him," I growled, my bitterness over that rising keenly.

"So you think that between the stars and Darius himself, they're entirely to blame. None of it falls down on you?" he asked. And he was right, I wanted to punch him.

I pushed my tongue into my cheek as I tore my gaze away from his and looked out over the campus. "What should I have done differently? Just roll over and take all of the shit he put me through? Let him humiliate me, victimise me, taunt and bully me, burn off my clothes, tell lies about me to the press, team up with his friends to hurt my sister, go out of his way to make me miserable, call me all kinds of cruel things and try to *drown* me and then say to myself, well he had his reasons so never mind, I'll just let him take ownership of me too?" My words were heated and burned across my tongue. My anger, frustration, rage, disappointment, all of it rolled up into one hard pit in the centre of me where my heart should have lain and lashing out at the slightest provocation.

"I don't think you should let him off the hook for it. But I think you need to take responsibility for your part in things too. Darius is a product of this world, these people who surround him, the monster who made him. How do you think you would have faired with a father like Lionel Acrux? Who do you think you would be if the Savage King had never died and he'd moulded you into his image?"

"How am I supposed to answer that?" I growled. "But it's not like me and Darcy had it easy. We were bounced from place to place, never wanted, constantly sent away. We had no one to raise us with any kind of consistency, yet we didn't grow up to be total assholes. *She* certainly didn't anyway."

"I know that you bear the scars of your life before Solaria on your soul. They moulded you just as Lionel moulded Darius. But despite the fact that Lionel worked his hardest to create Darius in his own image, he still fights back against his father. He still tries to protect his brother no matter the cost. And in everything he did to you, no matter how fucked up it might have been, he was acting with the belief that it was the best thing for Solaria. Ask anyone who was alive during the Savage King's rule and they'll tell you what a horrifying place our kingdom was to live in while we were governed by the rules of a mad man. Aside from that, Darius has been preparing for years to challenge his father and take his place on the Celestial Council by force. He wants to do that so that he and the other Heirs can make even more progress within this kingdom. That's why he fought so hard to stop you from seizing it from him. It doesn't excuse his faults, but it does explain them."

"And it doesn't change what he did to me," I growled stubbornly. "He never apologised, you know. Not once. Not until it was too late and we were standing beneath the stars being asked whether or not we wanted to be bound for life. Then all of a sudden he was filled with regret. But how am I supposed to know if that was regret for what he did to *me* or if it was regret for what he did to his mate?"

"You're one and the same."

"No. We're not. Because I said no. Because I might have a thousand faults of my own. I might be stubborn and selfish and unforgiving at times. I might be harsh and hard and damaged, but I have enough self respect to know that I'm worth more than some overdue apology blurted when there was no choice but to make it."

"You're right…but do you remember the night I asked you to get stardust for our flying lessons from Darius? I told you he would say yes if you asked so long as you went before midnight."

"What of it?" I muttered.

"Do you remember I warned you that there were two paths your conversation could take depending on the two of you and what choices you made?" he pressed.

"Vaguely."

"And did you heed that warning? When you went to him, did you try and stop your conversation from heading down the darker path?"

"From memory, he acted like a complete douchebag from the moment I entered his room."

"I'm pretty sure he tried to talk to you reasonably," Gabriel countered.

"Do you just vision snoop on all of your friends' private conversations or is that a special treat you've reserved for me?" I asked, narrowing my eyes.

"I get my visions for a reason, and the only reason I *snooped* was because I knew that could have been a turning point for you one way or another. It was important." Gabriel shrugged like he had no qualms about his sneaky, snoopy visions and I narrowed my eyes on him.

"So you knew we were going to be Elysian Mates?" I asked, my heart pounding at the thought of that. If he'd known and hadn't warned me, I'd wring his fucking neck and pluck all of his feathers before lighting them on fire while he cried over it.

"No. Of course not. No one can predict those kinds of star bonds, the heavens hide that from us. Believe me, I know – I spent a lot of time trying to predict them a long time ago."

"Why were you so interested in us then?" I demanded.

"The stars offered me enough to know that your relationship with Darius was important. Not just for you, but for the whole of Solaria. It still is, even now. You're both destined to rule this kingdom and one way or another you'll have to figure that out one day."

"So what? You're saying that if I'd been reasonable too, talked to Darius instead of freaking out over the idea of him hurting me again then this whole thing might have turned out differently?" I scoffed. "Because of one conversation?"

"Wars have hinged on less. Fate is a fickle and temperamental beast."

I frowned as I thought back on that night. Darius had told me he cared about me and I hadn't wanted to believe it. He'd seemed so close to apologising for everything, the words almost seeming to stick in his throat and for the longest moment I'd really believed he was going to speak them. But he didn't. And I hadn't waited around for him to find the courage to do it.

"We fought," I said, bitter tears stinging the backs of my eyes. "He insulted me again and I just lost it with him. He wanted me to admit that my feelings for him had changed, that on the night of the Lunar Eclipse when we almost kissed it meant something *more.*"

"But you slammed the door in his face and told him nothing had changed," Gabriel said sadly like knowing I'd done that hurt him too. "And you told him you still hated him."

"Well what the fuck else was I supposed to say?" I snarled. "Are you telling me I should have just cut myself open, shown him my heart and let it bleed for him? Made myself vulnerable to him after everything he'd put me through when he couldn't even say he was *sorry* for any of it?"

Gabriel sighed like my words caused him pain and he shook his head sadly. "You both could have made different choices there. If he'd apologised, if you'd been honest…you would have been together that night. It would have changed so many things."

I scoffed because I didn't believe it. Or maybe I just didn't want to. Maybe I *was* too stubborn, but what difference did that make now?

Gabriel hesitated before he went on, seeming to see the way my blood was boiling and rage was fuelling me. "After you were together in the Shimmering Springs, you told him it didn't matter to you, you made little of it, told him it didn't change anything."

I ground my teeth. I knew why I'd said that then. Darius had been looking at me in a way I couldn't put a name to and I'd been terrified that he was about to say or do something cruel again. And I couldn't take it. I was too raw in that moment, too vulnerable, desperate for it to mean nothing and mean everything all at once that I'd gotten there first with venomous words and lies held before me in a shield to try and protect myself.

"I assumed it meant nothing to him. That I was just some conquest," I muttered.

"He was falling in love with you and you ripped his heart out," Gabriel said quietly. "There is no greater pain in this world than that. Believe me. I know. I've lived it."

"So am I supposed to feel guilty now?" I demanded. "Responsible? After everything? All of it? He never said that to me. Never told me-"

"He told you. You just didn't want to hear it," Gabriel interrupted.

"I don't want to hear *this*," I snapped, getting to my feet as the tears threatened to fall. "I don't have to hear it."

"Yes you do," Gabriel growled, standing too. "Because you need to accept that you're to blame in this too. You both failed the tests the stars set you-"

"I don't-"

"In the throne room, when you were with him there, he *told* you, as clearly as I'm telling you now that he wanted you, he said he wanted to claim you as his own, he said he wanted everything from you, that you-"

"Do you just have visions about my fucking sex life?" I snapped.

"It's not about sex," he said with a grimace like the idea of seeing me and Darius going at it horrified him. Which it should have because the idea of him vision-perving as well as vision-snooping was so far beyond gross I could have puked. "I don't see that. I see the parts that matter, the things you say and feel and I *know* how much you both care-"

"Enough!" I shouted as the tears finally broke past my defences and spilled down my cheeks. "That's *enough*. I don't care whose fault it was or how many chances we had not to end up here. We *are* here. That's the end of it. So fuck fate. Fuck the stars. Fuck destiny. Fuck Darius Acrux. And fuck *you*."

I leapt off of the roof before he could reply, throwing up a hard air shield behind me to make sure he couldn't follow as I beat my wings hard and took off across campus. I didn't know where I was going, I just knew that I needed to get the hell away from Gabriel Nox, my so called bestie.

Wasn't it bad enough that I had to live with this shit for the rest of my life? Did I really have to turn it all over and over? Couldn't he just leave me to blame Darius for all of this and at least take comfort in my own innocence? I didn't need him piling blame onto me too. And I really didn't need to be thinking that he might just have a fucking point.

Gah! Fucking psychic Harpy asshole.

A rush of magic swept over my skin and I shivered as I realised I'd just flown straight through the magical barrier which surrounded campus.

I knew I should turn and head back but as I swept over the green hills beyond the academy, I couldn't bring myself to do it. I just needed a bit of head space to think.

I might not have wanted to listen to Gabriel's accusations, but they were worming their way into my head all the same. And despite a petulant little voice in the back of my skull screaming that I'd had every reason not to trust in Darius's words when he'd expressed his feelings to me. That I'd learned time and again never to trust anyone aside from me and my sister - especially pretty assholes filled with beautiful promises and cruel intentions - I was starting to have doubts.

I'd learned a long time ago to take actions more seriously than words and Darius's actions had always proved me right to hate him. Hadn't they?

Memories of waking up in his arms trickled past my anger and the way that had felt made me bite my lip. If there had been any time when I'd sensed the bond between us most keenly it was then. In the quiet moments where we didn't try to be anything, didn't say anything, didn't even really *do* anything, where we were just *us*. Like when we power shared or danced, when we climbed the diving board after the Halloween party or played in the snow at Christmas...

There was pain in those memories, but there was a sad kind of beauty too.

The tears had fallen still once more, but my wet cheeks stung in the cool wind as I flew.

A grassy hilltop opened up beneath me and I tucked my wings as I dove towards it.

I landed lightly, retracting my wings as I looked around at the green space with the setting sun in the distance. I couldn't remember the last time I'd been alone like this. It was so peaceful.

I took a deep breath and dropped down to sit on the grass. It was cold and the ground was damp, but it only took a little flare of fire magic to cure both issues and I turned my gaze to the orange and pinks that stained the sky as I thought back all the way to the beginning. To the first time I'd laid eyes on Darius Acrux, and tried to figure out all the places it had gone wrong and how much of it was really on me.

"Roxanya?" a woman's voice came from behind me and I shrieked in fright as I leapt to my feet, throwing an air shield up around me a moment before fire burst to life in my palms.

My eyes widened as I recognised Catalina Acrux, Darius's mother, with her perfectly styled brunette hair and perfectly pushed up tits in a designer dress and killer heels which sank into the wet ground. Although as my gaze fell on them, she flicked her fingers and the mud hardened beneath her to give her better purchase.

"What the fuck do you want?" I snarled, holding my ground despite the fact that I wanted to bolt. Was her psycho husband hiding in the trees somewhere? Were they planning on grabbing me again? I looked around surreptitiously, not seeing any signs of that, before snapping my gaze back to her. "And where the fuck did you come from?"

"I managed to pay off a few staff members to alert me if you were to leave campus," she admitted sheepishly. "And I'm fairly adept in tracking spells. I was on the path to joining the FIB before my marriage to Lionel was arranged and..." She stopped talking suddenly, almost seeming to be choking for a moment then just shook her head like nothing had happened.

"Why?" I demanded.

I didn't know a whole hell of a lot about Catalina's magical abilities, but I had no doubt she was strong. Lionel only would have married the best candidate for producing his Heirs after all. And though I was sure being beautiful helped her case, I had no doubts she was a lot more than that beneath all the layers of bullshit.

"I need to know if-" she pulled up short again, her nostrils flaring as she seemed to struggle with something.

"What?" I narrowed my eyes at her as her gaze locked on mine and she swallowed thickly.

"Why?" she asked eventually and I didn't need her to ask any more than that to know what she meant.

I released a slow breath as I looked into her eyes and saw pain there, true pain for her son and what he was going through. I guessed her porcelain perfection did have a heart hiding within it somewhere and that made my gut twist in a way which I hadn't felt in a long time. But it was hard not to feel a pang of jealousy and longing at the idea of having a parent who gave a shit. I would have traded anything for one when I was growing up.

"You're married to a monster. Can't you imagine any reason why I might not want that fate for myself?" I growled, the pain of my decision pressing in on me keenly after Gabriel had jabbed at my wounds.

"Darius isn't his father," she breathed.

Part of me wanted to agree with her and part of me didn't. Hell, I was so torn up over Darius that I didn't know what I should be feeling about him anymore. Was this the stars punishing me and making me pine for him, or was I already this hooked on him before I'd said no but I'd just been too stubborn to admit it to myself?

"Did Lionel…" she pursed her lips then began again. "Did he warn you off or tell you something about Darius which made you feel like you had to say no?"

My jaw ticked against the answer to that one. Yes, Lionel did tell me to keep away from his son. In fact, he used his Dark Coercion to compel me to break Darius's heart and the memory of that ate me up inside. Because I didn't want to face the fact that despite the way my Phoenix powers had protected me from that bind he tried to put on me, I'd still ended up doing exactly as he'd commanded. And the idea of playing into his plans just made me want to spit with rage. But was I going to discuss that with his wife who'd just rocked up here to accost me in the middle of nowhere? Not so much.

"Don't come and corner me like this again or you'll find out just how well your defences hold against Phoenix fire," I warned. My wings burst from my back in a blaze of red and blue flames which lit the hilltop so brightly that I was almost blinded by it for a moment.

I spread my wings in preparation of take off, but Catalina moved even faster than I'd anticipated. A spear of wood punched a hole in my shield with a carefully targeted attack and she thrust her arm through it, grabbing my wrist as she cried out for me to wait.

My heart leapt and my Phoenix flames sprang forth to protect me, racing from my skin at the point where she held me and slamming into her body.

Catalina gasped, her dark eyes flying wide as my flames collided with her but instead of burning her flesh, they dipped beneath it and my heart pounded as I was suddenly gifted a connection into the very magic which ran through her veins.

Our eyes met in shock as my Order gifts pulsed beneath her flesh, burning, chasing, dancing under her skin like the flames were hunting something and I was merely left to watch them.

All of a sudden, the flames met with a wall of darkness which stood before them like an endless sea of nothing, barring their way on. There was something so alien about it, so *wrong* that my instincts pushed at me to destroy it immediately.

My Phoenix flames roared as they tore through the wall in Catalina's mind and she cried out as the darkness within her was devoured. The moment my fire had destroyed the wall, it raced on, soon finding another and another as Catalina's grip on my arm tightened.

A tear slid down her cheek then a second as my Phoenix flames swept beneath her skin and burned away every dark and corrupt thing they found lurking there.

Once it was all gone, the flames returned to me and I was left panting, shaking with fatigue as my wings sagged low on my back.

"What was that?" I groaned, the remainder of my air shield shattering as I slumped down onto my knees with fatigue pressing in on me.

"You…I'm free," Catalina gasped, releasing her grip on me as she backed up, her hands clasping her chest as a radiant smile captured her full lips.

"Free of what?"

"The Dark Coercion Lionel placed on me…each and every command he ever bound me with is just…*gone.*" Her eyes were shimmering with emotion and she suddenly dropped to her knees sobbing as she fought to adjust to what had just happened.

"He had you Coerced to do things?" I asked in confusion.

The suspicious part of me wanted to be wary of her still, but it was hard to deny the raw emotion coming from her now or the walls of darkness I'd destroyed within her mind.

"He's had me under his spell for a long time," she sobbed. "He stole my children's love from me. He made me cold and brittle with them…he took them…he…" Catalina looked up at me suddenly, her dark eyes which were so like Darius's pinning me down and holding me hostage. "He can't find out about this. Promise me you'll tell no one."

"I'm not doing that," I said, shaking my head as her eyes blazed with determination.

"Let me go back to my son, Roxanya. I need to get back to Xavier, to figure out a way to cut him free of that place. If Lionel doesn't know that he's lost his command over me then I might be able to get him out of there."

"What's he doing to Xavier?" I asked, my heart thrashing at the desperate look in her eyes.

"Xavier has a shameful secret," she whispered fearfully.

"I know about him being a Pegasus," I growled. "And I don't see any shame in that at all."

Catalina's lips parted like she hadn't expected that, but she brushed past it quickly enough. "Lionel is up to something. I don't know what, but it's to do with Xavier and his Order, I'm afraid of the lengths he'll go to to keep this secret hidden."

"You think he's going to hurt him?" I asked, my gut twisting anxiously. Lionel already made his sons' lives hell, so if she was this afraid then maybe she feared he'd do more than just hurt him and the idea of that made my heart pound. Xavier had carved a place in my heart, I hated the idea of him being locked up in that house with that monster and if he was in real danger for his life then I wanted to do anything I could to help him.

"Lionel can't bear the shame of Xavier's Order. He's satisfied with hiding him for now, but that can't go on forever. One day soon, people are going to start asking questions about why he left high school. Or why he won't be attending Zodiac next year and… I'm afraid that he's planning to kill him." A choked sob escaped her. "I managed to put some protection in place for him before, but Lionel is working tirelessly to undo it. Once he figures out how to negate what I've done, I don't know how much time Xavier will have left. Lionel won't ever allow knowledge of his true Order to be discovered. I have to find a way to get him out of that house and hide him. Please, swear to me you won't tell anyone that you freed me from his Dark Coercion."

Catalina extended her hand to me and I knew she wanted me to swear it to the stars. But I wasn't just about to agree to that without getting something more from her.

"On one condition," I growled. "I won't tell a soul about this, so long as you promise to keep me updated about anything and everything Lionel is doing with Clara. Anything and everything that might put my sister and me in danger. If he's planning to strike at us, I need to know. If he's doing something with the shadows then tell me that too."

"Yes. I'll tell you everything, I swear it," she growled fiercely and the only thing I could see shining in her dark eyes was a pure, raw determination to protect her child. And the ache that kind of devotion awoke in me couldn't possibly be refused.

I slapped my palm into hers and a clap of magic resounded between us. "And I swear not to speak of this to anyone in return."

"Give me your Atlas number and I'll message you whenever I can," she urged, holding her own Atlas out for me so that I could key it in. "I have to get back to the manor before I'm missed."

"Me and Darcy are getting stronger every day," I said as the two of us prepared to part ways. "One day we'll come for Lionel and show him exactly who the most powerful Fae in Solaria are." Shadows licked keenly beneath my skin at those words and Catalina's eyes shone with hope for a moment.

"Your choice with Darius was your own, wasn't it?" she breathed in a sad voice. "Lionel's Dark Coercion couldn't take root in you, could it?"

"It was my own," I agreed, a rough edge to my voice.

She sighed in disappointment, stepping back as she pulled a pouch of stardust from her pocket. "I wish he could have done enough to win your love, Roxanya."

She tossed the stardust over her head and disappeared before I could reply.

I swallowed against the thick lump in my throat and spread my wings wide before taking off too, beating a path through the sky towards the academy, wondering if things had really just changed as profoundly as it felt like they had.

MAX

CHAPTER THIRTEEN

Marguerite Helebor:
It's not hard to imagine why @Darius Acrux said no to the gutter whore but I'll be more than happy to help him move on.

Tyler Corbin:
Darius dumped your muffscruff a long time ago, but why not keep riding the desperation train and see where you get off? I'm just wondering how long it will be until he takes a restraining order out against your desperate ass. #ToryVegaishotterthanyou #desperatefordragondick #theheirdontcare #beingbittergivesyouwrinkles #iheardyouvegotmanticrabs

Marguerite Helebor:
Everyone knows that Darius and I shared the only true love he's ever felt #isteppedasideforhisbride #oncehehasheirswewillbetogetheragain

Tyler Corbin:
Who are you kidding @Margurite Helebor? You were pumped and dumped and I heard you were shit in the sack too #hititandquitit #nextdayregrets #ihopedariusgotansticheck #toryvegaiswaaaaaayhotterthanyou #yousuckinthesack #iheardhefellasleepduring

Darius Acrux:
@Margurite Helebor, I wouldn't fuck you again if you were the last Fae in Solaria and my dick would fall off if I didn't. Don't talk shit about my Mate. One more word and I'll destroy you #trymebitch

I looked up in surprise as Darius slammed his Atlas down on his desk and aimed a sneer across the Cardinal Magic classroom at Marguerite who looked like she was about to burst into- yep, she totally burst into tears. Darius literally never commented on FaeBook posts. Ever. She'd probably be best to run as well as giving us a show of the waterworks because I was willing to bet he was one second away from barbecuing her ass Dragon style.

Marguerite seemed to realise that too as Darius continued to glare at her, ice spreading out across the table from beneath his palms. She leapt up and bolted for the door but when she made it half way across the classroom, she slammed into an invisible barrier and fell back to the ground with a crack and screamed as her nose broke.

"Twenty points from Ignis," Orion said lazily from his seat without looking up from his Atlas. "For trying to leave my class without permission. And another ten for failing to spot my shield before you ran into it face first. It'll be ten more if you bleed on my floor, Miss Helebor."

Marguerite scrambled upright, healing her face through a sob before running back to her chair where she continued to cry into her arms. Orion threw a silencing bubble over her so none of us had to listen and a smirk tugged at the corner of my lips. That asshole could be savage when he wanted to be and I kinda liked it. Presuming he wasn't aiming that savagery at me.

"So, Darius, did Tory like her gift?" Caleb asked casually and I froze.

We had a silencing bubble up around us to keep our conversations private as usual, but it was still a bold choice to ask him that in a class full of students. I guessed he thought he was safe with all these witnesses if Darius turned murderous.

I mean, yeah we'd all been desperate to know how the limited edition super bike with the one of a kind paint job had been received ever since we'd seen it parked up in our lot, but none of us had dared to ask the question. Apparently Cal had a death wish today. Or maybe he just thought he could outrun Darius with his Vampire speed if he tried to toast him with Dragon Fire.

"It wasn't a gift," Darius grunted. "We had a bet and she won. I was just paying up."

Paying up didn't require a custom paint job with the Gemini constellation inlaid in diamonds over the engine, but fuck if I was going to point that out. His trust fund took a serious hit for that beauty for sure.

"So, how did she like her winnings?" Cal pressed and I kicked him beneath his desk, shooting him a frown as I tried to get a read on his emotions, but for once he was blocking me out. A twisted little smile was playing around his lips though so I had to think he was up to something.

Darius sighed and the weight of the world was in that sound. It hurt me. Genuinely. Like I could feel his pain slicing into my soul. He was so unhappy it was like he was drowning and I just couldn't think of anything that I could do to pull him back above the surface.

"She hasn't been to look at it yet. I set a detection spell around it to sense her magic when she does, but…I guess I should just be glad she hasn't shoved the key back in my face."

Seth whimpered sadly, pushing his hand through his long hair. Orion had set us work practicing facial illusions and I was giving a bit of attention to it while mainly focusing on my friend.

"Well, you know she'll love it," Caleb said with a shrug. "Why don't you just ask her to go see it with you?"

Heavy silence fell and for a moment I was half sure Darius would flip out and incinerate his desk, but instead he just turned a scowl on Caleb and answered his question.

"Because if we're alone together, the stars cause thunderstorms and earthquakes and Griffins to fall from the goddamn sky between us and fuck knows what else to force us apart, asshole."

"Yeah...how does that work exactly though?" Seth asked, deciding to chip in for some unknown reason. "Because you've been running with her every day and getting away with it."

"I don't run *with* her. I run behind her and for some reason she hasn't told me to fuck off yet. It seems like I can be within a few meters of her like that with just a few people around so long as we aren't really interacting. I guess the stars see it as me pining for her and are content to let me torture myself."

"So there are loopholes?" I asked, unable to stop myself. Besides, this was the first time he'd spoken more than two words to us about his situation with Tory Vega since it had happened and I was curious as fuck about it.

"I guess," Darius replied with a shrug.

"Like how you can talk to her and shit with other people around, the way you do in class?" Cal asked, tapping his finger against his lips like he was trying to figure something out.

"Yeah. So long as there's one other person there, I can get close to her, talk to her...but if I touch her, the thunderstorms and shit start up again." Darius turned back to his work, ending the conversation.

I scratched at the stubble lining my jaw wondering why the fuck the stars would come up with such a cruel fate for him. He might have had a lot of darkness in him, but he'd been given a shit father and a difficult life. An Elysian Mate could have been the answer to all the things he was missing – love, affection, devotion, but denying him her was so much worse than never offering it in the first place. And I knew that the two of them had had a choice in this, but the odds had been seriously stacked against them from the moment they were born. Celestial Heirs didn't marry royalty. Never had. Never would. Not unless they wanted to forfeit their own place on the Council to a sibling. But Darius had worked too hard to claim his position and Xavier had no desire for it. Besides, now that he'd emerged as a Pegasus there was zero chance of Lionel allowing him to ascend.

Caleb exchanged a look with me which said he was up to something and he let a tendril of cunning slip past his defences just to taunt me.

The door burst open and I looked up as Orion growled at the interruption, my heart falling still as I saw who had arrived.

Principal Nova strode into the room with a polite smile on her face and a girl following behind her. Not just any girl. Mildred fucking Canopus. Darius's second cousin and fiancé.

She was built with the full size of a male Dragon shifter, her broad, muscular frame damn near rivalling my own. She had a lion's mane of frizzy brown hair which stood up in all directions and had a polka dot bow clipped to the top of it. Her lower jaw protruded further than her upper, making her look a bit like a shitzu, and her upper lip had a coating of fine hair which I could see even from my position at the back of the room.

"Oh, shit," I breathed as Darius fell scarily still.

He'd said his father had been making him spend time with Mildred at the weekends, going out for dinners and letting the paparazzi catch them on purpose, that kind of thing, but he clearly hadn't known she'd be coming here too.

Mildred's eyes did this weird wandering thing like she could never quite settle on what to focus on, though at that moment they managed to hold their position on Darius quite easily as she spotted him.

"Snookums!" she cried as Nova began to explain that we had a new student joining our class.

"Fuck this. As if my life didn't suck enough, he has to twist the fucking dagger in my back by sending her *here*?" Darius growled and the rage that slid from him was enough to make my own blood pump hot.

She raced across the room with her arms held wide like she thought he'd leap up and embrace her. There were more than a few assholes filming his reaction already, and if he gave her anything less than an enthusiastic greeting then Lionel's whole plan to paint them out as this great love story defying the odds was going to fall to shit. And that could only hurt Darius.

Before I could think of anything to do to help him, Mildred suddenly tripped and crashed to the floor. I caught a glimpse of a green vine tangled around her foot as she hit the ground hard, her chin slamming down on the floorboards so that undercut jaw of hers sliced into her hairy upper lip. A hint of smug satisfaction fluttered against my senses from Seth as he flicked his fingers to destroy the earth magic he'd conjured before hiding his smile beneath his hand as he gasped like he was shocked by what had just happened.

"Canopus!" Orion barked as she scrambled upright. "Your desk is at the front of the class where I can keep an eye on you and see if you're able to keep up with the other students here or not. You can greet your fiancé on your own time!"

Mildred began to protest but he flicked his fingers, scooping her up on a gust of wind and dumping her onto the empty desk at the front of the class.

"Thanks," Darius murmured, his gaze slipping between Seth and Orion at the front of the class.

"I thought you might be able to be Miss Canopus's Liaison, Lance?" Nova asked him as she moved towards his desk, totally ignoring the way Mildred had just entered the room.

The rest of the students were all starting to whisper excitedly, their eyes flipping back and forth between Darius and Mildred. My Atlas started pinging with notifications as more than half of them uploaded the news of our new student to FaeBook and I wondered if Tory Vega was sitting in class somewhere reading about this and feeling as shitty as the guy she'd turned down.

For a moment, I really hoped she was. I hoped she was there with her heart shrivelling and tears burning her eyes in payment for the shit she had cursed the two of them with. But then I remembered the way her emotions mirrored Darius's whenever I caught a whiff of them and I found I couldn't even harbour my animosity towards her like I used to. She was hurting over this too. And as fucked up as the whole thing was, as much as I wished she'd made the other choice, I could understand why she'd said no. Especially as she hadn't grown up here. The concept of fate and Elysian Mates and curses was still so new to her that I doubted she'd even had a full comprehension of what she was condemning them to with her refusal. But she was clearly paying the price now.

We worked in silence through the rest of the class and five minutes before the bell rang, Orion asked Darius to go and run a message to Professor Washer over in the Water Elemental Lagoon. It was clearly a bullshit mission designed to let him escape Mildred as there was no chance of him making it back here before class ended, but there wouldn't be much escaping after lunch when we had our next lesson.

Darius left without a word, sending us a message on the group chat to say he was going flying during lunch and he'd see us later. I made a mental note to take a few subs to Tarot for him to eat and started to pack up my things as everyone began to file out.

"Altair, Rigel and Capella, I need a word if you wouldn't mind waiting," Orion called out. "And Canopus, we need to sort out your House allocation before you leave too."

Mildred puffed up her broad chest as she strode over to Orion's desk and I couldn't help but stare at her funny strut as she approached him. Darius had told us a few weeks ago that he was pretty sure she injected herself with performance enhancing Faeroids to help her bulk up. She didn't like being smaller than the male Dragons and believed that stacking on the muscle (and accompanying body hair) made her presence more domineering, which in her opinion suited her role as future wife to an Heir.

For years, the three of us had been ribbing Darius about his betrothal to this strange girl, the whole thing seeming like a fucked up kind of joke that would never really come to pass. But now that Lionel was pushing them together more and more, had moved up their wedding date and kept getting the press to write articles on them, it wasn't exactly funny anymore.

"I understand you have Fire and Earth magic," Orion said as Mildred came to stand before his desk and the three of us hung back.

"Yes," she replied, straightening her spine proudly.

"Then I'm going to have to insist you choose House Terra. We don't allow the students to have sex while you are in our care and knowing that you are in a relationship with Mr Acrux, I can't in all good consciousness allow

177

you be put in the position of temptation."

I bit down on my tongue at that declaration. Yeah, I was pretty sure there was a no sex rule in the student guidebook somewhere but the students at this school were fucking like rabbits in every cupboard, corner and clearing in the woods at every opportunity and he knew it. The teachers never enforced that rule and clearly knew we didn't adhere to it, offering out sex ed classes instead of detentions. But as Mildred was new, she wouldn't figure that out until she was in House Terra and couldn't switch back. It was a twisted kind of genius.

"But Uncle Lionel said that he'd get me a room right next door to my snookums and-"

"Absolutely not. It wouldn't be appropriate. How would I explain an unplanned pregnancy to him? No. You will head to House Terra after classes this evening and Mr Altair will sort you out a room."

Mildred pouted as Cal tossed her a salute with his middle finger and she stomped from the room in frustration.

"I hate you a tiny bit less now," Seth purred as he grinned at Orion and the asshole even grinned back.

"I think in this particular situation, it's a good idea for the four of us to work together to help protect Darius from Mildred and whatever the fuck else Lionel decides to throw at him. Don't you agree?" Orion asked.

"Hell yes," I growled.

"Good. And on that note, I thought I might as well tell you that I'm trying to research a way to break this curse that Darius and Tory have put upon themselves. If there is any way in hell for them to get another shot at this then I'm going to find it."

"But everyone knows you don't get another shot," I said helplessly. "That's it. They're bound to be apart forever, pining and yearning and never loving another and-"

"There have been so few cases of people becoming Star Crossed that I refuse to bow down and believe it that easily," Orion growled. "So are the three of you going to help me out or what?"

"But how?" I asked, wanting to do that more than anything while feeling endlessly helpless at the same time.

"I can handle the research," he said. "But what I need you three to do is help him win Tory over. Because there's no point in me finding a way to make the stars change their minds and give them another chance if she still doesn't want him."

"She does want him," I growled. "I can feel the heat between them from a mile off."

"She might want to fuck him, but she doesn't want to love him," Seth said darkly. "And that's the problem, isn't it?"

"How are we supposed to make her love him?" I asked. "She doesn't even like us, let alone value our opinions."

"And the two of them can't even get close to one another without the fucking ground and the sky trying to force them apart again," Caleb added.

"Well, those are the problems I need you three to figure out," Orion snapped. "Or don't you care enough about this to get your hands dirty for it?"

"We care," I growled, my heart lurching with the thought of us being able to change fate for him.

"Good. Because you're three of the most powerful Fae alive. And I believe that if we all set our hearts to this then we might just be able to achieve it." Orion looked between the three of us, holding out his hand in offering.

"You want us to vow to it?" Seth asked in amusement.

"Yeah, I do. I want us all to swear we will do *everything* in our power to overcome the odds for the sake of our brother. So what do you say?" Orion asked.

"Hell yes," Cal agreed, slapping his palm into Orion's fist before I clasped mine over the top of it with a grin.

Seth and Orion exchanged a loaded look before he laid his hand on top and we all swore to it at the same time.

Magic rang between and we grinned before stepping back. We might not have had the best chance of success with the stars stacked against us, but it felt pretty fucking good to be doing *something*.

Orion shot out of the room with his Vampire speed and the three of us followed on after.

"I've got an idea, but it might be insane," Cal said slowly as we began to walk.

"What's that?" Seth asked.

"There are holes in the way the stars force them apart. I'm not convinced they monitor them as perfectly as it seems. But I need to look into it more. Maybe I'll ask Gabriel for some insight into the future to let me know if I'm on to something or not."

"Okay. But getting them close to each other will only help if she doesn't think of him as the worst person she knows," Seth said thoughtfully. "I think he needs some help planning a grand gesture."

I snorted a laugh at that, wondering if he'd have any success there. I mean, the bike had been a pretty big gesture but I was guessing Seth had something a little more public in mind and I just couldn't see Darius going for that. Especially with his father monitoring his every move and holding Xavier's safety to ransom.

"Well, I don't think Tory Vega is going to listen to me if I start spouting Darius's finer qualities to her," I said slowly. "But I happen to know a Cerberus who she just might care about enough to listen to."

"You just want to use Grus so that you can try and get in her pants again," Cal teased and in fact, he wasn't fucking wrong there. But it was also a solid plan. She was Tory's friend. She was anti Heir. If I could get *her* convinced over Darius then Tory would be a walk in the park.

"No, it's a solid plan. But if I happen to end up with Grus in my bed again as a part of it, I definitely won't be complaining."

The others laughed as we stepped out into the sun beyond Jupiter Hall and I felt a lightness in my chest at the thought of executing this plan. Sure, it was probably one in a million that it would work. But we had to try. I couldn't just watch Darius suffer for the rest of his life without doing everything I could to fix it. So now all I needed was to get Geraldine alone.

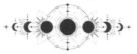

I sat on my own on one of the upper levels of the Venus Library, working on my advanced star charting assignment with one eye on Grus and the Vegas and some of their little Ass squad friends.

They were sitting around one of the group tables on the lower level of the library as they studied. None of them noticed me here. I'd figured out their little routine and come to set myself up here right after dinner, using concealment and distraction spells to make myself damn near invisible. They would vaguely know there was another student sitting up here working, but as they had no reason to look any closer than that, I was pretty sure none of them would figure out it was me. Besides, I didn't need any of my friends, followers or wannabe groupies to distract me tonight – because I was on a mission.

The rest of their friends slowly filtered out of the room, calling goodbye and blowing air kisses. The hat kid lingered, casting looks at the Vegas that made me wonder if he was crushing on one of them before he left too and eventually it was just the three of them and me left in the darkened library.

They stayed there, moving through different tasks and assignments, talking in low voices and laughing from time to time.

I tried not to look at Tory too much. There was a darkness to her which made my skin prickle. A deep sadness that had my Order gifts pressing against the surface of my skin and pushing me to go and feed on her magic. It was a primal kind of need, seeing a Fae as powerful as her in emotional turmoil.

My Order was termed a parasitic Order by classification and I guessed in black and white terms that was correct, but Sirens weren't just leeches made to suck emotion and magic from others. There was an innate need in us to provide peace and calm, to soothe others with our gifts and help them with the burden of their emotions when they got too much. There was a reason I liked feeding on pain and sadness which had nothing to do with enjoying the suffering of others and everything to do with that instinctual need in me to help them. And right now Tory Vega needed that kind of help. If she'd let me, I could soothe away that heartache and fill her with a sense of calm that would at least let her sleep well for one night. But I knew she wouldn't accept without me having to offer. Even Darius wouldn't let me help him like that. He was too fucking sure he deserved to feel like this that he refused to let me ease the burden of it at all, insisting on feeling every heart wrenching, gut churning minute of it for himself no matter what pain it caused him.

Finally, the Vegas called it a night and headed off, leaving Grus behind as she wandered into the stacks to return a book she'd been using.

I slipped out of my chair, gripping the wrought iron railing before me as I hopped up onto it and jumped over. I used air magic to slow my descent and dispelled the concealment spell that surrounded me before heading down the row that Grus had taken.

She was singing beneath her breath as I closed in on her in the far back corner of the room, swaying her hips to a beat in her head and drawing my gaze to her ass for a long moment. It was dark down here, the light from the lamps back in the main part of the library barely reaching out to illuminate the quiet corners like this.

I moved up close as she slid the book back onto a high shelf, leaning my shoulder against the stack and watching as her skirt rode up, revealing the tops of the thigh high socks she'd paired with her uniform.

"Are you putting on a show for me on purpose or are you just this hot without trying?" I asked in a rough voice.

"Bouncing bananas, you slippery eel!" Geraldine cried in surprise as she whirled around to look at me.

Shock, fear, excitement, lust – She slammed her mental walls up tight, but I'd caught it and that was more than enough encouragement for me.

"Sorry, Gerry, I didn't mean to startle you." I gave her a lazy smile as my eyes drank her in and she looked me over too. I'd abandoned my tie and blazer up at my work table and had unhooked several buttons, leaving some of my chest on show and I practically growled as her gaze lingered there for a long moment.

"Apology duly noted and accepted. Good night." She made a move to pass me and I shifted into her path.

"We need to talk," I said.

"I'm afraid I have matters to attend to that don't require a tricksome tuna-"

"I'll wear a buttery bagel as a cock ring for the day if it will make you stop and listen to me for a moment. I'm asking for your help, Gerry, and I don't do that lightly," I growled, interrupting her.

Geraldine pursed her lips like she sensed a trap and I had to force myself not to groan with frustration.

"I have told you, I have no intention to twist with the fishes for a second round and-"

"It's about Tory and Darius. But it's nice to know your mind goes straight to my dick whenever you see me."

She sighed dramatically. "Speak the words of my lady if you have anything useful to say. I have a date with the spangly stars tonight and must make it up to the observatory by midnight."

"Alright, I'll get to the point. Me and the other Heirs plus Orion have decided to see if there's anything we can do to force fate's hand into reconsidering."

"You mean to defy the heavens?" she breathed. "But how? Once they have decided a fate such as this-"

"Orion's working on the actual star bond shit. Me and the boys, we're looking at it from a more personal point of view. Meaning, we intend to help the two of them to work past their issues one way or another. But I've got about as much chance of convincing Tory Vega to start up a country and western band while wearing a clown's outfit as I do of getting her to listen to me about this. Which is why I need your help."

"You mean…that for no reason other than the pursuit of true and honest love, you wish to fix what cannot be fixed and defy the stars themselves?" she breathed, her eyes widening as she looked at me in a way that I couldn't quite describe. It was like, she was seeing something in me that she hadn't thought was there before and I kinda liked the way her deep blue eyes were shining.

"Well…yeah, I guess so." I shrugged, tucking my fingers into my pants' pockets as her lips parted, her gaze raking over me.

I felt weirdly exposed with her looking at me that way and I cleared my throat uncomfortably.

"So you propose a truce? You and I coming together in the pursuit of true love? Fighting against the heavens for what is right and just?" she breathed, making the whole thing sound like a mission for one of King Arthur's knights instead of me just trying to look after my friend.

"Yeah. So what do you say, will you help me convince her that Darius isn't all bad, that he might deserve a second chance so that if Orion can find a way to make the stars-

Geraldine stepped forward suddenly, catching my face between her palms a moment before her mouth landed on mine.

I groaned with longing as she pushed me back against the bookshelf, grabbing her waist and dragging her against me as I fell into the depths of her kiss.

Her lips parted for my tongue and she moaned hungrily as I twisted us around, pressing her back against the shelf as she finally gave in to what I'd been craving from her.

I didn't know what it was about this girl, whether it was the challenge she presented or the fact that I knew what a scandal it would cause if anyone found out about us, but I couldn't stop myself from wanting her. It was like that night of the Lunar Eclipse had opened my eyes to something in her which I just couldn't deny. And I needed it so desperately that I didn't care about the consequences.

Her hands moved down, unhooking more of my shirt buttons as she explored the skin of my chest. My own hands slipped lower, cupping the perfect curve of her ass before finding the hem of her skirt and teasing it up.

I trailed my fingers higher, groaning with need as I found the edge of her panties and caught them in my grasp.

I dropped to my knees before her and she reached out to push her fingers through my mohawk, her eyes hooded with desire as I slid her panties down.

She stepped out of them without hesitation, her thighs parting for me as I pushed her skirt up with a growl of desire. This time, I was gonna blow her mind so thoroughly that she wouldn't possibly be able to consider denying this heat between us again. I was going to shatter and destroy her, build her back up in pleasure and have her begging for more and more and more by the time I was through.

"Ravish me, you devilish doughnut," she commanded and I swear my dick got even harder as she uttered that ridiculous fucking phrase.

Her grip tightened in my hair and she pushed my head between her thighs in a clear command which I was more than willing to follow through on.

I groaned as I tasted her, my tongue lapping hungrily against her as she moaned loudly in encouragement.

"Oh blasted baguettes, take me to the mulberry bush," she moaned and I had no fucking idea what that meant but I liked it.

I kissed and licked her, devouring her hungrily as she continued to drive my head between her thighs, her nails digging into my scalp in a way that made me growl.

She was panting, begging, cursing in her own special, ridiculous way and I was so fucking into it that it felt like I was losing my damn mind. She tasted so good that I didn't think I'd ever get enough but as my tongue circled against her clit over and over, I could tell that she was about to fall into the abyss for me.

"Pickled cucumbers at a picnic, that feels as good as a dandelion blowing in a summer's breeze and *oh!*" Geraldine cried out so loudly that I was sure if anyone else was still in the library they'd have absolutely no question about what had just happened to her.

"Fucking hell, Gerry, you're something else," I growled as I looked up at her where she panted against the bookshelves.

"Stand up, you succulent squid," she commanded breathlessly and I seriously didn't understand why my dick felt like it might just burst at those words but it did. Apparently I had a fetish for all of the insane shit this girl said and there wasn't one part of me that wasn't into it.

I captured her lips again and she sighed with longing as she melted against me. I tried to stoke the flames of her lust even more with my gifts, but her mental walls remained as impenetrable as ever and I actually found I liked that. She wasn't turned on by what I was, she didn't want to feel the pleasure one of the most powerful Sirens in Solaria could push into her body. She didn't even want to try and capture me for my position as Heir. No, everything she gave me and everything she took was about nothing more than me and her. And there was a profound kind of purity in it that made me want to drown in that feeling forever.

Her hands made it to my belt and I groaned as she unbuckled it, loosening my fly before dipping her fingers beneath my boxers and caressing my cock.

"You are a big seabass, aren't you, Maxy?" she purred hungrily, stroking me in a way that felt so fucking good that I couldn't even reply.

She pushed me back and dropped to her knees before I'd even realised what was happening.

"Fuck, Gerry, I want you so much, I can't-"

She slid my dick between her lips and drew it all the way to the back of her throat with a moan of longing that had me cursing.

It felt so fucking good, I didn't even have words for it. Her tongue caressed and swirled around me as she drew back before suddenly taking me all the way in again. And again.

Her fingernails dug into my ass as she devoured me and I groaned as my shaft thickened between her lips, my balls aching with the need for release as she held me completely at her mercy. I was seconds away from coming and as much as I wanted to hold back, I couldn't, I was completely under her spell and I could only groan as she pushed me towards oblivion.

A faint ringing started up back in the direction of the desks and she suddenly pulled back.

"Oh, by the light of Venus on a summer morn, I'm late!"

"What?" I panted, looking down at her with my thoughts scrambling as she leaned forward to press a kiss to the head of my cock.

"I must bid you adieu, Maxy," she announced, leaping to her feet and snatching her panties from the floor. "But I look forward to working against the stars with you for my lady's true love."

"Are you seriously going to leave me here with my dick out again?" I demanded, but she'd already run off.

I groaned loudly, looking down at my raging hard on as she disappeared and wondering what the fuck I'd done to the stars. Because surely they were mocking me too.

DARCY

CHAPTER FOURTEEN ·

Istood outside the Earth Observatory with my nose in a large tome. Orion had leant me and Tory every book he'd found on Phoenixes and we'd been making our way through the collection, trying to hunt for clues on what other gifts we might hold. So far, we hadn't discovered anything new, but as I turned the page there was a whole section on Phoenix fire and its effects on different materials.

"Hey look at this." I swung the book around to show Tory and she lifted her eyes from her Atlas to glance over it.

"Great, we can melt shit," she said with a smirk and I laughed, flipping the book back around.

"Not just melt shit, we can imbue our power within stuff too. Look."

She moved to stand beside me and Diego and Sofia shuffled in close too, peering down at the page as I read a passage aloud.

"Some ancient objects such as the Quarrel Chalice and the Polar Crest of the Kestrian Dukes have been tested to discover the lingering power of Phoenix fire within them. The chalice, thought to be over three thousand years old, still flickers with Phoenix flames when filled with water and the Polar Crest is thought to shield its owner from mental invasion. These items have also shown little to no wear in all the years that they have existed. And after thorough testing, are thought to be indestructible."

"Ooh," Sofia cooed. "How does the magic work?"

"It doesn't say." I pouted, turning the page.

"Wait, what's that?" Tory pushed the page back over, tapping a small annotation which must have been written by the previous owner. I squinted, bringing the page closer to try and read the scrawling handwriting.

"Heat with stardust. Permeate. Forge. Cool," I whispered and glanced up excitedly.

"It's instructions," Diego said with a look of awe.

"Well whoever wrote it isn't winning the instructions of the year awards," Tory said. "Who needs an indestructible cup anyway?"

"Good point," Diego said. "I could use some indestructible shoes though if you fancy making any of those?" He gestured to his black shoes which the soles were hanging off of.

"By the stars, Diego," Sofia laughed, kneeling down to cast a fixing spell on them so they were as good as new. "Why don't you just buy new ones?"

"Thanks." He beamed as she rose to her feet. "My parents don't um... well I think maybe they forgot to send money to my account this month. And the last one..."

Tyler suddenly pounced on Sofia from behind, planting a sloppy kiss on her cheek as he slung his arm around her shoulders. "Did I just see you sucking off your ex, Sofia?"

Sofia elbowed him in the gut and he wheezed through his teeth. "I fixed his shoes, idiot."

"Good, but if you're into *horsing* around Diego, maybe the three of us can have some fun sometime?" Tyler offered and my lips popped open which was nothing in comparison to how far Diego's jaw dropped.

"Don't be an ass, Tyler." Sofia rolled her eyes. "If we're gonna do that again, let's try to keep my ex out of it. No offence, Diego."

"None taken," Diego said, his cheeks turning beetroot as he glanced away from the two of them.

"Wait. *Again*?" Tory questioned Sofia with a grin on her face and I couldn't help but laugh.

Sofia giggled, waving a hand as Tyler stuck his tongue into his cheek.

"It's a Pegasus thing," Sofia explained innocently.

"We're still working out the lead stallion in our herd," Tyler said like that made things clearer. "Once I win out, Sofia will wanna be all mine. But in the meantime..." He shrugged. "Stallions gotta do what they gotta do."

"Which is what exactly?" Tory folded her arms, not letting them get away with it.

Sofia's cheeks started taking the same route as Diego's as she shoved Tyler playfully again.

"Don't be shy, it's just the way of our Order," Tyler teased, his skin beginning to shimmer. "I'm quite enjoying working to impress you. Tell them."

"Well..." Sofia tucked a lock of blonde hair behind her ear. "In the herd we've formed, I can fly the fastest and my horn is way bigger and shiner than even Liselle's and apparently that means I'm extra fertile so...the guys are kind of vying for my attention right now."

"And I'm on par with Brutus and fucking Davros," Tyler said with a shrug.

"But you're a couple? Doesn't that bother you?" I asked him.

"Nah," Tyler said. "I plan on beating all their asses and becoming the Dom."

"The Dom?" I frowned.

"The lead male," he said proudly then nuzzled into Sofia. "What do you think, baby, am I gonna rule the herd one day?"

"Hm, well I think I'm doing such a good job on my own right now that maybe our herd doesn't need a Dom," she teased. "You might make a good sidekick though."

"I kinda like being your Sub," he whispered in her ear like we weren't standing right there.

"Sofia, you're like eighty percent more kinky than I would have pegged you for," Tory laughed.

She giggled again, waving her hand to dismiss her but she was fooling no one now.

"Chop chop – into class, come on!" Professor Zenith called as she strode inside and we started filing into the building after her.

We took the large elevator up to the observatory on the top floor and I gazed up at the glittering star map above us. We grabbed seats near the back of the room in our usual routine. Zenith always tried to make us sit in the weird ass chairs positioned at the front of the auditorium just for us, but since Tory had been Star Crossed, she didn't push the issue. She just sobbed whenever she saw Tory up close and ushered her to the back of the room like she was doing her the greatest kindness. Which in a way, she was. But the sobbing was uncalled for.

When everyone was settled in their seats, all eyes fell on Zenith as she rested her hands on the podium in the middle of the observatory. Her shoulders were shuddering and her head was bent over. I shot a frown at Tory just before Zenith sniffed loudly then turned her gaze to the stars above us. "Today we'll be discussing..." She drew in a long breath like she was trying to keep her emotions in check. "Mate bonds," she exhaled heavily and all eyes in the room swung towards Tory, making her shift uncomfortably in her seat and drawing a protective growl from my throat.

"In our previous classes, we have discussed such bonds as Nebula Allies, Astral Adversaries and...and..." her voice cracked and she released a mournful sob that echoed around the room. I glanced at Tory with an eye roll and she actually shot me an amused grin back.

"Nutcase," I mouthed.

"Loony ass," she agreed.

"Elysian Mates!" Zenith wailed. "And o-of course we all know the most t-terrible effects of r-refusing such a b-bond now m-more than ever." She blew her nose loudly into a handkerchief and I pursed my lips. I mean *really*. Did she have to put on such a display and draw so much more attention to Tory than was necessary? "As you'll remember from our previous classes," she cleared her throat, her spine straightening as she continued as if she hadn't just broken down in the middle of the classroom. "Elysian Mate bonds are the most rare of all the bonds. A bond from the stars is a gift indeed. To refute that gift…well, to refute it would be insanity." She slammed her hand down on the podium, the sound making my heart jolt and Diego actually leapt in his seat beside me.

Zenith sniffed again, running a hand through her long, raven hair. "I can't imagine the thought process of someone who would actually say no to such a blessed, divine gift from the stars themselves. Can you?" She rounded on the front row. "Can any of you tell me why someone would do such a thing? Commit such a *travesty*?"

"At least she's subtle," Tory breathed in my ear and I smothered my laugh under my hand.

Kylie's arm shot into the air. "I know why, Professor."

"You do, Miss Major?" Zenith asked with actual hope in her reddened eyes. "Then please enlighten me."

"I think Darius Acrux would rather wake up next to a woman who looks like a Heptian Toad in their shifted form for the rest of his life rather than lay a finger on a filthy Vega. I can't see the stupidity in that at all to be honest," she said sweetly and I shot forward in my chair in a fit of rage for my sister, flicking my fingers and making her desk burst into flames. She screamed, leaping out of her seat and trying to steal the air from the flames with her magic, only resulting in fanning them so they flared in her face.

"I'll help you, Kylie!" Tory raised a hand, casting a tsunami of water over her head to put it out and Kylie slammed down into her seat, absolutely drenched while the students beside her ran for their lives.

"That's enough!" Zenith called out to the frantic classroom. "Miss Major, dry out your things," she demanded. "And ten points from Aer for provoking the Vega girls."

"Are you serious?!" Kylie balked, wringing out her sopping wet hair as she started using her magic to dry everything.

"It will be another ten if you don't sit down and button your lip," Zenith demanded and Kylie cursed under her breath as she dried her stuff out. Her friends slowly returned to the seats around her while me, Tory, Sofia, Tyler and Diego fell apart with silent laughter.

When Zenith had the class back under control, she gathered her notes then waved her hand and all of the chairs started reclining.

I relaxed back in my seat, sharing a final grin with Diego before turning my head to the glittering ceiling.

"There are more bonds in the world than just the Star Bonds. Bonds that are far more common and which most of you will likely encounter in your lifetime," Zenith explained and the moon appeared above us, full and round and glowing. On the other side of the ceiling, the sun ignited as a deep orange and yellow orb. "The sun and moon rule all other bonds. Your Order is either that of night or day. Light or dark. For example, Werewolves are most famously known for their links to the moon as they draw their power from it too. But did you also know that Orders such as Vampires, Cerberuses, Minotaurs and Medusas are also ruled by the moon when it comes to Mate Bonds?"

My ears pricked up at that and I already had a thousand questions burning at the tip of my tongue.

"As for Orders ruled by the sun, well a few of them are Dragons, Nemean Lions, Harpies, and our very own recently arisen Phoenixes of course." She started clapping, but no one joined in and she quickly kept talking. "But what does this mean for you all? Well, firstly you will find yourself attracted to those of similar power levels to yourself. Then, if you find a mate within your Order or another Order of the same inclination, you may be Moon Bonded or Sun Bonded if the stars deem it in your fate for you to be together."

"What if you like someone from the opposite side? A moon ruled Order falling for a sun ruled Order?" Elijah called out and I bit my lip, wondering that very same thing. Were me and Orion destined to ever be mated somehow? I certainly couldn't imagine being with anyone else. But I didn't need the sun, the moon or the stars to tell me that.

"Well that is where things get interesting," Zenith explained and the sun and moon moved across the sky, crossing over one another so they seemed to blaze as one entity. "You can be mated by both. It is what we term a Soluna Bond. Both celestial beings lend power to bind the mates together, but it is no more powerful than a regular Mate Bond."

"What about a bond within Orders though?" Jillian called out. "As a Nemean Lioness, I'm planning on finding myself a King one day, but they usually have more than one mate."

"Yes, many Orders have names for their own special kinds of pairings. The Moon and Sun Bonds are not quite so limiting as the Elysian bond- barring the famous exception we discussed a few weeks back. They can extend to polyamorous relationships as is common with Orders like the Nemean Lions. It doesn't affect their way of pairing, if anything it compliments it."

"What about the Werewolves?" Kylie asked. "I heard they pair off monogamously when they find their true mate." There was a pout to her voice that made me roll my eyes. Maybe if she stopped chasing after Seth, he'd come around to the idea of the two of them again. But from the way he totally dismissed her these days, I had to doubt that thought.

"Yes, Werewolves are similar to the Pegasuses in that their pack will live polyamorously until the leader has found their mate. An Alpha Werewolf will seek other Alphas of the same power level, either in their Order or otherwise. The same goes for a Pegasus Dom – or Dominant. Once the leader has found their partner, the rest of the herd will then seek their mates until the unit is in harmony. It can take years for a pack or herd to find harmony however, especially as the groups grow or change," Zenith explained. "If you happen to mate with someone of your Order, there will be a special name for that bond such as the Nemean Lions' King and Queens, the Wolves' Alphas, the Basilisks' Cobras, the Pegasuses' Dominants, the Vampires' Count and Countess, the Dragons' Idols. But no matter who you are mated with, you will still be bound by whichever entity rules each of your Orders, either Sun or Moon or both. Unless you have been chosen to be bonded by the stars of course," her voice waivered on the word stars. "In which case this is the only bond that will matter, the only one which will present itself to you in your lifetime. The only chance for happiness…" She trailed off and I took Tory's hand, squeezing. I knew she didn't want people fawning over her, but her fingers held onto mine in the dark where no one could see. It was the only kind of comfort she could bear. The hidden kind.

"Now, I want you to all take out your Astrology 101 textbooks," she instructed and the lights grew brighter as the chairs elevated us back upright. Tory released my hand and I flipped out the lap table, placing my Atlas down on it as I took out my Astrology book, noticing I had one new message waiting for me.

I picked it up as Zenith started explaining the exercise, my focus entirely lost as I subtly opened the message and read it.

Lance:
What lesson are you in? I'm supposed to be filing paperwork on the new security regulations for Nova, but I've got a certain Blue haired Fae on my mind…

Darcy:
Hmm, sounds like you need some help ;)
And I'm in Astrology. I just learned about Mate Bonds. Am I going to be your Countess?

I smirked as I pressed send and his reply came in lightning fast.

Lance:
If you wanna start biting me a little harder, you can definitely be my Countess…

Darcy:
Agreed.
Maybe I can come and meet you after class for a snack…

Lance:
I can't wait that long and I'm gonna make a real mess of this paperwork if I keep messaging you.

Darcy:
Tut tut. Are you jerking off at your desk, sir!

Lance:
Well it's difficult not to get distracted. I've got my eye on a beautiful Cardinal Magic hardback with a leather bookmark pushed between its supple pages.

Is it cheating if I stick the tip in?

I burst out laughing and received looks from around the room as I fought away the blush burning into my cheeks.

"You're so busted," Tory taunted. "I know exactly what you're doing."

I bit down on my lip, showing her the text and she fell into silent giggles with me. She was the only one in the world I'd show that message to. And it felt so good to have a little moment of lightness with my sister again.

Zenith didn't care if we howled to the moon in this class, she'd never reprimand us, despite the fact that she took house points from anyone else who rose their voice above a low chatter.

I glanced down at my Atlas again, finding another message waiting for me.

Lance:
Couldn't do it, Blue. You're the only first edition I want.

I poised my thumb to reply with a stupid smile on my face when an alarm blared around the room, the bell drilling into my ears.

"Oh my gracious!" Zenith gasped. "Everyone up, out out out!" She ushered us towards the elevator.

"What is it?" Jillian demanded as she nearly fell over Kylie's bag in her haste to move.

"It's the Nymph alarm, it must have been triggered by the wards at the outer perimeter!" Zenith wailed. "Everyone get outside and line up for the count. That's it, hurry along now. Not to worry."

I moved along the aisle, swinging my bag over my shoulder as I tucked my Atlas and textbook into it, my heart hammering to a wild beat.

We made it downstairs and spilled out onto the path beyond the observatory, crowding together against the wall.

Zenith pushed her way through the group, moving in front of us as she started counting heads. "Everyone - stop moving! No – ah, please stop moving."

"Make way!" Washer's voice caught my ear and I turned as he raced down the path from the direction of Lunar Leisure in nothing but his speedos. He was dripping wet and the bulge in his tight budgie smugglers jostled from side to side as he raced towards us. He shoved through the crowd and I received a wet hand to the boob as he pushed me out of his way.

"Argh," I exclaimed, stepping back as everyone got the message and gave him a wide berth. "Even in a crisis he still has time to be a pervert." I lifted my hand to dry the wet hand mark he'd left on my shirt and Tory shuddered beside me.

We drifted to the back of the group and I spotted students standing outside the buildings nearby, getting rounded up by their teachers. Zenith finally managed to do the count then the bells stopped ringing around campus and her Atlas pinged. She took it out and her shoulders slumped dramatically.

"False alarm everyone," she announced. "Looks like it was triggered accidentally. Back inside, come on, in you go."

Relief washed through me as we started queuing towards the door at the back of the line. We soon made it inside and started moving towards the elevator as everyone grouped into it. A whoosh of air lifted my skirt up and arms surrounded me the same moment that a hand clamped over my mouth. The world blurred and a second later I found myself in a dark store cupboard, crushed against a trolley full of books as a hard chest pressed to my back. I didn't even need to smell the cinnamon in the air to know who it was. His hand slid from my mouth and I laughed breathlessly.

"Are you crazy? What if Tory thinks I just got kidnapped? Or what if someone *saw*?" My heart thrummed madly and I couldn't even focus on getting the answer to that question as Orion's hard-on pressed into my ass.

"I left a post-it note on her arm and no one saw, I'm too fucking fast," he said with a dark chuckle. "Now stop talking." I reached behind me in the dark, but he caught my wrist to stop me touching him, evidently able to see in here when I couldn't. The scent of new stationary and textbooks reached me in the small space and there was hardly any room to move.

"What happened to not being reckless?" I panted as the heat of his body called to me, sending a deep throb between my thighs.

"What happened to not talking?" he growled in his teacher voice and my pulse skyrocketed.

"You set off that alarm, didn't you?" I said in realisation and he forced me harder against the trolley that was jammed against the wall, his breath burning hot on my ear.

"That's it, Miss Vega, now you're going to be punished for disobeying me."

A tremor of excitement ran through me and I sucked my lower lip in anticipation of his so-called punishment. He kicked my legs wide, pushing my skirt up and running his palm over my ass as my heavy breaths filled the air.

"Do you think you're going to enjoy it?" he asked and I nodded shamelessly as he trailed his fingers around to the front of my panties and pinched my clit through the material.

I gasped, resting my head back against his shoulder and his fangs grazed my throat as a primal growl rumbled through him.

"I can always surprise you," he whispered against my skin and I tilted my head farther to the side, wanting the kiss of his teeth.

"Do it," I said, mostly because I wanted to goad him into whatever surprise he had in mind.

He took his hand from under my skirt and returned it a moment later. I couldn't see what he was doing, but when he pushed his hand into my panties, he had something cold and hard in his grip that grazed against my sensitive flesh and sent goosebumps fluttering across my body.

I gasped, pressing firmer back against him, but he didn't budge an inch. "What's that?" I asked.

"Do you know what a Delicia Crystal is, Blue?" he purred in my ear and I shook my head.

He grazed the crystal between the centre of my legs and pleasure skittered out from it in echoing waves. A moan left me and he'd barely even touched me. *Ohmagod.*

"It enhances pleasure," he said in a dark tone before repeating the same movement and my legs trembled from the sweet bliss radiating over my skin from the crystal.

"Lance," I begged and he pushed it inside me, grazing his thumb over my clit at the same time.

I cried out half a second after he cast a silencing bubble, my whole body flooding with waves of magnetic energy that all centred on that one object inside me. It was achingly smooth, but must have only been a few inches long. As good as it felt, I wanted more. I needed more.

I ground back against Orion and he groaned headily, stroking his thumb across that delicious spot once again as the crystal sent another current of pleasure twisting through me. He yanked my panties down and I kicked them off, moving my hand behind me and running it up the hardened bulge in his pants. "I need you."

"Bend over," he said in a gravelly voice.

I did as he asked, digging my teeth into my lower lip in anticipation as I rested my elbows on the books stacked on top of the trolley.

The sound of his zipper rolled down and he pulled the crystal free a second before he slammed himself inside me. His hand pressed down beside mine as he braced himself and I reared forward and bit into the back of it like I'd promised I would.

He slid the crystal higher onto that sweet spot and started pounding into me at a merciless pace as the magical item sent pleasure racing out from it in every direction. I was lost to the intensity of being claimed this way, my thoughts exploding and flashing with light.

Orion groaned with the feel of it too and I tasted his blood on my lips, the colliding sensations driving me wild. Everything was happening so fast, my mind was a blur and I was already collapsing into my downfall, shattering into a thousand pieces.

Pleasure ripped through me like a hurricane and I cried out as it continued on and on, the crystal amplifying it tenfold until I couldn't think straight. My body no longer belonged to me, my muscles bunching of their own accord as I lost all control of myself to the invading, all-consuming pleasure. I was shaking and moaning as Orion clung to me hard enough to bruise my flesh. He finished with a powerful thrust and his fangs sank into my neck, a deep groan resounding through his body.

He took the crystal away and I sagged forward as my lungs laboured for air and I tried to regain control of my trembling body. It felt like I'd just survived an earthquake located solely between my legs.

"Was that better than the Cardinal Magic hardback?" I panted through a laugh and he pulled his fangs free of my neck, chuckling as he stepped back.

I turned around, leaning down to tug up my panties with flushed cheeks.

He rolled up his fly then his mouth pressed to mine in a long and deep kiss that had my toes curling all over again. "That was even better than the collector's edition of Advanced Numerology, beautiful. And that little slut knows how to make my spine tingle."

I slapped his chest with a wild laugh. "You're one dirty, book talking Vampire, you know that?"

"I know that." He kissed me again. "And you're one sweet, bitey little Countess." He flicked a switch and a lightbulb illuminated above us. His hair had fallen forward into his eyes and his shirt was untucked, his teacher look firmly ruffled. And I liked that a lot. Especially being the one who'd caused it.

He admired the bite mark on the back of his hand with a smirk. "Wish I could keep it."

"New tattoo?" I suggested with a teasing grin and he actually looked like hc was considering it for a second before I jabbed his arm. "Heal it, idiot."

He sighed, rubbing his thumb across the mark until it was gone then reaching out to heal the little puncture wounds on my throat. "One day, Blue, I'm gonna wear your teeth marks wherever I go."

"I'll wear yours too, Lance." I grinned. "Just three and a half more years to go."

"Yeah," he sighed. "Are you sure I'm worth it?" He cocked his head to the side, a sudden vulnerability in his eyes and my heart slammed against my ribcage like it wanted to dive through the walls of my flesh and slap him for even questioning it.

"Every day." I tapped him on the nose and his face split into a grin. "You should go. I'll wait until you're gone before I leave."

"Alright." He took hold of the door handle then smirked at me. "The crystal is in your blazer pocket by the way. In case you miss me." He winked then shot out of the cupboard in a blur and the door swung slowly shut behind him.

I shook my head at him, trying to fight the endless grin on my face. *Well dammit if I don't miss him already.*

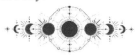

I approached the Heirs in The Howling Meadow with Geraldine and Tory either side of me. The sun was beginning to set and the air held the hint of spring to it, calling to us on the breeze. Our Elemental Combat lessons weren't getting any easier. Neither me, Tory or Geraldine had managed to put an Heir on their asses yet. And it was infuriating as hell. With each lesson, I'd hoped to get closer, but sometimes I took such a beating that I swear I wasn't even scratching the surface of their defences. But I wasn't deterred. Because one day, whether it would be tomorrow or next year or in five years, I was going to be skilled enough to knock the shit out of them, dammit.

We reached the boulders where they were gathered, the four of them shirtless and taking it in turns to brawl with each other with fists. Not a drop of magic in sight. I might have been spoken for, but I still couldn't ignore the stacks of shredded muscle slamming into each other before me. And I was half a second away from calling Orion over to have a go when I remembered I was here for a reason and I probably couldn't get away with asking for that.

"Seth!" I called and he turned towards me just as Darius took a swing at him, his fist slamming into his jaw and sending him flying into the dirt. *Oh hell yes.*

I smirked, wanting to bask in his loss, but he scrambled back to his knees running at Darius like a psycho and throwing his shoulder into his gut. They crashed to the ground with a tremor that rocked the earth beneath my feet and Orion appeared in a blur of movement, stopping at my side and blowing his coach whistle so loud I winced.

"Assholes! Despite the grunge hair Capella is sporting and the fucking worst mohawk of the century Rigel seems to think is cool, this is not a fucking mosh pit at some prissy indie rock gig. So get your asses up and start fighting like Fae or you'll all be in detention for the rest of the week."

I tried not to bat my lashes too hard at Orion, but holy hell when he used that voice and blew that whistle, and looked...*mmm.*

Tory elbowed me in the ribs with a restrained grin. "You look one second away from drooling."

Geraldine was evidently close enough to hear as she started laughing and clutching her side, and Orion and Caleb snapped around to look at me in surprise.

"What?" I asked innocently, shooting Tory a glare and she bit her lip to stop herself from laughing too, although I'd seen her staring at the guys as well so she wasn't exactly Miss Innocent right now.

"Oh give my queen a break!" Geraldine lamented. "There's enough mammoth man muscle, tight peach-cupping shorts and tantalising testosterone in the air to bring even fine ladies such as us to our knees. But I for one, will not stand for such an advantage in our brawls."

"I'm not putting my shirt back on, Gerry," Max said with a smirk, folding his bulging arms across his chest. "Not unless you beg me."

"By the gleam of my shiny waxed lady balls! Who said anything about putting your clothes on?" She laughed, taking hold of the hem of her shirt and whipping it off, revealing her huge breasts in a delicate blue bra with a seashell clasped at the base of her cleavage. Max's eyes practically bugged out of his head as she directed him further into the field for a fight. "I challenge you to a duel, you mouth watering barnacle of a boy."

"Barnacle?" he muttered, but didn't seem too bothered about the rest of it as he jogged after her into the meadow.

Orion glanced at me with a sharp expression and I guessed he was pissed at me for staring. But if he'd actually seen inside my brain, he would have found a completely innocent scene where he stripped off and got down and dirty with the Heirs. Totally above board. I didn't want anyone but my Vampire. But if he *happened* to tussle with a few muscular assholes, then far be it from me not to settle in for the show.

I noticed Mildred watching us from group two, pinning Jillian Minor down by the throat and baring her jutting teeth at us. Ever since she'd joined Zodiac, I swear all she did was look like she was about to shift into her Dragon form and eat someone. Or maybe she wouldn't even shift and she'd just take a bite right out of one of us. Most likely Tory.

Smoke spewed from her nostrils and her moustache rippled in the breeze it caused. It might have been funny it if wasn't weirdly terrifying.

"Come on then, babe," Seth beckoned me over. "Let's see how far up in the air I can throw you this time."

My cheeks heated as I marched toward him with fierce strides. In the last lesson, he'd captured me in a tornado for like twenty goddamn minutes. I'd been so dizzy afterwards, I'd puked. And Kylie had captured it all on camera and plastered it all over FaeBook. Not my finest moment. But this time, I was determined to leave a mark on him at the very least.

Tory headed after Caleb for a spar and Darius moved to chat with Orion while they watched. My jaw was grinding as I took up a fighting stance across from Seth. His smug face had a date with the dirt and I was more than happy to be the damn taxi driver.

"You really hate me, don't you?" he taunted, not even bothering to lower into the stance as he flexed his muscles, waiting for me to attack.

I didn't answer, trying to focus on every cast I knew as he started to circle to the right, forcing me to move left.

He yawned provocatively then flexed his arms above his head, giving me an open target. If he was going to be an idiot about it, I wasn't going to miss the opportunity. I threw out my hand, releasing a powerful gust of air, but he blocked it with a flick of his wrist, sending it whooshing out into the field and knocking over several students in group four.

Seth dove into action, throwing out a palm and sending a spear of wood tearing through the air toward me. I cast fire, burning it into ash, but he kept throwing them, the spears flying forwards with a ferocity that should have terrified me. But I wasn't afraid, I was furious.

I burned through every earth attack with yells of rage, keeping any of them from landing. But while he cast the onslaught of spears, a vine caught my leg, ripping me up into the air to dangle from it by one ankle.

He howled up at me and laughter carried from the surrounding crowd as people turned to watch. With a growl, I sent a tide of water crashing down toward him but it cascaded over a perfect dome of air above his head. I froze it in an instant and while he was blinded, I reared up toward my ankle and severed the vine with a flash of fire. I caught myself on the air, twisting around so I hit the ground on my feet, only stumbling a step before I launched my next attack at the frozen dome before me. I burned through it with a scream of rage and the dome dripped away to nothing on the floor, revealing an empty space where Seth had once stood.

Someone tapped me on the shoulder and I whipped around in alarm, meeting a powerful shot of air as it left Seth's palm and crashed into my face. I hit the ground, tasting blood and failure on my tongue. He leapt on top of me with another howl, casting vines around my arms to pin me down while taking a solid hold of my throat to prove his point.

"Yield," he growled and I clenched my jaw, refusing to say that fucking word for the thousandth time. He squeezed harder, his brows pinching together. "*Darcy*," he demanded.

"Fine," I spat. "I yield."

He released me immediately, standing up and offering me his hand, but I smacked it away as I got to my feet and wiped the blood from my split lip. Marguerite, Kylie and their little gang jeered me from across the field and my cheeks burned as I strode away, needing to just cool off for a second.

I stalked away from the group and into the longer grass, rage clawing at my heart.

In a flash of movement, Orion appeared in front of me but I tried to shoulder my way past him, not wanting any pity. He caught my arm, whirling me around to face back the way I'd come and casting a silencing bubble around us.

"Breathe," he demanded and I did. "Speak," he commanded next.

"I hate him," I snarled. "I know what he did for you and I know that confuses things, but it doesn't make what he did before that okay. And I hate that I turn up here three times a week just to get put on my ass again and again and ag-"

"Calm down," Orion growled and I looked up at him, heated anger invading every part of my body. His eyes softened into two obsidian pools and I found it slightly easier to keep breathing as I stayed locked in their gaze.

"I am calm," I said, though I wasn't.

"You want to run before you can walk," he said, inching closer, but not enough so that it crossed any boundaries if anyone was looking. "You need to be more patient."

"I'm trying," I huffed. "But I feel like I'm getting nowhere."

"Are you fucking with me? You moved up into the top combat class in your freshman year. Your only competitors are the Heirs now. You're not giving yourself enough credit. The way you got out of that vine hold took real skill, Blue. Real fucking skill." He fixed me with an intense look and I nodded, trying to accept that I was improving. But it was so hard when I rarely even landed a blow on the Heirs. And I *really* wanted to land a hit on that long haired jumped up Wolf boy.

"I just feel like I don't even get close to taking him out." I fixed my glare on Seth as he climbed to the top of a boulder, pounded his chest like a gorilla and howled to his pack who echoed it from within all the other groups.

Orion reached out to my busted lip, healing it quickly and wiping the blood away with his thumb. He placed it straight in his mouth, casually sweeping a hand through his hair at the same time like that was a perfectly normal thing to do. And I guessed he could get away with it as a Vampire. It was also weirdly hot as hell.

"Patience little predator," he said with a smirk, dropping his hand to his side. "Your skill will get there. But that's only half the fight."

"What's the other half?" I narrowed my eyes.

"Your prey," he purred in a devilish tone that made a smile pull at the corner of my mouth. He gestured to Seth who was leaping from boulder to boulder now like he was invincible. "Knowing who you're fighting is key when you're dealing with powerful Fae. It's not just a case of brute force. The devil is in the detail. And your pretty boy Werewolf prey has weaknesses. Find them," he commanded.

Seth cupped his hands around his mouth at that moment and called out to us, "Hey sir! Why don't you have a round with me while Darcy dries her tears?"

Orion moved a finger so subtly I almost missed it and a gust the strength of a hurricane sent Seth flying off of the boulders. He just caught himself with his own air magic before he faceplanted the ground.

"I'll take that as a no!" he called as he got up, striding over to Darius and starting up a fight with him instead.

"Why'd you miss that opportunity?" I asked with a frown. "I could have used the inspiration."

"No," he growled in a serious tone, catching me in his gaze. "I could have smashed his head in the second Darius told him to back off of us, but I held back. Because you know what's more satisfying to me than beating the living hell out of him, Blue?"

I shook my head, my throat too tight as I absorbed the passion in his expression.

"*You* doing it," he breathed with a seductive grin. "He's all yours, beautiful. I want you to make him scream. I'm gonna be right there with a fold-out chair and a bag of freshly popped popcorn to enjoy the show. But I won't be the one breaking bones – and trust me I really want to be that guy, but not this time. Seth Capella has written his fate in the stars. She's coming for him like a monster in the night. And her name is Darcy Vega."

My heart shone, at least that was what it felt like. I wanted to throw my arms around him and thank him for being the best guy I'd ever known. But it wasn't exactly good timing with the whole school watching. He had most definitely earned himself the best sex of his life tonight though. Which was gonna be hard to top, but I was happy to get imaginative.

"You're actually a really good teacher," I commented.

"She says like it's a surprise," he mocked and I laughed.

"Well, it just took me a while to realise that you're not just a dick to everyone because you hate the world."

He arched a brow. "Am I not?"

"No… you *care* Lance Orion."

He held his heart like I'd mortally wounded him, stumbling back a step and my laughter grew. "Don't insult me."

"Alright, keep up your heartless act then, but I've got you pegged, Professor."

He leaned in closer with his smile vanishing like a ghost in the night. "I'll admit this one thing, I don't always *hate* being a teacher."

I gasped, acting as dramatically as he had, pressing the back of my hand to my forehead like I was going to faint.

"Don't ever tell a soul," he said intently and I laughed, miming locking my lips and throwing away the key. He nudged me to get me walking back towards the Heirs and my whole body felt lighter as I approached them.

I sighed as I headed back towards the Heirs, smiling as Geraldine yelled, "For the magnificent queens of Solaria!" and leapt onto Max's back, her huge breasts slamming into his head as she flooded them both with a downpour of water.

"I love that girl," Tory said as she jogged over to join me, her arms and throat lined with bruises. "Caleb," she explained with a huff and Orion reached out to heal her.

She smiled at him in thanks and I glanced between the two of them with warmth in my soul. The fact that Tory had given him that little friendship bracelet – which he religiously wore every day without comment – was the cutest damn thing ever. I'd hugged her so tight when I'd found out about that she'd had to forcibly escape from me after five whole minutes of squish time.

I spent the next half an hour watching Seth fight and taking note every time one of the Heirs got him on his back. He led with his left foot, but his right hand was dominant when he cast. He was cocky, self-assured but there was weakness in that sometimes. Occasionally, he threw attacks which were too big, and so long as his opponent managed to shield against it, there was a small window of time where Seth had to take a second to recover. That window was gold.

"We're gonna be stronger than them one day," Tory said, lifting her chin. "It's just a matter of time."

I looked to her, that fact ringing truer in my skull than it ever had before. Her gaze hooked on mine and a moment passed between us where something just clicked together. Something so damn obvious it was strange to only realise it now. We'd decided to fight them. We weren't just working our asses off to beat them one time in some Elemental Combat class. We wanted to keep beating them again and again. And that could only mean one thing.

"Do you want it?" I whispered, the air seeming to stir strangely like the stars were leaning in to listen. "Because I do. It feels so right."

"Yeah," she said, her lips parting in realisation. "I want it too. I really do, Darcy."

"So let's take it," I said, surprising myself with the strength in my voice.

I could feel Orion's eyes on me, but I couldn't look away from my sister. This moment was *ours*. And it needed to be screamed from the nearest mountain. Or the top of the nearest boulder as the case may have been.

I snatched Tory's hand into my grip and she ran with me as we raced towards the boulders and climbed up to the peak of the highest one.

"Listen up!" I yelled and the Heirs stopped fighting, frowning over at us.

Orion casually flicked his fingers in my direction and when I spoke again, my voice amplified over the entire meadow.

"You've seen us get beaten time and again," I called and the Heirs laughed, smirking at us like we were about to embarrass ourselves. Geraldine thumped Max in the arm, giving us her full, undivided attention with her eyes glowing brightly. "But one day soon, we won't be beat."

"We're the most powerful Fae in this kingdom!" Tory shouted, her voice filled with power as it was amplified by Orion's magic and her hair swirling around her in a wild breeze, making her look fierce as hell. "And we may have been hurt, beaten, bruised, *drowned*." She glared down at the Heirs. "But we're never going to stay down."

The Heirs shared anxious looks and my heart swelled as I met Orion's gaze, his eyes brimming with pride. I loved him fiercely in that moment. Truly. Madly. Always.

"So we intend to claim our rightful place in the kingdom!" I announced. "Bring on the press, the photoshoots, the interviews, we're ready to step out and be the real princesses that we are."

Tory caught my hand and I lifted her arm into the air on instinct. "We're going to fight for our throne!" she cried.

"And we're going to win it!" I finished.

Geraldine broke down in tears, dropping to her knees in the dirt and clapping like mad. The rest of the A.S.S came swarming to the base of the boulders, jumping in the air and cheering like crazy. Gabriel clapped from across the field, a knowing smile on his face like he'd been waiting for this to happen today. And I guessed he had.

I let my gaze slide over to the Heirs again, eyeing Max's sneer, Seth's scowl, Caleb's darkened gaze and the tight-jawed silence Darius was sporting. They said nothing to each other. And maybe that was because they knew this moment had been coming too. That they'd realised we couldn't be beat. And one day in the future, we were going to face them one on one in a bid for our rightful place on the Solarian throne. It was written in the stars.

Orion blew his whistle to sound the end of the class and a wide smile split across my face. We climbed down into the sea of bodies, getting accosted by hugs and claps on the back. Geraldine waded her way toward us, dragging in ragged breaths like she couldn't get enough air in her lungs between words, "My – queens – are – finally – ascending -" she managed to get out then dragged us into her arms, sobbing loudly for the whole world to hear. "I'm prouder than a pecan in a tin of raisin berries!" she wailed. "And I'm happier than a clam riding a sea turtle!"

Most of the students had already departed by the time the A.S.S. started dispersing. Everyone tried to lure us into a party, but my legs were numb and even Geraldine was fighting a yawn with every excited word she threw at us. Orion lingered behind us with Darius, talking to him in a silencing bubble as the other Heirs peeled away, Caleb, Seth and Max jogging off ahead of us with their back muscles flexing and Seth howling angrily at the sky.

"Well, this has been the most wonderific moment of my entire life. But I must call it a night as I am positively flamboozled," Geraldine sighed, pulling her shirt on. "What a wild and wet evening it's been. Good night my queens. I look forward to versing you in all the customs of the how to claim the throne. By the grandest grapes in Ginkleford, what dreams I'm going to dream tonight!" She waved flamboyantly and headed off down another path in the direction of Earth Territory with a skip in her step.

Darkness was starting to fall and the shadows were thick between the trees, but there were no shadows in my heart tonight, there was too much brightness in me to let them in.

Tory flung an arm over my shoulders and I leaned against her with a groan of exhaustion, but a smile still bit into my cheeks.

"I can't believe this is only our first year," I said.

"Yeah, but imagine us this time next year. We'll be kicking ass. I'll be eating breakfast off of Caleb's washboard abs after I've knocked him out cold. Just because I can."

"Is that your plan?" I teased with a laugh, but she didn't return it and I felt the shadows in her for a moment, reaching out to try and join with mine. But they were buried so deep right now, there was almost none to find.

"Nah," she said offhandedly and I wrapped my arm around her waist.

"I love you, Tor," I breathed, just because sometimes people needed to hear that. And maybe I didn't say it to her enough.

"Love you too, Darcy," she whispered.

A shadow spilled onto the path ahead of us and the two of us cried out, throwing up our hands in defence as my heart lurched into my throat. A combo attack of water and air exploded from us and the figure tumbled through the air, slamming down onto their back several feet away. A hat laid on the ground just where they'd been and I swore as I realised who it was.

"Shit, Diego, don't jump out on us like that!" Tory reprimanded as I scooped up his beanie and hurried forward to give it to him.

He was lying awkwardly on the ground, groaning as he rubbed the back of his head. "Lo siento chicas," he wheezed as he sat upright and Orion appeared in a flash, jerking him to his feet by the collar of his shirt.

"You're gonna get yourself killed diving into the path of two fucking Phoenixes, you fool," he snapped.

Diego shrugged him off, taking his hat from me and yanking it on with a scowl. He seemed jittery, bouncing up and down on his heels as we gathered around him and Darius cast a Faelight, letting it float up above our heads and bathe us in a low amber light.

"What's up with you, Duncan?" he demanded, narrowing his eyes as an angry heat spilled from his body, telling me exactly how he was feeling since we'd laid our claim.

Diego glanced between us all, his eyes settling on mine last and evidently whatever he found there was enough to make him speak. "My parents have added a memory to the web," he breathed and Orion immediately cast a silencing bubble around us while Darius started casting some other spells which I guessed would deter anyone from coming this way.

"Show it to us," Tory said immediately and Diego nodded, rolling up his sleeves and extending his arms into the middle of the circle.

I took his hand while Orion gripped his forearm and Darius and Tory took hold of his other arm.

Darkness pushed beneath my eyes, thicker than should have been possible as I was yanked away into the abyss. The shadows started whispering, calling me into their depths as I sank deeper and deeper, Diego's presence guiding me into the very base of them.

The strange, white cloud appeared ahead of us and memories crackled amongst it, flashing and flickering in and out of focus. A memory grew brighter and brighter within them all and I gasped as I was sucked right into it like before.

My lungs compressed at the sight waiting for me.

Clara stood on a hill in a blood red dress with Lionel at her side in a black cloak. Around them stood hundreds upon hundreds of Nymphs in their monstrous forms, all the way down the hill, their heads bowed, a low and raspy chant leaving them, dragging its way through my ears.

"You will hunt the land on my command!" Clara called. "You will leave no stone unturned in your search. For the High Lord Lionel Acrux. Your king. Who will do right by you when you do right by him." The shadows poured out from her in every direction, seeming to tumble right into the very bodies of the Nymphs. At a swish of her hand, they moved and every fibre of my being hummed with terror.

This was an army of the most fearful creatures I'd ever known. And they were under the control of Clara, of the monster who'd almost torn Orion from this world. And of Lionel Acrux too. The Dragon master. The most powerful Fae in Solaria. And soon, no doubt, to be the one and only king.

I was suddenly yanked out of the vision and my heart stammered as I found myself staring across at Tory, a mirrored look of shock on her face.

"Fuck," she breathed which just about summed up the expressions on everyone else's faces around the circle.

"What do we do?" I turned to Orion with anxiety warring in my chest and his brows stitched together.

"If my sister can control the Nymphs…" he trailed off and I wished Diego wasn't there so I could reach for him, comfort him. Seeing her standing on that hill beside the man who'd destroyed his life must have been ripping his heart out.

"We're fucked." Darius growled, dragging a hand through his hair as he turned his back on the circle.

"I'm sorry, I…" Diego shook his head, at a loss for what to say and I squeezed his arm.

"Lance," I breathed and he looked to me with real fear burning in his eyes.

His throat bobbed and his jaw tightened as he forced his emotions down and raised his chin. "No one leaves campus," he commanded, looking between me and Tory. "And no one goes anywhere alone even *on* campus, understand me?" He fixed me in his gaze and I nodded.

"Las estrellas están contra nosotros," Diego whispered, turning his gaze to the heavens like he was praying.

"Walk Tory back to your House," Orion commanded Darius and he nodded stiffly.

"Just keep far enough away to avoid the earthquake," he grunted to her, then took off down the path and Tory gave me a grave look before heading away with him.

Orion started marching forward, the tension in his posture making my heart drum like crazy. "Follow," he barked when we didn't immediately do so and we jogged to catch up with him as he headed towards Aer House.

My head was pounding by the time we got to the tower and Orion left us there without a word. My gut knotted and frayed. He wasn't okay. I needed to be there for him.

I ran upstairs with Diego, saying goodnight to him as I hurried into my room with hope in my chest. My heart sank into my gut as I found it empty. And I knew in my bones that Orion wouldn't come to me tonight. He was going to disappear into the dark and drown in his pain alone.

I sank down onto the edge of my bed, my body shaking from everything that had happened in the past hour. We'd announced our intention to claim our throne, only to learn that there might not even be a throne to claim soon. Not when Lionel had so much power. Not when he was in a position to take it from all of us and force the entire kingdom to heel.

Our fight wasn't with the Heirs right now. And it might not ever be. Not unless we stopped Lionel Acrux from taking the throne.

TORY

CHAPTER FIFTEEN

Good morning, Gemini.
The stars have spoken about your day!
A recent decision will cause sparks to fly in all aspects of your life during
the coming weeks and you may be tempted to regret your choice. But take
heart, if you stay steadfast in your resolve, this storm will blow over and
you will find yourself much happier on the other end of it. Though change
can be daunting, making decisions and sticking to them is always character
building. And with a bit of hard work, this choice may just work out in your
favour.

I blew out a breath and almost laughed. I was a motherfucking *Princess.*
I mean, I guess I always had been but now that I'd stood up with Darcy and
claimed it, it felt more real somehow. Maybe I should have been holding court
and walking corgis while eating tiny cakes or something. Instead, I was just
going to go for my morning run as usual.

An article had been published in The Daily Solaria today entitled *The
Vegas officially announce their intentions to claim the throne.* Tyler's Mom
had even had some pictures left over from the last photoshoot we'd done with
her, and alongside the interviews we'd given over the phone last night they'd
completed the eight page spread. The two of us were pictured in beautiful
gowns while sitting in enormous wooden thrones and with a little addition

from photoshop, the old photos had been updated to give me authentically black ringed eyes and the two of us were sporting some rather extravagant crowns. We looked hot as fuck and totally badass too with full resting bitch faces and challenging glares.

I should have been nervous about it. It was basically a red rag to the Lionel Acrux bull, but fuck it. I was done hiding in the background, letting him talk shit about us and spread lies in that rag The Celestial Times. From now on, we intended to release a counter interview every time an article was published about the Heirs, the Council or Darius's fucking wedding. Any and every time they made a show of power, we'd make one right back.

My gut churned at the idea of Lionel trying to strike at us, especially now that we knew he wielded such power over the Nymphs. But I'd stayed up talking the whole thing over with Darcy late into the night and we'd decided to press forward regardless. Lionel had never left us alone before we made this decision anyway and we knew there was nothing to stop him from trying to strike again. In fact, we were hoping that by officially announcing our intentions, we'd actually be gifted some protection from him. It would be even more suspicious if we had a sudden accident now and we were hoping that he'd be forced into the position of waiting for us to make an official challenge.

I wasn't going to waste time worrying about how long it would take us to hone our skills enough to do that. The point was, one day, we would. And come hell or high water, we'd see that asshole fall.

His control over the Nymphs was its own separate level of terrifying, but it also might work in our favour. What he was doing went beyond trying to claim more power – it was treason. He'd infected himself with the shadows and aligned himself with the mortal enemies of Solaria. So the plan we had for dealing with that was even simpler than trying to claim our birth right – we were going to expose him.

If we could get irrefutable evidence of his allegiance with the Nymphs then we could turn Solaria against him, not to mention the fact that the other Celestial Councillors would be forced to take him down. And Lionel may have managed to make himself strong enough to face the other Councillors one on one in the Fae way and win. But if he'd broken the law then that was a whole different kettle of fish. It was the one and only time that the other Councillors would band together to use their combined strength to defeat and arrest him. And the idea of him being carted off to prison in magical cuffs that cut off his access to his magic made me all kinds of happy.

I dressed in a matching white sports bra and leggings combo and headed down for my run.

My heart began to beat a little harder as I closed in on the door at the foot of the stairs. Every day, without fail, Darius had been waiting to run with me when I stepped outside. It had been six weeks now and he'd shown up every single day. But...I got the feeling that was about to end. Yesterday we'd stood up and laid claim to the throne after swearing we didn't want it since the day we'd first arrived at the academy. It was the root of all the issues I'd ever had with Darius and the article which had been published today was nothing less than a declaration of war. A political war, but a war all the same. And I just knew that was going to be the end of whatever tenuous relationship we'd been nurturing with these runs.

After he'd escorted me back to Ignis House last night, he'd stripped off, shifted and took off flying without even looking at me, much less uttering a word.

It had hurt, but then I could hardly complain about it considering the rejection I'd given him. And if he'd decided that this was the final nail in the coffin for us then I could accept that too. It wasn't like these moments we'd been sharing could do anything other than pave the path for some kind of awkward friendship anyway. And it was never going to be easy for me and Darcy to befriend any of the Heirs with the constant rivalry between us.

No, Darius wasn't going to be here this morning. And that was just fine by me. We'd always been destined to fight on different sides of this war anyway.

I bit my bottom lip, raised my chin and stepped outside.

Darius was leaning against the wall in his running gear like usual, his eyes brightening as I stepped out and my gaze locked on his.

"You're here," I breathed before I could stop myself and his eyebrows rose in surprise.

We never spoke to each other in the mornings. Not once. He waited for me, we exchanged a look, I ran, he followed, he got my coffee for me in The Orb then he left. That was it. Every day. I didn't even know what to make of it or what it meant to me. Except that being faced with the idea of him not showing up this morning had forced me to admit to myself that it meant *something*.

"Why wouldn't I be?" he asked, his rough voice sending a shiver down my spine.

We weren't close to each other, but we were alone and distant thunder rumbled in warning. I ignored it for the moment but I knew we didn't have long before the stars made more effort to push us apart.

"Because…well, I just thought, the article, the throne…"

"I've always known who you were, Roxy. The only difference is that you've realised it now too. You're a Princess, one of the two most powerful Fae in the whole of Solaria. You were always going to challenge me eventually. Just don't start thinking I'll roll over for you because you've decided you like the idea of wearing a crown."

My lips twitched at the challenge in his tone and I raised a hand, spinning earth magic to my command until I'd constructed a crown out of twisting green vines with little red roses dotted all over it. I placed it on my head and smirked at him tauntingly, taking a step closer before I could stop myself. "You have to admit it looks good on me, though."

Darius gave my entire body a lingering look that dragged up from my feet to the crown on my head and my flesh scorched everywhere his eyes landed.

"It looks even better on me," he countered, raising his own hand and fashioning a beautiful crown of ice which sparkled in the morning sun as he placed it on top of his black hair.

Fuck, I didn't realise I had a Prince Charming fantasy until right now. Although that wasn't right, Darius was no Prince Charming, more like a prince of darkness and he'd already corrupted me beyond recognition.

Thunder crashed overhead and thick raindrops spilled from the sky, but for a long moment neither of us moved.

"Ice melts," I pointed out.

"Flowers wither," he countered.

"I guess we're both screwed then."

"I was already aware of that."

Lightning flashed through the clouds and I bit my lip as I turned and sprinted away from him. His footsteps chased me up the path and I ran even faster as I headed off down the familiar route.

The rain continued to pound down on us until we'd passed through Fire Territory and into Water, but I just waited for it to stop then siphoned it out of my clothes with my magic. The stars left us to it as we finished up our run and by the time we'd made it to The Orb we'd both tossed our crowns away. It was just a shame that the real thing wasn't so easy to forget about.

Darius moved forward to open the door for me but he hesitated before opening it as he stepped close, reaching out to pull a red rose petal from my hair.

"You'd better be ready, Roxy," he purred in a deep voice which made my toes curl even as the ground trembled in warning beneath my feet. "Because the wolves are about to descend now you've staked your claim."

My lips parted to ask him what he meant by that, but he pulled the door wide for me and I gasped as I was met by a tumult of noise.

The Orb was full of the usual breakfast buzz, but the sound of excited chanting and cheers washed over me as heads turned my way and I was suddenly accosted by the sound of my name being screamed from countless lips.

Justin Masters caught my hand and tugged me into the crowd and I glanced back at Darius as he watched me go with an almost resigned look on his face. He turned and headed to the far side of The Orb where a just as raucous crowd were screaming their support for the Heirs.

There was a divide right down the centre of the room and it looked like everyone was picking a side.

My pulse raced as Justin swept me into his arms, placing a kiss on my cheek before lifting me up to stand on a table beside Darcy who was looking just as overwhelmed as I felt.

"This is insane!" she shouted so that I could hear her over the chant that Geraldine had started up.

Vegas for the throne!

The true queens are home!

Vegas for the throne!

The true queens are home!

"Why do I feel like our lives just got a whole lot more complicated?" I yelled back and Darcy laughed in a way that was bordering on hysterical.

"No going back now," she said.

"No going back," I agreed as I turned to look out over the sea of bodies that filled The Orb.

My gaze fell on the four Heirs who were standing up on a table amongst a cheering crowd of their own. Mildred was screaming her support alongside Marguerite, Kylie and countless others, but I was surprised to find it was a fairly even split. Even with all the shit Lionel and the Heirs had spread about us to the press, there were plenty of people willing to ignore them and throw their lot in with us.

I expected hatred, animosity and outright hostility when I met the Heirs' gazes, but that wasn't what I found. Instead, they were all looking at us with a challenge in their eyes and a hint of anticipation too. Like this was what they'd been waiting for. And they were ready to give as good as they got.

Bring it on then, assholes.

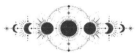

The last few days had been…bizarre.

For a start, no one knew about Lionel and the Nymphs so even though our little group was still reeling from the information and desperately trying to figure out ways to divide him from his newfound army and supposedly save Clara too, nothing had changed. Though that last part was all Lance and the rest of us were too nice, or maybe too chicken shit to point out that the girl was batshit with a capital B and needed putting down pronto. The idea of that tore at me after everything we'd done to help him get her back and I could totally sympathise with his desire to believe his sister still resided in her shadowy soul, but I was having a hard time seeing it.

Clara hadn't just been seduced by the shadows, wielding them in her Fae form the way we were all learning to do. She'd literally been devoured by them and sucked into the Shadow Realm for years. I mean, what did she even eat while she was there? No one ever mentioned that, but it seemed pretty important to me. I'd seen enough of the barren wasteland which housed the shadows to feel confident that there wasn't a toastie maker just sitting there waiting to be fired up. You couldn't order up a Dominos either. And people needed food to survive for years somewhere. Which made my theory irrefutable in my opinion. No food, no Clara. Whatever that *thing* was that Darcy and Orion had dragged up out of the Shadow Realm, it wasn't his sister anymore. It may have worn her face and stolen her memories, but it wasn't her.

Even our spies in the Acrux Manor hadn't given us any reason to suggest otherwise. Not that anyone knew about Darius's mom reporting to me now as well as Xavier messaging him. But it would be kinda hard for me to explain why she was helping me without being able to reveal what I'd done for her in return. And the last thing I needed was to break a star pact and goad the stars into cursing me with years of bad luck. Those assholes had it out for me as it was.

I expelled a heavy breath and forced myself to forget about all of that for now. As insane as it was, we knew that the world was in the process of being taken over by a psycho lizard king and his shadow whore - Catalina's words, not mine – but there was nothing we could do about it. I had to admit that I kinda loved Darius's mom. Weird, I know. But we were kinda becoming…text buddies. I guessed she was pretty lonely stuck in that fucking manor while still having to pretend to be bound by Lionel's Dark Coercion. So she'd been using every little excuse to message me about all kinds of things, a lot of which she couldn't even pretend were related to information on what Lionel and Clara were up to. She was desperately afraid for Xavier and couldn't even risk approaching him any differently now that she was free in case Lionel realised that he wasn't controlling her anymore. In my opinion, the idea of him stealing her ability to love and care for her children from her was actually the worst of the things he'd done to her.

But today I had something more important to do than worry about all of that. Today, I had to win a cheer off.

I stood in the locker rooms at the Pitball arena, diligently tying the pink ribbon intended for my hair into a choker around my neck as Bernice knelt behind me and drew on my ass cheeks with the face paint.

My entire mini squad were in the process of doing the same thing. Everywhere I looked, hair ribbons were becoming chokers, smoky eyes and blood red lips were replacing the sticky pink lipgloss Marguerite's squad usually plastered on and ass cheeks were being decorated. Perfect.

Bernice finished her paint job on my ass and stood up beside me with a grin, rearranging her cleavage in the navy crop top with the silver ZA printed on it.

I glanced around at the group of girls as they all beamed with excitement.

In fact, I was smiling too. As much as I hated to admit it, cheerleading was actually *fun*. And these girls were all pretty cool. Bernice was like my soul sister. Snarky comments and bare faced insults tumbled from her lips in a way that was so cutthroat that she often drew a surprised laugh from me. As a squad, we laughed a lot and we'd worked our asses off to perfect this routine. Much to my surprise, I actually cared about winning this thing for more reasons than just kicking Marguerite and Kylie's asses. I wanted to cheer at the upcoming Pitball match against Aurora Academy, screaming my sister and Geraldine's names as they played.

"Is everyone ready?" I called, drawing the attention of my squad as I prepared to give them their pep talk.

But before they'd finished calling back to me in excitement, the locker room door opened.

"Make sure your fannies are tucked away!" Washer called as he strutted straight into the room wearing a Lycra all in one suit which I guessed was intended for cycling. The thing was red with a silver zip running down the centre of his chest which of course wasn't even closed half way. It had cut off sleeves and ended at his knees but with how tight the fucking thing was, he might as well have been naked.

"We're just heading out to the pitch," I said through gritted teeth as he wiggled his way through the group, brushing his hands over the girls' arms as he passed and drawing faint sighs from them as he exerted his Order gifts over them.

Since he'd been allocated to assist Orion with overseeing Pitball and Cheer practice, we'd been subjected to these kinds of visits way too often and if I had to listen to him suggest we add more bending and splits to our routine one more time, I was gonna scream.

"I just wanted to come and offer my services for your performance," he said with a wide smile. His teeth were too white in his orange face, but it seemed to be a choice he'd made. "I just feel like the finale would really pop better if you were all wet for it."

"What?" I asked with a frown.

"You know, a water display at the end. Just a little squirt or two and you could all be flicking wet hair around as you pump and grind to the music and-"

"We can't exactly change up our routine at this point," I said through gritted teeth.

"Okay," he agreed, sounding disappointed. "But maybe you girls can use it in your next one?"

"Maybe," I agreed in a tone which clearly said *no fucking way*, barrelling on before he could make any other gross suggestions. "Right, girls – let's go fuck up those bitches!"

Yeah, my pep talks rock.

The girls whooped in excitement as they all ran out into the stadium, heading onto the pitch and I jogged out amongst them.

We found Marguerite's squad, Team Twinkle, already assembled before a section of the stands where Orion had gathered the Pitball team to watch us. Professor Prestos and Principal Nova were waiting too, each holding clipboards to score our routines.

"Oh good, the Heirs got front row seats," I muttered as I spotted them and Bernice snorted a laugh.

"Well at least you can show that Dragon what he's missing," she joked.

Her words instantly made my gaze flick to Darius and the heated look he was giving me made me want to straighten my cheer uniform self consciously. I didn't, because I refused to give a shit about what he thought, but still.

Washer swept forward to claim a seat beside Seth in the front row and I exchanged a smile with Darcy as I spotted her front and centre next to Geraldine.

Marguerite turned to look at us as we moved beyond her squad to take our own seats.

"Get comfortable watching from the sidelines, Vega," she snarled, her upper lip curling back. "Because this is the last time you'll get to wear that uniform."

"Don't say that," Caleb groaned. "Seeing Tory in her cheer uniform is a damn important part of our practice sessions. Isn't it Darius?"

I tried to fight it but I couldn't help but glance at him again and I was instantly sucker punched by the filthy look in his black ringed eyes. It really shouldn't have been legal for him to look at me like that because then I just ended up remembering where those looks had led us before and how that wouldn't be happening ever again and – *gah.*

"Yeah. It is," Darius agreed, running his hand over the stubble lining his jaw as he sat there in his letterman jacket. Apparently the team wasn't going to practice at all today and this session had been given over to our competition, so he was wearing jeans and a black shirt which clung to his muscular frame beneath it. Not that I appreciated anything about the way he looked. But if I had, I'd have to admit he looked good enough to lick.

"It's kind of sad how desperately you're trying to get his attention after he turned you down," Marguerite said loudly enough for everyone to hear. "And it's kind of pathetic the way you keep lingering around him like a bad smell dressed up in desperate."

Errr pot and kettle? Seriously, is this bitch for real?

"What's the matter, Marguerite? Are your manticrabs biting or are you just stressed out because you know the Vixens are about to wipe the floor with you and your basic bitch routine?" I taunted.

Marguerite tossed her red hair and stepped towards me, raising her voice to make sure everyone heard what she was going to say.

"I just don't see how you ever could have thought he'd say yes to you," she said. "I mean, sure, you're a *Vega.* But what does that even mean? That you're the daughter of a man who brought chaos, death and terror to his people during his reign. You didn't even grow up in Solaria. You're practically a *mortal,"* she spat like there could be nothing worse than that. "You don't know anything about being Fae. You were raised in a gutter and learned to spread your legs to get what you needed from men who you tricked into falling for your shit with your trashy clothes and near constant position on your knees for sucking cock. You're scraping by here on your power level alone, but no true Fae would ever follow a cheap pair of trashy whores who don't even know our customs let alone how to claim their power with class. It's no wonder Darius said no to you. Can you imagine how embarrassing it must be for him to have his Mate go around screwing every guy on campus? You're a cheap, ignorant, gold-digging bitch. And everyone in Solaria is praising their lucky stars that he had the good sense to say no to you."

Anger prickled along my skin at her outburst and I opened my mouth to tear her a new one, but before I could, Darius spoke.

"Roxy said no to *me,"* he said in a low voice which cut Marguerite short. "Not the other way around. And I'm pretty sure I told you not to talk shit about her once already."

Marguerite balked, her face paling as her lips opened and closed like a goldfish. She stammered something which might have been the start of an apology, but he didn't give her the chance to speak it.

"I don't know where you get off claiming to have something going on with me anyway. I barely even dated you and I certainly didn't take an interest in anything you had to say. I fucked you because I was bored. And I dumped you because I hadn't realised that getting into your pants would be even more boring. So keep your fucking mouth shut about me and Roxy otherwise we're going to have a problem."

I flushed hot all over, my jaw grinding as I tried to figure out how I felt about him jumping in like that. I'd never been the girl who needed saving by the valiant knight.

"Asses in seats, Vixens," Orion said lazily as he waved my squad towards the stands to watch Team Twinkle do their routine. "Contrary to popular belief, watching cheer squads dance about is not actually a hobby of mine and there are other things I'd like to do with my evening once this is wrapped up."

"Maybe I should be the head judge then, Lance?" Washer suggested enthusiastically casting a hopeful look at Nova like he thought she might give him the position. "I've been something of a cheer enthusiast my whole life and I know all the ways their flexible young bodies should be bending and flexing and moulding into the moves. So, if you want to swap, I can-"

"Is someone gonna get the music playing or what?" Orion barked, totally ignoring him and I was swept along in the midst of my squad as we took seats in the second row up behind the Pitball team.

I ended up in a seat right behind Darius as Kylie fiddled with the sound system to set it up for their routine.

"I didn't need you to jump in and rescue me," I muttered, unable to bite my tongue as I looked at the back of his head.

Darius turned in his seat and rose an eyebrow at me. "I was just telling the truth. I'm not asking you to thank me."

He rested his arm on the back of his chair and my knee brushed against it, sending a shiver dancing up my leg.

"So you were just in the mood to point out how terrible she is in bed?" I asked, ignoring the pang of jealousy that went through me at the thought of him and her.

"Yeah."

"Was she really that awful?" I asked because morbid fascination was a bitch and apparently I was in the mood to torture myself.

"It was like sticking my dick into a sack of potatoes and shaking it around to see what happened," he deadpanned. "I would have had to question my own performance if it wasn't for the way she was screaming."

"Is that so?" I refused to blink at the subject matter, but my fingernails were most definitely cutting into my palms. I just had to hope he couldn't tell.

"Yeah. She sounded like a pig with a carrot stuck up its ass. I didn't even finish."

A laugh tumbled from my lips before I could stop it and suddenly all of the other Heirs, Geraldine, Darcy, Orion and well everyone actually, were swivelling in their chairs and staring at us.

"Liar," I hissed.

"Am I?" There was a smirk playing around his lips which drew my attention to his mouth and suddenly I was too hot in my skimpy outfit and memories of the two of us tangled together on the throne at the Palace of Souls were slipping to the front of my mind.

The first beat of the music started up and everyone looked away from us as Team Twinkle began their routine to Can't Stop The Feeling! by Justin Timberlake, but Darius stayed looking at me for a moment longer.

"Well, at least I have her beaten in that department," I teased. "You definitely finished with me."

"Yeah. I could come just thinking about you," he agreed. "And I do pretty frequently."

My lips popped open and I almost let him render me speechless before forcing myself to respond in a low voice. "Well that's handy, seeing as we'll never be touching each other again."

The smirk fell off of Darius's lips and shutters slammed down behind his eyes as his expression darkened. "Thanks for the reminder, but I'm well aware."

He turned away from me before I could try and take it back. I hadn't meant it as a taunt or an attempt to drive the knife in further. I'd just blurted out the first thing that had come to mind. And it wasn't the first time I'd done that to him and hurt him. I felt like I was so preprogrammed to go on the defensive all the time that I almost couldn't stop the shit that poured from my lips sometimes. Just like when I'd told him that us being together meant nothing to me. The urge to be honest and tell him how much this was hurting me too swelled in my throat. I almost did it, but I couldn't. It was weak and selfish of me, but I'd never been good at being vulnerable and I wasn't even sure what the point to it would be now.

My gut churned guiltily and I released a breath. Maybe Gabriel had a point about me needing to own more of my shit. I probably owed him an apology too.

I stared at Darius for another moment but as Marguerite leapt into the air, my gaze was drawn to her squad instead and I let it drop. It wasn't like it mattered anyway. I'd made my choice. It was better that I continued hating him and he hated me too. Even if that thought just knotted me up inside and left me aching.

I noticed Caleb watching me still and glanced at him as he offered me a dazzling smile. I frowned a little as I returned it, wondering what he was after and he flicked his fingers, a single leaf spinning from them before he tossed it into my lap.

I glanced down at it, seeing the words which he'd formed on it.

Do you want to come on a hunt with me again soon?

I raised an eyebrow at him, wondering what he was thinking. We'd basically agreed that we weren't going to be hooking up again and the hunt stuff had really just been foreplay for us. But I had to admit that I was tempted. I missed the rush I got from the hunt, trying to escape him as adrenaline coursed through my veins. And really, the biting wasn't that bad. But if I won I'd have to think up a different prize…maybe I could convince him to give me some tutoring with my earth and fire magic…

I pushed my magic into the leaf, changing it so the the word *maybe* stood out on the waxy surface instead then flicked it back at him before focusing on Marguerite's routine.

Team Twinkle were good. I hated to admit it, but they were. They worked seamlessly together, jumping, spinning, shaking their colour changing pom-poms and combining magic with all kinds of impressive gymnastics.

"Tuck that hiney!" Washer called enthusiastically. "Flip that dipper!"

I bit my lip as I watched them, nerves warring inside my stomach like a hoard of angry wasps.

"C'mon Minor, I know you can spread your legs wider than that – get it right over your head!" Washer yelled.

I exchanged a look of disgust with Bernice as she gave me an exaggerated shudder.

As the routine came to an end, Kylie and Jillian shot up into the air, spinning as they came back down and landing perfectly just as Marguerite threw a fireball up over their heads. As the flames began to fade, the words *Go Zodiac!* flared within the fire.

Team Twinkle were all beaming with triumph and shaking their pom-poms or jazz hands respectively as the music faded and I had to wonder whether or not our finale would be appreciated.

The Pitball team all clapped, a few guys from the sub bench whooping their support as they moved over to congratulate the mean girls. I was guessing they were the manticrab spreaders, but I couldn't say I particularly knew any of them.

"Come on then, Vixens, let's see if you can top that." Orion pointed us forward and we headed down to the pitch as Bernice hurried over to start our track.

We'd gone for something a little different to the usual peppy routines. Our song had a fast beat and plenty of spots which encouraged tricks and flashy magic. It was really more of a show piece than a dance, but I didn't mind admitting the whole thing was shit hot.

I took my position in the centre of the squad, not a pom-pom in sight as we all leaned on each other and waited for the music.

My heart was pounding with a combination of nerves and excitement as the girls all closed in around me. On the one hand I knew this was just some stupid routine for a club I hadn't even wanted to join, but there was something freeing about doing something for no other reason than having fun and I was actually hoping really damn hard that we were about to win.

U Can't Touch This by MC Hammer started up and the music took over as we all leapt into motion, dancing in perfect synchronisation in moves that were pretty well suited to a night club but worked all the same.

Two of the water Elementals threw a sheet of glimmering ice crystals before us and we sprang into a set of flips, twists and cartwheels. Every time the backup singers called *wooaah*, a different pair of squad members were thrown into the air, shooting flames, ice, or flower petals from their palms. Then the air Elementals shot above everyone else.

I stayed in the centre of the pack, twisting and grinding between the other girls to the music as I sent a combination of all of my Elements flying at different times in the routine.

As the music hit the breakdown, Bernice and Alexa tossed me up into the air and I shot above the rest of the squad, using my air magic to propel me up with a mixture of flames, ice crystals and petals all falling from my fingertips as I spun on the spot. I descended just as the verse kicked off again and the other girls all flipped and cartwheeled around me.

"That's it! Legs behind your head!" Washer cried, but I only had eyes for Marguerite as I moved between two of the other girls and we formed a line with all of our hips locked together, winking at her as we ground our hips in a way that may have been bordering on pornographic. But if she was going to go around calling me a whore all the time, I didn't want to disappoint.

The girl at the far left of the line threw her hands up, casting fire which she tossed behind her head to the next fire Elemental in the group. So on and so on until it had bounced over all of us, where the girl at the back of the crowd shot it up towards the roof.

I threw my hands up, blasting a ball of Phoenix fire into it which exploded overhead into a red and blue fireball. Sparks of molten gold rained down on us as we all turned our backs on the stands, bent over and flipped our skirts up to expose the face paint on our asses as the music came to an end.

Silence greeted us as the Pitball team were all gifted a view of the words *Zodiac kicks ass!* scrawled across our actual ass cheeks and I exchanged a grin with Bernice.

"Fuck me," Caleb breathed half a second before Darcy and Geraldine both began whooping in excitement and clapping enthusiastically.

By the time we straightened and turned around, everyone else was clapping too and the grin on my face felt suspiciously real. Like…maybe I was actually *happy* in that moment.

My squad all began screaming in excitement, leaping on me and crushing me beneath them as I couldn't help but laugh too. That routine had been totally badass. If they didn't pick us then it was a damn travesty, but at least I knew we'd performed it to perfection. The rest was up to the stars and as I was pretty sure they hated me, that didn't bode well, but whatever, we'd done all we could.

Silence fell as Orion, Nova, Prestos and Washer began to discuss our routines, making little notes on their clipboards.

It was kinda ridiculous but I found myself aching to win.

"It was a little...suggestive," Washer said in a disapproving voice that carried and my mouth fell open. *That fucking ball sack.*

"Zodiac has always pushed boundaries though," Nova said, her gaze sweeping between us and Team Twinkle who had moved to stand on the pitch a little way from us to wait for the decision too. "We don't follow standards, we set them. And they'd certainly draw a crowd."

"It's not every day you can show off Phoenix fire skills," Orion added with a smirk as he glanced my way.

My heart pounded as the four of them exchanged looks and Nova nodded as she pointed at something on the clipboard.

"The Vixens took it," Orion announced, but I barely heard him as the girls surrounding me all shrieked like banshees, leaping on top of me and squeezing me so hard that I was in danger of popping.

I laughed along with them as we rolled on the ground and for a moment I felt light and free and just...*happy.*

The darkness whispered to me with promises of oblivion as I lay in my bed. The lingering happiness from our win had faded away to let them in again and after that fleeting moment of freedom, the pain had hit me tenfold. I'd been hoping to make it through the night without giving in. But...

My fingers twitched and shadows coiled between them, drawing a sigh from my lips as they kissed my flesh.

I need to learn how to wield them better anyway.

But I was going to have a night off. I'd decided on it and I meant to stick to it.

That was before the nightmares though, before the pain tried to drown me while I slept again...

If I could take one night off from them I'd know I wasn't getting addicted, that was the bargain I'd struck with myself.

That was before the agony came back though. And half a night without them is still proof that I don't need them...

The shadows slid up to coat my arms and I sighed at their gentle caress. They knew just how to soothe the darkness in me. And I didn't need much, just a taste to take a bit of the pain away.

A moan escaped me as the shadows slid over my skin, my back arching against the bed as they delved inside me, feeding on my pain, offering me solace for a moment. But I could still feel that well of sadness in my heart which bled for Darius Acrux and I didn't want to feel that.

My fingers chilled as I called on my water magic, forming a blade out of ice so that I could offer up a little more of myself.

I needed to bleed for them, just a bit, just enough to take the edge off and then-

I dropped the blade I'd created suddenly as something brushed up against my skin, calling me back out of the dark with a promise of safety unlike anything I'd ever really known.

I gasped as I sat up, the shadows receding as I tossed the covers back and my skin prickled with heat.

I hadn't closed my shutters last night. Hell, I'd barely even remembered to shower, let alone caring about that, but this particular slip in my standards was actually a slap in the face. That moment of happiness with the cheer squad had cost me dearly. Coming down from that high had put me into a really dark place again.

The stars shone brightly in the navy sky outside, twinkling innocently as they looked back at me like they hadn't cursed me to a fate of misery and loneliness.

My lip curled as I glared at them and I got to my feet, stalking across the room to throw the shutters over to block them out.

Screw the stars. Screw fate. Screw every fucked up thing that led me here, chewed me up and spat me out. Screw the throne and the Council and this academy. Screw being a fucking Vega.

I released a long breath as I fought to regain control of my temper before I ended up breaking something.

Shadows coiled around my hands, twisting further up my arms as they whispered promises of oblivion and freedom in my ear again.

I inhaled deeply as I closed my eyes, teetering on the brink of their embrace. How easy it would be to dive into them, just for a little while, just long enough to forget...

A soft noise caught my attention and my eyes snapped open as I whirled toward the door.

My pyjamas consisted of a pair of black panties and the mortifying reality that was Darius Acrux's old T-shirt. Fuck the stars for making me pine for him even now. They knew just as well as I did what reasons I'd had for my decision. Yet I was to be punished alongside him for this failure. What kind of fate was that?

I padded across the soft carpet towards my door, my magic brimming to the surface of my skin as I heard another low sound from beyond the wood. There was someone out in the corridor, I was certain of it.

I reached the door, my fingertips caressing the handle as I considered opening it to see who had disturbed my sleep, but something stayed my hand.

The desire to return to my bed consumed me for a moment and I almost turned away before my Phoenix fire flared beneath my skin and burned all thoughts but my own from my mind.

I was done listening to the stars.

I reached out hesitantly and pressed my hand to the wood before my face.

I gasped as heat washed against my palm, a fierce and hungry magic licking the other side of the door as its owner stood so close that I could feel the deep well of their power.

"Darius?" I breathed and the magic flared as if in surprise, but no answer came to me.

My heart pounded with an ache so pure that it burned me right down to the depths of my soul.

I leaned forward until my forehead pressed against the wood, exhaling deeply as I dropped the walls surrounding my own power.

I groaned as his magic flooded past my barriers, my fingers pressing against the wood more firmly as if I might be able to claw my way through it to him. It was ecstasy and agony all rolled into one. I wanted to bathe in it until I drowned and never again have to spend a moment suffering for the choices we'd both made.

He still didn't speak, but there was no denying his power was there. I could almost feel his fingers pressing to the wood just as mine were, like the thin barrier of this door didn't divide us. But it did. Just like everything else did.

"What are you doing here?" I breathed, my voice barely a whisper and yet seeming like a scream in the darkest of nights.

He didn't reply and my heart pounded fiercely as I lingered between the desire to open the door and tell him to leave again. I didn't do either.

All the things we'd never said to each other hung in the silence and all the things we should have said too. But they kept company with all that had passed between us and so much of it was dark and cruel and ugly that I didn't even know where to begin with it. Neither of us did. We never had. Which was half the problem, though not all of it by a long shot. And now none of it even mattered anyway.

My lips parted and I tried to force the words I needed from my throat, but I wasn't even sure I had them.

"Darius, I..."

His magic withdrew suddenly and I shivered as I was left cold, leaning against my door in the wake of his presence.

I drew in a shuddering breath and a tear slipped down my cheek.

I might not have had the words but he'd come here, come so close that maybe I needed to be the one to make up the difference.

I shifted back, wrenching my door wide and opening my mouth to call out for him to stop-

There was no one there.

My heart pounded to a dangerous tune as I looked back and forth along the corridor.

I'd been so sure that he was right here, but as I stepped into the empty corridor with every intention to call his name, I found nothing but shadows waiting for me.

Another tear tracked along my skin as I backed into my room again.

The space inside felt colder than before.
And I doubted I'd find sleep again.
But I had found the strength to resist the shadows once more.

ORION

CHAPTER SIXTEEN

I lay on my couch watching the sun set beyond the window, the light rippling through a bottle of bourbon that sat on the coffee table. I hadn't touched it. Not yet. Every night since I'd seen the soul vision of Clara standing at Lionel's side, commanding an army of Nymphs, I'd been tempted to drink myself into a stupor. But there was one unmistakable thing stopping me from opening that bottle. Blue.

I was no good to anyone half cut, least of all her. But I played with temptation all the same, placing that bottle where I could see it. I didn't know why I liked to torment myself. Maybe it was to test what I was really made of. If I could truly remain as the man I'd become since Blue had arrived in my life.

The thought that she was temporary made me afraid. Because who I'd been before didn't come close to deserving her. And at least now I was *trying* to be better. To be enough. But sometimes, the shadows called to me in the dark, whispering my sins, my failures. And maybe deep down, I was never going to feel worthy of her.

Apparently I was in the mood to suffer as I'd dug out the shoebox of Clara's things which I'd kept after I lost her. I fished through it, running my fingers over the gold coin she'd won on a bet with a Dragon in her senior year, the lovingly worn box of Tarot cards she'd used for every Arcane Arts class, the charm bracelet she'd made herself from ice then had an earth Elemental cast it to silver. Lastly, I tugged the diary from the bottom of the pile, grazing my fingers over the leather binding and letting my heart bleed for a moment.

I'd never opened it. Her secrets were her own. Even in death. Or at least, that was where I'd thought she'd been all these years. Somewhere beyond the veil. I'd convinced myself she was at peace, and all that time she'd been in a literal hell. Alone, suffering, with nothing but the shadows to keep her company. No wonder they'd taken root in her. But it still broke me.

I couldn't entertain the idea that she couldn't be saved. Even after what she'd done to me. But there was so much doubt in me now that if I let my focus slip for a second, my hope began to unravel and I started to sink into despair.

I closed my eyes, drawing on one of my happiest memories. Of me and Clara playing under the willow tree at my family home. Of my father calling our names while we laughed and hid behind the fronds. I'd been six and Clara seven. She'd pressed her fingers to her lips and we'd dropped to our knees, peeking under the branches where my father's feet could be seen pacing.

"Hm, the Nymphs have stolen away my children," he teased, pretending he didn't know exactly where we were. And at the time, we really believed he didn't know we were there. *"I'll have to call the FIB."*

"The FIB," I gasped, looking to Clara. She had a wildish look, her hair sticking out in every direction, her freckles brightened by days in the sun. But I was always darker, the sun gilding my skin in a sheen of gold every summer with barely any effort at all.

"Shh silly, he won't really call them," Clara whispered, clutching my hand as we lay in the dirt.

Father started talking like he was on the phone. *"Yes, my dear children have vanished. It's definitely Nymphs. Will you come quickly?"*

Clara's mouth popped open and she looked to me in fear. "We're going to be in big trouble."

I chuckled, stifling my laugh with my hand. I liked trouble. I'd even heard my elementary school teacher talking about me once, saying I was going to cause trouble with the girls when I was older. At the time, I'd thought she meant my sister. And I'd vowed to always be her guardian from that day, because out of everyone in the world, I never wanted to cause trouble with her.

Clara clutched my hand and her eyes sparkled with mischief. "Let's pounce on him."

I laughed, nodding. "I'll go first in case he gets angry."

She shook her head. "You don't have to protect me, Lancey."

"I don't have to, but I want to," I said firmly, getting to my feet and she beamed as I picked up a stick and wielded it like a sword. I charged out between the willow fronds but Dad was ready, whipping me off my feet on a tendril of air magic so I hung upside down in front of him.

"Yah!" I jabbed him with the stick and he barked a laugh, reaching out and tickling my sides until I couldn't breathe with laughter.

He finally let me down and Clara ran out to hug his side. "We didn't really get kidnapped," she said, batting her long lashes as she gazed up at him.

Dad's hair was an unruly nest of darkness, his eyes inky and deep like mine. Mom said I'd look like him one day. She said I'd make a fine husband one day too, but I didn't want to be a husband, I wanted to be a Vampire. I wanted to run as fast as Mom and Dad and carry Clara on my back like a monkey.

Dad picked Clara up, putting her on his shoulders and she shrieked with laughter. *"Well that's a relief,"* he said. *"I didn't fancy charging into a Nymph nest to save you this afternoon. But I would have of course."*

"Would you come for us if we were captured by a hundred Nymphs?" I asked.

"Absolutely, Lancelot," he promised, ruffling my hair. He always called me that. He said it was a knight from a mortal story and it suited me because I was brave like him.

"How about a thousand?" I narrowed my eyes suspiciously. A thousand was an awful lot of Nymphs.

"Without a doubt," he said easily.

"What about ten thousand?" I demanded. That was far too many Nymphs to take on alone.

"My boy, I'd come for you if you were held by a million Nymphs. There's no lengths I wouldn't go to."

"Why?" I frowned.

"Because I love you and your sister. And that's what you do for the people you love," he explained and I nodded, my heart swelling. Because I understood that. I'd take on a million Nymphs for her and my parents too. But I was definitely going to need a real sword.

A knock came at the door and I jolted out of the reverie, getting to my feet and hoping Brian hadn't decided to pay me a visit. He could probably feel my misery stretching out into his house, so I really had to lock it down before he convinced me that a hug with him was a great idea.

I pulled the door wide, finding Gabriel there with a bottle of orange Faenta and a sideways smile. "Thought you could use the soda to take your mind off of that bottle of bourbon, Orio."

I released a breath of amusement. "Did you come to join my pity party? You just missed the childhood flashback I'm afraid, but you're just in time for the apathy cake and a round of musical grumps."

I stepped aside to let him in and he arched a brow at me with a smirk, moving into the house and kicking the door shut. "At least you're still sarcastic, brother, the day you lose your wit is the day I'll lose hope for you entirely."

"Good to know." I strode back to the couch, dropping down and Gabriel poured us each a glass of soda before joining me.

I drank the sweet, fizzy pop as Gabriel picked up Clara's diary. There were very few people in the world I'd allow to touch that, but luckily he was one of them. Otherwise his face would be reeling from the impact of my fist right about now.

"Don't read it," I said. "It's Clara's."

"No, it isn't," he said immediately, his fingers brushing over the leather binding like he was getting some reading on it.

"Of course it is." I snatched it away from him, planting my empty glass on the table. "It was with her things."

"It's not hers, Orio," he said in a serious tone. "Open it."

I frowned, my jaw tightening as I flicked open the first page and my lungs compressed at the words I found there.

Property of Azriel Orion.

"It's my father's," I rasped in disbelief.

"His diary?" Gabriel asked but I didn't know so I shrugged in answer, wetting my mouth as I turned the page.

The words were encrypted, appearing as a jumble of nonsensical symbols and as I traced my thumb over the page, I felt the magic still binding them. "By the stars, I've had this all these years and never thought to check it was really Clara's."

"Can you break the encryption?" Gabriel asked, leaning closer to get a look so his dark hair fell forward over his brow.

I closed my eyes, trying to feel out the magic he'd used on it. My mind snagged on a certain sensation and I blew out a breath, opening my eyes and resting back in my chair. "It needs a password. I'd have to speak it aloud, but I have no idea what my father would choose. Any chance you can *see* the answer?" I asked, but he shook his head.

"Maybe if I'd known your father, but I can't read those kinds of details from a stranger. Try your name," Gabriel encouraged, his eyes glittering with intrigue.

"Lance," I said, frowning at the page. "Clara, Stella..." Nothing.

I frowned, placing the notebook on the coffee table. My head was too fucked right now to figure it out. But maybe I'd be able to crack it in time.

Gabriel rested a hand on my shoulder and cast a silencing bubble around the room.

I frowned, looking to him for an explanation and he sighed, giving me a guilty sort of smile.

"What's going on?" I demanded.

"I've withheld some information from you."

"What information?" I growled, my heart rate rising.

"It's nothing bad, just don't lose your shit, okay?" he asked and I pressed my tongue into my cheek, waiting. "I know about you and Darcy Vega."

I felt like I'd been punched directly in the heart. Despite the fact that he was my friend, my Nebula fucking Ally, my defences still flew right up. "Gabriel, it's – there's-"

"Save it." He clapped my shoulder. "I've heard all of it in my visions a thousand times. You don't need to explain. When I say I know, I mean, I *know*. You're in love."

The blood was definitely draining from my face and I stared at him in shock and maybe some relief too. I hated hiding Blue. Despised it. And to share the truth with another of my closest friends in the world felt like a weight lifting from my shoulders.

"No one can know," I said, my voice thick with concern. I'd tried to keep this between me and Blue for so long and now I feared how quickly the secret was spreading. Even if it was to people we trusted. One slip of the tongue and that would be it for us.

"Of course," he said gently. "And just so you know, I don't judge you or anything. Frankly, it was inevitable."

"Wait," I breathed, my heart thumping harder with a note of hope ringing through my body. "Can you see the future? Can you see if it will work out for us?"

Gabriel's brows stitched together and he stared into my eyes like he was trying to peer into my soul and find the answers I sought. "There's so many paths," he said heavily. "I don't know...I can't be sure. I'm sorry."

I looked away from him, my teeth grinding to dust. "It's alright," I forced out, though I felt pissed in that moment. Mostly at the stars for not giving me any comfort at all. If I knew things would be okay for me and Blue, life would have been a hell of a lot less stressful.

"I'm happy for you," he said, leaning back in his seat again. "Really fucking happy, Orio. You've had a shit lot in life."

"Thanks," I said on a breath of laughter.

"Could be worse, right?" he joked and I rubbed my eyes. Could it be worse right now? Lionel was getting in to a position to take the throne. And my own sister was helping him. The Nymphs were banding together with them and the stars only knew how long it would be before the death toll started rising. Part of me wanted to tell Gabriel all about it. His Sight wouldn't be able to detect the Nymphs movements or anything to do with them, so there wasn't any chance he knew already. But I didn't want to drag him into this mess. Though I imagined the whole world was going to get dragged into it soon enough.

"There's something I need to talk to you about," I said slowly, knowing I'd been putting this off because dragging it all up felt like cutting open a vein. But Gabriel was a good friend. And I knew I could trust him with anything. So I told him all about Clara, the night I'd brought her back from the shadows, the dark magic I'd used. All of it. And when I was done, it felt like a ten ton elephant had lifted from my chest.

"That's why I couldn't *see* you that night," he breathed, his elbows on his knees as he rubbed at his eyes. "Fuck, Orio, I'm so sorry I wasn't there. I should have-"

"You didn't know. And at the time...I didn't want to put all of this on you."

"You know I'd be there for you through anything," he growled, turning to me with anxiety in his gaze.

"I know, Noxy," I said with half a smile. "I guess I was just trying to protect you. But it seems I'm fucking terrible at protecting people." I thought of Clara with a pang in my chest.

He frowned grimly. "You're better than you think."

My Atlas buzzed and I took it out, finding a message waiting for me.

Darius:
Father has summoned us.

Those four words sent adrenaline tumbling into my limbs. I'd wanted to go to Acrux Manor and tear my sister out of Lionel's arms since the night she'd returned from the Shadow Realm. But now…now I knew things were more complicated than that. She wasn't in her right mind, but maybe if I could get close to her, break through the power that held her in its dark grip, I could bring her back from it. I could make sure she really was still in that body.

I shot Darius a reply, rising from my seat and Gabriel stood with me.

"You have to go," he said before I could say a word then he moved forward and wrapped his arms tightly around me. "When you want to talk, I'm here. Always."

"Thank you, Noxy." I clapped him on the back and he headed for the door, exiting a moment later.

I shot to my room, changing out of my professor bullshit into jeans and a blue button down before rifling through the box of Clara's things and taking out her bracelet. There were silver charms on it which represented each member of our family, plus her friends, her life before she'd started working with Stella and been led astray by Lionel.

I had a feeling the path her life had taken hinged on the moment she'd agreed to be Lionel's Guardian. He'd gotten his claws in her from that very second and he'd never let go. I doubted he'd planned for any of this to happen, but it had sure worked out in his favour. He had a devoted servant who could wield the shadows and control all the Nymphs in the world. *So if I could just break that loyalty, bring her back, remind her who she really is…*

I pocketed the charm bracelet and used the back door to leave the house. I met Darius on the edge of Campus where I'd left the hole in the defences. His eyes were ringed with darkness and I knew he was plagued by plenty of his own demons these days. We wordlessly slipped through the gap in the fence and I wrapped my arms around him as we stood beneath the bushes that shaded the perimeter. He clutched onto me and the knot in my chest eased as the bond between us deepened, thrumming in my ears and making me want to get nearer and nearer to him.

"Let's just run off together into the sunset," Darius joked. "We can forget all about the Vegas and buy a house in Starshine Bay."

"We can have two kids. Boys obviously. Girls are trouble," I played along and he released a chuckle as we stepped apart.

"Are you ready for this?" he asked, his face falling grave once more.

I sighed, turning my head to look up at the stars and wondering what they had in store for me tonight. They twinkled so innocently and I swear I could almost hear the laughter passing between them. All of this must have looked so amusing from way up there in the heartless sky.

"I'll never be ready," I admitted, dropping my gaze to him. "But I have to go. I want to try and reach her."

"She's not herself," he said in a dark tone that made my pulse beat angrily beneath my flesh.

He'd told me that a hundred times since he'd been home and seen her. And though I knew it was true, I still couldn't believe I wasn't going to recognise my own sister when we got there. A foolish part of me was hoping she'd see me, run into my arms and apologise for everything, tell me the shadows had claimed her and she hadn't been in her right mind.

I bit down on the inside of my cheek. "Let's go," I forced out and Darius threw a handful of stardust into the air.

We arrived on the edge of the Acrux property and two guards in black uniforms stepped forward in front of the iron gate with magic flashing in their palms.

"It's me, assholes," Darius growled as a Faelight illuminated above us to check.

"Good evening, Master Darius," they said in unison which was creepy as fuck, then they moved to open the gates.

I guessed old Uncle Lionel had upped security on the place. And if you were planning world domination, I supposed watching your back was a sensible move. I wished he wouldn't though, then I could drive a draining dagger into his heart. It would be pretty difficult to land the hit though, considering it must have been about the size of a Tiberian Rat shit.

My heart pounded to a war beat as we walked up the long driveway side by side. I'd been here so many times in my life, but never with so much apprehension as now.

My hands were balled into fists by the time we reached the huge wooden door and Darius reached out to rest a hand on my shoulder. "I'll be with you."

I turned to him with a razor sharp lump in my throat, gratitude spilling through me though I wasn't able to find the words to voice it before the doors pulled open before us. Jenkins bowed low, ushering us inside with murmured pleasantries and I pushed a hand into my pocket, winding my fingers around Clara's charm bracelet and trying to draw an ounce of hope from it.

Footsteps caught my ear and my gaze caught on Xavier at the top of the sweeping staircase in his sweats.

"Fuck, it's good to see you both," he said, taking a step down the stairs before hesitating.

"And you, Xavier, how are you?" I called.

"Master Xavier has decided to stay in his room for the night," Jenkins said, looking to him with barely concealed irritation. It was obvious he'd decided no such thing, but I could take a pretty good guess at who had commanded him to.

"Go back to your room," Darius encouraged, a note of worry in his voice. He didn't want Lionel showing up and finding his youngest son ignoring orders, though it felt good to see him pushing back. "We'll come see you before we leave."

Xavier nodded, shooting a glare at Jenkins before heading off back down the hall.

"This way, Master Darius, Mr Orion." Jenkins murmured, leading us to the smoking room before scurrying away.

Inside, Lionel was standing beside the fireplace and I had to double take the woman beside him, expecting it to be Catalina. But it wasn't. My sister wore a low-cut black dress that hugged her figure and made the shadows stand out in her eyes.

A breath snagged in my lungs a second before she rushed at me, sprinting with the full speed of our Order. Darius cried out as I braced to meet her, but before I could do anything to protect myself, the weight of the shadows immobilised my body, my arms locking against my sides as Clara crashed into me. *Fuck!*

"Clara!" Lionel barked a warning as I feared for my life, hunting for any signs of my sister in her eyes as she threw her arms around me, making my back slam into the door.

"Baby brother!" she cried, lunging toward my face and I snarled in warning a second before her lips stamped to my cheek. Then my forehead, my nose, my eyes. My breathing came raggedly as I searched her face, pain slicing me apart. *Is it her?*

"Clara, do you really know me?" I breathed, hope making my heart lift.

She stepped back, peering into my eyes as she batted her lashes. Everything about her was so familiar and yet terrifyingly alien. Her face was hers, and yet it wasn't. Her cheeks were hollow where they'd once been full and her eyes...they were tainted by an ever-swirling sea of darkness. She released me from the shadows and a beat of strained silence stretched between us. I had to take a chance, had to be fearless.

I dug into my pocket, silent as I took her hand and placed the charm bracelet in it, aware we had an audience. And aware my sanity was taking a dive right now. But it was the only plan I had.

"Do you remember this?" I whispered, wishing we could have a moment alone as Lionel's shadow drew ever closer.

Darius wasn't moving in the corner of my eye and I had a feeling Clara was holding him in check with the shadows too. And that made my confidence waver.

"So pretty," she breathed, turning it over in her palm. "Is it for me?" She glanced up with hope in her gaze and my neck prickled.

"It's yours already. I kept it for you."

She held out her wrist so I could put it on and I did so, my lips firming into a tight line as I waited for some recognition to cross her features.

"This one's yours," she gasped suddenly, taking the Orion constellation charm between her fingers. "And this one's for Dad." She brushed her thumb over the silver willow tree.

My throat thickened as I nodded, my heart pounding solidly in my ears.

She looked up again with tears brimming in her eyes and for a moment she was just my sister again. The girl who'd played Vampires and Werewolves with me when we were kids. Who I'd held when she'd fallen and scuffed her knees. Who I would have done anything for.

She blinked and that girl was gone, a disturbing grin pulling at her mouth. "Oh Lancey it's beautiful!" She turned, spinning towards Lionel and draping her arms around his neck as she dangled her wrist in front of his face. "Look what my little brother brought for me."

"I'm speechless," Lionel deadpanned, his eyes on me. "We won't be having any trouble now will we, Lance?"

"No trouble," I said in a growl that wasn't entirely convincing.

Clara waved a hand and Darius let out a heavy breath as he was released from her spell, marching to my side in solidarity.

"Clara was quite famished when she returned from the Shadow Realm," Lionel said, an edge to his tone. "It's a pity you didn't think to include me in your plans to rescue her then perhaps things wouldn't have been so...messy. It's almost as though you didn't want me to find out."

I didn't answer, because he knew the truth. I wasn't going to lie to his face and make up some bullshit story that we hadn't gone behind his back and wielded the shadows to bring Clara home. I was already in his shit books. And I didn't think I'd be getting out of them any time soon.

"Stop being so pouty everyone," Clara demanded, combing her fingers lovingly through Lionel's hair and chills ran through my body.

Please tell me this is not fucking happening.

My suspicions were horribly confirmed as Lionel's arm wound possessively around Clara's small waist, tugging her against his hip.

Rage flashed white hot beneath my skin and my upper lip peeled back on a snarl before I could even think about stopping it. Lionel eyed me with his Dragon form flickering behind his eyes, a dangerous glint to them.

"You understand the pull of a Guardian bond," Lionel said, almost mockingly. He was goading me and I wasn't Fae enough not to rise to it.

"What exactly do you mean by that?" I hissed, my shoulders squaring as my gaze dragged over his hands where they touched her.

Darius caught my arm as I stepped forward but I jerked out of his hold, my lungs heaving as I waited for the axe to fall.

"Oh dear," Clara said in a sing-song voice that didn't sound like her at all. "Are you upset about mine and Daddy's little affair, Lancey? We can't help it. It's *love*."

"Get your hands off of her!" I pointed in Lionel's face, knowing I was asking for a world of hell, but fuck him. Fuck this son of a bitch for laying a finger on my sister.

"Watch your tone, *boy*," Lionel snapped. "You need to get used to the way things are now. And frankly, you should be on your knees begging for my forgiveness after the stunt you pulled bringing her back without telling me."

I caught Clara's arm, trying to pull her away from him and Darius fisted a hand in the back of my shirt to try and stop me. I threw a blast of air at Lionel, making him stumble away and the look in his eyes in response was pure murder. He came at me like a beast, catching hold of my throat with a palm that was scalding. My flesh seared and I hissed between my teeth as Clara locked down my body with the shadows, not letting me fight back. And that hurt more than anything else she'd done so far.

"Father, let him go," Darius demanded, but Lionel ignored him.

"Monster," I spat in his face.

"You raise your voice to me again, Lance, and I'll show you just how much of a monster I can be," he snarled then threw me to the ground with a blast of air. His shiny shoe slammed down on my chest to keep me there and I stared up at him with hatred seeping through every pore in my body. "Clara is with me now. Get used to it. She protects me as you protect my son."

"I might protect him, but I don't *fuck* him!" I roared and he stole the air from my lungs with a swipe of his hand.

He leaned down, a sneer pulling at his features. "I don't care what you do with him so long as he stays out of trouble. You will not comment on mine and Clara's relationship again, are we clear?"

The seconds ticked by, turning to a minute, two. I fought for air, starting to convulse beneath him as his shoe pressed harder down on my chest.

"Father," Darius growled. "Enough."

"I'll decide what's enough," Lionel purred, a hint of pleasure flitting through his gaze as he watched me suffer beneath him. This was what he lived for. He was a fucking sadist.

When I was about to black out, he stepped away from me and released his hold on my lungs. I gasped heavily, clutching at my chest as I struggled to get enough air down. Darius dropped to my side, worry lining his features as he subtly released healing magic into my body.

"Get up. Move. We have guests waiting in the ballroom. This talk is over. Take this as a warning. But remember, Lance Orion, I can find another Guardian for Darius if needs be. And I am running out of patience with you," Lionel hissed and Clara giggled as they headed away toward the ballroom.

"Fuck him," I rasped as Darius helped me to my feet.

"Yeah," he agreed in a low tone. "But don't piss him off again, Lance. He follows through with his threats and I can't lose you." His brows pulled together and I sighed, pressing my forehead to his.

"You won't," I swore, trying to swallow down the bitterness in my mouth at knowing Lionel Acrux was screwing my damn sister. *Fuck fuck fuck.*

"Come on," Darius sighed and I followed him from the room with a heart that felt as heavy as lead.

We entered the party from hell in the ballroom as I fought to keep my composure. The vast hall was thronging with Lionel's family and followers and Catalina was floating amongst them in a dress that showed off her fake tits like a trophy display as she made polite chit-chat with her guests.

"Oh fuck my life," Darius said under his breath just before Mildred Canopus stepped out of the crowd in a vivid pink dress and hurried toward him with open arms.

"Snookums!" she exclaimed, drawing attention from everyone nearby and they turned, smiling serenely like they were witnessing a true display of love.

She wrapped her muscular arms around Darius's neck and he placed a hand on her back, the low cut of it meaning he touched bare, mole-ridden flesh with little hairs sprouting between his fingers. Call me an asshole, but she was one serious dog of a girl because of all those Faeroids she took. Her frizzy brown hair had been twisted up into an elegant bun and her thick neck was adorned with a gold choker that looked like it was about to pop off and take someone's eye out.

A few people actually clapped and one woman had the audacity to wipe a tear from under her eye as Mildred placed a kiss on Darius's cheek. My insides churned and my muscles bunched as Darius schooled his expression, trying his best to look charmed by his horrid fiancé. If there was any justice in the world, that girl was not going to end up marrying my best friend. I'd marry him myself if that was what it took to keep him from ending up with the Ogre. I could at least have had some compassion for her if she'd had a half-decent personality. But she was vulgar and arrogant, her bulky form just an extension of her big head.

"Drinks," I announced, dropping an arm over Darius's shoulders and not entirely subtly elbowing Mildred in the tit as I stole him away with a spurt of Vampire speed. I didn't care who I pissed off tonight. I was not in the mood to be fucked with.

I found us a waiter and snatched two glasses of champagne from it, holding one out to Darius.

"Thanks," he said, shuddering before draining the drink in one while I mimicked him, my eyes latching onto Clara again as Lionel introduced her to his guests.

My gaze hooked on the bracelet around her wrist with a tide of sadness in my chest threatening to overwhelm me. What should I do now? One moment she'd almost seemed like herself and the next, she'd been a stranger. And a psychotic one at that. But if that single flash of her I'd seen in her eyes had been real, that meant she was in that body somewhere, drowning in the shadows, her morals crushed, her inhibitions stolen. And Lionel was taking full advantage of that.

"Evening, sweetie," my mother's voice dripped through me like melting ice and I turned to find her directing a sugary smile at me.

"Stella," I said curtly.

She was wearing a grey silk dress, her ebony hair quaffed stylishly and her lips painted blood red like she'd just finished feasting on someone's neck.

"You must be so glad to have your daughter back, Aunt Stella," Darius said in a mocking tone. "Or do you miss being Father's number one bit on the side?"

"Keep your voice down," she hissed, casting a silencing bubble around us. "Are you going to let him talk to your mother like that, Lance?"

"I don't tell Darius what to do," I said hollowly. "And if I did, I certainly wouldn't go to the bother of telling him not to speak to you like trash. Not when you've proved time and again that's what you are." I kept a mean as fuck smile on my face while I spoke to her. It was strange to think I'd ever held any love in my heart for this woman. That I could be related to her at all. I wasn't a good man, but I wasn't a deadened lump of coal either. No, that special kind of coldness was saved just for mother dearest.

"How can you say such things to me?" She pouted and I rolled my eyes.

"Don't turn on the waterworks," I growled. "I have zero tolerance for it."

Stella clucked her tongue angrily then stalked away and I hoped she didn't plan on coming back for the rest of the night. If she tried to manipulate me with crying one more time in my life, I was not going to be responsible for my actions. I would have thought she'd realised that bullshit didn't work on me by now. But apparently I was going to be subjected to it forevermore.

"Heads up," Darius murmured and I turned to find Catalina approaching us. Her eyes were glued to Darius and she moved quickly toward him, wrapping him in her arms.

"How are you?" she breathed and I swear there was more emotion in her plastic face than I'd ever seen before.

"Fine," he said, squeezing her formally then stepping back.

Catalina reached out to caress his face then gave me a warm smile. Like, one that wasn't made of stone. And I frowned as she patted my arm then walked away. She didn't even try to flirt with me like she usually did - thank the stars. I'd spent way too many hours in the company of Catalina while she talked on auto-pilot, whispering compliments in my ear. And always the same ones too, just to drive me to complete insanity. Handsome, enamouring, lovely, powerful. And sometimes she'd throw in unbelievable and sexy too, just to really make my blood curdle.

"She seems to be in a good mood," I muttered, swapping our empty glasses for full ones as a waiter glided by.

"Maybe father gave her a shot of lightning from his collection to get her heart beating again."

I chuckled. "Is he still receiving lightning jars from Dante Oscura?" I asked. The storm Dragon from Alestria was a friend of mine, especially so because he hated Lionel's guts as much as I did.

"Every month," Darius said with a tut. "Speak of the devil."

I glanced over my shoulder, spotting Dante muscling through the crowd. He was a huge man with dark hair and equally dark eyes, his shirt untucked and a gold chalice in his hand which he'd gotten from the stars only knew where. I smirked at him, moving forward to embrace him and clapping him on the back. At least there was one good thing about this party.

"Good evening, fratelli," he said in his Faetalian accent before embracing Darius. "You two look as miserable as a fucking Pegasus shitting rainbows."

236

"You're telling me you're enjoying this shit show?" I asked and his smile withered away.

"About as much as I enjoy getting fucked up the ass with a spiky dildo."

"Which you've no doubt tried, you kinky fucker," Darius jested and Dante laughed.

"No one goes near my ass with anything. Rule number one of my marriage." He glanced over his shoulder with a groan as Darius's older cousin, Juniper, came swooping towards us, guiding her three kids along too. She wore a spangly orange dress which showed off her fake cleavage and clashed with her equally orange hair.

"There you are, my big Dragon boy," she said brightly. "The kids have missed you."

Dante scruffed their hair vaguely. "Have you been good girls?" he asked.

"They're boys," Juniper said sharply and Dante swigged from his chalice. If I hadn't known that Lionel had forced him to father these three little brats in the hopes of adding a collection of Storm Dragons to his family - psycho that he was - I might have felt sorry for them. Except for the fact that they had trust funds the size of the Wingolian Canyon and I'd seen the oldest one eating worms last summer while the other two watched.

Suffice to say, they were the sort of kids who could turn you off having one of your own. But the fact that Dante took zero interest in them was a little strange. He wasn't the type to ditch out on his family. In fact, as a Dragon born of Werewolves he had so many cousins, siblings, aunts and uncles that he always made time for, I couldn't really understand why he didn't include these three boys too.

As far as I understood it, he'd made some deal with Lionel to father these kids to get him off his back. Not that I was meant to know that. But Dante trusted me and Darius enough to share the truth. It wasn't like we were in a position to do anything about it. Though hell if Lionel didn't have a lot to answer for. And one day soon, I was going to ensure he bled for it all.

"Right yeah, Jason, Jiles and Jax, isn't it?" Dante asked like he genuinely didn't know and genuinely didn't care.

"Bertie, Escobar and Hubert," Juniper corrected.

"Mother says you're a drunk and a philanderer," the oldest one piped up and Juniper clapped him over the head.

"Did she now?" Dante looked to Juniper with electricity crackling around him. I'd seen him use his storm powers before and he was not a man to be messed with.

Before she could try to explain herself, someone dinged a glass with a spoon and all eyes turned to Lionel as he prepared to make a speech.

Silence fell and I turned to face the bane of my life, wondering what wonderful things he had to say to the room.

"Good evening family and friends," Lionel said warmly. "Tonight we are here to celebrate the return of a long lost family member, Clara Orion.

237

After she went missing years ago, we have never stopped worrying about her and I am nearly brought to tears to announce that she has finally come home." He looked about as close to crying as I was to shitting my pants.

Applause rang out and Clara bowed dramatically before wrapping her arms around Stella. Lionel gave no more explanation about her whereabouts, but I had no doubt a well thought out story would be filling the newspapers tomorrow morning. "Secondly, I would like to address the news this week that the Vega twins have announced their intention to claim the throne of Solaria."

Tension rippled through the room and my hand tightened around my glass.

"I want to assure you that the two girls who have been living in the mortal realm their entire lives are spouting nothing but pretty, hopeful words. As much as I wish them my best, there is little to no reason to think they could pose any real threat to the throne at all. Tomorrow, I will be meeting with the other Celestial Councillors to discuss our sons' coming ascension and we will start to prepare them for their eventual takeover of our four seats. The ones we have held peacefully since the rule of the Vegas' cruel and merciless father, the Savage King."

A smattering of applause filled the air and I shared a look with Darius. Lionel was planning no such thing. He was going to steal the throne right out from under them and force the whole world to bow. Including every single person in this room.

"As a show of good faith, my very own daughter-in-law to be, Mildred Canopus, has offered to run a club for those in support of the Heirs at Zodiac Academy to ensure the true next in line are given the encouragement they deserve from their peers."

Mildred moved up beside him and Lionel wrapped his arm around her meaty shoulders. "She will ensure the society is run smoothly and help quiet the rumours amongst those doubters who have sadly been conned by the Vegas into believing they really could pose a challenge to our wonderful Heirs."

Another round of applause and I was about ready to puke.

"Where is my boy?" Lionel called, a fake as fuck cheery look on his face.

Darius painted on a smile as he moved to join his father and Dante inched closer to me.

"Does this look as fake to you as it does to me?" he murmured so only I could hear.

"Faker," I growled in agreement.

"Lionel's up to something, right?" Dante breathed and I glanced at him before nodding. "I do hope you have a plan."

"Sort of," I muttered.

"If you ever need a hand, you know where to find me," he said with a serious look, his eyes flashing with lightning for a moment.

A chant started up in the room as everyone sang *kiss kiss kiss kiss*. And I looked to Darius as Lionel pushed him firmly towards Mildred, my heart shrivelling for him.

He leaned in and pecked her quickly, but Mildred snared his head in her hands, pressing her pink-lipsticked lips - complete with carefully combed moustache - right against his mouth. If anyone noticed him bristling, they didn't mention it as they parted and photographers snapped pictures of him with lipstick smeared across his mouth. And no doubt a few stray hairs too.

I clenched my jaw and nodded to Dante. "I might just take you up on that one day."

"Just say the word," he breathed. "You know the rest of my family will help too."

"Will you be attending the Aurora versus Zodiac game?" I asked, hoping I could get a chance to talk with him when we weren't in a house full of our murderous enemies.

"Wouldn't miss it for the world. My cousin Rosa's gonna kick ass." He winked, polishing off his beer and looking like he was ready to make his escape from funsville. "See you soon, mio amico."

Darius made it back to me and we glanced around the hall at the party goers. "I think we can make our escape now," he said and I gave Clara one last lingering look before nodding my agreement.

"Let's check in on Xavier before we get the fuck out of here," I said, not wanting to hang around, but I worried about that kid. He was basically Lionel's prisoner these days. And I knew Darius lost sleep over it. Besides, he could use the company for a while.

"Definitely," he said eagerly. "At least Father's still hiding him and not forcing him to endure this slice of hell."

I patted him on the back with a heavy sigh as we made a passage towards the door and I swear I could only breathe easily once I got out of that room of pretentious, primped pricks. I just wished I could pluck my sister out from amongst them and take her somewhere safe. Somewhere I could try and fight the darkness that had her in a cage. I just hoped it was the type of cage I was able to break her out of. Because I couldn't let myself accept the alternative.

DARCY

CHAPTER SEVENTEEN

I woke early, Orion's soft breaths making me hope he was having peaceful dreams. He'd come to me in my room last night, wrapped me in his arms and held me like the world was ending. He told me everything and I tried to kiss away his pain, hating that there wasn't more I could do to help. What he said about Clara made me worry she really was lost. But I wanted to hope she wasn't for his sake. He needed me to.

I slipped out of bed, heading for the shower and was soon dressed for the day in my uniform. Then I moved to my desk to finish up my Tarot assignment. Gabriel said we were going to be moving on from Tarot this week. We were going to be learning the Arcane Arts instead and studying different ways to predict the future while we continued to practise with the cards. Apparently Tarot was a lifelong skill I needed to cultivate. Any insight you could get into your own fate was an advantage in society, but so far it was difficult to get a reading that gave me anything concrete. I guessed that was the way of fate though. It was up to interpretation, as changeable as the wind. I supposed I just had to get better at learning which way the wind was blowing.

When I'd finished the paper, I took up my Atlas, reading over my horoscope for the day.

Good morning Gemini.
The stars have spoken about your day!
Mars's movements predict an incoming war. Not just for you, but for all Fae.
Prepare for a divide to come and to find yourself being asked to lead. Trust

your judgment today.

You will know what to do in all situations.

My brows arched at that and I couldn't help but grin. *Well if that wasn't just the most straightforward the stars have ever been.*

A confidence filled me that I couldn't ignore. I felt self-assured by having fate on my side today. And apparently I couldn't make a wrong move.

"Blue," Orion murmured in his sleep and I turned around as he reached for me in the small bed.

My heart tugged and I hurried over to him, slipping back under the covers and he pulled me against his chest.

The tension in his features eased and I kissed him gently to wake him. His eyes cracked open and a lopsided smile pulled at his mouth. "I hate the days I don't get to wake up with you," he said, his voice rough from sleep. "For a second I thought it was one of those days."

My heart melted like wax and I pushed the hair away from his forehead with a smile. "I don't like those days either," I whispered. "How are you feeling?"

He grunted. "Like the world is about to be fucked up the ass with a giant Dragon dick."

I laughed hollowly, my stomach knotting up but he continued before I could say anything in response, wrapping me tight in his arms.

"One day soon, I'm going to shrink you down into a pixie-sized Fae and put you in a jar that I can keep in my pocket."

I smacked his shoulder and he growled in amusement. "Maybe I'll shrink you into a tiny little Vampire who can suck on my thumb while I go about my life kicking ass."

Laughter rumbled through him. "Alright, no shrinking. But I'd really prefer it so I can protect you always."

"That's not protecting, that's caging."

He sighed. "Dammit, I can see your point. I'm not so good at this boyfriend stuff. Most of the time I wanna latch you to my side and break the bones of any boy who looks at you."

I grinned. "I could break their bones myself if I needed to, so you don't need to worry," I teased.

"I keep forgetting how powerful you are," he murmured, his hands sliding up under the back of my skirt and yanking me closer by the ass. "It gets me all kinds of hard."

"How many kinds?" I laughed, but just as his mouth landed on my neck, a knock came at the door.

"Shit," I breathed. "You'd better go."

He kissed me quickly with a groan of irritation then shot out of bed, dragging on his clothes. He tugged up the hood of his sweater and moved to the window, pushing it open and checking the coast was clear. "See you later, beautiful." He dove outside, lowering himself on a gust of air and my heart beat wildly as I got out of bed, straightening my skirt and unlocking the door.

My lips popped open at the sight of Gabriel there in his smart work attire and a knowing smirk on his face. Orion had told me he knew about us and though I should have freaked out that a member of the faculty had that information, it wasn't like that with him. I knew he'd keep our secret.

"He didn't have to leave on my account," he said in a low, teasing voice and I bit my lip guiltily. "But I do want to talk to you in private, so this works out just fine. Can I come in?"

I nodded, stepping back to let him inside with a curious frown. I shut the door and looked to Gabriel, finding it weirdly normal that he was visiting me here like a friend.

"What's up?" I asked.

"You need my help with something," he announced with a grin. "And I've had a vision showing me exactly what items you require."

"What are you talking about?" My brows pulled tighter together.

Gabriel fished through the stack of Phoenix books on my desk, picking up the one I'd been reading the other day and flipping it open to the page on Phoenix fire imbued objects. He tapped the page as he showed me it. "I saw how to do this. And I saw what you dreamed of making."

Heat flushed into my cheeks as I moved forward to survey the page. "It was just an idea…"

"A fucking awesome idea," he pointed out, smirking. "It's just what Orio needs to cheer him up."

"So you'll help me?" I asked, excitement flitting through me.

"Yes, but you need to get some stardust from Darius. I'm rationed too hard for the amount we need. A full pouch."

I sucked on my lower lip in concern and Gabriel evidently read my thoughts as he continued.

"Darius will help if you explain what it's for. But just make sure you ask him before breakfast today, his mood is going to take a dive after that."

"Before breakfast?" I balked, glancing at the clock on the wall. That gave me like ten freaking minutes.

"Better get a move on," Gabriel laughed and I pulled my door open, throwing my bag over my shoulder as he followed me out.

"See you later!" I called, running for the stairs as his laughter continued to follow me. Fate was such a bitch.

I raced downstairs, nearly knocking several students over before I made it outside and jogged towards The Orb. I knew Darius had been running with Tory every morning so they must have been almost finished.

I spotted them racing up to The Orb, way ahead of me and I pushed myself harder, casting the wind at my back to give me every advantage.

Darius opened the door for Tory and she slipped inside.

"Darius!" I called out and he turned his head just as he moved to follow her.

He spotted me racing towards him and a frown creased his brow as I slowed to a halt, panting heavily.

He folded his tattooed arms across his tank top, his brows raised as he waited for me to explain.

"I need your help," I said breathlessly.

"What's wrong?" he demanded instantly catching my hand and pulling me to one side of the door.

"Nothing's wrong," I said, my cheeks heating. This had seemed a little dramatic, but I really wanted to give this gift to Orion. And if this was my best shot at getting stardust then I would suck up looking like a hot mess right now. "I need a pouch of stardust."

His eyes narrowed in suspicion. "Why? It's not safe to leave campus."

I raised a hand to cast a silencing bubble around us. "I'm not going anywhere." I proceeded to explain to him what I needed it for and when I was done, he was smirking.

"I'll give it to you at lunch," he agreed and I actually had the urge to hug him for a second. I refrained, considering that he was still, at heart, a douche. But I knew he was *trying* to be better. According to Orion anyway. And I guessed I'd seen some evidence to support that.

"I need to grab coffee for Roxy." He moved to step away, but I caught his arm, wondering if I should do this. But my sister lit up every morning when Darius brought her coffee. I'd watched it a thousand times. To the naked eye, you wouldn't notice it at all. But I knew her so well, and that look she got around him held a secret only I could read.

"You know what's a shame? Tory loves those little chocolate wafers in the dessert section at lunchtime. She especially likes them with her coffee, but they don't provide them at breakfast."

His eyes brightened and his lips hooked up into a grin. "That is a shame."

"Imagine if you were a big ass Dragon who everyone listened to all the time? Even the kitchen staff..."

"Imagine," he agreed with a snort of laughter.

A weird moment hung between us where I actually sort of liked the asshole, then I gave him an awkward smile and he headed away into The Orb. I took a moment to fix my hair using the reflection in the door before following.

Was that the right thing to do?

The stars did say I couldn't make a wrong move today. So I guessed it had to be.

Still...I didn't know if I should be encouraging Darius's behaviour or not. What was that really saying about me? That I wanted them to be together? Holy shit, I couldn't mentally walk down that road. There were so many reasons why they shouldn't have been a couple. And yet, all of them had to do with politics and one scaly green Dragon daddy who was trying to take over the world Pinky and the Brain style. Put that aside and they were a match made in heaven. The problem was, they were both so doggedly stubborn that I knew if I even vaguely suggested that Tory should try and figure out a way to counter the stars, she'd dismiss it. It had to come from her. And even if it was impossible to achieve, I just hoped she tried. That they both did.

I pushed through the door and my ears were immediately assaulted by a horn blasting through the room. My gaze locked onto Mildred Canopus as she climbed onto a table beyond the Heirs' couch just as Darius dropped onto it beside his friends. Her hand was raised and the foghorn noise seemed to be emitting from it to get everyone's attention.

"Listen up!" she demanded, the noise falling dead.

Everyone in the room was staring at her and I drifted towards the A.S.S tables, sitting down beside Tory sipping her coffee.

Mildred placed her hands on her hips as she surveyed everyone through her beady eyes. "There's a new society starting at Zodiac Academy and *I'm* running it. So if you support the Heirs and want them to claim the throne and not the Vegas, then you can sign up right here and *now*." She stamped her foot on the table and I spotted her Atlas at her feet apparently ready to take names. Several people rushed forward and started forming a queue to join her. "As of this moment, you are either part of the Heirs Officially Ruling Everybody Society, or you're part of the Almighty Sovereign Society. You will choose. There is no in between. Do not be a cock-munching coward of a Fae. No one leaves The Orb until they've made their choice!"

"Is she for real?" I muttered to Tory whose face was pinched with hatred as she stared over at Mildred and the people drifting closer to her, though there weren't that many who'd bothered to get up.

Chatter filled the room as everyone decided what to do and Mildred stamped her foot again. "Tell them, snookums." Her voice suddenly became as sweet as pie as she looked over at Darius.

The other Heirs glanced at him and his jaw ticked with annoyance. He nodded stiffly and a tsunami of people got out of their chairs, racing towards her to sign up.

A noise like an angry bulldog escaped Geraldine and I turned to find she was climbing up onto our table with fury in her eyes.

"The Heirs Officially Ruling Everybody Society?" Geraldine spat, rolling up her sleeves like she was about to go apeshit on Mildred. And I was definitely buying a ticket to that show. "You mean you're the *HORES*?" she laughed and the A.S.S all joined in.

I shared a look with Tory, snorting a laugh. It was like Geraldine didn't even realise what her club name spelled. But I had to admit, this was possibly even funnier.

"It's pronounced Hor*es*," Mildred shot back with a snarl. "And don't you talk to me, you filthy Heir traitor."

"I'll talk to you exactly however I fancy, Mildreadful!" Geraldine cried then pointed at the crowd sweeping toward her feet. "You there! You nincompoops all flocking to that horrid hagfish! Who are you really in support of? Four beastly barracudas who strut around this place like they already own the world, or the classy cuttlefish who swim elegantly through our waters, showing nothing but grace, poise and exude an air of true royalty!"

All eyes swung between us and the Heirs and some people started backing out of the queue for Mildred's club and a new queue formed behind Geraldine. Tory and I tried to keep our faces straight as Geraldine beckoned everyone around the room towards her, her legs bending into a half squat, up and down, up and down as she waved people over.

"The four Heirs represent each of the Elements. Together they create harmony, a perfect balance. Darius is brave and noble, and his heart is made of iron, he'll rule with fire in his soul at my side and bring Solaria to greatness!" Mildred cried in retaliation. "Seth can be as ruthless as a storm or as gentle as a summer breeze, his passion for unity will bring Solaria together as one family. Max's spirit is as wild as a river and his power to feel his people's pain and love will be what heals our kingdom. And Caleb's connection to the land will make our crops prosper and feed his hungry army which will protect us all from faraway powers. To choose two girls who have no experience in ruling, no guardians to have taught them the way of our world, not even had a head start in their magic training would be as good as flushing our lives down the shitter!"

"That was so close to being eloquent," I muttered and Tory barked a laugh.

More students surged towards Mildred, chanting the Heirs' names, but I could see Geraldine wasn't going to stand for it.

She started clapping to a steady beat and the A.S.S all joined in as she gestured to them. My lips parted as Geraldine opened her mouth and started singing to the beat.

"They came from over the hill to slay, the monsters, beasts and bullies. The princesses came with their shiny crowns, two beauties in their flowing gowns. And so they shouted, away away away!"

"Away away away!" the A.S.S. sang in response like they knew the words and my jaw dropped.

"The monsters said we're here to stay, raising forks and sticks and sharpened picks. The princesses came with their silver blades, two beauties with their loyal maids. And so they shouted, away away away!" She started up a dance, stamping her foot twice to the left, then twice to the right before jumping up and clapping above her head.

"Away away away!" Tory and I joined in between our laughter as Justin Masters produced a flute from his bag and started piping out the tune. *Oh my god this is actually happening.*

Geraldine reached out to us and I shrugged at Tory before climbing up to join her on the table. She started the dance again and I copied her, picking it up as Tory joined her other side, laughing as Geraldine continued the song.

"The beasts they laughed with their hearts so black, they pushed, they fought and they attacked. But the princesses came with a swirl and a swoosh, and pushed those beasties in the Lake of Multush. And so they shouted, away

away away!"

"Away away away!" I cried with everyone else, wiping tears of laughter from my eyes as more and more people crowded around our table and joined in.

"The bullies they smiled and they jeered the town, they jibed, they battered and made everyone frown. The princesses showed them the strength of their souls, no bully could make a dent on their walls. And so they shouted, away away away!"

We clapped above our heads in time with Geraldine and everyone continued on singing that last line again and again, pointing over at the Heirs who were staring at us with their jaws slack like they couldn't quite believe what was happening. "Away away away!"

I clutched my side as we all felt apart with laughter and Geraldine wrapped us in her arms. "Holy onion balls, I haven't sung my heart out like that in a yazzilion years!"

"I loved it," I laughed then someone tugged on my skirt and I turned, finding a swarm of people below us.

"Where do we sign up?" they called to us and I looked to Geraldine as her face split into the brightest smile I'd ever seen. Mildred still had about half of the room around her and the Heirs were busy signing every spare space of flesh or workbooks that were thrust at them, but there were smirks playing around their mouths too.

Mildred sprang down amongst them, throwing her arms around Darius and he jerked backwards before he could stop himself. My heart twisted as she moved into his personal space and he was forced to take a kiss on the corner of his lips and wind his arms around her. I guessed Gabriel had been right, he really was going to be in a foul mood for the rest of the day. And I couldn't help but pity him.

Seth caught my eye with a dark smile on his face and my heart pounded harder as Max and Caleb turned towards us with resilience in their expressions.

They thrived on this challenge. And it turned out that I did too.

Keep away from our throne boys. Away away away!

TORY

CHAPTER EIGHTEEN

Catalina:
I need your help. I don't have anyone else I can ask.

I was sitting at my desk in my room trying to work on a Numerology assignment but since that message had come through, I hadn't been able to think of anything else. Because it came down to this – was I going to help Mommy Acrux with her little problem?

I hadn't even replied yet so I had no idea what she wanted my help with, but I needed to make a decision before I did. Did I trust her? And how far was I willing to go for her?

I tapped my pen against my lips as I wondered. Catalina had been messaging me every day since we'd swapped numbers. She gave me information on Lionel and Clara's comings and goings and revealed anything they'd let slip but there hadn't been a single, solid thing that she'd told me which would make any real difference to us. I understood that Lionel kept her out of his plans, but still, she hadn't exactly given me any irrefutable evidence that she was actually on my side.

There was something in me that still wanted to trust her though. Call it my gut, my instincts, whatever, but I just had this feeling that she was genuine.

Tory:
What's wrong?

Catalina:
It's Xavier. Lionel has employed a man called Mr Gravebone to Reassign his Order. He's been coming and going all week but I thought he was a tutor.

Instead he's had Xavier locked up for hours at a time while he brainwashes him to believe he's a Dragon instead of a Pegasus. I need you to do what you did for me and burn the lies out of his head.

Well that's seven shades of fucked up.

Tory:
What difference does it make if he believes he's a Dragon? He'll still turn into a Pegasus when he shifts.

I frowned to myself as I leaned back in my chair. It didn't make any sense to me. Someone could brainwash me into believing I was a cat and I might go around sleeping in the sun and licking my own ass. But I wouldn't be a cat. I'd just be a crazy girl with some embarrassing hobbies.

Catalina:
I think Lionel plans to have him act like he's a Dragon and fake some photographs for the press. Eventually if the secret becomes too hard to hide I think he'll kill him and pretend it was an accident. Once Xavier has gained control over shifting, Lionel will Dark Coerce him never to shift in front of anyone so he can go out in public. I heard Mr Gravebone say he was making good progress. Please, I can't bear the thought of someone messing with who he is on the inside. I've already failed him so many times.

Tory:
I can try. How am I supposed to get to him though?

Catalina:
Come to the manor tonight. Lionel is at a Council meeting in the city because of the war with the Nymphs. He won't be back until tomorrow evening and Clara went with him.

A shiver ran down my spine at that suggestion. Was I seriously going to walk into the lion's den willingly? Sneaking over to Acrux Manor late at night when no one knew where I was going sounded like suicide to me. And yet…I just couldn't help but trust in Catalina's words. Which meant that Xavier really was in trouble. And even though I'd only met him a few times, I'd felt a real connection with him. But the truth of his Order was a secret that was going to bury him before long and even if I could help with this issue, it wouldn't be the end of it.

I pushed out of my chair and quickly stripped out of my uniform before changing into high waisted jeans and a crop top, twisting my hair into a messy knot on the back of my head. Nothing about my outfit choice said that I was on a secret mission, which was perfect.

I shot Darcy a text as I kicked on my boots, but I wasn't going to hold my breath for an answer. She was staying with Lance tonight which basically made her uncontactable. But it was probably best I did this alone anyway. At least that way if this was some kind of seriously convoluted trap then there would only be one of us walking into it.

I took the stairs down to the Ignis House common room and my stomach did an inelegant backflip as I spotted Darius holding court beside the huge fireplace.

I raised my chin and headed straight for him, ignoring the way he made my heart thunder. He looked up as I approached, his eyes widening slightly as he realised I was coming straight for him.

"Can I have a word?" I asked, pleased to find my voice steady even if the rest of me was shaking a little.

"Leave," Darius barked and every single one of the group surrounding us leapt to their feet and disappeared.

"Bossy much?" I asked as I dropped into the seat in front of him and tossed a silencing bubble up around us.

The common room was pretty packed so the stars were content to let us talk.

"I assumed you'd want privacy for whatever it is you want to say," he replied with a shrug as he leaned forward, elbows pressing on his knees.

"Well I suppose it helps to keep your ego propped up to send people scurrying at whim," I teased.

Darius didn't bite and I sighed. Was it completely insane for me to miss our little to and fros? Did it mean there was something wrong with me to be disappointed that he hadn't made some crack about me in response? Maybe I really was broken if I was grieving the way he used to rile me up, but I couldn't help it. I missed how he could get me all hot and bothered with a single arrogant remark.

"You know, you don't have to hold your tongue around me all the time now," I said with an ever so slightly petulant pout. "It's no fun goading you if you don't bite back. Besides, you must *want* to rip into me, at least a little considering the fact that I did this to us."

"I was under the impression that I was to blame for our situation," Darius said in a low voice, ignoring everything else I'd just said.

"Yeah, you are," I agreed, though my voice lacked conviction and I hated to admit that ever since Gabriel had called me out on my shit, I'd been thinking about my part in all of this too. "Anyway... I didn't actually seek you out for this. I was wondering if I could borrow some stardust?"

"No," Darius replied instantly and I bristled.

"Okay then, I'll just drive. Thanks a lot." I got to my feet, but he was suddenly in my face.

"It's not safe for you to leave campus, Roxy," he growled. "You know that."

"There's something I need to do tonight," I replied just as firmly. "And I'll be doing it with or without your help."

251

"Then I'll come with you," he demanded.

"And have the heavens come crashing down on us and the earth crumble at our feet until we're dragged down into the fiery chasm beneath? No thanks." My blood was pumping and I was struck with the desire to call him a pig headed, controlling, lizard asshole but I bit down on my tongue, wondering if there was a better way to handle this than just biting his head off and storming away.

"You can't just decide to pick up and leave the safety of-"

I reached out and caught Darius's hand, looking up into his black-ringed eyes as he paused mid rant to gaze down at me in confusion.

"This is important, Darius," I breathed. "*Please.*"

His frown deepened and his fingers curled around mine. The nervous tension in my stomach felt like my organs were having an orgy and I didn't even care when the foundations of Ignis House trembled and other students cried out in fright.

"I just don't want you to get hurt," he growled in a low voice that sent a shiver dancing down my spine.

"I won't," I promised, hoping I could keep to that vow. "There and back again within an hour. I wouldn't ask if I had any other choice."

Darius looked at me for another long moment before finally releasing my hand and pulling a silk pouch from his back pocket. "Do you know how to use this?" he asked, concern lining his features.

"Click my ruby heels together and think of the place I want to go with all my heart," I joked.

"Something like that. Call me if anything goes wrong."

"Okay," I agreed, ignoring the fact that the idea of calling on him for help should have been insanity in the light of the fact that I liked him offering.

A spark leapt from the fire and landed on the coffee table beside us, exploding into flame and making me yelp as I leapt back and put some room between me and Darius. *Stupid star twats!*

Darius took control of the flames with a growl of frustration and guttered them with a flick of his fingers. He pressed the stardust into my hand and I gave him a tight smile before turning and running down the stairs to the exit.

As I made it outside, I shot a quick text to Catalina telling her to expect me soon then called on my Order form, unleashing my wings. I took a moment to concentrate on banishing the flames from them so that I wouldn't be spotted flying across the campus so easily.

Without the fire coating them, the feathers of my wings were a deep bronze colour which shone like an oil spill with the deep red and blue tones of my inner flames glimmering in them when they caught the light. I flexed them out behind me and took off, heading for the gap which Orion had left in the shield surrounding Zodiac.

I landed quietly, looking around to make sure that there was no one close by as I slipped through the gap in the fence and out into the world beyond the academy.

I didn't waste any time as I pulled the pouch of stardust from my pocket and tossed some of it over my head while thinking of Acrux Manor.

The stars swept me up in their embrace, transporting me through them in a blur of silver light before depositing me onto the gravel drive outside Acrux Manor right before a huge, iron gate.

"Who goes there?" a man shouted and I looked up to find two guards leaping from their hut with magic stunning guns aimed at me.

"Don't you recognise a Vega when you see one?" I asked lazily, feeling like a total douchebag for playing the princess card, but needs must. "I've come to see Lionel."

The guards exchanged a look and slowly lowered their weapons. "Lord Acrux isn't here. Perhaps you should make an appointment with him to-"

"I can leave a message with his wife easily enough," I said impatiently. "But I'm not going to be leaving it with the hired help. So just let me in."

They exchanged a look at my entitled tone, but I'd spent plenty of time around the Heirs to be sure I had it down.

"We will find out if Lady Acrux wishes to receive you," the guard said with a slight bow of his head as his friend scuttled back into the hut.

I pulled my Atlas from my pocket and put on a good show of looking pissily impatient as I scrolled through posts without really looking at them.

Mildred Canopus:
Has anyone seen my beloved @Darius Acrux tonight? We had plans for a sweet serenade by Aqua Lake but he seems to have forgotten and his Atlas has died. #helpmereunitewithmylove

Tyler Corbin:
I saw him hiding himself in a grave-shaped hole he'd dug in The Wailing Wood and threatening to off himself for real if you found him.

Stephanie Wiltshire:
I heard he's been hooking up with Tory Vega behind the Pitball Stadium #thestarscantstopthembanging #loveerrerrerrerrwillfindaway

Denisha Pillay:
I saw him covering himself in Griffin shit and hiding in a bog #takingthepooburnoveryourcompany #wouldratherrollinshit #ihopeheneverhastomarryyou

Ashleigh Clare:
I heard he has to get @Max Rigel to suck all of the repulsion out of his body to even be around you and he couldn't find him tonight #cansomebodypleasethinkofthechildren #lifesnotfairyoudontdeserveanheir

Erica Collins:
I reckon he's hiding under @Diego Polaris's hat #evendandruffisbettercompanythanyou #doyouthinkhesleepswearingit

Brianna Hayes:
Have you checked your butt crack since the last time you sat on his knee? #isawawholeherdofpegasusdropoutofthereonce

#ibetthattakesapowershowertoclearitout
Deema-Yara Mohiar:
I saw him kissing a steaming turd by the Shimmering Springs – I guess he just thought it was you #hedchoosepooooveryou #iheardyoureaturd

I stifled my laughter at the comments so that the guards wouldn't see my resting bitch face crack, but I had to admit that I didn't totally hate the way everyone was against the idea of Darius being shackled to that bitch. Even if half of them were just as disgusted at the idea of him being bound to me, at least I didn't have to survive people gushing all over the happy couple all the damn time.

After another minute, the gates swung open and the guards bowed as they directed me through them.

I stalked up the drive with my head held high and my heart pounding. I was going to have to conduct a cover story for coming here so that Lionel didn't get suspicious, and I was just hoping that I could do that without having to actually see him. Maybe I could pretend I came to call him out on commanding me to break Darius's heart. Play the heartbroken card and say I'd come to beg for a second chance or some shit. Yeah, that would probably work. It would be mortifying and all, but if Catalina passed that message on to him, I knew he'd do nothing more than take pleasure in my pain and refuse my request.

The doors opened before I reached them and the snooty butler peered out at me. Hopkins or Smithkins or Buttkins or something.

"Good evening, Miss Vega," he simpered, bowing in a way that felt mocking somehow.

"Hi," I replied, sweeping past him and ignoring him as I looked up at the huge staircase with the golden handrail.

"Lady Acrux is currently awaiting you in her parlour," he said before gliding onwards up the stairs.

I guessed that meant I was supposed to follow so I did, trying not to let the cold feeling of this place slip under my skin. There was something about the Acrux Manor which chilled me to my core. No love lived here. Only pain and shadows.

We kept going, taking long corridors lined with paintings of Dragons and douchebags until we reached another staircase which I recognised from the time I'd spent sliding down it on trays with Xavier. We headed up until we reached the level below Xavier's room in the top of the tower where Buttkins opened a door for me.

Catalina Acrux sat waiting in a beautiful parlour with a huge bay window which must have offered a view out over the lake at the end of their property during the day. She was wearing a silk gown and her dark hair was perfectly styled as she sipped a cup of steaming tea and surveyed me over the rim.

"What have I done to earn a visit from a Vega?" she asked curiously as she waved me towards the chair opposite her.

I moved towards the table which was laid out with a pot of tea and a cup for me too. There was a little three tiered cake stand filled with sumptuous looking cakes, macaroons and biscuits there too. I had to hand it to their kitchen staff, they knew how to work under pressure. You'd never know I'd rocked up unannounced and taken them all by surprise.

"I'd rather talk alone," I said as I moved to take the chair.

"Of course. You're dismissed, Jenkins," she said and the butler backed out of the room, narrowing his beady little eyes suspiciously. I was pretty sure I was going to keep thinking of him as Buttkins.

Catalina threw a silencing spell over us and glanced towards the door in warning. So, Buttkins couldn't be trusted? I guessed that was to be expected in this viper's pit.

"Thank you for coming," Catalina breathed, reaching across the table to squeeze my fingers for a moment. "I don't know what else I can do."

"I'm still not sure I can help," I admitted. "But I'll definitely try."

"That's all I can ask." She picked her Atlas up and sent a message to Xavier, summoning him to join us.

I reached out and took a biscuit from the little stand and devoured it in two bites as Catalina watched me. It was fucking delicious. Going hungry in the mortal world had definitely left me with a taste for good food and there was no way I'd be letting those little treats go to waste.

"Have you seen much of Darius?" she asked and I stilled. We talked a lot via text, but there was an unspoken rule that we didn't discuss *him,* and I would have preferred to stick to it.

"Every day," I admitted. "Meals, classes, the common room. It's kinda like getting punched in the heart every other hour."

I wasn't really sure why I'd admitted to that and I looked away from her before she could get a read on the pain it caused me. Because I didn't have a right to be hurting over it, did I? It had been my choice that put us in this position after all.

The door opened before she could push me on the subject and I looked around with a smile as Xavier stepped into the room.

He fell still as he spotted me. His dark hair was a mess, he was barefoot and the grey sweatpants he wore had a stain on the leg. He was also shirtless which gave me a look at the lean muscle lining his frame and the defined V which dipped beneath his waistband.

"Well shit, Xavier, have you spent the last two months working out or something?" I teased and a faint blush lined his cheeks as he stared between me and his mother.

"What...why are you here?" he asked, not seeming to know if he should be pleased to see me or not.

"I wanted a word," I said, exchanging a glance with Catalina.

She seemed to be waiting for me to make the move though so I beckoned Xavier closer and pointed to the chair beside me.

He approached, his eyes narrowed suspiciously as he lowered himself into the seat and pushed a hand through his hair self consciously.

"Did I interrupt your nap?" I teased.

"No. I just…didn't really expect to see anyone today so I didn't exactly bother getting dressed." There was a hollow tone to his voice which made me frown and my heart twisted painfully as I wondered how many days he spent alone like that.

"Your mom asked me to come and see if I could help you with-"

"Why did you say no to Darius?" he blurted, his brow lowering as he gazed at the black rings in my eyes. "I know he was an asshole to you and he did a lot of things that he shouldn't have but that was all about power, the throne, the fucking crown. And I didn't think you cared that much about any of that."

"I don't. Or I guess, I didn't. Being Fae kind of goes hand in hand with claiming power though, doesn't it?" I asked, tightening my jaw as I refused to balk at the subject.

"Fine. Whatever. I get that side of it. But what I don't understand is how you could have said no to loving him. Because when I saw the two of you together I could see how much you liked each other. Even when you were denying it or fighting or whatever, it was still there. And I just don't get how you could stand there beneath the stars, look him in the eyes and say no. Why would you curse him like that? Why would you curse yourself?"

I wanted to shrug off his question, but the accusation in his dark eyes demanded an answer and I blew out a breath as I gave it to him.

"Because all I've ever wanted is to be loved like that but I was afraid that if I let myself love him, he'd use it to hurt me. Too much has happened between us and…I just don't trust him." I raised my chin as the two of them looked at me like my words caused them physical pain. "Anyway, I don't want to talk about Darius. I came here for you."

I reached out and took Xavier's hand in mine before he could stop me, tapping in to my Phoenix fire just like I had when I'd burned the Dark Coercion from Catalina.

He gasped and tried to pull back but I held on tight, my magic keeping him in its grip as it burned through him, hunting down whatever Mr Gravebone had been putting in his head. But the only thing I found was a single wall of Dark Coercion which I recognised as Lionel's magic. I tore it down then pulled back, releasing his hand as he stared at me with wide eyes.

"What the hell was that?" Xavier asked.

"Phoenix fire. I used it to take the Dark Coercion from your mind, but I can't find whatever Gravebone has been doing to you. It's not any magic that Phoenix fire can locate anyway." I offered Catalina an apologetic expression and her face dropped with concern.

"I…you mean I can talk about my Order now?" Xavier asked. "I can actually tell people about it if I wanted to?"

"He Dark Coerced you not to tell anyone you were a Pegasus?" I asked, my gut lurching at that idea.

"Yeah, well, if he could Coerce me never to shift again I'm sure he'd have done it, but as that's something I can't always control I guess he couldn't." His gaze slid to Catalina like he wasn't sure how much he should say in front of her and her composure suddenly broke.

A sob escaped her as she threw her arms around her son apologising again and again, explaining in murmured whispers for all the years she hadn't been allowed to show him any love or softness as his face scrunched with confusion which was slowly replaced with a dawning comprehension.

It broke my heart to watch them. Xavier seemed so uncomfortable in his mother's arms and yet so relieved to be there all at once. Like he didn't know what to do with that kind of affection. But he craved it all the same.

I knew exactly what it felt like to hunger for the love of a parent, but I'd never had one who I could try and claim it from. Xavier and Darius had been denied this love for years and years while both wishing they could express it. All because some monster had decided he owned them. That somehow he had a right to decide this for them and used his power to enforce it.

And he was still doing it. Hiding Xavier away, cutting him off from the outside world and forcing him to deny who and what he was just because it didn't fit with Lionel's idea of perfect. Well fuck perfect. There was no such thing. And all of life's beauty was in the imperfections anyway.

"He's never going to let you out of here is he?" I asked. "He's never going to let the world know what you are or who you are. Is he?"

Xavier looked up at me hopelessly as Catalina sobbed in his arms.

"He owns us," she said. "He owns everyone really. We just feel the full sway of his power more than most because we're trapped here with him."

"Bullshit. He doesn't own everyone. He doesn't own *me*. And he doesn't own you either."

I pushed out of my chair and crossed the room to the huge bay window, unlatching it and throwing it wide. The cool evening air whistled in around me, blowing loose strands of hair across my face as I inhaled deeply.

"What are you doing?" Catalina gasped.

"Do you trust me, Xavier?" I asked.

"Why?" he countered suspiciously

"Because I'm going to set you free. Come here." I beckoned and he got up, walking towards me cautiously as I pulled my Atlas from my pocket and set it recording.

"This is Xavier Acrux and he's got something fucking amazing to show you," I said, smirking at him as I raised my other hand.

"Do I?" he asked in confusion.

"Fuck yes. His Order just Emerged and he's something way cooler than a big old lizard – no offence to Dragons, I'm sure your scaly balls are great and all but it's just not as badass as being a fucking Pegasus."

Xavier's eyes widened in horror as I flicked my fingers at him and threw him straight out of the tower window with a gust of wind. We were on the ninth floor so he had plenty of time for fear to shock his Order form from his flesh and spread his wings way before he could hit the ground, but I was ready to catch him with my magic if he didn't manage it for any reason.

Xavier cried out as he fell but his screams suddenly became whinnies as the huge, lilac Pegasus burst from his skin, shredding through his clothes as his wings unfurled and caught on an updraft.

I caught it all on camera, laughing excitedly as he levelled out then beat his wings and started flying up and up and up towards the clouds which were lined with silver as the moon shone through them.

Catalina rushed forward like she meant to rip my Atlas from my hands, but as her gaze fell on her son out of the window, her lips parted and a beautiful smile graced her mouth.

Xavier shot into the clouds and out of sight and I finally ended the recording.

I typed out a FaeBook post with the video attached and glanced up at Catalina with my thumb hovering over the post button. I had over a million followers on there now, and if I hit that button, the word would be well and truly out.

"The only reason Lionel maintains his hold over him is because it's a secret. Pegasuses are one of the most common Order forms there are. Unless Lionel wants to alienate all of them, he'll have to come out in support of his son. The only power he holds here is in keeping it a secret. Once it's out, it's out."

"He'll kill you for exposing this," she breathed, her eyes wide with fear.

"I'm pretty sure he plans on killing me anyway," I said with a shrug. "At least if he kills me for this, it was for something that matters."

"I-"

"Tell him I came here and spoke with you about Darius. Tell him I made some excuse to get you to leave the room and by the time you came back I'd done this. Put all the blame on me. I mean that."

"Okay…" she said hesitantly and I met her eye.

"Do I need to make you swear it on the stars?" I growled.

"No. I'll tell him. Thank you, Roxanya."

"It's Tory. Only Darius calls me Roxy and I can't make him stop, but I don't want anyone else making a habit of it," I said. Although at this point if Darius started calling me Tory it would probably just be weird. Not that I'd ever admit that I was okay with the Roxy thing.

"Okay. Thank you, *Tory*."

I smirked at her and hit post.

Catalina gasped as Xavier's secret went viral and I glanced down at my Atlas as reactions and comments began to pour in before I locked the screen.

Shit, what if Daddy Acrux really does kill me for this?

"Run, Tory," Catalina breathed, real fear dancing in her eyes. "Run for the gate and get back to the academy before he comes back. If he finds you here-"

"Consider me gone." I barked a laugh as nerves made my heart flutter.

Catalina smiled at me before ripping her dress off, knocking her hair free of its perfectly styled bun, flashing me those gloriously fake tits and leaping out of the window after her son. She transformed as she plummeted and my lips fell open as a stunning silver Dragon burst from her flesh.

She beat a path up towards the clouds just as Xavier dipped beneath them with an excited whinny.

I quickly raised my Atlas and snapped a picture of the two of them dancing through the sky before I took a running jump out of the window too.

My wings burst to life at my back and I flew hard and fast along the drive until I soared over the gates, beyond the anti-stardust wards where I landed quickly, my boots skidding in the gravel.

I grabbed the stardust from my pocket and winked at the startled guards half a second before I tossed it over my head and the stars whisked me back to the academy.

I stumbled as they deposited me and suddenly strong arms locked around my chest from behind, making me scream in surprise.

A hand slapped over my mouth and I stilled for a moment as the scent of smoke and cedar overwhelmed me.

Darius dragged me back through the hole in the wards, pulled me through the fence and shoved me up against a huge tree at the edge of campus before he took his hand from my mouth.

His hands landed either side of my head as he penned me in, glaring down at me with an angry as fuck Dragon peering out of his eyes, his pupils transformed into reptilian slits and a hint of smoke slipped between his lips. He was only wearing sweatpants and I got the impression he'd flown here to ambush me the moment I returned. *I guess he didn't like my FaeBook post.*

"What the fuck were you thinking?" he demanded.

"Whoa, chill out dude," I said, pressing my hands to his chest to push him back. He didn't move a single inch and I just ended up with my hands pressed to his rock hard muscles, his heart pounding frantically beneath my right palm.

"Do you know what you've done?" Darius snarled. "Father could kill Xavier for this! He could-"

"He won't," I snapped angrily. "He can't. Don't you see that? The only power he held over Xavier was in keeping his real Order form a secret. Now everyone knows, he's free. Killing him wouldn't change the truth. And he can't very well alienate every Pegasus in Solaria by making his Orderist bullshit public knowledge. He'll have to let Xavier leave the house, join a herd, *fly."*

Darius was staring at me like he didn't know whether to kill me or kiss me and as my gaze fell on his mouth, I found myself aching for the latter. *Fuck the stars.*

"She has a point," Caleb's voice came from the shadows behind the massive Dragon who was taking all of my attention and I turned my head to find him, Seth and Max all watching this exchange with interest. That would explain the stars not smiting us or whatever other bullshit they might want to do. Though I was guessing I should really stop touching him...not that I did.

"You did this to...*help* him?" Darius asked like he couldn't understand why the fuck I'd do that and I narrowed my eyes at him.

"I'm only an asshole like, ninety percent of the time," I said, rolling my eyes at him. "The other ten percent I'm a fucking saint. So yes, I did it to help him. Turns out I only hold two members of your family in low regard."

"You pushed my brother out of a fucking window," he growled.

"I would have caught him with my air magic if I had to. Besides, this way Daddy Acrux can't try and claim he was in on it. It's a genius plan and you know it. Plus, your mom told me to post it so I don't have to explain myself to you."

"Mother?" Darius scoffed. "She hardly notices anything beyond appearances. The last thing she'd encourage is a scandal like this. She-"

"That's not true, she loves you, she just..." I trailed off as the deal I'd made with Catalina stayed my tongue. I'd sworn not to tell a soul about the way I'd freed her from Lionel's Dark Coercion and I wasn't going to take even more punishment from the stars by breaking my word.

"Just what?" Darius demanded.

Phoenix fire burned hot beneath my skin and my palms twitched against his chest as a thought occurred to me. One I really should have considered before now if I hadn't been so caught up with studying, the shadows, cheer practice and just plain old pining away for this monster before me to think of it.

"Do you trust me?" I asked, my fingers shifting on his skin just enough to draw his attention.

"Why?"

"I want to try something. Something I did for your mother. But you'll have to stay still while I do it."

Darius looked at me for a long moment and a faint tremor in the ground beneath my feet let me know that the stars had realised just how close we were to one another. Even with company they didn't like us to touch each other, though it seemed to take them a lot longer to notice if we were.

Darius exhaled angrily but his eyes shifted back as he managed to rein in some of his temper, their deep brown colour ringed with black once again.

"I trust you," he growled and the other Heirs muttered something behind him, but I didn't care to hear it because there had been a sincerity in his words which reached out and touched my soul. He meant it. For whatever reason, despite everything we'd been through, he was still able to put his trust in me.

I offered him the hint of a smile as my Phoenix fire reared up to the surface of my skin before I guided it into his flesh where I touched him.

His muscles tightened beneath my hands, his eyes widening as he looked at me but he didn't pull back, waiting as the liquid fire tore beneath his skin and sought out any signs of Lionel placing restrictions on his soul.

It only took me a moment to find one then another and another. I gasped as I found more and more and more of them. So many binds and restrictions on things he could say and do that I couldn't even count them as I tore them all down, burning through them one after another.

My hands began to shake and my legs trembled as I blazed through my gifts, but I refused to stop until each and every piece of dark magic was shredded from his soul.

I gasped as I burned through the final one, my knees buckling as I fell against him but he caught me before I could hit the ground.

"You…" Darius lifted me into his arms, staring at me with wide eyes like he didn't even have words to explain what I'd just done for him.

"What happened?" Max demanded as he moved closer, trying to get a look at me while Seth and Caleb jostled him.

Thunder crashed through the sky overhead and as I looked up above Darius's head, I realised we were being sheltered from the storm by a huge air shield.

Lightning slammed from the sky, crashing into it and Seth cursed as he just managed to take the brunt of the blow with his magic.

"Put me down," I murmured.

"You can't even stand," Darius snarled.

"I'll take her," Caleb offered and a ferocious growl tore from Darius's lips as he reached out for me.

Caleb bared his teeth right back for a moment then managed to school his expression.

The ground beneath our feet was shaking even harder now and with a curse, Darius closed his eyes and handed me over to Caleb.

Everything began to calm down almost instantly and Darius growled again as he looked at me in Caleb's arms.

"Just chill out, man. I'm only holding her," Caleb huffed.

"Tell us what the hell she just did to you," Seth pressed, his gaze fixed on Darius as he reached out and brushed a hand over his arm in a comforting gesture.

"She…I think she…but I don't understand how-"

"Phoenix fire burns through bullshit," I supplied. "I just released him from every Dark Coercion spell Lionel has ever placed on him."

The Heirs all turned to stare at me like I'd just told them an alien named Clive lived up my butt and I sighed as I leaned my head back against Caleb's shoulder. I felt like I'd just gone ten rounds in the ring against a Dragon with toothache. My eyes were hooded already and I was pretty sure that if we stood here much longer I'd fall asleep.

"Thank you, Roxy," Darius breathed and the look he was giving me made my heart do a weird squeezing kind of thing as I bit down on my bottom lip.

"Well, like I said. I'm only an asshole ninety percent of the time," I joked, not really knowing what to do with the way he was looking at me. "But, if it's all the same to you guys, I just want to go back to my bed and-"

"Take her back to my room," Darius said, his gaze flipping up to meet Caleb's. "Make sure there's a fire roaring in the grate so she can restore her magic while she sleeps. I'll sleep at the Hollow tonight. There's things we all need to discuss."

"Fuck yes," Seth said enthusiastically as Max laughed darkly and I had to wonder just how many secrets Darius had been forced to keep from the other Heirs and what exactly was going to change now that he didn't have to keep them anymore.

"I'll meet you there," Caleb said, tightening his grip on me as Darius handed over his room key.

Darius hesitated right beside us and reached out to run his fingers along the side of my face. "You were right you know," he breathed as if the others weren't surrounding us and as I looked into his eyes, it almost felt like they weren't. "I'm not good enough for you."

I didn't even have time to respond before Caleb shot away from him, leaving the safety of Seth's air bubble and tearing off into the storm with me in his arms.

I scrunched my eyes up against the hammering rain as we sped through it and before I knew it, we were outside Darius's door and he was turning the key in the lock.

"I'd rather just go back to my own room," I protested but Caleb ignored me, shooting straight inside and placing me on my feet beside the bed.

In a blur of motion, he shot around me, yanking off my boots, jeans and crop top before dumping one of Darius's shirts over my head on top of my underwear then scooping me straight into the enormous bed and tucking the blankets right up beneath my chin.

"Caleb!" I snapped, but he just laughed.

"I've seen it all before anyway, sweetheart," he joked as he sped off again, yanking the window and shutters closed before using his magic to light a huge fire in the grate.

The warmth of it washed over me and I sighed as my inner Phoenix bathed in the magic of the flames.

"I don't wanna sleep here," I muttered as Darius's scent enveloped me and a whole host of regrets came whispering in my ears. But I was so exhausted from using my gifts that I just couldn't stop my eyes from fluttering shut.

Caleb laughed softly. "I'll lock the door and push the key back under it so you can escape in the morning."

"Asshole," I murmured.

"Always," he agreed, flicking the lights off and the door clicked shut before the sound of the key turning in the lock followed.

I was too tired to argue further but before I gave in to sleep, I snagged my Atlas from the nightstand and forwarded the photograph I'd taken of Xavier and Catalina flying together in their Order forms to Darius. He deserved to see evidence of his mother's love after all of these years and the knowledge that they'd all been denied that bond for so long made my heart ache for them.

A moment later, a message came through from him and I smiled to myself as I read it.

Darius:
Thank you, Roxy. This means more to me than words can convey.

My cheeks flushed at his reply and I bit my lip as exhaustion pulled at me. I sighed to myself as I nestled down in his bed, trying not to linger in the memories of sleeping here with his arms wrapped around me, feeling like nothing and no one in the world could ever hurt me so long as I just stayed right there. Maybe I should have listened to those instincts. Because his bed didn't feel the same without him in it. And for the first time that I would admit to myself, I had to wonder if I'd made a terrible mistake when I said no.

XAVIER

CHAPTER NINETEEN

I ran on the treadmill at full speed, pushing my body to its very limits. I'd taken the beating of a lifetime last night. There'd been so much blood, I'd feared for a second Father wasn't going to stop. But I shouldn't have doubted, because now that my Order was exposed to the world, he couldn't kill me. Not anytime soon at least. Tory Vega had given me the protection I needed. And not just that, she'd saved me from any more sessions with Gravebone too. His mind tricks had made me question my own head, but since last night, I felt like myself again.

I never had chosen the Dragons in my hypnosis, but he'd gotten frighteningly close to persuading me that way. Closer than I liked to admit. I just hoped that asshole took a long walk off a short pier sometime soon and fell into a fiery pit of lava.

In an hour, the press were going to arrive along with the other Councillors and the Heirs to celebrate my Emergence. It was laughable. In fact, after my mother had healed me from Father's attack last night, I'd laughed my fucking ass off. Because now he was going to be forced to let me out in public. He was going to have to send me to school. To Zodiac. It was only a matter of time before I'd be Awakened in the summer and ready to start my education in September. I'd move out of this house, this hell.

My gut twisted suddenly and I banged my fist against the emergency stop, the treadmill slowing to a halt beneath me.

I took in heavy breaths, my mind latching onto Mom. She'd stayed with me late into the night, apologising for everything. I didn't care that I was nearly a grown man, I'd curled up into her arms and drank in the feeling of her surrounding me, trying to make up for every lost hug we'd missed out on. But then she'd gone away. And now we had to act as if she wasn't healed. Because that was what she was. My father was a disease that ate into the minds and hearts of others. His desire for power had corrupted him a long time ago and his need for control meant he'd fought to mould us into the ideal, mindless little puppets he needed us to be. *If people really knew what he was like, if they knew what he'd done...*

I swallowed the hard ball in my throat and stepped off of the treadmill as I caught my breath. Leaving this house and going to Zodiac Academy was something I'd hoped for my entire life. But that was when I'd thought that Mother was as heartless as Father. Now...how could I leave her here in good conscience?

The answer was simple: I couldn't.

So I needed a plan, some way to get her out of this life before I was carted off to school in September and she was left to the misery of Acrux Manor alone.

I headed out of the gym and was soon showered and heading back to my room. Mother had laid out a fine white dress shirt and dark trousers on my bed for the photoshoot. The Acrux family crest was embroidered on the breast pocket in gold; two dragons reaching toward a single flame above them, their tails intertwined where our surname was printed.

I dressed in the smart clothes and headed to the mirror on the wall, using some product to push my curling hair back. I never usually bothered, but today was a special day. One I was determined to enjoy. I wanted to see my father's skin stretching back over the shiniest smile he could muster for the cameras. I wanted to feel the discomfort hiding behind his eyes, sense the blood rising in his neck when his friends congratulated him. I was going to bathe in every delicious moment of it. I'd take a hundred beatings for that. Today was mine. And I was going to own every second and commit each one to memory. I knew things weren't going to be plain sailing from here. But they were surely going to get better. They had to.

"It's not fair!" I heard Clara cry from somewhere down the hall.

I moved to my door, stepping into the hallway to find Father dragging her along by the arm. He was dressed in a black suit that was more fit for a funeral than a celebration. But then again, I supposed this was a kind of death to him. A death of his absolute control over me. *Ha. R.I.P.*

"You will do this, Clara, it's not a request," Father snarled and she threw a blast of shadows at him, throwing him back a step. His hand came at her so fast, she had no time to stop him as it crashed against her cheek, sending her head wheeling sideways.

My heart beat harder as I watched, not moving an inch in case they spotted me and dragged me into whatever this fight was about.

"Daddy!" Clara wailed, cupping her reddened cheek. Then she dropped to her knees, wrapping her arms around his legs and hugging tight. "Don't do this to me, please! I don't like the dark!"

"There is a light in the attic, foolish girl," he snapped. "You cannot be seen by the press, you don't hide the shadows well enough. One slip and we'll be exposed." He caught a fistful of her hair, dragging her to her feet and hauling her along as she bawled like a child.

They rounded a corner and my heartbeat steadied as I hurried forward and headed downstairs. At least I didn't have to deal with her today.

I ate a bowl of cereal in the kitchen before refilling the bowl and having another one, because why the hell not? Might as well celebrate. I wished I could dance with Mom and hug her in front of everyone today. And the thought ripped and pulled at a long suffering wound in my chest. After all the animosity I'd harboured in my heart for her, now my insides were all twisted up, my love for her expanding and chasing away those dark feelings I'd aimed toward her. If only I'd known she'd been a slave to Father too, maybe I wouldn't have felt so alone since Darius had gone to school.

My phone started ringing and I took it out in surprise, finding Sofia calling. My heart jammed into my throat and I half choked on the cereal in my mouth.

One startling truth rang in my ears like a gong. *She's figured it out.*

We never called each other. The only way I'd heard her voice before was through her videos on FaeBook which I may or may not have saved to my phone and watched like some creeper. But seeing her smile and laugh with her friends had felt like she was smiling and laughing with *me*. Which yeah, was sad as shit. But I'd found comfort in it. I wasn't remotely prepared to answer that call and hear her voice aimed at me for real.

I left the bowl on the side and raced into the pantry, pulling the door closed and rushing past the shelves of food. The call was going to damn well cut out if I didn't answer in the next ten seconds.

Shit what do I say?

Am I going to sound like a douche?

What if she hates my voice?

I cleared my throat. "Hello Sofia," I practised in a deeper tone than usual. *Idiot.* "Hello. Hi. What's crack-a-lackin'?"

Answer it asshole!!!

I pressed the button and held it to my ear, saying – nothing. Yep, I said nothing. Just remained quiet and listened to her breathe.

"Philip?" she asked tentatively and I pressed my back to the far wall, sinking down to the floor beside a sack of potatoes. Which was weird because I kind of felt like a sack of potatoes in that moment.

"Hey," I said. And I sounded normal. Definitely normal.

"You're not Philip, are you?" she asked. By the stars, she sounded sweeter than in any of her videos. That voice was husky, innocent yet seductive. And I *might* have been getting hard for her like a twelve year old boy with his first ever boner. *Real fucking smooth.*

"No," I answered in a slightly strained voice, apparently only able to give one word answers. But what was she going to think now? What if she didn't want to talk to me anymore? Darius wasn't exactly a BFD (Big Friendly Dragon). And she was definitely Team Vega, so maybe she didn't care for him or my family.

"You're Xavier Acrux," she said, her voice quavering a little.

I wasn't sure if she was afraid or just about to break down into tears because her bubble had been burst when she'd learned that I wasn't Philip the low level Pegasus who was entirely inoffensive with his existence.

"Yeah," I rasped. *More words, idiot, more words*! I barrelled on. "Does that change things?"

A beat of silence passed which might as well have been a lifetime.

"No," she answered. "At least, not if you don't want it to?"

"No – of course I don't. I'm sorry I lied, I just..." A thousand explanations rang through my head, but I didn't have to say any of them before Sofia answered.

"I get it. You're an Acrux. Your father wanted you to be a Dragon."

"Yeah," I sighed. *Man* it felt so good to talk to her. Her voice was a silken thread that seemed to weave itself into my soul and soothe every dark shadow it found there. "He's going to pretend it's the best news ever now. Tory saved my ass."

"I'm gonna give her the biggest hug for you."

"Thanks," I laughed, pushing a hand into my hair as my heart raced. I didn't know why I felt like such a bundle of nerves, but talking to her was like taking an injection of pure adrenaline. "I should be able to come to Zodiac next year," I blurted then instantly regretted it. What was I even trying to say by telling her that? That we could meet? *Date?* No chance. She was a year older than me anyway, why would she want that?

"That's amazing news," she gasped and a shit-eating grin took over my whole face.

"Is it?" I asked.

"The best," she laughed and that sound – *fuck,* that sound.

"Xavier! The press are here, where are you?!" Father's voice boomed through the walls as he used magic to amplify it and my heart stuttered.

"Shit, I've gotta go," I muttered.

"Okay, talk soon?"

"Real soon. And watch out for an article in The Celestial Times tomorrow," I said with a low laugh.

"Can't wait."

"Bye," I breathed then hung up, getting to my feet and staring down at my hard on with a sigh. I was so not camera ready right now.

"XAVIER!" Father bellowed and yep, that did it. My boner sank like a ship hitting a rock at sea and I rearranged my pants as I headed out of the door into the kitchen.

My heart thumped against my ears as I hurried through to the entrance hall, finding Jenkins opening the door and Mother and Father standing at the top of the stairs, looking like a picturesque couple as he wrapped an arm around her waist. The Celestial Councillors all strode inside followed by Seth, Caleb and Max. Darius appeared a step behind them, his eyes searching the space then landing on me.

He rushed forward, wrapping me in his arms and I laughed as he clapped me on the back.

"Are you alright?" he asked in a low tone.

"Better than I've been in a long time," I muttered then flashes of cameras fell over us as the press descended.

"Can we get a few photos of the Acrux family on the stairs?" a blonde woman called and I exchanged a smirk with Darius before we moved to the foot of the steps while Jenkins ushered the Councillors through to the lounge. The Heirs didn't leave though, creating an arc to one side of the room as they watched the shoot with interest.

Father's hand landed on my shoulder suddenly and I fought the urge to flinch, glancing at him with a polished smile. He returned it and I couldn't remember any other time he'd directed a smile at me.

"Now just the High Lord and his youngest son," a bearded man asked and Darius peeled away with my mother as Father stepped down to stand at my side.

He put his arm around my shoulders and tugged me close to his side. I fought the urge to laugh at the absurdity of it as the group of photographers gathered closer, looking excited as they snapped photo after photo.

I could see Darius and Mother in the corner of my eye, speaking within a silencing bubble as she clutched onto his hand. They were being careful not to make a scene, but the look in their eyes said that they were both desperate to bridge the gap that Father had forced between them with his Dark Coercion. Darius had already text me to say he'd be coming home the next time Father had to stay in the city and the three of us planned on spending some time as a proper family for once, without anything keeping us from loving each other the way we should. And I was looking forward to that with a desperate ache in my soul.

We posed for several more photos as Father kept his fake smile in place through pure determination and I relaxed as they finally called an end to them.

I thought that would be it, but a woman with steely eyes who I recognised as the head of The Celestial Times, Portia Silverstone – a woman whom my father always worked so hard to keep sweet - directed us outside.

"Let's see that Pegasus form then, dear boy," she asked. "We've got a few props for you set up out here…" She headed out of the door and the photographers snapped a few surreptitious photos of the Heirs before following and Father's grip on my shoulders tightened painfully.

I couldn't help a snort of amusement as we made it outside and found that Portia had set up a scene under the ash tree to one side of the drive. A bucket of carrots laid beside it and a large, checkered picnic blanket had been spread out next to it.

"Don't be shy, Xavier," Portia encouraged and Father released me, his arms falling stiff at his sides. "Let's see you shift."

My cheeks heated from the attention, especially as I started pulling my clothes off and the photographers had a field day over my new set of abs.

"We should book him in for a less family friendly shoot in Zodiass Weekly," I heard one of the reporters mutter and another laugh escaped me.

A youngish girl who I guessed was an intern ran forward with a towel before I whipped my dick out and I offered her a smile. "Thanks. I think I'll build up to the full nude shoot," I joked and her cheeks coloured with a blush.

My brows arched at that. I'd always been the less cool, less hot, less interesting brother in the family. And I hadn't really cared about that. But the way she was looking at me made me wonder if that was still going to be true after today. *Holy glittering Pegasus shit, what the hell is happening right now?*

I shot a glance at my father before I attempted to shift, nerves warring through me. I'd never done this under so much pressure before. What if I screwed it up? What if I burst into my form too vigorously, skewered Portia Silverstone on my horn and shit a rainbow in the process?

Don't be a dick today, stars. Pretty please with a cherry on top.

Father was smiling so hard, I wondered if he was going to break a tooth.

A smirk pulled at my features as I turned away from the crowd then leapt forward, letting my Order take over and spill through my flesh. It felt incredible. Blissful.

I shook my head and glitter tumbled from my mane as an excited whinny broke free of my throat. I trotted around to face the reporters and camera flashes blinded me. I reared up, enjoying the attention for once and giving them a show with a full on neigh.

The Heirs stood beyond them, clapping and whooping. Seth howled like crazy and Max crowed like a cockerel. Darius had the biggest smile I'd ever seen him wear and Caleb was just outright laughing as he stared at my father.

"Wonderful, Xavier!" Portia cried. "You are quite the stallion. The biggest I've ever seen. Are you proud of your son, Lord Acrux?"

"So proud I could burst," Father replied, his eyes dead, his smile still intact.

"Were you expecting him to be a Dragon? Was it a surprise?" the blonde woman called.

"It was quite the surprise," Father agreed, a bead of sweat rolling down his brow which he quickly dabbed at. "Astounding how the stars work, really. With so much Dragon blood, it should have been impossible. But here we are."

A whinny escaped me again as laughter crashed through me and Portia clapped excitedly before ushering me towards the picnic blanket.

I walked over, the scent of the carrots making my mouth actually water. I'd always liked them, apples too, was this why? I was always destined to be a Pegasus?

"Beautiful Xavier, now let's see your father feeding you one of the carrots," Portia encouraged and the Heirs' laughter rang in my ears.

I looked to Father as he strode towards me with his grin starting to look painful and he swiped a carrot out of the bucket, holding it out for me.

I chomped down on it as more cameras flashed and Father reached out, seeming unsure where to pet me for a moment before settling on my neck with one firm clap. Glitter tumbled down to the ground and plastered his hand. I could see how much he wanted to wipe it off as his arm dropped heavily to his side and his fingers flexed. It angered me how disgusted he was by me, by my kind. But I wasn't going to let that ruin my day.

The photographers had the time of their lives directing us into various stances, then finally freed my father from his moment in hell, calling the Heirs over to have pictures taken with me while he headed inside.

Seth stripped his shirt off with a whoop and the rest of the Heirs followed, laughing their heads off as they positioned themselves around me in ridiculously over-the-top poses.

Caleb lay on the ground before me with a carrot between his teeth while Max ran a hand down my back, smearing his chest with glitter and the others soon hurried to get themselves covered in it too. Darius stood by my head and I nuzzled into his face the moment the cameras flashed. This was going right up there with the top best moments of my life.

"Are we done?" Darius asked the press eventually. "I want to go flying with my brother."

My heart pounded madly at the thought. Flying with Mom last night had been euphoric and I'd envied Darius of his wings for so long, I was more than ready to do it all over again with him.

"Absolutely," Portia said with a beaming smile. "We won't intrude any further on this special day."

They started packing up their gear and the Heirs moved around me, petting my back and making happiness spread through every part of my body. Shivers ran through me from the contact and I never wanted it to end.

"He needs a herd," Max commented.

"We can be his herd today, huh Xavier?" Seth asked and I nodded my head excitedly.

"I bet you can't keep up with me," Caleb challenged with a smirk and I stamped my hooves impatiently as Seth stripped down and leapt forward into his enormous white Wolf form.

Max whistled at the intern who turned beetroot as she glanced back at him. "Can I borrow your backpack, love?"

She nodded wordlessly, dropping it from her shoulder and tipping everything out of it before tossing it to Max.

"Thanks," he said.

She nodded, darting away with her things bundled in her arms and I whinnied a laugh as Max gathered up Seth's clothes then held the bag out for Darius's.

My brother stripped down, tossing them in it and moving away from us before diving onto the lawn in his enormous golden Dragon form, an ear-splitting roar leaving him that made the earth quake.

I reared up in excitement, charging away from the other Heirs as Darius spread his wings and launched himself into the sky. I spread mine too, running faster across the grass and leaping off of the ground with two wing flaps as I climbed after him towards the sun. We tore into the clouds and there was something so achingly wonderful about the brush of them over my body. When I was Awakened, they'd be what I needed to recharge my magic and I could almost feel their connection to my soul humming through me already.

I flew beneath Darius in his immense shadow before circling up to fly at eye level with him. If Dragon's could smile, he'd be doing it right now. His gaze burned with a thousand emotions as glitter tumbled off of my body, leaving a gleaming trail through the sky as we started swooping and soaring around each other.

He soon took a nose dive towards the ground and I tucked my wings, following his every move and using the drag of his powerful body to pull me along with even more ease.

His wings stretched out as he pulled up just a few meters from the ground and Seth threw his head back, howling up at us from below with Max on his back whooping and pumping his fist.

Caleb raced along at their side, grinning up at us as we followed them towards the group of trees beyond the lake. I dropped down onto the grass, my hooves thundering along, galloping feeling just as good as flying as I kept pace with Seth. His flank rubbed my side and a zing of energy danced through my limbs. I needed this. I needed a herd, a group, a family. And I loved that they were offering me that, even if just for one day.

I wonder if Father will let me meet with others of my kind before I start school.

Darius flew up above the trees as we tore into them and we finally slowed to a halt beside a bubbling stream, shifting out of our Orders.

"Heads up!" Darius called as he plummeted from the sky in his Fae form and let Seth catch his naked ass on a gust of air as if he'd done it a thousand times.

Max tossed us our clothes and I pulled my pants on, leaving my chest bare and the others did the same as we dropped down onto the rocks, bathing in the sunlight filtering through the branches. I was hot as hell from the run and the heat of spring was finally starting to seep into the world too. It really was a new beginning for me. Not just for the trees and the flowers. This year, I was going to get to bloom with them.

"That was awesome," I exclaimed, grinning around at them.

"You're one fast horse," Seth commented. "You make me hungry for the hunt."

"Me too," Caleb laughed. "I was looking at that sparkly neck salivating, Xavier. You'd better get ready to defend yourself at Zodiac."

"I'll eat anyone who touches him," Darius commented, leaning back on a boulder with a smirk.

"You don't have to look out for me." I rolled my eyes.

"I'll always look out for you," Darius said with a shrug. "But I'm sure you'll be ready to kick ass by the time you enrol if you keep working out like you are."

"I wonder if he'll get two Elements like you," Max wondered aloud. "You're a fire star sign, right?"

"Of course," I said. "Mother and Father must have had our conceptions planned right down to the hour." I grimaced and Darius mirrored me.

"If I ever have kids, I'm gonna let them be whatever the stars decide," I said firmly and Darius glanced away with a tight expression, making guilt rack my heart.

"Sorry...fuck Mildred," I muttered and he nodded.

"You've got Dragon blood Xavier, you won't get off that lightly with Father anyway. He'll force you to do whatever he wants," Darius said sadly and I glanced around the Heirs, wondering how he was able to say that.

"Wait, you..." My lips parted as they all looked to me with sad smiles. They knew. And that could only mean one thing. Darius's Coercion was gone, just like mine had vanished when Tory had burned through it with her Phoenix fire.

"So you know everything?" I asked warily.

"Everything," Caleb said grimly as he cast a silencing bubble around the group. "We tried to talk to our parents, but there's not any evidence to prove it yet. They're being cautious though. My mom has had her suspicions about Lionel apparently. She said he disappeared for a while the morning of the Nymph attack at the Palace of Souls. She followed him, but he had a decent alibi and after they fought together against them, I guess she dismissed it. But now...hopefully they'll take this seriously."

"What if we went to the press and just told them everything?" I suggested hopefully.

"Father's got this all locked down too well, Xavier," Darius said with a sigh. "Until he makes a move on the Councillors and reveals his cards, there's nothing we can do but try to undermine his plans in the meantime. And at least the other Councillors can prepare for his next move to take the throne."

"Well, look at all these pretty boys hanging out in the woods."

The voice made my blood chill and I swivelled around, finding Clara hanging upside down from a branch in what looked like a wedding dress with a lace corset and a flowing skirt.

"What the fuck?" Max rose to his feet with his hands raised and Caleb dispersed the silencing bubble as he got to his feet too, a low growl rumbling through his chest.

Clara dropped from the tree, flipping upright and using the shadows to help her land softly. Caleb, Max and Seth inhaled sharply at the sight. Even though they knew about this, seeing Clara for the first time must have been disturbing. She was like a beautiful monster, her skin laced with shadow, her power emanating from her body almost loud enough to hear.

I moved to get up but she grabbed hold of the shadows inside me, keeping me still as she dropped into my lap and pushed her fingers into my hair. "Daddy locked me up in the attic, isn't he a bad, bad man?"

"Go back to the house, Clara," Darius demanded as fire flickered in his palms.

Her touch was icily cold and my stomach churned as she raked a fingernail down my neck. "But I'm hungry." She lurched forward, her fangs driving into my throat and I hissed, my jaw locking tight as she drank deeply from my veins.

The Heirs moved closer with danger in their stances and I shook my head to warn them off, not wanting this to descend into a fight. She yanked her fangs free again and grazed her fingers over my neck to heal the wound then giggled softly, getting to her feet.

She moved towards the others, brushing her hands over their naked chests and licking her lips. "I bet you all taste *wonderful*."

"You try and bite anyone else and we won't be responsible for our actions," Darius snarled. "Now go back to the house."

"But I want to *play*." She pouted. "And I found such a pretty dress to wear and none of you have even told me how nice I look in it. I think it was your mother's."

She released her hold on the shadows within me and I growled as I rose to my feet. "Father will be furious."

"He's *always* angry," she laughed. "And he has to catch me first anyway, but you wouldn't tell on me, would you Xavier?"

She rounded on me again with darkness in her gaze and Seth caught her arm to try and hold her back. She threw out a blast of shadow and he shielded at the last second, making the dark tendrils spread out over the dome of air like a spiderweb. Clara laughed then directed it at Caleb instead who met it with a tangle of roots that burst from the ground, deflecting it away from him.

"Go back to the house!" Darius snapped, raising his hands as flames flared in them.

Clara laughed manically like this was some game we were playing with her, rushing forward and closing his fists as she took hold of the shadows within him. He bared his teeth and she smiled sweetly.

"Don't shout at me, Darius. I don't like to be shouted at," she whispered.

A tremendous roar sounded from back at the manor and a twisted smile spread across my face. "Father knows you're not in the attic," I breathed and her cheeks paled a little. Which was saying something considering she was practically translucent.

She pressed her finger to her lips then raced away into the trees with her laughter tumbling back to us.

"I guess you heard about Clara," I said to the Heirs, folding my arms. "Father's new psycho pet."

The three of them looked from me to Darius, concern burning in their eyes.

"So we need to deal with her before Lionel," Seth said thoughtfully.

"That's how you win against a pack, cut the leader off from the strength of their inferiors."

"Yeah, plus if we get rid of her, Lionel won't have power over the Nymphs," Max added and hope suddenly lit a path through my chest.

We all fell into a conversation about how to fight back. How to win. And with the strength of the Heirs on our side and the Vegas too, I had the most incredible feeling that the future might not end up so bleak after all. We had a long way to go before I could truly believe that. But at least I wasn't alone anymore.

DARCY

CHAPTER TWENTY

I filed into the Tarot classroom for our first Arcane Arts lesson since we'd upgraded to learning about all kinds of fortune telling. The layout had changed since Astrum and Washer had run Tarot. The tables had been rearranged over the Christmas break into a crescent to face the front desk and the shelves had been lined with delicate silver and bronze instruments, plus crystal balls, scrying bowls and beautiful pendulums.

Gabriel was leaning against his desk as he casually spoke on the phone to someone. "-be home a little late tonight, I've got something to do. I know...." He laughed. "How hard is the baby kicking?...It matters because if it kicks like a pissed off-" He cast a silencing bubble as he noticed everyone in the class was raptly paying attention to him and he turned his back to us as he continued the conversation. Gabriel had told me and Tory about his wife being pregnant and I was pretty excited to meet her after everything he'd said. They were going to have us over for dinner one night soon and I couldn't wait.

I sat beside Tory who looked like she hadn't gotten much sleep again last night as she yawned heavily, taking out her Atlas and Tarot deck.

"I really hope I'm going to predict that I'm about to be sent back to bed for rest of the morning." She flipped over the top card of her deck and The Fool stared up at her. "Dick," she muttered and I laughed as she tossed the cards back into her bag.

"At least the cards give you actual predictions," Diego said with a frown. "I suck at this class."

"Maybe fortune telling isn't your gift, but you're good at other things," Sofia said from beside Tory.

"What's my gift then?" Diego asked and the three of us sat in thoughtful silence for a moment.

"Um…" Sofia tapped her lips and my brow creased as I tried to think of something, feeling like a terrible friend. He was still attending a few different kinds of Order Enhancement classes to try and figure out which one he belonged to. He now reckoned the sun was responsible for recharging his magic so he'd narrowed it down a little, but somehow he didn't strike me as a Nemean Lion or a Harpy.

"Your hat!" Tory announced proudly and I trapped a laugh in my throat, swallowing it down as Diego hung his head.

Gabriel dispersed his silencing bubble, turning to us with a stupid smile on his face from his conversation.

"Are you having a baby, sir?" Kylie asked from across the room, giving him the big eyes. I noticed a shiny gold badge on her chest with the word H.O.R.E.S. printed on it in bold, black letters. *And I thought being an Ass was bad.*

"Yes, in the summer," Gabriel said proudly.

"Aww!" Jillian squealed, holding her heart where she also had a Hores badge pinned. "Is it a boy or a girl?"

"We thought we'd keep it a surprise, my wife has banned me from predicting it," he said with the sort of smile that said he knew exactly what sex the baby was. "Right, today we're going to let the stars decide our pairs." He swiped up a gold pot from his desk and shook it about a bit before moving to the end of the row and holding it out to Tyler. "Pick a name."

Tyler reached into it, taking out a folded piece of paper and unfurling it. "Tory Vega," he said brightly.

"Good, you can all move once you've been partnered." Gabriel walked along the line and when he reached me, I dipped my fingers into the pot.

I plucked out a folded piece of paper, opening it and my heart sank. "Kylie Major," I said with zero enthusiasm.

"Ergh, *sir*, make her pick again," Kylie demanded.

"The stars have spoken," Gabriel said harshly and I sighed as he threw me an apologetic look before moving on.

When everyone was partnered, I gathered up my stuff and headed over to take Jillian's seat as she vacated it. She threw her shoulder into me as she passed and I growled, whipping my head back to look at her and casting a vine from the ground to snare her ankle. She stumbled with a shriek, catching herself at the last second and throwing me a scowl. I batted my lashes innocently before dropping down beside Kylie.

She kept her eyes pinned on Gabriel, her lips pushed out in a pout as I laid my Atlas on the desk.

"Today, we'll be interpreting each other's dreams using the guide written by the famous Dreamologist, Adelaide Som, over two hundred years ago," Gabriel explained. "No better guide has been produced since her pioneering work on dreams where she used her gift of The Sight and her Siren Order to study over twenty thousand Fae, following their dreams from inception through to materialisation. The guide is on your Atlases in the Arcane Arts list of references."

I located it on my Atlas and found a huge alphabetical list of all kinds of symbols found in dreams.

"Write down the last dream you can remember in as much detail as possible then swap with your partner and interpret each other's," Gabriel instructed. "It is often difficult to study your own dreams as we're so swayed by things like desired outcome. If you're hoping for something to happen, you'll often ignore the bad signs subconsciously and hunt for the answer you want. This can be dangerous, especially when looking for signs on a life or death situation. Of course, your partner may need more details about your life circumstances to draw accurate conclusions, so try to be honest with one another. In your junior year you'll learn how to detach from your emotions to be able to do your own readings, but only the very accomplished can master it."

We remained silent as we both took out notepads and I wrote down a dream I'd had last night.

Me and my sister had been out walking in a beautiful forest when a dark shadow had suddenly blotted out the sun, then a pack of five wolves had started circling us, moving closer and closer. But when they got near, they didn't bite like I'd expected, they turned to cubs, rolling onto their backs so we'd tickled their tummies and played with them in the wood.

I hadn't really thought much of it apart from the fact that it was kinda weird and kinda cute at the same time.

When I was done, I ripped out the page and passed it to Kylie while she wordlessly passed me hers.

I dreamed that I was on a beach, running out towards the water, but it kept getting further and further away. Then the ground became boggy and I was sinking and couldn't turn back. The water finally stopped moving away and the tide came crashing over me in a wave.

"That sounds like a nightmare," I commented, searching my guide for the word beach.

"It was," she muttered.

I found the term and read the description. "Was the beach deserted or were there people there?"

"There wasn't anyone there," she said quietly.

"Okay, well that means you need to take some time to yourself apparently."

"What about the rest of it?" she demanded, clearly not paying any attention to my dream as she stared at me impatiently.

I fought an eyeroll and looked up meanings for a wave. "How big was the wave that washed over you?"

"Really big, like a tsunami." She shuddered.

"That means you're about to release some pent up emotional energy," I read out, looking to her and to be fair, she did look like she was about to blow a blood vessel just from sitting next to me.

"And what about the bog in the sand?" she pressed.

"It means…" I found the word bog and one of the meanings mentioned being stuck in it. "That you're struggling with an unpleasant situation that you can't see a way out of."

Kylie huffed then turned to read my dream.

"Does that make sense to you?" I asked, wondering if I'd done it right.

"Yeah," she murmured. "Total sense."

I doubted I was going to get more out of her than that and I guessed I didn't really care anyway, but the look on her face did have me wondering what was bothering her so much.

"Walking through a forest in your dream means your soul is entering a new phase of enlightenment," she read out, then barrelled on as she found the next interpretation. "A shadow over the sun represents a dark change in your world…and the wolves…" She pursed her lips. "Probably means you're a grade A bitch with a Werewolf fetish."

"Excuse me?" I growled, but she just shrugged, her eyes pinned on the guide.

"A wolf symbolises a guardian in your life, so however many there were - like five did you say?"

"Yeah," I said, still pissed about the bitch comment.

"So you've got five guardians and I guess your sister does too, but then the cubs mean you're unsure of the wolves' true intentions. But I guess I can clear up one of their intentions for you because my Seth is only screwing you because he thinks it's funny that he can have a Vega princess who's supposed to be his enemy. It's obvious."

My brow pinched and I was about to lash back when I suddenly realised that she'd never been set straight about the rumour Seth had spread about us. And now that Darius had told him to back off, there was no reason for me to keep up the pretence.

"I never screwed Seth," I said firmly. "He blackmailed me into saying that."

"Ha!" She whipped around to face me with her eyes flashing green and snake-like with her Medusa form. "Why would Sethy bother? You obviously spread your legs as often as your sister does. It's not like he'd need to lie."

My hand whipped out before I could second guess myself and I slapped her across the face. She never saw it coming and her jaw dropped as she glared at me. "Don't talk about my sister like that."

"Sir!" she screeched. "Darcy just hit me!"

Everyone in the classroom was looking at us and I clenched my jaw, turning to Gabriel as I awaited my punishment. Whatever it was, it was definitely worth it.

"Did she now?" Gabriel mused. "And do you expect me to step in and fight your battles for you, Miss Major?"

Tory shot me a grin from across the room and I couldn't help but return it.

"Argh, I hate you," Kylie muttered and I scowled.

"Now, I want you to replay your dream in your mind and hunt for the more subtle symbols hidden within it that you may have missed," Gabriel called out. "Were there clouds in the sky or none? Was the ground beneath your feet soft or hard? Was it summer or winter? Think carefully, because this is where you'll find real depth to your fortune telling. Everyone close your eyes and do it now."

I shut my eyes and tried to walk through the dream again and remembered there had been little white flowers under the trees around me.

My Atlas buzzed and I cracked an eye, sliding it subtly off the desk and into my lap. I tapped on the screen and brought up Orion's message, leaning back in my chair so no one else could see.

Lance:

Come to mine for dinner tonight. There's a staff meeting at six so I can leave the door open for you while the place is empty.

I grinned, about to reply when Gabriel swooped over towards me. "You have detention with me tonight remember. Seven 'til eight."

I frowned, remembering no such thing, but he gave me a pointed look and I realised what this was about. My gift for Orion. "Of course," I said as my heart lifted. "I'll be there."

He nodded as he moved away, hiding a smirk as he scratched the corner of his mouth.

I glanced back down at my Atlas to find another message.

Lance:

I forgot to buy dessert but luckily I have a can of whipped cream and a voracious appetite for you. So I won't go hungry at least. Selfish fucker, aren't I?

A laugh escaped me and Kylie shot me a glare. I quickly deleted the messages and brought the dream guide up again, schooling my features.

"By the moon, you're so obvious. You could at least just admit you ruined my relationship and are still screwing my ex like the heartless bitch you are. What did he text you exactly?"

I rolled my eyes. "He didn't text me and I would rather screw a cactus than Seth Capella," I shot at her.

"*Liar,*" she hissed with poison in her tone and for a second I thought her hair was going to explode into streams of furious snakes.

"I'm not a liar," I snapped. "I don't want anything to do with him."

"You know what's worse than a whore with no class? A whore who can't even admit she's a whore," she snarled,

"Says the girl who's wearing a Hores badge, Kylie," Tyler called across the room. "I heard you have Seth's name tattooed on your vag with the words *insert here to make me howl* and an arrow pointing to your butthole. Is that true?"

I burst out laughing with the rest of the class and I swear even Gabriel snorted.

"Shut up!" Kylie snapped then glared at me as if I'd been the one to say it, and I sensed more than rage in her. There was genuine hurt too. It was enough to make me bite my tongue and turn away. She clearly wasn't going to listen to anything I said anyway. So why bother?

The lesson went by painfully slowly and Kylie interpreted every other symbol I remembered from my dream as meaning that I was a whore. So it wasn't exactly productive.

Relief filled me as the class finally ended and I headed out of the room with Tory, saying goodbye to Diego and Sofia as we made our way to Earth Elemental Class with Tyler. I changed Lance's name on my Atlas to Starboy so if anyone ever did catch sight of one of my messages, they wouldn't know who it was from. Not that I kept any of them for long. I also sang Starboy by The Weekend and Daft Punk in my head while I did it. Not that I knew ninety percent of the words. But I had the chorus down. Sort of.

Kylie marched past us with her head lifted proudly in the air and Tory flipped her the finger.

"That girl needs to get a life. As if you'd fuck that asshole. He made your life hell. You've got higher standards than I do."

Tyler snorted.

"I think she's just so in love with him she can't even see the bad in him," I said with a frown. Not that I was giving her a free pass, but I'd seen that look in her eyes. Her heart had been crushed when he'd broken up with her.

"Well holding a grudge is like drinking Faesine and expecting your enemy to combust in a fiery blaze," Tyler said. "And that bitch drank a gallon."

Tory and I laughed, but I was distracted as I spotted Seth and Caleb up ahead as we arrived in Earth Territory at the entrance to the caves.

Seth was doing a handstand on Caleb's freaking shoulders while the Vampire Heir ran around to see how long he could hold on for. The class was forming an audience outside, cheering and laughing as Caleb leapt into the air and Seth came tumbling down. He caught himself with a gust of wind, landing upright in front of his friend and bowing low while everyone applauded.

"Again, again!" a couple of junior girls cried, clapping as they bobbed up and down on their heels.

"Hey Vegas!" Caleb called as he spotted us. "Bet you can't do this!" He leapt up to stand on Seth's shoulders from a standing freaking jump then double flipped over his head and landed in front of him with a smirk as another round of applause broke out.

"The true queens could out flip your acrobatic asses any day!" Geraldine cried, placing her hands on her hips as she muscled her way through the students toward us.

I shared a look with Tory and she grinned the same time I did as a decision passed between us.

We dumped our bags and blazers on the ground, pushing through the crowd to the circle of space between them.

"I'll throw you in the air," I muttered to Tory and she nodded keenly, the challenge igniting in her eyes. Her cheer routine had proved exactly how prepared she was for this. And my Pitball sessions had gotten me good at propelling myself up in the air to block the Pit, so we were the perfect team.

I knelt down, cupping my hands together like I was going to give her a boost up a tree the way I had when we were kids and she crossed her arms over her chest with a smirk. She stepped into my grip and I boosted her skyward, throwing my air power into it and she shot up high above our heads, spinning around wildly in the air and making her skirt fan out around her to raucous applause from the crowd.

I guided her down to land softly and she immediately dropped to her knees, holding her hands out and linking them together for me. Caleb and Seth were watching us keenly, their eyebrows raised.

"Er, I'm not so graceful, Tor," I muttered.

"You can do it," she pushed and the fire in her eyes made me nod, not wanting to doubt myself in the moment of excitement.

I stepped into her hands, hoping I wasn't about to look like a handful of spaghetti tossed into the air. She propelled me upwards and I used the momentum to flip over backwards, my heart hammering as I zoomed back towards the ground.

I landed on the springy earth as Tory softened it and gasped as I only stumbled one step. *Hell yes!*

Cheers rang out and Geraldine was leading the Terra members of the A.S.S. club in a chant of *Vegas for the throne!*

I glanced over at Seth and Caleb who were sharing a conspiratorial look which made my heart dip.

"Child's play. Now let *us* throw you," Seth said with a dare in his eyes. "Bet you can't get three flips in before you hit the ground."

"Psh. That would rely on us trusting you," I said. "Which we don't."

"Yeah, thanks but no thanks," Tory said, tossing her hair over her shoulder.

"Come on, you could just save your own asses if we decided to drop you," Caleb said. "I'll throw you with my Vampire strength, Tory. It'll be fun. You can control the entire landing."

"I'll sweeten the deal for you Darcy," Seth said, stepping closer to me. "If you get three flips in and land without stumbling, I'll let you have a free shot at me. No shielding."

My lips popped open and I found myself walking straight towards him without question. Did I want to punch his damn face in? I sure as hell did. So was I going to pass up that opportunity for anything? No chance.

"But only if Tory does it too," Caleb agreed and Tory laughed, moving toward Caleb as he placed his hands on her waist. That was sister love right there.

Seth stepped forward and gripped my waist and the fresh, wolfish scent of him ran over me. His hair was pulled up into a topknot today and his mouth was tipped into a devilish smile. I hoped I wasn't walking right into a hunter's trap here, but I could use my own magic to slow my fall anyway.

In the corner of my eye, I felt Kylie's glare burning a hole in my head and I was pretty sure she would have actually melted my brain if she could have. She was getting the wrong end of the stick though. The wrong end of the entire tree actually. I was doing this for the punch that I was going to land on Seth's face. Nothing else.

"Ready, babe?" he asked.

"Always," I replied easily, like my heart wasn't pounding like a jack-hammer.

"Three full flips, no cheating," he breathed.

"I don't cheat and I don't lie either. Unlike you who's let his ex continue to believe we hooked up. That's just cold, Seth."

His brows arched and he tossed a look in Kylie's direction. "I didn't think she cared. We broke up ages ago."

I tutted. "You don't even know the damage you cause, do you? Sweeping through life smashing people's hearts while you're looking in the other direction. Do you even have a soul in that hollow chest of yours?"

He curled his hand around my back, yanking me closer with a feral growl. "You know I do or a certain someone wouldn't still be breathing right now."

My heart jammed into my throat. I had no answer to that.

"Are we doing this or what?" Caleb called.

Seth nodded, lifting me off the ground and preparing to throw me. "Have a nice trip. Don't hit your face on the dirt too hard."

I ground my teeth in determination and someone in the crowd shouted, "Go!"

Seth threw me with the full force of his air power and I shot up so fast, it took everything I had not to scream. A blur in my periphery told me Tory was close, but I couldn't focus on her as I started falling, gazing down at the ground over a hundred feet below us with a swoop in my belly.

I threw my head back and forced myself to flip, falling faster and faster. I spun over once, twice, three times, four then threw out my hands to catch myself before I hit the floor.

I have to land this right dammit.

I pulled up a foot from the ground and lowered myself gracefully, landing firmly on both feet just as Tory dropped down beside me.

Cheers rang in the air and I whooped, jumping on Tory and hugging her tight.

"Give him hell, Darcy," she said in my ear and I whipped away from her towards Seth with a fierce desire for vengeance in my veins.

"Fight, fight, fight, fight!" everyone in the class started chanting, thrilled by the bloodlust in the air.

Seth tapped his chin with a jibing grin like this wasn't gonna hurt him one bit. But you didn't grow up in foster care for half your life amongst the dodgier half of society without learning how to throw a good punch. And now that I'd been strength training in Physical Enhancement, I had the power to maim too.

I thought of every vile thing he'd done to me and threw my fist as hard as I could with a yell of defiance. My hand crashed into a solid air shield and a scream of pain escaped me as my knuckles busted and crunched.

An *oooh* rang out from the crowd and Seth started laughing his ass off.

"You asshole," I snapped.

"Woah, woah, it was just a joke," he said, reining in his amusement fast.

Tory hurried forward, wrapping an arm around me but I shrugged her off, fixing Seth in my gaze as a growl ripped from my throat.

"Screw you, your word means nothing," I spat.

"Not true, it was just a laugh. You have to admit that was funny," Seth said, looking to Caleb hopefully.

"Dude, I don't think the joke landed," Caleb said, running a hand down the back of his neck before turning to me. "We play pranks like that on each other sometimes."

"Hilarious," I deadpanned, raising my good hand and causing a storm to swirl around me. I was going to rip Seth apart.

"That's enough now, students!" Professor Rockford called. "Everyone inside."

"Here, let me heal it," Seth offered and I jerked away from him.

"Don't touch me," I hissed and a whine escaped his throat.

"Calm down, babe. I'll heal it and you can throw your punch."

"Seth plays rough that's all," Caleb said apologetically. "Break his nose, it'll make you feel better."

"No," I spoke to Seth, a dark energy rising in my blood as the shadows swirled inside me. He'd humiliated me one too many times. And if he thought he could just start treating me like one of his little pals with his oh so funny pranks, then he was going to think again. "In fact, I don't want any free hits from you anyway. When I defeat you, it's going to be because I'm stronger, more capable. And you're going to look up at me from the dirt and wish you'd never become my enemy."

Seth's gaze lit with a hungry kind of gleam and he moved into my personal space with a wicked smile. "You got one thing wrong, babe. There's nothing I like more than a worthy opponent. So come at me with everything you've got, because I'm starving for that fire in your eyes. I know you've got what it takes."

He headed past me and Caleb offered us a taut frown before striding after him. Geraldine rushed forward, capturing my hand in hers and releasing a channel of healing magic under my skin. I sighed as my knuckles mended, turning my head to glare after Seth.

"Thanks Geraldine," I muttered.

"No problem my dearest dandelion. That rapscallion needs a good bish and a bosh. What I wouldn't give to butter the wrong side of his bagel." She shook her fist in his general direction and Professor Rockford clapped her hands to encourage us along.

"He's got it coming," Tory whispered to me and I nodded, feeding on that seed of hate in me that was growing deeper roots and blooming into something truly deadly. I knew what he'd done for Orion was something I could never forget, but that didn't cancel out every bad thing he'd ever done to us. And I was determined to make him pay.

"I'm going to earn it," I said firmly. "Then my revenge will taste all the sweeter."

CALEB

CHAPTER TWENTY ONE

"**I** want the world's biggest cake," Seth announced excitedly. "And a mountain of presents. And balloons. And streamers. And party games. And drinking games. And we probably need a theme. Or maybe some kind of performers, like fire girls or maybe earth teasers, or how about-"

"Do I get any say in this?" Max asked, rolling his eyes. "Because the last time I checked it was a joint birthday party and yet I'm hearing a whole hell of a lot of things that *you* want to have at it without much consultation with me."

I snorted a laugh. Every year we had the same thing. Seth and Max were born within five days of each other, Seth right at the end of the Aquarius cycle and Max at the beginning of Pisces. And every year they had a joint party. And every year they spent the entire lead up to it arguing over the details before swearing that next year they'd have separate parties so that they didn't have to compromise on what they wanted so much.

This year they'd agreed to make the party air themed before realising that it's pretty difficult to make air decorations or really do anything with it party wise and so the arguments over what else to have had begun.

We were all sitting around the fire in King's Hollow while we discussed it, though Darius had barely contributed two words so far.

"I don't know why you always leave all of this to the last minute," I said in exasperation, leaning back in my chair. "The party is in a week and you still haven't even sorted the guest list."

"We don't need to sort the guest list, it's obviously a Hores exclusive event which will make the Ass brigade cry into their pillows with the knowledge of how much they're missing out," Seth said with a shitty little smirk. He was sitting beside me on the couch and was clearly feeling very Wolfy today as he kept brushing his hand over my arm and had nuzzled right up so that he was leaning on me. Generally speaking, my Order didn't go in for the touchy feely shit the Wolves liked, but I usually didn't mind it with Seth somehow.

"Right. But you still haven't picked a venue," I pointed out.

"How about out on the lake?" Max suggested. "I could freeze a section of the water beside the bank and we could create a palace out of ice and earth together exclusively for the party. We've got that practical magic assessment coming up anyway so we could use it to showcase our talents as well and kill two birds with one stone."

"Gah, that sounded great until you turned it into work," Seth huffed dramatically, flopping down onto my lap with an arm draped over his eyes.

"Seriously?" I complained and he shifted about with his head resting in my crotch and peeked out at me from beneath his arm.

"I'm stressed, I need body contact, don't reject me now, dude," he said, throwing a fake little whimper in for added effect and I rolled my eyes.

"Fine. But I'm not stroking your hair for you," I deadpanned as he grinned widely.

"Probably best you don't or you might get me hard," he agreed and I didn't even know if he was joking, but I laughed as if he was.

Darius got up and headed to the ice cooler to grab himself a beer. It was Saturday so I guessed it didn't matter if he was on his third beer...even if it was eleven am.

He'd been like this a lot the last few days. Quiet, brooding, detached from the mundane conversations we were all having.

I had a plan to cheer him up as my part of the deal with Orion and the other Heirs to try and break this curse on him and Tory, but I was still worried about whether or not it would work.

There were several issues with it. One: I'd been paying a hell of a lot of attention to the way the stars reacted whenever they got too close to one another and I was hoping I'd figured out the loopholes in it but there was really no way to test that before the main event, so I just had to hope my guesses were right.

Two: Tory had pulled away from me in the last few weeks and I wasn't sure if I'd be able to get her to trust me enough to follow along with my plan. But I also couldn't reveal it to her, or anyone else for that matter, in case the stars were listening in. Did stars have ears? No idea. But they definitely seemed to have eyes so I was going to keep my plans secret until the time came just in case.

Three: Darius did not play well with others, and he was a double grumpy fucker recently – I got why, but it just made my job harder – convincing him to try out my idea was going to be like scaling a mountain. But, I had the faintest glimmer of hope that if I could overcome each and every one of those obstacles then I might have been onto a fucking brilliant idea. Hopefully. Presuming it didn't blow up in my face. But for now it was all I had, so it was worth a shot.

"Can we at least agree on chocolate cake?" Seth asked, peeking out from beneath his arm and throwing Max the puppy dog eyes.

"I wanted vanilla," Max said, punctuating that idea by pushing feelings of desire and temptation over all of us until my stomach growled and saliva pooled in my mouth.

"Vanilla does sound good," I admitted, wondering if I could get some from the kitchen staff ASAP.

"Asshole," Seth grumbled. "Now I want vanilla too."

"Sounds like you've made a decision then," Darius said in a hollow tone. He did not seem to be in the party spirit. Not one bit.

The rest of us exchanged looks as he focused on his beer.

"So...how's Xavier doing now?" Seth asked tentatively.

It was always hard to say what way Darius's moods would go when he was like this. He could turn full Dragon asshole, bite our heads off, rip into us a bit and then tell us to fuck off. *Or* he might just open up. And this week, since Tory had snuck off to his manor and tossed Xavier out of the Pegasus closet for the whole world to see before unlocking all of the barriers in his mind, he'd been more prone to the latter.

"Better," Darius replied, a smile hooking up the corner of his mouth as he looked at us. "He's been allowed to do more interviews and the papers are all speculating about which herd he might join so Father is going to have to allow him to go meet with them. He's like the kid I grew up with again, he's got so much light back in him now. And it's made such a difference having Mother back to herself – at least behind closed doors. He's not alone in that house anymore. We've gotten something back with her which I didn't even realise I'd been missing so desperately... And all because Roxy had bigger balls than any of us."

"She's something else alright," I agreed and he shot me a look which said he was still a bit pissed at me over the hook up thing. But he'd also accepted it. It made me feel like shit but there wasn't much I could do about it without a time machine and even then, I wasn't sure I'd take it back. Tory had been hurting so much when I'd gone to her that night. She'd *needed* me, not just wanted. She'd needed something to pull her back from the brink of despair and I'd been it. It wasn't pretty or simple or easy, but it was life. And life just got messy sometimes even when you didn't mean for it to.

"How was she when you went back to your room the next morning?" Seth asked.

He'd been aching to ask that all week, practically bouncing off of the walls with his desire to know while Max banned him from asking. But was there really any point in us holding back around Darius now? He'd told us everything the night that his Dark Coercion was lifted and I was still reeling from all of the information about his dad, Clara, the shadows, the Nymphs... it was all too fucking much. And worse than that, there wasn't anything we could do about it.

We'd warned our parents of course but with no evidence to back us up, they couldn't make any moves against Lionel. They could only watch and wait and hope to be ready when he sprung his trap. Not that they'd been entirely convinced that everything we'd told them was true anyway. And I had to admit that I would have doubted it if Darius hadn't shown us the shadows himself, but I wasn't going to make him show my mom that. They'd arrest him along with his father if they found out he'd been infected with them. None of us had discussed whether that might mean he was stronger than the rest of us now and I didn't want to either. Darius was my brother. He was nothing like his father and I didn't for one second doubt him enough to worry about what he might do with that power. He'd never try to unseat us. Our bond was as unbreakable as sun steel.

"She'd left by the time I returned. Which is probably a good thing as the stars would have just forced us apart anyway," Darius muttered.

"So that was it?" Seth asked in disappointment. "No sexual tension filled moment where you found her in your bed? Or your shower? Or maybe laid out naked on the rug beside your fire-"

"She left a note," Darius growled, pulling a folded piece of paper from his pocket and tossing it on the table so that we could read it.

Thanks for being a gent and letting me steal your bed.

P.S.

I used your jacuzzi and it's still the most ridiculous thing I've ever seen.

"What does that even mean?" he asked in exasperation.

"That she…likes your jacuzzi tub?" Seth suggested.

"I just don't know what she wants from me," Darius growled. "You know she basically told me she doesn't like me biting my tongue around her all the time. Like, she *wants* me to goad her or argue with her or something."

"Maybe you should just try and talk to her about this whole situation?" Max suggested. "You could sit with us but use a silencing bubble to keep it private if you wanted, or-"

"I can lip read though. Just so you know," Seth put in and I snorted a laugh.

He shifted on my lap and shot me a smirk as I looked down at him.

"I dunno. I need to go and check in with Xavier and Mother anyway. You mind if I ditch out on the party planning?"

"No worries, man. We've got the party under control," Max said easily and Darius offered us an apologetic smile as he headed out of the room to make his call.

"I feel like we're stuck on a merry go round with this shit," Max muttered. "How are you guys doing with the plan?"

"I think I'm ready to execute mine," I said. "But to have any chance of it working I need them both in a good mood. More amenable to my suggestions."

"I'm winning Geraldine around…slowly," Max said. "She's all for true love but she also seems to want more of it to come from Darius than Tory, and with this defeatist shit he's got going on…"

"So we need to make him want to fight," Seth said. "I've tried to convince him to do all kinds of gestures for her, but he's not biting. In fact, he full on told me that oiling himself up and putting on a strip show with a rose clasped between his teeth was a stupid fucking idea. He even tossed my massage oil in the trash. And that shit was a new bottle."

"Your idea was for him to put on a dance for her?" I said through a laugh. "In what world can you see Darius doing that? Or Tory enjoying it for that matter? Besides, any asshole can make a fool of themselves, it's not exactly *deep* is it?"

"Oh you want me to go deep, do you, Cal?" Seth teased, raising his eyebrows at me suggestively and I rolled my eyes at him as a prickle raced along my skin.

"Stop flirting with me, asshole," I joked, shoving him so that he almost fell out of my lap.

"Stop smiling so much when I do then," he replied, giving me a dirty grin as he settled himself back in over my crotch.

"Whatever," I replied dismissively. "But you need to up your game if you want Darius to earn some brownie points with Tory anytime soon."

"That would be a lot easier if he actually believed there was a chance that they could be together in the end," Seth huffed. "Which is pretty hard to convince him of seeing as it's never been done before and I don't even really believe it myself."

"Well start believing," Max snapped. "Because he needs us to. I don't care if it's impossible or hopeless or like trying to believe that Griffin farts taste like cherry pie. Just do it. For him."

"Alright, alright, keep your panties on. I'll come up with something. I can do deep and meaningful. My plan will be the shit," Seth announced. "You two just crack on with your parts and leave it to me."

"Well, I need to get him and Tory in a good mood if I want to execute my part of the plan," I said with a shrug. "Which happens less often than Christmas at the moment, so-"

"You know what will put them in a good mood?" Seth said, shifting upright out of my lap to sit beside me again as he grinned excitedly. "A party!"

"I thought you were having a Hores only party?" I asked.

"Yeah, and Darius isn't going to enjoy a party with Mildred in attendance," Max added.

"Okay, so what if we just invite Tory as like a…peace offering type thing. Well, not peace but like in acknowledgment of the fact that once we beat her and Darcy out for the throne we will be open to having them as sub councillors or whatever," Seth suggested. "Then she comes, she parties, she's having a great time, Darius is having a great time-"

"Mildred appears and ruins everything," I interjected.

"Then let's make sure Mildred never makes it to the party," Max said with a dark smile.

"Oooh," Seth cooed enthusiastically, rubbing his hands together like a villain in some cheesy movie.

"I have been worried about her doors and windows," I said with a smirk. "I'm concerned they might be prone to sticking. And if she lost track of her gold and happened to have run through her magic in Elemental Combat before the party kicks off, she'd have a bitch of a time trying to bust out of there."

"Yes, yes! Hell to the fucking yes!" Seth shouted with a howl of excitement. "We ban the troll from the party, make sure Tory Vega is looking shit hot, get Darius in the best mood of his life and then shove them together. They dance, they have fun, there's so many people around that the stars don't get pissy. This plan has it all."

"Apart from the Vega in question," Max added. "We have to get her to come first."

"Right, yeah, that. Let's go convince her now," Seth said, pushing to his feet.

I smirked as I got up too, but I wasn't really convinced we'd get Tory to agree to this. Why would she want to come to a party with a bunch of people who were openly opposing her? I shot her a text all the same to find out where she was and smiled as she replied quickly for once, telling me she was in the library and not to disturb her unless I was bringing snacks. Snacks I could do.

"Okay, she's in the library and wants food if we're dropping by. Not that I mentioned you two assholes would be with me, but I'm sure she'll forgive me so long as I don't bring sushi."

"You go get the food then and we'll meet you there," Seth said, waving a hand at me to shoo me along. "And get me some Oreos. And milk. Don't forget the milk."

"Okay, asshole, but you'd better make good on your side of this plan because I'm starting to think me and Max are the only ones making an effort and you don't want the stars to curse your ass for breaking your oath."

Seth rolled his eyes as Max chuckled and I shot away from the two of them, swinging by The Orb for the food before speeding to the Venus Library where I leaned against the door as I waited for them to catch up.

They narrowed their eyes at me as they jogged up the path, taking in the bag of snacks and trying not to show how much it bugged them that I could literally beat them anywhere at anytime. Being a Vampire was the best and they knew it even if they'd never admit it.

"Here goes nothing," Max muttered as he pushed the door open and we headed inside.

We spotted Tory sitting in a corner with Darcy and Geraldine as they poured over a series of star charts.

They didn't acknowledge us as we approached but as I perched my ass on Tory's work, she was forced to look up at me.

"Did you bring the snacks?" she asked and I smiled brightly as I offered her the bag of food. She took it with a word of thanks and started handing stuff to the other two girls as they eyed us suspiciously. "What's with the backing singers?" She bobbed her chin at Max and Seth as they stood behind me and I glanced at them too, wondering if we were going to just ask her outright or build up to it.

"We wanted to ask you to come to our birthday party," Seth said, going all in as usual, pushing his hand through his hair as he offered her a smoulder. "Both of you," he added, glancing at Darcy. That hadn't really been the plan, but it made sense. It would be pretty obvious that we were up to something if we only invited Tory.

"As if the Princesses of Solaria would want to waste their time at a party filled with scoundrels and ragamuffins," Geraldine scoffed before turning back to her work dismissively.

The twins exchanged a glance and Tory leaned back in her chair as she popped open the carton of milk I'd grabbed for Seth and started dunking his Oreos in it. His jaw ticked with irritation, but he didn't comment on it which was a pretty impressive show of self control for him.

We waited for her answer while she chewed and I started tapping my foot with frustration.

"No," she said with a shrug and Darcy snorted a laugh. "Do you wanna get your ass off of my table? It's just that we've got our snacks now so we don't really need you to hang around..."

I bit down on a smile as I turned to face the other guys with my eyebrows raised, asking for a bit of help.

"Why wouldn't you want to come to the best party of the year?" Max pushed. "We're having a band, fire dancers, air gymnasts-"

"I thought we said we were having water strippers?" Seth hissed in an undertone.

The twins looked about as tempted to accept the invitation as they'd be if we were offering to take them to a funeral.

"Why would we want to go to a party filled with you and your Hores?" Darcy asked, rolling her eyes at us like we were just too fucking annoying to deal with.

"*Because,*" Seth growled. "Me and Max are turning twenty. It's a big deal-"

"For you, maybe," Tory muttered dismissively and Geraldine started laughing like it was the funniest thing she'd ever heard.

"Take your unsavoury invitations and skidaddle, you hooligans," she commanded with a waft of her hand.

"What if we invite your friends too?" Max suggested, his eyes firmly fixed on Geraldine. I wondered vaguely if he'd even realised how hooked he was on that girl. "You can come too, Gerry, and all the other Asses."

"Be still my beating heart, what a beautiful suggestion," Geraldine cooed. "I feel so honoured to receive this most wonderous of invitations. And look how stunningly crafted it is-" She unfolded an imaginary invitation and

Tory and Darcy grinned as she proceeded to pretend to read from it. "Their un-royal un-holinesses Maxy boy, king of the trouts and Sir Seth, ruler of mutts, formally request your attendance at their birthday party. There will be unsavoury characters around every corner and the chance of having your drink spiked with unmentionable potions. Not to mention amorous dongles galore, ready to invade any unwitting lady garden they can find. Please don't forget to bring a toothbrush and spare pair of panties just in case you fall for any of their baloney under the light of that tricksome minx Venus and end up on your back beneath one of them before waking up filled with morning after shame."

Even I had to laugh at that and Max grinned as he leaned towards her. "So you *are* expecting to end up beneath me then either way?"

Geraldine rolled her eyes dramatically. "Heavens forbid I get near your slippery eel again."

"But…don't you think this could be a good thing, for what we discussed? I've even heard that Mildred isn't going to be able to attend so we can call a ceasefire for one night only. Please, Gerry…" Max gave her an imploring look and Geraldine cast a glance at Tory before sighing dramatically.

"Well, I suppose we have nothing better to do, do we girls?" she asked, changing lanes so suddenly that it gave me whiplash. I guessed Max really was making progress with getting her onboard for Mission: Defy the Stars.

"Erm, I can think of a thousand better things to do," Darcy contradicted.

"A million," Tory added.

"*Please,*" Seth pushed, giving them the puppy dog eyes. "It's our birthdays…"

Tory pursed her lips and looked between all of us before her gaze landed on me. "No Mildred?"

"No Mildred," I confirmed.

"No slipping us potions?" she added.

"I swear, we won't do a single thing to hurt you for the entire night." I painted a cross over my heart and she glanced at Darcy who shrugged.

"Fine. But as I don't trust you for shit, I'll take a magical seal on that deal." Tory held her hand out to me and I smirked as I slapped my palm into hers.

"I swear that we will all have an amazing night without a single act of assholishness passing between us," I said.

"To not being assholes," she agreed and clap of magic rang out between us with a flash of white light as the deal was struck.

We headed away, leaving them to their work and I exchanged smiles with Max and Seth. Now all that was left to do was make sure her and Darius agreed to the next part of my plan too and it was on. Simple.

SETH

CHAPTER TWENTY TWO

I ran with my pack, lifting my head as I howled as loudly as I could, the noise ringing all across campus. We'd been up early and the crescent moon was sharing the sky with the rising sun, the two most beautiful celestial beings in the solar system united just in time for my birthday. Coincidence? Hardly. They were here to celebrate just for me.

Max's birthday was in four days, but mine was on a Saturday so it was the perfect choice for the party. And I was only a little bit smug about that.

I finally turned my pack back into The Wailing Wood and slowed to a halt where we'd left our clothes beneath an ancient oak tree to the side of the path. My Wolves gathered around me, nuzzling my neck before I shifted back into my Fae form and pulled on my sweatpants then pushed my feet into my sneakers.

Everyone was soon dressed, though most of them had arrived in their pyjamas so Alice was in a slinky pink nightdress as she approached me, running her palm down my chest.

"Happy birthday, Alpha." She leaned in to kiss me, but I gave her my cheek as a yawn ripped through me. She frowned, running her hand even lower. "Let's go back to your room and treat you." She bit down on her lip seductively and I was tempted for a moment. But lately I was getting kind of bored with having my every need met at the drop of a hat. Being treated like a king was great and all, but sometimes I ached for a challenge. And I seemed to be aching for it more and more lately.

"You go have fun, I'll catch you at the party later," I said with a wink and she looked as shocked as if I'd slapped her. They all started howling and whining and I scowled. *"Go have fun,"* I commanded in my Alpha tone and they whimpered as they shrank back then grouped together as they headed the path. "And you can join in today, Maurice!" I called as an afterthought and he looked back at me, his eyes wide and full of actual tears.

"Are you sure?" he asked.

I'd been making him stand outside the room while we fucked like rabbits for weeks on end as punishment for him taking over my pack after I'd gotten fleas. But as it was my birthday and I was feeling super nice today, I figured it was time to end his long spell of blue balls.

"Yep, go nuts," I said and he howled like crazy, jumping up and down while the others immediately welcomed him deeper into the fold. The rush of power that gave me wasn't quite as sweet as I'd wanted it to be. Maybe now I was twenty, I was getting used to being top dog all the time. But when you were at the top, there was nowhere else to climb. And that was just a little bit...boring.

I wanted to work for stuff in my life again. Hence why I was goading Darcy Vega at every chance I got. She had no idea how close she was to getting past my defences in Elemental Combat. I'd been thoroughly fucking shaken on more than one occasion by her attacks, but my cocky smile and unfaltering bravado gave her no idea that my shields had sometimes been a second from shattering or that occasionally, her attacks were so skilled, it took every ounce of concentration I had to defend myself. And I relished it. Fighting Tory didn't give me quite as much as of a buzz because her sister had it out for me so bad that she was practically on fire with it.

I'd been fighting with the Heirs my whole life and I loved that, but there was nothing like a new opponent. One I had to figure out, assess, conquer. This fresh challenge lit me up from the inside out. I was actually rooting for her in a small way. Though I could never tell anyone that. Because yeah it was a thrill, but the implications of that reality were not fucking good.

She was a Vega. If she beat me, that was it. It officially made her a worthy opponent. One who everyone in the kingdom would acknowledge. And I was going to fight my ass off to make sure that didn't happen. But the determination in her eyes and that desperate need in her to hurt me couldn't be ignored. Had I deserved it? Well, that was debateable. And it was also a debate I wasn't gonna get into with myself right now.

I whipped out my phone, shooting a text to Caleb with a smirk on my face.

Seth:
What are you doing?

Caleb:
I was *sleeping.*
P.S. Happy birthday. I have a present for you.

I bobbed on my heels as excitement ran through me.

Seth:
Well why don't you come and give it to me?
If you can hunt me down that is…

I pressed send, training my ears on the woods around me. He might be coming for me already, cheating bastard that he was.

Caleb:
Run for your life.

A laugh escaped me but I didn't run. I moved to the oak tree and started climbing until I was up in the branches, gazing down at the path below with a grin on my face.

My blood was pumping and adrenaline made my heart skip. This game was more than just a bit of fun for Caleb. I relished every second of it. But my favourite part was when he caught me and we fought like wild dogs.

The wind blew and sent my hair flying around me.

My muscles bunched as an instinctive prickle ran up my spine. I cast a solid wall of air below me and released a breath of laughter, loud enough for him to hear if he was close by.

He appeared in a blur and crashed into my air shield so hard, he was thrown to the ground on his back with a yell of rage.

I dropped from the tree, laughing my ass off as I fell on top of him, wrapping my hands around his throat. "Yield."

His mouth hooked up at the corner and he threw a solid punch to my side. "Happy. Birthday. Asshole," he said with every punch he landed, laughing with me as he shoved me off of him. I tried to get up but he dove forward with hunger in his eyes, grabbing my arm as he tried to sink his teeth into my wrist.

I bashed my other fist against his head and he snarled as he dove onto me, wrestling me into the mud as he tried to get near my throat. Our laughter had thoroughly died and I growled ferociously as I fought back, rolling us over and throwing heavy punches into his gut as we both scrambled to get the upper hand.

His dark blue eyes were alight with the bloodlust and he caught a fistful of my hair as I weighed him down, wrenching my head backwards as he lurched toward my neck.

"Fuck," I exclaimed as his teeth sank into a vein, my breathing quickening as he immobilised my magic.

He wrapped an arm around me and in a burst of speed, carried me to the oak tree and slammed me back against it, his fangs sinking deeper into my neck.

His body pressed flush to mine and a groan escaped my throat as his muscles hardened against me, unable to help getting off on this. He crushed me against the gnarled bark even harder and I wrapped my hand around the back of his neck, gripping him firmly as he fed. He was the only Vampire in the whole of Solaria I'd ever let drink from me. And I was starting to get a taste for these games, even the biting. *Shit does that make me a masochist?*

"Cal," I growled, my other hand running up the smooth plain of his back.

He pulled his fangs free, lifting his head to look at me and a line of blood spilled from the corner of his lips. I had the serious urge to lick it away and the look in his eyes at that moment said he might not mind that at all. But he was my friend, an Heir. I may have had more than the odd fantasy about him, but I never acted on it. Not since that one time where we'd shared a girl and *accidentally* kissed each other (or that was the way Caleb told it). We'd been absolutely fucking wasted. But we weren't drunk right now. And the way his body felt against mine was good enough to send the blood in my veins rushing really far south.

"I think you just sent a hurricane through my fucking throat," he rasped.

"Wouldn't be the first time," I taunted and he barked a laugh, making my gaze drop to his mouth again. He had morning stubble and bed hair. It was my favourite look on him. Effortlessly fucking gorgeous. It was a serious shame he was straight. Well, at least when he was sober.

His throat bobbed and I was aware our chests were still pressed together and there was no reason for that now. I still had my hand on the back of his neck and I dropped it, wondering if he'd step away, but he didn't.

"Where's my present then?" I asked, arching a brow and he finally stepped back, dropping my gaze.

He cleared his throat, pushing a hand through his unruly blonde curls. "Here." He shoved a hand into his pocket and tossed me something.

I caught it out of the air, looking down at the greyish rock in my hand. My jaw dropped as I felt the hum of power emanating from it. The call of the celestial being it belonged to. This stuff was rare. Rarer than a diamond growing on a Heptian Toad's ass.

"Moon rock?" I gasped.

There was a lottery every year in Solaria and the ten winners were permitted to visit the moon. You had to be one lucky son of a bitch to get a ticket and it didn't matter if you were the richest asshole in the world, AKA *me*, you couldn't buy your way into it. I'd tried to bribe the Fae who ran the expeditions a thousand times. Written him countless letters, visited him (alright stalked him and knocked on his door at four am – twice) and fucking begged him to give me a ticket.

No Werewolf had ever been. And we were *made* for the moon. Practically moon-born for the star's sake. But him and his fancy little magic that managed to transport Fae to the moon – which he kept a classified fucking secret though I'd tried to discover it on a gazillion occasions – was kept firmly locked down and guarded. So no moon trip for me. But I knew what this was in my hand because I'd seen those smug just-been-to-the-moon assholes waving them at the cameras on television every year while I seethed.

Caleb nodded then reached into his pocket again and took out a silver ticket that glittered in the morning light. He held it out to me and I couldn't even lift my hand to take it as I met his gaze.

"No way," I breathed, eyeing the words printed across it. My heart stopped. Actually ceased to fucking beat.

"Way," he laughed.

"No fucking way!" I pointed an accusing finger. "I swear to the stars, Caleb Altair, if you're screwing with me-"

He slapped the ticket into my palm. "I bought over three hundred thousand lottery tickets," he said with a simple shrug like it meant nothing. "In fact, I've been buying that many every year since you lamented on your sixteenth birthday that you'll never get to stick your dick in a moon crater. Figured it had to pay off eventually."

"You did this for me?" I choked out the words and he shrugged again.

"The moon's your favourite thing in the world, man. And I never know what to buy you."

I launched myself at him, wrapping my whole body around his and licking his fucking face because oh my stars, I was going to the fucking moon!

I howled and howled so loudly that Caleb had to clamp his hands over his bat ears.

"When!?" I bounced up and down and he shoved me playfully with a bark of laughter.

"In August," he said with a smirk and I hugged him again because shit, this was the best present anyone had ever gotten me. And Alice had bought me a vibrating butt plug once that had changed my life.

"This is everything," I told him stepping back. "Everything."

"Good." He beamed like an asshole, then clapped me on the shoulder. "You ready to party until we pass out tonight then?"

I grinned, feeling like I was never going to frown ever again. "You have no idea." And this incredible, momentous moment of my life made me decide on something else too. If I was going to visit the moon, then I was going to make her proud of me first. So I needed to talk to Darcy Vega.

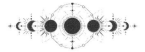

I spent the afternoon decorating the ice castle on Aqua Lake with Max, covering it in flowers and vines and growing huge lily pads around it where people could sit and make out or whatever. It looked fucking awesome. Even more so when I was heading back there in the evening in a nice shirt and pants; the whole place was lit up under the night sky by a thousand Faelights glowing in the windows. Darius, Caleb and Max were waiting on the lakeshore and students were heading across the ice into the castle's depths where music thumped.

The three of them dove on me as I arrived and I tussled with them, grinning as Max shoved a shot into my hand. A bartender stood nearby handing them out to everyone entering the party.

"To being one year closer to claiming the throne," Max said, raising his own shot glass while Darius and Caleb grabbed shots of their own.

I drank down the gingersnap rum then howled to the sky, ready to have the night of my life. The bartender ran around us, grabbing the shot glasses and replacing them with our favourite drinks in cups made of actual ice without a single word.

My eyes were drawn to Caleb and I gave him a surreptitious once over as I sipped my vodka and Redtaurus. He was wearing a black button down which his muscles were bulging against and a pair of distressed jeans. His eyes shone with that glint that said he was going to get up to mischief tonight and I was definitely here for it.

"So how did it go locking Mildred in her room?" Darius asked and Caleb smirked.

"She headbutted the door like a charging bull, dude. No lie."

Darius grinned darkly as we all burst out laughing. We had to do whatever it took to make him happy. He was family. The Heirs were a special pack to me. One where there was four Alphas and no bullshit. It was bliss.

We headed into the party where the central ice chamber was so perfectly fucking decorated it took my breath away all over again. I may have wielded earth to add the archways of flowers and the indoor garden in the next chamber over, but Max's magic really was something to marvel at. The dance floor glittered with rough crystals that ensured everyone kept their grip on it and to one side of the room was a steaming pool where students were splashing around with drinks in their hands. I could take credit for the bar, the whole thing carved out of a' huge tree I'd grown and shaped.

A round of wild applause filled the air as everyone spotted us and I waved my hand to cast a confetti of blue petals over the crowd. I emptied my drink before someone passed me another one and I was soon getting a light buzz going. We headed to the central room and the walls of ice glittered with purple, blue and pink lights. A DJ was blasting out tune after tune and students were already cramming onto the dance floor, going crazy for the music.

My gaze snagged on the Vegas dancing with the Asses across the room. Geraldine was grinding up against Justin Masters, wearing a flamboyant pink top hat to match her tight pink dress. I had to hand it to Max, the girl had a hot body. She was athletic in the way that made you wanna find out how flexible she was. Though I couldn't make much sense of the crazy stuff that spilled out of her mouth most of the time. Max seemed to dig it though. And he clearly wanted to dig it right then as he headed toward her and we all followed.

"Hey Gerry." He plucked her hat off of her head, flipping it onto his own and she rounded on him with a scowl.

"Give that back you overgrown seabass!" She tried to grab it, but he took hold of her waist as she did so and spun her around to the music. She fought for all of two seconds before letting him pull her closer and starting to grind shamelessly against him while muttering something about a devious dogfish.

"Hey babes." I nodded to the Vegas as they danced with their friends, completely ignoring us like we didn't exist. Though Tory's eyelinered eyes kept shooting toward Darius really unsubtly. She wore a two piece skirt with a floral top and Darcy wore a dark blue maxi dress which matched her hair. They looked hot enough to melt the whole castle.

I tossed back another drink and got a zing of confidence shooting through me. Not that I needed the confidence hit for most things. But there was something I'd been planning to talk to Darcy about all day which required me unloading a few of the emotions I kept locked down deep in my chest. And that shit was going to need the alcohol.

"Hey, can I have a word?" I swooped in to make my move, dropping my arm over her shoulders and trying to steer her off the dancefloor.

"You can have two." She ducked out of my hold, spinning to face me with a glare. "Back off."

"Please." I gave her my big wolfy eyes and she didn't even melt. Not even a little bit. And that was just unheard of. "It's my birthday." Totally pulled the birthday card. And I was not ashamed.

She rolled her eyes then folded her arms. "What is it?"

Winning.

"Come on, it's too loud in here." I gestured for her to follow me and she glanced over her shoulder at her sister, sharing some sort of silent twin message before heading after me through the crowd.

I led her down a corridor of ice with glittering lights strung above and a couple making out against a wall like they were having a *who can eat the most face* competition.

We stepped out onto a balcony which was like something right out of a fairytale, the view over the lake enough to steal your breath away.

"In." I directed the students who were hanging out there and they all scampered inside like mice, leaving us alone.

Darcy watched them go with a little unease in her eyes then straightened her spine as she faced me.

I leaned against the railing, pushing a hand into my hair as I jerked my head to beckon her closer. "Come on babe, I won't bite you." I gnashed my teeth playfully which earned me an even darker look.

I sighed, twisting to face the view and trying to tug out a few of those emotions I was always trying to pretend didn't exist. The problem was, whenever I unpacked them it felt like my heart was being kicked in with a steel-capped boot. And I hated feeling that way so much, it was just a whole lot easier to leave them undealt with. But I was going to try for once. Because…well, because it was my birthday and maybe I wanted to move into my twenties with one percent less guilt weighing down my organs. Plus I wanted to impress the moon. So there was that.

"Do you like the castle?" I asked her, gazing down at the water below. Max had used his magic to wield hot tubs out of ice that floated on the surface which was just about the most impressive water magic I'd seen. They weren't melting even a little bit.

"It's beautiful…but totally over the top." I sensed her moving closer and fought the urge to turn my head, sure she'd back off the second I did.

"Twenty is a big deal. I'm not a teenager anymore," I said with a shrug.

"Still an asshole though," she commented and I snorted a laugh.

"I'm just a creature forged by circumstance."

She tsked and annoyance flared inside me. If she knew the pressure I was under. If she had any idea what it had taken for me to get to where I was today…

"You'd have done the same, you know. If you were brought up like I was." I tried to disguise the bitterness in my voice, but it leaked in a little. I still wasn't looking at her and didn't plan to. Maybe it wasn't because I thought she'd run away though. Maybe it was because I was scared of what I'd see in her eyes. Hate. Contempt. Disgust.

Darcy Vega's eyes could cut into my flesh as keenly as a knife. And that was reason number three hundred and fifty eight of why I hated her back. Why I'd wanted to punish her from the second we'd met.

"You're wrong," she said coldly. "I'm not like you. Even if I'd been brought up in Solaria-"

"Bullshit," I snapped, trying to rein in my temper because *dammit* I wanted to try and talk rationally for once. Not bite and snap. I was making an effort and already royally fucking it up.

I turned to her at last and she lifted her chin. And there they were, those dark green eyes which held my downfall in them. The ones which were an ocean of goodness. I couldn't compete with that. It was the one thing I lacked in barrels.

Maybe I wanted to believe she would be just like me if she was brought up here, that her moral compass would have been swung to due south by society, by her parents, by the way of the Fae. Because the idea that that wasn't true meant one thing only. I was a bad person. A cruel, fuck up of a guy who wouldn't have been good even if I'd had mortal parents who'd molly coddled me instead of the ones who'd left me on a mountain to fend for myself when I was five years old. I loved my parents fiercely. But even with all their affectionate ways, they'd raised me harsh and cold. I'd been an Alpha in the making ever since I'd stepped off that mountain. They'd seen something hard in me and wanted to make it harder. And I'd let them because maybe I'd seen it too.

"Believe what you want, Seth," Darcy said, sounding tired of me. I'd probably be tired of me too if I was her. "Did you bring me out here just to try and convince me I'd be an asshole if we traded lives?"

A whine left my throat and I clutched the railing, forcing my gaze away from her again and trying to set free the emotions I needed to offload. To slit open the wounds I so desperately wanted to heal. Maybe this wasn't about putting on a good show for the moon. Something was plaguing me about her lately. That if I didn't deal with all the shit that had happened between us, I was never going to be worthy of the throne when I claimed it. I'd just be an unworthy fuck up who didn't deserve to rule his people. So it needed to be done. But I just couldn't...*dammit why is this so hard?*

After so many years of stifling and repressing my emotions, it was all locked down too tight. But I had to try.

"I don't want you to hate me," I forced out, my shoulders tensing, stealing a glance at her. She looked suspicious of course. "So...that's what I wanted to say," I finished weakly. Fuck, that was the worst apology ever. In fact, it wasn't even an apology. It was a statement. But even as I tried to think of a way to actually say sorry, the word got stuck in my throat and I heard my mother's voice ringing clearly in my head.

Don't ever let your enemies see you have a heart.

The box of emotions inside me ceased to rattle and I drew in a breath as I became numb all over again.

"You don't want me to hate you?" she echoed hollowly. "After you cut off my hair? Humiliated me? Hurt me? After you blackmailed me and my boyfriend?"

"*Boyfriend,*" I tsked, unable to stop myself as a surge of anger rose in me. I rounded on her with a snarl and butted against a solid air shield she'd cast around herself. But I wasn't aiming to hurt with magic anyway, I was going to do it with words. "You're living in a fantasy, Darcy. You're a Princess of Solaria. You and your *boyfriend* are going to end in a fiery fucking blaze if you don't stop it before it's too late."

Her eyes flared with fury. "Is that a threat?"

"It's a warning," I growled. "Don't be an idiot."

"I don't need advice from you," she snipped. "I know what I'm doing."

She went to storm away, but I cast a wall of air in front of the doorway so she couldn't and she turned back with her teeth bared. She was looking more and more like a true Fae these days. There was hardly any fear showing in her expression anymore. And when she got the last of it under control, she was going to be a force to be reckoned with.

"I *know* better. I know this world. And I know what they'll do to him when it goes to hell," I growled. "And do you know what will happen to you?" I stalked closer and that venom in her eyes seeped over my flesh, making it sizzle and burn.

"What?" she demanded on a breath.

"You'll fall from grace. You won't get backing for the throne. The papers will rip you apart. Seizing power is pointless if no one in the kingdom will work for you and help you rule the entirety of Solaria. Are you willing to lose your chance at that because of him?"

It wasn't like I wanted her to rule. Maybe I should have been encouraging her to keep fucking Orion and wait patiently for her imminent downfall. But I just didn't have it in me to swallow the truth. She deserved to know what she was risking.

A moment of tense silence stretched between us and I got to see what she was truly afraid of. It was written in every corner of her beautiful damn face. She wasn't scared for herself, she was scared for him.

"Leave Lance alone," she warned in a powerful voice. "If you want to take me on, then do it with everything you've got. But leave him out of this."

"Might not be my choice to make in the end, babe," I said with a shrug, dropping the wall of air.

She stared at me for a long moment and I opened my mouth to go on but she walked inside, taking out her Atlas, no doubt to text her Professor and tell him what a fuckwit I was.

And the award for the worst apology ever goes to...

TORY

CHAPTER TWENTY THREE

I hated to admit it, but the Heirs really knew how to throw a party.

The venue they'd created for the celebrations was seriously cool. The huge room crafted from a combination of earth and water magic took my breath away and I couldn't help but marvel at everything. From the walls built out of crisscrossing vines and layers of glimmering ice to the waterfalls which cascaded over boulders glimmering with veins of precious metals inside them, it was breathtaking.

The building was half on the lakeshore and half over the water itself, the surface of the lake frozen into a dance floor painted with patterns in the frost. At the far side of the room, a portion of the floor was missing and there were two pools filled with people who had chosen to go for a dip. One side had been imbued with fire magic so that the water was hot and perfect for the countless people lazing in it while the other was ice cold and gave access into the rest of the lake where Sirens in their shifted form were diving in and out of the water.

A bar had been set up using what looked like a tree that had been grown into the perfect shape to provide all manner of cocktails as the bartenders put on a real show of mixing them, adding magic to more than a few of the recipes as they went.

Geraldine dragged me through the dancing bodies over to the bar as she wafted a hand dramatically to cool herself down.

"Well, if I don't just feel like a turnip in a sack of potatoes," she gasped. "Sorry to be a Betsy Buzzkill but I just need a breather for a moment."

I laughed as I followed her to the bar and she barked at the people gathered there so that they moved aside to make room for us. And I mean she genuinely barked like a dog, channelling her Order form and damn near giving me a heart attack as the huge sound rang out from her lips.

"Two Footloose Faradays," she ordered and the bartender grinned as he began mixing her order.

"What's that?" I asked, watching as he added tequila to grapefruit juice then threw in some other dashes of colourful drinks and a few raspberries too before casting a spell over the canister then closing it up and beginning up an impressive routine of tossing it into the air and spinning around as he caught it again.

"It's a magical cocktail which helps you to lower your inhibitions," Max's voice came from behind me and I turned to look as him and Darius moved to stand beside us at the bar. "And can you make enough of those for all of us?" he added, catching the bartender's eye.

My mouth dried out as I looked up at Darius and he looked back at me with enough heat in his gaze to set my core burning molten hot.

I'd chosen a cute skirt and top combo in a bold flower pattern which left my midriff on show. The top buttoned in the front and I'd left a few open to offer up a view of the girls in my push-up bra which Darius clearly noticed as he closed in on me.

He took a spot right beside me at the bar with Max on his other side and my gaze drank in the sight of his muscles straining against the confines of the black button down he was wearing. Several buttons were undone at his throat and I tried not to think too much about what hid beneath them.

"You look incredible tonight, Roxy," he said in a low voice which sent a shiver running right down my spine.

"You scrub up pretty nicely too, Dragon boy," I teased with a seductive edge to my voice.

I didn't know why I was bothering to flirt with him considering our situation, but it was impossible to resist with him looking like that.

The bartender lined up four of the pale pink cocktails in tall glasses before us and I glanced at mine hesitantly. After the last magical drink I'd consumed had resulted in me grinding up against anyone and everyone I could get near, I was hesitant to repeat the incident. Especially as I remembered being all over *Diego* of all people. *Bleugh.* Even drunk Tory wouldn't have made that mistake. *Just imagine screwing him with that creepy grandma soul hat on. Ew.*

"Happy birthday," I said, shifting my gaze to Max and giving him a smile which was pretty close to genuine. "Are you having fun?"

"I am," he said with a wide smile, his gaze slipping from me to Geraldine as she totally checked him out. He was wearing a red button down and had a silver crown sitting on top of his mohawk with the words *birthday boy* scrawled across it. "Here's to me," Max said as he lifted his drink to his lips and took a long swig of it.

"Bottoms up!" Geraldine announced as she drank hers too, swallowing again and again until the whole glass was gone. "Down the hatch milady!"

I laughed at her and she bounced her hip into mine, knocking me sideways so that my arm brushed against Darius's and I glanced up at him again as I shifted away quickly.

"Aren't you drinking yours?" I asked as his pale pink drink stayed sitting on the bar beside mine.

"I'm concerned about what I might be tempted to do if my inhibitions are lowered," he replied, his gaze dropping to my mouth for a moment before hooking on my eyes again.

"Oh, I see," I said, nodding my head. "So you're chicken shit?"

He expelled a breath which was almost a laugh and shook his head. "Hardly."

"Is it more like you can dish it out but you can't take it then? It's okay to give me a potion that made me grind up against a bunch of random dudes in my underwear so that you could sell me out to the press and tell lies about me, but you don't wanna risk your own precious reputation on doing the same?"

Darius pursed his lips, but Max spoke up before he could.

"Technically *I'm* the one who put that potion in your drink and Darius actually tried to stop Seth from sending the footage to the press - but he was too late."

"Oh you devilish scoundrel!" Geraldine chastised as I looked up at Darius in surprise. I hadn't known that, I thought it had been all him if I was being totally honest. Though he clearly knew all about the plan and didn't try to stop it until after the fact so I still had a right to bear a grudge. "That move was beyond low! You don't see my ladies using tricks and lies to win this fight, do you? They are the epitome of poise and decorum and-"

"Would it make you feel better if I drank this then?" Darius asked me, cutting her off. "An eye for an eye and all that."

"It's hard to say," I replied, tossing my long hair over my shoulder as I glanced down at the drinks which twinkled with pink light as the magic swirled within the liquid.

Darius reached out and grabbed his drink as if I'd challenged him to, draining it in one as I watched his throat bob with each swallow. He took mine next and lifted it to his lips, ignoring the bartender's warning that drinking two would have more potent effects.

"So?" he asked me as he placed the glass down. "Have I paid my dues over this incident?"

"I'll be needing a half naked picture of you grinding up against some people you'd never want to hook up with before I'd say that," I hedged, my lips twitching in a smile. "And you'd want to get that posted online for good measure."

"Fair enough, but Father won't like it," he said, dead serious as he looked out into the crowd for someone who would fit the bill and began unhooking some more of his shirt buttons.

My lips parted in surprise as I realised he was really willing to do it and I wondered if the drinks could have taken effect that quickly or if he actually felt bad enough about doing that to me to try and make us even.

I was almost tempted to let him go through with it, but my gut tightened at the thought of Lionel punishing him for this game and I reached out to stop him, my fingers curling around his bicep as he looked down at me with a confused frown.

"Forget it, I was only joking," I said with the hint of a smile.

A girl stumbled as she walked past us, tripping over her heels and falling right between us so that my hand was knocked off of his arm. She smacked into the bar and cried out in shock a second before shifting into her Sphinx form and tearing through her dress.

"Fuck biscuits," she cursed on a hiccup.

Her underwear had actually survived the transformation which meant I had to try really damn hard not to laugh my head off at the sight of her huge lion ass wrapped in a black thong with her tail poking out the side of it.

She staggered away as some of her equally drunken friends hurried to help her while murmuring apologies and I looked back at Darius as we exchanged a smile. On occasion, the way the stars chose to part us was hella funny.

He looked like there was something else he wanted to say, but I caught Geraldine's hand and slipped away from him into the crowd before the roof could cave in on us or something as I tugged her back towards the dancing.

Darcy and Sofia spotted us and they moved to join us in the middle of the dancefloor where we carved a space for ourselves and danced to the beat of the music as I lost myself in the warmth of my friends' company.

The time slipped by and eventually someone rolled out an enormous cake with twenty tiers covered in candles as everyone moved to sing happy birthday to Seth and Max.

They both grinned as the chorus of voices filled the space and for a moment it didn't feel like we were taking part in some battle for the throne. It just felt like we were a group of teenagers enjoying a birthday party exactly like everyone else in the world would. I mean sure, most people didn't have twenty tier cakes and a table so overloaded with gifts that it had actually caved in, let alone over a thousand people in attendance, but blowing out candles and singing that song was universal.

Cake was handed out and I took a huge bite of vanilla goodness with a moan of appreciation as I grinned at my friends, icing smearing across my cheeks.

"I have a new game I want to play with you," Caleb's voice came from behind me and I turned to look at him as I sucked icing from my fingers.

"Is that so?" I asked, arching an eyebrow at him.

"Yeah. But it's a surprise," he said, leaning close to me and licking my cheek to get some more of the icing.

I laughed in surprise, batting him off as I wiped my cheek to remove his saliva. "What are you up to?

"How about you just come with me and find out? We made a deal, so you know it's nothing bad," he reminded me, his navy eyes twinkling with a secret.

I glanced at Darcy and she shrugged. "Go have fun if you want to," she said and I didn't miss the undertone which said she thought I might hook up with him. But was I really going to go there with Caleb again? I hated to admit it, but the only person I really thought about like that these days was Darius. But that was an impossibility now. So was I going to just become celibate because I couldn't have him? The scariest thing about that question was that I didn't even know the answer.

If the stars have stolen sex from me then is life even worth living??

"Look, just come with me and see what I've got planned," Caleb urged. "If you're not up for it you only have to say the word and I'll shoot you back here in the blink of an eye."

"You seriously won't tell me?" I asked, looking up at him again, my heart beating a little faster in response to the wild look in his eyes.

"I promise you'll enjoy it," he replied. "But you'll have to trust me, sweetheart. Can you manage that?"

I looked into his navy eyes, a playful smile toying around my lips as he suckered me in to whatever game he was playing. "I suppose I can. At least while you're bound by our deal," I replied slowly.

"Come on then." He offered me his hand and I took it, waving at Darcy and letting him tow me out of the party.

He didn't release me and I noticed a few lingering looks at our intertwined hands, but he didn't let go and I didn't care about what people thought of me anyway. I was already the sex addict who Darius Acrux had said no to, so what difference did it make if they thought I was sucking Caleb's dick too? It wasn't like I hadn't done it before anyway.

He led me along the lakeshore, looking back over his shoulder at me with a grin that was so filled with trouble that adrenaline surged into my veins. The music faded away behind us as we followed the path around the curve of the lake and Caleb kept shooting me excited glances as we went which had anticipation pooling in my core.

I wanted to lose myself in whatever trouble he had planned. The smile which was currently stamped on my lips wasn't easy to come by recently and Caleb had always been able to make me laugh. It was so hard for me to feel happy ever since I'd become Star Crossed with Darius, and even if he only helped me forget for a little while, it was still better than lingering in what ifs.

Caleb pulled his Atlas from his pocket as we walked, typing out a quick message on it and giving me a furtive look as he angled it so that I couldn't see what he was writing before hitting send and pocketing it again.

A few moments later it pinged in his pocket and he glanced at the reply he'd gotten, once again holding it so I couldn't see before smirking as he put it away.

I figured he was hoping I'd ask who that had been, but I didn't. It didn't make much difference to me anyway and I wasn't going to give him the satisfaction of refusing to answer.

He suddenly turned off of the path, moving towards a group of boulders clustered on the lake shore and I frowned in confusion as he led me around them and revealed a door hidden between the stones.

"What is this place?" I asked as he released my hand to open the door.

A long, dark staircase stretched away ahead of us, leading down to somewhere beneath the lake.

"This is an amplifying chamber," he explained. "It's a place created with an entirely equal blend of all four Elements, making the space inside entirely neutral. The natural amplifying qualities of the water above makes it easier to take a peek at what the stars have in store."

"So you want to take me fortune telling?" I asked in surprise.

"No," he said, smirking like a fox who'd just found his way into the hen house. "Put these on and I'll explain more once we're inside." Caleb pulled a set of bangles from his back pocket which I recognised from the fun house at the Fairy Fair. They would cut off my access to my magic if I wore them.

"Why do you want to-" Caleb's hand landed over my mouth and he glanced up at the sky for a moment before pushing the power restricting bangles over my wrists. He scooped me into his arms in the next breath and shot down the dark stairs before I had a chance to object.

I gasped as we plunged beneath the earth, moving down and down until finally racing along a passageway which must have led beneath the lake itself.

The world flipped upright again and I bit my lip as I looked around at the space we found ourselves in. We stood in a bubble formed of smooth stone beneath our feet and thick glass above our heads where I could just make out the movement of dark water against the other side of it. Around the edges of the room orange flames flickered in a circle and the air I drew in between my lips was sharp and fresh like the morning after a storm.

"This place is designed for Fae to look at the stars not the other way around, and it will mask our presence from them for the most part," Caleb explained, his smile widening. "The other way the stars can track us is via our magic, so while we're blocking yours, I think they won't know what you're up to."

"Why don't we want them to know what I'm up to?" I breathed, looking around at the magical space and feeling that equilibrium between the four Elements hanging in the air with a shiver of pleasure.

The black walls sparkled with silver mineral deposits and I realised that they'd been placed with care, replicating countless constellations all around us.

Caleb took a step closer to me, capturing my lips with his and making my heart skip a beat as he caught me off guard. I wanted to pull back but for a long moment I didn't, wondering if I even had any reason to want to stop this. Darius might have been different recently, but it didn't matter, did it? Even if he managed to pluck a star from the sky for me, I couldn't be with him now that I'd made my choice. It was all too little too late.

I still pulled back though, looking up at Caleb as he smiled like he'd expected that. "I'm not sure this is a good idea," I said in a low voice.

"You're thinking about Darius, aren't you?" he asked with a weird smile which said he was pleased about that.

"I…" I wanted to deny it but it was true no matter how unfair that was, how pointless. Caleb pushed my hair back over my shoulders and rested his hands on my upper arms as he waited for my answer. "Yes," I admitted. "I'm always thinking about him."

"Good."

I frowned as I tried to figure out why the hell he would think that was a good thing and Caleb ran his hands down from my shoulders until he'd encircled my wrists with his fingers and his grip tightened. He drew my arms behind my back, pressing my wrists together before creating a vine with his earth magic which secured them in place.

"I don't understand," I admitted.

"I've been spending a lot of time trying to figure something out and I think I might just have cracked it," he said slowly. "But I'm going to need you to keep trusting me for another few minutes. Can you manage that?"

My pulse quickened as I leaned back to look up at him, my eyes widening with anticipation and a touch of fear as I wondered what the hell he was talking about.

"Okay," I agreed slowly as I found something reassuring in his gaze. "But why do you want to tie me up?" I asked with a faint smile. The vine was tight enough to hold me in place, but I was fairly sure I'd be able to break it if I really wanted to.

"That's just the start." Caleb smirked at me as he reached up to his neck and slowly loosened his tie.

I watched him with my bottom lip between my teeth as he undid the knot and slid it free of his collar. He really was something to look at. Like a Greek Adonis brought to life with his golden hair and chiselled features. And for a moment I wished that I wasn't so caught up in Darius, that the stars would just release me from this curse and let me consider pursuing something with him instead. Or someone else, *anyone* else. Why did I have to pine for Darius forevermore as well as knowing that I'd denied myself my one true shot at love?

Caleb walked behind me again and I stayed still as he wound the tie over my eyes, blocking my view of the chamber and only leaving the faint orange glow of the fire lingering at the edges my vision.

"Caleb…" I said slowly, a hint of warning in my voice. I wasn't sure I liked being so vulnerable with him like this.

My voice echoed slightly against the cavern walls and Caleb stepped away from me, making me feel entirely alone down here beneath the earth and water.

"I promise you'll like this," Caleb said, surprising me as his voice came from right beside me instead of behind.

He ran his fingers down the side of my neck for a moment, caressing the spot where my pulse pounded beneath the skin before moving away again.

"If at any point you want us to stop, just say the word," Caleb murmured in my ear, his lips brushing against the shell.

"Us?" I asked, my heart beating a little faster as I frowned beneath the blindfold.

Caleb's only reply was a dark chuckle which sent goosebumps rushing along my sensitised skin. Footsteps approached and I stilled, straining my ears to try and figure out what was going on beyond the frantic pounding of my heart.

"Relax, sweetheart," Caleb whispered, his breath washing over my mouth a second before he ran his finger in a slow line along the length of my nose then brushed my lips in a feather light touch.

Electricity sparked right through to the base of my spine and I inhaled sharply, wondering where the next touch would come from.

The footsteps came to a sudden halt and I caught the sound of someone letting out a breath in surprise before the sound was abruptly cut off.

"Caleb?" I asked, my voice bouncing back to me from the cave walls, but there was no response.

I squirmed a little against the restraints holding my wrists. They were tight enough to keep me still, but I was aching to try and break loose. I almost gave into the temptation to do just that, but I fisted my hands instead. He wanted to put me on the back foot, he was probably half expecting me to bail out of this game already. But I wasn't going to back out.

I gritted my teeth and waited. A few seconds later, footsteps approached me again and I quickly realised there were two sets of them.

I fidgeted a little more, wondering why he'd brought someone else here and if I was being utterly stupid to put my trust in him like this. He was an Heir. This could easily be some trap. But he'd made that deal with me and so far, I was still fairly confident in my ability to escape my bonds if that was what I wanted. And for some reason, I wanted to find out why he'd chosen to do this to me.

"Sorry, sweetheart," Caleb murmured in my ear, making me flinch a little at his proximity. "I had to cast a silencing bubble to explain what was going on. I didn't want to ruin the fun by giving the game away too quickly."

"I don't understand," I began, frowning into the fabric of his tie which still hid the world from me.

"You will," he promised, his fingertips brushing across my neck and excited energy skittered through me.

"But-" I began just as another hand skimmed along the length of my jaw, a rough thumb teasing a line along my bottom lip and making my skin burn with a desperate *need*.

My heart pulsed with surprise. That wasn't Caleb. This hand was rougher, his touch firmer and the heat radiating from his skin sinfully familiar.

I opened my mouth to say something, to make some protest at the idea of the two of them moving around me while I was tied before them like some prize to be won. But before I could align my thoughts into words, Caleb's cool fingers teased through my hair from behind me, pulling it back over my shoulder.

The second hand traced a line with his fingers down the side of my face, skimming a path along my neck and on until he dragged it across my breast beneath my shirt. My nipple hardened in response, a jolt of energy flooding straight between my thighs as my breath caught.

I didn't want to give a name to my suspicions, but goosebumps were erupting all over my skin and a soft moan escaped my lips.

Not knowing where he was or how he might touch me next was making my heart pound like crazy and my breaths came deeper in anticipation of what he'd do.

Caleb's fingers slid through my hair and trailed down my spine, my back arching as the second guy painted a line with his fingers from my chin to the top button of my shirt.

His fingers plucked at it gently and my breathing hitched as he dropped it again, leaving it in place.

"What are you doing?" I asked, my voice breathy from the game already. "I don't know if I want to-"

"Come on, Roxy," Darius whispered in my ear and a shiver ran down my spine as my guess was proved right. "Show us what you're made of."

Before I could reply, his lips brushed against mine and every inch of my body set alight for him. I didn't have a chance to react at all before he moved away from me again and I was left in the dark and the cold, my skin aching for his touch.

This was a bad idea. I'd made my choice. There was no going back on it. But there was something about us being here, hidden from the world without me even being able to see him, that made me want to forget all that. Just for a moment.

"What do you say, Tory?" Caleb asked, his fingers brushing across my hands where they were still tied at the base of my spine. "I have a theory that with the bangles hiding both of your magic and me thrown into the mix while we hide down here, the stars won't be able to figure out what we're doing."

"And the blindfold?" I asked, my breath catching as I tried to buy myself a moment to process that idea.

"Because it's hot as fuck," Caleb said and Darius growled like he agreed with that.

I bit my lip, wondering if this was insanity just as Darius ran his fingers down the side of my neck, making me shiver with need.

"So, do you want to play?" Caleb asked, his voice sounding from my right.

My heart pumped harder, my breaths coming deep and heavy as I considered what they were offering me. It seemed crazy. After everything that had happened between us, especially me and Darius, I should have been screaming at them to get the hell away from me. But maybe I was a glutton for punishment or maybe I was addicted to the darkness because if there was even the slightest chance that I could have him, then I wanted it. My lips parted, my heart thumped solidly in my chest and a single word left my lips.

"Yes."

A kiss captured my mouth and I stumbled forward a step, recognising

Caleb as his hand caught my jaw and he turned my head to the right so that he could reach me better.

Darius growled like he didn't like that and his mouth landed on my neck, his stubble grazing my skin and I moaned as the two of them caged me in with their muscular bodies.

A hand slid to my top button, and my heart thundered adrenaline through my body as I realised I couldn't tell whose it was. Another hand made it to my bottom button and started working up my shirt to meet the first.

Caleb's tongue slid over mine and his grip on my face tightened as he stepped around me, turning my head to maintain our kiss as he moved to stand against my back, kissing me over my shoulder.

His body pressed against mine and I pushed my ass back, feeling the hard length of his arousal driving against me through the barrier of our clothes. My hands were still pinned in place at the base of my spine but I flexed my fingers, rubbing them along the length of him and drawing a groan from his lips as he broke our kiss.

I turned my head forward just as the final button of my shirt was released and the cool air of the chamber washed over my exposed skin.

"You're so fucking beautiful, Roxy," Darius growled from somewhere just out of reach in front of me, watching me while I couldn't see him.

Goosebumps speckled my skin as Caleb's hands slid around my waist, his mouth coming down on my neck.

His fangs brushed against my flesh and a gasp escaped me, my back arching in anticipation of what I knew he was about to do.

He bit down and I cried out at the sharp slice of his teeth but Darius's lips landed on mine a second later, filling me with heat and devouring my pain. I melted against him, my heart hammering a wild tune as the heat of him slid through every inch of my body.

His hands skimmed up my ribs until they found my breasts over my pink bra and a groan of longing escaped him as my nipples hardened at his touch.

The ground wasn't trembling, there was no sound of thunder, nothing to suggest the stars knew what we were doing and the thought of that was a thrill in itself.

My gut clenched as Darius's kiss deepened and I gave myself to him, knowing that I shouldn't, that this decision had already been made. But with his hands on my body and his mouth against mine it was hard to remember why. Everything about him felt so right when he was touching me, his heart beating close to mine...

An echo of pain raced through my chest at the idea of what he could have been to me. What he should have been. If everything had been different.

I kissed him with a desperate need to stifle that pain. I could taste the same desire on his tongue, that ache to make this more than just a stolen moment, to undo all of the things that had put us here and force the stars to change our fates.

Caleb withdrew his fangs from my neck and swept a thumb over the sore skin as he healed the wound away but I could barely feel it anymore, lost to the sensation of Darius's mouth against mine.

One of Darius's hands slid into my hair and my soul ached for him, my heart longing to be his in a way that wasn't possible. I drew back from the pain of his closeness, pushing my ass back against Caleb as I broke my kiss with him.

Darius let out a low growl, letting his own pain show as he acknowledged what I'd done, but I had to do it. I could take this pleasure from him but I had to keep my heart blocked off. I'd made my choice. I couldn't forgive what he'd done to me and my pupils were ringed with black to prove it.

I flexed my fingers along Caleb's dick again, tipping my head back to give him more access to me as Darius began to trail kisses down my throat, over my collar bone and on to my breast.

He dragged my bra aside as his mouth closed on my nipple and a moan escaped me as Caleb's hand found my other breast at the same time.

The two of them tugged and teased me, my breathing growing heavier as the combination of the two sensations sent my body wild.

Darius released my nipple and shifted lower before me, the sound of his knees hitting the stone floor reaching my ears as his mouth moved over my stomach.

My breath caught as he hooked his fingers into the waistband of my skirt. He dragged it down achingly slowly, his rough palms teasing across my thighs as he tugged it lower.

It dropped down to my ankles and I stepped out of it, leaving me before them in my stockings, stilettos, underwear and open shirt. I was aware that their clothes were still on even though with the blindfold and my hands restrained it didn't make much difference, but my heart beat a little faster at the knowledge that I was so exposed while they weren't.

I shifted my bound hands higher behind my back, awkwardly managing to hook my fingers through the loop in Caleb's belt and drawing a dark laugh from him as he moved away from me before I could do any more.

"Impatient little thing, aren't you?" Caleb teased, breathing against my ear before biting my earlobe playfully.

"Take your clothes off," I insisted breathlessly and the two of them laughed at my demanding tone, though Darius's grip on me tightened like he wanted to drag me away from Caleb and claim me for his own. I knew this wasn't natural for him, he wasn't programmed to share like this but he was clearly willing to push against his instincts for this chance to be with me and my heart beat harder just thinking of that.

Darius caught my left ankle in his grip, tugging gently until I shifted my weight onto my right foot and let him lift it from the ground. His fingers pressed against my calf through the fabric of my stocking as he slowly slid his hands higher, lifting my leg and forcing me to bend it.

His mouth landed against the inside of my knee through the silky material of my stocking and he began to carve a trail of kisses up the inside of my thigh, sending an ache of need right through me as he drew closer to exactly where I wanted him to be.

Caleb pulled me back against him more firmly, balancing me as Darius hooked my leg over his shoulder. Caleb's hand continued to toy with my breast, his mouth skimming down my neck as Darius passed the top of my stocking and my pulse thundered as his lips pressed down on bare flesh.

Darius's mouth fell on me over the barrier of my lace panties and a moan escaped my lips as I shifted my hips against him. His stubble grazed the sensitive skin at the tops of my thighs and his hands moved to grip my ass and hold me exactly where he wanted me.

His mouth closed over me, his teeth dragging against the thin material and sending a spike of pleasure through my body so intense that my knees almost buckled.

"*Fuck,*" I breathed, tipping my head back against Caleb's shoulder as his mouth moved across my jaw.

I could feel him smiling against my skin as he watched me fall apart under Darius's movements.

Darius continued to toy with me over my panties and I strained against the vine binding my wrists, wanting more, needing to touch them properly too.

Caleb slid his other hand down my side, hooked his fingers through the edge of my panties and a flash of heat flared along my skin as he used his fire magic to destroy them.

I gasped in surprise as Darius pressed forward instantly, dragging his tongue straight up the centre of me and sending heat tearing right through my core. I swore again, leaning more of my weight against Caleb as his grip on me tightened to keep me in place, his fingers digging into my hip almost painfully.

Darius moved faster, licking, circling and even biting me a little as he sent my body wild. I was panting in Caleb's arms, the darkness beneath the blindfold meaning my whole world was centred in on the movements of Darius's mouth between my thighs and I was sure I'd never felt anything so intensely before in my life.

Caleb stopped teasing my breast, shifting his hand down my side and sliding it beneath my raised thigh.

My heart started racing in anticipation of what he was about to do but I could only lean against him, my fingers still rubbing along the length of his dick where they were bound behind me.

Darius ran his tongue up the centre of me again just as Caleb pushed two fingers inside me and my back arched as I was overwhelmed by the two of them working together to destroy me.

I swore again as Caleb moved his fingers in and out and Darius kept up his sweet torment with his mouth. It was too much, my heart was pounding too hard, my whole existence narrowing down to what they were doing to me and nothing else.

I wanted to drag my fingers through Darius's hair or fist my hands in Caleb's shirt, but the vines on my wrists were keeping me still and I couldn't concentrate enough to free myself. I'd given myself up to the mercy of monsters and there was no turning back for me now. I could only arch my back as my body pulsed with need and they worked together to ruin me.

I cried out, my voice echoing off the glass roof as the combination of the two of them drove me to a climax so hard and fast that I could barely keep myself upright as it tore through my body.

Caleb withdrew his fingers, snaking an arm around my waist to hold me up as Darius drew his tongue across me in languid circles, drawing every inch of pleasure from my flesh before he leaned back.

He slid my leg from his shoulder and I managed to take my weight again as he pushed himself to his feet, moving his mouth up my body until he claimed my lips once more.

He kissed me roughly, possessively, demanding that I give myself to him and making me want to do just that despite all the reasons I still had to deny him. His hands wound around my waist as he dragged me flush with his powerful body, pulling me away from Caleb like he wanted to steal me away entirely. And the deep growl that rumbled through his chest sounded a hell of a lot like a warning too.

I yanked against my restraints again, needing to touch him as well, my jaw tightening with frustration at them until I managed to break one hand free.

I rotated my shoulders as I freed myself, letting my open shirt slide off of me as Caleb chuckled again, his hands sliding across my stomach, painting heated circles on my flesh.

I leaned into Darius's kiss, reaching up to skim my hands down his neck before making quick work of undoing his buttons so that I could explore his chest with trembling fingertips. I tried to paint the lines of his tattoos from memory, my eyes straining against the darkness of the blindfold.

Each touch took me by surprise as the two of them moved their hands over my body and my uneven breathing was met with theirs as I shoved Darius's shirt from his shoulders.

The longer I kissed him, the more my heart ached for him, making it harder for me to deny what the stars had wanted for us. This heat that burned between us, the twisting of my soul when I was close to him like this made it so clear. And in that moment all I wanted was to let myself be his. Even if I knew it couldn't last.

Caleb skimmed his hands down my spine and the fabric of his shirt whispered against my skin.

I broke my kiss with Darius, turning half way towards Caleb so that I could remove his shirt too. Caleb kissed me as I worked and Darius growled deep in the back of his throat, making goosebumps rise along my skin. This thing that was happening between us obviously wasn't easy for him; Dragons didn't share what they wanted. And he'd made it clear that he wanted me for himself. Seeing me in Caleb's arms was clearly driving him wild with a mixture of lust, jealousy and rage and a twisted little part of me enjoyed being the object of his desire and torment like this.

The heat of their bare chests pressing against my skin from both sides was consuming me, setting a fire burning in me which they were stoking out of control.

Darius ground against my side, pressing his lips to my neck as I continued to kiss his friend, his dick so hard that it dug into my hip, demanding my attention.

A spike of adrenaline ran through me at the knowledge of how turned on this was making him. He might not like watching me with Caleb, but it was driving him to compete for my attention and the thought of it set my blood pumping with anticipation of what he might do next.

I continued to kiss Caleb, my tongue dancing across his as I reached out to loosen Darius's belt. I unhooked his fly and pushed my hand beneath his underwear, taking the long, hard length of him into my hand with a moan of longing. I began stroking and teasing him, my hand moving up and down as he groaned hungrily against my neck.

I shifted my other hand down to Caleb's waistband, slowly unhooking his fly too as I pushed my fingers into his jeans.

Darius growled possessively again and the sound of it turned me on so much that heat flooded through my whole body. His fingers were digging into my flesh as he drew me closer to him, demanding more of me, all of me. And I needed more of this. More of *him*.

I broke my kiss with Caleb and turned to meet Darius's lips, his mouth coming down on mine hard and fast, need pouring through that connection as he tried to devour everything I had to give. Stamping his mouth to mine in a way that tried to claim me soul deep.

He kissed me with enough passion to light a forest fire, my broken heart swelling and pounding for him as every touch he gifted me burned me up until I was afraid I'd be consumed by the flames.

Darius dropped his pants, the soft thump of them hitting the stone floor sounding ten times louder to my heightened senses.

He dragged me around to face him fully, yanking me away from Caleb for a moment and I let him, wrapping my arms around his neck as Caleb shifted behind me. Darius grabbed the backs of my thighs and hoisted me into his arms as the sound of Caleb's jeans hitting the floor followed too.

My arms wound around Darius's neck as I kissed him, drowning in the feeling of this moment, my heart fracturing with the knowledge that it couldn't last.

Caleb's fingers danced across my back as he unhooked my bra and I let him slip it from my arms as I leaned back against him. He shifted to grip my ass, holding my weight as Darius positioned himself between my thighs. I moaned in anticipation, needing to feel the fullness of him inside me like I was drowning and he was air.

Caleb ran his tongue down the length of my neck as the two of them held me in suspense and I arched my back, demanding more.

Darius pushed inside me with a possessive growl and a powerful thrust that stole my breath.

I cried out as I was overwhelmed by the feeling of him claiming my body and Caleb's grip on my ass tightened, pushing me down onto Darius even harder.

My ankles locked behind his back and he thrust into me again, compelling another moan from my lips as I fisted my hands in his hair.

Caleb's chest was pressed against my back, his breaths coming quickly as he got off on watching us fucking right in front of him. But it wasn't enough, I reached behind me, gripping the hard length of his dick in my hand and matching Darius's thrusts with my movements along the length of his shaft.

Caleb groaned in my ear, kissing my neck as he slid his hands around the front of me, one teasing my breast while the other circled that perfect spot at the apex of my thighs as Darius started to move faster.

"Holy shit," I cursed as the two of them started to build a flood of energy in my body which was so intense it had my head spinning.

Darius kept pounding into me, his mouth finding mine and silencing my cursing as I fell into the fire of his kiss.

My body was tightening around him, my cries of pleasure bleeding out between our joined lips. Caleb was breathing more heavily against my neck and I could feel his body tensing as I continued to work my hand up and down around his dick.

Darius's grip on my hips was so tight that it was bruising and I relished the pain, wanting him to mark my body in every way imaginable.

We were all building together and my head spun as I lost myself in the feeling of their bodies against mine. I couldn't see anything but the faint orange glow beyond my blindfold. Every inch of my skin was alight with pleasure, every place they touched burning and tingling with need.

I gripped Darius's hair and kissed him like I'd die if I didn't. Because that's what it had felt like these last few months, like I was slowly wasting away without him, drowning, suffocating, dying. My lips were bruising, my flesh trembling and my muscles tightening around him as the two of them drove me to climax again.

A tidal wave of pleasure crashed through my body and I cried out, breaking my kiss with Darius as I felt him swell inside me as he followed me into oblivion, his grip on me tightening as my name spilled from his lips. My moans of pleasure were enough to finish Caleb too and his head fell against my shoulder as I stroked him through the final throes of it.

The three of us stayed locked together for several long seconds, none of us quite ready to relinquish the moment.

I reached up slowly, tugging the blindfold from my eyes and blinking in the dim light as I found Darius staring at me like he'd never seen me before and he never wanted to look away again.

He lowered me to the ground and we untangled ourselves from each other.

I bit my lip, heat colouring my cheeks at what we'd all just done as I quickly recovered my clothes from the floor. I pulled my skirt into place and started buttoning my shirt before I looked back up at them.

Caleb was smirking to himself as he straightened his fly and stepped back a bit.

Darius was staring at me, his pants on but his shirt still off. He stalked closer and I stilled, my heart leaping at the intensity in his gaze.

"You can't tell me you don't feel that when we're together. The way my heart pounds, my soul burns, my whole body aches...I *know* you feel it too," he breathed, catching my cheek in his rough palm and forcing my eyes up to meet his, the black rings in them taunting me with the choice I'd made. "Why did you fight it before?"

I looked into his eyes for a long moment, pain scorching through my chest. "Because I'm almost as afraid of this feeling as I am of you," I replied, offering him the truth for once.

My gaze slipped over his shoulder to Caleb as he shrugged his shirt back on. "You two are fated to be together," he said, not seeming the least bit uncomfortable with the situation. "If the stars don't realise what we did and you want to do this again then I'm more than up for that – because that was fucking unbelievable," he said with a grin. "And I feel like I owe you guys for all the times I got in the way of you. But I'm not going to try and stand in the way of destiny."

"We were made for each other, Roxy," Darius growled, tipping my chin to bring my gaze back up to his.

He leaned forward to kiss me and after what we'd just done I didn't see the point in stopping him. My heart lurched and I melted against him, letting him draw me close and dropping the walls around my heart for one fleeting moment.

It was an agony of the sweetest kind. My heart thumped endlessly against my ribs, my skin came alive with want and need and I curled my fingers into his hair, drawing him closer, never wanting to let him go.

He kissed me desperately, sweetly, painfully, all the need and longing he felt for me clear in the depth of that kiss as his tongue moved with mine and his lips tried their best to claim me.

"I know I don't deserve you, Roxy. But I don't think I can give you up even though I know that's true," Darius breathed against my lips and a tear slid down my cheek.

"It's too late for that," I murmured, the painful truth of that consuming me for a moment.

The ground began to tremble beneath our feet and I glanced away to find that Caleb had left us to it. The stars must have figured out where we were, their curse coming back full force after we'd managed to steal a moment from them.

"The stars might have decided that you can never be mine," Darius said roughly, refusing to move away from me. "But I *am* yours. No matter what. I don't care where we end up or who we're with, I'll always be yours. And I'm going to fix the damage I did to us even if the stars don't care. I'm going to prove to you that I could have been worthy of you if I'd just listened to my heart sooner."

"It won't change anything," I said, my voice cracking as I bit down on my bottom lip and tried to force the tears to stop.

"If it changes the way you look at me then that's enough," he replied, his eyes full of pain as I took a step back.

I wanted to stay, to talk to him, to tell him…I didn't even know what, but the chamber rumbled ominously and I glanced up at the glass dome which held back the weight of the lake fearfully and backed away again.

I broke away from him and turned my back as I hurried out of the tunnel and started running up the stairs. Caleb was nowhere to be seen and I guessed he'd really decided to leave us to it. I was just glad he wasn't there to see me cry.

Tears streamed down my cheeks and pain blossomed like a fresh wound in my heart as I ran.

I could feel Darius's gaze on me as I left him behind, but I didn't turn back. I knew if I did my resolve would shatter like the fragile thing it was.

I couldn't let Darius Acrux have my heart. No matter how much I ached for him. We were doomed anyway. Star Crossed. And even if we weren't, I just couldn't trust him with it.

DARCY

CHAPTER TWENTY FOUR

Idressed for the Aurora game in my navy and silver Pitball uniform with nerves making my belly flutter. It was like a bunch of nauseous butterflies had taken up residence right in the pit of my gut. Tory was on one side of me pulling on her cheerleading uniform and Geraldine was on the other doing lunges in her bra and panties to 'limber up' – or so she'd put it.

The sound of the crowd carried from the stadium above us and my heart juddered every time a horn went off or a wave of excited cheers rang out.

Oh my god, so many people are here to watch.

I'd been working my ass off in Pitball training, but nothing could have prepared me for the pressure of a game that actually mattered.

The press were here. It was my first match of the season. I was going to be watched like a hawk. Ridiculed if I fell on my ass. *Oh hell, I'm so gonna fall on my ass.*

The door opened behind us and several of the cheerleaders shrieked as Darius strode in wearing his Pitball uniform, making a beeline for Tory.

She was only in her skirt and sports bra, looking to him with her brows arching.

"Flans on a Friday!" Geraldine exclaimed mid-lunge. "This is the ladies room and Jacinta has her Petunia out!" She pointed at Jacinta who was struggling to get her panties up her legs, getting entangled as she stared at Darius's back in alarm.

Darius rolled his eyes, ignoring the chaos around him as he fixed Tory in his sights while I fought a grin at the two of them. I couldn't believe what Caleb had done for them and I was so happy that there was a way they could be together sometimes. Even if that did involve a threesome with two Heirs, at least she was enjoying herself. *Get it, Tor.*

"Cheerleaders sometimes support a certain player on the field," Darius said as he pushed his hand into his pocket and took out a navy ribbon with the word *Fireshield* on it. "Will you cheer for me today, Roxy?"

He held it out for her and I swear she actually blushed. "I'm cheering for Darcy and Geraldine too."

"We don't mind," I said immediately. "Do we Geraldine?"

"By all the rocks in Saturn's rings, of course we don't!"

Tory shrugged in answer, a smile playing around her mouth and he leaned forward and wrapped the ribbon around her throat and tied it in place.

"They're normally worn on the wrist," Geraldine whispered to me overly loudly. "This is most romantic."

"Good luck," Tory said and he nodded before heading out of the room.

I bit my lip, looking to her for a comment while Geraldine rested a foot up on the bench, pressing her elbow to her knee and perching her chin on her knuckles as she gazed wistfully at my sister.

"What?" Tory asked innocently.

"You know what," I teased and she fought a grin, glancing over her shoulder as if checking to make sure he was really gone. Then she cast a silencing bubble around the three of us and her expression became anxious.

"It's not that I don't like the sweet side of Darius, but…" she started.

"But what?" Geraldine gasped.

"What is it?" I pressed gently when she didn't elaborate.

She sighed, looking a bit guilty. "I just miss our back and forth. This isn't him. It's just a nice version of him. I want the *real* Darius, not some watered down version. And I need to be sure the real Darius isn't going to hurt me again. Like what happens when one day I piss him off and make him lose his temper again?"

Geraldine's jaw almost hit the floor, but before she could try and convince Tory otherwise, I spoke. Because I knew my sister, and I was starting to get a fairly good read on Darius too. And she had a point. He was on his best behaviour right now, but that couldn't go on forever. If they were going to find some way to make this work, she needed to know what long-term Darius looked like. And besides that, she lived for being kept on her toes.

"So piss him off and see how he reacts," I said.

"I've tried," she sighed. "He doesn't rise to me anymore. It's infuriating."

I nodded, thinking on it for a moment. Then an idea struck me that was completely insane but would definitely get a rise out of the Dragon.

"What about the gold we buried?" I suggested with a mischievous smile. "You could remind him you've still got it."

"My ladies, I must remind you both that riling a Dragon is not a safe expedition. I once sat on Angelica's favourite scrying bowl and she broke fourteen windows across campus with her roar."

Tory laughed, dispelling her silencing bubble as she pulled on the rest of her uniform. "Don't worry, Geraldine. I have a plan. I'll see you soon."

"Where are you going?" I called in surprise as she jogged away. "You have to cheer in less than fifteen minutes!"

"I'll be back!" she yelled then darted out the door and a laugh escaped me.

I was soon dressed for the game and so was Geraldine and we wished the cheerleaders good luck as they headed out of the room and made their way into the stadium to tumultuous applause. The sound brought my nerves back on in full force and I knotted my fingers together.

A knock came at the door then Orion's voice cut through the air. "Everyone into the men's locker room for a pre-game talk. Now."

The girls hurried out of the room and I jogged after Geraldine, the last one to exit. Orion stood beside the door in his black coach uniform and the second I stepped out, he blocked my path. "I need a word with you, Miss Vega." He pointed back into the room as the girls disappeared into the men's locker room across the hall.

I backed up with my heart pounding madly against my chest and as the door swung closed, he whipped me around to crowd me in against it and cast a silencing bubble around us.

"Nervous?" he asked with a smirk and I nodded.

He pressed his mouth to mine, kissing me deeply and making my heart pound for a whole different reason.

He released me, resting one hand above me on the door which made his bicep flex. "You'll do great. You've been killing it in your practise sessions. You're the best Pit Keeper we've had in years."

"Are you just saying that to get into my pants, Coach?" I teased and he chuckled darkly.

"No, Blue. I'm saying it because it's true." He smiled and my heart started to slow as I drew comfort from his confidence in me.

"Thanks. So are you wearing a cheer ribbon for me today?" I taunted and he leaned in closer with mischief in his eyes.

"Yes, but I had to wear it somewhere no one would see. So it's tied in a very special place."

I burst out laughing, gripping his waistband. "Are you telling me it's tied to your-"

"You can find out exactly where it's tied after the game, but only *if* you do well." He plucked my hand off of him with a stern stare that sent a shiver through me.

"Okay, sir," I said breathily. "Let's go beat Aurora then." I pushed away from the door and he disbanded the silencing bubble with a chuckle before we exited and headed across the hall into the men's locker room. The noise inside was deafening as the nine other team members were locked together in a circle, their arms over each other's shoulders as they chanted. "Zodiac will not be beat, Zodiac can take the heat!"

After the disaster that was the Starlight game – no thanks to me and Tory – Zodiac had fallen behind in the school tournament. We needed this victory to secure a place in the semi-finals. And I was determined to get it.

Max broke the circle, gesturing for me and Orion to join and we linked arms with the group as everyone starting running to the right. We ran faster and faster as we continued the chant, the circle locked tight together until everyone was laughing and breaking apart.

"Acrux, remember what we said about Aurora's Fireside?" Orion demanded as the team gathered before him.

"He uses fire to blind anyone on his flanks, so come at him from behind or in front," Darius said promptly.

"And what about their Waterback, Evergile?" Orion demanded of Darius's friend Damian.

"She's got weak ankles," he said with a grin.

"Who are their strongest players, Grus?" Orion swung toward Geraldine and she lifted her chin high.

"Their Captain and Earthraider, Oscura, their Airstriker, Paulito, and one of their Keepers, Fallow," she said immediately.

"Precisely." Orion nodded. "So I want all defence taking out those players in every round to keep this game swinging in our advantage." He pointed at me and Justin Masters. "Keepers, let me hear your tactics."

"Keep a two meter defence beyond the Pit. Don't leave the Pit unattended unless we hit the final round and are down more than a point and need to get their players out for minus points," I said then Justin took over.

"If anyone gets close enough, use the one meter, no-magic Pit Zone to our advantage by letting them step into it before taking them out."

"Good," Orion said. "So who's ready to beat Aurora?"

"We are!" I shouted along with everyone.

"Then why are you still fucking standing here?" Orion demanded with a smirk and we fell into line.

As Captain, Darius led the team out behind Orion and I took my place near the end of the line between Seth and Justin.

Adrenaline rumbled in my veins like an oncoming thunderstorm. I was excited and terrified in equal measures.

The roaring of the crowd sent another swirl of nerves through my stomach as we headed out of the locker room and up towards the pitch.

Applause exploded against my eardrums and lights blinded me as we jogged onto the field and I took in the incredible sight of so many thousands of people standing in applause for us. Our cheerleaders were finishing their routine and MC Hammer's U Can't Touch This came to an end just as they whipped their skirts up and bared their asses to the crowd, sending the Zodiac fans into chaos. I spotted Tory amongst them as they stood upright again, all jumping on one another in celebration and a grin of pride pulled at my lips.

The stands at the far end of the field were filled with Aurora fans in their black and plum colours and even they were clapping for our cheerleaders' routine.

We lined up opposite the Aurora team and I took in the pale boy opposite me with Pit Keeper scrawled across his chest. He gave me a challenging look and I offered him one in return before swivelling my head toward Professor Prestos as she jogged onto the pitch in her black and white referee uniform. Orion and the bald, broad Aurora coach headed away, taking seats at the very edge of the pitch beyond the forcefield that protected the audience.

Prestos held the starting Pitball out, gesturing for the two captains to step forward and a tense silence fell in the stadium as Darius moved to stand in front of the Aurora Captain. She was tall and beautiful, her dark hair twisted into a French braid down her back. Her eyes were as dark and as fierce as a sea storm and power emanated from every corner of her body. This was Rosalie Oscura, the best Earthraider in the school league, or so Orion had told us. She was born to the infamous Oscura gang who ran a city called Alestria in the south of Solaria. Not someone to be messed with. Well, not until she faced our team anyway.

"Fuck me," Seth breathed and I looked to him, finding him giving Rosalie the hungriest eyes ever. He looked like a wolf about to stalk a deer, but Rosalie didn't look like prey to me. She looked like a predator through and through. "Alpha," he growled to no one in particular and I snorted a laugh.

"You know you're talking out loud right?" I muttered and he blinked, turning to me in surprise.

"Werewolf," he breathed and I couldn't help but laugh again. "Pretty."

"You've been reduced to single words," I pointed out. "Maybe you should ask her out after the match."

"Yeah," he agreed, blinking out of his stupor. "Maybe I should."

Rosalie turned her head in Seth's direction, her gaze skimming down him approvingly. He puffed his chest out like a douche and she rolled her eyes before turning back to the referee.

"Good luck with that," I taunted, totally rooting for her to turn him down. He needed some of that air let out of his head.

"I don't need luck, I'm an Heir," he said proudly then the whistle blew and my senses sharpened as Darius and Rosalie collided as they fought to get the Pitball on the ground between them.

"Go on Darius!" I shouted with everyone else. His pure bulk was a challenge for Rosalie, but she was seriously skilled, throwing hard punches and winding her leg around his as she aimed to uproot him. He tried to tackle her, throwing his shoulder into her stomach but she just flipped over the back of him with incredible agility and snatched the ball from the ground with a laugh of victory.

I broke apart from the rest of my team as they sped forward to try and get the ball from her. But that wasn't my task. I had to get to the Pit. And fast.

My pulse elevated as Justin raced at my side and the Aurora Pit Keepers charged along just behind us. Orion put one hell of an emphasis on sprints during practise so we had the edge, racing like the wind towards the Pit and whipping around right on the edge of the no magic zone to face the game.

The Aurora Keepers took up tactical positions either side of us, ready to block our attacks as Rosalie raced toward us with the four Heirs on her heels.

Seth cast air shields in front of her to try and stop her, but she threw spears of wood at them, breaking through each one with her ferocious strength. I had to marvel at her skill as Darius caught a fistful of her jersey, setting it alight and she whipped it over her head, dumping it without even slowing for a second. The crowd went crazy and Seth and Caleb crashed into one another as they were momentarily distracted by her curves and the rose vine tattoo spiralling up under her push-up sports bra, sending each other crashing to the ground.

Gah - idiots!

I raised my hands, holding out for the very last second before I cast my shield. I wouldn't be able to recharge my magic until half time so every single drop I spent had to be useful.

Justin was bobbing on his heels to my right, heat emanating from him as he prepared to cast fire. We'd done this a thousand times, Orion had drilled it into us and despite the roaring crowd and pounding adrenaline in my veins, my body took over. I knew what to do and I wasn't going to let the pressure of the game get to me.

Max cast the ground to ice beneath Rosalie as he gained on her and she started skidding like mad before turning her hand to the earth and making a bridge burst from its depths that led right toward us. She ran up it with a yell of determination and combo attacks flew at her from our defence team members. Geraldine's ice shards scored across her arms and blood poured as she reached the end of her bridge, diving off of it above me and Justin.

I acted fast, my pulse throbbing in my temples as I threw my hand to the left, casting a billowing inferno of flames that sent the Aurora Pit Keeper flanking me screaming and running away. With my other hand, I built a shield of solid air and a flood of magic fell down on it the second I got the dome in place as the entirety of the Aurora team tried to break it and leave the Pit open for Rosalie.

Rosalie threw the ball, a javelin of wood leaving her palm a millisecond beforehand so it crashed into my shield and broke a hole in it big enough for the ball which sailed through after it.

I growled in determination, twisting on my heel and throwing air behind me as I leapt up to meet it. Rosalie landed gracefully, throwing out a hand to stop me but Caleb ran into her from behind, the two of them smashing into the no magic zone ringing the pit and hitting the ground as he wrestled to keep her down.

The ball slammed into my chest and I wrapped my arms around it with an *oomph* and my feet hit the mud on the other side of the Pit. I stumbled forward, my knees smashing into the ground as my heart thundered in my ears. The clock was ticking down to ten seconds and the crowd were screaming so loud, I couldn't hear anything else. I wasn't allowed to score, but Geraldine was just a few feet away, tearing up the earth as she sprinted forward with the look of a rabid dog as she opened her hands to catch it.

I tossed the ball to her, casting an air shield around her and saving her from a blast of flames from the Aurora Fireside just as she caught it. She dove forward with a scream, slamming it into the Pit and the noise from the Zodiac crowd totally deafened me just as a buzzzz announced the five minute round ending.

Geraldine scooped me up from the ground, throwing me into the air with her incredible strength and I laughed as the Heirs ran forward, piling on top of us and knocking us down into the mud.

"And Zodiac take the first Pit!" Prestos announced in her amplified voice and I laughed wildly, gazing up at the scoreboard through the tangle of muscular arms and legs weighing me down, finding us at one and Aurora at minus one from Caleb taking down Rosalie.

"Vega one, Oscura none!" our school were chanting and I laughed as Darius peeled me off of the ground and clapped me on the back.

"Good save," he said with a grin before jogging off to take up a position in the fire quarter. A grin bit into my cheeks as the other Heirs and Geraldine congratulated me then I headed back to stand in front of the Pit, feeling like I could take on the entire world.

Bring it on, Aurora.

MAX

CHAPTER TWENTY FIVE

I charged across the pitch, my fists coated in ice as I locked my gaze on the Aurora Fireshield who was thundering after Cal as he raced for the Pit with an airball in his hands.

I threw a blast of ice at the ground beneath the Fireshield's feet, a dark smile gracing my lips as he stumbled and I shot forward for the kill. But before I could reach him, my foot caught as vines snaked around my ankles and I crashed to the ground heavily, rolling through the mud with a curse of frustration.

I threw my hand out, a blast of air tossing the Aurora Earthraider flying away from me and she laughed as she tumbled, mud splattering up the back of her jersey and staining the name Oscura which was printed on it.

I cast a blade of ice into my palm and slashed through the vines before leaping to my feet and turned my eyes back to the ball.

The Fireshield took Cal down in a savage tackle just as I spotted them, but he managed to hook the ball away from him before it could be stolen.

With a cry of determination, Geraldine sprinted for it, throwing a tidal wave of dirt into the faces of the opposing team members as she leapt up and snatched the ball from the air.

I charged around the pit to flank her, throwing a solid air shield up around her as the Aurora players battered it with fireballs, water blasts and air strikes of their own. But they couldn't match me.

Geraldine raced for the pit, throwing a tremendous blast of water at the Aurora Pit Keepers. One of them managed to protect themselves with an air shield and the other fell back into the Pit with a scream half a second before Geraldine slammed the ball down on top of her.

The whistle blew to signal the end of the round and us winning the point and I bellowed our triumph to the stands as Geraldine took off on a victory lap of the pitch. She was screaming in celebration, arms raised in the air as she fist pumped excitedly over the point she'd won and I just watched her with a dumb as fuck grin on my face. Or at least I did until she grabbed the hem of her jersey, ripped it off alongside her sports bra and continued her victory lap completely topless.

"NO!" I bellowed as I charged across the pitch to intercept her, my blood pumping hot as fury charged my limbs.

I cast air at my back so that I shot towards her even faster and within moments, I'd wrapped my arms around her and tackled her to the ground.

"Great warthog balls! What are you doing you cumbersome sea cucumber?!" she gasped as she looked up at me and I kept my chest flattened to hers to shield her from view.

"Stopping you from flashing the entire school," I ground out in frustration. "And my dad by the way, in case you hadn't noticed that he was here too."

"Of course I am aware that your mother and father are here you ten ton terrapin! But why on earth should that matter to me?" She wriggled beneath me, but I refused to move.

I wanted to snap that that woman wasn't my mother, but of course I couldn't. "Isn't your dad here too?" I ground out, not answering her question because she might have had a point. There was no reason why I should care what my dad thought of her...I just kinda did. "And I'm trying to protect you here, by the way."

"Are you saying I should be ashamed of my buoyant Brendas? Because I'll have you know that the Fae body is a glorious thing and I won't have you try and shame me, Maxy boy-"

"You can't seriously think I have anything other than appreciation for your bouncy Bettys or whatever you wanna call them. I just don't want them on show for any and every asshole in sight," I growled.

Geraldine laughed beneath me. "Don't tell me you want me all to yourself, you oily octopus," she scoffed and for a moment I could only frown down at her as she mocked me for that idea. Because obviously I didn't want that. She was the leader of our opposition and seriously annoying with her constant insults and jibes directed towards me and the other Heirs. Not to mention the fact that she drove me to insanity most of the time.

"I think you dropped this, carina," a deep voice came from above us and I looked up to find Lionel's pet Storm Dragon, Dante Oscura, standing over us holding Geraldine's jersey out for her.

"Well, aren't you the gentle Fae," she purred, bucking me off of her with a sharp thrust of her hips which took me by surprise and knocked me into the mud.

"I wouldn't say that," Dante purred in that fucking Faetalian accent of his that always made girls act stupid.

Geraldine stood to pull her sports bra and jersey back on as Dante looked out over the pitch, whistling at his cousin as she moved back into her starting position. She waved enthusiastically at him as he yelled out to her. "Beat 'em to a pulp, Rosa!"

"I hear you were quite the beast on the Pitball pitch in your day?" Geraldine asked him as she finally covered herself up again and his mouth twitched into a smile.

"You make me sound like an old man, carina. But yeah, I would have wiped the floor with your team when I played. If I hadn't had to take charge of the family business, I might have gone pro."

"Daddy took me to a Blueshine game and I saw your wife playing with-"

"We need to get back to our starting points, Gerry," I snapped and Dante offered me a grin which made me want to punch his pretty boy face.

"Chop chop," he said, clapping his hands to herd me along as he backed up to take his Pitside seat again beside Professor Nox. "I want to watch Rosa kick your ass for a second time."

"Pfft," I grunted dismissively as I jogged back onto the pitch with Geraldine and headed for my spot in the water quarter.

"Well isn't he quite the specimen," she cooed as we ran. "I bet he could give Darius a run for his money in a *most smouldering Dragon* competition."

I frowned at her but she was already running away from me, moving into the earth quarter to take up her starting position and I gritted my teeth.

Why is she looking at other guys at all?

"Let them have it Max!" my dad bellowed from the stands as I waited for the starting whistle and I looked up at him with a grin, ignoring the sour trout face on my step-mom.

The whistle blew and a ball shot out of the Water Hole in front of me covered in pale blue ice. I threw a gust of wind at the two Aurora water players, sending them both tumbling away as Gary Jones leapt up and snatched the ball.

I gave chase with a snarl so that I could defend Jones as they raced for the pit, forcing all thoughts of Geraldine from my head.

I held onto my anger though, aiming it solidly at the Aurora Academy team as I took them down one by one with savage tackles and brutal magic attacks.

We were three points up, but that was by no means a big enough lead to start getting cocky. So I got my head in the game and prepared to fight to the death.

TORY

CHAPTER TWENTY SIX

The half time whistle blew and I smirked at Bernice as the Pitball team moved off of the field and we headed forward to start the cheer off against the Aurora Academy cheerleaders.

As the hosting team, we were going first and I twisted the solid gold ring on my index finger as I cut a direct line out towards our players. It was a chunky thing with a Dragon's head carved into it and was far too big for me, but that didn't really matter. I'd paired it with a ring on my middle finger which held a sapphire the size of a quail's egg and one on my ring finger with an onyx stone carved with an image of the sun on it. I'd wanted to add necklaces, bracelets and even a gold and diamond tiara to the mix but I had looked kinda ridiculous wearing all of that so the rings were going to have to do. It didn't matter that they were too big – a simple sticking charm made sure they weren't going anywhere until I released the magic.

The rest of the cheerleaders fanned out as they slapped the players high fives or offered them hugs if they weren't too filthy and I greeted Darcy and Geraldine enthusiastically before setting my sights on Darius.

I hurried over to him as he made it to the edge of the pitch and he turned back to look at me in surprise as I approached him.

Most of the Celestial Councillors had shown up to watch the match today but luckily, Lionel wasn't able to attend. Xavier and Catalina sat in the VIP box, waving down at us enthusiastically and I waved back before giving Darius my full attention.

The entire right side of his face was covered in mud, not to mention the rest of him and his torn jersey fell open to reveal the firm cut of his abs and that perfect V which dipped beneath his waistband.

"You're killing it out there," I told him truthfully, flashing a sweet smile which instantly had him narrowing his eyes in suspicion.

We hadn't exactly talked much since the whole three way thing and I was really curious about how he was feeling about that. But I was even more curious as to how he was going to react when he realised I'd been playing with the sack of treasure I stole from him oh so long ago. There were plenty of times when I'd thought about the little stash we'd hidden out in the woods and wondered why he hadn't asked for it back and there was only one reason that made any sense – he assumed I didn't have it anymore. I didn't know if he thought I'd sold it or destroyed it, but I was about to remind him that I still had it and see how nice he was when his temper flared. I was pretty sure there was a guide book or two out there about not poking a Dragon, but I guessed I was just too stupid to care.

"Thanks. Are you looking for me to make some cheesy statement like I'm thinking of you every time I tackle someone?" he teased and I laughed, tossing my hair. He frowned at me and I had to admit that might have been overkill, but whatever.

"Nice to know I'm on your mind every time you have someone pinned beneath you in the mud," I purred.

From the corner of my eye, I noticed Mildred rising to her feet in the stands with a face like an angry Koala which had been hit by a car. I didn't have long before she came over here to stake her claim on her Dragon, but I didn't need much time.

"I think I've made my desire to pin you beneath me pretty clear," Darius replied in a low voice which had my toes curling, but I wasn't here to flirt, I was here to poke a Dragon.

"Good luck for the second half," I said in a sweet voice, reaching out touch his bicep, making sure that the gold rings pressed against his skin.

Darius looked down the moment he felt his magic stir in response to the gold and his eyes widened in surprise which was quickly followed by a flash of fury as he recognised the jewellery from his stash which I'd stolen.

I whirled away from him with a dark laugh before he could do any more than suck in an angry breath and I jogged out to join my squad just as they started up a chant.

V – E – G – A!

She'll wipe the floor with you today!

Veeeeega! Veeeeega!

I fell into the moves of the chant, clapping my hands as some of the others rustled pom-poms and Darcy offered me an appreciative smile from the side of the pitch. We had little chants like that for all of the team members, but we often forgot to call out for the Heirs.

The music suddenly dropped and 7 Rings by Ariana Grande burst from speakers around the stadium as we moved into a full routine filled with dance moves and tricks. The song choice turned out to be perfect for taunting a gold obsessed Dragon as well as performing a badass routine to and I couldn't help but smirk like a psychopath throughout.

Darius stood glaring at me from the side of the pitch even when Seth tried to drag him into the locker rooms and my heart thundered at the pure fury in his eyes.

Remind me again why I thought poking the Dragon was a good idea because he looks ready to shit a brick!

I turned my eyes from him, grinning out at the crowd as I moved between my girls, running forward as I performed a set of hand springs which ended in me throwing a huge blast of multicoloured petals up into the air so that they fell over the crowd.

The other girls swarmed around me, casting their own magic in sweeping arcs over our heads, fire and water colliding and cancelling each other out in clouds of steam which the air Elementals whipped up into a mini tornado which caught a lot of the petals in it before throwing them all over the crowd again.

I ran forward and leapt up into the air with Phoenix Fire bursting from my outstretched palms, arching up toward the open roof high above us before I executed a perfect flip and used my air magic to land it.

The crowd erupted into cheers for us as I grinned at them, but my gaze was drawn back to Darius as he glared at me with his jaw tight and his Alpha Dragon bristling beneath his flesh.

Was this a terrible idea? Maybe. But did I need to see what he'd do when I backed him into a corner? Damn right I did.

Orion appeared beside him, cutting a dark glance my way before grabbing his arm and forcing him to head on down to the locker rooms for their half time pep talk and magic recharging.

A nervous laugh spilled from my lips as Darius finally tore that furious gaze from me and I wriggled my fingers in farewell as he backed away, the gold rings flashing in the light.

The look in his black-ringed eyes was filled with darkness and violence and the shadows inside of me were having a fucking field day over that, but I pushed them down hard, refusing to rise.

Darius might have been trying to remain calm and considerate towards me up until now, but he didn't have to. And it wasn't like I wanted an all out war – I was just sick of him tiptoeing around me.

He'd been doing a damn good job of keeping that beast within his flesh asleep around me since I'd cursed us, but now I'd woken it again, I was actually a little excited to let myself get burnt.

DARIUS

CHAPTER TWENTY SEVEN

I raced across the pitch with Max right on my heels in the second half of the game, chasing down the Aurora Earthraider, Rosalie Oscura, as she sprinted around the pit, howling at the sky like she already thought she'd won it.

We were in the final round of the game, the timer ticking down the last minutes and Zodiac were six points up. She was trying to buy time as every member of her team went on the defence and tried to score points by pinning our players in the mud.

Orion was bellowing at me to run faster and out of the corner of my eye, I spotted three of their teammates overwhelming Justin Masters and slamming him into the dirt. Our lead was down to five points and the little Wolf I was chasing howled again.

She was fucking fast, I'd give her that, but as Seth and Cal circled the other side of the pit to cut her off, she had to know she was done for.

"Come and get me boys!" she hollered, slowing down for a moment as we closed in on her.

I raced forward but suddenly, the ground beneath my feet disappeared as she carved a huge chasm into the earth all around her and the four of us dropped down into it immediately.

A snarl of rage escaped me as I cast water beneath my feet, using it to blast me up and out of the crater again as she raced away once more.

Seth sent vines to trip her, but she danced over them with a bark of laughter before tossing up a wall of dirt to block the fireball Cal shot her way.

I didn't bother with magic, letting the other three aim their power at her as I ran for the kill.

She charged towards the pit as Darcy stood before it, arms wide as she cast a wall of air to block the ball. Rosalie threw her free hand out and suddenly, the earth beneath Darcy's feet collapsed, causing her and all of the Pit Keepers to fall down into the Pit which was now twice the size it had been.

She threw the ball with a howl of glee half a second before I slammed into her and pinned her down in the mud with a deep growl.

I turned to see if she'd scored the Pit but as the ball shot towards it, it collided with an air shield, bouncing back off again as Darcy managed to maintain it despite her fall.

Seth howled wildly as he leapt up to catch the ball and Darcy dropped the shield half a second before he slammed it down into the Pit and the whistle blew to sound the end of the game and our victory.

"Are you going to stay on top of me all evening, stronzo? Because if that's your plan, we could do with getting rid of some of these clothes," Rosalie purred as she wriggled beneath me.

I snorted a laugh as my attention moved back to the girl I was crushing and I stood, offering her a hand up as I grinned my fucking head off. The moment she was standing, I released her and ran across the pitch with a roar of victory as my team all leapt on each other in celebration and we jumped up and down in a tangle of limbs.

Seth howled to the sky and every member of our team joined in a second before Lance jumped onto the pile too and we all fell back in the mud laughing.

I caught Darcy's eye as she grinned at me and a deep laugh escaped me as I pulled her in for a hug. "Nice work on that shield, Gwen," I teased, scrubbing my knuckles into her hair as she shoved me off.

"Nice work on that tackle, Dari," she joked back just as Lance leapt on me.

"You fucking beauty!" he snarled, grabbing my face between his hands and placing a rough, scratchy kiss on my forehead as he straddled me in the mud.

The other Heirs all started piling on top of us one after another and when we were finally done exchanging hugs and congratulations, we stood to accept the applause from the crowd.

Rosalie Oscura was running back and forth on the far side of the pitch, howling excitedly as the students from Aurora Academy went wild for her. And I guessed for the lowest funded academy in Solaria, coming that damn close to beating us was almost as good as winning. They'd definitely stepped up their game in the last few years and we'd have to be even more prepared for them next season.

The cheerleaders were all up, jumping around and calling out our names and I caught Roxy's eye as she shook a pair of sparkly pom-poms at me and called my name out along with the rest.

My gaze snagged on my rings on her fingers as she continued to flaunt them at me and a growl rumbled through my chest.

I took off across the pitch towards her as Nova's voice rang out announcing the final scores as if no one could read the scoreboard for themselves.

"I want my treasure back," I said in a low voice, gravel coating my tone as my Dragon shifted beneath my skin. I came to a halt right in front of her and she gave me a killer smile which said she'd been dying for me to ask.

"I don't know what you mean," Roxy replied sweetly, moving to stand in front of me with her hands on her hips, pom-poms and all.

My gaze lingered on the ribbon she still had tied around her neck. I'd never asked a girl to cheer for me before and when she'd said yes, I'd had to fight hard not to grin my fucking head off and sweep her into my arms. Ignoring the fact that the stars would get pissy obviously. And I'd thought that she was happy about it too. So why had she chosen to do this shit with the treasure now? Why was she so fucking insistent on drawing out the rage in me, the worst parts of me, no matter how hard I tried to shield her from them?

My gaze trailed down over her navy and silver cheer uniform before I could help it and my gut tightened as I noticed the letters DAR painted on the side of her toned waist. *Did she really paint my name on her skin? And why do I like the idea of that so much?*

Roxy tossed the pom-poms and folded her arms as she waited for me to reply and I managed to read the rest of the letters which curled around her side CY. *Right. Idiot. Of course she wouldn't paint my name on her body.*

"You know exactly what I mean. Where's the rest of my treasure?" I demanded, taking a step forward. But before I could reach her, Xavier and Mother appeared, throwing their arms around me in congratulations.

Roxy offered me a taunting smirk and slipped away into the crowd before I could stop her.

Where the fuck is she going?
What the fuck is she playing at?
And where the fuck is my gold??

By the time I'd received a round of congratulations from what felt like every single fucker at the school and said goodbye to my family, she was long gone.

My jaw ticked as anger trickled through my limbs, seriously dampening my post-win buzz. Taking a Dragon's gold was like taking the moon from a Werewolf. It was just wrong on so many levels and I couldn't let it lie. Not now. Not knowing that she still had it. I'd tried to make peace with the idea that it was gone before now, but this was taking things too fucking far.

I was more than a little relieved when the team finally headed down to The Orb for the after party. We were still filthy, our uniforms torn and bloody from the match but it was tradition for us to turn up like this, bathed in the filth of our glory.

We arrived in The Orb as a team, the rest of the school screaming and cheering us, the divide between Heir and Vega supporters forgotten for once in favour of something much more important. Pitball.

There was music blaring and people were dancing and drinking everywhere. My gaze instantly locked on Roxy as she danced above the crowd in the centre of the room, her cheerleading uniform clinging to her body like a second skin.

For a moment I couldn't help but think about the time we'd stolen from the stars beneath the lake after Seth and Max's party. It had been a beautiful form of torture which had haunted me daily ever since. I only wished it could have been ours alone. Or that I could have spoken with her properly afterwards. We hadn't discussed it since, though Cal kept making offhand comments about setting something up again. But I didn't even know if she wanted that. She'd been the one to say no to me after all. So maybe she'd just been taken by surprise that night and the ache she was forced to feel for me by the stars had combined with the drinks we'd had to make her give in to temptation. Or maybe it had been Cal. Though it hadn't felt like that. It had felt like her attention was on me most of the time. But maybe I was just bullshitting myself because I still couldn't bear the idea of them together.

An arm landed around my shoulders and a full Dragon growl escaped me as Caleb yanked me against his chest with a broad grin. His eyebrows went up in response and he released me before I could bite his damn head off.

"Thinking about it again, then?" he teased, pushing a hand through his mud stained hair.

I grunted in agreement, not trusting myself not to snap at him as I fought to wrangle my own anger back. It wasn't his fault. I knew what he'd done was for us and I knew there was no chance at all of me having her to myself with the stars haunting us, but I just...

"*Fuck,*" I cursed, swiping a hand over my face. I couldn't cope with my jealousy alongside my rage over the fucking treasure and the never ending agony of knowing that I would never be able to call Roxy mine anyway.

"If it's got you this knotted up, we don't have to do it again," Cal said with a frown, pushing a beer into my hand. "I was trying to help, not make you feel worse."

My heart dropped at that suggestion and the shadows suddenly reared up within me, offering a pit of oblivion to dive into to escape this hopeless feeling. Part of me wanted to agree with him. To say I didn't want to try and do it again because I couldn't take having him there with us too, that it cut me open and made me bleed all the time I was with them. But then I considered the alternative. Not having her at all. Never getting to feel her body against mine or kiss her full lips or make her heart pound to a rhythm that matched my own. And surely that was worse. But either way, it broke me. Either way, she wasn't really mine at all.

"I know." I blew out a frustrated breath. "It's not...I'm not angry with you really. I'm angry with myself. If I'd just done something different, so many things..."

Caleb's blue eyes darkened like he could actually feel my pain and he reached out to grip the side of my face as he made me hold his gaze. "We're going to fucking fix this, Darius," he swore. "Orion's going to find a way and by the time he does, she won't be able to deny her heart anymore. You'll have proved to her exactly the kind of man you are and the kind you can be for her and then-"

I pulled away from him, shaking my head as my heart crumbled and shattered again and I was forced to grit my teeth against the agony of forever alone without her.

"It isn't going to happen, Cal. I don't believe there's going to be some convenient do over for us," I said darkly. "I'm going to do everything I can to make things right between me and her because she deserves that much. She deserves to know how much I care about her even if she can't ever be mine. I don't want her thinking the man the stars chose for her was nothing but a monster. But I *am* a monster all the same. And no matter how much I make up for, that isn't going to change. There's darkness in me that will never find the light. So she's better off away from me anyway."

I pushed past him before he could reply and carved my way through the crowd towards our couch.

People slapped me on the back, called out my name and offered me drinks as I went and I tried to offer them smiles in return, but I was pretty sure I was closer to hitting a glower.

As I finally made it to our red couch, I fell still. Roxy hadn't been dancing on a table like I'd thought, she was standing on the back of the couch. Directly above my usual spot at the end of it.

Anger licked along my limbs as I looked up at her in that micro skirt and her long socks and she turned to look down at me with the biggest fucking smile imaginable on her face. It wasn't a kind smile. It was goading, knowing, taunting, *dangerous*. The kind of smile I shouldn't have liked but really did.

"What are you up to?" I demanded.

I may have vowed not to fight back against her in our combat classes, but she was seriously treading a fine line by doing this. Everyone knew this couch belonged to us. As stupid as it was, her jumping all over my territory like this was practically a declaration of war. If I let it pass with all of these witnesses then it was political suicide. I had to prove to everyone that she was still beneath me, but I refused to lay a hand on her and she knew it. I just didn't understand why she was pushing me like this.

"Here he is!" she cried. "Player of the match!"

The crowd cheered and I frowned. She wasn't here to pay me compliments, she was up to something. But I didn't know what yet.

"Get down," I demanded and several of the students surrounding us backed up like they could sense a fight coming. But that wasn't going to happen. I refused to let her back me into one no matter how fast my pulse was pounding.

Roxy tapped a finger against her lips dramatically. A finger which held a Dragon ring that had been in my family for eight generations. My blood lit with Dragon fire and the taste of smoke coated my tongue for a moment.

"And give me back my treasure," I added in a dark tone.

349

"Oh! That reminds me..." Roxy hopped down from the back of the couch into my spot and reached for her bag which lay on the floor beside it. She rummaged around for something while I folded my arms and waited her out.

When she sat up again, she had a pendant hanging from her neck beneath the ribbon I'd given her. It held a stunning fire ruby the size of an egg, cut in the shape of a heart. It was worth over a million auras. She'd also placed a crown on her head which had actually been a gift from a Vega Queen to my great, great grandmother. She'd pushed gold bracelets and bangles over her wrists and was wearing even more of my rings too.

A deep growl rattled through my chest as she sat back in my spot with a taunting grin and my fingers curled with the desire to punish her for daring to touch my gold. A Dragon's treasure was more precious than all the stars in the damn sky and only a fucking fool would dare to touch it, let alone dress themselves up in it like she was right now. If she was anyone else, she'd have found herself charred to a crisp already. As it was, the thin grip I was holding on my rage was slipping out of my control.

I lunged at her and she screamed in surprise as my hands landed either side of her head on the thick red cushions and I bared my teeth right in her face.

"Give those back!" I snarled and from the corners of my eyes I could see people running.

My skin was flaring so hot with fire magic that they were probably all getting burned as the heat rolled off of me. But not Roxy. Fire couldn't hurt her. Maybe it was fate for her to be a Phoenix, the only creature immune to the worst of my power. Maybe the stars had always wanted me to be unable to hurt her.

She stared up at me with her big green eyes for the longest moment before laughing darkly. "Make me."

Suddenly the heat between us had nothing to do with fire magic and everything to do with me and her. This fucking wrecking ball who'd come crashing into my life, tearing apart everything I thought I'd known while refusing to shift from her course one single bit.

I growled again as I reached out and grabbed her, lifting her out of my spot before spinning around and sitting in it myself and dumping her in my lap.

"I told you I'm not going to hurt you, Roxy," I purred, just for her to hear as she steadied herself by pressing her palms against my shoulders as she was forced to straddle me while my fingers curled around the bare skin of her waist. "So how about we play a game instead?"

We were drawing an audience, but in that moment I didn't give a shit. I was either going to flip out and go full Dragon on everyone here or I was going to defy the stars and this girl in my arms by holding her close despite the fact that my instinct was to demand blood. I may have held darkness within my flesh, but I refused to be ruled by it ever again. I was my own man and I was going to make my own choices. Which meant I'd never hurt her again.

"What's that?" Roxy breathed, her pupils dilating so that there was more black than green in her eyes.

"Let's play chicken with the stars. We sit here and let them do their worst to tear us apart. The first one to get out of this seat wins."

Thunder crashed in the sky outside as if to make my point even clearer and Roxy looked up at the roof in alarm as the flaming sconces which hung from it shuddered ominously. The stolen pendant swung at her throat before falling to sit between her breasts and making me stare for the longest moment.

"Fine," she agreed, looking back down at me again, her eyes lighting with the challenge. "But if I win, me and the Ass Club get your couch."

I snorted dismissively. "Well if I win, I get every last piece of my treasure back."

"Done." She smirked at me as the ground began to tremble and the determination in her eyes made me wonder if we might just end up killing ourselves with this game. I wasn't sure if either of us had it in us to lose willingly.

"What's going on?" Seth's voice came from behind me but I didn't bother to look at him, my gaze firmly captured by the girl in my lap.

The ground shook more fiercely which effectively made her body vibrate against my dick as she straddled me in that tiny skirt and I grunted as she gave me a knowing look. I couldn't deny that I'd had more than a few fantasies about getting her in a position like this with that cheer outfit on and me still wearing my Pitball uniform. It was a pretty cliched fantasy, but a hot one none the less. Especially with the way she looked in her uniform.

"Problem, Darius?" she teased, shifting her hips again as my dick hardened between us. I should have been too angry to be turned on, but with her it always felt like this. Like we were dancing the line of love and hate with the only thing consistently present being lust.

"You whore!" Mildred's voice jolted me out of our moment of insanity and I looked up just as she charged at us, her gaze firmly set on Roxy in my lap like she fully intended to tackle her off of me.

I shifted forward at the last moment and she hit me instead, knocking both of us off the couch and I dropped my hold on Roxy as we fell to the ground.

By the time I'd pushed myself upright, I found Roxy pinned beneath Mildred as she swung a fist straight at her face.

"Stop!" I commanded, but Mildred didn't even bat an eyelash at me. Her lips were curled back to reveal that under cut jaw and her beady eyes flared with fury.

Her fist slammed into Roxy's jaw and blood flew as she snarled in rage beneath her.

I took a step forward to intervene, but Max's hand landed on my shoulder and he whirled me around to look at him before I could.

"It's Fae on Fae, man, what are you thinking?" he asked with a frown and I could only glower as I looked back to the fight, forcing myself to remain still.

It might have made me ache to hold back but he was right, I couldn't get involved in a fight between two Fae. And if it had been anyone else, I never would have considered it. But Roxy always made me want to break the rules.

"You jumped up, crown touting, cock sucking, whore!" Mildred slammed her fist into Roxy's face again, not even bothering to use magic as she screamed insults in her face which included way too many references to me being her beloved.

"What's the matter, Mildred?" Roxy snarled. "Is it just that you can't suck cock properly with that mis-matched jaw of yours or is it that you know Darius is only marrying you because his father is forcing him to?"

"When I take my beloved to the bedroom he will be screaming so loudly that he won't even remember the name Vega!" Mildred howled as she punched Roxy again.

"Yeah, screaming in horror," Roxy spat and I almost fucking laughed aside from the fact that she was about to get her face smashed in by that beast of a girl.

"We'll see if he's so tempted by you when I'm done pulverising that pretty face of yours and I cut your perky tits off for good measure!" Mildred howled.

"Not the tits!" Tyler Corbin gasped from the other side of the crowd as he filmed the whole thing.

My heart pounded. Roxy might have been tough, but Mildred was four times the size of her. She needed to fight back with magic if she was going to stand a chance, but as she swung her head forward and cracked the bridge of Mildred's nose with a savage headbutt, I got the feeling she wasn't going to use it.

Roxy swung a fist into Mildred's throat to follow it before driving her knee up between her legs as hard as she could.

"Ooo right in the vag!" Tyler called and a laugh caught in my throat.

"Yes, Tor!" Darcy screamed as she pushed her way to the front of the crowd. "Show her how we fight where we come from!"

As Mildred reared back, Roxy lunged forward, rolling them over so that she was on top before swinging her fists down into Mildred's ugly face with a brutality that made my heart race.

She was wild and vicious, blood pissing down her face from her own injuries as she used my stolen rings to batter Mildred again and again. I wouldn't be surprised if she didn't end up with Dragons imprinted all over her face from the shape of the jewellery.

Mildred gave as good as she got, punching Roxy in the sides, the chest, even trying to bite her fist as she punched her.

"Holy shit," Seth breathed as he nuzzled against my arm. "This would be so hot if it wasn't, you know, *Mildred*. But if I imagine her being literally any other girl then I'd be so turned on right now."

I swallowed a lump in my throat as I refused to agree out loud, but he was right. There was something about Roxy as she fought like that, her lip curled back with determination and absolutely no mercy in her. They might have been fighting like mortals having a bar brawl, but with a crown on her head and blood painting her flesh, I didn't think she'd ever looked more like the Savage King's daughter before. She really was a Fae Princess. And I liked it.

Mildred cursed and screamed, throwing fists like sledgehammers so hard that I was pretty sure I heard ribs cracking, but Roxy wasn't going to give in.

She swung her arm back one final time and with a scream of rage, she hit Mildred so hard in her pug face that she blacked out.

A laugh tumbled from my lips before I could stop it and Roxy looked up at me with a wild determination in her eyes as she grinned like a damn warrior.

The crowd were cheering and Geraldine led the Ass squad in that annoying as fuck song about princesses as they all celebrated her win, but I ignore them as I moved forward to offer Roxy a hand up.

"I'll toss Mildred back in her room, heal her and cast a sleeping spell on her so that she can properly recover," Cal announced as he moved around us and I couldn't help but smile at him.

It might have annoyed the fuck out of me that he'd been with my girl, but he really was a good friend. A true brother.

He threw Mildred over his shoulder like a sack of potatoes and shot out of the room as Seth howled in excitement.

"Come on," I said to Roxy. "I'll clean you up and heal those wounds."

"Okay." Roxy followed me back to the couch and I sat her down in my spot before throwing a ring of fire and a silencing bubble up around us to give us some pretence of privacy.

"Doesn't this count as us being alone?" Roxy asked as I dropped to my knees in front of her and she pulled her busted bottom lip between her teeth.

That shouldn't have been hot, but it really fucking was.

"I'm going with no," I replied, but as the ground trembled beneath my knees I had to admit it did.

"Maybe you should just-"

"I'm going to look after you," I growled, leaving no room for negotiation. "So just let me."

Her lips parted, eyes flared, fingers gripped the edge of the couch and I was sure she was about to tell me no, but instead she just nodded.

I reached out and curled my fingers wound around her waist as I pressed healing magic from my skin into hers, closing my eyes so that I could concentrate. She had cracked ribs and healing bones was more difficult than damaged tissue.

She fell still as I shifted my hands over her flesh and I tried to ignore the way the floor quaked beneath me. We couldn't stay in this bubble for long, but I wished that we could. I wished we could just build a bubble where the stars couldn't see us and stay in it forever. Although I guessed if I offered her that she'd just say no again.

I sighed as my magic depleted, using the last drops of it to heal her and clean the blood from her skin after burning through so much in the game.

A soft touch against my hair made me open my eyes and I looked up at her as she pushed the crown onto my head.

"Mildred knocked me off of the couch first," she explained in answer to the question in my eyes. "So you win. Besides, you need a big head like yours to pull off a crown like this."

I snorted a laugh as the ground trembled so violently that I was almost knocked back onto my ass.

Roxy quickly pulled the rings and bracelets from her hands and offered them to me too and I pushed them into my pockets wordlessly.

But as she reached up to unclasp the blood ruby pendant from around her neck I caught her wrist to stop her. "Keep it," I said, my gaze slipping to the priceless heart where it lay against her flesh. Dragons didn't give treasure away. Ever. It was inherited through the family or we bought more of it, but we *never* gifted it to anyone. It went against everything we stood for and the fierce possessiveness of our natures. But for some reason that I couldn't fully comprehend, I wanted her to keep that necklace. "It looks better on you anyway."

Her eyes widened but before she could reply, I dropped the wall of fire and stepped away from her. Darcy hurried forward with wild eyes, looking between me and her sister for a long moment like she'd expected us to be arguing or something. But the last thing I was going to do was call Roxy out for beating Mildred's ass for me. She'd absolutely been working in my interests and I wasn't even going to pretend to be pissed about it.

"Are you okay, Tor?"

"Darius fixed me up like new. Did you see the bit when I kneed her in the vag?" Roxy asked as she grinned and Darcy started laughing.

"It was classic, you've gotta come see Tyler's slow motion footage of you punching her in the throat too!"

The party was in full swing around us again and I couldn't help but feel a little more like joining in as I watched Roxy walk away from me. She glanced back once and my heart leapt as she offered me the smallest of smiles.

Roxy Vega might never be mine, but sometimes I found I didn't mind pining for her as much as I should have.

SETH

CHAPTER TWENTY EIGHT

I'd been trying to get Rosalie Oscura's attention all evening while she made friends with Darcy, Tory and the A.S.S. crew and I lingered around them like a hungry animal. Caleb was giving her his best smoulders, his best pick up lines and his best smirks, and she wasn't buying any of that either. And yet, every now and then, she'd walk past me, brush her hand over my arm and give me the come-fuck-me eyes that made the Alpha inside me rear up and want to claim her as mine.

I'd never met another Alpha Wolf who matched me so closely, I could sense it in everything about her. The way she walked, the way she carried an air of power that I wanted to know the taste of. My instincts made me taunt her, push her for a reaction, but she gave me none. She was as cool and as unaffected as a cucumber in an ice bath. And fuck if that didn't get me hot.

"So you're from Alestria," I tried, planting myself in front of her as she headed to the buffet table to grab another drink.

She tossed a lock of that delicious ebony hair over her shoulder, her cheeks still smeared with mud from the match. I wanted to smear more of it on her while we wrestled in the dirt and I made her submit to my superior strength. But I didn't think she was going to go for that just yet.

"Do you always state the obvious to other Fae?" Rosalie asked, batting her long lashes in a way that was clearly designed to pull me in and yet the rest of her face said *fight me.*

I stepped closer to her with a growl, wanting to break through this little game she was playing. "How many Alphas have you met in your life who could match you in every way?"

Her eyes slid past me to where Caleb was fixing himself a drink and glancing over at us with a carnivorous look in his eyes. As I gazed at him, she moved into the arc of my body, her sweet scent enveloping me as she pressed a hand to my chest and tip-toed up to speak in my ear.

"No one can match me in *any* way. But it looks like you and your bestie wanna try, lupo de mine," she purred and her accent got me hard in an instant.

I turned my head towards her with a smirk but she was gone in an instant, sashaying her hips as she headed over to Caleb and directed him to get her a drink, playing the innocent act. He actually fucking did it as well.

I surveyed the two of them, swigging my own drink as his hand slid onto the small of her back and she laughed at something he said. Then she turned her gaze to me and bit down on her lower lip, making me ache for her. Fuck it, not just for her - for both of them. I could have watched this show all day. But I really would have preferred a leading role in it.

The party soon thinned out and someone – who may or may not have been me - announced a game of truth or dare. I was soon riding a buzz as everyone agreed and wondered if I could dare Rosalie to kiss Caleb so I could mentally record that image forever. Unfortunately it was my turn to be asked.

"Truth or dare?" Rosalie shot at me with a smirk.

"Truth," I announced, maybe a tiny bit wasted and still high off of winning the game despite the fact it was definitely three in the morning and the party was down to eight people. Well seven if you took note of the fact that Milton Hubert was passed out on the buffet table. Someone had glued a line of gummy bears to his monobrow and that someone had most definitely been me.

We were sat in a circle with me and the other Heirs on the couch, Tory, Darcy and Geraldine on the coffee table opposite and Rosalie Oscura cross legged in an armchair she'd pulled over. Turned out, the girl wasn't just hot. She was funny and smart and got my dick hard in ways I needed to explore. Tonight preferably. But her attention kept swinging between me and Caleb and I couldn't figure out who she was most hot for.

"What's the last good deed you did?" Rosalie asked me. We'd been playing the game for an hour while Jack Johnson tunes rolled through the speakers, the party mellowing out. But I didn't want to call it quits yet. I was having too much fun.

I thought on her question and the answer made my eyes slide to Darcy. She chewed on her lip in that way that said she expected me to spill her dark secret at any moment.

"I can't tell you, it's a secret," I said earnestly and everyone turned to me with narrowed eyes. Caleb was sitting beside me and he threw an arm around my shoulders, yanking me close.

"We don't keep secrets," he said firmly. I hated keeping anything from him. It felt like shit. But I had one secret of Darcy's that could open up a whole can of big fat ugly worms that needed to stay buried. In the can. Or the ground. Whatever. The fact was…

I sipped on my rum and wondered what I'd just been debating.

"I love you man," I told Caleb with a smirk then pinched his cheek hard. "Isn't he pretty, Rosalie?" I turned his face towards her and she gave him a once over before nodding her approval.

"Yeah, real pretty, stronzo. Now answer the question."

"Told you, I can't," I said and Darcy's shoulders relaxed.

I didn't know why she was so worried about me telling people. It wasn't like I was a bad guy. Oh wait, yes I was. Except I didn't *want* to be bad. Really, what was the difference between being bad and good anyway? It just came down to people's opinions. All situations were neutral until someone formed an opinion about them. So to a lot of people, I was a great guy. But maybe that didn't matter if the people you cared about thought you were bad. Not that I cared about Darcy or anything.

"Fine. You have to do a forfeit shot," Rosalie announced and Caleb bounced happily in his chair.

Darius and Max weren't even paying attention, just staring at their little crushes with hearts in their eyes. Tory Vega and Geraldine Grus though? Max's step-mom would cut his balls off and wear them as earrings if she found out he was pursuing a Grus. And Lionel, well…nuff said.

I took the shot and my head spun for a second. I was going to be obliterated tomorrow. But tomorrow didn't exist yet, so whatever.

"Tory truth or dare?" I pointed at her because I had a cunning plan (alcohol always made me extra cunning). To play my part in Mission: Defy The Stars, I had been trying my hardest to make Darius do a grand gesture for Tory.

He'd shot down literally everything I'd suggested so far. From serenades to candlelit picnics and trips to the Polar Capital to see the northern lights. He had zero game. But what I'd finally realised was, he not only didn't want to do any of that shit, but Tory would have hated it too. And after she'd pounded Mildred's face to a pulp earlier, I'd finally realised what they both loved. Violence. Dirty, mortal fist fights and blood being spilled in vengeance. So my plan was simple. I was going to set Darius on anyone who had wronged her – besides us obviously. And I knew of one person in particular thanks to Max's Siren trap which had pulled her darkest fears from her.

I just had to phrase this right…

"Name the person you hated most *before* you came to Zodiac," I asked, saying it casually like I wasn't fishing for anything.

"Zane Baxter," she said with darkness in her eyes. "My ex-boyfriend."

"Interesting," I said, rubbing my shoulder against Caleb's and giving him a *I'm so clever expression* which made him and Tory frown. Darius glanced between us in confusion too because I hadn't had a chance to tell him my master plan yet.

By the stars Caleb's lips look good right now. I could just…

"Truth or dare?" Tory tossed back at me even though I'd just had a go.

"Dare," I said simply, sure she was about to try and get the truth out of me for what I'd just asked.

She sipped her drink, looking to her sister for ideas.

"Make him post a video on FaeBook singing that princess song!" Darcy cried, grinning from ear to ear.

"Ha! Yes," Tory agreed, looking to me with a challenging stare.

"Oh my snake pit!" Geraldine slapped her thigh with a laugh. "Yes, you must – you must!"

"What's the song?" Rosalie asked excitedly, sitting up in her chair and looking so edible, I just wanted to eat her good. And lick and bite her. *All* the mouth things. I was so fucking glad the Aurora team were staying for the night. I wanted to wake up with her moaning for another round with me tomorrow. And another and another and another…

"Seth." Caleb elbowed me and I gave him a slanted smile. *Hm, wouldn't mind waking up with him tomorrow either. Damn, why does rum always make me so horny?*

I groaned dramatically as Rosalie whipped out her Atlas to record me and Tory leaned on Darcy's shoulder as they both started laughing their asses off.

Well if I was gonna do it, I was gonna commit. I pushed Caleb's arm off of me, using his knee to help myself up then leapt onto the nearest table, walking down the length of it to give myself room for the performance. If there was one thing Capellas did well, it was put on a show.

Rosalie hit record and I had oh-so-sadly forgotten most of the lyrics. What a tragedy. I'd have to make my own up.

"They came from over the hill to lay, the monsters, beasts and bullies. The princesses came with their shiny bits, two hotties with their bouncing tits. And so they begged, come play, come play, come play!" I stomped my feet just like Geraldine had in time with the tune and everyone started laughing, even the Vegas. But not Geraldine. She rose from her seat, planting her hands on her hips, her face twisted in offence.

"Those are not the words you malfunctioning mutt!" she yelled and I sang louder over her as Rosalie continued to record it with a bright grin.

"The monsters said we're here to stay, raising hard and long and throbbing dicks. The princesses came so hard they swayed, and so did all their loyal maids. And so they begged, come play, come play, come play!"

The other Heirs took up the echoing chant and Rosalie lifted the camera higher, laughing as she panned over to them then back to me. I did the Geraldine dance again and she charged toward me, climbing up onto the table with a growl of fury. Max ran forward, catching her around the waist and trying to spin her in time to the tune.

"Unhand me you common carp! I will not let this lowly dog befoul the song of the Vegas!" she yelled, but she was drunk as hell and seemingly unable to wrangle her magic as Max started dancing her around the couch in circles. Caleb was wiping tears from under his eyes and every time Darius laughed, smoke puffed from his nose.

"You guys are pazzo," Rosalie laughed and I shot her a wink.

"The beasts they laughed with their cocks in hand, they danced, they sang and they ruled the land. And the princesses came with a sigh and a moan, and made those beasties really groan. And so they begged, come play, come play, come play!"

"If you sing the final verse, you dirty Daniel, I will decapitate you with a cuttlefish and bury you face down in a sewer so you can never see the moon again!" Geraldine roared and the Vegas really lost their shit, laughing like maniacs while trying to smother it as Geraldine grew more and more red faced.

"Sing the final verse," Caleb started chanting and Rosalie got up, falling into my vacated seat as she joined in the chant with him. She bit down on her lip as she rubbed up against Caleb and I forgot what I was doing mid-dance and nearly fell off the table. Fuck they looked hot together. I could really have enjoyed a sandwich tonight with a lightly toasted Vampire bread and succulent Wolfy middle.

"Sing it, asshole!" Darius demanded, a grin on his face. It felt so good to see him happy that a puppyish yip escaped me as I righted myself on the table.

"Anything for you, you beautiful Dargon. Dargron. I mean, Draron," I slurred. "Dammit, how hard is it to say Dragarn? Dargon! Oh fuck my life."

"Sing it Seth!" Rosalie howled and yeah, I was gonna be making her howl my name louder than that soon.

"Final verse," I announced as Max continued to sweep Geraldine around the room, practically carrying her as she swatted and thumped him.

"One more word, Seth Capella, and I shall not only castrate you, but I will castrate your sons and your sons' sons. There will never be another Grus in all of existence who will not proudly display a pair of Capella balls on her nightstand!"

"What if I have daughters?" I goaded her, snorting in amusement as she spun around to face me in Max's arms, causing his hands to land right on her huge tits. She didn't even seem to notice and he certainly didn't seem to have any intention of removing them.

"Then...then..." she faltered, thinking on it. "We shall steal their Lady Petunias and create a garden of Capella misfortune!"

"How will Seth have kids if you castrate him?" Max asked, noticeably squeezing her boobs while he had green light access to them.

"Oh that tricksome terrier would find a way, I'm sure," she said, pointing an accusing finger at me.

"Sing it!" Tory demanded and Darcy fell apart again as Geraldine slumped back into Max's arms as if she'd fainted.

"Ohhhhhhhh," I howled the first note as Rosalie continued to record this shit show to the end of time. "The bullies they smiled as they seized the crown, they won the war and made everyone bow. The princesses said sorry for all the lies and the tricks, by kneeling down and sucking their dicks. And so they begged, come play, come play, come play!"

Rosalie swung her Atlas towards the Vegas and Darcy pulled herself together enough to speak. "And that was tonight's fake news everyone. See you when we beat their asses."

Caleb tried to grab her Atlas but Rosalie turned it off with a smirk. I leapt off of the table, gazing down at her with a dark smile as the others started getting up.

"Oh, are you leaving?" I asked with a whine.

"It's nearly four am," Darcy said through a yawn which was totally fake. She had a wild look in her eyes and I could guess exactly whose door she was going to go knocking on tonight.

Darius and Tory drifted closer together and Darcy linked arms with both of them in the middle and my heart tugged as I realised she was doing it so they could stay close to each other. It was a fucking shame the stars were little glittery pricks sometimes. Of course, the stars seemed to be very much shining on me tonight because Max and Geraldine headed towards the exit too. She'd apparently forgotten about being offended by me as she wrapped her legs around Max's waist and kissed the face off him as he clutched her ass and walked her towards the door blind. He bumped into every fucking table on the way. Every. Fucking. One.

"Night then," I called with an eyeroll and Milton Hubert snored like a warthog, reminding me the three of us we weren't entirely alone.

"You're in my seat, babe," I said to Rosalie, stepping right up to the couch and gazing down at the dark-haired, dark-eyed, shit-hot delicacy sitting beneath me.

"But it's such a comfy seat," she purred. "Would you really move me out of it into that lonely old chair all the way over there?"

I crouched down with a smirk so we were at eye level. "You can stay, but you have to share."

"How good are you two at sharing?" she asked, glancing between me and Caleb and my throat thickened.

"I'm real good," I growled. "How about you Caleb?"

His mouth hooked up at the corner and he yanked Rosalie into his lap to make room for me. I dropped down into my spot and she rested her bare feet in my lap. Right on my fucking cock. Which instantly got hard for her. Her brows rose and she wet her lips as her hand slid onto Caleb's cheek, her fingers scraping against his stubble.

"Caleb?" she pushed, turning her head to run the pad of her tongue along his jaw as her feet shifted in my lap and made me groan with desire.

Caleb heaved a sigh and slipped out from under her, rising to his feet and shooting me a look I couldn't decipher. "Nah, not tonight," he said, faking a yawn.

Rosalie moved to straddle me, leaning forward to tease my lower lip between her teeth. Fuck. Me. This girl. I glanced over her shoulder towards Caleb, hoping he was watching as she dropped down to grind against my dick.

"Are you staying here then Seth?" Caleb asked and I got the strangest feeling he didn't want me to.

"Well, he'll be all on his own." Rosalie sprang out of my lap, picking up her letterman jacket and pulling it on, stretching her arms above her head.

"What's the saying? Two's boring, three's a party? I was kinda hoping for a party." She winked then headed toward the door and slipped out of it. Just like that. Gone.

Fuck.

"What's wrong? You didn't like her?" I got to my feet, moving closer to Caleb and nuzzling against him.

He slung his arm around me and I moved closer still, the warmth of him drawing me in and making an unknown part of me ache. And it wasn't my dick for once. Despite the boner. So that was saying something.

He looked to me with his jaw tight and his fingers dug into my flesh through my shirt. "Just...after everything with Tory...life's complicated enough right now, you know?"

I nodded, winding my arm around him too so we were awkwardly half hugging. Then I figured fuck it and moved into him properly so we were chest to chest. And dick to dick unfortunately for him as I was raging. But I could tell he needed this right now.

"I know," I said for a thousand and one reasons. The first on the list being him. And the way my heart was pounding and my skin was dancing with heat and every part of me felt too alive.

His hands slid around me and I felt the powerful beat of his heart against my chest. I suddenly didn't care that we were alone. I could just be with him like this for a moment. It was the only place I wanted to be right now, gripping him tightly and breathing in his fresh, sandalwood scent. And with that knowledge came a terrifying realisation I knew was true despite the haze of alcohol fogging my brain.

Yep, it's official. I'm into my straight best friend. Thanks for the headfuck stars.

ORION

CHAPTER TWENTY NINE

I watched Blue as she filed out of the Cardinal Magic classroom with her sister, dropping down behind my desk with a tug in my chest. The urge to call her back consumed me, but I had another class and I needed to talk with Diego about his grades. *Fucking Diego*.

"Polaris!" I shouted as he made it to the door, glancing back at me with a look of concern. And he should have been fucking concerned. "A word."

The rest of the class vacated the room and he tugged on his hat nervously as the door swung closed and I leaned back in my seat, stacking my hands on my stomach.

"Sit down." I raised a finger, whipping a chair from behind the nearest desk with a gust of air magic and parking it in front of my desk.

Diego scurried forward and dropped onto it, his eyes full of contempt as he waited for me to speak. Couldn't really blame the kid for hating me. I wasn't his biggest fan either. Weakness disturbed me. But normally, I could hone Fae like him, find strengths in them regardless of their power level and help them cultivate their own advantage. But there was something off about Polaris. He was a low level air Elemental, but he should have been progressing more than he had.

I wasn't easy on him, but that was only in an attempt to coax a rise out of him. I wanted to see the Fae that the stars had deemed worthy of this academy when he'd passed The Reckoning. I hadn't just been shocked that he'd made it this far, I'd been fucking astounded. With every test and challenge I gave the class, he *just* managed to scrape by so that I didn't have quite enough of a reason to report his shortcomings to Elaine Nova. It wasn't even that I wanted him to fail, but this middle ground of hovering just above failure wasn't going to cut it with me any longer.

I opened my drawer, taking out his last paper on the uses of the Cardinal Magics for Fae enhancement in society and dumped it in front of him.

"I don't grade papers," I told him. "I simply give a pass or fail then offer you a more difficult assignment on the same topic if you fail. Most of those who fail the first time, excel on the second paper. You do not." Failing his papers this continuously simply meant he was likely to fail his end of year exams and end up out of the school anyway. But The Reckoning was designed to weed out the weak. Most freshman students who had made it this far didn't fail their first year examinations. It was nearly unheard of. And I certainly wasn't going to take the blame for it when Elaine came asking about why Polaris had flunked.

"I'll try harder, sir," he said, bowing his head as his cheeks coloured.

I slammed my hand down on the desk and he looked up at me again in alarm. "Not acceptable. You've had weeks to try harder. Months. Your spells are sub-par and your papers aren't good enough to wipe my ass with."

His blush deepened and he tugged on his hat again. "It's just I…it's…I have confidence issues."

"No shit," I said dryly.

When he turned the colour of a beetroot I sighed, leaning back in my chair, figuring this angle was not working. Which was extra fucking annoying because it was the only angle I was used to playing. Being hard on Fae spurred them into fighting back, going from strength to strength. I'd never had a student it didn't work for, so I was stumped. "Talk to me about your issues. I can't help you if I don't know what you're struggling with. You have the same opportunities everyone else in this class does, Polaris. And you can't have any less brain cells than Jillian Minor. So what is holding you back?"

He shifted in his seat, his posturing stiffening. I gave him a few agonising minutes to come up with a response before I held back a growl in my throat, struggling to stick with this different tactic. It would feel about as comfortable as shoving a pineapple up my ass, but I was going to try and be… nice. *Shudder.*

"I know you dislike me," I said calmly. "But contrary to your beliefs, I'm not actually out to get you. I don't lay awake at night thinking up ways to disturb and ridicule you. I have a lot better things to be doing with my time. And the fact that I'm sitting here with you now, offering you this chance should be proof that I'm on your side. I don't want you to fail this year unless you deserve to fail it. So are you worthy or not?"

Diego sighed, tugging his chair closer and resting his hands on the desk. He slid one across to me, not meeting my eyes as he offered me his palm. "I'll show you why I'm struggling," he rasped. "It's easier that way."

I hesitated before casting a wall of air in front of the door to stop anyone walking in then gripped his hand. I closed my eyes and felt him yank me down into the shadows, diving into the darkness where nothing but a heavy silence awaited us.

He took me deeper into the abyss until that strange, white cloud of memory appeared out of the black. Flashes of light rippled through it then a scene grew brighter until it consumed me entirely and I stepped into the body of whoever the memory belonged to.

The porch was dirty and paint was flaking off the walls. I recognised Diego's mother, Drusilla, as she dragged a young boy out of the door with her hand fisted in his dark curls. Diego couldn't have been more than five, his tiny hands clutching onto his mother's arm as she hauled him across the porch, shrieking at him. "You worthless little shit, how dare you speak back to me?"

Her brother Alejandro stalked out after her with a snarl. "You can sleep under the porch tonight like the *perro* you are." He shoved Diego down the steps and he stumbled before falling onto his backside and staring up at them in horror. He didn't even cry. Like he'd been on the receiving end of their temper a thousand times.

"Now now, Drusilla, Alejandro, leave the boy be," an old woman's voice came from whoever's body I was seeing this through and I assumed it must have been his grandmother. "He's young."

"Don't question the way I mother him. That child was born with something missing in him." Drusilla stormed inside and the old woman stood, hurrying down to comfort Diego as the tears finally flowed and he nuzzled into her arms.

"Don't mollycoddle him, madre," Alejandro growled from the porch. "He needs to toughen up or he'll never be one of us."

The memory changed and I saw Diego again, a little older this time, as he carefully pieced together a wooden plane, gluing each part in place with a smile on his face. There was dirt on his cheeks and his clothes looked worn, but at least he seemed happy. The room was pretty bare and spoke of the kind of poverty we never saw walk through the doors of Zodiac. So I had no idea how he'd come to afford his spot here.

"It's beautiful, mi nieto," his grandmother spoke, clapping her wrinkled hands together. "Isn't it beautiful, Miguel?" She turned and I saw a pale man sitting in a chair with a drink in his hand and a blank expression on his face. He didn't respond and Diego's grandmother tutted as she turned back to face her grandson. "We can put it in the window."

"Why would we want that in the window?" Drusilla strode into the room with a sneer. "Is this what you let him do when I leave the house?" she demanded. "Make pointless things while I'm out trying to secure our future?"

"What else is he supposed to do? The boy is bored," she answered, clucking her tongue.

"There are chores to be done!" Drusilla yelled, storming forward and snatching the plane from the table.

"Mamá!" Diego cried and she rolled her eyes.

"This is almost as useless as you are. What is the point in having a son if all he does is make pointless things? Isn't that right, Miguel?" She rounded on Diego's father and he nodded like a robot.

"Yes, my dear. Absolutely."

"Teach your boy to be useful then or I'll be done with the lot of you," she snapped, dropping the plane to the floor and stamping her foot on it before striding from the room.

The memory changed again and Diego must have only been a little younger than he was now. He sat beside his grandmother's bed as she coughed and gripped his hand.

"Promise you won't leave," he demanded of her through teary eyes. "You're the only one that makes this place bearable."

"I'll never leave you truly," she said in a dry voice. "You must be strong."

"That's not good enough," he begged. "You have to stay."

"Diego," Drusilla's sharp voice came from beyond the darkened room. "Stop bothering your abuela."

"He's no bother," the grandmother rasped.

"Ha, that's all he is," Drusilla replied before pushing the door open and gesturing for Diego to leave.

"Do you need me to drag him out of there?" Alejandro's voice sounded from the hall.

His grandmother squeezed Diego's hand then the memories faded and I was tugged out of the darkness. I dragged in a breath as I found myself back in my classroom and I released Diego's hand, finding him hurriedly wiping tears from his cheeks.

"She died a week after that. But all her memories are in the web. I can still visit them whenever I miss her." Diego wouldn't meet my eyes and my heart knotted at his expression. "It got a lot worse after she was gone. Mother and Uncle Alejandro got work for Lionel Acrux and I thought things would finally be okay. They always complained how we needed the money. But they got more cruel, more hateful. I was mi madre's biggest regret and my uncle always thought I was lacking. And when they sent me here, they hoped I'd be of use at last to spy on the Vegas for Lord Acrux. But I never managed to give them anything of much use and now that I'm working against them, I…"

"What?" I pressed, surprised by the softness of my tone.

He met my gaze and there was just a broken boy in his eyes that made me wonder how I'd never seen it before now. "Mi madre will pull me out of Zodiac soon enough, Professor. I don't try because…there's no point. I was never here to be good at magic. I was here to work for them. And when they realise I'm no use here, that'll be it."

A beat of silence passed between us and I leaned forward, resting my elbows on the table. "You know, my mother was hard on me too. Especially after my father died. Once I came to Zodiac, I broke free from her. This place opened up a whole new world for me. A free life. I didn't have to answer to her anymore. I didn't have to be who she wanted me so fucking desperately to be."

Diego's brow creased. "But my mother will never let me stay."

"You're already here, your tuition is paid. How can she make you leave? Especially if a certain Cardinal Magic teacher has a word with Principal Nova."

His lips parted as he stared at me, some of that hate he directed at me falling away. "I can't have anyone knowing why-"

"No one has to know any details. Besides, you're eighteen, Diego. She doesn't control you anymore, so long as you don't let her."

He nodded slowly, hope filling his gaze. "Did you ever…earn your mother's respect? After taking your own path?"

I frowned, my gut twisting at remembering going through this exact struggle when I was younger. I sighed, shaking my head. "No. I disowned my mother for many reasons." I thought of Clara and a familiar sting of pain invaded me. "Look, sometimes we want to see the good in people we care about so much that we pretend it's there, living under all the layers of cruelty. But the fact is, Diego, some people are toxic. And if you keep them in your life, they'll poison everything good in your world until you end up being just like them. And that's a far worse fate than going against the grain and making your own path. Even if that means you're alone."

He absorbed that for a second. "It's so hard to shake everything she's said to me my whole life. I don't care what my uncle thinks of me. But it's harder with mi madre. Sometimes…I think I really am useless," he said, his voice breaking on the word.

"Well, Diego, I think there's one thing that proves that isn't true, don't you?"

He frowned, unsure what I was getting at.

"You passed The Reckoning," I said, pride inching into me at knowing what he'd been through to get here at all. And that was the shocking twist of the day. "The stars have deemed you very fucking worthy of a place at Zodiac Academy. So what are you going to do with the chance they've given you?"

He stood, knocking his chair over in his haste. "I'm gonna work harder." He snatched his failed paper and strode towards the door, pausing before he left. "Thank you, sir."

I shrugged, disbanding the air shield to let him out the door. He strode away with a fucking skip in his step and I had to check myself for a second because did I just make friends with Diego fucking Polaris?

I scraped a hand through my hair, sitting back in my seat with a bemused smile as I hooked my Atlas off of the desk. Blue had been friends with him since she'd first arrived. Maybe I should have just trusted her judgement because she clearly saw people's hearts when she looked at them. *Fuck, I love that girl.*

I shot her a message with a smirk, fantasising about exactly what I was going to do to her later just as my senior class started filing in, bursting my bubble.

Lance:
Meet me at the library archives tonight. 10pm.

"Why are you smiling like that, sir?" Shabnam Hosseini asked me, giggling with her friends.

"Get out of my fucking classroom!" I barked, pointing at the door and her jaw dropped before she hurried to obey. "Has anyone else got any pointless questions they'd like to air? No? Good. Now sit the fuck down!"

Ah, today is a good day.

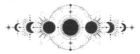

I left the library door unlocked for Blue while I headed into the darkened back aisles and lifted the secret hatch that led down into the archives just before ten o'clock. I'd wanted to show her this place for a long time, but the librarian was often here into the small hours of the morning as if she had no life. Which, to be fair, she didn't. Tonight, however, I knew for a fact that she'd gone away for the evening to visit her sick brother in Lapeli. *Score.*

Students were allowed down here, but most of them either didn't know about it or didn't ask the librarian for the pass they needed to access it. It was a simple spell that ensured anyone who came down here was accounted for. Because if a single one of these scrolls or tomes were damaged or went missing, it could cost the school thousands of auras and regardless of that, each precious scripture in here was irreplaceable. I disbanded said spell as I pulled open the hatch with a smirk on my lips.

Adrenaline streamed through my veins as I headed down the steps that led beneath the library, using a fire crystal to light the ancient sconces lining the walls as I moved through the stone arches, the path of them leading me to the centre of the room. There, between four arches, was a circular space with a mosaic floor and above it, the ceiling domed. An intricate mural had been painted there hundreds of years ago, the beautiful image featuring The Orb at the heart of it shining like the sun and an incredible scene around it picturing every Order there was and ever had been. I moved the desks out from under it where I often spent time studying and left the floor clear. Then I set to work laying out a pile of blankets before placing the jars of everflames Darius had gifted me a few years back around the edge of the blanket.

When I was done, I scored my thumb down the stubble of my cheek, eyeing the set up and wondering if this was a stupid idea. A tug in my chest told me Blue had just stepped through the detection spell I'd left at the library door and my heart pounded to a manic beat. If I'd told myself last year, I'd be standing here laying out blankets and everflames for a student, I'd have laughed my fucking ass off. But Blue was no ordinary student. And I'd accepted the insanity of this a long time ago. I'd stopped asking myself what was going to happen long term. I lived for each moment. And I knew I was getting more reckless. But seeing her in classes, unable to touch her, kiss those lips that were as soft as sin, drove me to the brink of insanity. I was a man unhinged. And the one thing I knew for certain, was that I didn't ever want to get my right mind back.

The sound of footsteps approached and I turned, finding Blue walking towards me in a pale green wrap around dress that was tied at her waist and clung to her figure, making my eyes drag down her hungrily. Her lips were painted darkest red and her hair was blown out of place by the wind.

"Come here," I growled, my patience having spent its last dime several hours ago. I needed her in my arms, needed to touch her, smell her, taste her. I wanted to forget all the nos that lived beyond these walls and soak in the single yes that was us. The one we'd decided. Defying the law.

She gave me a shy smile as she approached and another growl rumbled through my chest. I loved making her shy. Adored the pop of colour in her cheeks and the fluttering of her breath. The way her pupils dilated and how she tugged her lower lip between her teeth like she needed to bite something just to keep away from me. But she wasn't going to be anywhere more than an inch from me tonight.

We'd stay here for a couple of hours then I'd run her back to her room between patrols. Since the Nymph threat had grown, there were always teachers walking the perimeter. But I knew exactly who was on duty and where they'd be.

"Stay here," I said, swallowing against the hard ball in my throat before heading past her and hurrying back to the hatch. I pulled it down, locking us in and using my air magic to manoeuvre the rug back over the top of it through the cracks either side of the hatch. Then I headed back to Blue with my heart pounding, feeling like a teenager with his first crush. I'd never had that all-consuming first love everyone talked about during my school years. I'd thought it wasn't for me. But I guessed the stars had decided to keep me waiting a little longer. And now I had it, I was determined for this love to be my one and only. My last and everlasting.

As I approached, I noticed she had a large bag hanging from her shoulder.

"Did you bring your school books to study like a good girl?" I taunted and a playful grin pulled at her mouth.

"No, sir. I brought a gift for the best teacher I know," she purred in a seductive voice that had my dick hardening.

"A gift?" I questioned, lifting my hand to trace the curve of her jaw with my thumb.

Everything about her beauty was delicate, seemingly breakable. Maybe that was why me and the Heirs had underestimated her and her sister so foolishly when they'd first come here. And maybe that was one of the reasons she got my heart racing. She appeared small and fragile, the perfect hunter's delight. But knowing she held a maelstrom of power in her veins was even more of a turn on. Plus her wit, her tenacity, her intelligence, her unending optimism. All of those things were enough to get me hot for her individually, but together? Well, maybe she'd always been a forgone conclusion for me.

Her optimism had been tested greatly of late, but it had never failed her. We often discussed her sister and Darius being Star Crossed. I'd been spending a lot of time down here hunting for answers about undoing their curse, but I hadn't found a single hint of the possibility that it could be. Yet Blue had never once doubted it. She was unfalteringly determined to find an answer. And I coveted that about her. It gave me hope for them too.

Blue slid the bag off of her shoulder, smiling nervously as she unzipped it and took out a long wooden box which was carved with the Orion constellation in the grain.

She handed it to me and I was surprised by the weight of it as I took it, hurrying under one of the arches to rest it on a desk and open it.

"Gabriel helped me make it. I got the idea from one of the Phoenix books you gave me," she explained and curiosity bled through me as I undid the silver catch and flipped it open.

A bed of black silk lay within it and I shifted it gently aside, my breath hitching as I laid eyes on the most beautiful sword I'd ever seen. The metal glinted like diamonds and the hilt was engraved with two stunning wings wrapped together around a single heart. I took it out and energy buzzed through my limbs.

I turned to Blue with a wide, boyish grin and whipped the blade through the air between us. My breathing stuttered once more as the entire sword ignited in red and blue fire, the blade itself shimmering like it had turned to molten silver.

"Holy fuck," I gasped and she laughed.

"Do you like it?" she asked like there was an actual possibility that I couldn't like this. It was incredible. Fucking unbelievable. "It's indestructible," she explained, stepping closer. "It was forged with Phoenix fire. You just have to run your thumb between the wings to put out the flames."

I did as she said and the fire extinguished, but the blade seemed to glimmer for a long time after. The power in this weapon was immense, I could feel it ringing through my bones.

"It's magnificent," I breathed. "Thank you. Though I've got no idea what I've done to earn it."

"You've done a thousand things to earn it, Lance. You make me so happy, you've taught me to trust again, you've helped me become a true Fae."

My heart thundered at those words. They made me shine like a damn Pegasus on a rainbow high.

I placed the sword back in the box, fucking giddy as a kid as I thought about using it on the next Nymph run.

I turned to Blue and pointed at the pile of blankets with a smirk taking over my features. "Sit."

I had a bottle of champagne waiting beside two glasses next to her and I picked it up, popping the cork and making her jump in surprise as she kicked her shoes off and dropped down in the centre of the blankets.

She stared up at me with a grin, looking like the most edible thing I'd ever seen. I tipped a measure of champagne into my mouth and she watched me with undisguised lust.

"Take your dress off," I commanded and her eyes widened. I'd been waiting all day to have her and now she'd given me a fucking sword, I was going to say thank you in the best way I knew.

She opened the tie on the little wrap around dress she was wearing, her gaze fixed on mine. She curled her bare toes against the blanket as I watched her, drinking champagne and swallowing the fizzing bubbles on my tongue.

When the dress hung open either side of her, I took in the dark blue underwear she wore, the lace giving me a view of her puckered nipples through her bra. My dick was straining against my fly as I kicked off my shoes and stepped onto the blanket, gazing down at her beneath me as she shrugged out of the dress and tossed it aside.

I couldn't help but get off on the position of power that standing over her gave me. It was how I was made. Vampire. Fae. Man. I wanted to bend her to my will and make her praise my name like the stars themselves. I wanted her to renounce her faith in every one of them in the sky and name me as her one and only god. But Blue wasn't a pious little thing who knelt at my altar. She was a goddess in her own right. And however hard I pushed her, she'd always push back.

"Lie down," I instructed and she hesitated, giving me that look that said she wasn't entirely approving of my bossy tone. She wanted to fight me, I could see that instinct in her eyes. But if she didn't play along, then I'd have to be firmer.

"Why don't you come down here?" she insisted, ignoring my demand and shifting onto her knees before me. Her dark blue hair pooled around her, shimmering in the light of the fires burning in the sconces around us. She was almost entirely irresistible to me as she looked up and batted those long lashes. But we were going to play on my terms tonight. I wasn't going to be persuaded otherwise.

I lowered the bottle between us and held it to her lips. "Do as I say or you'll be punished." I poured the champagne haphazardly over her mouth and it spilled down her chin and onto her breasts as she swallowed the small amount she'd gotten.

Her throat bobbed and mischief entered her gaze. Always the rebel.

She reached for my waistband and I let her run the palm of her hand up my solid length. I was as hard as steel for her. Had been since the second she'd arrived. No girl had ever driven me this wild. I only had to scent her on the wind and I was ready to fucking pounce.

I caught her wrist with a dark smirk then brought it to my lips and sank my fangs into her veins, being rougher than usual so she let out a little squeak of surprise. Her blood was a drug I took willingly. It washed through me like an electrical storm, raising every hair across my body as I got lost to the taste of her. When I yanked my fangs free, I rubbed my thumb across the wound to heal it before letting go of her, taking in the sight of her parted lips and the need in her eyes. A need I was going to fulfil until she couldn't remember her own name, let alone mine.

I lowered to a crouch before her, taking another long swig of the champagne. "Now, lie down, Blue."

She went willingly this time, resting back on the soft bed I'd made, her chest heaving. I devoured the view of her spread out for me, my own breathing matching the rampant pants of hers. I was a slave to this body, this girl. I wanted to possess every part of her, invade her and lay siege to every corner of her being.

I used my water magic to chill the bottle, causing ice crystals to form on the glass. Then I ran the edge of it along her side, following the curve of her hip as she flinched and shivered.

"Still," I growled. "Or I'll restrain you."

She gave me a look that said she wasn't totally adverse to that idea and I chuckled darkly. When I reached her bra, I rolled the bottle between the swell of her breasts then tipped it up and splashed a healthy measure of the champagne all over her. She gasped, rearing up, but a whip of my air magic forced her back down again.

I placed the bottle beside us, moving over her and straddling her hips as I leaned down and ran my tongue between her cleavage, lapping away the alcohol as she moaned my name. Her hand fisted in my hair and I caught hold of it, slamming it back down onto the blanket as I lifted my head to snarl at her in warning. "Don't touch me unless I say so."

She nodded, her eyes dancing with the thrill of this game and a grin tugged at my lips.

"Open your mouth," I commanded and she did so as I brought the bottle to her lips, pouring a measure inside then lunging forward to devour it with my tongue. She moaned as she kissed me and I growled as I lost some control, the flavour of her mixed with the champagne making me heady. This girl would be the ruin of me. But I was too far gone to care. I'd let her destroy me brick by brick because if I had to fall, I was more than happy for it to be by her hands.

I ground my hips against her stomach so she could feel how much I wanted her and her fingers hooked into my waistband as her tongue met mine with desperate strokes.

I pulled back, capturing both her hands with a wicked look. "Looking for trouble, beautiful?"

She blushed and I wished I could bottle that colour. I'd paint it on my walls and wear it on my damn skin. She was too divine a creature and I was utterly captivated by her when she looked at me like that.

She licked her lips, no doubt tasting the last of me and the champagne on her tongue.

"Are you going to punish me, Professor?" she asked sweetly and fuck, I was about to lose my mind. I needed to be inside of her, feeling her heat, her aching flesh as she wrapped herself around me. I could sense myself giving into that urge inch by inch.

I nodded with a sinister smile, lifting my weight off her and flipping her over beneath me, making her gasp in alarm with the strength I used. I pressed my knees into the blanket on either side of her and yanked her hips up, sitting back as I brought her perfect round ass to my lips and sank my teeth into her flesh. She cried out as I marked her with my fangs then caught a fist full of her hair as I reared over her. The blue glittered around my fingers and looked so damn good in my grip. I brought my mouth to her ear, grinding my aching cock into her ass as she panted my name.

"Good girls get rewarded," I purred. "Are you going to behave?"

She nodded.

"Say it," I growled.

"I'll be good."

"Then stay where you are." I moved behind her as she remained on all fours, her back peppering with goosebumps as I sat back on my heels and brushed my fingers over her flawless skin. I unhooked her bra and she shrugged out of it, shivering as I circled my fingers between her shoulder blades.

I hooked my fingers into her panties and she swore as I pulled them down, tugging them over her ankles and making her toes curl up tightly as she was bared to me.

I palmed her ass, releasing a wave of healing magic over the bite mark and her hips started to sway with urgency. It took everything I had not to unzip my fly and thrust myself into her. But I wanted to take it slow, make her endure every ounce of pleasure I could give before I took any for myself.

"Are you wet for me, Blue?" I asked.

"See for yourself," she said breathily and I laughed. Always lippy. Even when I had her at my mercy.

I slapped my hand hard against her ass and she gasped in surprise before I rubbed the reddened mark to soothe it. "Answer me," I insisted and I could picture her blush from here.

"Yes," she whispered and I slid my hand between her legs, feeling the evidence of her arousal with a groan.

Fuck, she's so ready for me.

I placed one hand on the base of her spine then pushed two fingers into her without warning, making her back arch as she cried out. I pumped them slowly, getting off on her moaning and begging for more. I built up a relentlessly slow rhythm that was enough to drive her crazy, but never enough to push her over the edge. She wasn't going there until I said so.

"Lance, please," she panted and my mouth pulled up at the corner.

I pulled my hand free and grabbed her hips suddenly, flipping her back over and grabbing the bottle of champagne. I poured the ice cold liquid between her legs and her hips bucked as she let out a cry of alarm. I pressed one palm down on her stomach to keep her still, dropping my mouth between her thighs and lapping up the champagne as she cursed like a sailor.

I feasted on her, nipping and sucking, licking and devouring until she was right at the edge of oblivion. I teased her clit between my teeth then used the tip of my tongue to soothe the pain and push her nearer to bliss. Her thighs tightened around me and my name fell from her lips again and again, echoing around the chamber and branding this place as ours forever.

I feasted on her mercilessly, drawing her closer and closer before slowing my tongue and making her beg and beg and beg. It was the highest form of power and I was losing my mind over it.

"Please – god – please," she cried, but she wasn't going to come like this. I wanted to fall apart with her and I was so desperate for her, I knew I was going to last about as long as she was at this point.

I moved over her and she clawed at my shirt, her eyes wild with need. I let her pull it over my head, losing all control as she slid her hands between us, unbuckling my pants with frantic fingers and taking my solid shaft into her hand.

"Fuck, Blue," I gasped as she skimmed her thumb over the head of my cock and I swear I was gonna blow any second.

She guided me between her legs, lifting her hips in a desperate offering and I claimed her with a forceful thrust that made her scream. I caught her wrists, holding them above her head and slamming into her with the speed of my Order. She was coming apart, clenching around me and I was just as close, panting heavily as I drove us both toward nirvana.

Her lips crashed clumsily against mine and the taste of her sent me over the edge at the same moment as her. She clung to my back with her nails tearing into my flesh as I spilled myself inside her and groaned curses as pleasure seized me. An explosion of ecstasy took place everywhere in my body. My head was bursting with light and her body felt like an extension of mine as our magic tumbled together, colliding and joining, making another wave of pure pleasure tear through me. I didn't feel like I was on the same plane as I had been two seconds ago, I was lost to her. My beautiful blue-haired warrior.

My forehead fell against hers and the sweet scent of her flesh brought me back to reality. I stared down into the infinite depths of her dark green eyes and placed a kiss against the corner of her mouth as I fought to catch my breath.

Everything in my life was brighter with her. It was good and sweet and perfect. I didn't know what I'd done for the stars to gift me this girl. I could never have offered them enough to earn this good fortune. And I wasn't going to squander it. I knew what I had. And I'd protect her until my dying breath. And even then I'd still fight to keep her safe beyond the veil. Whatever it took. Always.

DARCY

CHAPTER THIRTY

After my night with Orion, my head was left spinning and my body weakened by so much pleasure that I could barely walk straight. He'd carried me back to my room just before sunrise. Exhausted, shattered, whole.

I slept for a few hours and when I woke, I was still smiling. I didn't think I'd ever get rid of this smile. And I didn't want to.

I shimmied to the edge of the bed and pushed a hand into my bag on the floor, hunting for my Atlas and wondering how the hell I'd woken up before my alarm considering how little sleep I'd had. But somehow I didn't feel tired, I felt energised. High on freaking life. Orion was like a shot of adrenaline that made my heart sing and my mind swim with endless happiness. I hadn't wanted to part from him last night, but I knew he couldn't sleep that well in my small bed and it had been too risky to head back to the staff quarters that close to dawn. We'd gotten some sleep in the archives, but we'd also had an insatiable appetite for each other that just hadn't quit.

I huffed as I poked my head over the edge of the bed, trying to see into my bag as I searched for my Atlas. I couldn't actually remember seeing it since dinner yesterday and I sighed as I realised it wasn't there. I must have left it down in The Orb.

Getting out of bed, I headed to the shower and was soon ready for the day in my uniform. I used a handy little vanity spell Sofia had taught me to conceal the bags under my eyes before heading out the door with my bag over my shoulder.

By the time I got to The Orb, the tiredness was starting to set in and I yawned broadly as I headed over to join the A.S.S. at our usual table. Tory was there already and I dropped down beside her with another yawn as she raised an eyebrow at me. I offered her a twin look which gave her the answer and she snorted a laugh as I swiped a bagel off of the mountain Geraldine had laid out for us, hiding a grin.

"What dastardly deeds did you get up to last night, Darcy Vega?" Geraldine demanded, leaning in conspiratorially. "It's unlike you to be late to our morning feast."

A blush hit my cheeks and I shrugged, unable to give any kind of honest answer.

"Cod in a cornfield! Do you have a young gentlefae who has stolen your affections?" she asked excitedly and Sofia and Diego looked to me too with a keen interest.

"I er..." I tucked a lock of hair behind my ear. "Well, there might be someone I guess."

"Do tell!" Geraldine demanded, slamming her hand down on the table and making a bunch of bagels tumble down the mountain.

"I can't," I said, chewing my lip. "It's a secret." At that moment, my gaze snagged on Orion at the far end of the room sitting at a table with Nova and Washer. He rarely came to breakfast and it made my heart thunder as he caught my eye and a smirk danced around his lips before he looked away again. Lips that had been all over my body last night. A mouth that had made me scream a hundred times.

I cleared my throat, taking a bite of my bagel to try and distract myself from how good he looked today in a crisp white shirt and navy tie.

"I would take your secret to the grave and beyond, my lady," Geraldine swore, marking a cross over her heart.

I smiled guiltily, wishing I could be honest with her. I knew she'd keep the secret, she was just so damn loyal, she wouldn't dare breathe a word to anyone. But this wasn't something I could implicate my friends in. It was bad enough that Tory knew, despite the fact that I was so glad she did. It was so nice to be able to talk about it at last.

"I know," I said, about to come up with some explanation when Geraldine gasped like a wasp had flown into her mouth as she pointed frantically at the door behind me.

I turned in confusion and my heart dipped as I spotted the group of four FIB agents striding into The Orb in their black jumpsuits with high-powered magical weapons strapped to their hips, including a gun and what looked like some sort of taser.

"What are they doing here?" Tory murmured as excited chatter filled the room.

"Nymph attack?" I guessed, sharing a concerned look with her as they strode towards Principal Nova.

She jumped from her seat, seeming just as alarmed by their appearance as everyone else. But they didn't acknowledge her, two of them grabbed hold of Orion's arms and yanked him out of his seat. *What the fuck??*

"Professor Lance Orion, you are hereby detained by the Court of

Solaria for fraternising with a student who is none other than a Princess of Solaria."

Noise exploded around the room and eyes turned towards me and Tory, but I couldn't see anything but a blur as my world spun and everything became terrifying unsteady. My heart squeezed like it was in a razor sharp vice as I struggled for breath. *This can't be right, there must have been some mistake.*

"Oh my stars, does Tory Vega's sex addiction know no bounds?" Mildred piped up and Tory gripped my hand under the table as eyes swung toward her. *Shit, no, no, no.*

Every single nerve ending in my body screamed. Panic warred through my body like a flashfire.

I had to stop this.

I had to explain.

But how?

What could I do?

Think Darcy, fucking think!

Nova looked to Orion in alarm and one of the agents slammed some sort of notice down in front of her.

"Wait, just wait a fucking second." Orion yanked his arms free, swivelling to face the agents with his shoulders rigid. "What proof do you have?" he demanded and I stood up, knowing I needed to do something.

I felt eyes on me from everywhere as whispers snaked their way into my ears.

"What's she doing? Surely Darcy Vega wouldn't have fucked a teacher?"

"Why would Professor Orion screw a Vega?"

"Maybe she gave blowjobs for good grades."

Tory tugged on my arm, trying to make me sit down, but I couldn't. I was numb. My mind was taking a moment to catch up to what was happening as dread took hold of me in an unyielding grip.

"Lance, what's going on?" Nova demanded, looking rattled. Washer gazed from Orion to me and Tory with wide eyes, looking like he was desperate to confirm which one of us the agents meant.

"A video file was sent to the bureau just one hour ago showing you being overtly intimate with a student," one of the male agents explained before grabbing Orion's arm again.

Fuuuuuck.

My head screamed. My lungs screamed. All of me was screaming except my actual voice. I stood there silent, struck dumb by this news. That someone, some *asshole* had recorded us together. But who? And how? I thought of my missing Atlas and everything started to slot together. The message from Orion...the library...the archives. Someone had known. Someone had set us up.

"Blathering bandicoots!" Geraldine exclaimed, but I couldn't look at her or any of the other faces aimed my way.

Darius was out of his seat in a heartbeat, marching towards the FIB agents with the air of a soldier marching into battle. "What exactly are the charges?"

"With respect, this is none of your concern," a male agent said, bowing his head for a moment before turning back to Orion.

"It's my concern if I make it my concern. Do you know who I am?!" he bellowed.

"Of course, Mr Acrux." The man dipped his head again. "But this is the law. And I have a job to do."

Darius snarled, snatching his Atlas from his pocket and violently tapping out something on it as he muttered under his breath.

My gaze pinned on Orion and Orion alone. Fear sliced into me, tearing apart the fragile sense of security we'd built together. The lie we'd told ourselves that this would never happen. But now it had and I couldn't think. I couldn't breathe.

Orion turned ghostly pale and I could see the resignation on his face as the agents spoke to him in a low tone I couldn't hear. He wouldn't meet my gaze and I couldn't handle it a second longer.

I marched away from my table and strode towards the agents as people stood up around The Orb, their Atlases angled at me from everywhere as they filmed the whole thing. A few people were even climbing onto tables to get a better look.

"Let go of him," I demanded and the nearest agent glanced over her shoulder at me with a serious expression.

"Step back, madam, you will be issued with a court date within twenty four hours. You will have your say then and only then."

"This is ridiculous," Darius hissed, his eyes still pinned on his Atlas as he typed out message after message to his contacts.

"A court date?" I gasped, terror winding its way around my organs as Nova's horrified gaze slid between me and Orion, the reality dawning on her that this was actually happening.

"There must be some mistake," Washer tried, stepping forward, but the female agent gripped the taser on her belt.

"Step back, sir," she growled and fear fuelled my movements as two of the men started hauling Orion toward the exit.

"No – wait!" I cried, panic burrowing into me and making a home. I couldn't let him go. I couldn't let them take him. "Stop – just listen to me!"

Orion glanced over his shoulder, his face drained of colour and his eyes full of a desperate kind of fear. "Stop, Blue," he whispered firmly, just for me. But I couldn't. I wasn't just going to stand here and let them take him away from me. The moment he stepped out of that door, I didn't know what would happen. But I was so petrified of whatever it was, that I simply had to try and face down fate.

"Wait please!" I caught the sleeve of the guard holding Orion's right arm, tugging hard. He tried to shake me off and rage spewed through me. Fire blazed beneath my skin and blasted out of me before I could stop it. The agent yelled in pain, stumbling back as he poured water down his blazing arm to douse the flames.

Shit. No. Fuck.

He took the taser from his belt, aiming it at me and Orion roared a command to stop before what felt like a thousand bolts of electricity slammed into my veins. I hit the ground, tasting blood as I bit my lip and pain exploded through every inch of my body. It stopped as quickly as it had started and my vision cleared, but my body felt drained and I couldn't access my power for a long second.

I blinked up through the fog of my mind as my ears rang and my heart hammered. Orion yanked himself free of the guard holding him and headbutted the asshole who'd tasered me.

Blood pissed down from the guy's broken nose and all four agents dove on top of Orion in a heartbeat. He was thrown face down against the nearest table and students screamed and gasped as they scattered to give them room. They wrestled his arms behind his back, locking him in cuffs which glowed blue as they secured them, then they dragged him upright.

Tory was suddenly at my side, helping me to my feet. "Darcy, you have to stop," she said, her voice breaking, but I refused to listen. I couldn't let them take him.

Darius was beside her with reptilian slits for eyes and rage spewing from his expression. "I'll fix this," he swore before striding after the agents.

I shrugged Tory off and ran after them as they made it out the doors. Students were spilling after us to watch the show and I didn't know what I was going to do, but I had to do *something*.

"Lance!" I cried, my voice sounding like glass shattering into a thousand pieces. He didn't look back. *Why won't he look back?!*

"You cannot come with us, Mr Acrux," an agent said apologetically as Darius marched beside them.

He growled dangerously then shoved his way through them toward Orion, whispering something in his ear before turning away and marching back towards the crowd.

I ran forward, desperate to try and stop this, but a shadow fell out of the sky and Gabriel landed in front of me with anxiety in his eyes. He pressed a hand to my shoulder with an intense look. "You have to stay here, it will only make things worse otherwise."

"Why didn't you *see* this?!" I demanded as I tried to step around him, but his wing stretched out to block me.

I was about to fight him with magic when he caught my hand and tugged me close, a look of fervent emotion in his gaze. "I came as soon as I could. I was at home, I wasn't focusing on him to receive this vision. But as soon as I got near the academy…" He shook his head. "I'm sorry."

I shoved my way past him, ducking under his wing and starting to run after Orion with my heart in my throat. Fear tangled with every thought I possessed and turned me into a wild animal. *They can't take him. I won't let them.*

But Gabriel raced after me, his arm locking around my shoulders. "Darcy, this will make things so much worse for him if you go. Please trust me."

I fell still, my rampant heart slowing as I accepted his words and tears tracked down my cheeks.

The agents marched Orion away from me and I screamed after him, begging him to look back. But he didn't.

The Heirs appeared beside us as Tory rested a hand on my back. Darius was on the phone within a silencing bubble, pacing frantically back and forth as he spoke with whoever was on the other end of the line. My eyes locked with Seth's and the second it happened, I knew. I fucking *knew* he'd done this. Because who else would? He'd even warned me of this very thing happening on his birthday, told me how much it would fuck up my chances for the throne. So he'd bided his time. Waited for his moment to strike, taken my Atlas when I'd been distracted and found that message Orion had sent so he knew exactly where to find us. How to trap us. Now he'd gotten what he'd always wanted and ripped my heart out still beating.

Gabriel's grip eased enough for me to wriggle free and I ran towards Seth and pointed an accusing finger at that bastard of a Wolf who sought to destroy everything good in my life.

"You did this!" I shouted, feeling Atlases aimed at me from every angle.

Before he could answer, Principal Nova muscled through the crowd, her face pinched in distress. "Miss Vega, go to my office. Now!" she bellowed, making the whole school fall silent with her powerful tone.

My lower lip quivered and terror coursed through my limbs. This was it. It was all fucked. Every day we'd spent together had been foolishly, blindly spent in ignorant bliss. But Seth had been plotting all along to destroy us. Of *course* he'd never let us win. He'd never just let us be happy. And I hated him more than I'd ever hated anything. It spilled into my veins like an insidious poison that ate into my bones.

I'd kill him. I'd fucking *kill* him.

Seth stared at me in shock and Gabriel caught my arm again as my gaze fixed on the Wolf I vowed to destroy and Tory took hold of my other hand. The two of them gave me serious, pleading looks that burned into my core.

"We'll bring her," Tory announced to Nova who nodded stiffly then she turned back to me with tears in her eyes. "Come on. You have to go."

My throat thickened and I knew I wouldn't get near Seth now. But I silently swore on every star in the sky, I would obliterate him for this.

I let them guide me away from the staring crowd, away from the whispers of *whore* and *slut* and even worse accusations than that. I was numb as I moved, tears tracking silently down my cheeks as I tried to figure out an answer to this. There had to be a way out. There had to be a chance for us yet. This couldn't be it. We were meant for each other. I felt it down to my soul. I *knew* it to be true.

Gabriel slid his arm around my shoulders and Tory clutched my hand harder, neither of them saying anything until we arrived outside Nova's office and my legs started to shake.

"There's still the court date," Gabriel said softly. "They'll hear both of your stories." He winced suddenly and I lurched toward him, clutching his shirt in my fists.

"What do you see? Is there a way out of this?" I begged, searching his eyes as I hunted for a glimmer of hope.

His Adam's apple rose and fell and he cupped my cheek with his hand. "There are many possibilities. It depends..."

"On what?" I demanded, my heart cracking, ready to fall apart. I needed something to hold onto to keep it together. I had to have a shred of hope.

"On both of you, on the stars, on the mercy of the Court," he said heavily.

"But there is a chance?" Tory asked for me and I was glad because I couldn't draw enough breath to ask it myself right then.

"I..." Gabriel sighed, giving me a look that said he was about to be brutally honest with me. "He will be punished, there is no doubt about that. But the degree to which he is punished will depend on too many factors that I can't clearly see. The only hope for the two of you is a lenient judge and even then..." He shook his head. "He will be power shamed, Darcy. He'll lose his job, they'll strip him of his place in Solaria."

I sank down to the floor, losing all the strength in my body as this terrifying reality crushed me on all sides. He was going to take the fall for this. It didn't matter what they did to me, I didn't care. But he was a good man, he didn't deserve to lose everything because of me.

"Up," Nova's voice clipped as she arrived. "Inside. *Now*, Miss Vega."

Gabriel helped me to my feet as Nova unlocked the door to her office, gesturing for me to enter and telling the other two to wait outside.

As the door closed behind me, silence pressed in on my ears, deafening after the loudness of the crowd. All I could see was Orion's face the moment he accepted it. That dark truth settling over him, like he was realising what a fool he'd been for ever thinking this wouldn't happen. What fools we'd both been. But this wasn't his fault, or mine. It was Seth Capella's. And I was going to ensure justice was damn well served.

"Sit," Nova snapped and I dropped into the seat before her desk as she stood on the other side of it, turning her back to me as she faced the window.

The tension in her posture told me how furious she was. But I didn't care about her rage, all I could think about was Orion being hauled to some prison cell somewhere. Alone. And it made every part of me hurt.

"I'm going to ask you some questions, Miss Vega," she said coldly. "And you are going to answer them concisely, do you understand me? I don't want to hear your explanations, those are for the Court now. But what I do need is to get a clear picture of exactly how much damage this is going to cause our school."

My throat tightened and I forced out the words, "Yes, Principal."

"How long have you been having an affair with Professor Orion?" she asked, a sharp note of rage in her voice.

I bit my tongue, refusing to confirm anything until I knew what was on that video. A tear rolled down my cheek and I quickly wiped it away.

Her spine straightened in annoyance, but she didn't turn around.

"Did he force you to have sexual relations with him?" she asked, her voice suddenly filled with sympathy as if she'd just realised the possibility of that.

"No," I snarled immediately.

No matter what came of this situation, I was never going to let anyone think he forced me into this. I'd scream it from every mountaintop in Solaria if I had to. I loved him. And he loved me too. But it started to seem impossible in that moment. It sounded like a pretty dream I'd painted. The two of us, teacher and student, making it work. When did that ever work?

"Are you aware of the law in Solaria prohibiting teachers from having intimate relationships with their students?" She twisted around and her eyes spewed hellfire at me. "And are you aware that, dependent on what comes to light in court, you may have brought your position at this school under question?"

I took in a ragged breath, but she barrelled on before I could answer, slamming her hands down on her desk and glaring at me.

"Do you understand the seriousness of this situation, Miss Vega?!" she boomed and I nodded, wiping the wet trails from my cheeks as I tried not to fall apart.

She fell silent, surveying me through her soft blue eyes that currently looked as sharp as razors. "I will make a decision on your place at Zodiac after the trial has been held."

I nodded, a sliver of fear driving deep into my chest. Because losing Orion was the worst thing in the world, but to lose my place here too. My home. It was unthinkable.

"What will happen to Lance?" I whispered, my hands curling into fists as the shadows snaked up from a dark pit inside me and offered to bury my pain. But I wouldn't let them have it. Not even now, when the hurt inside me made me want to drown in their soothing embrace. I needed the sharpness of it to fight this war. I was going to cling to every venomous drip of it and aim it at the boy who'd caused this. The Werewolf who'd decided to destroy me the moment I'd arrived at this academy. And he'd finally found a way to do it.

Nova gave me a cool look which chilled me to my core. "He's no longer welcome in my school. And he will be lucky if he doesn't end up in prison."

"Prison?" I echoed, horror knotting up my veins. "I know he broke the law, but he's not a bad person-"

"The Court of Solaria will decide exactly what kind of person he is, Miss Vega," Nova said with her upper lip peeling back. "Lance Orion has been a good colleague, a spectacular teacher, but he has chosen to scorn his prestigious job in favour of fucking a student. I do not have any pity for that."

Those harsh words out of her mouth shocked me into silence. Then she pointed to the door, looking bitterly disappointed in me as she turned her gaze to the wall.

I rose from my seat, trembling all over as I opened the door and stepped into the corridor. Tory's arms surrounded me and I fell apart. Every piece of strength inside me dissolved into nothing and I tumbled into the deepest pit of despair I'd ever known.

TORY

CHAPTER THIRTY ONE

I lay curled up in bed with Darcy all night while she cried and raged and eventually fell silent. She wasn't asleep. Neither of us had gotten any of that, but we were together. And I wasn't even sure what else I could offer her right now.

Her room slowly lightened around us, but I just stayed with her wrapped in my arms until she finally stirred.

"Darius will get him off lightly," I murmured for the thousandth time. "Orion's his Guardian. Even Lionel will help, I'm sure of it."

"Even if they do, how am I supposed to be with him then?" Darcy asked in a flat voice which sounded so unlike her that I eased back so that I could look at her.

Her green eyes were dull and lifeless as well as puffy and bloodshot from a night spent in tears, but the set of her jaw was stubborn, angry. She'd avoided lessons all day yesterday and I'd stayed with her, knowing she couldn't bear to face the world right now.

"You'll find a way," I promised. "We can figure out somewhere for you to meet in private, or maybe Darius can get you stardust, or-"

"We were never allowed to be together," she said, her gaze darkening as she pushed herself upright and I followed to sit beside her, pulling a pillow into my lap. "The whole world was against us, even the law."

"I know," I said, reaching out to take her hand. "But you love each other. There has to be a way to fight for that."

Darcy looked at me for a long moment, her jaw tightening as shadows flickered in her eyes. "What would you know about fighting for something like that?" she snapped at me and I flinched at the acid in her tone.

"I don't under-"

"The stars picked a perfect mate for you and all either of you ever did was fight and goad each other and force each other away."

"This isn't about me and Darius," I breathed, my heart thrashing in my chest. Darcy never lost her temper with me like that, but I wasn't going to bite back. If she needed me to be her punching bag for this pain she was feeling then I would be.

"No. It's about the way me and Lance *always* fought to be together. We've always had to. Fate has always been against us, but we knew it was worth the risk. We owned our feelings and acted on them. When have you and Darius ever done that?" she snapped.

"It's not the same," I said defensively. "Lance never hurt you the way Darius hurt me. Darius made my life hell, he tormented me and attacked me time after time. He tried to *drown* me-"

"I know," she ground out, the emotion in her gaze clear. "But it's not like you're entirely innocent in all of the things that have happened between you, is it? You goaded and taunted him too. Besides, you got revenge, you set his room alight, you even made him turn on Milton, you fought back against all the shit he put you through. But you also slept with him, drew him in and then pushed him away-"

"Because I couldn't just forgive all of his shit," I snarled, my own temper fraying as she called me out. "He never apologised to me, never gave me any real inclination that he cared at all-"

"Bullshit!" Darcy shouted and I flinched. "He might be a fucking bastard and a ruthless asshole, he might have done all of those horrible things to you and maybe he even deserved a life spent pining for you. But you can't say he never tried to show you how he felt. You just refused to hear it. And you refused to see it. Because you're too fucking stubborn for your own good. Even when you wanted him you refused to admit it to yourself, you just hid behind hate and sex and came up with every excuse under the sun to deny your own heart."

"You know why I couldn't just offer up my heart to him," I said in a low voice as her words cut through me like gunfire. "I couldn't just give him the chance to hurt me with it. I couldn't-"

"That's what love is, Tor," Darcy said in exasperation. "It's taking a leap of faith. It's opening yourself up and letting your walls down and allowing someone to see every dark and broken corner of your soul. It's truth and honesty with yourself and them. It's raw and brutal and terrifying and *real*. You can't just claim to want it, but refuse to allow yourself to be vulnerable to it. That's not how it works. If you love someone, truly love them, you'll bear your soul to them and let them be the keeper of your heart no matter how fragile or damaged it might be. And if they love you then they'll do everything in their power to keep it safe, to nurture and protect it and heal over all the old wounds. So when you said no to him in that snow storm, you weren't even hurting him. You were hurting yourself. And that's what kills me the most about all of it."

"Darcy," I breathed, my heart aching with pain as she tore apart every stubborn, rational, hateful reason I'd been holding onto to stay away from Darius Acrux.

"That's what I have with Lance," she snarled. "It's messy and terrifying and to anyone else it wouldn't even come close to perfect. But it is perfect, Tor, he's everything to me. And now he's been torn away from me and there's *nothing* I can do about it. Everything has been against us from the beginning. But there was never anything stopping you and Darius from being together apart from the two of you. If either of you had just pulled your heads out of your own asses and been *honest* with each other then none of this would have happened to you! And that *kills* me. Because I would give anything to have that freedom with Lance." A choked sob escaped her and I shifted forward, reaching for her to pull her into my arms again.

"No," she hissed, flicking her fingers at me with a blast of air magic so that I stumbled off of the bed, dropping the pillow to the floor. "I don't want you here telling me everything will be okay. If you want to fix something then go and tell Darius how you feel. I don't want to sit here with you moping about me and Lance while you refuse to even *try* and fix your own shit."

"I can't fix it, Darcy. It's too late!" I protested as her air magic shoved me back towards her door.

"You might not be able to be together. But you can be honest with each other," she said forcefully. "And if you want any chance of moving on from this fucking mess you've made for yourselves then you'll be brave enough to do that."

"It's not about being brave-"

"Yes it is! You're so caught up in proving how strong you can be and improving your magic that you're forgetting that true strength comes from facing down the things you're most afraid of. So Fae up, Tory. And go face your problems."

Her magic knocked the door open behind me and before I could reply, I stumbled out into the corridor and the door slammed in my face again.

I stood gaping at it as I hesitated, not knowing whether I should just knock her door down to get back to her or do what she wanted, but at the sound of the door locking, I gave in.

I blew out a deep breath as Darcy's pain threatened to drown me and turned to jog away down the stairs.

Shadows flickered over my vision and danced along my fingertips as they called me to them. I could just go back to my room and let them have me for a few minutes. Just sink into the euphoric oblivion of their embrace so that I didn't have to feel any of this.

The more I used the shadows, the more they called to me and the greater my control over them grew. There was a dark kind of comfort to be had in them and after spending the night with Darcy without using them, I could hear their call more sharply than usual. I knew I should be worried about what Orion had said about how addictive their call could be, but I wasn't. I was only dipping into them at night and even then it wasn't for all that long. The more I used them, the greater my control over them grew. And as they could be exactly what we needed to defeat Lionel, I wasn't going to let him get ahead of me with them. The shadows licked around my wrists and I pushed them back with a grunt of effort. No matter how tempting they may have been, using them while standing in the middle of Aer Tower was a bad idea.

See, I'm in total control.

I didn't want to think about the words Darcy had thrown at me, but they were ringing around my skull, forcing my attention to fix on them whether I wanted to or not. I knew I was stubborn and pig headed and unforgiving, but having the closest person in the world to me cut me with those weapons hurt.

No, it wasn't hurt. It was a bitter kind of acknowledgement. Because as much as I might have hated having her strike me with those words, I couldn't really deny them. But was I really going to track down Darius and do what she said?

I huffed in frustration, jogging down the steps in Aer Tower until I made it to the foot of the stairs.

I'd stolen some of Darcy's clothes last night so I was dressed in a pair of leggings and an oversized sweater instead of my uniform.

I paused outside as the cool morning air gusted around me, tugging at my hair and making a shiver race along my shoulder blades as the urge to shift tugged at me.

It was still early, the sun low in the sky and birdsong filling the air. In fact, at this time I'd usually be out running with Darius...

My gut twisted as I realised I'd missed our run for the first time in over two months. I'd had somewhere more important to be, at Darcy's side, but I chewed my bottom lip as I wondered whether or not he'd shown up expecting me, only to find I wasn't there. Surely he'd have figured out why. But the idea of letting him down kinda...made me feel bad.

I wondered if he would have gone without me or if he'd have just gone back to his room.

Why do I even give a shit?

I stalked away from Aer Tower, growling with frustration as I shoved my hands through my hair, tugging at the knots in it as I tried to figure out what to do. Did I really care enough about hurting his little Dragon feelings to track him down and explain my absence? Was I seriously considering doing what Darcy had told me to do and facing him with everything I'd never even admitted to myself?

Gah. Fucking Dragon asshole!

I tugged Darcy's sweatshirt off and rolled my shoulders back as I dropped it in the long grass by my feet. I was wearing a razor back crop top beneath it so my wings had room to spring free as I called on them and I sighed as my Phoenix fire burned away the last echoes of the shadows. It was like waking up as the shadows receded and my mind cleared, the cool air shivering around me as the heat of my flaming wings affected it.

I took off right away and started flying along our usual running route, wondering if he would have gone without me as I kept my eyes on the path.

I slowed down as I soared over The Wailing Wood, my gaze catching on several colourful bodies as I spotted a Pegasus herd moving between the trees at a slow pace as they grazed.

Just as I was about to fly on, I saw him, my heart leaping as he ran along the track at a fast pace, his shirt off and skin gleaming with sweat as he sprinted up the track.

I beat my wings hard to get ahead of him then dropped down between the trees, landing on the path and banishing my wings just as he crested the hill before me and fell still.

The corner of his mouth twitched as he looked at me, a question lighting his dark eyes.

My gut churned as I looked at him, my heart pounding and my palms growing slick. He looked good enough to eat with sweat coating his golden skin and making the light shine on his tattoos as his muscles tensed from his workout. My gaze slid over every perfect curve of his abs down to that irresistible V which disappeared beneath the low slung waistband of his black sweatpants.

I forced myself to stop eye fucking him and looked up at his face. His black hair was messy and the stubble on his jaw thicker than usual and the dark rings beneath his eyes made me wonder if he'd even slept at all. I guessed the stress of Orion's arrest was hitting him almost as hard as Darcy and I hesitated for a moment, wondering if I should really be coming here to talk to him about this now.

"What's wrong?" he asked, his gaze slipping for a moment as he looked at the ruby pendant hanging around my neck. I hadn't taken it off since he'd given it to me and I shifted uncomfortably as he gazed at it. Why would I keep wearing it if it didn't mean something to me? And if I was being really honest with myself, I knew it did mean something. The stone warmed between my fingers when I held it and the feel of it reminded me of his fire magic so intensely that it gave me goosebumps. I'd woken up with my fingers wrapped around it more than once.

He looked back to my eyes and my heart thundered as I tried to force my tongue to bend around the words Darcy had told me to speak to him. But it was damn *hard.* After everything we'd been through, everything he'd done and I'd done, I just...

"Why didn't you ever just apologise?" I asked him, lifting my chin as my voice caught in my throat. Because if I was seriously going to consider being honest with him about how I felt then I needed him to do the same.

A frown tugged at his brow and he moved closer to me before pausing again just far enough from me that he couldn't reach out and touch me. The ground trembled beneath my feet and he growled as he glanced down at it, the stars instantly working against us even when I just wanted to talk to him.

I stumbled as the ground bucked again and huffed irritably as I strode around him and nodded towards the Pegasus herd at the bottom of the hill he'd just crested.

The herd moved between the trees further down the path and I led the way to stand between them as I moved off of the path and pressed my back to a huge oak so that we were no longer alone and the stars would leave us to talk. I tossed a silencing bubble over us and offered Sofia a tight smile as I spotted her in her pink Pegasus form. She glanced between me and Darius and nodded her horsey head before stomping her foot on the ground to signal the rest of the herd to stay around us too.

I need to tell that girl I love her more often.

Darius moved to stand before me and I looked up at him as I waited for my answer.

He scrubbed a hand over his face and sighed as he took me in.

"My father raised me to be brutal, ruthless and merciless in my quest for power and dominance," he said eventually, holding my eye so that I couldn't look away. "When you and your sister returned to Solaria, it was the first time that I'd ever been forced to face a threat like that. Someone who might actually be able to stand between me and what I was born for. Father and the other Celestial Councillors put a lot of pressure on us to make sure that you would never rise. We thought if we could get you to withdraw from the academy, prove to everyone that you had no chance of ever matching us then we could just forget about you. Move on. Claim the throne the way our parents had after your father was killed and just carry on like you'd never returned at all."

"I understand that. But it doesn't answer my question," I said in a low voice, fighting to hide the hurt of all the things he'd done to me, though I was sure I was failing miserably.

"I guess, I…" He took a step closer to me so that I was forced to tilt my head to look up at him, the air between us heating with his fire magic as mine rose to the surface of my skin to meet it. "I just didn't think any apology I made could be enough to right all the things I'd done to you. And if I'm honest, I didn't think you had any interest in hearing it even if I tried."

I swallowed a thick lump in my throat, wetting my lips as I tried to figure out what to say to that. His eyes chased the movement of my tongue and my heart pounded as he closed in on me again. I leaned back against the tree, the rough bark rubbing against the bare skin along my spine as he caged me in. But I didn't have the slightest inclination to escape him.

"I shouldn't have said it meant nothing to me after we were together in the Shimmering Springs," I breathed, my voice so low I wasn't sure he'd catch it, but the way his eyes flared with heat said he had.

We stared at each other for the longest moment. All of the hurt and pain and the echoes of every horrible thing that had ever passed between us sitting there in that space.

"I should have realised that you were meant for me sooner," Darius said in a rough voice that betrayed just how much this distance between us hurt him.

"Some part of me did realise it," I replied. Because I couldn't deny the pull I'd always felt towards him, that ache in me which begged me to forget every horrible thing he'd done to me and just claim him for myself.

But as easy as that might have sounded, I wasn't that girl. I'd been hurt too many times before in too many ways.

"Me too," he breathed in this hopeless kind of way which didn't detract from the heat that was building between us at all. "But I was...weak I guess. I took the route my father wanted. The easy route."

"It will always be easier for you to hurt me than be there for me. It's who you are. You're a power hungry creature who would sacrifice *anything* to get what you think you're owed out of life." That bitter edge to my tone was back. That spite and anger, the blame.

Darius didn't flinch away from my words, but the way his brow furrowed made my heart ache, like he saw some truth in them too and hated that fact.

"I know. But if you'd said yes to me I would have spent my life trying to make it up to you," he breathed, shifting closer to me so that I was overwhelmed by the size of his huge body. His muscles flexed with tension and his dark gaze burned with all the things he wished he could have had with me. My gaze hooked on that black line surrounding his deep brown irises, that mark which bound him to me and bound him away from me all at once. And as he looked into my eyes, I knew he was looking at the same thing. This mark the stars had branded onto us the moment we'd failed their tests. His forehead was almost touching mine, the space between us falling away inch by inch as he drew closer, leaning his forearm on the tree above my head as he boxed me in.

"How could I have said yes to you after everything you'd done to me?" I breathed but not angrily, my limbs were trembling, my heart pounding and my soul aching for his. "I lie awake at night and think about it, think about *you*, wishing I could have made the other choice. But I couldn't. As much as this is killing me, I know it's killing you too. And there's a fucked up part of me that revels in that, in knowing that I'm causing you pain just like you did to me."

Darius reached out slowly with his free hand, his fingertips trailing a burning line across the side of my face before painting a mark down the side of my neck. I shivered at his touch, still craving more of him despite all of it.

"I deserved it," he said in a low voice, my heart leaping in surprise at those words on his lips. "I deserved it, Roxy. And I'm sorry. Really, truly sorry for all of it. I know that doesn't matter now and I know there's nothing I can do to change this, but I need you to know it. I need you to feel it." His hand landed over my heart and my flesh burned and ached for him even as my broken heart pounded beneath his palm. I was sure he could feel the shattered pieces of it fighting so hard to stay together, feel every bruise and burn and wound on the battered thing which still pounded for him. Even after everything. All of it.

Thunder rumbled through the heavens as the stars gave us a warning but neither of us so much as flinched, not caring what they thought of us and what we were doing.

"I'm sorry too," I whispered, because I could see it in his eyes. I could feel it in his flesh.

He was broken as well. This man who'd tortured me, cut me open, battered and bruised me all for a throne I'd never wanted in the first place was burning up over this rift between us. He was sorry and he was hurting and there was nothing either of us could do to fix it.

He drew in a deep breath, his forehead pressing to mine so that the cedar and smoke scent of him overwhelmed me.

I could feel eyes on us from all around the clearing as the Pegasus herd looked on and the ground beneath our feet began to tremble and quake, but I didn't care. Let them watch us. As far as I was concerned, we were the only two people in the world in that moment.

"It doesn't change anything though," I said slowly, even though the words tore into the small piece of me which had fought so hard to survive Darius Acrux. "I made my choice. We don't get another shot."

Darius gazed intently at me as he continued to lean forward with his forearm pressed to the tree above my head, his other hand sliding back up over my chest, caressing my neck before he was holding my cheek in his grasp. He cupped my jaw with his fingertips and teased them into my hair, causing goosebumps to blossom all over my flesh.

His magic shifted to the surface of his skin and the deep heat of it called to my own power like they were one and the same, destined to be together always. My walls fell away and his magic tumbled beneath my flesh, filling me up and burning in the best possible way.

A soft moan escaped me and his dark eyes flared as he kept me captive in his gaze. Being this close to him hurt in the sweetest way and made my broken heart bleed.

We were standing so close to each other that I could feel the heat of his body pressing against mine. My hands seemed to move of their own accord as I reached for him, my palms sliding up and over his hard chest before landing against his pecs like I intended to push him away. But I didn't. I just touched him as his magic washed through me, blinding me, intoxicating me, branding my soul as his from the inside out.

My gaze was still hooked on his eyes. Our foreheads still pressed together and his lips so close to mine that I could almost feel the movement of them as he spoke.

"I love you, Roxy," he said in a rough, dark voice which held no room for lies or falsehood, no space for tricks of cruelty. Only the truth. I could feel it just as keenly as I could feel the rush of his magic beneath my skin.

A tear slipped from my eye, searing a burning trail along my cheek as it spilled from my flesh and fell between us.

How many times had I ached to hear someone say that to me? How many times had I wondered if anyone even *could* love me like that? I might have denied it to myself more times than I could count, but I'd been aching for this for a long time. Needing it more than I'd ever wanted to admit, more than I'd ever needed anything. And not just from anyone. I needed it from *him*.

"And I know it doesn't change anything. That it *can't* change anything," he growled. "But I'm going to prove it to you. I'm going to do everything I can to make it up to you, for the rest of my life if that's what it takes. I'll never forgive myself for bringing this curse on us. And I'm never going to stop loving you either."

I didn't know what to say to that, I didn't know how to process it, what to do with it. Did I love him? How could I love a beast who'd tortured me? What would that make me if I did? Just a broken, fractured, beaten, *stupid* girl who'd fallen for her tormentor. But maybe I was all of those things. Maybe I was worse because I'd hurt him too while placing all of the blame on him. Maybe we were just two sides of the same coin.

His lips brushed against mine and another moan escaped me as I tilted my chin to meet him.

It was the faintest touch of his mouth to mine and yet it felt like an earthquake was taking place in my soul to rival the one rocking the ground at our feet.

My lips parted and he leaned in, his body pressing against mine and his presence overwhelming me until he was all I could see, smell, feel, *taste* and it was just too good to pull away.

A crash of thunder sounded overhead as my arms slid around his neck and I moaned as he drove me back against the tree, his lips moving with mine as a desperate kind of hunger passed between us.

The Pegasus herd whinnied and squealed as lightning flashed bright enough to show through my closed eyelids and my heart pounded as I drank in the fragile moment before it burned out.

A huge groan sounded and the earth beneath our feet shuddered as the sound of more panicked Pegasuses reached us and people started shouting our names.

Tears slid down my cheeks as I kissed him harder, my whole body tangling with his as I threw an air shield up over our heads, pouring my magic into it as I fought to buy us just a few more seconds.

He kissed me like he'd die if he didn't, like the only reason his heart was beating at all was so that it could be mine, and I kissed him like the world could cave in around us and I wouldn't even care so long as I was still in his arms when it ended.

Lightning flashed beyond my closed eyelids again and we were surrounded by screams and whinnies, a stampede of hooves racing to escape us as an echoing groan tore from the trees to our right.

Something slammed into the shield above us with a force so hard that I gasped, falling back out of Darius's arms as the two of us looked up to find the enormous trunk of a fallen tree bearing down on my magic right above our heads.

"I meant what I said," Darius growled passionately before stepping back, breaking the contact between us and fracturing my shattered heart once more.

He backed away and I did too, holding his gaze as we made it to opposite sides of my air shield and out from beneath the falling tree.

I released a shaky breath before dropping my shield and letting the tree crash to the forest floor where we'd just been standing.

It hit the ground with an echoing boom which sent dirt and gravel flying up in a cloud between us and stole my view of him across the clearing.

By the time the dust settled, he was gone. And I was left with a desperate ache in my heart which I knew would never go away.

Darcy

CHAPTER THIRTY TWO

It was waiting for me when I exited the bathroom. Someone had pushed the letter with the Court of Solaria seal on it under my door and I dropped to my knees with my heart cramming into my throat as I opened it up and read it.

Dear Miss Gwendalina (Darcy) Vega,

You are hereby summoned to the Court of Solaria on March 30th for the trial of Lance Azriel Orion for breaking Law 303 of the constitution. In accordance with said law (outlined below*), you are required to provide a statement to determine the fate of the defendant.

The High Court Judge's ruling will also decide if any motion need be taken against you.

Please note: your position at the prestigious Zodiac Academy has now been brought into question.

You MUST appear on the date of your court summons or a default judgement will be passed on you based on the evidence provided in court.

Regards,

Ravis Darkice

High Court Judge of the Court of Solaria

Griffin, Libra, Justice of Fae

*Law 303 of the Education Sector of Solaria: Any teacher or teaching aid in the position of authority over Fae studying at their institution of employment are prohibited from engaging in sexual relationships with their students on punishment of arrest and prosecution.

I wiped the tears from my eyes before they could fall, finding I didn't have the strength to stand up. Everything hurt. And the shadows kept calling to me, begging me to dive into them, to take some relief from this pain. But I refused them again and again. I needed this burning agony, this rage. Because I was going to turn it against Seth.

I'd skipped lessons all day again, unable to bear facing the world. I still didn't have my Atlas so I couldn't check FaeBook, but I could have guessed I was plastered all over it by now. The rumours about me and Orion would be rife. The story thrown out of proportion a thousand times. Maybe the reason I hadn't left this room yet was because the second I did, this would all be real.

Guilt ate at me for snapping at Tory. I hadn't meant to say the things I did. Well, certainly not in the way they'd come out. But I just wanted the best for her so badly and it hurt me that she'd thrown away any chance at love when she'd defied the stars. I would have given anything for the stars to choose me and Lance as Elysian Mates. But it wasn't to be. The stars had been laughing at us all along. And maybe Tory was right after all. Fate was bullshit. The fact that the stars would offer us something so sweet only to rip it away again made me sick to my core.

But I wasn't done fighting for us yet. I had to talk to Orion. I had to find a way to call him. To know that he was alright. To plan a way out of this together.

I pressed my hands to my eyes, willing away the tears that threatened to start falling again.

It was almost seven o'clock and everyone would be heading down to The Howling Meadow for Elemental Combat class. I was going to walk out of this room and face my demons. One in particular, in fact. Seth Capella. That was what gave me the strength to get off the floor.

I headed to the mirror, wiping my eyes and using a vanity spell to hide the blotchy mess my face had been reduced to. I wore a mocha coloured crop top and matching yoga pants. And I decided not to bother with a sweater as I strode to the window and shoved it open, planning to fly. I leapt forward into the cool breeze and my wings burst free of my back in a fiery inferno, seeming to burn hotter with my anger as I swept around Aer Tower and headed over the trees, my eyes falling on all of the students gathering down below in the meadow.

I set my gaze on the boulders in the middle and plummeted towards them, dropping out of the sky like an arrow let loose from a bow. People started pointing as they spotted me and I clenched my jaw, determinedly ignoring them as I landed in front of Seth, not even stumbling a single step. All four of the Heirs were shirtless and covered in a dusting of dirt like they'd been fighting in the mud already.

"Darcy," Tory said in surprise, a note of hope in her voice as she rushed to my side. "Are you alright?"

"No," I answered truthfully, a crowd gathering around us as I faced the Heirs.

"By the eye of the storm on Jupiter," Geraldine breathed. "Perhaps we should go for a ramble in the forest, Darcy? We could all have a heart to heart."

"I'm fine right here," I said firmly, stepping toward Seth and his brows pulled together. "Well?" I demanded as a hush fell over the class. Even Washer had stepped up to watch, apparently not planning to direct anyone away from staring at me. "Aren't you going to say something? Aren't you going to cheer and laugh and congratulate yourself for being such a fucking clever boy?"

Darius kicked away from the nearest boulder, his forehead creasing. "Seth?" he asked, like it hadn't occurred to him that his beloved friend would be the one to throw Orion to the wolves. But who better to do that than the Alpha of the pack himself?

"You think I told the FIB?" Seth balked and mutters broke out in the crowd as the news that he'd known about me and Orion moved from ear to ear.

I released a bitter laugh. "I know you did. Who else would do it? My sister wouldn't have done it and Darius is Lance's best friend. So who does that leave, huh? Just a heartless Wolf with a sad little vendetta against me which he can't fulfil like a man. Like a *Fae*," I spat, raising my hands in preparation to fight him. I wanted him on his ass, but more than that, I wanted the truth. I wanted the whole school to know that this piece of shit had wronged me. And that I was going to destroy him for it.

"Why would I give you up?" Seth asked innocently and Max and Caleb moved back a few steps, sensing the fight that was going to break out.

"Maybe you should stop throwing the blame around, Darcy," Kylie's voice cut into me and I whipped my head in her direction, my wings casting her in an orange glow as they flared hotter. "You're the one who spread your legs for grades. Maybe you should point the finger at yourself."

I bared my teeth, stepping in her direction and she backed up into her friends with a look of fright in her eyes. Whatever I looked like right now, it must have been enough to strike fear in her heart. But she wasn't who I'd come here for.

I turned to Seth and Tory gave me a nod of encouragement. She knew I needed this. If it didn't have to be Fae on Fae, I had no doubt she'd beat his ass alongside me. But this was my fight. And I was going to win it even if it cost me every drop of magic I had to give.

"I didn't do it," Seth lowered his voice so only I could hear, stepping closer and reaching for my arm.

I yanked it away from him, horrified that he'd consider touching me. Lying to me. After everything, could he not even just admit that he was the one to get Orion arrested? That *he* was the one to dig through my flesh with sharp claws and tear my heart out?

"Fine, you wanna fight?" He raised his hands as the wind twisted between his fingers. "Then don't hold back."

I let my wings fall away then threw out my hands, forcing a huge surge of magic into them and releasing a tornado at him that launched him through the air. The crowd backed up as the storm tossed him to the ground with a hard whack, but he was up again in seconds, throwing his fist into the earth with a smirk on his features.

My heart drummed against my ears as the ground split in two and I started running toward him, trying to close the distance between us before it tore apart completely. A savage snarl ripped from my throat as the dirt tumbled away into a huge abyss beneath me. I threw out my palms, casting cushions of air to catch me, jumping from one to the next as I raced across the space dividing us with adrenaline zipping through my veins.

His long hair whipped around him in the breeze and his eyes were set on me in a way that was goading and hungry. I despised that look. Like he wanted this. I was going to make him regret every single second of that thought. He'd be bleeding and begging by the time I was done.

When there was just a meter parting us and the huge chasm echoed below me, I leapt into the air with a yell of determination, casting ice blades into my palms as I fell towards him.

A vine wrapped around my ankle before I made it and I was yanked down into the pit, falling and falling, a strangled scream stuck in my throat before my back impacted with the dirt. I was twenty feet below ground and staring up at Seth as he stood on the edge of the chasm, a twisted smile on his face.

"Fuck you!" I cried, sending the ice blades spearing from my hands towards him with another wave of rage crashing through my chest.

They shattered into shards as they collided with his air shield, but he'd been distracted long enough that I was back on my feet, causing the air to pummel him from behind so he was thrown head first into the pit with me. My heart soared but he caught himself before he hit the ground, landing lightly on his feet.

I dove at him with the force of a hurricane at my back, tackling him with the ferocity of a rabid animal.

He hit the ground and I straddled him with victory singing in my ears, grabbing his throat and throwing a fist into his face. An air shield covered it and I swore as my knuckles impacted with it, but I didn't give up. I kept slamming my fists into it, covering them in flames as I battled to break through the shield and they started to bleed. He laughed wildly, getting cocky, but that was when the shield cracked and my fist slammed into his cheek, sending his head whipping sideways.

"Fuck," he gasped then threw me off of him with sheer force, rolling over and pinning me down into the mud with the hard plain of his chest, his hands latching around my wrists and holding them still.

"Why did you do it?!" I demanded, battling to get my hands free as I hunted his eyes for a crack in his façade. This bullshit lie he was feeding me. And why? What difference did it make now?

"I didn't do it," he snarled, coming nose to nose with me, not blinking even once so all I could see was the depths of his earthy brown eyes. "I kept your secret. I never told anyone. I never even planned to."

I encouraged fire to bloom down my arms where he held me and he let go with a dogish whimper, lurching upright to sit over my hips. I cast a vine from the ground, latching it around his throat and yanking him backwards so his spine hit the dirt once more. I was on my feet in seconds, holding my hand above him as I tightened the vine mercilessly, my breathing coming raggedly as he suffered beneath me.

The shadows stirred under my flesh, urging me on, whispering terrible, deadly, enticing things that I wanted to lean into in that moment.

Then the ground swallowed Seth whole and he disappeared into the mud, making my lips pop open as I hunted for him.

Dirt suddenly fell over me in a tremendous flood and I gasped, staring up above me as Seth stood at the top of the pit, covered in mud and casting a tumult of dirt down as he tried to bury me alive. He must have made a tunnel in the earth right to the top – *asshole!*

The weight of the earth slowed me as it pressed up to my thighs already, but I wasn't beat yet. I clawed my way out then lifted one hand in the air and used the wind to drag me out. I shot towards the sky, my eyes pinned on Seth as I raced towards him. He leapt back a moment before my feet touched the ground and I collided with the air shield surrounding him. He smirked that awful smirk which turned my blood to ice and a growl poured from my lips.

"Go on Sethy! Put the teacher fucker in her place!" Kylie called and her little friends started laughing.

I threw everything I had at Seth's shield, spears of wood, a raining shower of ice shards, a storm of air, but it didn't give.

"Did Orion take pity on you, Darcy?" Marguerite's voice called, setting my cheeks on fire. "Did he let you suck his cock and let you pass Cardinal Magic so no one would see what a loser you are?"

Tory waved a hand at her and Marguerite was knocked to the ground with a gust of air, her face smashing into the dirt.

"Woops, careful Marguerite," Tory smirked.

I blinked to try and refocus, pouring more magic at Seth's shield as I continued to blast it with everything I had.

He stepped back, watching me silently as I hounded forward with every spell I cast. It occurred to me that he couldn't fight back. He was using all of his magic to keep that shield in place. So if I could only shatter it...

Exhaustion was gnawing at my muscles, making everything feel heavy, but adrenaline kept me going. And I realised Tory and my friends were cheering me on, screaming and clapping on the side lines. My heart lifted slightly at the sound and I focused my mind, trying to figure out how I was going to break his defences.

The answer came to me clearly. Fire. It was the most violent of Elements. And it lived in my core like a molten slice of the sun.

I cast two whips of fire in my hands that were as blindingly white hot as my rage. I knew I was running into the last reserves of my magic, so I had to make this count. I wielded the two huge whips with anger coursing through every inch of my flesh then brought them down on Seth's shield with curses pouring from my lips at the effort it took.

I felt the bitterest and sharpest of all the emotions, hate, malice, anger, hurt, all tangling together like I'd swallowed a hundred sharp objects and washed them down with cyanide.

Seth's expression wasn't goading anymore, his features were contorted in concentration and effort as he battled to keep his shield in place. I struck at it again and again, my arms aching, sweat pouring down my spine as I gave this everything I had. I did it for Orion and me and Tory and even Darius. I did it to spite the stars and to cut down my enemy who'd made it his personal mission to ruin me the moment I'd walked into this school.

With one huge, final, splintering whip, his shield gave out and the fire wrapped around his limbs, upending him and searing huge burns across his bare chest. I doused it in a heartbeat, my final move decided as I poured the last of my magic into ice, letting it encase every part of his body right up to his neck, binding him in a freezing chamber until he couldn't move a single muscle except his tongue. Enough to give me my victory.

"Yield," I demanded, the world falling quiet around me as I stood over him, panting, battered, bruised. But triumphant.

Seth bit down on his tongue, saying nothing and I let the ice sharpen to a collar of knives around his throat.

"Yield," I hissed, the shadows whispering in my ears, telling me to end it. They wanted his blood to spill and part of me did too. They latched onto that darkness in me and added kindling to it, coaxing it until it was a blaze I couldn't ignore.

"Yield, you idiot!" Darius barked and Seth groaned.

"I yield," he huffed and my friends went crazy, diving on me and pulling me into their arms. But I couldn't stop staring down at Seth as I melted the ice from his body and he rose to his feet. It felt good to beat him. But it wasn't enough. It didn't bring Orion back. It didn't fix anything.

I lifted my head to find the whole school looking at me, some in awe, some in horror. I grabbed Tory's hand, pulling her out of the crowd and giving her a look that begged her to come with me. She nodded immediately, stripping off her shirt so she was left in her crop top and we took off into the sky without a backwards glance.

We raced across The Wailing Wood and I spotted King's Hollow in the distance, the roof of the treehouse calling to me. The Heirs wouldn't be heading there until the lesson ended and the wards around it kept it private from weaker Fae, so I led Tory that way until we landed on top of the slanted wooden roof and sat with the evening birdsong filling the air around us.

I dropped my head into my hands and tried to take even breaths, but I couldn't seem to manage it.

"That was incredible, Darcy," she said, resting a hand on my back as I hid behind a waterfall of blue hair.

"Why don't I feel any better?" I asked through my teeth. My heart was drowning in a vat of acid. My hopes and dreams had long since melted in it too. And when I thought of Orion, the pain of it made me sick all over again.

"Because beating Seth doesn't bring him back," she said gently and I nodded, clawing a hand into my hair and tugging to try and force myself to feel anything but the hurt in my chest.

"He can't go to prison." I looked up at her through watery eyes, desperation lacing my tone. "He can't. He -I-"

She pulled me into her arms and I held onto her, clinging to the other half of me. My twin, the night to my day. She was in pain too, and somehow in her arms it felt a little lighter. Like she was carrying some of mine and I was carrying some of hers.

"We'll figure it out," she promised and I nodded against her shoulder, trying to find some sliver of a possibility to hold onto. But everything seemed so bleak.

Silence stretched between while we just clutched onto each other and the sky turned to dusk, then to total darkness, and the stars glittered pitilessly down at us.

"I spoke to Darius today," Tory broke the quiet at last and I pulled back from her with my lips parting.

"I didn't mean what I said, it was out of order-" I blurted, guilt swelling up inside me.

"No, you were right," she cut over me, nodding firmly. "I needed to hear it. And you're the only one I could have heard it from."

I gave her a sad sort of smile. "What happened?"

"I told him the truth. How I feel and all that shit. And he...told me he loved me," she breathed and tears pricked my eyes for a whole different reason.

"That's great, Tor," I said earnestly, though I knew it couldn't change anything now. Not unless we found a way to fix this. And I swore on everything in this world, that I would. I took her hand and we dropped back to lie on the roof without a word passing between us, gazing up at the cruel sky.

"Do you think the stars hate us?" I whispered like they could hear me,

407

my eyes automatically seeking out Orion's belt and wondering if wherever he was, he could even see the stars tonight. Or if he was locked in the dark like some criminal, some heathen.

"Maybe," Tory breathed.

"Maybe they're the souls of all the spiteful Fae who came before us, stubbornly clinging to the sky instead of passing beyond the veil. Maybe they want to punish the world for the miserable lives they left behind."

"I hope not," Tory said, her fingers squeezing mine. "But if they are, then we can still defy them. They don't control us."

I wanted that to be true for her sake, for Orion's. But a quiet part of me knew it wasn't true. In a world where the zodiac ruled our lives, our paths were just a roll of the dice. And once the dice had landed, our fate was set in stone. I just hoped our dice were still rolling. And there was a chance for us all yet.

DARIUS

CHAPTER THIRTY THREE

There were many things my father had taught me which I wished I could scour from my brain, but in some things, I had to admit he was right. Though I didn't appreciate his methods of educating me on them.

On my eighth birthday, Mother had been throwing one of her grand parties to celebrate and half the damn kingdom were invited, very few of whom were actually my age. As the youngest of the Heirs, the others had been teasing me about my birthday mattering the least and I'd made the mistake of muttering complaints about the entire affair within earshot of Father.

Even then, I really should have known better, but I could admit that being born to be one of the most powerful men in the kingdom had made me into a bit of a brat at times. He'd moved to stand over me, his hulking form blocking out the sunlight as I sat pouting by the marquee and casting me in shadow as he'd sneered at me. *The key to being the most important man in the room is in knowing it's true right down to the very fabric of your soul, Darius.*

He'd driven his point home by making me choose one of the servants at random and I'd picked a Fae called Osmond who was four times the size of me and had been employed to tend the gardens at our manor for my entire life. He was a man I'd been fond of, who'd played ball with Xavier and me from time to time if our father was away for work. He was kind and had plenty of friends and I was young and stupid and didn't realise that whoever I picked would be in for something bad.

Father called him into the house and brought him to the music room where the open space was built with perfect acoustics in mind.

At eight years old I was a big kid, my Dragon blood showing through even then, but I was still only around the size of most thirteen year old boys.

Father had wrapped me in a silencing bubble with him and explained just how much more important my life was than pretty much every other Fae alive. He told me that that meant I could take any of them and do whatever the hell I wanted to prove that point and they would thank me for my efforts while kissing my feet.

I was still in awe of my father then, naïve enough to take him at his word and act on his commands eagerly as I tried to win his approval, but that was the first time I hesitated to follow through on what he wanted.

He hit me so hard, I was deafened in my left ear and blood coated my tongue as I fell against the wall.

You are under no illusions that I'm the most important man in the room now, aren't you, Darius? So go and show that Fae how important you *are.*

I'd lifted my chin and stalked into the music room where Osmond was waiting. He offered me this strange, sad kind of smile which I couldn't understand at the time but I realised now was something between acceptance and pity.

In my coldest voice, I'd commanded him to his knees before me because he was far too tall for me to attack effectively while on his feet.

The first strike of my fist against his jaw had rocked pain up through my arm and a spike of fear through my chest. I'd glanced back at Father where he stood watching lazily from the doorway and he'd raised a single brow at me as if to ask if that was all I had.

The next punch I landed was harder and then harder again. I kept hitting Osmond until he fell to the floor before me and my knuckles were split and bleeding, then I started kicking him. My muscles burned with strength and this incredible feeling of power as he took each and every strike I dealt him just because of who I was.

When I was out of breath and speckled in blood, I finally fell still and looked down at him in triumph, though guilt twisted through me too. Father had approached slowly, his polished shoes echoing on the hardwood floor as he closed in on me and my victim.

Do you want to pay the man for helping you learn this lesson, Darius? he'd asked, pulling a thick wedge of auras from his pocket. I could see enough hundred aura bills to know there was well over ten thousand there. But the look in father's eyes said that that was another test too.

I'd reached out carefully and taken a single aura from his hand, dropping it onto Osmond dismissively and the smile Father had given me in return was all monster. He was thrilled.

He'd healed my ear but left my knuckles split and bloody for the party to prove to me that I could do anything I wanted and no one would ever dare question me. Because I was more important than them.

No one aside from the other Heirs asked why my fists were busted and Father bought me more gifts than any child could possibly need, including my first motorbike and a Faerarri. And for too long I'd been proud of that act.

Osmond still didn't raise his head in my presence to this day and now when I looked back on that lesson, I knew that the worst part of it all was the value I'd put on his life. A single aura. It was somehow worse than if I'd offered him nothing.

It was a lesson I wished I'd learned in any other way, but it was a valuable lesson all the same. From that day on, Father had enforced my superiority complex by teaching me to belittle and ignore other Fae as easily as breathing. And it might not have been a pretty lesson to learn, but there was some truth to it. In almost every situation I ran into, I *was* the most important man in the room. And I had no trouble at all in reminding other Fae of that.

I strode down the grey corridor in the Fae Investigation Bureau building in central Tucana with Mr Kipling keeping pace three steps behind me where I didn't have to look at his sombre face. He was the best lawyer I knew, more than capable of handling any and every little problem which came my way. From persistent stalkers who I wanted off my case, to covering up any accidental murders I might have to deal with. Luckily that last one hadn't been an issue for me yet, but if it ever was then I knew who to call. He was a Griffin, smart as a whip and one of three brothers who ran a legal empire based on fixing anything and everything a Fae might need. And best of all, they weren't affiliated with my father. Dante Oscura had pointed me in their direction years ago and if they were good enough to keep half of the infamous Oscura Clan gang out of prison then I was more than confident that they would be able to help Lance too.

We strode through the waiting room where other Fae sat in hopes of gaining an appointment and I ignored them entirely.

Several uniformed officers stared at me in shock as I strode straight through a set of security doors and three of them actually tried to stand in my way. I knocked them aside with a blast of water magic and encased them against the wall in ice for good measure without even slowing my stride. Each of them were well trained and more than capable of fighting back, but they didn't. Because I was Darius Acrux, the most important man in the fucking room.

Kipling breathed heavily behind me which was enough to let me know he was loving this power play. He was a man of few words, not wasting time on anything he didn't deem necessary, but over the years, I'd learned to read his ticks and tells. And I was pretty confident he liked me. He was the oldest brother of three and was the one I dealt with most. With my constant issues with the press, admirers, straight up stalkers and so on, we spoke pretty damn regularly. He was only in his late twenties but something about him made him seem so much older, like his soul had seen and done so many things that it had lost all the lustre of youth too young. He was tall and heavily built with a square jaw and cold, calculating eyes. In fact, the three brothers all looked so similar that it was hard to pick them out of a line up, but this one was the leader. Just.

I kept going until I reached the commanding officer's door and threw it open without knocking. Agent Hoskins shoved himself to his feet with something akin to a snarl on his face. He was a big bastard, a Manticore with a reputation that had the criminal underbelly of Solaria pissing their pants in their sleep. But I wasn't afraid of him.

"Save it," I snapped before he could try and reprimand me. "I'm here for a meeting with Lance Orion. I brought his lawyer and I suggest you don't keep me waiting if you like this job."

Hoskins puffed himself up as his muscles tensed defiantly. "Lord Acrux, I-"

"*Lord* Acrux isn't here and I assure you, I'm a lot less amenable to bullshit than he is," I growled, my eyes shifting to Dragon slits as I stalked towards him and used every inch of my height and bulk to intimidate him. He might have been big, but no fucker could rival an Acrux Dragon for muscle mass. "You will go and get Lance Orion *now,* or you're going to find yourself with one hell of a problem on your hands."

The head of the FIB swallowed thickly as he held my gaze for five long seconds while the weight of my power settled over the room so potently that it made the hairs prick up along the back of my neck. He finally dropped his eyes to somewhere around my chest and inclined his head to show submission.

"I'll have him brought to an interview room. If you can just wait-"

"*Now,*" I snarled and he blanched just enough to let me know he was afraid of me. Good. He should be afraid.

Hoskins lifted a phone on his desk and quickly dialled out to get some other agents to bring Lance out to meet with me.

"If you can just wait for Agent Bravas to come and escort you to-"

"You'll be escorting me," I snapped before turning my back on him in the most insulting way I could manage and striding back out into the corridor.

Kipling was hiding the edge of a smile as he followed me from the room and all of the agents beyond the door were trying their damn hardest not to point and stare as their boss hurried around me to lead the way on like a whipped little bitch. No doubt they'd all suffer his rage once I was gone but for now, I had his balls firmly cupped in my palm.

We headed down long, grey corridors and through locked doors before I spotted Lance walking towards me, herded on by a group of six agents.

They ushered him through a door before I could do more than meet his eye and I strode in a moment later to find him sitting in a bare room with a table and three chairs laid out for us. His hands were manacled in magic blocking cuffs which one of the agents was about to chain to a bolt in the centre of the metal table.

I flicked a ball of fire at the agent, striking his hands and making him drop the chain with a shout of pain before he could lock it in place.

Every other agent in the room lurched to whip guns from their hip holsters and I growled loud enough to make them shit themselves.

"If any one of you aims a weapon at me, I'll gladly cook your ass in Dragon fire for treason and piss on your smouldering bones for good measure."

Mouths popped open, guns were lowered, wide and terrified gazes were levelled at me from all around and I growled again to make my point.

"Get the fuck out," I snapped and they all fucking ran to do so without even waiting for Hoskins to okay it.

"Attorney client privilege states that this conversation remain private and cannot be spied on," Kipling said in a curt voice as he turned to face Hoskins in the doorway and pulled a small, cylindrical device from his pocket. He pressed it to the wall and raised a solitary eyebrow. "You have three hidden cameras and an amplification spell cast on this room." He slid the device back into his pocket with a calculating look. "That's a major infraction. When was the last time you were given food, Mr Orion?" he added without looking at Lance.

"They gave me a slice of bread last night," he grunted.

"Three square meals a day, a clean cell, a shower and fresh clothing are mandatory requirements for Fae incarcerated in a holding cell while awaiting prosecution. This isn't Darkmore Penitentiary, Agent Hoskins, Mr Orion has Fae rights which must be adhered to. Innocent until proven guilty."

"I'll get him a proper meal and a change of clothes for his return to his cell," Hoskins grunted reluctantly.

"He will require a suitable, *clean* mattress, warm blankets, constant access to toilet facilities and water at all times. I'll be checking in to make sure he has all of those things," Kipling said in a flat tone as he turned to place his briefcase on the table.

"Consider it done," Hoskins grunted.

"Oh, I do," Kipling agreed. He pulled out his curofile and I couldn't help but watch the magical object with fascination as he opened the white binder and lifted a freshly inked page from the top of it before pressing his finger to the base of the paper and imbuing it with his magical signature.

Kipling crossed the room to stand before Hoskins and held the page out to him. "Agent Hoskins, you have been served on behalf of the FIB for failing to provide due care and comfort to a suspect under your charge and for attempting to spy on legally protected conversations between myself and my client. I'll see you in court."

Hoskins gaped at the legal document in his hand and Kipling threw the door shut in his face.

I exchanged a dark smile with him as he set about securing the room from any more magical spy work with a series of complex spells and turned my gaze to Lance instead.

I threw my arms around him and he grunted as he leaned into my embrace, unable to hug me back due to his cuffed hands. My heart leapt and pounded in relief as the ache in my chest eased from having him so close.

He looked like shit and smelled like he hadn't showered. His hair was a mess, he was wearing the clothes he'd been arrested in and there were huge bags beneath his eyes.

"How are you?" I asked him as I drew him close, running my hands up his back.

"How's Blue?" he asked in return.

"Fucking furious," I replied. "She beat the shit out of Seth in front of the whole school. He's been howling all fucking night and day since."

A merciless laugh escaped him. "That's my girl."

"I asked him outright if he did this," I added because Seth would be lucky to be alive if I believed he had. "But he swore he didn't. I know you don't have a high opinion of him, but he's my brother just like you are. I believe him."

Lance scoffed and pushed out of my arms, dropping into the chair on his side of the table and I tried not to let the sting of that rejection show.

"Who else then?" he growled. "Who else knew?"

"I haven't been given the name of the witness as of yet," Kipling said formally as he finished up his magic and took a seat opposite Lance.

I caved and sat too, folding my arms to stop myself from punching something over the fucking injustice of the situation. I didn't know who else it might be, but whoever it was had made themselves an enemy of mine.

"As soon as you find out, I'll kill them," I promised.

"A full character assassination will take place of course," Kipling nodded as if I'd meant that instead of bloodshed, but we all knew I hadn't. "In the meantime, my brothers and I spent the entirety of the last seventeen hours watching the video evidence. It was a six hour tape, so it took a while but during that time we managed to individually catalogue each law break and how we will fight against their use in this case."

"You watched hours of my girl and me having sex?" Lance snarled protectively and he looked damn close to leaping out of the chair and throttling Kipling just for having seen it.

"If it appeases you, you may wish to know that my brothers and I have very specific tastes sexually and neither you nor Miss Vega fulfil them, so I can assure you the work was in no way gratifying. I prefer men in their fifties or older with considerably more body hair than you. My middle brother only enjoys sex with inanimate objects and my youngest brother likes Medusa women in shifted form."

"Oh," Lance said, cutting a glance to me which said he was half relieved and half freaked out by that. I liked to know everything about the people I employed, so I already knew all of that anyway but the plain faced way Kipling discussed it was definitely weird as fuck.

"So, as I was saying. You have the full use of me and both of my brothers for the duration of your case. Both of them are listening in now by the way and relaying ideas to me."

"You're on the phone to them?" Lance asked with a frown as he looked for an earpiece and I almost smirked.

"No. We underwent a...*procedure,* several years ago which links our psyches. It was immeasurably painful, destroyed most of our ability to feel empathy and removed all forms of privacy between us. But it makes our work as a unit so much more cohesive that we all agree it's worth the sacrifice."

"Aside from when your middle brother starts humping a grapefruit or something and you're linked in for the show, I guess," I joked to lighten the tension in the room and Kipling just shrugged.

"He's been more interested in sponge cakes recently, but we are getting off topic," Kipling deadpanned.

There was a beat of silence where I almost laughed before realising it wasn't a joke and Lance cut me a look like he was wondering if these guys were really the right men for the job. But he also knew I'd only ever get him the best so he didn't comment.

"So," Kipling began, drawing another sheet of paper from his curofile. He'd explained the magic of it to me once. Basically, his brothers each had one of their own and any document they created was magically duplicated into the other files no matter how far they were from one another. So while this Kipling had been listing out all of the infractions Agent Hoskins had made against Lance, his brothers had compiled the file and sent it over for him to use. It was seamless and pretty fucking spectacular magic. "We can dismiss the charge of sexual biting. Miss Vega is your Source and that was a well-known fact. There are no rules in the school contract you signed or anywhere else to say that you had to bite her in a specific place. So it doesn't matter that you bit her breasts, inner thigh and buttocks. That will be dismissed."

Lance shot me a look and cleared his throat. "Okay. What else?"

"We have, four counts of full coitus, two counts of cunnilingus, one count of fellatio. A single spank which I think we can dismiss as an accidental fall-"

"Fuck me, Lance you couldn't have just had a quickie, could you?" I muttered as Kipling went on and Lance ran a hand over his face with a groan.

"Four hundred and three kisses-"

"You counted the kisses?" Lance blanched.

"One hundred and sixteen pecks to the lips. Eighty four kisses to the lips with tongue. Thirty seven to her left breast, forty five to the right, eight to-"

"By the stars, is that really necessary?" Lance growled.

"We are extremely thorough in our work. It may interest you to know that the cunnilingus is likely to work in your favour if we have a mainly female jury. They tend to see that as an act of selflessness and love as opposed to the work of a sexual predator. Unfortunately, the fellatio somewhat detracts from it, but depending on the moral standards of the male jury members, it might balance out. Especially once they see how willing Miss Vega is in the tape-"

"You're not playing that tape in court!" Lance yelled suddenly, leaping to his feet, slamming his fists down on the table and shoving away from it in a rage. "I won't have countless assholes ogle her like that. I'd sooner just plead guilty and take my punishment!"

"I'm afraid the tape will be played regardless of plea," Kipling said calmly as if Lance didn't look about five seconds away from ripping his throat out. I guessed he had plenty of experience working with gangsters and killers to have learned not to flinch under such rage. "Like I said, the best we can hope for now is to convince the jury that this was love, not abuse and get them to be lenient. I won't lie to you though, Mr Orion. The prosecution will paint you out as a sexual predator who manipulated his way into the bed of one of the most important people in Solaria. They will be looking to prove that you tricked and brain washed her, convinced her to believe she loved you and made her spread her legs for you so that you could use her to claim more power and place a pawn on the Solarian Throne. You will lose your job, no question. You will be power shamed, I guarantee it. The best we are hoping for here is house arrest and magical confinement for an extended period of time. I'd guess ten years but I'll fight for two. And we can always use appeals to lower it if I don't get that outcome. But I'll take any of those outcomes because what the prosecution will be fighting for tooth and nail is a prison term. Supermax because of your power levels and the fact that the girl you abused is a Vega."

"Darkmore?" Orion breathed, his gaze sliding to me again as fear spiked through my chest.

That place wasn't a prison. It was hell on Earth. An underground hive filled with the worst criminals in all of Solaria and beyond who were sent down there to rot in the dark. I'd even heard rumours that they kept a genetically engineered monster down there to make sure the inmates had no chance of escaping. And there were no rules there either, no laws to protect inmates. Only ways to control them. Less than half of the inmates survived their full sentence to be released again. I'd do anything and everything in my power to make sure Lance didn't end up there.

"Don't even think about it," I snarled. "You're *not* going to prison."

"Darius," Lance said suddenly, looking up at me with real fear in his eyes. "You have to swear to me that you'll look after Blue. Promise me you'll keep helping her with the shadows. Swear to me that she will not fall prey to your father or his hateful quest for power!"

I moved to grab him, clasping his head between my hands as he looked at me with wild eyes. "You're not going to prison," I growled again.

"Promise me!" he bellowed, shoving me back a step as he snarled at me. "She's all that matters to me! I need you to swear it. You'll protect her, teach her, fix your shit with Tory and make something work between the Heirs and the Vegas so that you can overthrow Lionel and Clara."

"Okay," I gave in at the desperation in his tone. He needed me to swear it, but I refused to give up. "I swear to look after her, so long as you swear to do everything you can to get yourself out of this mess."

I looked around at Kipling like he had all the answers and Lance nodded as that hollow look crept into his gaze again.

Kipling cleared his throat like the outburst hadn't even happened. "Then let's start from the very beginning. I'm going to need all of the details to get the right spin on this."

"Okay," Lance breathed as he sank back down into his chair and I followed as I took mine too. "I'll tell you whatever you need to know."

I flew back to campus in my Dragon form, a bag filled with my clothes clamped in my jaws as the sun began to set and the orange light made my golden scales sparkle.

I did a circuit of the grounds and as I passed Aqua Lake, a blast of fire caught my attention from the shore.

My gut plummeted as I spotted Caleb and Roxy sitting together on the stony beach, but as Caleb threw up more fire which he shaped into words, a completely different kind of shiver ran through my limbs.

Round 2?

I circled the lake and tucked my wings as I flew down to join them, slowing my speed and landing heavily on the bank behind them as I dropped my bag.

Roxy got to her feet and turned to look at me, laughing at something Caleb said but I didn't catch it. And that wasn't annoying as fuck.

My attention swivelled between them as they laughed together and my heart pounded in a desperate kind of way. I ached for her to look at me like that, carefree and happy, enjoying the moment without any drama or pain.

But as she turned to look at me again, her laughter fell away and she bit her lip nervously. I stilled as she approached, looking down at her as she strode straight towards a Dragon who was bigger than a bus like I was a fucking house cat. I hadn't spoken to her since I'd told her I loved her and I didn't really know what I was going to say. But I had to think that if Caleb had suggested that the three of us repeat what we did a few weeks ago, he must have asked her first. And as much as it hurt me to know I couldn't have her to myself, if this was the only way I could have her at all then I was willing to make the sacrifice. Because I woke up aching for her and I spent the day thinking of her and every glimpse I caught of her, every word we exchanged, it wasn't enough. I needed more. And if this was the only way I could get that then I'd make my peace with it somehow and just ignore the parts of my heart which burned with agony at the thought of him touching her too.

I breathed out slowly and she was engulfed in smoke for a moment, a soft laugh escaping her just before her hand landed on my scaly nose.

"I definitely like you better like this," she teased as I leaned down and let her stroke me, her palm running right up between my eyes. I wondered if she had any concept of how few people had ever gotten this close to me in my Dragon form.

"Because he can't talk, right?" Caleb joked as he moved closer too, pushing a hand through his unruly blonde curls.

"Yeah," Roxy agreed and I snorted smoke in her face again. Her other hand swung out as she coughed against the smoke and she lightly slapped me on the snout to tell me off.

"Did you just slap a fucking Dragon?" Caleb asked, his eyes sparkling as he looked at her with a little too much appreciation for my liking.

"It's easier to believe he's not a monster when his fangs are on show," Roxy said, cutting him a bright smile which made a growl rumble through my throat. She turned to look at me again and I practically sighed as she ran her hands over my scales once more. "How fucked up is that?" she murmured and if I really was a house cat I might have been purring.

"Almost as fucked up as having to have a chaperone *every* time you want to hang out with him," Caleb teased and I grunted again before shifting back into my Fae form.

Roxy gasped as her hands landed on my chest instead of my face and her gaze instantly fell to my dick.

"Do you wanna just stand there staring or take a picture to look at later?" I teased.

"I choose the picture," she replied instantly. "Maybe you can get all oiled up and send me one?"

Caleb barked a laugh and offered her a high five as she withdrew her hands with a grin and stepped back.

"Don't tempt me, Roxy, if sexting you is on the cards then I'll do it constantly," I warned as I grabbed a spare pair of sweatpants out of my bag and pulled them on. I didn't want to wear the damn suit I'd worn to see Lance again.

She opened her mouth to reply, but the ground began to shake beneath us as she did. "Why is that happening now?" she asked as she took a step back again to put more distance between us.

I glanced at Cal in confusion. The stars had never had an issue with us being together so long as we weren't alone and he was standing closer to me than Roxy was. So what was their problem? She'd only touched me for a moment.

Roxy kept backing up until she was right at the water's edge and the quaking ground finally began to fall still.

"So...are we going to go and take a closer look at the stars in the amplifying chamber?" Cal asked, his gaze snagging on Roxy's bare legs beneath her little denim shorts for much longer than I liked. I wondered if he was hanging out with her like this regularly again or if he'd only invited me to join them because he'd seen me flying through the clouds above them. The idea of that made my heart race in a terrifying kind of way. Because I'd suggested it once to both of them. Back when the hopelessness was consuming me and the guilt of what had happened between us was tearing me apart so much I could hardly think. I'd told them to be happy together if that was what they wanted, knowing that it would destroy me if they did while feeling that I deserved to be destroyed anyway. But could I really handle that? Could I really face that reality day in day out?

No. I was pretty sure it would kill me.

Roxy seemed like she wanted to say something, but the ground started rumbling again and a crash of thunder overhead made me look up to the heavens.

I drew in a sharp breath as I spotted the Gemini, Leo and Taurus constellations lit up brightly above us despite the fact that the sun hadn't even set.

"Shit," Cal muttered. "They figured it out."

I looked back at Roxy just as a tear slipped from her eye, her gaze caught on me like there was something she wanted to say. But whatever it was, she abandoned it as the next tremor rocked the ground at our feet and she suddenly shifted into her full Phoenix form.

My eyes widened as her entire body was coated in flames, beautiful burning wings blazing from her body before she took off so fast that the blur of her motion was left imprinted on the backs of my eyelids.

I watched as she flew away from me with more pain in my heart than I felt I could bear as the quaking ground finally fell still.

I dropped down onto the bank, hiding my face in my hands as I growled in frustration over the loss of something I'd never really had.

A moment later Cal sat beside me with a heavy sigh, throwing his arm around me as he rested his head against my shoulder.

"I'm sorry, man," he muttered. "I was afraid they might figure it out the first time. That was why I went to all the effort of keeping it secret, hiding your magic with the bangles, even the blindfold..."

"The blindfold was fucking hot," I muttered. I didn't think I'd ever gotten hard as quickly in all my life as I had when he'd presented her to me all wrapped up like that and waiting. Hands tied behind her back, blindfold on, she'd looked entirely vulnerable and utterly corruptible but as badass as they come all at once.

"I'm sorry it's fucked now though," he said.

I sighed heavily. "It was fucked anyway. Even if we could make it work long term with you in the mix, how is that fair? For us to be fighting to be together when the stars have made the entire world fight against it. And to pull you into that shit too, tangle you up with us and whatever the fuck it is we're doing..."

"It wasn't exactly a hardship," he said with a shrug, but there was an edge to his voice which said that wasn't quite the truth.

I shifted away from him, turning to face him so that I could look into his navy eyes and I psyched myself up to ask a question I wasn't sure I wanted the answer for.

"We need to talk about Roxy," I said slowly.

"You mean Tory," Caleb said with a smirk. "You know she hates it when you call her Roxy, right?"

"No. She doesn't hate it, it gets under her skin but that's exactly where I like to be. Besides, you're wrong, her name is Roxanya Vega and she was born to be a Solarian princess. Calling her Tory is just a crutch to allow yourself to forget that."

Caleb snorted a laugh. "I'd have trouble forgetting that."

"You're skirting the issue," I muttered.

"I know." He held my eye and I huffed, hating the irritation I was feeling towards him. He was my brother, the least I could do was speak honestly with him.

"So, was a part of the reason you wanted to involve yourself because you want her too?" I asked.

Cal frowned, started to shake his head, stopped, looked up at the sky and sighed heavily.

"I...no, I don't really want her for myself. Not now," he said slowly. "There was a time when I used to daydream about it. Me and her being something...different. I dunno. She keeps me on my toes, she makes me laugh and the sex was fucking-" I growled at him and he smirked as he shrugged. "You've been there, man, you know exactly what the sex is like with her."

"This conversation is likely to end in your death," I muttered as I tried to rein in my anger and jealousy and just deal with the fact that I should have gone after her when I'd first seen her instead of waiting and letting this situation play out.

Cal snorted a laugh like I was joking even though it was pretty clear I wasn't and he pushed a hand through his curls again. It was just one of those things he did without thinking, but I'd seen the way girls looked at him when he did it and with this particular subject of conversation, it really annoyed the fuck out of me.

"So why are we having it?" he asked.

"Because..." He waited me out and I forced myself to go on. He was my brother and we needed to clear the air on this subject even if neither of us liked the outcome. "The worst thing about being Star Crossed isn't even knowing that I'm never going to have love or happiness in my life like that. It's about knowing that *she* isn't. So I guess what I'm asking is, if I wasn't in the picture, if she didn't have black rings in her eyes...would it be you and her?"

Caleb drew in a deep breath as he looked at me and I could tell he was really considering his answer before he gave it.

"Me and Tory," he began slowly. "It was fun, like crazy fun. She never just fell at my feet like most of the girls who are so desperate to bag an Heir that they forget all about their dignity. I could never tell if I'd be getting a yes or a no from her and then when she started letting me hunt her, it awoke this feral part of me which I hadn't even known I'd been missing. We laughed together and have chemistry that just makes everything so hot and she seriously doesn't know when to stop pushing my fucking buttons and that was pretty fucking liberating."

I bit my tongue on every angry, bitter, jealous thought which ached to tumble from my lips and waited for him to finish as my heart pounded with this dull ache which I was afraid would consume me entirely if it got its way.

"But it was also...kinda hard work," he said, offering me a grin. "She literally never messaged or called me except in response to me doing so first. She refused to meet up with me nine times for every time she said yes. When we went to the Fairy Fair we had a fucking brilliant time, but I had to work my ass off to figure out what she'd like to do and then when I took her on that date..." He groaned and dropped his head back as I chuckled at the memory too.

"I can't believe you fucked it up so bad," I said.

"I can't believe you never took her out yourself," he shot back and I sighed. "Seriously, you had that whole perfect date planned out, you can't tell me it never occurred to you."

"Only in a fantasy kind of way," I admitted. "I was aware enough of all the reasons she had to refuse me to know that it wasn't worth actually asking."

Caleb gave me a look which really only could be described as pity and I narrowed my eyes at him.

"*Anyway,*" he said. "Coming back to my point. If I'm totally honest, no, I don't think me and her could have gone long term. I like hanging out with her the way I like hanging out with you guys - she's great for a laugh and can drink me under the table, she winds me up damn near constantly, her blood tastes like ecstasy. Then I got sex thrown in too."

"That sounds kind of like the perfect girl," I muttered.

"Maybe if it had been easy, but...I think I was always just a place holder for her. While she really had her eye on you." He smiled at me in a way that didn't hold any anger, just acceptance. "And at least now I know why."

"So there's not a part of you that thinks or hopes that now that me and her can't-"

"No," he cut me off. "I don't want this to sound harsh man, but I don't want to be her consolation prize. And I don't want you to have to give up on her either-"

"I don't want to talk about this insane idea you and the others have about us defying the stars," I growled.

"Why not?" he demanded, refusing to let me turn away from the subject. "You seem to want to fight for her, you want to prove to her you're more than the monster she thought you were. What's the point of that if you don't believe there's any hope for you?"

"Because that's what love is," I said in a low voice, running my finger over a bare patch of skin on my right forearm thoughtfully. "It's giving everything without expecting anything in return. It's sacrificing your heart and happiness for someone else and it's owning all of your mistakes and trying to make them right. Not because you expect to get something in return for it. But because the person you love needs to know how you feel."

I got to my feet, intending to leave but Caleb shot upright too, catching my arm before I'd even made it a step away.

"Doesn't she deserve to have love then?" he asked. "Doesn't she deserve to wake up every day in the arms of someone who loves her? To have laughter and happiness and a hundred fucking Dragon babies if that's what she wants?"

"She does, but-"

"But nothing," he snapped. "That's why all of us are working so damn hard to figure out a way around this for you. Because we believe you *both* deserve that. So stop selling yourself short. Stop selling her short. And decide right here and now that you're going to fight for your girl. *Really* fight for her. Not just achieve this bullshit mission to right all your wrongs against her. Prove to her that you deserve her and then climb up into the fucking sky and tear the stars right out of it for her if they still don't agree."

The ferocity in his eyes made my heart pound harder as his words lit an ache in me which was so fucking tempting that I didn't even want to try and resist it.

"You want me to fight against the will of the stars for her?" I asked, though for some insane reason that didn't sound as terrifying as it should have. Terrifying was *not* fighting, it was accepting this fucking hell as our fate. It was giving in and letting the stars and my father and some fucked up version of fate choose my life for me.

"Isn't that what you want?"

My tongue felt leaden in my mouth, my palms slick and my heart racing as I thought about that. Did I want to fight with every goddamn fibre of my being for Roxy Vega to be mine?

"Yes, it is."

ORION

CHAPTER THIRTY FOUR

I was up early. Not that I'd slept. The world was a twisted mess that didn't allow for sleep anymore. After everything I'd been through, everything I'd worked for, my life had fallen apart in the space of thirty seconds. And it was taking everything I had just to keep it together.

I clawed at my hair as I paced back and forth in the six by six cell of sun steel bars, my wrists still cuffed to contain my magic. They let me have a few minutes every day in an empty room designed to contain my power so that I could use my magic and not get sick. But I *was* sick. I was sick with anxiety. And I'd been up all night trying to work out a way out of this. But I still had nothing.

I dropped down on the bench at the back of the cell, ignoring the agent who was sitting at his desk across the wide space, his feet perched up on it as he watched some comedy show on his Atlas with a laughter track that was eating into my skull.

I rested my elbows on my knees and dropped my head into my hands as I tried to focus, tried to block out the incessant laughter and the guffawing chuckle that came from the agent in response.

Today, in less than two hours, I was going to be walking into the Court of Solaria to face the judgement of the people. And I wasn't fucking ready. Even after everything I'd talked through with Kipling, nothing he'd suggested outright fixed this shitshow. Nothing I said on the stand was going to make it go away. It was already decided, I just didn't know how bad my punishment was going to be.

I kept my mind from straying to Blue despite the fact that she possessed me, begged my thoughts to go to her again and again. But as soon as I let her slip in, the guilt weighed down my heart so hard I fell into an abyss of misery I'd been careless enough to let this happen and now she was going to be ridiculed because of me. And the worst thing of all, was the slicing, ripping, endlessly agonising possibility that I was never going to hold her in my arms again.

I kicked off of the bench, pacing once more, trying to drive it all out so I could come up with a solution. Darius might have hired me a top of the range lawyer, but it wouldn't make a difference in the long run. He might even get me the reduced sentence he promised, but I didn't give a fuck about that. I cared about Blue and what this was going to do to her. I was going to be latched to her reputation forever, dragging her name through the mud, damaging, possibly irrevocably, her chances of seizing the throne. The papers would tell lies, they'd make her out to have been cheating her way through my classes, they'd shame her until no one had any faith in her. They'd probably already started.

My breathing grew ragged and I found it hard to drag in air as I continued to labour back and forth, back and forth.

"Would you ever stop that fucking pacing?" the agent shot at me, wiping crumbs off of his large stomach from the huge cookie he'd just eaten. He had a paper bag of them on his desk which apparently counted as this prick's breakfast.

I snarled it him, but my fangs didn't snap out. I'd been under the influence of Order Suppressant gas since I'd arrived.

"You're like a damn animal," he muttered to himself.

"Sorry to interfere with your pleasant fucking morning, asshole. It's just the rest of my life that's going to be weighed in the balance this morning. Nothing important," I spat.

He sat upright in his chair, his face morphing into concern as he turned to his cookie bag and looked inside it as if searching for something. "Oh sorry, mate," he announced suddenly, dropping back into his seat. "I'm totally out of fucks to give. So sit down and shut up."

I ground my jaw, my gaze narrowing in on his throat. I'd been given blood through a fucking straw twice since they'd put me in here. And if that wasn't the most degrading thing about all of this then I didn't know what was.

I thought over everything Gabriel had told me when he'd come to visit a few days ago. The Sight had given him a hundred paths and he couldn't clearly see any way out for me. But he said that if I was in the 'right state of mind' I would be able to save Blue. I just didn't know what that meant. And now I was down to my final hours and I had no plan. No fucking idea what I was going to do.

After an hour, I was taken through to the showers to wash and I was soon dressed in the dark grey suit Darius had provided me with. Kipling had suggested it. Apparently grey was less arrogant than blue and black just marked you as guilty before the jury had even begun. I smelled bullshit, but whatever. I was going to take whatever advantage I could get at this point. A suit wasn't going to save me from the judge though. And it wasn't going to save Blue either.

After I was dressed, I was led through to an interview room and frowned at the bastard clutching my arm, sensing three other agents following threateningly behind me. "What am I doing in here?"

He pushed me down into a seat at the table, chaining my wrists to it by the magic restricting cuffs. "You have a visitor," he said then strode from the room.

I shifted my hands, making the chains clink. The tie around my throat felt uncomfortably like a noose and I was tempted to loosen it. The door opened and Francesca walked in in her dark FIB jumpsuit, her hair braided tightly into a knot that gave her a more severe look than usual.

In all of this, I hadn't even considered what she thought of me. She'd been a good friend through my years at Zodiac, but I suddenly realised that she hardly knew the guy I'd become since then. How little of me I'd really shared with her after Clara had been lost to the shadows. And now she probably thought she didn't know me at all.

"Lance," she breathed, the word holding so much bitter disappointment in it that my jaw locked in response. "How could you be so stupid?"

Her tone was soft, but I could see a war of emotion in her eyes as she dropped into the seat opposite me.

"Aren't you going to say anything in your defence?" she pushed, her cheeks colouring as her temper rose.

"I think I'll be saying enough in court," I said dryly.

"For the stars' sake!" She bashed her fist down on the table as tears brimmed in her eyes. "A student, Lance, really? And not just any student, a Vega *princess*."

The muscles in my jaw worked harder as rage collected like water against a dam in my chest. "Things aren't always as black and white as they seem, Francesca," I growled, a warning in my tone.

I didn't want to discuss this with her now. I was going to be cut open, my heart ripped out and placed on the weighing scales in less than an hour. I didn't need the judgement in advance.

"Then how about you clear things up for me then, huh? Is that why you brought her on the Nymph run? Because she was in your bed when I called?" Her upper lip peeled back and a growl rumbled dangerously in my chest.

"I will explain myself in court," I said evenly, trying to hold back the anger pouring from me. She'd always been a good friend, but if she couldn't back me on this, I couldn't see how we were going to get past it.

"Explain yourself now," she demanded. "Us....we – I thought we-"

"What?" I snarled and she glanced away from me with her lips pursed.

"I always thought it would be *us*, Lance. We always had so much fun together."

"That's all it was. You knew that from the start," I growled, furious that we were even having this conversation right now.

"Please tell me you don't love her." She rose from her seat, her gaze deadly and probing.

"I won't tell you that," I hissed and she shook her head at me.

"Don't flush your whole life away for her," she said in a quiet tone.

"Tell the court she manipulated you. Blackmailed you. Be *smart*, Lance. You can't be with her either way."

I was out of my seat in a second. "Get out!" I roared as her eyes widened in alarm. "Get the fuck out!" I pointed at the door, yanking my hand to the extent of its chain and tears flowed down her cheeks as she hurried to exit, the door clicking shut behind her a second later.

Fuck her. She had no idea. No clue.

The door swung open again and the cookie-munching guard returned, unlocking the chains and hauling me out into the corridor with a group of agents, before guiding me away in the opposite direction to the cells and through a set of security doors. I was led out onto the street where a black armoured van awaited me. My heart ticked faster as I was towed into the back of it and my ankles were chained to the bench I sat on.

"Wait, I will be riding with my client," Mr Kipling appeared, climbing into the back of the van and settling himself opposite me, planting his briefcase down beside him.

The doors slid shut and the dreary morning light filtered in through the window behind him.

"Are you ready, Mr Orion?" he asked, dusting off his knees as he sat before me, his posture ramrod straight.

"Yeah," I said, a dark acceptance settling over me.

"Run me through the plan," he prompted and I sighed.

"I'll tell the court the truth. That this wasn't pre-meditated. That we fell in love. That we believe we could be Elysian Mates and that the stars have been guiding us together."

"Good, and how will you answer questions from the prosecution?"

"Emotionally," I gritted out.

"Not angrily though," he pointed out. "You need to present yourself as the victim of love. Of the stars."

"I know," I growled, rubbing my eyes.

"We don't have room for errors today, Mr Orion. You really must get this right. It will mean the difference between house arrest and a stint in Darkmore."

I chewed on the inside of my cheek, nodding my head robotically as he continued to go over the details. When he was done, the van slowed to a halt as if he'd timed his speech to coincide with the exact length of this trip. From the strange ways he behaved, I wouldn't be surprised if he had.

Kipling rose to his feet, straightening his tie. "If you follow my instructions to the letter, this will go perfectly. And after you're released from house arrest – in two years if I win the plea - we can start negotiating your terms on being let back into society. All in all, you're probably only looking at six years as an outcast from the moment of being power shamed." The door opened and he stepped out of the van, leaving me with my heart flaking away like sawdust in my chest.

Six years.

I'd be thirty two. Blue would have long since graduated. She would have moved on from me. From us. She'd probably resent me after a while. Her biggest mistake. This could fuck with everything she'd worked so hard for. I'd just be the dark smudge on her history. The name everyone brought up every time she did a press conference, the discrepancy that would never go away. I'd hang around her throat like a fucking anchor until the end of time.

An FIB agent moved into the van to unlock me from the bench, pulling my arm to lead me outside where I was surrounded by five more of them. Photographers started crying out, the blinding flash of cameras making me squint as I was guided towards a colossal set of imposing steps leading up to an even more imposing building.

I couldn't hear the questions the press were shouting at me, I couldn't hear anything but a droning din in my ears as my fate closed in all around me.

For once, I could see my future more clearly than ever before. There was only one path I could take now. I may as well have trodden it already. And as I reached the arching silver doors at the top of the stairs and they were pulled wide and gaping like the mouth of a beast about to swallow me, I took the last breath of crisp, free air before my fate was sealed within these walls.

DARCY

CHAPTER THIRTY FIVE

I was too hot in the back of the fancy chauffeured car Darius had organised to take us to court. He sat beside me, his hands knotted in his lap as we both gazed though opposite windows.

My heart beat differently than it used to. Ever since they'd taken Orion away, it was like it couldn't keep pace with my breaths, like it was coping with too much pain to work properly.

A tear dropped down onto the white dress I wore. Below the knee, loosely fitting, long sleeves. Darius had been meeting with the Kipling lawyers all week and every time he came back, he had new advice for me. And this was one of their tips. I was supposed to look innocent, lovelorn. Apparently crying was a good thing. But the only real advice I'd been given for questioning was to tell the truth. Be heartfelt, honest and make sure the world knew that we were in love. That this wasn't some fling or some pitch for grades as plenty of my classmates were happy to believe.

I wiped the tear from the skirt of my dress, rubbing angrily at it when the mark didn't vanish and Darius laid a hand on my arm.

I glanced over at him with a sharp pinch in my chest. I hadn't been allowed to bring Tory. And it felt like an impossible task to face this day without her. I had to rely on Darius to be at my side through this. And despite everything that had happened between us and the Heirs, I was glad he was here. I was glad Orion had him to rely on too. And I was comforted by the fact that Darius had done everything within his power to give Orion the best chance possible in his trial.

Darius retracted his hand, running it through his hair with a heavy sigh. "Are you ready for this?" he asked and I frowned, shaking my head.

"I don't think I could ever be ready for this," I breathed. "The worst thing is, I always knew this was a possibility, I just never took it seriously enough. I should have stayed away from him. I should have-"

Darius shifted across the seat and pulled me under his arm. I stilled for a moment as my cheek pressed to his chest and his arms folded around me. Then I wrapped my arms around him too and drew strength from having someone to go through this with. Even if it couldn't be my sister. Darius loved Orion. He was heartbroken about this too. His despair might have been channelled into working his ass off to help him get the right lawyers, the right information to fight in court, but underneath it all, he'd been hurting like I had.

"He doesn't deserve this," I choked out. "It's all my fault."

He held me tighter and the scent of smoke filled the air as the Dragon in him rose to the surface. "This isn't your fault. Lance has never spoken about any girl the way he speaks about you. It was inevitable that you'd end up together."

I pulled back as he released me, hunting his eyes for the truth. "Do you really believe that?"

He nodded firmly, his jaw set, his mind made up and an inch of my heart was given to him in that moment. I could have said a thousand bad things about Darius Acrux, but the best ones shone brighter, outweighing them so they were all I could see.

"You've been a good friend," I said. "He couldn't ask for a better one."

Darius's eyebrows knitted together. "I hope it's enough."

"You couldn't have done more." I squeezed his arm reassuringly and he seemed to accept that.

The car pulled up outside a massive building built of matt white stone, reaching up towards the sky with the flag of Solaria hanging proudly from a pole above the doorway. The flag was black with a golden mountain at the base of it, rising up to the sun, the moon and the twelve zodiac constellations above. The press were gathered at the base of the steps beyond a cordon which held them back.

I wet my lips, wondering what the kingdom would think of Darius and I arriving together. It was a show of solidarity that was separate to any feud we had beyond Orion's trial. And one I hadn't even considered the political implications of before now. I found I didn't care. And Darius clearly didn't either. The driver stepped out, opening the door for Darius and I slid across the seat to follow him onto the sidewalk.

The noise from the press was deafening, cameras were pointed at us, the rattle of shutters clacking in my ears as questions were cried out to us.

Guards surrounded us as we moved up the steps side by side and my heart clenched into a tight fist as we reached the arching silver doors and headed inside. A large, marble atrium awaited us, but we were whisked across it before I could take in many details, guided directly through another set of doors and my breath snagged in my lungs.

The court room was the most intimidating place I'd ever stepped foot in, including the throne room in the Palace of Souls. But maybe that was partly because my whole world was about to fall apart in here.

We walked through aisles of white stone benches stretching out either side of us, full of people here to watch the trial. Ahead of us was a huge marble wall which rose to the judge's bench and to the right side of it was a set of steps that curved up to a witness stand, the imposing seat carved into the stone itself. To the right of that was a raised seating area where all twelve members of the jury were waiting. Men and women, old and young. There were a few more women than men, but my gaze didn't linger on them long as my gaze moved magnetically to the two, tall black tables in front of the benches.

Orion stood behind the one on the left with his lawyer. I could only see the back of his head, his chin dipped to his chest. As I drew closer, he turned like he could sense me there and Darius gripped the crook of my elbow like he expected me to run to him. And maybe it was a good move because every fibre of me wanted to.

Orion's eyes were hollow and his mouth was a sharp line. His features were tightly drawn with worry and I desperately wanted to hold him and tell him it would be alright. The shame of knowing I'd be the cause of whatever sentence he got today was suffocating.

My throat closed up as Darius guided me down the aisle to the front bench on the right and I dropped onto the cold stone, the position giving me a clear view of the judge's seat ahead. It was an intimidating chair that looked as though it was made of iron, the crest of the Solarian Court stamped into the back of it, picturing an astrology circle with the twelve constellations symbols within it.

The prosecution lawyer stood behind the black stone table to my right, thumbing through her notes. She had a fiery perm and a fitted pant suit that hugged her bony figure, her cheekbones blade sharp.

There was an icy chill in the room that clung to every inch of my skin. The only warmth around me was the steady, angry heat radiating from Darius with every breath he took.

"All rise for his honour, the High Court Judge Darkice," a man in royal red robes spoke from the corner of the room.

I stood up with the rest of the court as the judge appeared from a black door behind his seat, noticing that Darius didn't move to stand. The man's robes were red too, but had gold embroidery and a crest that marked him as the judge. He sat down in the high backed chair and picked up a silver gavel, banging it against the block which sparked with a flash of purple magic. The noise rang cleanly around the room, sending my heart into overdrive.

"Court is now in session," Darkice announced. "Please be seated."

I dropped down, everyone but Orion and the two lawyers remaining on their feet.

My tongue scratched the roof of my mouth like sandpaper. I needed water, I needed air.

"The trial of Lance Azriel Orion for breaking law three oh three of the seventeen eighty four education act will now commence. Defendant, how do you plead?"

A beat of tense silence passed that made my skull feel like it was about to cave in.

"Not guilty," Orion's voice filled the room and the jurors surveyed him keenly, some of them looking like predators hunting for weaknesses, others curious, and the rest keeping their cards close to their chests.

I was hit with a burst of relief at hearing him say those words. It meant he was going to fight. And with Darius's best lawyer standing at his side, maybe…just maybe he had a chance.

"I now ask that all evidence is presented to the jury," Darkice instructed. "Mrs Whitclaw, will the prosecution please present their case."

The woman with the perm moved around her table, walking up to the jury and turning so I could see her face. She looked professional, ruthlessly so. And I just had to hope she wasn't as good at her job as her appearance suggested.

"May I turn your attention, ladies and gentleman, to the screen just to your right," she spoke in a powerful voice. A wall jutting into the room beside the jury's seats hid the screen from view of the public, and my heart crushed into dust as I guessed what they were about to watch. "The six hour video has been cut into four admissible points of evidence for this trial," Whitclaw explained and I tried to fight the clawing embarrassment that those twelve strangers were going to watch that tape of me and Orion down in the archives, not to mention the judge and both lawyers who must have already seen it. "And I wish to highlight some key moments which I believe are of notable importance."

She waved her hand at the screen and I was painfully thankful that the rest of the room couldn't see it, but that didn't save us from my moans filling the room or the breathy noises both of us were making. The clip played out each command Orion had given me that night and a blush burned so deeply into my cheeks, I didn't think it would ever go away. People were whispering somewhere behind me and my gaze slipped to Orion, finding his body rigid, his hands curled into tight fists. Mr Kipling was talking into his ear and I had no doubt he was trying to keep him calm as Orion nodded, his eyes squeezing shut.

The clip finally ended and Whitclaw turned to the jury. "From this footage, it is quite clear that the relationship between Mr Orion and Miss Vega was dominant and submissive, fitting the teacher student roles and suggesting that their relationship never evolved beyond that fantasy. This is perfectly demonstrated by the phrase Mr Orion so clearly uses in the first segment of the footage stating that he would punish Miss Vega if she didn't do as he said. Therefore, I think it is clear that this relationship held no depth, no divine pull from the stars and was easily avoidable."

"Objection," Kipling clipped. "Mrs Whitclaw cannot make assumptions about the divine pull of the stars without further evidence."

"Sustained," Darkice agreed and I released a shaky breath. "Proceed."

Mrs Whitclaw shot Kipling a vicious look before moving onto the next clip. I sat through each of them with a burn in my brain, wishing I could block it all out as my skin flamed hotter and hotter. She used everything against us, making our relationship sound like nothing more than a dirty tryst that Orion had manipulated me into, abusing his power in the school to make me submit to him.

Finally, Kipling took her place and I had to listen to the entire four clips all over again as he explained everything in the complete opposite manner. Telling the jury that the fact Orion gave me cunnilingus (*dear fucking god*) twice was a sign of his undying and selfless affection for me, that the way I kissed him, cried his name and gave him fellatio in return (*please kill me now*) showed my devotion to him, and how we told each other we love one another proved I wasn't just a girl who'd been taken advantage of by her teacher.

By the time it was over, I couldn't tell who had made the strongest case. Both had been convincing as hell, but neither the jurors' faces nor the judge's gave anything away.

My fingers were knotted together in my lap, sweaty and cold. Darius continued to steadily expel heat as he sat quietly, taking it all in, saying nothing, never looking away from the jury like he was trying to decipher their thoughts. Or maybe he was planning to hunt down each and every one of them if they voted against Orion and make all of them pay for their mistake.

Mrs Whitclaw moved before them again and her apple green eyes found me amongst the crowd. "Your honour, I call Gwendalina Vega, informally known as Darcy Vega, to the stand."

If I'd been anxious before, it was nothing in comparison to this. Heat spread everywhere, but somehow none of it warmed my outer flesh. I was frozen and scorching and I couldn't find it in me to move.

Darius stood from the end of the aisle, his gaze meeting mine and I found the strength to get up. He was all I could see for a long second and he gave me a firm nod of encouragement, his faith in me iron clad.

I headed past him with countless eyes boring holes in my back as I walked towards the witness stand. It seemed far higher up close and I slowed at the base of the steps that led to it as a man in red robes moved before me, holding his palm out flat in front of me. I knew what to do, Darius had told me, so I lay my palm on top of the glittering, smoothly polished meteorite in his palm.

"Do you swear on every star in the sky that you will tell the truth, the whole truth and nothing but the truth lest you be cursed by the heavens themselves?"

"I do," I said, my voice coming out surprisingly strongly. And maybe that was because I wanted this. I needed to have my voice heard. I wanted to convince every single person in this court that what Orion and I had was love, as simple as that. And he didn't deserve to be punished for something we never could have predicted let alone ignored.

"And do you understand that if your statement is brought into question by the proceedings here today, through evidence, witnesses or otherwise, his honourable High Court Judge Darkice is within his rights to submit you for

Cyclops interrogation?"

"I do," I said, my throat so dry it ached.

He stepped aside and I climbed the steps. I lifted my thumb to my mouth, sucking and casting a little water down my throat to ease my parched tongue.

I made it to the seat, dropping down and staring back over the entire court. My eyes swung to Orion and a knife seemed to drive itself into the pit of my heart. He looked desperate and hopeless.

I had to do whatever I could to make this right. I had to fix this. I had to make the judge and jury listen to me, really listen, and really believe what I had to say.

Mrs Whitclaw stepped in front of me, taking a slow breath as if she was measuring her words before she spoke. "Miss Vega, you are Mr Orion's Source, correct?"

"Yes," I agreed.

"Objection," Kipling called, making my heart stutter. "The fact that Mr Orion bit Miss Vega cannot be used as evidence against him due to his Order."

"The whereabouts of said bites, do however pose bearing in this trial," Whitclaw shot back, lifting her chin.

My heart pounded harder as I waited for the judge to speak.

"Overruled, Mr Kipling. Will the prosecution please proceed." He nodded to Whitclaw and she barely concealed her smug smile as she took a step towards the stand.

Despite being below me, it felt awfully like she was ten foot tall with a knife to my throat. "Which part of your body would you say, Miss Vega, that Mr Orion bit you most regularly *before* you became intimate with one another?"

I swallowed the swarm of bees that seemed to be piling up in my throat as I answered. "The neck."

Whitclaw swung towards the jury like a cat with a mouse between its paws. "Interesting, wouldn't you say, that a Vampire would bite his Source on the neck even after they were claimed? A Vampire usually bites the neck when fighting or…when sexual desire is involved."

"Objection," Kipling said firmly.

"Sustained," Judge Darkice said and goosebumps tumbled down my spine. "Please rephrase your question, Mrs Whitclaw."

"Would you agree, Miss Vega," she rounded on me again, changing tact. "That there are several far less sexual places on the body that Mr Orion could have bitten you? Perhaps you could name some, hm?"

I despised the way she was talking to me. The way she was trying to plant answers in my mouth to feed her case. But I wasn't going to play her game.

"I think the neck is as convenient a place as any, Mrs Whitclaw," I said firmly. "In a school uniform, really his only choice would be my neck or my wrists, unless you think he'd be better getting on his knees to bite my ankles?"

"Of course not," she said, a bright gleam in her eye like she'd won something. "But it is *interesting* that you mentioned the wrists." She said the word *interesting* like it was a threat. This woman was fast becoming my number one enemy. And that was saying a lot considering how many I had these days.

She turned to the jury again, her high heels clipping over the marble floor as she approached them. "It could be argued that a Vampire who works in education would be quite used to biting his students. As such, he could easily keep a healthy distance between himself and said students by feeding from the wrist instead of the throat."

A few of the jury nodded their agreement and anger boiled up hot and acidic in my chest.

"He didn't bait me if that's what you're suggesting," I snapped, refusing to take my eyes off of her as I felt everyone staring at me. "I wanted Orion from the moment I saw him. And that want grew to like and that like grew to love. I tried to fight against it, but I felt drawn to him like he did to me. We couldn't help ourselves," I said passionately. Because it was true, and it wasn't right that I had to defend it, but I would. Until my dying fucking breath, I would. "We are in *love*. This isn't some dirty affair or some bid for good grades. I love him and he loves me too. It's as simple as that."

I turned to Orion and he smiled in a way that broke my heart. A tear tumbled down my cheek and I let it fall, let it be seen, because it was proof. And though I hated to be so exposed, I would bleed for Orion. I'd cut myself open to win this case for him if it was asked of me.

"Your honour." Kipling extracted a piece of paper from his briefcase, slamming it down on the table. "As is outlined in the Vampire Code, there is no rule stating that my client can't bite his Source wherever he pleases on her body. There's no law against it and it is conjecture to suggest one place on the body is more sexual than another. There are plenty of people in the world who have a foot fetish, finger fetish, or even a nose fetish. So you cannot take Mrs Whitclaw's line of questioning into account."

The judge considered that for a long moment then nodded, making a ragged breath escape me. "This line of questioning has been overruled and will not be taken into account as evidence. A Cyclops will remove the jurors' memories of this line of inquiry before a verdict is decided. Mrs Whitclaw, please proceed."

She moved closer to me again, that huntress look back in her eyes as she searched for a different angle. She wasn't done with me, far from it. "Please detail the first instance you were intimate with Mr Orion."

I took a breath, then another, trying to quiet the pounding of my pulse. "We were at Lord Lionel Acrux's manor at a private party," I said. "I went for a walk and bumped into him so we went outside together to get some air."

"And who instigated that arrangement?" Whitclaw asked, making me fall still.

"I…I don't know, I can't remember. We both wanted to escape the party that's all. So we went outside."

"And then what?" Whitclaw pressed.

"Then…Lance made me a drink and-"

"He gave you alcohol?" Whitclaw interjected and my heart raced.

"Just a wine," I said like it didn't matter. And it didn't, she was just looking for ways to use this story against him. I was allowed to drink, but she was making it sound like he'd poured alcohol down my throat.

I remembered the cocktail umbrella he'd put in it and a small smile pulled at my mouth. "He was sweet, we were laughing together, then he went for a dip in the pool."

"So he plied you with alcohol then he took his clothes off in front of you?" Whitclaw guessed and my heart stammered.

"It wasn't like that," I blurted.

"What was it like?" She raised a questioning eyebrow and my heart thundered in my ears.

I searched for the right words, not wanting to give her any more ammo. "It was…fate. I could feel it in every part of my body. The sky wanted it. I wanted it. We wanted each other." I chanced a look at Orion and I wished I hadn't because I almost came apart, his dark and penetrating eyes making me weak.

"What happened next, Miss Vega?" Whitclaw pushed, clearly wanting me to move on from this.

"He went under the water," I breathed. "He was under there for so long that I moved to the edge of the pool, ducking down to look for him. When he came up, he pulled me into the water."

"He used force to get you in the pool?" Whitclaw questioned and I shook my head sharply.

"No, he was playing around."

"Did he ask for your consent?" she pushed.

"No, but-"

"And what happened after he dragged you under the surface?" she asked, letting a little shock into her voice for show. Some of the jury were lapping it up, gazing at me in concern.

I wanted to leap from the stand and claw this woman's eyes out. She was twisting everything I said, turning that perfectly magical night into something nasty and premeditated. "He created an air pod at the bottom of the pool." I let myself smile so the jury could see. I wasn't going to let this bitch taint this story. "And we kissed."

"He kissed you or you kissed him?" Whitclaw asked.

"He…I – I wanted it."

"But who kissed who, Miss Vega?" Whitclaw demanded and I knew I had to give her the truth.

"He kissed me," I breathed.

"And then what?" she pushed.

"Nothing," I said firmly. "We went back to the party."

"And who did you tell?" she asked.

"No one."

"Did he threaten you to keep it quiet?"

"No," I growled.

"What did he say exactly?" she asked and my brain rattled as I tried to think.

"He said…" I racked my memory and it came to me. "He said, you know how it has to be. And I said that I did know."

"And did he explain what he meant by that?" Whitclaw asked, seeming aghast now.

"I…no, but I knew it meant that we couldn't tell anyone. That's obvious."

"Is it?" she questioned, that eyebrow popping up again as she turned to the jury once more. "It is *interesting* that Mr Orion would use such a phrase. *You know how it has to be*….quite a threatening phrase some might say. The words 'has to' implies that if Miss Vega broke that rule she would be punished. And as he used exactly such a phrase in the video evidence provided, stating that he would punish you if you disobeyed him, it seems quite clear that's what he meant."

"That's not what he meant," I snapped.

"Objection. It's conjecture," Kipling said simply. "Without hearing the way it was spoken, we have no idea how it could be construed. She cannot compare it to any instance in the video evidence provided and assume it to be so."

"Sustained," the judge agreed and my shoulders relaxed as Whitclaw was stuffed back in her box. "Do you have any further questions, Mrs Whitclaw?"

She eyed me like she was trying to pick at my skin and see the blood and muscle that lived underneath. "Just one, your honour." She moved closer and my heart struggled to pump blood for a long second. "Why, if he loves you so dearly as you claim, do you believe that Mr Orion did not quit his job at Zodiac Academy to be with you?"

My lungs compressed as I absorbed the question. There was a hundred answers to that. He'd been appointed his position there by Lionel Acrux himself, he had no choice but to stay there as Guardian to his son. He was training Darius in dark magic, he needed to be close to him, and to me and Tory too since we'd gotten the shadows. And regardless of all that, it was his job, his life, his home. I never would have let him give it all up for me.

"Miss Vega?" Whitclaw pressed as my lips opened and closed.

"He had responsibilities," I said firmly.

"What responsibilities?"

"He's Darius Acrux's Guardian, for one," I blurted.

"And for two?" She arched that damn brow again.

I struggled for anything I could say in court. I couldn't bring up anything about the shadows or dark magic or Lionel Acrux being a domineering buttcrack of a Dragon lord.

"No further questions, your honour," Mrs Whitclaw said and I sagged down in my seat, my gaze falling to my hands. I had the horrible, bone-deep feeling that I'd just let Orion down. And it was unbearable.

Mr Kipling came up to question me next, clasping his hands behind his back. He was so formal and yet he had a warm presence I far preferred over

Whitclaw's. And at least he was on our side.

He asked me all the same questions again plus more, letting me talk about Orion and our relationship in detail, asking about the time he'd taken me for a picnic at his home, the gifts he'd given me, including the rose quartz which was a symbol that we were exclusive. Then he declared to the jury that our love was plain for the world to see as Orion and I got caught in each other's eyes and I hoped that was true with all my soul.

I was finally released from the stand and made it back to Darius's side, my legs like jelly. I breathed a sigh of relief, leaning close to whisper in his ear as I sat down. "Did I do okay?"

"You did great, Darcy. No one can deny how much you love each other," he said, lifting his chin as if he was ready to go to bat for us if anyone did dare deny it.

"Your honour, I'd like to call my next witness to the stand," Whitclaw announced and Darkice inclined his head. "Miss Kylie Major."

I froze, confused as the sound of heels clicking down the aisle behind me made me twist around in my seat. Kylie was dolled up in a bright pink dress that had no business in a place like this. Her high heels were over six inches tall and her perfect make-up and flowing blonde hair made her look like she was about to attend a catwalk over a damn trial.

She vowed to tell the truth then rose to the stand, crossing her legs and showing off ample skin as she smiled patiently at Mrs Whitclaw. Inside, I was screaming. Because I knew why she was there. It suddenly clicked together like a puzzle in my head that featured something dark and grotesque.

Kipling was talking into Orion's ear again as his muscles bunched and flexed. I could see his jaw grinding and his rage was mirrored in my own heart.

"Miss Major, you presented this Atlas to the FIB on March twenty third, is that correct?" Whitclaw plucked a transparent bag out of her briefcase, holding it up for the jury, showing them the pink case of my Atlas inside.

I couldn't draw a single breath, my fingernails driving into the skin of my palms and splitting it open. Magic was washing through my veins with the force of a tsunami, desperate to be unleashed on that bitch sitting on the stand.

"Yes," Kylie agreed, nodding. "I found Darcy's Atlas in The Orb at dinner. She must have left it there."

No way. She'd stolen it. And this whole mess was her fault. *She'd* given them the evidence. Not Seth. That truth hit me like a heart attack and I rubbed my forehead as I tried to process it.

"And what did you do then?" Whitclaw asked.

"Well, I had my suspicions that Darcy Vega was sleeping with my ex-boyfriend. I have *loads* of friends who've seen her down on her knees for boys all over campus, but she'd been sleeping with my Sethy even when we were together."

"That's a lie!" I snapped, unable to help myself and Darkice banged his gavel.

"Silence in court!" he roared and my hands balled up even tighter until I made my palms bleed.

Kylie flicked her hair, not giving me her attention as she barrelled on. "I found a message from her from a codename called Starboy with arrangements to meet in the school archives. She'd been lying to me for months about sleeping with Seth, so I set up a camera down there and decided to out her for the liar she was."

"But she wasn't a liar, was she?" Whitclaw spoke in my favour for the first time, though I knew it wasn't because she was going to vouch for me.

"Well, I wouldn't put it past her for screwing my ex too, but I couldn't believe what I'd caught on camera. At first, I was shocked. But then it made a whole lot of sense," Kylie said thoughtfully and I wished I could grab a handful of all that blonde hair and rip a chunk of it out of her scalp.

"And why is that?" Whitclaw asked.

"Because Orion has always taken a liking to her. He calls her Blue like it's a cute little nickname or something. It singles her out from the other students in class, makes her feel important, I guess." She shrugged. "She wasn't doing so great when she first started at Zodiac, but weirdly her grades got better and better as she went on. Now it makes complete sense. She's been spreading her legs for a teacher!" She feigned her absolute shock and my insides shrivelled.

Kylie had always been a bitch, but to go this far to hurt me was just cruel. She was as venomous as her Order form.

"No further questions, your honour," Whitclaw dismissed her and apparently Kipling didn't have any intention of questioning her and giving her the limelight any longer than necessary as she clip-clopped her way to a bench at the back of the room with a smug as shit smile on her face. I wanted to tear her lips off and stuff them down her throat for what she'd done to us.

"It's now time for the defendant to make a statement in light of the evidence brought before us and reaffirm his plea to the jury," Judge Darkice announced and Orion strode toward the stand with his hands balling and unballing at his sides.

I didn't breathe until he'd taken the oath to be honest and sat down on the witness stand, my teeth driving into my tongue. I stole a look at the jury and found many of them sitting up in their chairs. Like they wanted to listen, like they cared to. All he had to do was tell the truth and they'd believe him. I was sure of it.

"Please make your statement, then the prosecution will proceed with the questioning," Judge Darkice instructed and Orion took in a long breath, his eyes finding mine in the audience.

The world seemed to fade so there was just us and far too much space separating our souls. I needed a moment in his arms, I needed his mouth against mine and his soothing caresses. I didn't know when I'd get any of that again, or be able to give them to him in return. But if he could just avoid prison, I knew Darius could find a way to get me to him. There had to be a way. We could make it work. We just had to climb this momentous hurdle and seek the light on the other side. Because no one would ever compare to him. No one would ever own my heart but that man. It was a truth cast in iron, impossible to undo. And if I had to wait months or years or an eternity for him, I would.

Orion visibly swallowed, an apology in his eyes before he turned his gaze from me towards the jury instead. A horrible lick of dread ran up my spine at his expression and panic flittered through me. *What's he thinking?*

"It's with regret that I laid a hand on a princess of Solaria," he spoke evenly and his words brought a sharp frown to my face. "And it's with even more regret that I admit that I used her for my own gain. I groomed her, manipulated her and ultimately, I used Dark Coercion on her to force her to be mine."

"No!" I screamed, rising from my seat as absolute horror encased me. Darius was up beside me too, fury in his eyes as he stared at his friend and a tumult of chatter broke out around us.

"Order, order!" the judge commanded, bashing his gavel down. "Sit down immediately!" A wave of air magic rushed across the room and I was forced back into my seat with everyone else.

"What's he doing?" I begged of Darius, fear slicing my heart to ribbons. But he didn't answer, just stared at Orion unblinkingly, desperation written into his features.

"Will the prosecution please approach the stand," Darkice commanded, his voice sharp as he glared at Orion.

I was shaking all over, staring at Orion as I begged him to meet my gaze. Darius suddenly grabbed my hand, squeezing tight and I clung to it with all my strength.

"Dark Coercion is a form of dark magic," Whitclaw purred, moving toward Orion like she was savouring the kill.

"No shit," Orion gritted out.

"So you admit that you cast Dark Coercion on Gwendalina Vega, Princess of Solaria? A girl who is protected by the highest of royal laws?"

"I do," Orion said with a nod that shattered my heart into a million sharp pieces. "She has no idea, of course. That's why she told lies here today. I convinced her that she loved me, I made her forget that I forced her hand, I made her want me and desire me. Everything she believes about our relationship is a farce that I concocted."

I shook my head, tears rolling down my cheeks as Darius's grip tightened on my hand.

"And why would you do that?" Whitclaw asked sweetly.

"Because I wanted her. I got off on the power and I knew I could use her to rise in society," Orion said with a shrug that was callous and cold.

He let the jury see him as a monster, painting himself as one. But I didn't understand why. I wanted to scream and fight and demand he take it back, but he'd ensured that no one would believe me. They thought I'd been Coerced to feel this way. And the idea that he could betray me so deeply made me want to vomit.

"So do you change your plea?" Whitclaw asked, victory in her posture.

"Your honour, I demand a moment alone with my client," Kipling insisted, his shoulders pressed back.

"I change my plea," Orion said before Darkice could answer him. "I plead guilty."

"He's lying!" I rose from my seat again, refusing to let this stand.

"Have him put through Cyclops interrogation," Darius demanded, pointing directly at the judge like he could threaten him into doing so. "Then you'll see the truth."

"Order in my court!" Darkice boomed. "If you do not sit down this instant, I will have you ejected."

Darius's hand was still locked with mine and we both dropped back down in unison as tears started washing down my cheeks.

This can't be happening. Please tell me this isn't happening. He wouldn't do this to me. To himself.

Orion's gaze was fixed on the wall, his jaw set in stone, his eyes infinitely dark.

Darkice straightened in his seat, drumming his fingers on the bench then bashed his gavel down on the block. "The defendant is power shamed and outcast from society indefinitely. He will serve a sentence in Darkmore Penitentiary of ten years on account of his manipulation of a Solarian Princess, and another fifteen for wielding dark magic to do so. Court adjourned." He rose from his seat, sweeping out the door behind him with the finality of an axe falling. *No.*

A group of FIB agents strode towards Orion and he lifted his cuffed wrists, letting him bind them without a glimmer of a fight. I got out of my seat, pushing past Darius and running towards them with so much rage in me, it was surely going to set me on fire.

"How could you do this!?" I screamed at him, grabbing one of the agent's arms as I tried to battle my way towards him. I caught Orion's hand somewhere in the throng and his fingers hooked around mine for half a second before I was forced back.

"Stand down," an agent commanded, marching away as he helped guide Orion toward the nearest door.

"Lance!" I screamed, tears searing my flesh as he went with them. Not looking back. Never giving me even a second to say goodbye as he cut out my heart and left it bloody and butchered in his wake.

His betrayal sliced deeper than a knife. He hadn't fought for us. He'd dived head first into the pits of hell without me. And for what?

I felt a cracking in my soul that spoke of the promise we'd made on the stars together. To always fight to be together. He'd broken it. And he'd broken me in the process.

TORY

· CHAPTER THIRTY SIX ·

I wandered through Fire Territory as the sun blazed overhead and the warmth of it tried to fight against the cold feeling which had sunk into my bones while I allowed the shadows to have free rein for a little while.

It was quiet out here, most people preferring the landscape of the other Territories to relax in on their Saturday afternoon over the barren, rocky terrain of Fire. But I'd been spending a lot of time out here during the last few weeks.

Darcy had taken to sleeping in my room every night, refusing to even mention Orion's name by day. She saved her tears for the middle of the night when there was no one but me there to see them. And when she finally cried herself to sleep and I didn't have to be strong for her anymore, I slipped out of my bed, lay on the floor and let the shadows have me.

When I'd started toying with the darkness Lionel Acrux had forced into my body, I'd only endured the shadows for a few minutes at a time. Sometimes I sank into them for hours now.

Orion's conviction hung like a heavy weight over all of us. Darcy was struck dumb with grief and Darius had reverted into the rage filled monster I'd once known. Not that he directed any of it at me. He didn't direct much of anything at me anymore. He still ran with me every morning, still got me my coffee and held the door for me. But there were no smiles. Not even when I slid my fingers though his and squeezed for the briefest of moments. Something in his eyes lightened whenever I did it, but the moment I pulled back, the walls went up again and he left me to it.

I knew he was grieving too and the Guardian bond between him and Orion was an agony of its own without them being able to see each other. He was hurting and I couldn't even try to comfort him because if I went to him, the stars forced me away again.

I took my Atlas from my pocket and sighed as I pushed the shadows back. They were slipping beyond the confines of my flesh, coating my wrists and fingers in a way that would be too obvious to hide if anyone saw me.

A grunt escaped my lips as all of my pain resurfaced as I banished them and I had to fight against the urge to dip back into them to escape it again.

I pursed my lips as I typed out a text and then forced myself to hit send before I could chicken out.

Tory:
I miss you

I waited to see if Darius would open the message right away and my heart lifted as the red ticks appeared to show he'd read it.

Three little dots began to flash on his side of the screen and knots warred in my belly as I waited for his reply.

A minute ticked by. Then another. Then the dots disappeared. I waited for the message to come through. But it didn't.

My heart sank as I watched the screen for another minute then I realised that he'd be able to see that I was online while I sat here staring and waiting for a message that obviously wasn't coming.

Why the fuck did I send that?

Embarrassment clawed at me and my cheeks flushed with colour as I locked my Atlas and resisted the urge to throw it away from me in favour of jamming it back into my pocket.

Fuck. My. Life.

Before this had happened, I'd had things to focus on; Darcy's happiness had lifted me up, banished some of my own pain. But now…

Well, now I had the shadows to steal it away.

They whispered sweet promises of oblivion in my ears and I fought not to listen. They were always harder to resist when I was feeling something unpleasant. Like attempting to be open and vulnerable with my feelings and having them completely ignored. Definitely unpleasant. And embarrassing. Humiliating. Devastating.

The shadows burrowed further into my skin and I sighed as I let them claim me for a moment. Just a moment. Long enough to forget about Dragons who had altogether too much sway over my heart and no chance of healing it anyway.

I rounded a corner and fell still as I spotted Marguerite Helebor and Mildred Canopus walking towards me from the Fire Arena. Their eyes fell on me and narrowed instantly as they stepped forward with intent in their gazes.

"Well if it isn't the number one, gutter whore," Marguerite said acidly, feeling brave with her big pal at her side.

I blinked at her through the fog of shadows as I tried to summon a fuck to give about her. But I was coming up blank and the shadows were hungry for a taste of her blood instead.

"I heard she's amazing in bed and gives blowjobs that can blow a guy's mind and that's why all the guys go crawling to her," Mildred sneered as she looked me up and down.

"That's not an insult," I said, my voice rougher than usual as the shadows coated it, hungry for a taste of her too.

"It is!" she cried, puffing her chest up. "Because that's all you are. A super hot, super fuckable, super brainless, super whore."

"Me and Darcy are top of our class," I deadpanned. "So I'll take all of your names aside from brainless. And whore suggests I get paid, which is bullshit."

"Oh is it?" Mildred demanded, stomping towards me. "Because I happen to know for a fact that that pendant hanging around your neck is a fire ruby, forged by the Dragons of old back before the Hectian Revolt. There are only seven of that age and quality in the entire kingdom. Each are owned and guarded possessively by Dragons due to their immense value. So excuse me if I brand you a super whore for taking a necklace worth one point three million auras from my snookums in payment for use of your super pussy while he waits patiently for a real woman. But don't get too comfortable warming his bed. Once he has a ride on his bride the night of our wedding, he'll forget all about you anyway."

She placed her hands on her hips and curled her lip back so that her lower jaw was even more prominent and Marguerite giggled like that was the best insult she'd ever heard.

I opened my mouth to bite back, but I was too stunned by her announcement that this necklace I'd been wearing for weeks could be worth over a million auras so I just gaped at her.

The two of them sauntered away like they'd won a point against me and my fingers closed around the heart shaped ruby as the inner heat of it warmed my palm and helped me to push the shadows off again. I seriously needed to question Darius on the value of this thing though. If it really was worth that much, I couldn't keep it.

I wandered into the Fire Arena as I thought on it, but stumbled to a halt as I came face to face with an angry Vampire.

Caleb lunged at me with his teeth bared and eyes wild and I threw an air shield up between us at the last moment to hold him off.

"What the hell, asshole?" I demanded as he crashed into my shield and fell back on his ass, growling with frustration.

"Sorry," he bit out, huffing a breath as he shoved his hand through his blonde curls and got to his feet. "I just…I've had a bit of bad news is all. And I'm thirsty. Don't worry about it, I'll go hunt down someone else."

He made a move to pass me but I dropped my shield and caught his arm to stop him. "What's wrong?"

He looked at me for a long moment then sighed as he decided to give in. "It's nothing really. My uncle Marlowe has gone mouthing off to the press about family shit again and it makes us look bad. He went through some…

stuff a few years back and he's a little unhinged. But Mom refuses to confine him after what he went through and then she tosses the clean up duty to me when he ends up talking shit all over the papers about political matters and aligning his views to mine and Mom's. And this time he's making me look bad which is really fucking annoying."

"Nightmare," I agreed sarcastically and he rolled his eyes at me.

"It's just a pain in the ass and the last thing I need at the moment. Plus I had to come here to complete some advanced fire magic work and I ended up tapped out which *should* have been fine because Seth promised to let me hunt him tonight. Except now he's gone and initiated some girl into his pack today instead which means he's off running with them all fucking night and probably screwing them all too and I'm *thirsty.*"

"Wow. I've never seen you throw a tantrum before," I teased as he shoved his hands through his hair and started pacing.

"I know. Mars is in my chart tonight too and it's the planet of war which basically equals insatiable blood lust for Vampires and now I can't even get my drink and I'm going out of my head and-"

"So hunt me," I suggested, cutting him off. "We used to do it all the time and you just tried to bite my head off anyway so you clearly want to. Plus, aren't I supposed to be your Source still? Seems like you've only got a taste for Wolf these days."

He shot me a look that was all predator and my heart leapt. "I assumed you didn't want to do it again after I asked you at the cheer off and nothing came of it," he said slowly. "Besides...I can't really play the game with you now. Seth's got me too used to hunting him down in his Order form and then we fight it out before I get to bite him and I've gotten used to being rough. So..."

"So what? You think you could catch me in my Order form?" I taunted. *"Please.* You'll be running around in circles trying to catch me while I laugh my ass off at you. Besides, I'm tough enough to fight you off now. Especially if you're all tapped out of magic."

Caleb's eyes flashed with excitement at that idea and the shadows fell back even further as adrenaline slid through my veins. This was exactly the kind of distraction I needed. Pure, honest, *fun.*

"I dunno," Caleb hedged, but he licked his lips as his gaze dropped to my throat again. "Mars is making me kinda edgy-"

"Oh. So you're a pussy?" I taunted.

"No."

"Chicken shit?"

"Fuck it. Fine. You're too fucking delicious to refuse again. But you'd better be ready for this, sweetheart."

"There's a problem though," I said, holding up a hand as he bared his fangs at me. "What do I get if I win? Orgasms are off the menu, so how about a lesson instead?"

"A lesson?"

"Yeah. I wanna learn that fire and earth combo whip thing you used to knock Darius off his ass in Elemental Combat the other night." I grinned at him and he groaned.

"You realise that would mean training up the enemy? Betraying my fellow Heirs and-"

"Do you wanna bite me or not, Caleb?" I demanded.

"Fuck it. Alright. But don't say I didn't warn you."

"Catch me if you can." I flicked my fingers at him and threw him away from me with a gust of wind so powerful that it sent him flying all the way to the other side of the Fire Arena as my wings burst from my back.

Caleb shot towards me again as I leapt into the air, his fingertips brushing my sneakers as I took off and he leapt for me.

Adrenaline burst through my veins and an excited laugh tumbled from my lips as I shot away, looking down as Caleb kept pace beneath me.

He was faster than me and my heart thundered as I flapped my wings harder, swooping around as many obstacles as I could so that he was forced to dodge them too.

I swept out of Fire Territory and zoomed across campus at high speed, laughter spilling from my lips as I headed for The Howling Meadow.

My feet touched down on the top of the highest boulder where the Heirs always hung out and a moment later, Caleb scaled them and tackled me.

His arms locked around me with crushing strength as his fangs lunged straight for my throat. I managed to throw an air shield up around my neck to block him as we rolled across the grass and I extinguished the flames on my wings to stop a fire from breaking out.

Caleb fought hard, snatching my wrist into his grasp and yanking it towards his teeth. Fire sprang to life along my skin, burning him so he was forced to release me.

He snarled ferociously as he lunged at me again, his weight falling on me so hard that my back was slammed into the ground painfully.

I swung a fist at his face, coating it in ice and catching him in the jaw as he scrambled to get a hold of any piece of me that he could bite.

I fought like a wild dog as he attacked like a beast and real fear coiled with excitement in me at the savage look in his eyes. I didn't know if he'd just gotten used to playing this way with Seth or if Mars really was sending his bloodlust crazy, but I was suddenly struck with the certainty that I didn't want him to get his teeth into me.

We rolled across the ground and I managed to end up on top as I coated his arms in vines and pinned him beneath me.

"Yield," I demanded but he only snarled at me, using his Vampire strength to rip his way out of the vines, lunging for my neck again.

I coated my fist in ice again and punched him in the jaw, knocking his aim off as his fang chipped a chunk of ice from my knuckle and a bead of my blood was spilled.

Caleb snarled as the taste of my power touched his tongue and he lunged at me with the strength of a charging bull, slamming me down beneath him once more.

He snatched my hand into his grip and his fangs crashed against the ice as he tried to break through it with pure force.

I gasped as I struggled beneath him and the hard plain of his body pinned me down, but without his magic he was at a serious disadvantage and there was no fucking way I wanted him biting me while he was frantic like this.

With a grunt of effort, I managed to slam my palm into his chest, loaded with air magic that threw him away from me. I scrambled upright as he shot back towards me, opening a chasm at his feet to trap him and keep him away.

The wild look in his eyes made my pulse race and for a moment it didn't even seem like I was looking at the Caleb I knew.

He scrambled over the edge of the pit I'd conjured with a hungry snarl and I leapt into the air taking off as fast as I could, aiming for the sky as I looked down at his snarling face below me.

I flew hard and fast, heading for The Wailing Wood as the sound of a Wolf pack howling in the trees caught my ear.

I lost sight of Caleb beneath me amongst the leafy branches and my heart began to slow as I swept across the trees.

The roof of King's Hollow appeared ahead of me and aimed for it to hide and wait out the game while he was left to hunt the woods for me.

Remind me not to taunt a Vampire when Mars is in their chart ever again.

My heart fluttered nervously as I landed softly on the roof of the massive treehouse and I looked down over the huge drop below as I checked to make sure Caleb was nowhere in sight before sinking down to sit and wait for my win.

The soft murmuring of voices reached me from the treehouse beneath my feet and I stilled as I realised Darius and Max were in there talking.

It was fine though, because I couldn't make out what they were saying so it wasn't like I was spying or anything.

Darius spoke again and I could have sworn I heard my sister's name.

Dammit.

I quickly cast an amplification spell on the area around me and their voices suddenly became loud and clear.

"-he was fucking thinking, but he's going to have to tell me soon. The bond feels like it's going to tear me in two if I don't see him and he finally accepted my request for visitation. I swear, I could fucking murder him for that alone. Fuck knows how I'm supposed to survive twenty five years of him stuck that far away from me," Darius growled. If I were to take an educated guess, I'd say he might just be drinking.

"If your dad is still being an asshole about it, why don't I see if mine can pull a few strings?" Max suggested but before Darius could reply, a shiver raced down my spine and I spun around just as Caleb leapt up onto the roof.

"Wait!" I gasped, lurching upright as he shot towards me and I tried to summon magic to hold him off.

His eyes were manic and bloodshot, sparking with the desperate need of his hunger and I didn't even recognise the creature before me. They said Vampires didn't shift like other Orders, but in that moment I was sure he had. Caleb had checked the fuck out and there was nothing but a bloodthirsty demon in his place.

My fingertips had barely even tingled before he slammed into me and I screamed as his fangs tore into my neck, pain blossoming through me more keenly than I'd ever felt as he pinned me in his arms.

I stumbled back, my foot slipping on the edge of the wooden roof as my limbs lost energy and suddenly we were falling. My gut lurched and I threw my hands out in some desperate bid to save us with my air magic, but it was no use. My power was utterly immobilised by his venom and I screamed as we fell through the branches of the canopy which slapped and scratched at my skin.

Caleb's grip on me loosened seconds before we hit the ground and he tore his fangs from my neck as he threw his hands out to save us.

We hit the ground hard and the most horrifying crack sounded as an explosion of agony tore through my body.

I tried to scream again, but suddenly I couldn't draw in any air and I was coughing and spluttering against something warm and wet which filled my airway and threatened to drown me.

"Help!" Caleb roared, his navy eyes meeting mine with a terrified kind of panic as he clapped a hand over my neck and pressed down so hard I feared he was going to choke me.

I tried to move beneath him but none of my limbs would respond, nothing would do as I commanded and I was still choking on whatever the fuck was blocking my airways.

"I'm sorry, Tory," Caleb gasped, as he looked down into my eyes. "I'm so, fucking sorry. Shit, *shit!* I'm sorry, I didn't mean to-"

An almighty roar cut the air in two a fraction of a second before Caleb was torn off of me with the force of a tsunami and thrown away across the clearing.

Darius's face appeared above me a moment later, his rough palm landing on my throat and he squeezed tightly as he pressed healing magic beneath my flesh.

The pain in my neck began to fade and I started coughing, blood coating my tongue as I managed to heave it up out of my lungs.

"I've got you, Roxy," Darius growled, his hands moving again as he used his water magic to pull the rest of my blood up out of my lungs so that I could breathe again and I sucked a breath down immediately as my vision focused once more.

I gasped as pain continued to blossom through the rest of my body and panic consumed me as I realised I still couldn't move at all.

"Where does it hurt?" Darius asked in a deadly voice as a tear slid from my eye.

"Everywhere," I hissed, biting down on another scream as Caleb started calling out more apologies.

"I managed to soften the ground a bit before we hit it with the magic I'd taken from her, but it wasn't much," he called. "I'm so sorry, I didn't mean to. I swear I didn't mean to."

He was cut off by the arrival of a huge white Wolf. I hissed in disgust as Seth shifted right beside me and flashed me a view of the underside of his dick.

"What the hell happened?" Seth gasped, dropping down next to me as Darius slid his hands over my hips and stomach, growling beneath his breath.

"Caleb knocked her off the roof and bit her real bad," Max muttered as he dropped down too.

"He's broken her fucking spine," Darius growled and the terror in his eyes would have frozen me in place even if I could move. "I've never fixed something this complicated before."

"You can do it," Max said confidently, placing a hand on Darius's shoulder to lend him magic if he needed it.

Seth released a worried whimper and placed his hand on his other shoulder to offer the same and Darius's brow furrowed in concentration as I felt his magic pouring beneath my skin.

The pain began to ebb away and I drew in a shaky breath as the feeling slowly returned to my limbs. First my fingers and toes tingled before the sensation slid further up and up until everything felt normal again.

Darius looked down at me with a sea of agony in his eyes and I reached for him, my fingers brushing across his solid jawline in the gentlest touch. Just long enough for him to be sure that I was alright before he lurched away from me with a roar of utter fury.

I gasped as he leapt at Caleb, throwing him down into the dirt before slamming his fist straight into his face.

"You will *never* hunt her again!" he roared as he battered his fists down over and over. "You will never put your fucking mouth on her, never sink your fucking fangs into her *ever again!"*

Max and Seth leapt on him with panicked curses, somehow managing to rip him off of Caleb who lay bleeding in the dirt beneath him.

"I'm sorry, man, I'm sorry, Tory," he gasped as he looked between me and the Dragon who looked dead set on killing him.

"Get the fuck out of here, Cal," Max snapped just as Darius tore his arm free and elbowed him straight in the face.

Caleb hesitated for half a second, but I was willing to guess he could see his own death shining in Darius's eyes. He threw one more, desperate apology my way before turning and shooting off through the trees.

Darius dislodged Seth with another roar and looked like he was about to take off after him just as Max leapt into his path.

"Aren't you forgetting someone?" Max demanded, pointing over at me as I managed to get to my feet.

I still felt shaky, a bit of an ache radiating through my hips, but it was endlessly better than it had been.

Darius whirled around, his face painted with emotion as he looked at me like I was the most precious thing in the world to him.

He moved towards me suddenly, backing me up against the huge tree which housed King's Hollow as he stood before me, looking like the whole world was caving in on him as he refrained from touching me.

"I'll go after Cal," Seth murmured, giving me a final glance to check I was okay before shifting back into his Wolf form and speeding away through the trees.

Darius didn't even spare him a glance, his gaze fixed on me as his dark eyes danced with emotion and terror.

He reached up tentatively, his hands painted red with my blood as he brushed the tips of his fingers along the lines of my face with the gentlest of touches, like he feared he'd break me.

I watched him in silence and my skin tingled from the feather-light caress of his fingertips tracing my jaw, my cheekbones, nose, brows, neck and lips like he just had to be sure it was all there, safe and accounted for.

He leaned forward slowly until his forehead was pressed to mine and I could feel a slight tremor in his body which betrayed just how much he cared, how frightened he'd been, how concerned.

"I'd take death over life without you," he breathed, his voice rough and broken by fear.

I reached up to lay my palm on his jaw too, my other hand landing on his arm. "Darius," I murmured, unsure what I was even going to say just as thunder crashed in the sky above.

"I miss you too," he interrupted. "More than any words could ever convey."

Thunder crashed again and he stepped back so suddenly that I almost fell.

Max moved to take his place, reaching for me calmly as Darius backed up. "We need to take you to the infirmary to get those bones checked out, little Vega," he said softly. "I can carry you if you can't walk."

"I can walk," I protested, glancing at Darius again as he watched me with nothing but horror in his eyes, like he was somehow responsible for what had just happened.

"Come on, let me. Or Darius is only gonna chew me out for it."

I sighed in acceptance as Max lifted me into his arms and the three of us headed to the infirmary in the centre of campus.

Darius followed on silently, not saying a word even when I goaded him about giving me a necklace worth a small fortune. But when I'd made a move to take it off and return it to him, he caught my wrists and shook his head firmly. "It's yours."

And something about the tone of his voice and the way he'd looked at me made me relent even when he went right back to silence.

CALEB

CHAPTER THIRTY SEVEN

I shot into my room in Terra House in a blur of speed and threw the door closed behind me as my heart thundered with this mournful kind of panic.

My hands were trembling and my breaths coming too fast as I reminded myself over and over again that she was okay, Darius had saved her, she was going to be fine.

But, *fuck*. I'd just thrown a Solarian princess off of a roof and damn near ripped her throat out with my teeth for good measure.

I glanced down at my trembling hands, spotting the wet gleam of Tory's blood coating my fingers. I'd been trying to save her. I'd wanted to help. But I was tapped out and run dry and *weak*. I had to admit that much to myself. I'd been jittery all day, Mom had messaged me several times to remind me about Mars being in my chart, but I'd chosen to ignore her. I'd chosen to fuck up completely and risk someone's life.

My fangs snapped out as I looked down at my bloody hands and a snarl ripped from my throat as I fought against my desire to lick them clean. This hunger in me, it was a cruel and heartless monster. It relished pain and suffering and bathed in blood. It didn't feel remorse or regret, it never hesitated in taking what it wanted. But I'd lived with it for years, bending it to my will, forcing it to only ever be wielded as a weapon when I desired it. And I'd clearly fooled myself into believing that that meant I had utter control over it. That I ruled it and it didn't rule me.

What a pretty lie that had been.

Because even now, after what I'd done, I could hardly stop myself from licking every drop of Tory's blood from my fingers.

With a determined snarl, I shoved open the door to my en-suite, reaching out to set the water running in my walk in shower before ripping my shirt off and kicking my shoes aside.

I took a step towards the shower, but fell still as that ache in my fangs made me look down at my bloody hands again.

I closed my eyes and inhaled deeply as I tried to force the desire away from me, but the scent of blood tinged the air and made my mouth water with need. My own blood coated my face from Darius's attack on me, but I couldn't bring myself to heal the wounds. I deserved them. Each and every one and more.

Just wash it away.

With a grunt of determination, I opened my eyes and stepped into the shower, not even caring that I still had my sweatpants on. All I needed to do was rinse it off. Once it was gone, this would all be over.

Steam coiled around me as the water continued to pour down the drain and with a groan of hunger, I reached out to push my hands beneath the hot flow.

The second the water touched my skin, the blood began to run away and I yanked them back with a ferocious snarl as I stumbled out of the shower and my back hit the tiled wall.

I slid down it as I pushed my fingers into my mouth, groaning loudly as the taste of Tory's power touched my tongue.

I gave in to the beast in me as I sucked and licked my hands and fingers, running my tongue down my wrists and catch every last drop as a trickle of her power washed into my veins.

My chest was heaving, my muscles trembling and my eyes closed as I lost myself to my demon and feasted on what it required.

"Cal?" Seth's voice called out to me as I gave myself to the dark and I peeled my eyes open as he pushed the bathroom door wide. He'd raided my drawers on the way in and had stolen a pair of my sweatpants to cover himself.

"You should go," I snarled, my fangs cutting into my tongue as I forced myself to remain where I was on the floor instead of lunging at him. "It's not safe to be around me right now."

"Bullshit, you'd never hurt me." Seth moved closer and the ache in my chest tightened.

The few scraps of magic I'd drawn from Tory's blood was nothing and this all consuming hunger in me demanded more. My gaze skimmed over his bare chest, searching out every point where his pulse flickered against his skin, before settling on his neck.

"I mean it, Seth," I breathed, pushing my back against the cold tiles as I fought against the urge to bite him with everything I had. "I'm not myself tonight, I'm tapped out, I'm worked up, Mars is banging a fucking war drum in my head which demands sacrifice and I *can't* hurt you too. Please just go."

"I'm not going anywhere," he replied roughly, stepping closer so that he towered over me. "So you made a mistake? Okay. How many of those have I made over the years? I couldn't even begin to count the amount of times that I've fucked up and you've been there for me."

"This isn't the same. If you stay here, I'm going to lose control. I'm going to bite you, and then-"

"Then you'll feel a hell of a lot better. You know you can't function when you're hangry." He smirked at me and a hollow laugh fell from my lips.

"This isn't like craving a sandwich."

"It had better fucking not be," he said. "I'm no sandwich. I'm like a goddamn triple chocolate sundae with sprinkles and syrup and the juiciest damn cherry on top. Don't compare me to a basic lunch, Cal, you'll hurt my damn feelings."

He leaned down and caught my arm, heaving me up to my feet and I let him because I didn't really know what else I was going to do, but the jittery panicked feeling in my bones hadn't lessened. I still didn't want to hurt him. I still wasn't sure I was in control.

Seth reached out and shut off the shower before pushing me back out of the door into my bedroom.

"Look how fucking civilised this is," he teased, moving around me to leap onto my bed. He landed on his back and bounced amongst the cushions as he grinned up at me. "You can have me any way you want me. Usually you've gotta fight tooth and claw to get a taste of this and I'm offering myself up on a silver platter here."

"Seth..." I began, but I wasn't even sure what I was going to say. My fangs were aching and that emptiness in my chest where my magic should reside wasn't going to feel any better until I filled it up.

"Come on, man. You can pin me down or bend me over or whatever the fuck you want. I'll be your sub for the night. You can even tie me upside down and drain my blood into a wine glass if you like?"

I cringed at that idea and he snorted a laugh.

"Too much?"

"Yeah," I agreed.

He slung his hands behind his head and watched me as he waited me out, but I didn't move. I couldn't. If I hurt someone else tonight, I felt sure I was going to snap. But I couldn't deny the desperate need in me for blood either. If I didn't give in, I'd end up heading out of this room sooner or later and hunting down the closest Fae and taking what I needed by force. So surely this was better than that?

Seth sighed dramatically and got to his feet before me, moving to stand so close that our chests were almost touching and the earthy scent of him enveloped me.

"Come on, Cal. I want you to," he demanded, meeting my eye with honesty shining in his gaze and something else which I wasn't sure I could put a name to.

My flesh was burning up with the need to take what he was offering. His body was so close to mine that I could feel the heat of him as if he were actually touching me.

I reached out slowly and gathered a handful of his long hair into my fist, gently winding it around my hand until I could use it to tug his head aside.

Seth inhaled deeply as he bared his throat to me and for a moment I was struck with the realisation of just how much he must have trusted me to show such vulnerability to me like that. Especially for a Wolf. They only ever bared their throat as a sign of submission and though I knew he wasn't submitting to me in any way other than this, the knowledge that I had such a powerful Alpha at my mercy willingly made my heart race.

I touched my lips to his neck, my fangs brushing against his skin and a shiver danced through his flesh as I prepared to take what I needed from him.

But just as I was about to bite down, the memory of Tory laying beneath me, her throat ripped open as she choked on her own blood overwhelmed me.

I drew back with a grunt of pain, refusing to risk hurting him like that as I released my hold on his hair and the ache in my chest grew tenfold.

I fell to my knees before him, fighting with all I had to just tame the bloodlust and refuse its call. My breaths came in harsh pants and I shook my head, refusing my nature as the beast in me howled for his blood.

"Bite me, Cal," Seth urged in a dark voice, snatching a fistful of my hair and pressing his wrist to my mouth.

I slapped his hand away with a snarl as I fought it, but the shaking in my limbs wouldn't quit and we both knew I was going to snap soon one way or another.

"Would you sit back and watch me if I chained myself indoors every night to stop myself from running beneath the moon?" Seth demanded, using his grip in my hair to force me to look up at him.

"Running beneath the moon doesn't hurt anyone," I rasped.

"Maybe not most of the time. But it can. When I give myself to the Wolf, my instincts take over, I'm an apex predator pure and simple. And if I cross paths with someone who runs from me, you can bet your ass I'll be chasing them down and going for the kill. You're the most powerful Vampire of our generation, Cal, and maybe sometimes that means you'll hurt people, but it doesn't mean you're a bad person. It just shows how fucking unstoppable you are. How strong and fierce and powerful. Now bite me before I cut a vein open myself and pour it in a glass for you."

The last of my self control snapped at his command and I lunged at him, my teeth sinking into the flesh right above his hipbone as he grunted in surprise.

His blood washed over my tongue and I groaned in pure, undeniable pleasure as the taste of it swept me up and pulled me out of my own pain.

My hands grabbed his hips as I held him in place but I didn't need to, he wasn't making any effort to escape me. Seth's grip on my hair tightened as he pulled me closer, his other hand grasping the back of my neck as his fingers slid across my skin and raised goosebumps on my flesh.

I growled desperately and a groan of pleasure escaped him too as I drank and drank, flooding my body with his power and finally finding myself in the dark.

I took more than I should have and he made no move to stop me as I feasted.

I managed to gather the resolve I needed to pull back, panting as I ran my thumb over the wound above his hip to heal it, my hand skimming over the tightness of his abs for a moment before I was pulling away.

With a burst of my Vampire speed, I got to my feet and shot away from him, coming to a halt with my back resting against the slatted doors of my closet.

Seth groaned as he looked across the room at me, swiping a hand over his face before turning away and taking a deep breath. I watched him as he paced back and forth for a few minutes, wondering what he was thinking as he carved a path into my carpet.

"You might just be the best person I know, Cal," he said, turning his earthy brown gaze on me as he moved towards me.

"Because attacking girls and throwing them off of rooftops is such a glowing accolade?" I deadpanned, my dark thoughts sweeping me up and making me relive everything I'd done to Tory tonight with a terrifying clarity.

"No. Because you're so selfless. How many guys do you know who would help their friend get with the girl they liked?"

"Darius and Tory are meant to be together," I muttered. "In fact, if I hadn't been getting in their way all this time then maybe none of this would have-"

Seth's hand landed over my mouth to silence me as he closed the distance between us again. "*Don't* do that," he snarled.

I frowned at him as he moved his hand from my mouth and shifted it to the bruise along my jaw where Darius had punched me. A trickle of healing magic slid beneath my skin and I sighed as he slowly moved on to heal my cheek, my black eye, my busted lip, then dropped his hands to heal the black and red bruises which were blossoming across my ribs.

"I'm such a fuck up," I said with a heavy sigh.

"You're not a fuck up," Seth growled. "You're the most thoughtful, generous, amazing fucker I know."

I snorted dismissively. "Maybe you look at me through rose tinted glasses."

"I don't," he snapped. "When I look at you, I promise you I see it all. The good and the bad, the light and the dark. And you're still the best person I know."

My heart twisted at his words and I reached out to pull him into a hug. "You're the best person I know, too," I murmured.

Seth fell still, his hands still on my chest as an achingly long moment passed between us.

He turned his head against my neck. His lips brushed my skin and I froze.

My heart pounded as he moved his mouth up my neck slowly, his hands gentle against my chest as my skin tingled where he touched me.

His lips brushed against the soft skin beneath my ear and I swallowed thickly as he pressed the lightest kiss against the corner of my jaw.

My free hand moved to clasp his waist as my fingertips brushed against his skin and he groaned beneath his breath as his mouth moved along my jaw, scratching at my stubble in a way that made my flesh prickle.

My heart was hammering wildly and the breath I inhaled caught in my throat as his mouth brushed the corner of mine and a shiver danced through every inch of my body.

He moved again and I found myself looking into his eyes, less than nothing between our lips as he hesitated.

"Seth…" I breathed, not really knowing how I was going to finish that sentence.

His eyes widened then darkened and for a moment I was sure I found pain in them before he locked it away again.

"Sorry," he murmured. "I shouldn't have…sorry."

He pulled back an inch and my grip on him tightened for half a second before I let him go.

He frowned at me like he wasn't sure what that meant and I shifted uncomfortably as I looked at him.

"Maybe I should just go," he said slowly, his voice rough as he looked at me with regret in his eyes.

"Maybe," I repeated as he backed up another step and he bit his bottom lip.

"Are you…okay now?" he asked hesitantly.

"I…yeah, I'm okay," I agreed.

He gave me a tight smile and turned away, dropping his sweatpants and shifting in the same movement.

He moved to the door, using his paw to open it and tossing one last glance back at me before he tore out of my room.

I watched him go with my heart in my throat and moved to close the door behind him.

My skin still tingled where he'd touched me and I was struck with the desire to call him back. But I didn't.

A frown tugged at my brow and my mind turned over and over as I tried to make sense of the way my heart was pounding out of rhythm.

I fell back onto my bed with a shaky breath and let my eyes fall closed. *What the hell just happened?*

A Wolf howled mournfully beyond my window outside and a tingle ran down my spine which had nothing to do with what I'd done today and everything to do with my best friend's visit.

DARIUS

CHAPTER THIRTY EIGHT

Seth:

Dream Team meeting in King's Hollow. Now. No excuses bitches.

I read over the message in our group chat as I finished up an Arcane Arts paper in my room and released a huff of frustration before replying.

Darius:

I can't be held responsible for what I'll do to Caleb if I have to spend time in his company at the moment.

Caleb:

I'm so fucking sorry, dude. But I get it, I'll just stay away.

Seth:

No! I've got a team bonding exercise in mind which we ALL need to be a part of. It's been twenty four hours. Caleb said sorry, Tory is fine now. I just saw her splashing around at the lake with her Ass buddies...

He added a short video to the group which showed Roxy in a tiny black bikini perched on Milton Hubert's fucking shoulders as she wrestled with Geraldine Grus who was on Justin Masters' shoulders too as they fought to get each other to fall in the lake. They were screaming and laughing as they played, but my gaze caught on Darcy who just sat on the beach watching them with glazed eyes. The clip ended just as Geraldine spotted Seth and started yelling at him for being a lecherous lupine and his laughter filled the speakers as he ran away.

He must have filmed that a few hours ago because a storm had rolled in since then and the day had turned decidedly grey and miserable beyond my windows.

Max:
Why the fuck is Grus always hanging around with that pompous Justin prick?

Seth:
I heard their parents are in talks about arranging their marriage…assuming he can't bag himself a Vega…

A deep growl escaped me at that suggestion and I pushed away from my desk as Max started sending all kinds of colourful insults about Justin over the chat.

Seth:
Well lucky for you guys, my plan will make both Roxy Vega and Geraldine Grus so fucking happy that they'll definitely wanna bang you.

Caleb:
Nobody says bang anymore, asshole.

Seth:
I'm bringing it back. So fuck you. Also, just get your asses to the Hollow now or I'm going to have to come beat your pretty faces in. Don't make me invoke the power code…

I groaned as he wielded that stupid fucking power code shit. We'd come up with it when we were seven and super excited about the idea of us ruling the world together one day. Basically, if one of us invoked the power code, we all had to show up. No excuses. I'd tried to get him to change the fucking name of it at least eight hundred times over the years, but he wouldn't. Fucking power code.

I yanked my shirt off and dropped my pants before throwing my floor length window wide and taking a running jump out of it.

I shifted and sped across campus to the Hollow with the rain pinging off of my scales. It was a miserable day which suited my mood just fine.

I arrived in no time, my claws digging into the wooden rooftop before I shifted back into my Fae form. I glanced over the edge of the roof at the drop to the forest floor and my gut knotted with anger as a blur of motion caught my eye.

I opened the hatch and dropped inside, grabbing a pair of jeans and boxers from the trunk at the side of the room and pulling them on just as Caleb shot into the room.

We looked at each other for a long moment and a growl echoed in the back of my throat as Max and Seth walked in.

"Enough!" Max snapped. "Tory wanted to play that damn hunting game and Cal warned her it was a terrible idea. They learned their lessons yesterday and now we just need to move on."

I growled again and Caleb looked down at his boots.

"What we need," Seth said with a cocky little grin. "Is to go on an adventure together."

"What adventure?" I grunted.

"One that I've been working on, oh so fucking hard. It's gonna make Tory *real* happy. And probably Grus too because she's all for Mission: Defy the Stars," he added, tossing a wink at Max.

"Really?" Max asked, running a hand over his mohawk as he tried not to grin.

"Yeah. Does the name Zane Baxter mean anything to you?" Seth looked my way excitedly and I frowned.

"Roxy's ex. The one who left her to drown in that car wreck," I muttered. If that asshole had lived in Solaria, I'd have ruined his life a long time ago.

"Yeah…you wanna go pay him a visit?" Seth waggled his eyebrows enticingly and my spine straightened as I looked at him with more interest.

"How the hell did you find him?" I asked.

"I've been taking little visits to the mortal realm for the last month, Coercing humans left right and centre to hand up the info on him. The fucker didn't have anything official linking him to his current residence because he's started himself up a nice little criminal empire, but I found him."

"Why?" I asked. I mean, I was all for going and messing with the fucker but I didn't get it.

"Because you wouldn't just do a strip tease or sing her a song like a normal lovestruck idiot so I had to think outside the box. And deep down, I think that a girl who the stars chose to be your perfect match must really want a badass kind of gesture over chocolate hearts and flowers. So I say we go kick the little gangster's ass for what he did to her and you can cut off his balls and put them in a box for her…or just take a photo, whatever you think she'd like best."

"Probably the balls," I said with a dark chuckle as I grinned at him.

"So it's a yes?" Seth asked enthusiastically.

"Fuck yes."

I opened up the chest and grabbed a pair of boots, a black T-shirt and a leather jacket from it and Seth howled as the four of us headed out. Max took a bag of stardust from the emergency stash we kept in the desk as we went and I moved to walk with him as Caleb followed beside Seth. We'd get over this, but at the moment I couldn't look at him without wanting to beat his face in, so I was glad I had a different asshole to focus on instead.

We strode across campus and slipped through the gap in the shield that Lance had left, my skin prickling as I recognised his magical signature and the

Guardian brand on my arm burning with a desperate kind of ache.

I was hardly sleeping, my studies were suffering and in all honesty I just felt like I was existing in this bubble of hopeless nothingness which I couldn't see an end to. If Xavier and my mom didn't need me, I wasn't really sure why I'd even get out of bed in the mornings. Sometimes I got so angry at Lance that I punched myself just so he'd feel it wherever the fuck he was. Why couldn't he have just stuck to the plan? What did he really think he was achieving by fucking up his entire life?

Self sacrificing fuckwit.

Seth took the pouch of stardust from Max with the smuggest damn look on his face that I'd ever seen and a moment later we were swept away through the stars.

My stomach swooped as the twinkling little bastards surrounded us and we tumbled through them for longer than usual as we crossed between the realms before they finally spat us out in a back alley in some city suburb in the mortal realm.

I drew in a shaky breath as I was suddenly freed from the shackles of my bond to Orion. The connection was still there, but it was dulled by the realms dividing us to the point where I could hardly even feel it anymore. And after weeks of aching for him to be close to me and sleepless nights dreaming of holding him in my arms, it was more than a fucking relief. He'd probably be panicking right about now, thinking I was dead as his connection to me was muted and a twisted sense of satisfaction filled me at that idea. I hoped he was suffering for putting me through this and then I felt like a total douchebag for thinking that. No doubt what he was going through was a hundred times worse.

"Fuck, I should have thought of this before," I groaned, rubbing a hand over the Libra mark beneath my leather jacket.

The only relief from the bond I'd managed to find until now was dipping into the depths of the shadows and I didn't like to do it too often. They fed too greedily on negativity and I knew they'd consume me if I started to use them as a crutch. I should have realised sooner that the mortal realm was the perfect place to escape to. Though I wouldn't have chosen this particularly shitty neighbourhood. There was trash all around us in the alleyway and the scent of stale piss hung in the air.

"That's the foster home the Vegas were living in when Tory met him," Seth said as we stepped out of the alley and he pointed across the street to the run down house.

I frowned as I spotted a kid sitting on the porch, smoking a blunt and scowling at us.

"Are you smoking again Brent?" a woman shrieked from inside. "I'll whoop your hide if I catch you!"

The kid quickly stubbed out his smoke and pushed the door open where the sound of more screaming reached us as she laid into him.

"Have new people moved in there now?" Caleb asked uncomfortably and Seth shrugged.

"Erm, no. Same registered owners. They have five foster kids at a time and err, I guess they go for the loud kind of discipline," Seth said as we all surveyed the house.

It was…a fucking dive. The white paint was peeling and one of the windows was half boarded over. There was trash everywhere and one of the old wooden chairs on the porch had collapsed. It looked like my idea of hell. Though I supposed I'd grown up in what could arguably be called a palace and I hadn't been happy for much of it, so maybe I didn't know shit.

"So, I had a fucking job of it finding the asshole, but I basically tracked down the high school the girls went to then used my charms to ask around about him and after the third guy practically pissed himself at the mention of his name, I Coerced the answer out of him and found out Zane Baxter is a gangster. Sounds like he's gotten an even worse reputation now than he had when Tory was screwing hi…dating him." Seth cleared his throat and I folded my arms as I waited for him to get to the point. "*Anyway* he doesn't live in the house she used to walk past on her way to school anymore but after a bit of digging I found him."

"That's how she met him?" I asked in a low voice. "He saw her walking past his door and just pounced on her?"

"I dunno man, I did some asking around and that's the story I got from one girl, but there's no way in hell Tory would confirm it even if I'd asked. If you really wanna know then just ask her about it when we get back." He shrugged at me and I rolled my eyes.

"Like she'd tell me."

"Maybe she would," Max said. "You could just ask and see."

"I can't even be alone with her, so how would that work?" I grumbled.

"Try texting, idiot," he shot back and I frowned at him as the others sniggered like that was so fucking obvious. And maybe it was.

"Or calling," Caleb added. "You're not together if you're just talking on the phone."

"Video chat," Seth added with a dirty grin. "You could totally have video sex."

"Shut up," I growled, but I couldn't entirely hide the grin on my face either. Maybe I *was* fucking dumb. It just seemed like such a step back to start messaging or calling her that it hadn't really occurred to me, but maybe it should have.

"Come on," Seth said, leading the way down the street as the woman inside the foster home finally stopped yelling. "And don't forget we can't use magic here, at least not in an obvious way."

"We know," Caleb replied, rolling his eyes.

We walked eight blocks through the rough area, drawing attention in our expensive clothes, though we must have been intimidating enough to stop anyone from trying to rob us.

"That's the high school they went to when they lived here," Seth said, pointing out the sprawling collection of huge grey buildings beyond the chainlink fence. It looked fucking depressing.

"They used to walk here alone?" Max asked in a low voice. "With no magic?"

I pursed my lips as I looked around at the streets. This neighbourhood wasn't just rough, it was fucking gangland. It was the kind of place where bad shit happened to nice girls and no one gave a fuck about it. The city of Alestria was like this in Solaria and the place was so lawless that Father and the other Councillors basically just left it to gang rule. Though I guessed with his Storm Dragon in his pocket he believed he had control over it anyway. How the hell had the Solarian princesses ended up here?

"Errr, yeah, I guess. Maybe add it to your list of Tory questions," Seth said with a shrug as we passed the school and headed on.

The further we walked, the more I began to notice marks spray-painted on the walls and doors of the houses. A black circle with a red skull in the centre. Ominous.

"Why didn't we just stardust closer to our destination?" Max muttered.

"Because I didn't wanna come here until now so I didn't know it to stardust in. This guy is a total fucker. He's like insanely dangerous...for a human. I didn't want him to see me and get wind of us coming," Seth said excitedly and I exchanged a smirk with Cal before remembering that he was on my shit list.

Sure enough, the further we went, the more eyes I felt on us, though so far no one dared approach. Max subtly constructed an air shield around us in case of gunshots but when it came down to it, we were going to do this like mortals. Mostly.

We finally turned a corner and Seth stopped beside a fence which ringed a large house with a load of pretty savage looking bikes parked outside it.

Gang members sprawled across the yard, their eyes falling on us as we looked their way. There were gang tattoos on each of them, the skull sitting in the circle, and more than a few of them loosened guns from holsters.

"Are you lost, boys?" a big fucker called out as he looked at us from the steps leading up to the wide porch.

"I'm looking for Tory Gomez's ex," I said in a low voice, using the name she'd gone by in the mortal world as I looked him dead in the eye.

His eyebrows rose in surprise at that name and another dude rose from a lawn chair as he looked at me. He was broad, covered in tattoos and had a pretty face which didn't really tally with his whole gangster vibe.

"Which one?" he asked with a smirk. "I used to date her. That girl was a fucking wild one."

"Not him," Seth muttered and my spine prickled at the fact that there was more than one of her fucking exes here. How many did she even have?? And was I a total fucking hypocrite because that pissed me off?

Probably.

"We're looking for Zane Baxter," Caleb added.

"Are you here to collect the bounty then? Because I don't see her," the big guy said, pushing off of the steps and fingering a hunting knife which hung from his hip.

"Bounty?" Max asked.

"Well…I guess that's not the right word. The boss only wants to talk to her, not hurt her," he chuckled and the rest of the goons joined in. "That girl and her sister just fell off the radar like ghosts when they left their last foster home."

"And why does your boss give a shit about where his ex went?" I asked, moving closer to him with the other Heirs at my back.

"Because I wouldn't exactly call her my ex," another voice called and I looked up as the door to the house opened and a huge guy stepped out onto the porch and looked at us. "I asked that girl to be mine and she said yes. I don't remember releasing her from that commitment."

He was tall and dark and had full sleeves tattooed on his arms as well as the gang symbol inked over his cheekbone. His eyes were icily cold and the way he looked at me let me know he'd figured out exactly why I was here.

I snorted dismissively at his words. These kinds of assholes liked to believe they owned the world just because they cast a big shadow in a small corner of it. But it was a huge fucking world and this was a small shithole of a corner.

"That girl doesn't belong to anyone," I growled. "Least of all some half rent gangster who thinks he shits gold when all he really is is a tiny little tadpole swimming upstream in a river filled with crocodiles."

"So you think you're a crocodile?" Zane taunted, grinning at me like he thought he was a predator.

"Something like that," I replied darkly, my eyes shifting to reptilian slits for half a second before shifting back again just as quickly.

He hesitated for a moment, his eyes narrowing as he tried to work out if he'd imagined that before he went on.

"And here's me thinking Tory ain't afraid of anything, but she sent her pet pretty boys after me without showing her face. You wanna tell me where I should send your heads so she gets them?" Zane asked, moving down a step as he closed in on us.

His gang got to their feet too, some of them pulling weapons from belts as a few kids raced out onto the street to keep watch for cops.

"Are you all so afraid of us, you've gotta use guns?" Seth taunted, grinning around at the gang like a psychopath. If they started shooting, we could shield easily enough but it would be a lot harder to avoid them noticing that kind of magic.

"Okay, I'll offer you a deal," Zane said moving to stand right in front of me as he pulled a revolver from the back of his jeans. He raised his chin but I was still taller and I smirked at him as he narrowed his eyes over the fact. "No guns. But the last one of you alive has to tell us where she is before you die."

"Alright," I agreed because there was less than zero chance of him winning this. "But when we beat the shit out of every last one of you, you've gotta make a little video for me, telling Tory how fucking sorry you are for leaving her to die in that car like the cowardly little worm you are."

His men all started grumbling at that comment, closing in on us from all sides. I'd counted eighteen of them out here already and there were more appearing from the house now they realised a fight was brewing.

"Deal," Zane hissed and I swung my fist right into his smarmy face with all the power of my Order.

I knocked him clean off of his feet and dove after him with a roar as carnage broke out all around me.

Seth howled as he leapt at a group of the gangsters and Max laughed as he dove into the fray too.

I punched Zane four times before the big fucker from the porch collided with me and the two of us were sent tumbling across the ground. He managed to get on top of me, slamming his knuckles into my jaw and drawing blood before I reared up and head butted him hard enough to break his nose. His blood spilled over my face and I laughed savagely as he fell backwards, shoving myself to my feet and kicking him to make sure he stayed down.

Caleb charged past me with a yell, dancing between several opponents just fast enough for them to miss every time they tried to strike him, but not quite fast enough to give away his supernatural nature. He swung punches that looked soft but packed the strength of his Vampire gifts and the gangsters fell back all around him with howls of pain.

A solid weight collided with me as I looked for a fresh opponent and I was almost knocked from my feet as Roxy's other ex clamped his arm around my neck and tried to choke me out.

I swung around and ran backwards until I crushed him between me and the wall of the house with a sickening crunch which instantly resulted in his grip falling loose. I left him to slump to the ground as I ran back to the fight.

Half of the gang were down and the rest were looking at us like they couldn't figure out what the fuck was happening.

As I looked across the crowd, one guy yanked a gun from his belt and fired at me. I dove aside before he'd even aimed properly and the bullet slammed into one of the motorbikes behind me instead. I rolled over, flicking my fingers at the bike with a deadly grin as I sent it up in flames, using the bullet as an excuse for the blaze.

The guy fired again, but I'd already constructed a wall of pure heat around me and the bullet melted into nothing before it got close.

Max leapt on him before he could fire again, snatching the gun right out of his hands and beating him around the head with it while crowing like a cockerel as blood flew.

Zane was back on his feet and he turned to me with a look of utter rage, grabbing a lawn chair as he passed it and swinging it at me full force.

I raised an arm to protect my face and the metal framework slammed into me hard enough to knock me back a step. But with my Dragon strength it was nowhere near enough to take me down like he'd hoped.

His lips parted and a frown pulled at his brow half a second before I slammed my fist into his face again. And that felt so fucking good that I almost groaned in satisfaction.

The rest of the fight was finishing up around me and I fell over fucking Zane with his fucking cocky attitude and his shit tattoos that looked like he'd done them himself and that smug fucking look on his fucking face that said he still seriously believed he had some hold on my girl.

He fought back hard, busting my lip and bruising my ribs, but he was no match for me and I soon had him bloody and battered beneath me.

I looked up and found the other Heirs closing in around me with triumphant grins as they finished up their parts of the fight. I felt closer to them now than I had since I'd been Star Crossed. And I realised that that was my own fault. I'd been pulling away from them because I didn't know how to deal with what had happened to me and Roxy, but they hadn't just let me retreat.

Even this fucked up little outing was planned to try and help me and I had to wonder how many people had friends who would go even half as far as this for them.

Caleb pulled his Atlas from his pocket and set it recording as I grabbed the front of Zane's shirt and dragged him back up to his porch where I sat him up against the door so that he could make his apology.

"Tell her you're sorry," I snarled.

Zane looked at me through eyes which were already swelling over and spat at my feet.

"Did she ever tell you about how we met?" he asked, laughing darkly, like he didn't even care if we killed him. And maybe he didn't. People like him didn't expect to live long lives. He probably expected us to finish him now that we'd won.

"I don't give a shit," I growled.

"She used to come walking past my house every damn day wearing tiny skirts and low cut shirts, whatever she could to catch my eye-"

I punched him hard enough to knock out a tooth and he laughed through the blood pissing out of his mouth.

"And you know how I got her to come over and see me?" he asked, grinning up at me.

I growled at him as magic tumbled to the surface of my skin but Max placed a hand on my arm, pressing his calming influence over me to stop me from killing the bastard.

"I whistled. Fucking *whistled* and patted my knee and she came trotting on over and sat right in my lap. Not even seventeen yet and bigger balls on her than half of the guys in my gang. That's when I decided to keep her. And as far as I'm concerned, she's still mine."

No amount of calming influence would have stopped me from punching him then. I rammed my fist into his gut and he lurched forward, wheezing against the pain as he clutched his stomach.

"If you were going to keep her then why did you leave her in that car to die?" I snarled and his gaze flickered with fear for a moment like he'd sensed what I really was.

"I wasn't going to die to save some bitch, no matter how hot she was," he muttered and Caleb punched him before I could.

"Tell her you're sorry," Caleb demanded, pointing the Atlas at him again.

"Fuck you," Zane spat, lifting his chin like he'd rather die than speak the words he'd promised.

I could see he wasn't going to do it, his damn pride meaning more to him than his fucking life. But he wasn't worth killing. Castrating? Maybe. But killing? Not worth the headache. Still, I wasn't going to leave here without Roxy's apology.

"*Tell her you're sorry,*" I commanded, my voice thick with Coercion.

Zane's eyes widened as his lips parted and his tongue was forced to speak the words though he didn't want it to.

"I'm sorry," he gasped, his eyes glazing over as if he was being transported back to that moment. His hands trembled slightly as he went on. "So, so sorry for what I did. I was weak and a coward and I have nightmares about leaving you there like that. I was just so scared…" A tear slipped down his cheek and I glanced at the other Heirs in surprise before releasing him from my control. I'd forced him to apologise, but the rest of that shit was him. Maybe deep down he wasn't a total fuckwit. But either way, he was a fucking coward who had almost caused her death.

"She's never coming back here," I said as Caleb cut the recording. "So you might as well get over her."

Zane just stared at me as I turned away from him and with a casual flick of my fingers, I sent the flames from the burning bike to hop onto the next one in line. And the next. By the time we made it back to the street, all of them were blazing and the injured gangsters were scrambling to crawl away from the inferno.

Seth offered them a cheery little wave as we walked away and held a hand up for a moment before grinning as he disbanded a concealment spell and his Atlas suddenly appeared in his grasp.

"I used air magic to suspend it above the fight," he said with a wild grin. "I filmed the whole thing."

We all laughed as he played the start of it back for us and I watched for a moment as the four of us tore through the gangsters like a pack of psychos. I knocked my shoulder against Cal's and he slung an arm around me as I smirked at him. I could forgive him for his stupidity yesterday for punching Zane on its own. He hadn't meant to do it and so long as he kept his fangs away from Roxy from here on out then we weren't going to keep having an issue. He gave me a squeeze and sighed in relief as the tension between us melted away and I felt some of the pain in my heart dissolve too.

I ran my hand over my face to subtly heal the damage from my injuries and used my water magic to clean the blood from my skin.

The others did the same, Max helping Seth and Cal with his water magic before Seth directed us into another side alley.

"You wanna make one more pit stop while we're here?" he asked enticingly.

"Where to?" Caleb asked.

"I thought we could go to the Vegas' old apartment and take photos of us there to tease them with."

"Why?" Max asked with a frown.

"Because I got the address while I was searching for shit on the assholes we just beat up and I think it would be a shame not to go see it. They moved to the other side of the city, presumably to be as far from that loser as possible. Come on, aren't you curious?" He gave us the damn puppy dog eyes and we all caved.

I had to admit that I was interested to see where they'd been living before they'd come crashing into our lives and changed everything. I'd never spent a lot of time in the mortal realm and definitely not in areas like this, so I was intrigued to discover more about the place that had shaped them into the Fae they were today. Whenever I tried to picture them growing up, I just came up blank and I already felt like I was getting a better understanding of Roxy's defensiveness just by gaining this glimpse into their lives. Seeing more could only help me understand her better.

Seth tossed a handful of stardust over us and within moments we appeared in a darkened stairwell which must have been part of an apartment block.

"Is this it?" Max asked, wrinkling his nose at the damp smell which hung around us.

"This is the address I got. I only came close enough to make sure I could find it again last time so I can't be sure until we go in." Seth shrugged. "Their old apartment is on the fourth floor. Orion sealed it up when he brought them to the academy in case they needed to come back for anything but as far as I know, it's still how they left it the night they arrived in our lives."

My heart ticked a little faster at the thought of that. Of getting a glimpse into the girl Roxy had been before she met me. Before I'd pushed and provoked her into showing me nothing but her claws and teeth.

We headed up the stairs and at the sound of our heavy footfalls, the other residents turned and fled, scurrying back to their own apartments as they hoped to avoid our attention.

Seth finally turned off and led us down a corridor with sticky carpet and a broken light to the door at the far end with an upside down seven hanging from it.

I felt the familiar essence of Lance's magic fluttering against my skin as a repulsion spell urged me to turn away and go for a piss. It wasn't particularly strong as it only needed to work on mortals so I broke it apart easily. Max reached for the door handle and unlocked it with a little bit of air magic directed inside the lock mechanism.

The door swung open and Seth giggled like a naughty school kid as he pushed his way inside first and the rest of us followed.

The apartment consisted of a single room which couldn't have been more than forty square foot with a tiny adjoining bathroom to our left.

There was a beaten up two seater couch pushed against the far wall beneath a window that was zigzagged with cracks and let in a steady trickle of cold air from outside.

Caleb tossed a Faelight up and the room brightened to reveal flaking green paintwork clinging to half of the walls and crumbling masonry exposed on the rest of them.

I swallowed a lump in my throat as the stained floorboards creaked beneath my boots.

"This can't be the right place," Max muttered as he crossed the space to the tiny kitchenette.

I watched as he pulled open a few cupboards and found nothing within them aside from a single tin of beans.

Seth was frowning around at the empty space like he was expecting to find something else hidden here somehow, but it was clear there was nothing.

A single chest of drawers stood to the left of the room with a partially broken drawer revealing a few items of clothing poking out.

"I think we should just leave," Caleb said in a quiet voice, his brow tight as he shifted uncomfortably.

I agreed with him. We were intruding by being here. This wasn't some joke, this was private, a look at their lives before they'd come to Solaria which they hadn't offered to share with us. Lance had told me they were living in a shitty apartment in a rough neighbourhood and struggling to get by, but my imagination hadn't been capable of conjuring this level of poverty. I couldn't understand it, couldn't figure out how the daughters of the Savage King had somehow landed in this shithole. What would have happened to them if Lance had never shown up?

"They don't even have a bed," Seth said with a whimper in the back of his throat. "Do you think someone took it or-"

"I think the couch folds out," Max murmured. "And there's a blanket, so..."

I glanced at the ratty blanket and the memory of burning Roxy's clothes off of her on her first night at the academy overwhelmed me for a moment. She'd been furious, and at the time I'd mostly put that down to the fact that she was naked in front of all of us. But I remembered her snarling something at me about the money she'd had in her pocket. It hadn't really meant anything to me at the time, money was nothing to me, I had more of it than I could ever need or spend and I'd never really known anyone who wasn't in the same situation.

But as I looked around this cold, dirty room with no food in the cupboards and a fucking couch for a bed I realised exactly what I'd done to her that night. I didn't know where she'd gotten that money, but I could figure it out. She'd already shown me that she was a competent thief and had been utterly unapologetic for the fact. And now I knew why. That was how they'd survived. And I'd looked down on her for it. When really I should have seen how strong that made her. When had I ever had to fight for my survival like that? I'd never once gone hungry in all my life.

Shame licked down my spine and my jaw tightened as the depths of my own total fucking clueless dickhead behaviour were revealed to me and I was filled with enough self loathing to coat my tongue with bile.

My gaze caught on a heap of paperwork which was abandoned on the coffee table and I lifted a page from it, glancing down at the photograph pinned to the top. The twins must have been around seven and despite their identical looks, I could still tell them apart. Darcy's arm was in a cast, her gaze soft and hopeful while Roxy held her other hand with a defiant look in her eyes and a pout to her lips that promised trouble. There was a summary of the care they'd received with one of their foster families attached to the picture and a brief recommendation for an experienced family to be selected to take them in next due to their *difficult* personalities.

I knew exactly why mortals would have found them difficult. Fae were built to push boundaries, fight for what they wanted and butt up against authoritative figures at every opportunity in their quest for power. The twins had been passed from home to home for being Fae. In our world, their behaviour would have been praised, but here they'd been subject to punishment and lost their chances at having a family because of it.

I glanced at the rest of the paperwork and realised this must have been the information Lance had gathered on them before coming to collect them. There were school reports, hospital records, more social services files detailing other homes they'd been in. Even a few police reports with mugshots of Tory Gomez and a brief description of things she'd been hauled in over, though it didn't look like any charges had ever been brought against her. I guessed it had only been a matter of time though. And then what would have happened to them?

I bit down on my tongue and shoved the papers together, pushing them into a thick envelope so that I could take them with me and give them back to Roxy. I didn't know if she'd even want them, but it didn't seem right to leave them here.

Caleb caught my eye and wordlessly grabbed a bag from beside the chest of drawers and filled it with their clothes. It was still pitifully empty when he was done and there wasn't anything else here.

"Let's go home," Max said in a low voice and Seth whimpered as he glanced around at the barren apartment one last time before pulling the stardust from his pocket.

"We're not telling anyone else about this," I said as we all looked at each other.

"No," they agreed and a moment later we were swept up by the stars and transported back to the academy.

DARCY

CHAPTER THIRTY NINE

Two weeks. I'd hidden like a rabbit down a hole for *two* damn weeks. And I knew it couldn't go on any longer. Especially when I'd received an email from Principal Nova last night stating that she was sympathetic to my situation, but I needed to get back to classes and face life like a Fae.

My Atlas had been returned the day after the trial, no longer required as evidence. I'd avoided FaeBook, the internet, instead spending hours poring over the Phoenix books Orion had given me while trying not to damage the pages with my tears. They weren't all tears of sadness either. A lot of them were rage. Confusion. Hurt. How could he have done this to me, to us, *himself?*

Not being able to ask him that question was driving me to insanity. I needed to know what the hell had been going through his head when he'd thrown his entire life away. He'd clearly decided on it during the space of the trial. Changing his plea to make me out to be some poor little student he'd forced into loving him. It was sickening. Enraging. *Humiliating.*

But I couldn't keep hiding from the world. I had to face it. Tory had been strong enough to show up on the first day of term after being Star Crossed, but when my world fell apart, I'd fallen apart with it. So it was time I scraped myself off the ground and took a leaf out of my sister's book.

The worst part of all of this was that Orion's lie was so iron clad that even if I screamed and shouted the truth, everyone would think I was still under his Dark Coercion, forced to believe I loved him forevermore. Another surge of rage clung to my soul as I thought of those words leaving his mouth. But then I pictured him alone in prison and my rage gave way to pain. And not just any prison, a maximum security prison for the worst Fae imaginable. Darkmore Penitentiary.

I stood in front of the mirror in my uniform, my hair hanging around my face which was painted in subtle make-up to hide the pallor of my skin which spoke of my lack of sleep.

I'd been sorely tempted to give myself to the shadows a thousand times since the trial. They were always there, winding beneath my flesh like my body was haunted by whispering ghosts. I never answered their call though. I knew the moment I did, I'd drown in them forever.

I eyed my blue hair with a twisting in my gut as it reminded me of *him* then I strode from the room, slinging my bag over my shoulder and locking the door before heading out into the stairwell. Groups of students paused as they spotted me, tugging on each other's sleeves and whispering beneath their breath.

"Good to see you back, Darcy," a girl I'd never spoken to in my life called to me.

I clenched my jaw, saying nothing as I headed down the stairs and words of sympathy rang around me. It was worse than being called a whore. Now they called me a victim. They believed Orion had preyed on me like some kind of monster.

My heart was thundering by the time I reached The Orb and I held my chin higher as I walked in. Geraldine leapt from her seat, her mouth opening as if she was about to make some grand speech and I shook my head at her firmly.

"Please don't make a show," I begged as I approached and her lips slowly closed as she lowered into her seat, her eyes brimming with tears.

"It is so good to have you back," she breathed, reaching across the table to take my hand.

I didn't let her take it, my brows stitching together as I grabbed a bagel and started buttering it just to busy myself. I couldn't eat it. I'd lost my appetite the same day Orion had cast himself into hell.

I felt Diego and Sofia's eyes on me, not to mention the entirety of The Orb, and I was grateful when Tory suddenly appeared in her running gear, dropping down beside me, her presence lending me strength.

A moment later, Darius arrived, placing down her coffee with one of the chocolate wafers she loved before walking off without saying a word.

Tory cleared her throat, picking up her coffee and taking a sip then everyone looked back to me with questions in their eyes.

"I'm only going to say this once," I told my friends, looking between them.

Tyler leaned in closer, chomping on a bagel like he was hanging on my every word.

"Orion didn't Coerce me, he lied," I said firmly.

"I told them the truth," Tory said. "And anyone who says otherwise can go sit at another table, isn't that right Geraldine?"

"It is absolutely correct," Geraldine said, puffing out her chest with pride. "There is no ounce of my being which would ever question the word of the true queens. If you say it is so, then it is so."

Sofia nodded firmly and even Diego seemed to agree despite the fact that I was sure it would have been easy for him to turn against Orion.

"And for your peace of mind, I will ask my most wonderous Aunt Brenda to keep an eye on him for you. She works as a healer at Darkmore and I have no doubt she would rise to the occasion to ensure he is taken care of if he has any bumps or scrapes."

"That's kind, thank you," I said, a rush of air tumbling from my lungs. I hadn't realised how desperately I needed my friends to stand by my side in this. But now I knew that they were, I felt foolish for staying away from them for so long. I could see in their eyes how much they cared for me. "I'd rather not talk about it any more than that, okay?"

"You hear that?" Geraldine called to the whole table. "Not a word is to be uttered about the recent events our Queen Darcy has faced or by the glowing backside of the moon, I will smite you!"

Everyone nodded their agreement and I offered her a smile of thanks. In the ranks of the A.S.S. I managed to get through breakfast without having to engage with any other student in The Orb who was looking my way. But I caught sight of people muttering, smirking, frowning, forming their opinions, starting their rumours. The events at court would have spread like wildfire by now. And I was going to have to accept that most people had probably already made their minds up about me and Orion.

As I walked to Jupiter Hall, my heart sinking as I thought about attending Cardinal Magic class without Orion to teach it, I decided I wanted to know what was being said. I knew it would hurt. But if I ignored it, I couldn't face it head on. So I took out my Atlas and Faegled my name, my stomach knotting as I tapped on the top article to appear - by Gus Vulpecula of course.

"Darcy, don't," Tory warned, reaching for my Atlas, but I side stepped away from her as we entered Jupiter Hall.

"I want to see," I said firmly, no room for negotiation in my tone.

She sighed, but didn't make another move to stop me.

My gaze fell on a picture of Orion at the top of the article and my heart thrashed against my ribcage. It was a mugshot, his eyes looking dead, his head tilted down, the tie he'd worn at the trial hanging loose around his throat. There were shadows cast over the black and white image that made him look monstrous, deadly. And the title of the article made me want to throw my Atlas into the nearest wall.

Zodiac Academy professor sentenced to 25 years in Darkmore Penitentiary for sordid predation of a Vega Princess.

As the people of Solaria held their breath to hear the outcome of the most televised trial in thirty years, the Court of Solaria confirms that Lance Orion, former teacher of Cardinal Magic at Zodiac Academy and esteemed Pitball coach, used

Dark Coercion (a form of manipulative black magic) to force Gwendalina (Darcy) Vega into an ongoing sexual affair which began just a few weeks after her enrolment at the academy.

With her already addled mind, it seems Orion abused the Solarian Princess in what can only be described as a sick and twisted plot. Details have emerged that he dragged her into a swimming pool the first time he forced himself on her, creating an air pod in the water where he could make his first move. No doubt, Gwendalina's history of mental illness made her even more susceptible to his suggestions and one can only pity the princess for what Orion put her through, all the while bewitching her thoughts and memories to make her believe she wanted his advances.

There is a growing concern coming from this terrible revelation that with her mind forever corrupted by her abuser, one can only wonder what kind of disturbed woman she will turn out to be beyond graduation. There are rumours that the Mental Health Institute for Fae have tried to call her in for assessment. But Miss Vega pointed them towards her P.A. for comment who, unfortunately for their efforts, turned out to be a raven.

As for Lance Orion, his past reveals the destructive route he's been on for many years, becoming cold to his widowed mother after she lost her husband in a magical accident and when her daughter disappeared years later (see page fourteen for news on the miraculous re-emergence of Clara Orion). Stella Orion gave this comment after her son's prison sentence was announced. "I am saddened and deeply hurt by this news. My son has not been himself for many years and unfortunately, I didn't realise how bad things had gotten. As a loving mother, I would have helped him through any problems he was having. I always had an open ear for my son, but perhaps there was always something missing in him."

I shut my Atlas off, stuffing it back in my bag as my hands tightened into fists.

"It's all bullshit," Tory muttered and I nodded.

"I know, but it's bullshit the whole world has swallowed," I growled. "And he did it to himself."

"Good morning, my dear," Washer's voice made me flinch and I recoiled as he reached out to touch me. Tory had told me he'd temporarily taken over our Cardinal Magic classes and he was about the last person in the world I wanted to see right now. "Great to see you're ploughing deeply into your studies again. But I would be amiss not to offer you my services." His tanned face twisted into a sympathetic smile as he glanced over at Tory. "Both of you must feel as though you've been dragged naked through a thorn bush lately. So if you'd like me to siphon away those dark emotions writhing inside you, then I am more than willing to assist you."

"I'd rather swallow a toothpick whole, but thanks," Tory said coolly and Washer tutted, turning to me again.

"But you my dear, you must be so troubled, not knowing your own mind. I can pick apart your thoughts, try to help you feel out what was real and what wasn't. We'd have to go through each of the times he touched you in quite vivid detail, but it would be most beneficial to get it off your chest."

"I know my own mind," I said firmly. "Orion lied in court."

I knew it was pointless saying it. No one was going to believe me. But not saying it felt like a betrayal to myself. I couldn't let the whole world think I'd been brainwashed, even though Orion had given me zero choice in the matter. And I wasn't going to give up trying to clear his name.

I'd talked it over with Tory a hundred times already and we'd decided it was time to let everyone know that Phoenixes couldn't be Dark Coerced. That our Order powers could block all kinds of invasive mental magic. But we couldn't just blurt it out and let the papers dismiss it. We had to handle it right. So Darius was working on an appeal with his lawyers which would allow us to prove it in front of a judge.

"My dear." Washer stepped closer, his musky cologne reaching to me from the patch of waxed chest I could see between the few buttons undone at his throat. "The first step towards healing is accepting what happened. Professor Orion seemed like a fine, *fine* man, but unfortunately it is never the ones you suspect that have a dark seed growing inside them."

"He did *not* abuse me," I snapped, my voice rising enough that the entire class turned to face me. "And the only pervert in this school is *you*."

Washer's lips parted in offence. "I beg your pardon? I do understand that you're dealing with a swell of emotions right now, but do not turn your ire against me, Miss Vega."

I pursed my lips, refusing to apologise. Why should I? He went around getting in people's personal space without their permission all the time. He was gross, and the fact that Orion was being called a creep by the whole world and not this guy was an actual joke.

Washer frowned pitifully, apparently giving me a free pass as he patted my shoulder and walked away to the front of the class. "Come on in, I'll be handing you over to your new professor today. She will be here any minute."

The door opened and people started muttering as they headed inside. My gaze hooked on Kylie giggling with Jillian and rage singed my insides as I took in her smirking face and the light dancing in her eyes. She was seriously damn pleased with herself for getting her revenge on me. Revenge for something I didn't even do. *Bitch.*

Tory scowled, stepping closer to me. "Want me to punch that smile off of her smug face?"

"No," I said through my teeth. "I want her to hurt far worse than that."

"Ooh, that's dark, Darcy," Tyler said, slinging his arm over Sofia's shoulders as they followed us inside. "I'm so here for it. Just make sure to gimme a heads up so I can have my camera ready when it goes down."

"I think she deserves a stint in hell for what she did," Sofia said with her upper lip peeling back.

They were all so determinedly on my side about this and it made my heart thaw out. They didn't doubt my story. They just blindly believed it. And I couldn't thank them enough for that.

"The stars will punish her," Diego said in a growl. "There's no justice in the world if they don't, chica." He laid his hand on my arm and I frowned at him in confusion, my heart tugging.

"You hated Orion," I breathed.

He dropped my gaze. "I think we were starting to see eye to eye. And Tory said she saw you together, she knows the truth. That's enough for me."

I was incredibly grateful to her for that and I reached out to squeeze her hand as we moved along the line.

We headed into class and I took my usual seat between Diego and my sister while Washer gathered up a box of things from the desk. Orion's desk. Things he'd obviously filled the drawers with. And I was hit with a blinding fear - *where has all his stuff been taken?*

Had his house been emptied out? His things thrown away or shoved in storage somewhere? My muscles tensed at the thought that his presence had been so swiftly and sharply removed from the academy when he'd given so much of his life to this place.

I took my Atlas out, shooting Darius a message with anxiety warring in my chest.

Darcy:

Do you know what happened to Lance's things?

Darius:

I've got them in storage. Don't worry, I wouldn't let any fucker touch his stuff. If there's anything you want to hang onto let me know.

Relief filled me and I released a slow breath as I sent another reply.

Darcy:

Thank you. How's the appeal coming along?

Darius:

The Kiplings are working on the documents. I'll let you know when I receive them and what will be required.

P.S.

Glad to see you back. Don't break alone. I know you have your sister, but I'm always here if you need to talk about him.

The weight of my heart lessened at his words and I offered him the only thing I could in return.

Darcy:

You too, Darius. Thank you for everything you've done for him.

"Ah, here she is," Washer announced and I turned to the door where a woman with raven hair down to her waist was stepping into the room.

She was beautiful, almost sickeningly so. Like every inch of her skin had been buffed and polished, her makeup impossibly flawless. It was as if she was wearing a Faechat filter that made her practically glimmer with beauty. Her almond eyes were delicately painted with eyeliner and her full, pouty lips were scarlet red. The knee length black dress she wore hugged her petite yet curvaceous figure, her boobs shoved up and displayed without modesty and a pendant hung around her neck with an aquamarine stone in it that matched her unusually coloured eyes.

"Class, this is Professor Highspell," Washer announced. "Although Professor Orion taught with a *firm* hand that we will all miss-" He paused as he sighed. "- I have no doubt that your new professor will make sure your needs are met, won't you Honey?"

"Honey Highspell? Is she some kind of escort for hire?" Tyler snorted and Highspell strode towards him, pushing her fingers into his hair then yanking backwards so he was forced to look up her.

"Watch that tongue of yours," she purred. "Or it might end up in trouble. And I always find a punishment that fits the crime." She chuckled flirtatiously then stalked up to the desk like a panther, waving her hand at Washer disinterestedly. "You may go."

He nodded, apparently not taken in by her allure despite him perving on ninety nine percent of the population. He kept his eyes fixed on her face instead of her obvious cleavage, smiling tightly before heading out the door.

Highspell leaned her ass against the desk, gripping it either side of her thighs with her long, manicured nails. Her eyes roamed over the class, moving from face to face as if committing each of them to memory. When she reached me and Tory, her upper lip pulled back almost imperceptibly. "I think it's apt for me to mention the elephant in the room," she said with a gentle smile. "Lance Orion, an upstanding citizen in Fae society whom I had the pleasure to train with for our teaching degree, has been convicted of a terrible crime. A

485

crime which he did not commit."

My lips parted and I exchanged a look with Tory, wondering if I was about to find an ally in this woman.

"After visiting him in Darkmore Penitentiary, I have come to understand the true story of what happened to him." Her eyes landed on me and there was no sympathy there at all. "He was manipulated by a girl with royal blood, a girl who has walked into this world alongside her sister and lied and cheated her way to being actually considered for the throne."

"*Liar*," I snapped and she whipped her fingers toward me, a hardened line of ice sealing my lips together as she turned her gaze from me onto Tory who looked ready to tear this bitch's face off. And I was seriously rooting for her.

I raised my fingers to my mouth, bringing heat to my fingertips to burn through the ice, but the magic was insanely powerful. I was desperate to unveil her as the liar she was. This woman hadn't visited Orion and he hadn't told her anything of the sort.

My heart crashed against my ribcage as fury bubbled under my flesh.

"Poor Lance thought Darcy Vega really did love him, but she manipulated him, gave her body to him and when he stood up in court, he sacrificed himself for her just like she'd always planned."

"Shut your mouth," Tory barked and Highspell's gaze fell on her.

"And you are no different, are you Miss Vega?" she said darkly. "Manipulating an Heir into falling for you only to cast him aside when the stars called you both together. I don't know how they do it, but these girls wield some sort of dark magic over powerful men and I will be watching you both very closely indeed to find out what it is."

I managed to burn through the ice sticking my lips together at last just as Kylie's voice rang around the room.

"I'm so glad someone finally sees it, Professor Highspell. I've been trying to expose them since they arrived," she said airily.

"What's your name?" Highspell asked.

"Kylie Major," she answered brightly.

"Well you'd have to be a talented Fae to achieve such a thing, Miss Major, and according to Professor Orion's notes you are sub-par." Highspell shrugged innocently and I could practically feel the heat burning from Kylie's reddened cheeks behind me. Apparently our new teacher wasn't looking to make friends with anybody. Even ass kissers.

She moved forward to perch on Tyler's desk, crossing her legs so her skirt rode up to reveal her long bronzed legs. She waved a hand at the board and a question appeared on it.

What is the difference between the Mutatio Orders and the Divisus Orders?

"Today, you'll be quizzed on everything you have learned from the beginning of term and I will rank you all at the end of the class. Take out your notepads and prepare to answer each question." She leaned down to speak to Tyler, her boobs thoroughly in his face. "Be a good boy and draw a map of the class with everyone's names on it. You can skip the first few questions." She winked before sliding off of his table like a cat and slinking her way to the front of the class again. "Begin," she commanded.

I ground my jaw as I worked through the questions, trying to keep my hands from shaking with anger. This woman was vile. I'd only known her five seconds and I would have taken Washer over her any day.

Tory's Atlas buzzed and she subtly slid it off of the desk, placing it in her lap as she checked the message she'd received.

"Oh my god," she breathed, then passed her Atlas over to me.

I watched the video Darius had sent of her ex-boyfriend, Zane, apologising to Tory, his face bloodied and bruised. I momentarily forgot the witch in the room as my heart lifted at seeing that bastard clearly having gotten exactly what he deserved. I passed Tory's Atlas back, finding her eyes glimmering with something that looked an awful lot like love. Trust her to get all gooey over Darius violently smashing her ex's face in. But it made me like him even more too and a grin tugged at my lips that she returned before quickly schooling it.

"I don't actually need him to fight my battles though," she huffed and I rolled my eyes.

"Vegas!" Highspell snapped and she marched over to us with her eyes turning to snake-like slits. "What do you think you are doing?" Neither of us replied and she hissed between her teeth, holding her hand out to Tory. "Give it here. Now."

Tory reluctantly handed over her Atlas with a scowl and Highspell stared down at the video on the screen for a moment before walking back to her desk and placing it there. She took her own Atlas out of her shiny, leopard print handbag and returned to stand before us, holding it up as if she was about to record us.

"Both of you stand on your desks," she commanded and I swallowed the burning sensation in my throat as I obeyed, climbing up and standing above her beside Tory.

"Watch a video in my class and you will have a video made of you in my class," Highspell said with a vicious smile. "You look like a strong man." She pointed at Diego and beckoned him up. "Come here and record this for me." Apparently Highspell didn't mind making friends with the boys in this class.

Diego frowned as he got up, moving to take the Atlas from her and giving us an apologetic look as he aimed it at us.

Highspell looked between us with that snakelike expression again and in my bones, I could tell she was a Medusa. She had that same aura about her as Kylie had, the dangerous glint of a hungry python in her eyes.

"As you are so hellbent on disrupting my quiz, you will have an extra round. Answer my questions incorrectly and you will be punished. If you fight back against your punishments, you will be in detention with me for the rest of the semester. And trust me when I say, it will be far more unpleasant than facing your punishments here like Fae," Highspell said, flicking a lock of that long, raven hair over her shoulder then raising her hands. My heart beat wildly out of tune as magic flickered in her palms. "How did the extinct Order of the Ophiotaurus recharge their magical power?"

I glanced at Tory, having no damn clue. We'd never been taught that and why would we have?

We shrugged in unison and she flicked her fingers at us and tiny shards of ice flew into my right cheek. I gasped as they nicked my skin and blood warmed my face. I glanced at Tory, finding her cheek cut open too and fury burst through my veins like an inferno. It was so difficult not to fight back. I wanted to destroy her for this. But a single look with my sister confirmed it wasn't worth the extra hours in detention with this cow.

I turned to Highspell in disgust, waiting for her next question, refusing to give her the satisfaction of complaining about the punishment.

Her eyes glimmered as she carried on. "Which spell would you use to bottle a Kithendium Glow worm?"

I bit down on my tongue, staring at her with a patient look. She wanted us bloodied on camera for her own satisfaction. All of the questions would be impossible to answer. So I stared evenly at her and waited for her to flick her fingers.

The second strike slashed across the bare skin between my knee high socks and the hem of my skirt. I reached out and took my sister's hand as we stared defiantly at her, refusing to acknowledge the camera which was shaking in Diego's hands.

The game continued on until our uniforms were ripped and blood seeped through the slashes. Blood dripped between my fingers as she finally let us sit back down, snatching the Atlas from Diego and tapping something on the screen.

"Maybe the comments on my post from your FaeBook friends will remind you not to be disruptive in my class." She released a light laugh then roamed back to the front of the room, tucking her Atlas back in her bag.

My pulse pounded in my ears, my jaw was grinding and heat invaded every part of me. It felt like the world was turning against us, taking every good thing and smashing it to dust. And I decided I hated the stars as keenly as I hated Professor Highspell.

The moment the lesson ended and me and my sister were announced at the bottom of the class rank despite the fact we'd gotten full marks, I was livid. She'd accused us of cheating and ripped up our papers saying we could work our way up the ranks fairly or not at all.

I peeled away from Tory and my friends, making my excuses before heading off across campus towards Aer Tower. The cuts on my skin still stung and blood stained my white shirt with patches of red. I had a free period before lunch and I didn't want to be around anyone for the next two hours. I'd had enough. Highspell's bullshit had brought my anger to the surface all over again and I couldn't take it. Sickness swirled in my gut as I started to come apart.

Not here. Not in front of everyone.

I was soon running into the tower, racing upstairs as emotion swallowed me up and the shadows started whispering, promising to drown it all away if I just gave in to them.

I tried to force it all down, but I needed some outlet and I found myself tearing past the corridor that led to my room, instead continuing to climb and climb until I made it into the stairwell that led to the roof. I sprinted up to the door, shoving it wide and the wind whipped around me, the sound of the huge turbine on the side of the building groaning in my ears.

I kicked the door shut and screamed at the sky, raising my arms in the same moment and releasing my magic in a flood. A hurricane of air poured from my body in a wild and chaotic storm. I grabbed hold of it and wielded the air to spin around the tower, forming it into a huge pillar of storm clouds which grew larger and larger as it rose up towards the sky and shrouded everything in darkness.

The turbine spun faster in the raging tornado that twisted around the edges of the tower and the wind sent my hair flying in the maelstrom.

Tears streamed down my cheeks as I let everything out. All the pain, the hurt, the betrayal.

How could you do this? How could you break every promise we'd ever made to each other? How could you throw it all away and not even say goodbye?

I ached for answers, burned for them. I needed to go to him, but how was I ever supposed to do that?

"Darcy!" a voice made my heart leap and I turned, dropping my arms as the storm continued to swirl and grow ever darker.

Seth stood by the door as it swung closed behind him, his face pinched with concern.

"Don't look at me like that," I snapped. "You have no right to."

"Come inside," he encouraged. "We can talk."

"I don't want to talk to you," I snarled. "Leave me alone."

His arms fell limp at his sides and he shook his head as his hair billowed around him in the storm. "I can't do that."

"Why?" I demanded, my heart tearing to pieces. The last person I wanted to see me like this was him. "What do you want from me? Isn't my pain enough? Don't you have your pound of flesh yet?"

My body shuddered as he took a step closer, his eyes glinting with hurt.

"I never wanted this," he said earnestly, shaking his head.

"Screw you!" I shouted, making my lungs raw. "You tortured me and Lance. So get out of my sight or I'll bring this whole storm down on your head."

Seth stepped closer and I raised my hands threateningly. He swallowed thickly, his gaze moving to the blood on my cheek and the reddened cuts across my body. "I know what I did. I'm not denying it."

"So just leave me alone, Seth," I snarled. "Do you really have to bathe in my misery any more than you already have?"

"No...I..." His jaw pulsed as he pushed a hand through his wayward hair. "I've suffered through this too, alright?"

"What is that supposed to mean?" I hissed as he took yet another step closer and magic tingled in my palms, ready to rip him apart if he got too near.

He seemed to be struggling with something as he opened and closed his mouth, then his eyes found mine again and a heavy breath left him. "Here's the truth." His shoulders dropped and he suddenly looked broken, his head dipping and shame colouring his angular features. "From the moment you walked into this school, I was primed to fight against you. You were my opponent, but I didn't expect...I didn't expect to like you too. To respect you every time you got up again. I hated that I couldn't hate you. And it was more than that..." He glanced away from me as if he couldn't bear to speak his next words.

"What?" I pressed, suddenly unable to look away, somehow sure I needed to hear whatever he was hiding.

"I envied you, Darcy. You and your sister," he forced out. "You grew up away from all this...this fucking *pressure*," he spat the last word. "You'd both avoided the weight that had pressed down on me my whole life then walked right into our world and had everything I'd suffered for handed to you. You have no idea what it's like to have every move you make watched, recorded, judged. And not just by the press, by my family. My brothers and sisters may love me, but they're constantly hunting for weaknesses, waiting for me to slip up so they can steal my place as Alpha and take the crown. It's our nature. But you...*you* most of all were so fucking innocent. So *good*. So unaffected by the world because you never had to bleed for glory like I did."

"I didn't have it easy in the mortal world," I said in disbelief. "And I never asked for this."

"I know that now, really...I do. But back then, every time I looked at you, I wanted to know what growing up without being corrupted felt like and every time I hurt you, I wanted to see the darkness in you to prove to myself that no one was that virtuous. But after everything I did, there was no black heart to find in you. You never became like me, even when the world tried to crush you." His throat bobbed as he bared his truth to me and I didn't know what to say before he barrelled on. "I've never figured out what I wanted from you, all I know is you possessed me, you drove me crazy. I thought for a while you were my equal, and that was why I obsessed over you. That maybe my instincts were driving me towards taking you as my mate. But then..."

"Then what?" I breathed, suddenly needing to hear it all. The very depths of his honesty.

"Then I found out about you and Orion and I just...snapped." He fixed me with a dark look that ate into my soul. "I thought he'd corrupted you. *Him*

490

of all people. The asshole professor who'd decided he hated me with a passion since you arrived. He'd been the one to make you bad. Not me. And I despised that. I couldn't swallow it. So I punished you. I wanted to get vengeance for all the suffering I'd put myself through over you. All the nights I'd wondered what it was that drove me quietly mad about you. Envy, hate, love? I didn't know which one it was or if all of them played some part in it." He stepped forward again so there was only a meter between us. "But after a while, I saw how Orion coveted you. How he hadn't made you bad at all, *you'd* made him good. And I realised it wasn't just some fling. The way you two looked at each other it was like…like an unbreakable thread was binding you together. Nothing anyone said or did would ever change it. Least of all me. And that was when I realised what I'd done. How I'd tried to tear you to pieces, tried to make out as if, somewhere deep down, you were as bad as me when all I was really doing was ignoring the fact that I'd become the monster I'd tried so hard to find in you."

His words hung in the air, kissing my skin, begging to be let in. But accepting them meant I understood why he'd done it. And I didn't want to do that. I didn't want to be the good girl he painted me out to be. I wanted to prove I was the bad one. The girl that could throw him off this tower for hurting me. But instead I just stood there, lost and rattled to my core.

Seth's eyes bored into me. "I don't think I'll ever be able to forgive myself for what I did to you, and I'd never ask you for your forgiveness because I don't deserve a drop of it. But for what it's worth, I am so fucking sorry, Darcy."

The wind roared in my ears and fresh tears spilled down my cheeks, turning icily cold the moment they met the air. I'd never wanted an apology from Seth. I didn't expect one, let alone one that made me believe he really meant it. But now those words fell from his tongue, I realised how desperately I had needed that apology. How much rage and hurt I'd kept in my heart over him. I knew it couldn't undo the awful things he'd done to me. But I could finally see remorse in his eyes. I could see a resentful boy becoming a remorseful man right in front of me.

Seth moved forward, closing the distance between us and capturing my chin between his finger and thumb as he tilted my head to look up at him. "There's one more thing I should have realised. You could never be my mate, Darcy Vega. Because we're not equals. You're far better than me in every way imaginable."

I didn't know if I fell into his arms or if he surrounded me in that moment, but suddenly he was holding me against his chest and I felt like he was the only solid thing in this storm that was keeping my feet on the ground. He was one of the few people who had witnessed the truth about me and Orion. He'd seen it first hand, and hearing him admit that what we'd had was undeniable soothed a piece of my fractured, suffering soul.

"Why did he do this?" I asked him, stealing the heat from his body as the wind froze me to my core.

"Isn't it obvious?" he sighed, resting his chin on my head. "He was protecting you, babe. By taking absolute responsibility for that crime, he ensured your name wouldn't get muddied in the press. You won't lose support for the crown. If anything, you'll win more sympathy for it."

A ragged sob escaped me as I realised he might be right and I fisted my hands in the back of his shirt as I buried my face in his chest. He brushed his fingers over my neck and healing magic washed through my skin, finding each of the stinging cuts Highspell had marked on me and knitting them over.

"That new professor is going to be a dead woman if she thinks she can get away with this," Seth growled, a fierce protectiveness filling his voice as his arms tightened around me.

It should have felt wrong taking comfort from him, but it felt awfully, frighteningly right. Like he would have my back through anything now. But that couldn't be true. It made no sense. We were still on opposite sides of a war. But I guessed that war would never come if Lionel seized the throne. He was an enemy to all of us now. Which currently made us allies.

"We need to deal with Kylie," he said in a low tone as the storm around us started to fall away. "That girl has grown far too big for her fucking boots."

I drew back, swallowing down the last of my tears. "Kylie Major is *mine.*"

He pressed his tongue into his cheek, a dangerous shadow entering his eyes. "You wouldn't deny me the pleasure of being a part of that show though, would you babe? I have a few words I've been dying to say to her for weeks. But I figured you'd want first dibs so I've held off."

I nodded, finding it strange to be on the same team as him for once. He lifted his hand, checking the flashy watch on his wrist. "It's lunchtime. She'll be in The Orb."

"Then let's go." I stepped past him and sensed him following as I headed into the stairwell, the last of the storm flittering out behind me. My heart turned to stone as I hurried downstairs and Seth Capella walked at my side like a prowling animal on the hunt for a kill.

When we walked into The Orb together, eyes turned our way and Geraldine stood up with her mouth agape and a sandwich falling from her grip.

I ignored the stares, hunting for Kylie and spotting her with Jillian, Marguerite, Mildred and a bunch of their mindless Hores. I made a beeline towards her as adrenaline rolled smoothly into my limbs alongside a wave of magic. Tory moved to walk beside me, wordless as she realised where I was headed and suddenly Darius, Caleb and Max materialised too like they were drawn magnetically to Seth's side.

Marguerite tapped Kylie on the shoulder to point us out as we approached, her face paling as she looked from the Heirs to me and my sister.

"Get up," I demanded of Kylie as we crowded around their table and her eyes widened as she rose to her feet in front of me, looking to Seth.

"Sethy, what's going on?" she asked innocently. "What are you doing with the Vegas?"

I'd spent the last two weeks thinking up all the horrible ways I wanted to destroy Kylie. And now she was before me, I knew exactly what I wanted to do. I wasn't going to lower myself to her standards and humiliate her, ridicule her, hurt her. Not in the way she expected anyway.

I grabbed a fistful of her shirt, dragging her nose to nose with me and she shrieked, her hair bursting into venomous snakes that lunged for my face. But I was ready, casting an air shield close to my skin so their fangs slammed against it, unable to reach me as her complexion turned green and her eyes sharpened to slits.

"Get off of me!" she yelled, shoving my shoulders with a blast of air magic, but I cast air into my own back to keep myself rooted in place.

"You cost me the love of my life," I said in a calm but dangerous voice. "He's in prison because you couldn't wait to destroy me the second you got the chance. And all over a Wolf I never laid a hand on. Do you understand what that makes you to me?"

"Your enemy?" she asked bitterly, looking to Seth again like she was expecting him to vouch for her.

"No, it makes you nothing," I growled. "Just a worthless, waste of oxygen who I now no longer acknowledge as existing."

"Why are you standing there beside that street trash over me, Sethy baby?" Kylie asked, her lower lip betraying her with a tremble.

"I'm not your baby," Seth said coldly. "Haven't been for a long fucking time. And even when I was, I wasn't just yours. Never have been. I made it clear I fuck around. I don't settle with one person until I find my mate. But you just kept denying it to yourself until I stopped correcting you."

"I am your mate, you just haven't realised it yet," she insisted, pouting in defiance.

Seth stepped closer with a growl. "I am an Heir to the Solarian throne. You haven't got enough power in your veins to fuel a bus. How could you ever think we would be mated? You're just a low born, low mannered, low class *snake*."

Her jaw dropped and though I'd pitied her in the past for Seth breaking her heart, I was done feeling sorry for her. She'd actively ruined Orion's life. And I wanted her ruined in return.

"That's not true!" she shrieked, still in denial and at this point it was just embarrassing.

"It is true," Seth snarled dangerously. "You were just a handy lay when my pack weren't around. And I am thoroughly fucking tired of your obsession with me."

She finally fell quiet, her eyes turning to me full of blame as if I'd somehow caused Seth's dislike of her. But she'd managed that all on her own.

In my periphery, Tory was squaring up to Marguerite and I could tell this might end in a brawl, but that wasn't what I wanted. I wanted to strip Kylie of the one thing she valued above all else. Her pride, the respect she had from her little friends, the circle of safety she surrounded herself with.

"Kylie Major is no longer visible to anyone who supports me and my sister!" I called to the room and Seth flipped his fingers so my voice was amplified ten times over.

I caught Darius's eye and he nodded with a dark glint in his gaze before I continued.

"You will not see her, hear her, or even smell the sickly sweet perfume she wears to hide the scent of evil on her," I spoke clearly, my voice ringing around The Orb and Tory let out a little laugh of triumph.

"That goes for anyone who supports the Heirs too," Seth suddenly boomed and I looked to him with a smile twisting up the corner of my lips. It was dark and savage and tasted new on my mouth. But it felt good to wield our power at long last over someone who deserved it. I thought of all the times she'd cursed me, laughed at me, of the time she'd spat on me. She thought I was beneath her, but she was going to get a rude awakening when she found herself at the bottom of the food chain in the next five seconds.

"If anyone is seen with her, they'll get the same treatment. She is officially *nothing*," Darius took over, a hungry glimmer of vengeance in his eyes.

Kylie's jaw fell slack as if I'd punched her, but it was really much sweeter than if I had. Her friends started backing away from her and Mildred strode resolutely to the other side of the room with her shoulders pressed back and her head held high. Marguerite glowered at Tory then me for a long second before looking to the Heirs, bowing her head and scurrying away with the rest of her friends.

Kylie was left alone, shifting back out of her Order form as she started to shake.

The Heirs turned their backs on her and we followed suit.

"Wait!" she cried with desperation in her tone, but I couldn't hear her. No one could. She was going to suffer alone and pay for what she'd done. Invisible, ignored, *nothing*.

TORY

CHAPTER FORTY

The Palace of Souls felt like home and that was so fucking unreal that I didn't even know what to do with it.

Spring break had been like a dream of escaping reality where me and Darcy had parked our relationship baggage at the door and made a damn good effort to leave it there. Mostly.

I may or may not have been messaging Darius a bit in the evenings. Or a lot. After seeing that video of what he'd done to Zane, I'd been pleased then pissed then unsure how to feel about it. I didn't want him to charge off and fight my battles for me and Zane was someone I'd clearly left in the dust for a damn good reason. But then, after a few days of stewing over his Dragon macho bullshit ways, I'd watched the video again, seen the actual remorse in Zane's eyes and felt...*good*. Vindicated even.

That asshole had sent me countless messages after I'd gotten out of hospital. Never once asking if I was okay but demanding I return to him, asking what my problem was, even chewing me out for the accident and trying to blame me for the argument that had caused it. Apparently, I should have realised that him letting another girl suck his dick was no big deal because he didn't kiss her or fuck her and he was thinking of me the whole time. Douchebag. I honestly didn't know what I'd ever seen in him.

Okay, that was a lie. I'd seen freedom in him. He was twenty one, starting up his own gang, he commanded respect on the streets and always had a roll of cash in his back pocket. I'd stupidly thought that a guy like him could take care of me and Darcy, offer us a place to belong. That was before I realised that relying on someone else to take care of me was a dumb bitch move and vowed never to do it again.

And he was hot. Not Darius Acrux hot. But I'd always had a thing for danger and darkness, and wrap that combination up in a bundle of muscle and you basically had yourself some Tory kryptonite. *Damn hot douchebags, I always knew they'd be my downfall.*

Anyway, I'd moved on from Zane the-fucker-who-left-me-to-die-and-only-had-an-average-sized-dick-which-he-didn't-know-how-to-use Baxter a long time ago. Even when I had nightmares about drowning in that car, he didn't really feature in them. It was more about being trapped and alone than *him* abandoning me in particular. So I hadn't had any grand plans of revenge for him. He really wasn't even on my agenda in any way, shape or form. But seeing him brought so low and forced to admit he actually gave a shit about what he'd done to me was pretty gratifying. And the idea of Darius beating the shit out of him for me was kinda hot. Not that I'd ever admit it.

So following a week of giving Darius the cold shoulder over treating me like a princess who needed her honour defending, I looked around my giant ass palace one evening, admitted to myself that the princess part at least wasn't entirely inaccurate, and decided to reply to one of the messages he'd sent me. It was a single word. *Thanks.* And it had kinda opened the floodgates for about a thousand messages since.

I now knew a hell of a lot about what it was like to grow up in a house with a tyrant, and he'd even opened up about some of the darkest shit that Lionel had put him through. I knew more details about his favourite Pitball team than I'd ever cared to know, countless funny stories about things him and the other Heirs had gotten up to over the years and much more besides. I'd traded him tales of shitty foster families, bike heists, the love I shared with my sister and a refusal to tell him how many ex boyfriends I actually had. Because there was no need for him to go hunting down all of them. For example, my fifth grade boyfriend Johnny Briggs really couldn't be blamed for dumping me – I *had* flashed my panties at his best friend behind the slide after all. No way he deserved to have a Dragon visit him while he slept.

I didn't let myself think about the reality of my situation with Darius when I was messaging him. Like the fact that this strange new relationship that was growing between us couldn't actually result in anything more than this. I didn't want to focus on the fact that I couldn't really have him or even admit to myself that I wanted him. His messages made me smile. And for now at least, that was enough.

Darcy seemed to have come to terms with her separation from Lance. At least in some small part. She was still devastated and heartbroken, but she was also managing to compartmentalise it, force it out of her mind as much as possible during the day. She'd admitted to me that she was still crying herself to sleep at night though. But she didn't want me to share her bed anymore. She wanted to learn to live with the pain of it on her own because there was a horrifying chance that this really would go on for years.

Each day we chose a new section of the palace to explore and now I hardly even got lost in the sweeping hallways and vaulted corridors. We'd decided to keep the Queen's quarters as our main residence while we stayed here and I didn't like to admit it out loud, but there was something comforting about being in the rooms that had belonged to our mother.

We were beginning to piece together more and more about our birth parents and had even faced reading some articles about the reasons for the Savage King earning his reputation. He was a monster alright. He'd been a ruthless and vicious leader, creating laws that were impossible to follow and punishing Fae who broke them with death.

But we'd also found a box filled with love letters he'd written to our mother hidden in their things and the tender way he spoke of her and even of his joy over her pregnancy made my heart ache.

It was so difficult to marry the two sides of him together and I still couldn't figure out what kind of a parent he would have been to us.

Our mother was easier to get a feel for. She'd run charities and funded projects in the rougher parts of the kingdom. She'd started scholarship programs so that promising Fae from poorer families could get into academies, and had funded women's shelters to help people escape from power abusive relationships. Though she clearly had a ruthless streak too. She'd swapped us for mortal children, knowing they would die because of it. She'd also intervened in some of the king's cruel plans, but stood by his side while he executed others. I didn't understand it. But I supposed what I did know about them for sure was that they loved each other and us. And maybe that was enough for me to make peace with some of my demons.

The palace was so huge that we'd eaten every single meal in a different room, terrace, veranda or garden since the day we'd arrived here and we still hadn't run out of options in nearly two weeks.

We were eating breakfast out on the Duke's Terrace (there were *six* freaking terraces in this place) on the last morning of our stay when a butler arrived to announce a guest.

Darcy looked up from her french toast and I shoved the last bite of my pancakes into my mouth just as Gabriel walked out to join us. His chest was bare and his wings were out and the butler looked like he might just choke on his own tongue as he looked at him. But after a week of tolerating my booty shorts, crop tops and sailor's mouth, the staff were starting to realise that we were never going to be the traditional kinds of princesses, so I guessed he was trying to adapt.

We both jumped up to embrace Gabriel and he grinned at us before taking a seat at the little wrought iron table in the sunshine as we looked out over the stunning grounds beyond the palace. There were gardens dedicated to each Element and season, a winding river with magical little boats which took you on a circuit of the grounds if you hopped into one of them. There was also a menagerie of various magical creatures, each housed within their own perfectly acclimated habitat and more besides that which we hadn't even begun to explore.

"Have you eaten?" I asked Gabriel as he turned his chair backwards and straddled it so that his wings had room.

"Not yet," he admitted. "I was woken by a damn insistent vision which demanded I come and see you two today."

I glanced at the lingering butler and leaned back in my chair. "Be a lamb, Jeeves, and get our friend some pancakes?" I said with a grin.

The servants had refused our insistence to stop waiting on us hand and foot and actually got pretty damn upset if we tried to do things for ourselves, so we'd eventually caved to the peer pressure. But I refused to take bossing them around seriously, so I asked for everything in the most douchebaggy way I could manage and layered on a heap of sarcasm for effect. I was actually pretty damn sure they loved it. But maybe not.

The butler scurried off and Darcy rolled her eyes at me. "Ignore Tory, she calls all the butlers Jeeves because she can't remember all of their names."

"Neither can you," I pointed out.

I swear, that guy was one of about fifteen butlers and it wasn't like they introduced themselves, they just appeared at random intervals with snacks and shit before disappearing again like ghosts. I was pretty sure they used hidden passages to get around, but I hadn't figured out a way into them yet.

"No, but I just smile politely and don't mention it," she said like that was so much better.

"So, what else did your vision tell you to do?" I asked Gabriel as I looked at him with a smile.

"Nothing," he replied. "But I couldn't shake the feeling that it was really important I come here today, so here I am."

I exchanged a glance with Darcy and a shiver ran down my spine. I could admit that I wasn't the biggest fan of divine intervention these days, but Gabriel's visions had rarely been wrong. They'd also rarely been able to help either of us and I knew Darcy was feeling a little bitter over the fact that he hadn't foreseen Kylie-the-cow planting cameras and fucking up her and Orion's lives. But I guessed it was hard for him to focus on visions about so many different things and people all the time. And I knew enough about the way The Sight worked now to understand that if he wasn't actively trying to focus on having a vision about something or someone in particular, then they didn't often come to him unbidden.

Darcy opened her mouth to say something else, but as she did, she fell still, her eyes landing on the steps which led down from the terrace to the immaculate lawn beyond.

"Do either of you see that?" she asked in a low voice.

I frowned as I looked more carefully and my heart leapt as I spotted a bare footprint on the top step, glimmering with a faint silver sheen in the sunlight.

"We need to follow them," Gabriel announced, pushing to his feet so suddenly, he almost upended his chair.

"Where to?" I asked as me and Darcy rose as well and the hollow look in his silver ringed eyes made my breath catch.

"*The answers*," he replied in a voice filled with power which at once sounded like him and not like him at all.

His shoulders relaxed as the vision released him and I reached out to take his hand as he looked down at us in confusion.

"Are you alright?" I breathed as he shook his head like he was trying to clear it.

"That…it wasn't like a normal vision. It was like the stars spoke through me." The frown on his brow told me how unnerving that had been and I squeezed his fingers as Darcy moved closer to him too.

"We don't have to do what they want," I said defiantly. "If you don't want to follow this path then I'm happy to tell them to go fuck themselves again."

"Because that went so well for you last time?" Darcy asked, arching an eyebrow at me.

"Burn," Gabriel teased as he looked between us and I rolled my eyes. Okay, she maybe had a point but that didn't mean I was just going to let those glimmery assholes dictate my entire life now because I was afraid of their vengeance. "But I actually think we should follow this path anyway," he added. "I don't know where it leads, but I have the feeling it will be… *enlightening.*"

I glanced at Darcy and she shrugged in acceptance as I nodded.

"Okay then, let's follow the creepy ghost footsteps. No reason to worry about that," I said and Gabriel snorted a laugh as the three of us headed down to the lawn.

More silvery footsteps appeared before us and a shiver ran down my spine as we crossed the winter garden filled with snow and ice white roses before emerging in the water garden filled with little pools and burbling brooks.

We left the palace far behind as we continued to follow the trail over small bridges in silence, an almost physical sense of anticipation consuming us.

We crossed the river with the boats floating lazily along its surface and the shimmering blue water caught my attention. We passed through an orchard and turned a corner at the end of it where we found ourselves at a huge archway fashioned out of flowering lilac wisteria which marked the entrance to the royal maze.

"The servants warned us not to enter the maze," Darcy murmured as we hesitated before it, the trail of footprints leading inside. "They said Fae have gone in there and never come out again."

"Apparently no one has reached the centre of it in over a hundred years," I added quietly.

I wanted to scoff at the silly rumours, but standing before the beautiful archway which led into the depths of the yew maze with walls so tall they blotted out the sunlight above us made me feel immeasurably small somehow. There was something about the maze that set me on edge and made my magic shiver beneath my skin.

Gabriel drew in a deep breath and shrugged, his wings rising and falling with the movement so that his black feathers brushed against my arm.

"If we want the answers, we have to go in," he said simply.

"The answers to what?" Darcy asked and he hesitated for a long time before replying.

"Everything."

"Well, that sounds promising," I muttered. *Fucking stars.* "I guess we're going in then?"

The others nodded and we followed the footprints in to the darkness which lingered within the maze.

We followed the footprints around several turns before they abruptly disappeared and the hedgerow behind us rustled as it grew over the path we'd just taken to get here.

"No wonder no one can find the centre of it if it *moves,*" I groaned. "Why don't we just fly up and over to the middle?"

"No," Gabriel said, shaking his head. "If we want the answers, we have to find the centre the proper way. Meet the challenge and rise to it."

"Of course we do," I muttered. Because the stars never let anything just be easy, especially for us.

"I think we need to take the next right," Darcy said slowly and before I could question her, I realised I agreed.

"So do I," Gabriel said and we all shared a look before moving to take that path.

There were no more footprints as we walked further and further into the maze, our instincts somehow staying in line with each other at every fork in the path. It was eerie, but something about it just felt *right.* The three of us together, heading into the dark.

We rounded a final corner and a soft gasp escaped me as we arrived in the centre of the maze where a huge weeping willow with pure, silver leaves stood waiting for us.

We walked forward as one, not hesitating for a moment as we pushed the fronds aside and stepped beneath them.

A stone archway stood within the shade beneath the tree with carvings etched all over it. There were Phoenixes and Harpies, Dragons, a Hydra and a sky filled with stars. All of it achingly beautiful and telling a story I couldn't quite understand.

Beyond the arch was a stone staircase with silver footprints leading down into the dark.

Gabriel took my hand on one side and Darcy's on the other as the three of us descended together.

Our footsteps echoed off of the hollow space beneath the ground and every breath we took seemed magnified.

We emerged in an empty chamber lit only by the light of a pool of silver water which sat at its centre, so still, the surface looked like a mirror.

As one, we moved to kneel before it, like our bodies were being guided

502

by whatever spirit had led us here.

We leaned forward to look into the reflective pool and my breath caught in my lungs as I stared down at myself. Except in the water, I wasn't wearing a crop top and booty shorts and my hair wasn't braided at my side. I was wearing a golden gown which looked fit for a queen and a silver crown inlaid with rubies sat on my head over the flowing locks of my black hair.

I glanced to my left and found Darcy dressed exactly the same as me in the reflection while Gabriel was in a fine black suit and shirt, an unadorned silver ring placed upon his black hair and a shimmering crystal ball clasped between his hands.

As I stared at the image of him, I was struck with the similarity some of his features held to ours. The straight slope of his nose, the arch of his eyebrows and the shape of his eyes.

"Gabriel..." I breathed as I turned to look at him beside me, but his focus remained on the pool as he slowly reached out and touched it.

Ripples shimmered and danced across the water and as I looked back down at it, I was suddenly sucked into a vision like the ones we'd experienced the last time we'd come to the palace.

This time, I recognised my mother the moment I saw her, though she only looked about our age. She was wearing weird leather armour like the kind of thing gladiators used to wear and she held a spear as she slipped between the trunks of huge trees in a lush green forest.

"That's a Voldrakian Marriage Trial," Gabriel breathed beside me and my frown deepened.

"A what?" I hissed.

"In Voldrakia, a kingdom to the south of Solaria, the elite members of society take place in trials designed to test the mettle of the Fae taking part. It's a bloody, brutal game where members of prestigious families put their children forward to survive two weeks in the wilderness, fighting to the death for the supplies necessary to survive. It takes place before their magic is Awakened and there are all kinds of perils in it from the monsters lurking in the woods to the other contenders who will all fight tooth and nail to survive. Whoever remains alive at the end of the trial will be betrothed to one of the other survivors. They then take on their magical education and are married four years later once they graduate," Gabriel explained in a low voice as we watched my mother stalking through the trees.

"That's...intense," I muttered, not mentioning the fact that the idea of the arranged marriage part of it freaked me out more then the death games bit.

"Different kingdoms do things differently," he shrugged as we turned our attention back to the vision.

The girl I was watching didn't look like a Queen, she looked like a warrior, set to survive anything and I felt a real sense of union with her in that moment. I knew what it was to fight for survival and the look in her eyes felt so familiar that it made my heart ache with a wish to have known her.

The vision shifted and changed, showing her fighting in the game, battling a monster coated in scales with deathly black eyes with her spear alone and winning. She made a camp, foraged for food, fought other contenders.

And then one night, a boy walked into her camp with a spear of his own and pressed it to her throat as she slept.

I was so caught up in fear for her that it took me a moment to look at his face hidden in shadows. But when I did, I almost cried out because I could have sworn that I was looking at Gabriel. As the boy shifted before the light of the fire, my pounding heart calmed a fraction as I saw enough differences in his face to know it wasn't him. But that only opened my heart up to a terrifyingly desperate possibility.

"The stars sent me to find you," the boy murmured and my mother stirred at the sound of his voice.

"I recognise you, Marcel," she breathed like they'd somehow met before, but I was struck with the most definite knowledge that they hadn't. Not in the flesh. Only in their dreams.

"I'm going to die tomorrow," he replied and there was no sadness in his voice, just a calm acceptance of the fact. "I'm going to trade my life for yours and the life of our son."

Our mother sat up and pushed his spear aside as she reached for him and he tossed it to the ground as he dropped to his knees beside her.

"Our son will change the world, he'll be the greatest Seer of his generation," Marcel breathed as he leaned down to kiss our mother and the conviction of his words let me know that he had no doubt of that whatsoever. He'd *seen* it.

"His life will be hard," our mother breathed against his lips as she pulled him down on top of her and a tear slid along her cheek.

"For a time," he agreed. "But he will know all the best kinds of love in the end. Even if he never knows ours."

Our mother cried silent tears as she kissed him again, the passion between them growing as their limbs tangled together on the bed of grass she'd created.

The vision blurred before we saw too much, but my hand slid into Gabriel's as my heart thundered to a deep and heady rhythm as the next vision played out.

The following morning, as they woke in each other's arms, they were surrounded by cries of triumph as a group of four huge boys leapt from the trees and circled them.

Our mother fought beside Gabriel's father fearlessly as they managed to cut down two of their attackers and adrenaline surged through my body as I ached for them to escape.

One of the other boys fell beneath their combined efforts but the last one lunged at our mother, throwing his spear just as Marcel leapt forward to intercept it. It plunged through his chest and our mother screamed as his blood coated her.

"Save our son," he demanded, holding her eye as he fought to stay on his knees and launched his own spear back at the boy who'd impaled him, forcing him to leap aside.

"I could have loved you in another life," our mother breathed, touching his cheek for the briefest second before she turned and fled with her hand touching her belly like she was cradling the tiny life which she knew had begun to grow within her.

Gabriel's grip on my hand was so tight that it was bruising and I could feel a tremor running through his limbs as he finally found out who he was.

His mother was our mother. He was our blood.

Our *brother.*

The vision blurred again and we watched our mother and the other victors of the games emerging at the end of the trials. The boy who'd killed Gabriel's father was among the survivors and before the day was out their families had promised them to each other, branding their backs with each other's star signs as our mother scowled in disgust at the choice which had been made for her.

A series of short visions followed, our mother's belly growing as life swelled inside her. Giving birth to a baby boy she named Gabriel as she placed a loving kiss on his head. We saw her running around the halls of her home with him, doting on him, playing with him, loving him with such clear intensity that it made my heart ache to watch it and tears spill down my cheeks.

His existence was hidden to protect him from the wrath of the man she was destined to marry. She was a princess in her own kingdom, but she wasn't allowed to make her own choice about the man she was destined to wed.

When she graduated her academy, she was tangled up in marriage preparations which happened to coincide with a visit from the King of Solaria.

I watched the visions of her meeting our father again, of gaining his trust by showing him the love she'd foreseen for the two of them. They snuck around the palace as they embarked on their affair so that her fiancé wouldn't find out about them while our father made arrangements to whisk her away to Solaria and marry her himself.

We watched as she introduced a four year old Gabriel to the Savage King and the man who had made our entire kingdom tremble in fear smiled with all the warmth of the sun. He took him in without question, played with him, taught him to ride a horse and took him flying in the sky on his back when he shifted into his Hydra form.

My heart ached as I watched moment after moment of the three of them together, the happiest of families behind closed doors. They told the world he was an orphan boy who they'd taken into their home as their ward, though our father planned to adopt him once his true Heirs were born.

It was achingly sweet and hauntingly sad. This perfect fairytale of a life which had been stolen from all of us. A brother who we'd never even known existed.

Of course it wasn't all dreams and fairytales and there was an undercurrent to the visions of things our father was doing in the kingdom. Of

Nymph attacks and plots our mother could see coming for them but couldn't uncover no matter how hard she tried.

Eventually the scenes of the happy family melted away and the visions faded as the familiar sense of our mother's presence slid from the room and the silver pool fell still again.

I drew in a deep breath as the magic of the place crackled around us but before I could draw back, a shiver danced along my spine and a soft sound caught my attention. It was like someone whispering in another room, the sound was there but the words were absent. Then a second voice joined in, a third, a fourth, until the air around us was filled with the whispered voices of the stars and goosebumps rose to cover my flesh.

A drop of liquid gold fell from the roof of the cave and splashed into the silver pool, causing a perfect circle of ripples to spread across its surface before the stars gifted us another vision.

I couldn't tear my eyes away from the pool as we were transported to the night our parents had died. Even before it began, I knew that that was what I was looking at, as if the whispers had told me despite the fact that I couldn't understand them.

Smoke tangled in the air and my breath caught as I forced myself to watch the inevitable play out.

Our mother and the Savage King were in their bedroom, standing by a hidden door at the back of the room as Astrum grasped a seven year old Gabriel's shoulders and listened to what they had to say.

"You have to make sure no one can find him," our mother insisted as tears tracked down her face. "You have to block his memories and his gifts too. He can't come into The Sight until the danger has passed or he'll be found."

"Mommy? I don't want to leave you," Gabriel said as he tugged on her skirt and she dropped down beside him as she dragged him into her arms.

"I wish it didn't have to be this way with all my heart," she sobbed. "But I promise one day you'll find your sisters. One day you'll have a chance to fix this kingdom and save our people from the threats that haunt it."

"Take this," the King commanded, shoving something into Astrum's arms which was hidden within a red cloth.

"But sire, I'm not worthy of it! I couldn't possibly wield-"

"If you even *attempt* to wield it, you will die," the King snarled, looking every part as savage as his reputation. "It's not for you. It's for my children. Hide it. Hide it well and scour it from your memory."

"Of-of course, your majesty," Astrum agreed, tucking the object beneath his cloak with trembling fingers.

"You can't ever let Gabriel or the girls know who is keeping them safe," our mother sniffed. "If they find out who you are while you're still alive, fate will twist and they'll be killed. I've *seen* it. They can *never* find out-"

"I understand, my Queen," Astrum replied, stroking my mother's hair fondly. "I will watch over your children and guard them until my last breath and they will never know who I am. I swear it on all the stars."

"You will swear it on more than that," the King snarled, grabbing Astrum's hand and gripping his face with the other. "You'll make a soul pact with me."

"Y-yes, sire," Astrum agreed, his eyes wild with fear.

"You will guard our children from afar with everything you have, but you will *never* let them discover your identity while you still draw breath. And you will hide the artefact in a place where my enemies will never find it and only my children can uncover it. Swear to this oath on penalty of your soul. If you fail in either mission, your very soul will be torn from the keeping of the stars and set to burn in pain and misery for all of time. Do you swear?" the Savage King demanded.

"I swear," Astrum replied, raising his chin as he held my father's eye and a flash of red and black magic passed between them, winding around their bodies before sinking into their flesh.

Our mother sobbed as the King pulled Gabriel from her arms, placing a kiss upon his head before he pushed him into Astrum's arms and forced them both to take the hidden passage.

Gabriel was shouting and trying to fight his way back to them but Astrum held him firmly, his face written in anguish.

"This is the only way," our mother sobbed as Astrum pulled him back and I could tell she wished it wasn't so.

She cried out in grief as the King closed the door between them and my heart twisted with pain for her as she said goodbye to her son for the final time.

I wanted to turn to Gabriel and pull him into my arms, but the visions weren't done with us yet and everything shifted again.

Two babies were screaming in their crib as our mother stood over them, wielding magic with ferocious strikes as she fought to protect them from more Nymphs than I could count.

Our father was on the far side of the room, fighting even more of them as he bellowed with rage and fought with a magic so powerful that the walls of the palace trembled.

I watched on in horror as more and more Nymphs swept into the the room and with a cry of pain, our father was overwhelmed.

Our mother's screams were deafening as the awful death rattle of the Nymphs filled the air and they fought to be the one to pierce his heart with their probes and steal his magic.

They all raced away from our mother in their desperation to claim him and as they fled, a man was revealed beyond them.

My heart froze into a solid lump in my chest as Lionel Acrux strode into the room and our mother fell still, her face written with shock.

"*You,*" she gasped as she stared at him in utter horror and I could tell that her visions hadn't shown her this. "I thought you were our *friend*, I thought-"

"That's where you went wrong, my Queen," Lionel purred as he closed in on her, his own power humming through the room as she fought to maintain her shield with the last dregs of her magic. "True Fae don't have *friends*. Just people we can use or people we can *destroy* on our way to the top. And I'm afraid it's time for you and your King to become the latter. You see, with your family out of the way, I become one of the four most powerful Fae in the kingdom. And then it's only a matter of time before I will find a way to claim the throne for myself alone."

"Why are you bothering to tell me this?" she gasped, her face stained with tears as the Nymphs finished her husband and began to circle close to her, sensing their next meal.

"Did you really think you could fool me with a couple of *mortal* babies?" Lionel sneered, flicking a disgusted look at the crib she was still shielding. "I'm not leaving the Princesses alive to grow up and challenge me again."

"I'll die before I give them up," our mother hissed.

"You'll die either way," Lionel agreed. "But luckily for me, you'll give them up despite your wishes."

"Never."

Lionel's smile deepened as he took a step closer to her and as he spoke again, his words were thick and laced with Dark Coercion. *"Tell me where you hid them."*

Our mother's eyes widened with panic as her lips were forced to part and her tongue spoke the words despite how hard she fought them.

Lionel smiled darkly as she gave up our location and with a savage blast of fire magic, he shattered the shield surrounding her and allowed the Nymphs to claim their prize.

He turned and strode from the room before she was even dead. I looked at her with pain wrenching my heart in two as a Nymph speared her heart with its probe but instead of the agony I expected to find there, the faintest smile graced her lips as if she'd won something despite her death.

"She knew," I breathed. "She knew we wouldn't die."

As the vision shifted for the final time, we watched the shadowy figure standing outside the house where our changeling family slept soundly in the mortal realm. Fire illuminated Lionel's face as he cast a burning orb into his hand and threw it at the house, encouraging the flames to blaze and blaze until there was nothing left but charred bricks and ash. He waited and watched then left in a flash of stardust with a satisfied smirk on his face just moments before we were pulled from the ashes by the firefighters. Not a miracle at all. Just two Phoenixes, reborn in flames and safe like our mother had foreseen. But he never knew. Not until we showed up eighteen years later.

The vision faded away until we were left staring at our reflections in the silver pool again and I fought to catch my breath as my brain swelled with all of the information we'd just been given.

"You're our brother," Darcy gasped as she turned to Gabriel.

I twisted towards him too and he looked between us, his face painted with so much emotion that it was hard to take.

"I was alone in the world for so long that I gave up on ever uncovering the mysteries of my past," he breathed. "I found happiness in creating my own family…but now… I *remember*. The visions broke the block on my memories and I remember my mother, your father… I remember holding the two of you on the day you were born and promising to love and protect you until the day I died."

I lunged at him as Darcy did the same and the three of us fell into a sobbing, laughing, happy, sad, utterly confused and yet completely fucking ecstatic heap.

I didn't know how to process half of the things that we'd just discovered, but I did know this: Lionel Acrux had been working with the Nymphs for a long time. He'd orchestrated our parents' deaths and followed us to the mortal world to try and kill us too. He'd been working on our deaths for a long time and had stolen more than just a life from us. He'd stolen our home, our family, and *kingdom*. And there was no way in hell I was going to let him keep it. One way or another, whatever it took, Lionel Acrux was going to meet his end. He was going to die.

But despite all of the horrors and pain of the things we'd just seen, there was something so pure and good there too. We'd found something we never even dreamed of. Another member of our family. And I swore on all the stars in the sky that I'd *never* let him be taken from us again.

DARCY

CHAPTER FORTY ONE ·

Coming back to Zodiac felt like sliding under the surface of an icy lake. I loved this place, but now everything about it screamed of Orion. And as I woke on Sunday morning, the familiar knot in my chest tightened as reality came swooping in on me the second I gained consciousness. Before the pain could swallow me though, I was distracted by a weight pressing down the end of my bed. I sat up and a scream escaped me as I spotted a guy curled up there. I started kicking him and he leapt off the bed with a growl. I stared at Seth in nothing but his sweatpants as he stared right back like he was as shocked to find me here as I was to find him.

"What the hell?!" I shouted.

He gazed around the room, rubbing his head and a flash of healing magic shot from his palm. "Oh shit...I think I know what happened."

"Well explain in the next five seconds or I'll-"

"It's okay," he said, lifting his palms in innocence, a whine escaping his throat. "I got a *bit* drunk with my pack last night. And then I started thinking about things..."

"What things?" I demanded. It was too early for this crap. What the hell was happening?

"You and Orion...and me being a dick...and you coming back to the academy last night and being all sad in here on your own and...well it's my nature to comfort people I care about and I guess I just...let myself in."

"Seth!" I admonished. "Are you serious? You crept into my room and slept in my *bed*? Do you realise how weird that is?"

He whined again, stepping closer. "Not really. It's my Order...I can't help it. I'd have slept with Darius every night since he was Star Crossed, but he'd flay me alive for it. In my drunken haze, I guess I knew I could get in here and…" He shrugged and I gaped at him, at a loss. "I'll go." He hung his head, trailing towards the door with a dog-like whimper that said he was hoping I might tell him to stay.

I frowned, not giving him that option and he sighed as he headed out the door, pausing before he shut it behind him. "I can teach you to cast better locks sometime, if you want?"

"Get out!" I snapped and he shut the door, releasing a mournful howl in the corridor.

Crazy damn Werewolf.

I slipped out of bed, firmly twisting the key in the lock and using the simple spell I'd learned in Cardinal Magic to lock it more firmly. Not that that did much good against trespassing Heirs apparently.

I strode into the bathroom, finding a wet towel on the floor and the scent of my shower gel in the air. *Did he have a freaking shower last night?*

There was an empty chip packet in the sink too and I fished it, tossing it in the trash and shaking my head. That guy had no boundaries.

I realised though, for the first time since Orion had been arrested, I'd actually slept most of the night. Sure, it had been almost one in the morning before I'd managed to drift off and it was barely dawn now, but I wasn't bone tired like usual. My time in the palace had helped. And learning that Gabriel was family felt like finding a piece of my soul that had been missing my entire life. It made so much sense. Of *course* he was blood. Of course he was our brother. But processing the other revelations in those visions was almost too much for my swirling mind to bear. Lionel had used the Nymphs to kill our parents then tried to kill us too. I couldn't say I was surprised exactly, but I was horrified at the lengths he'd gone to to try and secure the throne for himself. I knew now there was no limit on what he would do for the throne. And the body count could rise swiftly once he made his move to seize total power. The Heirs' parents were in mortal danger. And so were we.

I washed and spent some time cleaning my room just for something to occupy my mind and keep my thoughts from Orion. Not that it worked. It was like there was an arrow lodged in my chest so there was no chance of healing unless I pulled it out. But I didn't want to pull it out. I wanted to suffer through this pain because if I healed, that meant it was over. And I couldn't ever accept that fate.

Instead, I focused my mind on Gabriel as much as possible and the warmth of knowing we had one other surviving member of our family still in existence. For years, I'd dreamed of my parents and wondered what they'd be like, I never once considered what it would be like to have a brother. And now we had one, it was the most comforting feeling in the world.

By the time I'd cleaned my whole room and sat down on my bed, I was growing anxious again. I picked up my Atlas just for something to do, reading over my horoscope.

Good morning Gemini.

That stars have spoken about your day!

Uranus has moved into your chart and as such, you should be prepared for unpredictable changes. These could be good or bad, but as Pluto is influencing your sign right now, you may be best to prepare for the worst. A transformation is coming your way. But with the right attitude, you should be able to tackle the oncoming turbulence head on.

My brows pulled together. I couldn't see how things could get much worse than they were right now. But I supposed it would have been naïve of me to believe that. Lionel could still take the throne. My world could always fall into more turmoil. Growing up in the mortal realm had proved that much to me. Just when I thought our foster parents couldn't get worse, we'd be moved to a new house and met with a deeper kind of hell.

I clicked on FaeBook, scrolling quickly past the posts about me and Orion and pausing on one Tyler had posted.

Tyler Corbin:
Has anyone seen Kylie Major anywhere? She disappeared after an altercation with the Heirs and the Vegas the other day and I have no clue where she's gotten to... #missingmajor #ghostgirl #ithoughtismelledheryesterday #medusaloser
Victoria Pauley:
I have no idea, maybe a Dragon ate her for being a #whiningwilly
Jasmin Hosseini:
I heard she dissolved into a pool of tears and @Seth Capella bathed in them with his whole pack #saltysoak
Elke Henderson:
Side note: that shit was cold blooded! Are the Vegas and the Heirs teaming up now? I don't know who I support anymore #allofthemgetmehot #cantheheirsshare #whychoose
Amy Milton:
I heard she's hiding in Mildred Canopus's moustache #hairyhideyhole #combtokeepyourhome
Telisha Mortensen:
Maybe she blew away on a Pegasus fart and now she lives in a rainbow #maybeshellmarryaleprechauna #preshitterglitter #sparklefart
Kylie Major:
I'm right here assholes!!! @Seth Capella haven't I suffered enough yet?
Seth Capella:
Oh dear, someone must have hacked her FaeBook account because she wouldn't DARE reply to comments like she's an actual person.

Kylie Major:
Please baby!!!
Seth Capella:
Song: Click to play - Don't Call Me Baby by Madison Avenue*

I couldn't help but laugh. She was getting exactly what she deserved at last.

A knock came at the door and I frowned, wondering if Seth had come back and I stood up, unlocking the door and tugging it open ready to set some firm boundaries, but it wasn't him. Darius stood there dressed in a black long-sleeved shirt and jeans, his brows were knitted and his eyes full of some emotion I couldn't read.

"What is it?" I asked, my pulse escalating. He couldn't have come here unless someone had let him in the tower, but I doubted there was a single air Elemental in this building who would have refused him access. "Is Tory okay?"

"As far as I know," he said darkly. "This isn't about your sister. It's about Lance."

My throat balled up and my lungs ceased to work. "What about him?"

"I'm going to visit him. Now, in fact. And I figured you'd want to come too."

I felt like someone had reached into my chest and pulled my heart right out of it. "Of course I do," I said breathlessly, lurching toward him. "But how? Surely they won't let me see him."

Panic and hope and terror filled me in equal measures. I wasn't ready. But I'd never be ready. And I wasn't going to miss the chance, not for anything.

"I'll cast an illusion spell on you to get you in and I've paid off a guard who's on duty in visitation today. He'll disregard the warning spells that let him know your identity is being hidden, but we have to get there before his shift ends at nine."

I didn't know what to say. It was an opportunity I'd thought would never come. I could finally get answers from Orion, but more than that, I'd find out if he was okay. If he was surviving...suffering.

I moved forward and wrapped my arms around Darius, squeezing him tight. "Thank you."

His eyes darkened to pitch as I stepped back. "This is a one time only deal, you understand? I won't be able to get you in there twice."

I absorbed that fact, nodding my head as that truth settled over me like a ton of bricks. One time. This could be it for who knew how many years?

I had to find a way to get him out, but the Kiplings were struggling to find a loophole in the law that would allow Dark Coercion to be performed on someone for the sake of proof. It was utterly illegal no matter what the circumstances. And apparently Cyclops interrogation wouldn't be an option as my memories were now assumed to have been tampered with. But they still had hope. And so long as Orion agreed to the appeal, we'd at least be able to tell the judge the truth and prove Phoenixes could block legal mental invasion from Orders like Sirens.

Fear chewed on my insides as I pushed my feet into my sneakers and followed Darius into the hall. I was wearing jeans and a rumpled navy tank top and my hands smelled of cleaning products, but screw it. I wasn't going to waste a second in going to Orion.

The halls were deathly quiet as we headed downstairs and out into the cool morning air. The sun was hidden behind a sea of dark clouds and thunder rumbled ominously in the distance, though no rain was falling yet. I let my Phoenix fire push into my veins to banish the cold and keep goosebumps from rising across my arms.

We took off at a fast pace towards the north of campus and the secret gap in the fence that would let us out.

"How are you?" I asked Darius as we hurried through Earth Territory.

He grunted, glancing over his shoulder at me as I half jogged to keep up with his furious pace. "Not good. You?"

"Not good," I agreed with a weighted sigh.

"I'm furious with him truth be told," he muttered. "And this bond between us is making me pine for him like a fucking wolf cub for its mother."

I frowned, my heart wrenching for him. "Has your father said anything more about him?" I asked, the note of hope in my tone impossible to disguise.

"No," he gritted out. "I'm sorry, Darcy...I think he's going to let him rot in there and let us suffer through this bond."

"But he's your Guardian," I gasped.

"And I guess my father doesn't give a shit," he said quietly and barbed wire seemed to coiled through my chest. "He may even get me a new one to replace him, though I'd still pine for Lance for the rest of fucking time. And I'd rather cut off a hand than be bonded to some other asshole."

It wasn't fair. It wasn't right. How could Lionel just leave him in prison after all Orion had sacrificed for him? Willingly or otherwise. That Dragon asshole owed him that much.

"What did your lawyer say about the appeal?"

"That we can go ahead if we can get Lance to sign the document today," Darius said and my heart soared.

"We will," I said determinedly. "We just need to talk some sense into him."

He nodded stiffly. "Or beat it into him," he muttered.

We reached the fence and stepped through to the other side then Darius turned to me, his gaze raking over my face. "I'm going to make you look like Max, he's given his permission for you to use his identity today and removed his anti-mimicry wards," he said and my heart warmed at the thought. It was strange to be on the receiving end of the Heirs' kindness. Especially when I'd spent so long thinking they didn't have a kind bone in their bodies. "Close your eyes and hold still."

"Will it hurt?" I wondered, knowing I'd go through whatever hell it took anyway so long as it got me to Orion.

"No, but if you move while I'm doing it I could accidentally cut your nose off. So stay still or you won't be so pretty when I get you to Lance."

I breathed a note of laughter though he was clearly being deadly serious and I shut my eyes, falling as still as possible.

Heat licked over my skin, running across my scalp then the warmth continued to spread, making my skin tingle with pins and needles as it travelled all the way down to my toes. I became dizzy, but rooted my feet to the ground as the magic continued to flood over me.

"There," he announced and I opened my eyes, glancing down to find myself looking exactly the same as before.

"Didn't it work?" I frowned.

"You can't see it. It's an illusion for others, otherwise you'd be about three sizes too big for those clothes right now. I've changed your voice too so no one will be able to tell."

"So I look like Max to you right now?" I asked.

"Yep." He took out a pouch of stardust and I moved toward him, nerves taking hold of me as he tossed a pinch up into the air.

We were yanked through a galaxy of stars and my feet soon impacted with solid earth. Darius steadied me, then turned sharply away and I took in the huge metal fence that rose up above us like a wall, hiding whatever lay beyond it. It stretched away in either direction across an expansive plain of flat land. In front of us was a gate manned by two guards standing up in towers either side of it.

"Announce yourselves!" one of them barked, raising his hand with flames curling in his palm.

"Darius Acrux and Max Rigel," Darius called, his shoulders pushed back as I moved to his side. "We're here for visitation with Lance Orion."

The flames extinguished in the guard's hand and he signalled down to someone on the other side of the gate.

A moment later, a deep humming noise rumbled through the earth and the gate parted in the middle, opening inward to reveal a straight road with a couple of armoured trucks parked up either side of it. The road ran directly across the grassy land, cutting a path to an inner wire fence that looked at least half a mile away. Beyond that was a huge dome which seemed to glitter in the morning sun. The structure was immense and a glimpse of green could be seen within it even from this distance, but I couldn't tell what it was.

Darius led the way through the gates and magic tingled over my flesh as we passed through some barrier.

"Here, I'll take you down to the elevator," a young, blonde woman called to us in a black uniform, a badge on her breast pocket naming her as Officer Lucius.

She waved us into the back of the nearest armoured truck and I climbed in beside Darius with my heart thumping furiously against my chest. As she took off down the road, I tried to ignore the conflicting emotions warring inside me, knowing they were only going to drive me insane. I was desperate to see Orion, but nervous as hell and still so angry at him for sentencing himself to so many years in this place, I didn't know what to feel.

We soon passed through a second gate for the inner perimeter and another wave of magic crackled over the vehicle, making blue light spark across its surface. I gazed through the windshield to the dome looming ahead. It towered above us, a criss-cross pattern of magical energy spreading over the incredible space inside. From what I could see, there was a magical environment contained within it, a forest rose up toward us on the nearest side, the hint of rocky hills climbing up to the right of it and even a glimpse of snow further on. Clouds hung thickly in a makeshift sky beneath the dome, flashing with lightning and the grumble of thunder.

"Holy shit, what is that?" I breathed as the car veered around the side of it towards a large metal building standing about a hundred feet away from the edge of the dome.

"The Order Yard," Officer Lucius answered, as the truck slowed beside it, giving no more explanation than that as she directed us into the building.

I followed Darius out of the car, my pulse ratcheting up a level as we walked inside. Another officer sat behind a glass screen and a security door barred our way onwards.

"Ah Mr Acrux, Mr Rigel." He stood up, bowing his head to us both, but giving me a lingering look that suggested he knew what I was hiding. "Please step into the pod one at a time." He ushered Darius forward and the metal door slid open as he entered confidently before it closed again after him.

The door reopened a moment later and I moved into the empty space, another door barring my way on as I turned to look at the guard through the glass.

"Both feet in the boxes on the floor, Mr Rigel," he instructed and I arranged my feet, waiting for something to happen, but nothing did. "That's it. Okay, all done."

The door opened to my left and I headed through it, finding Darius waiting for me beside a large set of elevator doors. They opened as I approached and we walked into the shining silver space, turning back to face the doors just as they slid closed. The elevator descended at a rapid pace and my heart lurched in my chest as we drew closer and closer to Orion.

I noticed a strange tingling sensation in my chest and a chalky taste filled my mouth. I instinctively reached for my Phoenix, but it seemed to be sleeping, unable to be roused.

"My Order," I gasped and Darius nodded.

"It's Order Suppressant gas. They pump it into this place twenty four seven, so unless you take a daily antidote like the guards do, it's impossible to shift."

I didn't like that feeling at all. It was as if a part of my body had being severed clean off. "So Lance...he can't bite anyone?" The thought of him starving in this place was unbearable. It wasn't something I'd even considered

517

and it made me want to tear him out of these walls and never let them have him back.

"Not unless he's in that big dome up top. That's where they're allowed access to their Orders," Darius explained and a knot in my chest eased a little. At least he wasn't entirely cut off, but it still must have been hard to go without access to it in between his time out there.

I tried to get my thoughts in line for when I saw him. I had so many versions of what I wanted to say to him in my head, I had no idea what was going to come out of my mouth when I actually saw him. I chewed on my lower lip, getting more and more worked up.

The doors slid open and a short corridor stretched out ahead of us with a waiting room at the far end of it. Fae were gathered in the monochrome space, sitting on the metal chairs provided. People's mouths dropped open as they spotted us, exchanging looks with one another, a few of them bowing their heads while others stared, seemingly awe-struck. It was the strangest feeling in the world to be looked at like that. Tory and I didn't leave the academy enough to receive this sort of attention regularly. And I guessed for a moment, I knew what it was like to be an Heir.

A guard stood beside a door, checking his watch. "You'll be called in alphabetical order and will proceed to the room number I assign you," he announced then took out his Atlas, tapping on the screen. "Acrux, Darius and guest." He looked to us, dipping his head respectfully as we approached before pressing his hand to a scanner beside the door and it slid smoothly open. "Room thirteen." He pointed us down the corridor full of doors and we headed that way, my heart lodged firmly in my throat.

This is happening. I'm really going to see him.

The silence in the hallway made my skin prickle with unease. This place was cold and the air felt thin. Being so far underground was disquieting. Like this prison was a realm of its own, one I didn't want to wander too deeply into. And if I felt like that after a few minutes here, Orion must have been losing his mind.

We reached door thirteen and Darius opened it, blocking my view as I followed him inside. A heavy breath fell from my lungs as I found the room empty.

"Where is he?" I hissed.

"Just wait," Darius growled, looking about as anxious to see Orion as I was. His fingers were flexing and his muscles were bunched. He cast a silencing bubble and I felt it push out around me. "Don't speak to him until I give you a signal. I'm going to buy you some time in here alone, I have to cast ice on the cameras to make sure the video and sound is blocked. I've paid off the guard who'll be watching the feed, but it'll cost Lance a full cavity search."

"Oh my god," I gasped.

He shrugged. "He could have saved himself the inconvenience by not sending himself to prison."

"Holy shit," I breathed, my throat tight as he dropped the silencing bubble.

My heart was a desperate animal, clawing at the confines of my ribcage as I stared at that door. Waiting, waiting, waiting.

What if he's angry I came here? Or upset?

What if he's been hurt in this place? He's stuck with killers and degenerates, he could have been attacked or beaten or-

The door opened and I stopped breathing as Orion stepped into the room in an orange jumpsuit with four symbols on the breast. A pair of fangs, his two Elements and his number. One hundred and fifty.

His beard was overgrown and his ebony hair was falling into his eyes which looked sunken with lack of sleep. My heart practically beat its way out of my chest at seeing him like that. Looking so utterly broken. Like he was half the man he'd been the last time I saw him.

Darius rushed at him and the two of them embraced hard. I could almost see the bond between them blazing in the air as they gripped each other tightly.

"Fuck, I've missed you," Darius growled.

Orion groaned as he dug his fingers into his friend's back, the tension in his body making me hurt.

Darius suddenly shoved him back with a snarl. "You fucking asshole," he snapped. "What the hell were you thinking?"

Orion's eyes slid to me and my pulse thundered everywhere as he frowned, clearly surprised to see Max here, then looked back to Darius. "I had to," he said with a flash of resilience in his eyes, but he didn't expand on that.

"Yeah, well you can explain it to him first." Darius jerked his chin at me and Orion's brow pinched in confusion as his friend strode toward the exit. He threw me a nod as ice frosted over the cameras then he stepped out of the room and slammed the door shut behind him. The second it closed, I felt the illusion lift from my skin, fluttering away like butterflies.

"No," Orion gasped, taking a step back. "He brought you here?!" he roared and a tremor rocked through my body.

"Yes," I said, lifting my chin, trying to ignore the writhing ache in my chest as I forced myself not to run into his arms. I was so angry at him. And betrayed and hurt. But then seeing him look like this... like he'd been going through hell in this place, it made my anger fade enough that I could feel my heart shattering all over again.

"You've lost weight," he growled as his eyes slid down me.

I said nothing, my throat too tight.

"Don't let yourself suffer because of me," he said in a harsh tone.

The dam broke in my chest and anger won out over every other emotion. "Is that a command or are you trying to Dark Coerce me?" I asked icily.

His jaw ticked and he stalked toward me like a hunter starving for his next meal. His eyes scoured every inch of me, his throat bobbing and a tangible energy in the air swallowed me up.

He crowded me in against the wall, making my breath hitch at how little space parted us. He didn't smell like cinnamon anymore, he smelled like soap and misery. "It's a command. And one you're going to follow. Get out of here and forget this place. Forget me. It's over. Done. So move on."

His words were sharper than a knife, the hollowness to his voice making me long for the warmth he usually directed at me.

"You don't get to decide that for me." I blinked back tears, choking on my tongue. "You had no right to do this. You threw away everything, including your own life. *Why?"* I asked the question that had been haunting me for weeks on end. The one that had kept me up at night, the single word making me want to dive into the shadows just so I could forget it. But I hadn't. I'd stayed strong. And now he owed me this answer.

"You know why," he growled. "You're a princess of Solaria-"

"Fuck you." I shoved my palms into his chest with a blast of air magic that made him stumble back. The worst thing was how he didn't fight, he just stared at me with that look of acceptance stamped across his features.

I started to pace, my pulse thrumming everywhere and finally my anger came back in full force. "You had no right to do what you did!" I rounded on him, pointing at him in accusation. "We had a plan. You could have avoided prison if you'd just done what Darius's lawyer said."

"It's my life, Darcy, I'll do what I please," he said flatly.

I cringed at that name, shaking my head. I was always Blue to him, but he'd taken that from me along with everything else.

"So that's it?" I asked breathlessly, the wind crushed from my lungs. "We're done? Finished. Because *you* say so? And I never even got the chance to fight for us?"

His eyes darkened and he had the look of a wounded beast as he turned his gaze from me to the wall. "Yes."

"Is that all you have to say?" I lunged at him, throwing my hands into him with another blast of air. He staggered away, his back bumping against the wall as he didn't even bother to raise a hand to try and fight me off. The glowing cuffs on his wrists ensured he couldn't use magic, but that didn't mean he couldn't try to stop me physically. He just didn't seem to care enough to.

"That's all I have to say," he said in an empty tone with no emotion in it. Nothing. Didn't he care? Wasn't he even going to apologise for tearing my heart to pieces?

Of all the times I'd imagined seeing him again, I never could have predicted this arctic front from him. This apathy. It was worse than anything else I'd pictured.

My tears started flowing and I wanted to hide them away, but there was no force in the world which could stop them now.

"Why?!" I screamed again, my voice raw. "Give me the honest reason. I deserve that much."

Shadows swirled in his eyes and for a moment I feared he'd gone into them. He seemed so distant, so beastly. Like the man who'd loved me didn't even live in him anymore. He looked heartless and cold and exactly like the cruel creature he'd let the world think he was.

I approached him slowly when he remained quiet, the air alive with electric energy as I closed the space between us. And that was something of a comfort to know this compelling bond between us still existed, he was just refusing to acknowledge it. I reached out, pressing my hand to his chest as I got closer and closer, feeling the powerful pounding of his heart beneath my palm as I tried to hunt out the truth through it.

His jaw locked and his eyes focused on me so intensely that I couldn't draw in a single breath.

"Answer me," I whispered, a plea in my voice. I needed this. It was torture living without an explanation from him. Still, he remained quiet and another tear rolled down my cheek. "Seth said you were trying to save me. Is that true?"

"*Seth*," he hissed like his name was poison. "Why would you listen to Seth Capella?" There was a dangerous edge to his tone and I huffed a breath.

"So you want me to answer your questions but you won't answer mine?" I slid my hand up to cup the back of his neck, stepping closer so my chest brushed his ever so gently. I could have sworn the lights in the room flickered with how much energy bound us together.

I tip-toed up, aching to kiss him, wondering if he'd melt if I could just get past his defences. If we kissed, he'd remember why we were worth fighting for.

His eyes remained locked on mine, a desperation in his gaze I didn't understand the meaning of. Then he stepped out of my hold, brushing past me and turning his back on me, the biggest insult you could offer another Fae. And my jaw fell slack.

"Leave," he growled. "And don't come back. It's over, Darcy. Move on with your life."

"It doesn't have to be over," I gasped, terror wrapping its way around every organ in my body. "I don't care that you're here. You could be on the moon and I'd still find a way to love you."

"I don't want you to love me. I want you to leave and never come back."

Those words nearly brought me to my knees. Panic ripped at my soul as I stared at the man who possessed me, telling me to walk away. To never see him again.

"You don't mean that," I demanded, desperate to stop him from forcing me away.

"I do," he growled coldly, dismissively. "I mean every word. Get out."

I backed up, starting to shake as I reached the door. I gripped the handle behind me, unable to blink as I gazed at him in despair.

"Lance," I tried one final time, blinded by my pain. "Please don't do this."

"Get out!" He swivelled toward me, his gaze as dark as pitch as he pointed at the door.

My heart jammed into my throat and I turned the handle, wrenching it wide and shoving past Darius as I fled down the corridor. I needed to escape this place. I needed fresh air. I was going to suffocate if I didn't get it.

"Darcy!" Darius called, his footsteps pounding after me.

My blue hair flew around me as the guard admitted me back into the waiting room, his eyes narrowing as he took in my appearance. "Hold on-" he started, but I raced into the open elevator with Darius hot on my heels.

"You saw nothing!" Darius barked at him and the man's cheeks reddened before he bowed his head in submission.

The elevator started to rise and I pressed my hands to my face as Darius cast the illusion spell on me once more. The second the doors opened, I was out of them and when the guard finally let us outside, I dragged down a lungful of air, dropping to my knees on the dusty ground beside the building.

Darius fell down beside me, clutching my arm. "What happened?"

I couldn't get the words out, holding a hand to my chest as my heart felt like it was going to combust.

"What did he say?" Darius demanded.

"He said it's over," I forced out, wiping my tears away as I managed to catch my breath at last. I moved to sit against the wall of the building, the ground beneath me seeming unsteady. Everything was broken. All of it ruined. The world wasn't the same one I'd been in just moments ago.

Darius rose above me so I fell into his shadow, his features twisting into determination. "Wait here," he growled. "I'll speak to him. And I'll make sure he signs off on the appeal."

I nodded, cupping my head in my hands as I tried to slow my racing heart. The whole conversation replayed in my mind until I was breaking apart all over again, tears running down my cheeks. He wanted me gone. He didn't want me anywhere near him. Did he blame me for this? How could he? He'd made this choice. But maybe now he'd come here he'd realised what a terrible mistake he'd made. Maybe he would sign off on the appeal, but that wouldn't fix things between us.

Darius finally returned and before I could stop him, he threw his fist into the wall beside me.

"Darius," I gasped, getting to my feet as he dropped his arm to his side and blood dripped down into the grass. "What happened?"

"He's being a stubborn fucking asshole," he spat. "He won't sign off on the appeal. He's going to stay here and rot because he's a righteous prick."

"There must be something we can do." I clutched his arm as he looked to me with pity in his eyes. And I hated that.

"I'm sorry," he said heavily like he meant it from the depths of his being. "He's made his bed, now he's determined to fucking lie in it."

"No," I choked out and he dragged me into his arms, suddenly becoming the only thing solid that was holding me upright. "Darius," I sobbed. "Please do something."

He said nothing but his silence said it all. There was nothing he could do. He'd go to the ends of the world if it meant he could free his friend, but unless Orion made the choice to help himself, it was all pointless.

"He did this for you," he said quietly when I managed to draw myself together. "This fate means you can still rise in society without your name being sullied."

"I don't care what people think of me," I growled. "He took that choice away from me."

"I know," he said in a low tone. "But…we can't waste his sacrifice."

"What are you saying?" I stepped back out of his arms with accusation in my voice, my brows pulling together.

"It means, the best thing you can do for him right now, is give him what he's hoping for. Back off, give him time to stew in there until he comes to his senses. Don't send letters, don't try to call."

"But-"

"There's no other way," Darius said grimly. "If he thinks you've moved on, he might start listening to me. And in time…maybe I can get him to agree to the appeal." He didn't even sound convinced of his own words. I didn't know if he was saying them to placate me or himself. The chances of Orion changing his mind were miniscule. He'd chosen this fate. And I knew he was stubborn enough to see it through if that was what he'd decided.

A final tear tracked silently down my cheek as reality settled over me like a ten ton weight. The broken pieces of my heart sat jaggedly in my chest, piercing right through to my core. There wasn't a single part of me that didn't hurt.

That was it. My only option. I had to walk away from this place and not look back. I had to hold onto a hope that was so small, it barely shone at all.

The stars had turned against us so thoroughly, I wondered if they'd ever been rooting for us.

Me and Lance Orion were officially over. The most beautiful, pure love I'd ever known had been taken away from me just like that. And I didn't know how I'd ever recover.

TORY

CHAPTER FORTY TWO·

Good Morning Gemini. ·
The stars have spoken about your day!

In the wake of chaos comes calm and it may be tempting to bathe in that bliss, but be warned: when feeling safest, the dark is most likely to rise. Uranus is moving into your chart so be aware that sudden shocks and changes could be coming your way. Now is not the time to start feeling comfortable in your surroundings. Though sometimes the cosmic surprises brought on by this planet can be hard to adapt to, you will have to think fast if you want to avoid making the wrong decisions. Now is the time to be impulsive – but don't forget, nothing is ever as simple as it seems.

In the words of Geraldine: fuck me sideways with a Dragon dildo. I don't need anymore chaos in my life.

I sighed as I read over the message from the stars again. Those shiny asshats definitely had it in for me. What had I ever done to piss them off so bad?

I grumbled at my Atlas as Darius approached with my coffee, but instead of just leaving it on the table, he sat. He'd messaged me about missing our run yesterday because he had to visit Orion with Darcy and I obviously had no complaints about that, but it had kinda sucked not to start my day with him. And as classes didn't resume until today, I hadn't actually seen him until morning when he'd been waiting to run with me outside Ignis House. We'd gone on our silent run like usual and I'd found myself smiling for a ridiculous amount of it as I pushed myself as hard as I could and forced him to work to keep up. I didn't know why running with him meant so much to me, but I had to admit that it did. There was something about knowing he'd show up every day that just made me feel…important. And as much as I didn't want to admit that he had that kind of hold on me, I couldn't really deny it anymore. I was starting to care about the things he did and said and…*gah,* how was I supposed to actually talk to him face to face?

Blood rushed to my cheeks and for some reason, it took me way too long to lift my gaze from my Atlas to look at him.

This was weird. I knew it, he knew it, hell, the goddamn coffee knew it, and yet here we were.

The Orb was half full for the breakfast rush already so the stars were okay with this unexpected breakfast date. Not date. Obviously I didn't think of it as a date. It was just a Phoenix and a Dragon who had chosen never to be together sitting in a room filled with other people while food and drinks were consumed. Shit. If I had verbal diarrhoea in my head then how the fuck was I going to get a straight sentence out of my mouth without sounding like a goddamn douche canoe?

"Hi," he said, a knowing smile playing around his lips which was damn distracting.

Hate and sex I could do as easy as breathing. Saying hi to a guy who showed up every day to run with me and fetched my coffee was impossible though. Great.

Why hadn't I thought this through? Why hadn't it occurred to me that while I was pouring all of my childhood memories and secrets out via text that there was an honest to the stars demigod reading them? And why did a few weeks away from him and countless messages between us make me feel even more awkward in his presence? Surely getting to know each other better should have made it *less* weird? Instead, the weird had met Mrs Weird and had a bunch of weird babies who were currently having a party in my stomach which made the idea of consuming my coffee utterly unbearable.

"I was wondering if you'd been to see the bike you won from me yet?" he asked with a cocky little look on his face that said he knew full well that I hadn't. In fact, I'd shoved that key deep down into the recesses of my pantie drawer and refused to think about it at all. Aside from whenever I had to get panties out and spotted it of course. And sometimes when I was bored and fantasied about going for a ride…

"Umm, I've been a bit busy," I hedged, reaching out and snagging my coffee from the table so that I had something to do with my hands. I lifted it to my lips as he spoke again.

"And there was me thinking it had something to do with you not wanting anything from a jumped up lizard asshole who doesn't know his ass from his elbow and is only good for hate sex?"

I half gasped, half laughed and one hundred percent started choking on my mouthful of burning hot coffee. Like, I legit started hacking my lungs up and damn near spilled the entire mug in my lap as I struggled to set it down on the table. I leaned forward with my hand to my chest as I struggled to get control over my water magic and tempt the little drips of coffee back up out of my lungs before I managed to make an utter dipshit of myself. But as I sat up again and swiped my hand over my mouth for good measure, it was clear I was too late for that.

Darius was smirking at me in that way that used to get my blood boiling with rage but now, to my utter devastation, was making a motherfucking blush crawl over my cheeks.

"Asshat," I muttered without any venom.

"At least I'm consistent," he teased, his eyes lighting as he took in my shame and those little weirdos in my belly started up some kind of backflip routine.

"Well, I already knew you were a douchebag. I'm just trying to get my head around all of the other things I know about you now, too," I admitted.

"Like how good I am in the sack?" he asked, leaning forward and dipping his voice so that it wouldn't carry, but all that really achieved was to make the gravel in his tone more apparent and my toes curl inside my sneakers.

"I could have guessed that the first time I laid eyes on you," I quipped before realising I'd just admitted that I'd wanted him for that long.

The cocky ass smile on his face told me he didn't mind that one bit and I swear I could actually feel my blush growing. Tory Vega didn't blush. This was not like me. And those weirdos in my stomach were at it again and – *holy mother of shit, the weirdos are* butterflies. *Motherfucking butterflies! What the hell is happening to me??*

"Come on then, Roxy," he urged. "Tell me why you haven't been for a ride yet?"

My lips parted and I wasn't even sure what to say. That I hadn't figured out how to feel about the bike yet, let alone whether or not I was actually going to accept it and by just leaving it parked up without looking at it, I could just pretend it didn't exist at all and get away with not figuring any of those things out.

"I don't know how to deal with you when you're not being an asshole," I admitted.

"Don't worry about that, Roxy. I'm still an asshole," he assured me.

I bit my lip as I looked at him, casually dominating the chair opposite me, devilishly dishevelled after our run with his black hair a mess and the loose tank he wore revealing so much of his sweaty chest that I couldn't stop looking at it. He hadn't bothered to clean himself off with water magic yet and as much as I hated to admit it, Darius Acrux looked fucking lickable after a workout.

"Prove it," I dared before I could stop myself. Because I was really starting to enjoy getting to know all of his finer points, but I couldn't lie to myself about how much the darkness in him lit me up.

The corner of his mouth twitched like he could look right into my mind and see all of the depravity hiding in there.

I watched him as he lifted his gaze and looked around the room to the tables where some of the Professors had started to gather for breakfast together. Professor Highspell was perched on the edge of the table where Gabriel was sitting talking to Professor Rockford. Highspell seemed to be trying to draw his attention to the blood red pencil skirt she'd paired with a flouncy blouse which had half of the buttons open. Gabriel didn't seem to have noticed she was there, but she kept tossing her hair and laughing along to everything he was saying as she tried to catch his eye.

"Have you started on illusion spells yet, Roxy?" Darius asked me, his eyes twinkling with malice.

"A little," I admitted. "More concealment than actual illusions."

"I'll give you a demonstration then," he said and I watched as he casually twisted his fingers in a complicated pattern.

At first I didn't think anything had happened, but then something scuttled around the side of my coffee cup and my eyes widened as I took in the spindly spider which was bigger than my hand.

"The Baruvian Hellnet Spider doesn't generally live in this part of Solaria," Darius murmured as my eyes stayed glued to the creepy thing. I knew it wasn't real, but somehow it was hard to make my brain accept that. "It can move faster than a Manticore with a fire up its ass and has a particularly nasty bite. The pain of it is said to be so blinding that most Fae who feel it scream loud enough to tear their vocal chords. Not to mention pissing themselves."

"What are you going to do with it?" I breathed as I watched it scuttle across the coffee table before me.

With a casual flick of Darius's fingers, the spider leapt from the table and landed on my thigh.

I flinched, barely suppressing a scream as the very real feeling of eight little legs scrambling over my skin made my heart pound in panic.

"Am I making your heart race, Roxy?" he teased and I couldn't deny that it was true.

Darius stood and pulled his chair around the table so that he was sitting beside me with a clear view of the teachers while I stared at the insect on my lap and tried to convince my slightly terrified brain that it wasn't real.

The spider leapt off of my leg and began to scurry away from us beneath the tables. I glanced around at Darius as I felt him watching me instead of his creation.

"Impressive," I admitted. As much as it might have driven me insane that the Heirs were so much further along in their education than us, I could appreciate the fact that they worked damn hard to get so far ahead too.

"That's not the only way illusions can work," he murmured as he looked at me and I suddenly felt a hand touching my cheek.

Not just any hand. *His* hand. I recognised the roughness of his callouses and the heat of the fire that burned beneath his flesh despite the fact that his actual hands were clearly nowhere near me.

"That's incredible," I breathed. If I closed my eyes, I could have believed he was really touching me.

"You want incredible?" he teased and the feeling of his hand slid from my cheek down my neck, brushing my collar bone before finally caressing my breast. My nipple hardened and I practically started panting at the feeling of his hand on my body.

"*Darius*," I warned, but it didn't come out like a warning. My voice was all rough and pleading and the way his eyes darkened told me he liked that a lot.

A shriek of fear interrupted us and the sensation of his hand on me disappeared as he switched his attention to the commotion across the room.

Professor Highspell had leapt to her feet and I spotted the Baruvian Hellnet Spider scuttling up her skirt as she whirled around and tried to bat it off. She cast a shot of water at it and Darius smirked as it did nothing at all to the spider and only served to soak half of her skirt.

Everyone in the room was looking her way in shock and I was pleased to see Tyler filming as the spider ran up her chest and she screamed again. With a sudden lurch of movement, it dove towards her neck and sank its poisonous fangs in.

Highspell screamed so loud that it echoed off of the domed roof and a fucked up little smile tugged at my lips.

She fell to the floor and started thrashing about as the other professors tried to get close enough to help her.

Darius disbanded the magic with a twist of his wrist and as I turned to look into his eyes, the demon I used to fear was looking back at me. And that really should have been terrifying, but there was something about the monster I knew which had goosebumps rising all over my body.

Highspell's screams fell silent as the illusion disappeared and with the water she'd cast at herself I couldn't tell if she'd pissed herself, but I kinda hoped she had.

Darius pushed himself upright and placed his hands on the arms of my chair as he leaned down to speak to me, caging me in and making my heart pound.

"Nobody fucks with my girl and gets away with it," he growled, his lips brushing my ear for a moment and making me shiver.

He pushed away from me before I could reply and strode from the room. My gaze slid back to Highspell as she got her feet, panting and snarling as she looked around like she was hunting for something. Her eyes fell on me and the rage in them was enough to make me flinch. She clearly thought I was the reason for her humiliation and I guessed in a roundabout way, I was.

No doubt she was plotting her revenge for my next lesson with her already.

Perfect.

I'd have to remember to thank Darius for getting me even deeper onto her shit list. Though I didn't entirely mind seeing her humiliated in front of everyone so I guessed I'd let him off.

I pushed out of my seat and decided to grab breakfast to go, snatching a couple of pastries from the buffet table before slipping out of the door and heading back to Ignis House.

I needed to get changed into my uniform and head to the Uranus Infirmary for our first lesson on healing and I was more than ready to learn about that. Supposedly it was one of the hardest types of magic to master which was why they left it so late in the year to start us on it, but I was determined to perfect it. We managed to end up in way too many dangerous situations and with Lionel, Clara and the Nymphs out for our blood, we needed every advantage we could get.

I ended up being one of the first to arrive for our lesson and I grinned at Darcy as she approached me where I was waiting outside the teaching amphitheatre. It was on the third floor of the east wing in the huge building which looked like an old gothic manor house and a clean smell of mint and sage hung in the air.

"Ah! The princesses have arrived!"

I tried not to cringe as I turned to look at the middle aged professor as she pulled open the door to the classroom and ushered us in. She was wearing a pale blue robe with a white sash over the top of it and had an A.S.S. badge pinned to her lapel. She looked vaguely familiar and it took me a moment to remember that she was the healer who'd let us come and visit Geraldine after she'd been attacked by a Nymph.

"Just Tory and Darcy, please," I muttered as she smiled warmly.

"Of course," she agreed with a dramatic wink. "No preferential treatment here! I'm Mother Dickins and I'll be your healing guide, come, come."

She led us into the room as the rest of the class appeared and we found ourselves at the top of a small amphitheatre set up with seats circling a hospital bed and a table filled with medical instruments at the centre of the space.

Mother Dickens guided us down to a pair of seats in the front row and smiled at us fondly as she moved to the centre of the room to await the rest of the class's arrival.

"Sometimes I can't decide if I prefer the fans or the haters," I muttered to Darcy and she snorted a laugh.

"On first impression, I'd take her over Highspell," she shot back and I had to agree with her there.

My Atlas pinged and I pulled it from my pocket as we waited for the rest of the class to find their seats. My brows rose as I saw who had sent it and I opened it up with a hint of trepidation and a dollop of intrigue.

Seth:

Darius just told me he only sent you the apology video from our play date

530

with your ex. I told him you'd enjoy the action footage even more but he
didn't agree so I'm calling his bluff. Tell me this doesn't get you all hot under
the collar…

A video came through next and I tapped on it with interest as I chewed on my bottom lip. It was an aerial view of Zane's front yard as Darius and the other Heirs strode into a gang stronghold and proceeded to beat the shit out of all of them with their bare hands.

I held my breath as the footage played out, my gaze glued to Darius as he fought like a man possessed, taking down the gangsters one after another before turning his rage on Zane himself. As the row of bikes outside the house exploded in a fireball, I flinched, looking up to find that the class was ready to begin and everyone was looking at me.

Darcy caught my eye, raising a brow and I hurriedly locked my Atlas as I shot an apologetic smile at Mother Dickins. She didn't seem to mind and I had to fight to contain my grin over what I'd just watched.

There might have been something a little wrong with me, but watching Darius go all Dragon on some assholes who actually deserved it had given me fucking tingles. *Dammit.*

"Professor!" Kylie called from the back corner of the room where she was sitting alone with a ring of empty chairs around her. Even Jillian had abandoned her since she'd been outcast and knowing she was entirely isolated like that gave me a smug sense of satisfaction which just wouldn't quit. "Aren't you going to punish Tory for using her Atlas in class?"

"Did someone just fart?" Tyler asked, looking around like he was hunting for the source of the noise as laughter spilled out around the room.

"Is everyone ready to begin?" Mother Dickens asked mildly, looking around with a smile, her gaze skipping over Kylie like she wasn't even there.

Darcy's eyes flashed triumphantly as Kylie dipped her head and I snorted a laugh.

"Yeah, I definitely like her more than Highspell," Darcy whispered to me and I definitely agreed.

"Can anyone tell me how many different spells there are for the healing of a physical wound such as a graze, cut, burn, broken bone, internal bleeding, etcetera?" Mother Dickens called and several hands rose around the circular room.

She pointed to Sofia who beamed before answering. "One."

"Ten points to Ignis," Mother Dickens replied, giving Sofia a short round of applause. Everyone seemed unsure whether or not they should be joining in, so a few people clapped while others looked awkward and before anyone had really done anything, Mother Dickens had moved on. "That's it. *One* spell. And unless you choose to take Advanced Healing in your junior year, that single spell is the only one you will spend time learning in this class. Anyone care to tell me why?"

"Because once you know how to make a bendy bone hard again, you don't need to know anything else?" Tyler called out and several students laughed.

Mother Dickens flicked a finger his way and his laughter fell silent as he was trapped within a silencing bubble before she continued as if he hadn't spoken.

"Because healing is unlike any other form of magic. And almost all Fae agree it is the hardest magic of all. It comes from inside you, from the very *fabric* of your power. Most magic involves creating something from nothing. Your own power is given form by your intent and your ability. However, with healing magic, you need to learn how to tap into the very purest form of that magic where it lives and encourage it to blossom in harmony with the body of the Fae you are treating. Who knows why that is?"

No one seemed to have the answer to that and Mother Dickens smiled kindly before stepping back to the centre of the room where a small trolley stood beside the bed. It held various pieces of medical equipment like scalpels and tweezers and she grabbed a glass beaker from it.

"Why can a Vampire draw magic from blood that is bottled?" she asked, lifting her wrist to her lips as a pair of fangs snapped out.

"Woah," Darcy muttered and I raised a brow too. I was getting damn good at Order spotting and I totally would have pegged her for a cutesy Order like a Pegasus or a Cantrovian Rabbit. Not a damn bloodsucker.

We watched as she bit into her own wrist and decanted a glass of blood before healing the wound over again.

"Is it because our magic lives in our blood?" Diego offered.

"Yes! Ten points to Aer. Our magic is imbued in the very fabric of our DNA. The reason why we feel that hollow sensation in our chests when we're out of power is because our magic lives in our hearts. And our hearts move it around our bodies in our blood. Therefore, even decanted blood holds magic. Which is why Vampires drink it. And why the Nymphs attack the heart with their probes when stealing our power. The probe of a Nymph is, in fact, hollow. If you imagine a giant needle being used to suck the power directly from the heart of the Fae they attack then that gives you some concept of how they steal our magic."

"Could any Fae drink blood to gain magic then?" Diego asked. "Not just Vampires."

"Why not give it a try?" Mother Dickins offered, moving towards him with the glass of her blood held out.

Diego's lip curled back in horror and I had to fight really hard not to laugh as he tried to stammer excuses and she pushed the glass into his hand.

Mother Dickens eyed him sternly and with a hopeless look in our direction, he lifted it to his lips and took a sip.

I swear I threw up in my mouth a bit. I didn't know why it was okay when Vampires did it. In fact, it was freaking hot when Vampires did it half the time. But something about him raising that glass full of her warm blood to his lips had my breakfast swirling in my gut something chronic.

I watched his throat bob as he swallowed and Mother Dickens reached out with a single finger, pressing it to the bottom of the glass to make sure he kept drinking. His throat bobbed again and again as he eyed me wildly like he was asking for help, his skin turning a little green and I decided there was zero chance of me eating my lunch today.

"Ohmagod," Darcy muttered beneath her breath.

"Do you feel powerful?" Mother Dickens asked with a chuckle as she took the decanter back.

Diego shook his head and clapped a hand over his mouth and I shuddered. No fucking way would I have drunk that.

"Vampires seem like the Fae who change the least physically when in their Order form, but that is in fact entirely untrue. There are a lot of arguments that state that a Vampire actually changes their physiology the *most* of all Fae when in our shifted forms. From the outside, it may seem that only our fangs shift." She snapped hers out again to demonstrate, grinning in a way that looked utterly ridiculous on a Vampire before she retracted them once more. "However, *internally,* a Vampire's *entire* digestive system changes when we ingest Fae blood. Our stomachs have a separate chamber to collect the blood away from normal food and water. Then there is an entire network of organs something similar to the intestines, and veins which filter the blood and extract the magic from it. We have chambers in our hearts which can transform the shape of the magic we consume into the shape of the magic we can create with our Element. Meaning we can ingest the blood of a fire Elemental for example and then our bodies can transform that into the magic we use to create water. Other parasitic Orders have their own methods of doing this...but I digress."

The entire class was deathly silent as we listened to her in fascination and I was fast realising that there was still a whole hell of a lot about Fae that I had no fucking idea about.

"So, back to the point of this lesson – and all future lessons you will be having with me this year and next until you master it – standard healing. I'll need a volunteer."

I raised my hand instantly and more than a few people looked at me in surprise. Me and Darcy might have been topping all of our classes (aside from Cardinal Magic now due to Professor Twat Cougar) but I basically never offered up answers or volunteered for shit. But this was different. I needed to learn how to heal. It was vital. And there was no way in hell I was going to waste time in this class by holding back.

Mother Dickens smiled brightly as she beckoned me forward and hopped up onto the bed in the centre of the room as she waited for me.

I strode towards her, working to ignore all the eyes I could feel on me as I came to stand over her on the bed.

"Okay, Tory, I'm going to cut my hand open and I would like you to heal it for me. Place your palm over the wound, close your eyes and bring your magic to the surface of your skin in an utterly formless and *pure* stream of power."

I nodded as she reached for the scalpel on the tray of surgical instruments and she gently nicked the back of her hand so that a bead of blood ran to the surface of her skin.

I released a slow breath and placed my hand over the tiny wound with my eyes closed as I tried to summon my magic in the way she'd instructed. It took a few minutes but eventually, I felt my power nudging against hers. It wasn't like power sharing, it was more like dipping my toes into the top of a wave as it rolled away from me and wondering whether or not I should follow as it retreated.

"Good. Now, you need to meet the flow of my power seamlessly. My blood is here to heal this wound on its own. All I need you to do is add your power to the site of the wound and slowly add more and more of it until you give enough to allow the wound to heal. The reason it's so difficult is because your own magic must remain formless so that it can follow the path of mine. My body *wants* to heal, it's natural, and all you're doing is helping it to do so faster. Some Fae find that they can manage this magic on themselves because they don't need to find balance with another to achieve it, but they never learn to heal someone else."

I nodded, trying to take in everything she'd said while fighting against the urge to tell my magic what to do.

I stood there for a long time, trying to push my magic into hers and slamming against a solid wall time and again. Mother Dickens and the entire class just remained silent as they watched and I tried not to let the pressure of the situation get to me.

I pulled my attention away from the task, exhaling as I let my mind wander over the lyrics of a lullaby instead of trying to force it and all of a sudden, my power connected with hers and slid inside.

My palm warmed and I cracked my eyes open to see a glow of green light emanating beneath it as excitement trickled through me.

The magic came with a rush which made me heady, euphoric even as my power coaxed her body into action faster and faster before the magic suddenly finished its job and burned out.

I pulled my hand back and gasped as I spotted the perfect patch of skin where the cut had been.

"Bravo, Miss Vega!" Mother Dickens cheered and this time the class joined in when she clapped. "Now let's start building up your control until we can be confident you could heal a severed leg!"

Healing magic became our latest addiction and Darcy and I spent every evening that week cutting ourselves and letting the other heal it. Mother Dickens hadn't been lying when she'd said it was hard. Even a paper cut proved really damn difficult to fix most of the time. The magic was so different to anything else we'd learned that it felt like having to unlearn all of it again before we could even begin. Like trying to write in perfect cursive with your left hand when you normally wrote with your right. But we were going to master it. Determined to be able to heal ourselves or anyone we cared about whenever we needed to.

So after spending most of Saturday night awake studying before crashing in Darcy's room somewhere around four am, my alarm woke me and I glanced at the time with a gasp of shock.

I snatched my Atlas from the nightstand as Darcy yanked a pillow over her head and stared at it in horror as I realised it wasn't the alarm. It was the fucking snooze function. And I was already ten minutes late for my run with Darius.

"*Fuck*," I cursed, half falling out of bed and throwing open Darcy's closet as I stripped out of my clothes.

I grabbed a pair of red yoga pants and a pink sports bra, tugging them on and cursing as I realised they clashed horribly. But I didn't have time to change them. I needed to get the hell out of Aer Tower and back over to Ignis House before he left without me or gave up on me.

I took exactly thirty seconds to pee and brush my teeth in Darcy's en-suite and that was it.

I didn't have time to waste on anything else so I kicked my feet into a pair of her sneakers, threw her window open and dove out into the chilly morning breeze.

"Tory!" Darcy shouted irritably as my wings snapped open and the cold air whooshed into the room where she was still trying to sleep.

"Sorry!" I called back. "No time to close it, I'm late!"

I shot across campus as fast as my wings would take me, sped over The Wailing Wood, crossed into Fire Territory and sighed in relief as I spotted him leaning against the glass wall of Ignis House.

I landed a bit too fast and stumbled in my unlaced sneakers before slamming face first into Darius's chest as he lurched forward to catch me.

"Sorry," I laughed as I looked up at him with a grin and he fell still as he helped me steady myself. "What?" I asked, trying to blink the sleep out of my eyes.

"You've never smiled at me like that before," he said in a rough voice, reaching out to brush some tangled strands of black hair out of my face.

"Shut up, I smile at you all the time," I replied as heat touched my cheeks and I tried to run my fingers through my knotty hair.

Really should have taken a minute to brush it dumbass. Let's hope he assumes it's from flying.

"Not like that you don't," Darius countered, a smile tugging at the corner of his mouth too as his gaze ran over me. "You look...cute."

"I don't know what you mean. And I don't do cute."

Darius snorted at me. "You look like you got dressed in the dark..."

"Gee thanks, any more observations, Sherlock?" I asked, rolling my eyes at him but I was still grinning so there wasn't much bite with my snark.

"Well... You're not wearing any makeup."

"I...woke up late, so-"

"I like it," he said, his smile growing as he looked me over. "You look all sleepy and innocent. I could almost imagine you just woke up in my bed."

I was definitely goddamn blushing now and thanks to my lack of bronzer he was clearly well aware of it. The sky was darkening overhead already as we lingered, but I fought the stars for just another moment.

"If I'd spent the night in your bed, there wouldn't have been anything innocent about it," I taunted to get him back onto safer, less mortifying topics of conversation. Like sex.

"As much as I ache for the feeling of your body against mine – and I really fucking do – I think if I was allowed a single cheat against this curse that keeps us apart, I'd just want to be able to hold you in my arms," he replied. "Just to wake up with you there, knowing you were safe."

My heart pounded at his words, but a crash of thunder from the heavens stopped me from replying. I offered him a frustrated smile and turned away from him as I began my run.

Darius followed behind me, far enough back to allow the clouds to scatter again and I tried not to dwell on the disappointment that lingered in me as I upped my pace.

Did I just shoot over here at the speed of light without brushing my hair or putting any makeup on rather than risk missing out on our run?

I shook my head at myself as I tried to figure out what was going on here. I'd been purposefully ignoring this question up until now, but I seriously needed to consider what I was doing. Running with him every morning, messaging him every night. Exchanging little looks whenever we ended up in the same place and thinking about him way too often.

This felt a hell of a lot like the start of something instead of the end of it, but that wasn't possible.

Even if he wanted it. Even if *I* wanted it. We couldn't have it. The damn stars wouldn't allow it.

My mind twisted around and around as we ran on and I cursed the stars out with everything I had.

But why was I doing that? Hadn't I made my mind up about this? Hadn't I already made the only decision I could?

Darius might have been showing me more of himself now, he might have stopped hurting me and be trying to change but had he done enough to make up for all the pain he'd caused me? When I really thought about it, I still wasn't sure. But I *was* sure that he made me smile when he messaged me, that I looked for him whenever I arrived in a room, that he seemed to be trying to do everything he could to set things right. And that I fantasised about him more than I had about any man in all my life. Even Tom Hardy. Even. Tom. Hardy.

Fuck it.

We ran around Aqua Lake, circling the shore and heading on into The Wailing Wood. Darius kept pace behind me in silence like always, but I decided to drop back.

He glanced at me as I started running at his side and I cast furtive looks at him beneath my lashes from time to time as I continued along our route.

Students walked the paths, ensuring we were never actually alone for more than a moment or two but we weren't really with anyone else either. So far, the stars didn't seem to mind.

We kept running all the way through The Wailing Wood to Aer Tower and beyond until we reached the crossroads where the path we usually took headed back towards The Orb and a narrow track led up to the fields which ran along the cliffs above Aer Cove.

I hesitated at the crossroads, glancing at Darius for a moment as the damn butterflies made a return to my stomach before taking the narrow path up onto the cliff top. The path was empty with no one up on the cliff as far as I could see. If we ran up there, we really would be alone.

I glanced back over my shoulder as Darius paused, wondering if he'd dare to follow me. How far was he willing to push the stars on this?

He only hesitated a moment before jogging after me as I ran for the cliff top and a smile tugged at my lips as I put on a spurt of speed. If he wanted to run with me then he'd have to keep up.

My feet pounded up the track and I panted as my muscles burned in protest at the incline.

The sky grew dark overhead as we ran on and I glanced up to see thick storm clouds sweeping overhead despite the fact that there had been nothing but pale blue to see only minutes ago.

Fuck you, stars.

I gritted my teeth and kept going, ignoring a thin track which led back to the centre of campus and ploughing on.

Thunder rumbled overhead, but I pretended I couldn't hear it and kept running.

The clifftop loomed ahead of me and I fixed my gaze on it as the sound of Darius's feet hitting the trail chased me on.

Rain spilled from the clouds, peppering my cheeks and I didn't even bother to shield myself from it.

I kept running until I made it to the very top of the cliff then stopped.

I turned to face Darius as he came to a halt too.

"Do you think this is a good idea?" he asked slowly, looking up at the sky as the shower grew heavier and the rain washed over us. He wasn't shielding himself from it either and his tank was plastered to his skin as the rain pounded down.

"Why should we have to listen to the stars?" I asked, raising my voice to be heard over the rain.

"Because they govern everything," Darius said sadly like there was nothing to be done for it.

"They don't govern me," I growled.

Darius frowned slightly as I took a step closer and thunder crashed so violently that the ground trembled.

I waited to see what he was going to do and his jaw set as he moved towards me too. The rain slammed down over us so hard that I could hardly see through it. My hair was plastered to my back and a shiver ran through me, but I banished it with a flare of fire magic beneath my skin.

Darius stopped inches from me and I looked up at him as water gathered in my lashes and slid over my cheeks. He reached out to cup my jaw in his large hand and the thunder crashed again, lightning forking through the clouds above us as the stars fought to make us part.

"Are you sure about this?" he asked me.

"Fuck fate," I snarled because it was time I owned what was going on between us. "No one gets to pick my future for me. I choose what I want and I want *you.*"

The smile he gave me was bright and fierce and full of an emotion I was afraid to put a name to, but the way he was looking at me lit me up from the inside out.

"Fuck fate," Darius agreed darkly.

His grip tightened and he closed the distance between us, his mouth catching mine in a kiss that made my aching heart throb with the most painful kind of hope. I gripped his shirt in my fists and dragged him closer as I kissed him like the sky might cave in if I didn't, even though it was more likely that it would if I did.

Thunder crashed like an explosion overhead, freezing cold rain pelted down on us and lightning slammed into the ground behind us. But I didn't care. I would gladly take the rage of the heavens in payment for this moment in his arms.

Darius pulled me closer, growling hungrily as his tongue pushed into my mouth and he kissed me savagely, filthily, desperately.

I pushed up onto my tiptoes, my body pressing flush to his as I wound my arms round his neck and my heart pounded to a brutal beat like it wanted to force its way out of my chest and meet with his.

Lightning struck the ground so close that a crackle of electricity danced up my spine. I flinched, but my grip on Darius only tightened.

I dropped the barriers on my magic and Darius's power flooded through me on a tide of ecstasy as we merged our essences together. We were meant to be together like this, it was painted beneath my skin and through my veins, even my magic ached for him and yearned for the caress of his power.

Thunder boomed and I growled in defiance, lifting my hand to cast a shield of solid air magic around us, cutting off the storm completely. Darius's magic flowed alongside mine into the shield, the strength of our will blocking out the will of the stars.

The earth rocked savagely beneath our feet and we fell. Darius kept ahold of me as he hit the ground on his back and I tumbled aside for a moment, but I wasn't going to let them drive us apart. I shoved myself to my knees, crawling over his legs as he pushed up on his elbows and kissed me again.

His fingers slid through my wet hair and his stubble grazed my skin as he kissed me so hard it was bruising, punishing, branding and yet it wasn't enough.

My heart was aching, tears pricking the backs of my eyes as I fought to keep hold of him while the storm hammered against our magic, determined to tear us apart again.

I poured magic from my body to hold the shield as rain slammed against it so hard that the air rattled around us.

Darius dragged me against him and I could feel how much he wanted me in every hard line and ridge of his body.

We were both drenched, covered in mud and utterly incapable of giving one shit about it.

Lightning slammed into the shield and I gasped as it almost buckled, breaking our kiss as I looked up at the black sky above us. More lightning split the clouds apart, striking the ground all around us again and again, making the earth rock even more violently. As a second bolt hit our shield, I almost lost control of it and I could feel my power waning as I threw everything I had into maintaining it.

We only had seconds before it was going to collapse and I reached out to catch Darius's jaw in my grip, looking into his dark eyes with a pang of longing.

"I'm sorry I did this to us," I breathed. I might not have been sure everything between us was fixed yet, but I was beginning to believe it could be and I was starting to think I'd made the wrong choice when I'd been offered it

"It wasn't you," he replied, pain flickering though his gaze.

"It was both of us," I disagreed, tears mixing with the rain on my cheeks.

Before he could say anything else, another bolt of lightning slammed into our shield and shattered it. The force of its power sent us flying and I crashed down on my back in the mud five meters from Darius as he scrambled to his knees.

I pushed myself upright and we looked across the distance separating us as the rain pelted us again and a huge crash of thunder sounded in warning.

If we didn't stop this, we were going to get ourselves killed. And as much as I wanted to defy the heavens and refuse to bow to their commands, I couldn't just abandon Darcy like that.

Agony of a far too familiar nature splintered through my heart as I called on my Order form and flaming wings burst from my skin.

Darius watched me as the rain pelted down on him, his whole posture written with defeat as he waited for me to leave him behind again.

"I'm sorry," I breathed and he nodded just a little to let me know he understood.

I turned and ran from him before he could see me shatter, diving over the edge of the cliff as my wings snapped out and I beat them hard as I flew toward the storm clouds which had come to curse us.

I kept flying hard and fast, diving into the clouds and relishing the satisfying hiss that sounded as my wings turned the rain to steam all around me.

I let the Phoenix fire have me, coating my skin in it and relishing the full power of my Order as I flew into the darkness within the clouds, burning a path right through the centre of them.

I finally burst free, emerging above the storm and looking up at the sky as the last stars lingered in a sea of navy blue on the horizon.

I raised my hands and bared my teeth at them as I unleashed the might of my Order on the heavens themselves, hoping I could curse them just as they had cursed me.

Red and blue flames poured from me in a torrent so hot that the air shimmered all around me.

"You don't get to choose for me!" I screamed.

Thunder rumbled as the storm dissipated beneath me and for a moment I could have sworn the sky was mocking me.

Tears sprung from my eyes and I turned away from the sky and the stars and all the fucking secrets they held as I raced back down to the ground. They may have forced us apart, but my lips still tingled with the memory of Darius's mouth on mine. And if we'd managed to steal that much then I was going to figure out how to claim a whole lot more. I'd been a thief for a long time and if I had to take my destiny from the clutches of the stars while they slept, then I'd figure out a way to do it. I'd never set my mind on something and failed before. And this wouldn't be the first time.

ORION

CHAPTER FORTY THREE

I'd officially been in prison for three months. Three fucking months. And not a single day went by where I didn't think about her. Though I tried. I fought it like the moon battling the pull of the earth so it could remain in the heavy nothingness of the sky. But it was always hardest in the very first moments of the morning, laying in my bunk with the world pressing down on my chest so hard that it felt impossible to breathe.

I played it all over in my mind until it was an endless song of despair on repeat. The day of reckoning had come for us and I'd realised how terribly un-fucking-prepared I'd been to lose her. Even though I should have known all along that I would. She had been the most beautiful fantasy I'd ever known. But a fantasy was all it ever could have been. And that was blindingly obvious now, like the stars had drawn the curtains back on our illusion and laughed at us for ever thinking it was possible to remain in it. But I hadn't let them take us both down. Even though it had cost me twenty five years in the most ruthless prison in Solaria. It was a price I was willing to pay.

The moment I'd arrived here, I'd been placed in Cell Block A and forced to fight for a cell or else end up sleeping in the communal pen at the bottom of the three tiered block. The single good thing that had come from the trial was that I'd had enough energy in my veins to tear the world apart, so I'd beat the living hell out of the occupants of Cell forty eight on the second floor, not bothering to try and win a top floor cell where the clear leaders of this block resided. I wasn't here to try and take over from some long-term convict who'd seek to murder me in my sleep in revenge. I was going to live out my sentence alone, not mixing it with the monsters who lurked between these walls. But that solitary life hadn't been as easy to secure as I'd hoped. Being a loner who could hold their own against any fucker who sought to target me meant I'd inadvertently made myself valuable. I'd caught the eye of a few of the gang leaders who wanted to recruit me to their violent little crews. And I was having none of it.

I sighed heavily, wishing for something to distract me from my thoughts. I rolled onto my side and took my father's diary from the shelf beside my bunk, having hidden it between the pages of a book I'd borrowed from the library. Darius had paid off a guard to get it into the prison for me, but I'd still had no luck with the password that would reveal the writing. Every day, I whispered words to it, going through every member of my family, to simple things like food and drink he'd loved, the name of the raven he'd healed of a broken wing when I was a kid, the names of any friend or colleague of his I could remember. But still the words wouldn't reveal themselves to me. And I was running out of ideas.

A bell rang to announce the start of the morning count and I slid off of the bunk in my boxers, putting the diary away before moving to the cell door and ripping down the sheet I'd hung there. The cells were small with nothing but a toilet and a sink in one corner. A vent at the back of the space allowed the Order Suppressant gas to flow freely through the cells and ensure none of the inmates regained access to their Orders while they slept. Our magic was cut off at all times by the manacles on our wrists, apart from during our daily trip to the Magic Compound which was just a massive concrete yard with a power absorbing fence around it.

My favourite place here had quickly become the Order Yard up top. The fake landscape that had been created to nurture the needs of different Orders was something of a haven for me. It was a place I could hunt freely for blood then sit in a quiet part of the forest, finding real solitude away from the rest of the prisoners. My life was now defined by those moments. Going there felt like waking up from a dark dream I was constantly drowning in. For a short period of time, I fell into the needs of my Order, hunting for the most powerful blood in this place barring the five leaders who I wanted to avoid for obvious reasons.

First, there was Roary Night, a Lion Shifter from Alestria who had an invisible army in Darkmore called the Shades. You never knew who worked for him and who didn't, so avoiding him was difficult because he probably had people watching me at all times. I wasn't sure that he wanted me as a recruit himself, but he was certainly watching to see who I was going to align myself with. I knew his brother outside of this place, but that apparently didn't make us friends by any stretch of the imagination. Not that I was looking to make friends anyway.

Next, there was Ethan Shadowbrook, a Werewolf and leader of the cutthroat Lunar Brotherhood gang in here. He also happened to run my cell block, which meant I was on his radar fucking constantly. His nemesis, Amira Kumari, was the Alpha to the rival Wolf pack of the Oscura Clan. She'd proposed I switch cell blocks into hers and when I'd refused, she assumed I was aligning myself with Shadowbrook. Which meant she avoided me like the plague these days, despite the fact that I had done no such thing. I could have used my connection with Dante Oscura to get in with them, but I didn't see the point. Besides, if I aligned with the Oscuras, I'd then incur the wrath of the Lunar Brotherhood. So fuck that headache.

Next, there was Gustard La Ghast, a flat out psycho who ran a group of unFae fuckers who claimed their power sickeningly by flouting the Way of the Fae and fighting opponents ten on one. So far, I'd had few altercations with him, but his gaze had turned my way a few times when I'd come to blows with people in the Magic Compound. The fact that I was a double Elemental gave away my power level; it was printed on the breast of my jumpsuit for all to see. And my name was known well enough anyway. The Orions had been in league with the Acruxes for centuries. And when Fae tasted power on you, they wanted to take it for their own. Hence my current fucking predicament.

Lastly, there was Sin Wilder. He wasn't a leader of this place in the same way as the others were. He didn't rule intentionally, he ruled because he was a strong motherfucker who was as insane as they came. He didn't have a gang, he was a loner like me, though plenty of people served him to keep him sweet. I hadn't had much contact with him, but I felt we'd formed a mutual understanding. Incubuses were similar to Vampires in ways. As a parasitic Order, they preyed on sexual energy, but their nature was to live in solitude. He'd once broken a Fae's whole hand for sitting opposite me at my empty breakfast table. At least, that's why I assumed he'd done it considering the wink he'd aimed at me after. That was about as far as our interactions had ever gone.

"One-fifty!" Officer Cain barked as he approached. He was a trainee C.O., tasked to assess me in this place. He was a Vampire with short cropped hair and muscles that strained against his uniform. He had a nasty streak that had served me with several hits from his shock baton already. We hadn't liked each other since the moment we'd met. Vampires were instinctually driven to challenge one another when forced into each other's proximity, so his tactic of keeping me down before I could rise was one I had quickly grown tired of.

Without access to my magic or Order, I had no chance against him. But my nature made me hunger for the fight. I couldn't help but push at him. And I ached to show him how powerful I really was. That in the real world, he'd stand zero chance against me. But in here, he was the ringmaster of the Darkmore Circus and I was just a beast in a cage. My claws pulled out, my teeth filed short.

He moved in front of my cell, his storm grey eyes meeting mine as he lifted the scanner and held it to my face. The light flashed over me and the scanner bleeped to say I'd been counted, but Cain didn't leave.

"Sleep well last night, princess-fucker?" he asked in a mocking tone that made my hackles rise. His little nickname for me had me wanting to tear his throat out, fangs or not.

"Better than usual. I dreamed about the Belorian eating that smirk off of your face," I growled. The Belorian was a bio-weapon that had been created to roam the halls at night and ensure that if any inmate managed to escape their cells, they'd make a feast for the monstrous creature who lurked out there. I'd never seen it, but I'd heard its awful shrieking cries in the dead of night. I didn't have to get a look at it to know it was the stuff of nightmares.

"Careful, inmate," Cain snarled, baring his fangs. "Or you might wake up out in the halls tonight yourself. How hard do you think it would be for me to arrange that?"

I glowered at him and he smiled darkly to himself as he moved on to the next cell.

When the count was taken, we were let out of our cells to head to the showers and herded across the retractable bridge that led to the only exit on the bottom floor. A void stretched out ominously beneath it, the pit full of thick, black evermist vapour so anyone who fell into it was subject to excruciating pain the second they lost their footing and breathed it in. And people did fall – or get pushed. And even after a guard pulled them out, they'd be unconscious for six hours during which time they'd suffer the agonising burn of the poison in their blood until they woke.

A hand landed on my shoulder and a warning growl rumbled through me as Ethan Shadowbrook stepped to my side in his boxers, revealing the artwork of tattoos that covered his flesh. His dark blonde hair was shaved in at the sides and flopped loosely over the top of his head, yet to be styled for the day like it usually was. His pretty boy face didn't match the ruthless beast that lived in him. I'd seen him bite a man's head off in the Order Yard in his Werewolf form. Literally. It was the most dangerous place in Darkmore. Unmanned, unguarded, unwatched. Being a Vampire meant I could outrun ninety nine percent of the other inmates though, so I wasn't too worried about myself up there. I couldn't ignore the weekly death toll though.

"Morning, Lance."

"Ethan," I said curtly, shrugging his hand off of my shoulder and he let it slide down my back instead.

The tactile nature of the Wolves always made me uncomfortable. But following my instincts and shoving him away was a dangerous move not worth taking. Most of my block was taken up by his pack and of all the leaders in here, I needed to keep him off my case the most.

"I have a new offer for you," he said with a smirk.

"I told you, I'm not interested," I said firmly.

"And as I told you, *friend*, you won't have a choice eventually. Twenty five years?" He whistled a long note. "You'll be in here longer than me, better to start working yourself up the ranks now."

"I'm not inter-" I started but he cut over me.

"Yeah, yeah, you can't be bought and blah blah blah. But listen…" He slid his arm up and over my shoulders. We were about the same height, but the gesture said he was trying to make me feel like the smaller man. A tactic which was entirely fucking pointless. "I can get you something you can't refuse."

I remained quiet as he eyed me hopefully, expecting me to get curious and beg to know what it was. But he could have been offering me a key to my damn magic blocking cuffs and I still wouldn't have been interested.

"I've got a guy who can help with *this*." His hand landed on the crook of my elbow and he twisted my arm out to look at the Leo marking that bound me to Darius.

I snarled, yanking my arm away and glaring at him to back off.

"I've heard those bonds can be a bitch," he said lightly. "It must be driving you insane not being able to go and guard your little Dragon ward."

Insane didn't even cut it. I had dreams about Darius almost as often as I did about Blue. And they weren't all PG fucking thirteen either. It didn't help that Darius punched himself in the face every time he remembered to be pissed at me. It felt like his actual fist ramming into my cheek. I'd been mid-way through my breakfast the last time and had fallen off my fucking chair. Sin Wilder had thought that was hilarious while everyone else close by scattered like they didn't want to catch my brand of crazy.

Ethan went on as we headed into the showers and I hung my towel up beside his as we stripped off. "I've got a guy who can get these pills, numbs all kinds of emotions. Might be good for all that rage you're carrying too."

I rounded on him with a dark glare. "I don't want your pills. I don't want your friendship. I don't want to be a part of your gang. If I haven't made that clear yet, I must be speaking in tongues. Because it's really fucking obvious to me." I strode past him into the showers, moving to the far end where none of the other inmates had gathered yet. Ethan joined his pack and they started washing each other, lathering up in the soap like it was perfectly acceptable to start an orgy when other people were present.

I didn't waste time, washing and heading out to change into my jumpsuit for the day before making my way to breakfast upstairs. The Mess Hall was a sea of orange jumpsuits and ravenous beasts tucking into their food. The only reason I had any appetite at all these days was to keep myself strong. I spent every hour I could in the gymnasium downstairs to ensure I was strong enough to fight off the other convicts hand to hand. It had taken me four beatings, twelve broken bones and a punctured lung to remind me that I didn't want to die in here.

The first few weeks had been a special kind of hell where I'd had little will to do anything at all. My instincts had been to drink the pain into oblivion. But getting your hands on alcohol here was both difficult and fucking stupid. If I found a way to drink, I'd soon find myself weakened and forced to the bottom of the pecking order. And no matter how bad life was, how bleak and worthless it had all become, I still had my instincts. And fighting for position was always going to be ingrained in me.

I didn't want to dwell on the fact that when I left this place at the ripe old age of fifty one, I'd still be power shamed in society for the rest of my life. I wouldn't be allowed to fight for position. I'd be stripped of everything, forced to live on the outskirts of society. And somehow, I thought that would be even worse than Darkmore Penitentiary. At least in here, I could be Fae.

Beyond these walls, the little life left that awaited me was going to take a fundamental part of my existence away. I guessed I still had twenty four years and nine months to get used to the idea…

As I queued up for my breakfast, the inmate caterers conveniently ran out of fresh food so I was left with the only option of porridge. Again. It happened every day. No matter what time I came here. And I had the stars to thank for that. It was the thing that was causing me the greatest issue in here; I was facing the wrath of the stars for breaking the promise me and Blue had made to do whatever it took to stay together. So bad luck plagued me around every corner. Every move I made to keep myself off the radar was countered by gang leaders showing up at the worst moments, like when I was talking with their rivals or casting magic in the Compound that they could take as a threat. It was why I'd been in so many fights since I'd been here. It was why my lung had been punctured when a punch from a Minotaur asshole in the Compound had me landing on a trident some prick had been casting out of wood behind me. It was why Cain had been assigned to me, the guard I was forced to fight against because of my nature. And in return, I was punished repeatedly for it.

The stars had it in for me, but I couldn't even find it in myself to care. Because I deserved this bad luck for the hurt I was putting Blue through. I could weather it out for her sake. In time, she'd move on from me. Maybe she already had. And all of this hell would be worth it for that. I'd be out of her life for good soon enough. Then slowly forgotten.

A broken heart was the most painful thing I'd ever endured. But I'd never deserved to own the heart of Darcy Vega. And I'd had to give it back in the most brutal way possible. It was the only way I could see to save her. And it would be worth it when she rose to power and led the life she was meant to lead. If my own life had to be a casualty for that to happen, I was more than willing to sacrifice it. Even if I was going to pine for her for the rest of my days. Miss her with the very essence of my soul and ache for her until the world stopped spinning. I would stay here and I would suffer willingly to do what was best for her. And someday she'd understand why.

I sat on an empty table with my porridge, ignoring the looks thrown my way. I was still a subject of discussion around here. My trial had been well televised and the details had spread quickly after I'd arrived. Though most of the rumours had gotten out of hand. To some, I was an outright rapist while to others I was a hero.

Ethan Shadowbrook had decided how he felt about me within a week of me entering Darkmore after I'd beaten the life out of anyone who had made so much as a passing remark about Darcy. He'd announced I was too pretty to be a pervert and it was obvious I was in love with her. I hadn't bothered to try and convince him otherwise. It didn't really matter if people figured out the truth in here, it was the rest of the world that mattered. And apparently his statement was enough for more of the prisoners to start believing it too. Roary Night had walked right up to me and called Darcy a slut just to see my reaction for himself and I'd nearly disembowelled him for it. Which had cost me severely in my flying under the radar tactic. In fact, that tactic had been pretty fucking futile anyway when I thought about it. I'd garnered the attention of the most powerful Fae in this place, including the asshole guard who monitored me. I might as well have had a target painted on my head.

Maybe Ethan's right. Maybe I will have to choose soon enough.

Cain shot to my side in a burst of Vampire speed and I looked up at him with a scowl as he interrupted my train of dark thoughts.

"Guess what, One-Fifty?" he said with a smirk. "Your Mommy's here to see you. Only took her three months to bother."

I stood abruptly, knocking him back a step with my shoulder and he snatched his baton from his hip with a snarl.

"Watch it, One-Fifty," he warned. "If you wanna see your mommy then you'd better behave yourself all the way to visitation."

I released a dry breath of amusement. "I'd rather cut my tongue off and swallow it whole than see my mother, so feel free to tell her that when you ask her to fuck off."

Cain caught my arm with his eyes glittering darkly. "Even better," he growled. "I'll personally make sure you get to see her then."

My jaw clenched as he tugged me across the room to the exit and we were soon heading down the corridors to visitation where my flesh and blood was apparently waiting for me. My gut threaded with razor wire as Cain led me to the security doors, waiting there to make sure I couldn't turn back. The second I was on the other side of them, standing in the corridor full of doors that led to the visitation rooms, all I could think about was Blue.

I'd thought the most painful moment of my life was being dragged from the court room, but I'd been wrong. It was her coming here, seeing the hollowness of her cheeks, the broken look in her eyes, the thinness of her frame. I'd known this would hurt her, but I'd never expected her to fall apart so severely.

The most agonising part was, I hadn't been able to drag her into my arms and give in to the desperate, clawing ache inside me at seeing her. I wanted to fall to my knees and beg for her forgiveness and promise I'd banish that hurt in her eyes if it took me the rest of my life to heal it. Instead, I'd done the only thing I could do and forced her away, broken her harder. I could never show her an ounce of warmth again. Never give her hope for us. Because she needed to move on from me and live the life she was meant to before I'd ever come along to fuck it up.

Three months later, I still couldn't bear to ask Darius whenever he came here if she'd moved on. We had an agreement that he wouldn't mention her unless I asked. But asking could open myself up to a world of destruction I wasn't ready for. Because if Blue *was* moving on, I was going to have to accept that. And despite the fact that it was what I knew needed to happen, I was still terrified of the day when it was confirmed. Because I knew it was going to destroy me.

He'd told me Honey Highspell had taken over my class and how she'd taken a dislike to the twins and that made me want to decapitate her with my bare hands. The woman had been clingy as fuck during our teacher training and apparently she was now spreading lies that we were friends and she had come here to get the 'real' story about me. Of all the teachers in the world to take my position, Elaine couldn't have picked a worse one than her.

I was directed into room nine and steeled myself as I headed inside, wondering why Stella would bother coming here. Maybe to gloat or laugh or to make up some story she wanted to splash all over the press for the fame. I didn't know and frankly I didn't care.

She stood on the other side of the room in a smart navy dress and high heels, her dark hair styled into sharp points just below her chin.

"Lance!" she gasped, rushing forward and putting on a show for the cameras as she wrapped her arms around me and released a dramatic sob against my chest.

I didn't hug her back, in fact, I didn't move at all. "Stella," I said coolly. "What do you want?"

She stepped back then slapped me across the face with the force of her air magic, hard enough to imprint her fucking hand there. Great.

"How could you do such a thing to that poor girl?"

"Be careful what you say," I growled in a deadly tone.

She glanced at the cameras as if that was what I'd meant, flicking her fingers and casting some spell on them before she recomposed herself and slumped dramatically down into a seat at the table.

I slowly lowered myself into the one opposite, figuring I had nothing to lose by listening to the ramblings of my compulsive liar of a mother. Except a healthy few minutes of my life. But I supposed I had plenty of those to spare these days.

"How could you be so stupid?" she hissed, accusation filling her tone and pouring from her eyes. "A *Vega*?" she spat. "Have you lost your mind?"

Of course, Stella cared more about the fact that I'd wanted a Vega than she did about the world believing I'd Dark Coerced a student into my bed. And worse than that, she didn't even question the lie. She believed wholeheartedly that I'd be capable of such a thing. I guessed she thought the apple didn't fall that far from the tree. But little did she know, I was in an orchard on the other side of the fucking planet.

I remained quiet, weighing my options here. I wasn't going to waste my breath telling her the truth. If she and Lionel believed I really had Coerced Darcy then that meant they still thought I wasn't actively going against them. Not that I could do a whole lot in here now, but I would help Darius with anything I could to beat his father.

Stella sighed, dabbing under her eyes at invisible tears. "It's just so hard to see you here like this, bringing shame on the family name."

"Oh come on mother, I brought plenty of shame on the family name before they slapped the shackles on me," I taunted and her eyes sharpened, her teary act forgotten in an instant.

"I see not even prison has changed your attitude, Lance. It hurts me that you'd put your mother through so much stress. The press have been hounding me for interviews, do you have any idea of the pressure I'm under?"

"No, I reckon you lap up all the attention actually," I said, knowing exactly how much she'd enjoy playing the victim in this shitshow. The poor mother who never saw how troubled her son truly was, who'd offered him the world only to have it thrown back in her face. Classic Stella.

"Not at all! I have to try and explain why my boy would be disturbed enough to target a Vega princess," she lamented. "Do you have any idea how humiliating that is? That you, a guardian of Lionel Acrux's son, has been cavorting with a girl they say has an already addled mind-"

"That's a lie," I snapped, my voice ringing harshly through the room. She could say whatever the fuck she wanted about me, but I wasn't going to let her cast shade on Blue. "The newspapers are full of bullshit and you know it."

Stella rolled her eyes. "Whatever makes you feel better, baby boy."

I ground my teeth until they were turning to sawdust in my mouth. "What are you here for?"

"I...I'm trying to talk Lionel around to getting you out of here."

"No," I said dismissively. I didn't want to be transferred to some locked down house where Lionel could keep tabs on me twenty four seven. That was worse than being in this hell.

"Don't be ridiculous!" Stella cried. "You need to be somewhere more accessible to Darius. It is your *duty*."

I tsked, sitting back in my seat. "And what good will I be as a Guardian locked up in some house somewhere?" The idea of seeing Darius more regularly was sorely tempting, but I'd die before I gave my soul to good ol' Uncle Lionel on a silver platter. He'd own me for twenty five years. No fucking thank you.

Stella didn't have an answer for that, instead turning her gaze to the diamond encrusted bracelet around her wrist. "Clara's return has been difficult," she changed the subject so fast I almost got whiplash.

"How is she?" My voice dropped an octave as I thought of my sister, hoping maybe that the shadows had loosened their grip on her.

"She has practically replaced me as Lionel's right hand w-woman," Stella stammered, real tears shining in her eyes. This was what my mother cared about most. Power. And she'd always been willing to do whatever it took to get it. Even if she had to degrade herself in the process.

I cringed, looking away from her. It had been bad enough when she'd fallen into Lionel's bed on a regular basis, let alone Clara. I could hardly stomach it.

"You're just a pawn, Stella," I growled. "You're as dispensable as a fucking snot-ridden tissue. It's been as clear as day to me for years, so excuse me if I don't cry you a river."

"Your father would be furious if he heard you talking to me like that," she exclaimed.

"My father would be ashamed of the woman sitting before me if he was here today," I snapped.

It was arguable that my mother had lost her mind the day my father died. I knew she'd loved him, but whenever she spoke of him these days it was with false adoration and overly sweet recollections that didn't sound anything like the man who'd raised me as a kid. She'd made up some picture of him in her mind and decided it was true. But it wasn't *my* truth.

"Don't you dare try to use him against me," she demanded. "If he was still alive, he would be standing right at my side today as fiercely disappointed in you as I am."

I tried to ignore the dig, but it sliced right through bone and sinew in my chest, leaving a gaping wound behind. My father's love was something I quietly coveted, kept in a sealed box in my mind. It was untouched and unspoiled by everything that had happened since his death. But the possibility that my love of him had been a farce, that he'd been as cruel a Fae as my mother outside of the untarnished childhood memories I had of him was unbearable to consider. *What if I loved a lie?*

"He was a good man," I snarled, determined to believe it. "He would have understood why I was here."

"Oh what do you know? He died when you were a child," she said dismissively. "His blood ran darker than mine."

"I'd happily cut you open to prove yours is as black as tar," I said grimly and her eyes narrowed, anger twisting through her gaze.

"Well that might be impossible soon enough," she said with a smugness about her that made me frown.

"What's that supposed to mean?"

She stood up and I rose with her, stepping around the table as I expected her to try and run away without finishing that sentence. That was the kind of shit she liked to pull to make herself seem important. To leave me here with unanswered questions was one of her favourite kinds of mindfuck.

I caught her arm and felt the shadows stirring beneath my skin, reaching out to try and caress those living beneath hers. I'd kept them locked down since I'd arrived here, knowing that if the guards found out about them, I would be dragged before another judge, forced to spill the truth to the world through Cyclops interrogation and no doubt executed within the same fucking day.

"Well I suppose it doesn't matter if you know," she mused, batting her lashes at me innocently. "It's not like it makes any difference to you in here anyway."

"What doesn't?" I pushed.

"Lionel is drawing closer to finding a very special artifact," she said, her dark eyes brightening with a hunger that had nothing to do with her Order.

My pulse started to race as I waited for her to finish the dramatic pause and give me the answer. This had to be what we'd seen the Nymphs hunting for, why Lionel had tasked them to search the entire kingdom.

"The Imperial Star," she breathed and my heart jolted sickeningly.

"It's a myth," I shot back immediately, but the fervour in her gaze made me doubt it. As if they had some proof I wasn't aware of.

"It's no such thing. It's real. And we're drawing closer to it day by day. Once Lionel has it, he can wield it to ensure him and his loyal subjects are invulnerable to other Fae's power. No one in Solaria will be able to unseat him from the throne. All will fall beneath his unconquerable power." She pulled out of my grip, heading to the door and slipping through it without another word, leaving me with that bomb going off in my face.

The Imperial Star had supposedly fallen from the sky thousands of years ago, found by the first queen to ever sit on the throne of Solaria after she'd seen the blazing arc it had made through the sky as it fell. Once she had it, she started receiving visions in the night, whispers as if from the star itself that told her the ways of dark magic. She was the first Fae to learn it, wielding the powers to her advantage.

Then, from one generation to the next, she passed the star along to her heirs with the knowledge of the magic she'd learned. And when it came into the hands of her great grandson, he discovered another power the star had. It could hold magic within its depths. So before he died, he imbued it with a gift for his successors.

The legend said that the first gift was one of necromancy, giving the possessor the power to speak with the dead. With each passing generation, more gifts were added, the myth growing blurry until the stories told about the gifts became wild and exaggerated.

It was said that no one could wield the star without royal blood, but as the rumours of it spread far and wide, many sought to steal it. So a society was put in place called the Zodiac Guild, made of powerful Fae who were trained in the ways of dark magic to protect the Imperial Star and ensure it never left the hands of the royals. There were a thousand versions of how the star was kept, some saying it was embedded in the hilt of a sword or blade, others a crown, a ring, a chalice. And the legends surrounding its power were even more wild and varied.

There was one thing most versions of the story generally agreed on, and that was that the star held a gift to make its possessor invulnerable to magical attacks. So if it really did exist and Lionel got hold of it, it wasn't just a threat to our world, it would be the end of life as we knew it.

DARIUS

CHAPTER FORTY FOUR

As the school year drew to a close, exam season hit hard. There were Sphinx support groups for anyone suffering from a study addiction, constant Fae on Fae fights breaking out as people snapped under the pressure and a whole host of supposed study enhancing amulets, potions and spells were being sold around campus to any idiot gullible enough to buy them.

I'd retreated to King's Hollow with the other Heirs as often as possible to study away from distractions. Principal Nova had even granted us permission to take rare texts from the Venus Library so that we could avoid the fan clubs lurking in the stacks and I was just glad to be able to effectively avoid Mildred in as many situations as possible.

The only downside to our segregation was that I was seeing a lot less of Roxy than I wanted. I still ran with her every morning and even though I hadn't touched her again since we'd run up onto the cliffs and tried to deny the stars, it felt like a lot had changed between us since that day. She'd been the one to initiate that. And even though I was fully aware that she found it a lot easier to express herself physically than to open up emotionally, I now had every reason to believe she wanted both with me. It was a blessing and a curse.

With Lance gone, there wasn't anyone available to dedicate much time into researching a way out of our Star Crossed status. Especially as he'd been hunting the archives for answers and half the scripts down there were in ancient languages that none of us could read even if we had the spare time to look. So that meant that effectively, any progress that might have been made in undoing the curse on me and Roxy had come to a grinding halt. Not that I was convinced there even *was* a way out of this, but I'd embarked upon a feeling which might just come back to bite me in the ass, rip my heart out and leave me choking on my own heartbreak in the end - hope.

The more I considered the idea that we could find a way out of this, be together somehow, the more my soul ached for it to be true. And no matter how much the rational part of my brain didn't want to give myself to the feeling, I couldn't help it. Every time I learned something new about her, I just came up with more questions to ask. Every time I caught sight of her, I just ached for her even more ferociously than the last time. I was lost to this idea. Lost to *her.* And there really wasn't any coming back from that even if it really was all hopeless.

I'd asked her about the place she'd been living before coming to stay at the academy and she'd given me a half answer, calling it a dive and moving on without elaborating. It was eating at me that I hadn't told her that me and the other Heirs had been there. The bag with her and Darcy's belongings was sitting in the base of my closet, burning at my conscience every time I got clothes out. The problem was, I wanted to get her alone to talk about it with her properly and doing that was impossible. And I also didn't want to sabotage her exams by possibly upsetting her during them. So for now, I had to live with the fact that I was a lying asshole. Then I'd beg forgiveness when I could admit that we'd been there, and offer her the chance to have a full conversation with me about it. I just hoped she wouldn't be too upset by us intruding on her privacy and end up hating me all over again.

I'd been heading home more regularly recently too, wanting to check in with Mom and Xavier as much as I could. Fortunately, Father was away from home more and more often with Clara. He was searching for the Imperial Star but so far, he didn't seem to have had any luck in finding it. We were doing our own research into its location too, desperate to lay our hands on it before him, but as it stood, I hadn't found a single solid lead to follow in our search. I was growing afraid of the day he found it, because he was searching with such fervour that I could only imagine that him getting his hands on it would be disastrous. But unless we figured out how to find it first, I didn't know what we could do about it.

I knew I was going to have to challenge him soon. But now that I didn't have Lance to help me practice dark magic, I couldn't risk trying to progress that training on my own. I still met with Roxy and Darcy to practice with the shadows, but it wasn't the same. Dark magic was linked to the shadows, but the power of the bones and other spells of that nature had little to do with them. And I couldn't risk the girls getting too close to the destructive power of that kind of magic. It was outlawed for a damn good reason. I just wished I had some other way to gain an edge over Father. But if I challenged him before I was ready, the punishments he'd rain down on me would be immeasurable. And his rage would circle out to encompass anyone I cared about too. I couldn't risk his wrath falling on those I loved. When I struck at him, he had to lose. More than that, he had to *die.* And as much as it pained me to admit it, I wasn't strong enough to win that battle yet.

We were finishing up our final exam - written Astrology – and as soon as this was done, it was all over. Then I was staring a long, lonely summer back at

Acrux Manor right in the eye.

To make it worse, I knew I was going to rank last among the other Heirs in a lot of my subjects. Particularly in the written exams. The four of us easily outstripped every other student in every subject in our class, but it was always a battle between us as to which one would steal the top spot. But with Lance so far away from me, the Guardian bond itched and burned with a desperate need which I couldn't fulfil. It was like a gremlin breathing in my ear all the time, its rancid breath dancing beneath my nose and refusing to let me ignore it. Which was distracting to say the least. It had made studying damn difficult and even concentrating on my exams was proving close to impossible.

I was visiting him weekly, but it wasn't anywhere near enough to sate the bond's needs and my grades were going to suffer. Which in turn meant father would be furious. If the other Heirs bested me in too many subjects, rumours would start up about me being the weakest of the four. And though I knew that was bullshit and that the other Heirs would never try and take my position from me, Father hated any kind of scandal to do with weakness.

I sighed beneath my breath as I looked down at my completed paper and pressed my thumb to the bottom of the page to seal it with my magical signature. I caught Professor Prestos's eye to let her know I was done before getting up and striding out of the examination hall which was on the ground floor of Jupiter Hall.

The other Heirs were lingering in the sun outside as they waited for me and even the fact that they'd all finished before me was an indicator of how much I was lagging.

"We're free!" Seth howled as he spotted me and Max whooped in excitement as he shot himself into the air with a blast of air magic in celebration of the exams ending.

I laughed along with them, breathing a sigh of relief as I let the pressure of the exams slide from my shoulders. They were over. And even if I did end up ranking beneath the other Heirs, I'd still out do the rest of our class by a mile. I was capable of performing magic that even seniors couldn't attempt, and I'd proven it repeatedly throughout the practical exams as well as showing it in the written tests. So there was no point in me worrying beyond that.

"I can't wait for the party tonight," Caleb said with a wide smile as he tilted his face back to let the sun kiss his skin.

I shrugged out of my blazer and loosened my tie for good measure as they all began discussing the party which was being thrown at the Shimmering Springs. It was being hosted by Max as Aqua House had won the most points this year and he was insufferably smug about the whole thing.

"I'm taking Grus as my date," Max announced and we all looked at him in surprise.

"She said yes?" Seth asked, cocking his head like an excitable puppy.

"No. She has actually refused me about fifty separate times," Max admitted. "But I'm just going to show up at her door and demand she comes with me. I even got the green light from Dad to date her publicly...assuming

I can pin her down."

"How the hell did you manage that?" I asked. Geraldine Grus and her family were so pro royals that I wouldn't be surprised to find out she had Roxy and Darcy's faces tattooed on her ass cheeks.

"I just told him how good it would look if one the Vegas' biggest advocates suddenly jumped ship and started riding the Heir express instead," Max replied innocently.

"That's not what you want her to be riding," Cal quipped.

"And there's no way she's gonna switch her allegiance," I snorted dismissively.

"I know that…but my dad doesn't." Max grinned so widely that I didn't have it in me to tell him that this plan sounded like a terrible idea which would only blow up in his face once his dad realised that Geraldine was firmly Team Vega. I wasn't going to burst his bubble.

We headed toward The Orb and I trailed at the back of the group as I pulled my Atlas from my pocket and considered messaging Roxy. We generally didn't message each other until the evenings when we were alone in our beds and we could concentrate on our conversations, but the freshmen had had their final practical assessment this morning and I wanted to know how her exams had gone.

Fuck it.

Darius:
What are you wearing?

I wasn't really sure at what point that had become our standard conversation opener, but we hadn't actually started sexting each other. A part of me really fucking wanted to, but every time we got talking, I got so caught up in all the things she said that I never quite went there. And I was afraid the stars would notice if we crossed that line and stop us from messaging each other too. I couldn't risk it. They definitely hadn't liked it when we'd used Caleb to get around their rules and I couldn't bear losing this point of contact with her.

In answer to my message, she sent back a photo with the caption *this is either hilarious or mortifying, but I've had a few tequilas so I'm going to let you decide.* In the photograph, she was standing in the locker rooms at the Pitball stadium, pouting at the camera in an overly suggestive way as she wore my Pitball jersey like a dress.

My gaze roamed over her in it, taking in her knee length academy socks beneath it as well as the crumpled uniform tossed on the bench in the background. I swallowed a lump in my throat. I swear that girl was never hotter than when she wasn't trying to be.

Darius:
You should keep it, it looks better on you.

Roxy:

I'm choosing to take that seriously. I need a new shirt to sleep in anyway, your other one is getting seriously battered.

I frowned as I tried to figure out what she meant by that. Was she saying that she'd been sleeping in one of my shirts? Because it really seemed like she was. And the idea of that made me grin like an idiot.

Darius:

Consider it a gift. Speaking of which, when are you going to go and see your bike?

I knew I was asking her about the bike a bit too often, but it was niggling at me that she still hadn't been to look at it. I couldn't totally figure out why not. If she didn't want it, she could have just told me to take it back, but if she *did* want it then why hadn't she even been to look at the damn thing?

Roxy:

I have a gift for you too, so I guess we can swap...

I fell still as I read her message. Why did she have something for me? It wasn't my birthday. I hadn't done anything to earn a gift. I needed to send her a reply and I didn't know what to say.

"Why are you grinning like someone just offered to suck your cock?" Seth asked me and my head snapped up as I tried to school my features.

"I don't grin," I replied, rolling my eyes at him. "I occasionally smirk. That's about it."

"Well, what are you occasionally smirking about?" Cal asked, shooting forward and snatching my Atlas out of my hand.

I cursed him, but he just laughed as he shot away to read it.

"Why does it feel like you're gonna blush?" Max asked, reaching out to catch my arm as he tried to get a read on my emotions.

"Fuck off. I definitely don't blush."

"Tory's bought him a present," Cal cooed and I groaned as he started typing a reply to her.

"Give that back," I grumbled without bothering to try and snatch it. He was too damn fast for me to catch him if he didn't want me to.

"She's gonna meet us at the parking lot in half an hour," Cal said, tossing my Atlas back at me with a grin.

"Us?" I asked with a sigh as I looked down at the messages he'd sent. He'd called her sugar baby three separate times and ended each message with a row of ridiculous emojis and countless kisses. I considered messaging her again to explain that that wasn't me, but the laughing emojis in her replies made me think she'd guessed.

"Yeah. You need a chaperone, remember," Cal said, pointing up at the sky like the stars were listening in. And they probably were. Sparkly assholes.

"Why does that have to mean you douchebags?" I asked as we started heading for the parking lot.

"Because she's bringing her little Ass Squad too," he replied like it was obvious that we'd want to make this some huge group situation. Though I guessed we didn't have much choice about that as we couldn't be alone.

"Is Grus coming then?" Max asked instantly and Seth groaned dramatically.

"You seriously need to start playing it cool with that girl," he said. "You've totally lost your game when it comes to her."

"Her busty Barrys have him blinded," I joked, happy to move the ribbing off of me and onto Max.

"I can't help it," Max groaned. "She's like my own personal brand of fucking insane, curvaceous, utterly addictive Killblaze."

"You're comparing her to a drug addiction?" Seth scoffed. "The entire world is going to shit. You guys do realise that, right? We've told the whole school – no – the whole *kingdom* to pick between us and the Vegas and now we're off to hang out with them and exchange little gifts and Max is gonna go down on their chief supporter and it'll end up getting leaked to the press and then fuck knows what will happen."

"For someone who's complaining, you sound pretty damn happy about all of that," I commented.

"I'm ecstatic," Seth agreed with a wolfy grin. "The Vegas might be a total pain in our asses, but life has been so much more interesting since they came along."

We all laughed at that and we upped our pace as we headed to the parking lot.

No one mentioned the fact that if we somehow managed to succeed in this little plan to force the stars to reconsider me and Roxy, we'd have a whole new problem. But I guessed none of us wanted to consider the implications involved with me ending up with a Vega. There was no reason to think this would even work yet anyway. And if it ever did...well, we'd just have to figure out how the fuck we were going to cross that bridge when it came to it.

We arrived before Roxy and her friends so we took up positions leaning on the hoods of our expensive cars as Seth switched on the ignition of his white Faezerati and started up some music.

Cal shot away from us and returned within two minutes with a crate of beer and I accepted one as he tossed it to me, trying to join in the conversation as we waited for Roxy to arrive.

A tingle of magic rushed over my skin as her presence set off the detection spell I'd set up around the bike a moment before the elevator doors opened.

Roxy was still wearing my pitball jersey as she stepped out with Darcy and Geraldine who were both stumbling a little from the effects of their celebratory drinks.

"There you are you lickable lobster," Geraldine hiccoughed as she spotted Max, raising the tequila bottle in her hand to point at him.

Max grinned like all his dreams had just come true as she sauntered towards him, dancing to the music playing from Seth's car as if she were in a night club instead of a parking lot.

Roxy snickered at her and Darcy offered me a half smile as she skirted me to snag a beer from the crate before hopping up to sit between Cal and Seth on the hood of his car.

"I finally got you here, then," I said, stepping closer to Roxy as she watched me with interest.

"I'm weak," she admitted. "I knew the moment I looked at the bike I'd be drooling all over it and riding it all day and night. So if I wanted to have any hope of resisting, I had to avoid it."

"Is that how you feel about Darius too?" Seth called and I growled at him halfheartedly. This whole group hang out situation was seriously annoying already. I just wanted her to myself and the way she was looking up at me made me wonder if she was wishing for the same thing.

"Is there a reason you're wearing my Pitball jersey?" I asked as my gaze raked over her.

"We decided to have a private celebration in the Pitball stadium for the end of exams," she replied with a shrug. "We were playing a game of dares and Geraldine thought this was hilarious."

My lips twitched with amusement as I glanced over at Grus who was looking pretty damn pleased with herself. In fact, all of them were staring at us and I cleared my throat as I looked away again, wanting to get some measure of privacy.

I pointed out the bike on the far side of the lot with a jerk of my chin and Roxy fought a smile as she fell into step beside me.

I watched her from the corner of my eyes as she approached the bike. I'd thrown a cover over it, but I was wondering if I should have put a bow on it or something too. But she didn't really seem like a bows kind of girl and I wasn't really a bows kind of guy either.

She bit into her full bottom lip as she stopped before the bike and I reached out to grab the cover as the others all fell still to watch too.

I tried to ignore the feeling of their eyes on us as I focused on her and I whipped the cover off while my gaze stayed trained to her face.

Her eyes widened and her lips parted as she took in everything about it from the bodywork to the engine to the custom navy blue paint job and the diamonds inlaid in the shape of her constellation over the engine cover.

"Holy shit, Darius," she breathed as she stepped closer and ran her fingertip over the diamonds. "How much did this cost you?"

"I'd buy you fifty of them if I knew they'd all make you smile like that," I replied dismissively as I stepped closer to her.

"This is a limited edition, they didn't *make* fifty of them," she scoffed, smacking my arm lightly as her gaze stayed glued to the bike.

"You wanna take her for a ride?"

561

"I've had a bit too much tequila," she pouted.

"You can still start her up."

Her gaze lifted to meet mine and the smile she gave me was all danger as she moved to straddle the bike, placing the key in the ignition.

She started it up and the deep roar of the engine filled the space as she closed her eyes and moaned in appreciation. She looked so freaking hot straddling that thing in my Pitball jersey that I was hard for her instantly and I damn near groaned at the fact that I couldn't touch her.

She revved the engine a few times with a huge smile on her face before finally cutting it and letting our ears recover.

"I know I totally won this and I don't have to thank you for it or anything," she said as she looked up at me.

"But?" I asked.

"Thank you," she replied, her voice rough in a way that made my dick twitch.

The way her gaze kept slipping to my mouth made me wonder if she was aching to close this distance between us as desperately as I was. I reached out slowly and plucked at the edge of my jersey so that it shifted against her skin.

"I like you wearing this," I said as my gaze drifted over my name where it was splashed across her back.

"Is that so?" she asked, her eyes sparkling with amusement.

"Yeah. A bit too much," I admitted and her gaze dropped to my crotch as she bit her damn lip again.

I groaned as I had to force myself to release my grip on the jersey before the stars set her new bike alight or something.

"What did you get for him?" Seth called and I growled at him irritably.

"Can't you just be the kind of chaperones who just shut the fuck up and look at the wall or something?" I snapped.

"No chance," Max called back.

"Don't be a bothersome barracuda," Geraldine chastised and that might have even been worse.

Roxy snorted a laugh and slid off of the bike. Although she claimed to have consumed too much tequila to drive, she didn't seem drunk to me, so I was guessing she'd only had three or four shots.

"It's…a bit of a strange gift," she admitted hesitantly. "And you don't have to accept it if you don't want it."

"Why wouldn't I accept it?" I asked.

"Because it's kind of permanent," she replied.

"You've lost me," I admitted.

"Right. Well, before Orion was…" She cut a glance at her sister apologetically before going on. "Before he *left*, he gave us some books on Phoenixes and our gifts and things we might be able to do with them. And a lot of it seems like speculation or myths or maybe we just haven't figured it all out, but there was also stuff in this old script and – well, long story short,

Darcy figured out that we can imbue things with Phoenix fire. And then I did a bunch of research and managed to find this dusty old book which detailed the way Phoenixes can block out interference from other Orders and Dark Coercion. So basically, I made *this*." She pulled a large, gold bangle from her wrist which looked like a pair of Phoenix wings gilded in flame and spread wide to create a semi circle.

The Dragon in me rose to the surface of my skin as I instantly recognised the value of it and I had to work damn hard not to snatch it and growl *mine* at the whole room.

Roxy's green eyes danced with amusement like she'd read that desire in my gaze and a smile tugged at the corner of my mouth as I waited for her to go on.

"Erm, yeah, it's pretty and all but if you want the magic of it to work then you don't get to keep it. At least, not like this," she said.

"How then?" I asked as she pressed it into my hand and the warmth of the metal made my skin tingle.

"It's called a Phoenix Kiss. And it's basically a conduit," she explained. "I think I can use it to place an ounce of my Phoenix fire beneath your skin. But when I do, the bangle will fuse with your flesh and brand you, kinda like your Guardian mark-"

"It would bind me to you?" I asked.

"No. It will bind you to an ounce of my fire. I'd gift it to you and the brand would keep it safe beneath your skin. There's no link to me involved, I'd be giving up the flame I offer you for good. But without the magic of the brand, the fire would burn too hot and, erm, burn its way back out of you again…painfully." She smiled sheepishly and I barked a laugh.

"Why would he want to risk your fire burning a hole in him just to get a new tattoo?" Seth asked from behind me and I huffed at the interruption. Why couldn't they just pretend they weren't here?

"Because once it's living in you, it will work like it does for me. No one will be able to influence your mind. Not even-"

"This can stop my father from Dark Coercing me?" I breathed as my heart stumbled over itself.

"Yeah. At least, it should do, if I made it right…" Roxy gave me a shy kind of smile which didn't have an ounce of bullshit to it and I didn't think I'd ever been more furious at the fucking stars for stopping me from kissing her than in that moment.

"She made it right," Darcy interrupted. "She must have gone over that magic a thousand times before she was willing to give it to you."

"I just didn't want to do it wrong and accidentally burn a hole in you," Roxy explained, rolling her eyes.

"I would kiss you right now if the stars wouldn't smite us for it," I groaned as excitement surged through me and I had to physically restrain myself.

"Not near the pretty bike," she agreed though her gaze fell to my mouth again like she was sorely tempted. "So, you want me to do it?"

"Fuck yes." I made quick work of ripping my shirt off before offering her my right arm to do whatever she needed to.

The others all drifted closer, forming a circle around us as they watched but I ignored them, my gaze fixed on Roxy as she slid the bangle over my right hand and up my forearm until it was pressed to the bare patch of skin beneath the crook of my elbow.

"Ready?" she asked, looking up at me from beneath her lashes as if she was nervous.

"I trust you."

She leaned forward and pressed her lips to the bangle, her black hair falling all around her and concealing my arm as a deep burn pulsed through the flesh where the metal was touching it.

I grunted as the intensity of the flames picked up and the burn slid beneath my skin and into my veins before rushing through my body like a storm until I could feel it everywhere.

I was well used to all kinds of fire, but I'd never felt anything like it before. It was wild and tempestuous, savage and free. I could taste it on my tongue and hear it crackling in my ears. It was all consuming and never ending and yet somehow utterly euphoric too.

Roxy pulled back, looking up at me hopefully as her flames finally settled beneath my flesh until they weren't overwhelming anymore, just present. They danced with my own Dragon Fire and the sensation almost tickled as they skipped around my body.

"Well gobble my goose and call me Gertrude," Geraldine breathed and as I looked down at my arm.

Where the bangle had been, I found a new tattoo on my flesh instead. A pair of stunning wings which almost seemed to ripple with life as they curved around my arm.

"Did it work?" Roxy asked, her gaze cutting to Max as she stepped back again to put distance between us before the stars intervened.

Max caught my eye before placing a hand on my shoulder and pushing happiness beneath my skin. He fed me enough to make me grin, then I started laughing harder and harder until it felt like I'd never stop. But that wasn't right, I didn't want to laugh, and the moment I decided I didn't, I stopped. It wasn't like putting up mental shields. The Phoenix fire didn't work like that. It simply listened to my command, swept through my body and destroyed Max's magic like it was nothing but tissue paper trying to stay firm before a flamethrower.

I stopped laughing instantly and Max grunted as he pushed more of his magic into me. The others started laughing around me, all except Roxy and Darcy whose own fire burned through his command to protect them from it.

When he finally gave up, I was grinning for a wholly different reason than his power.

"You set me free," I breathed, staring at Roxy like she was some kind of mythical creature given flesh as I tried to figure out what the hell I could ever do to repay this. She'd just answered every wish I'd ever begged of the stars with a smile pulling at her lips and was offering me up a shrug in return like it was nothing.

"I wasn't going to let you head back to that house with that fucking monster for the summer and be at his mercy," she growled fiercely. Protectively. Like I was something she cherished and wanted to protect in the same way I ached to look after her.

I glanced at the others, but I didn't really care that they were here to listen to this. They already knew how I felt about her, so why shouldn't I just say it in front of all of them?

"I already told you I love you, Roxy," I growled and her eyes widened as she looked up at me in surprise. "But now I'm telling you I want you too. Only you. No matter what it takes to make that happen."

"Darius," she breathed, her gaze flickering to the others as they backed away a bit to give us some privacy. I could have thrown a silencing bubble over us, but what was the point? I didn't care if they knew how I felt about her. They were our family and despite all the reasons why they should have been encouraging us to stay apart, they'd been trying to help push us back together. Because when it came down to it, they cared about our happiness more than some fucking throne and I should have realised a lot sooner that that was more important too.

"I get it," I said as I stepped closer to her. So close that we were almost touching. "I understand why you made the choice you did. Forever is a hell of a long time to give to someone you don't trust. But what if forever was just a day? What if all we had was today and the clock was ticking down to midnight? What if giving yourself to me meant just that? Being mine until the strike of midnight. Would you be mine forever then?"

Roxy's eyes widened as she looked up at me, dragging her bottom lip between her teeth as my heart thrashed against my ribs and I could only think of all the reasons she still had to say no.

"Why would you want to spend forever with me after what I did to you?" she asked, and I frowned at her as I tried to understand how she could doubt that. "You were offered true love by the stars and opened your heart up to it willingly, only to have me crush it in my fist. So why would you want a second shot at this at all?"

"Because in my heart I know I deserved the answer you gave me," I replied honestly. "I wasn't worthy of your love then and I'm still not worthy of it now. But if you gave me forever then I'd spend every second of it trying to be."

She was looking at me as if she'd never looked at me before and I had to fight with everything I had to hold her eye and wait for her answer. Because I had to have it. I had to know if she was willing to try and fight this too or if I really had ruined everything beyond all hope.

Her eyes were wide and fearful as she looked up at me, but there was something else in them too. Something strong and fearless and unbroken despite everything she'd been through in her life at my hands and the hands of others.

"Yes," Roxy breathed, her voice shaky like she was afraid of saying it out loud. "I can't keep denying it anymore. I'm sick of denying what my heart wants."

"Forever?" I confirmed, moving so close to her that the sweet scent of her skin enveloped me and I never wanted to exhale again.

"Forever," she agreed, with a finality that weighed on us so heavily that for a moment I couldn't breathe.

"Then we need to figure out a way to force the stars to reconsider," I growled fiercely. I'd been fighting all my life for one thing or another, but there was nothing I'd ever wanted like the girl standing before me. And I was willing to fight for her until my dying breath.

The others started cheering and Roxy laughed as I rolled my eyes at them. The day that I could get her alone again would be an absolute dream compared to this goddamn chaperone hell.

"Gabriel," Roxy said, her eyes shining with hope as she looked up at me. "He can give us a reading."

My heart pounded as she grabbed her Atlas and sent him a message. Knowing she was as sure about this as me was making me feel all kinds of overwhelming emotions. And more than ever, I just wanted to wrap her in my arms and never let her go again.

"He's going to meet us in the amplifying chamber," she announced and I glanced at Caleb, but he was too interested in something Seth was saying to have heard her.

Roxy pushed through our friends and headed for the opening on the far side of the parking lot as she yanked my Pitball shirt off and climbed up onto the ledge in her bra and panties. She tossed a grin over her shoulder at me before she leapt out into the air and her flaming wings blossomed from her back as she took off.

I cursed as she sped away without me, kicking off my shoes and dropping my pants before folding them and clamping them between my teeth as I leapt out after her.

I shifted as I fell and I beat my wings hard as I raced after her while the others whooped and cheered behind us.

"Go yonder on a quest for true and brightest love!" Geraldine cried and I glanced back over my shoulder as she fell sobbing into Max's arms. He didn't seem to mind that at all and I shook my scaly, Dragon head as I charged after Roxy.

That girl was utterly fucking insane. But I had to admit she was growing on me a little.

By the time I landed beside the lake and shifted back, Roxy was already wearing my Pitball jersey again and she headed down into the amplifying chamber without waiting for me to pull my pants back on.

Gabriel was waiting for us in the Elementally balanced dome beneath the lake. I eyed him nervously as he waved a hand for me to take a seat opposite him beside Roxy without looking up from the deck of tarot cards he was shuffling.

"I can't promise that I'll be able to see anything," Gabriel murmured as he cut the deck and held it out for us. "Whenever I've tried to see anything about Elysian Mates before, the stars have been less than helpful."

"We just want to know if there's any chance," Roxy said as she reached out and took a card from him without hesitation. "Just the slightest indication that we could change this..."

Gabriel offered her a sad smile then looked at me. His gaze instantly narrowed and I got the distinct feeling that he was pissed at me.

"What?" I asked.

"You'd better mean this, Darius," he growled. "If you're not going to offer her the world then I'm not going to help you. And if you *ever* hurt her again, I'll hunt you down, cut your balls off and wear them as a necklace."

"Jesus, Gabriel," Roxy muttered and I glanced between them as they seemed to be trying to communicate via eyebrow motions alone. It was weird.

"Am I missing something here?" I asked.

"He's going to find out before the end of summer anyway," Gabriel said with a shrug, his eyes on Roxy. "And he will keep it secret until we're ready for the world to know."

"Know what?" I demanded.

Roxy sighed and cut me a look. "During spring break, we kinda figured out that Gabriel is our half brother."

"What?!" I yelled, my voice echoing off of the glass roof above our heads as Roxy arched an eyebrow at me. "You're a Vega?" I demanded, looking back at Gabriel like I'd never seen him before.

"No. He's our mother's son," Roxy said, rolling her eyes at me like I was being dramatic. "He's also the greatest Seer of our time and we aren't ready for Lionel to find out and paint a big fucking target on his back. So..."

"Shit." I stared between them for a long moment then just swiped my hand over my face. "Anything else you've been hiding from me?"

They exchanged another look and I growled at them.

"Nothing you need to know right now," Gabriel said, closing off the conversation as he offered me the deck. "Just focus on the question you came here to ask."

I blew out a breath and forced myself to calm down, focusing on Roxy beside me. On how much I wanted her to be mine and what I'd be willing to sacrifice to make it so.

As I reached for the cards, one of them sang for me and I pulled it from the deck instantly.

Roxy placed her card down and none of us were surprised to see The Lovers looking up at us. I placed The Devil down beside it and chewed on the inside of my cheek. That wasn't the end of the world, The Devil could represent restriction, but it could also mean addiction and I certainly felt like I was addicted to Roxy Vega.

Gabriel offered her the deck again and she placed The Tower down. Chaos, upheaval, personal transformations…the various meanings behind the card were the kind of things we could expect by trying to change our fate like this.

My next card was The Star which would have been good if it hadn't been reversed. Despair, disconnection…failure, *if* I was reading it right, which I didn't want to believe for a moment I was.

Gabriel's jaw tightened and he offered Roxy the deck again. The Wheel Of Fortune. In reverse. *Fuck.*

Roxy chewed on her bottom lip and Gabriel gathered the deck without commenting, shuffling them again.

"I warned you," Gabriel muttered, seeming irritated by the fall of the cards.

"Did you read an answer there?" I asked.

"Not really," he huffed. "Heartache, chaos, carnage – that's basically the recipe book for your relationship anyway. It's certainly not a yes or no."

Roxy released a breath of laughter as she drew another card. The Lovers.

This time Gabriel got her to draw every card and then he laid them out slowly, muttering beneath his breath as he interpreted them.

"It's not looking good," he admitted as he gathered the deck again.

"So how bad is it?" I demanded, but he just held the deck out for me without answering.

I went through another reading with him in silence and eventually he just huffed and gathered the cards up.

"Nothing," he replied with a sigh. "Nothing concrete anyway. It's like your fate is balancing on a knifepoint and until you tip the balance one way or another, I can't see how this will play out for you. I won't be able to get a better read than that unless something changes. And even then…"

"What?" Roxy demanded.

"I still don't know how much the stars will reveal. I think that this is just something you'll have to try and figure out together."

Gabriel's shoulders dropped and I huffed out a breath as I turned to look at Roxy. Her jaw was set in that stubborn way which I'd come to know as her *don't fuck with me* look. It was actually pretty hot when she didn't have it trained on me.

"I can try scrying," Gabriel offered. "And tealeaves. I'll get a crystal ball too and…"

I frowned at him as he trailed off and fell unnaturally still, his eyes glazing over as he was lost to a vision.

"Fire," Gabriel growled in a voice which echoed off of the walls around us and sent a shiver of dread coursing down my spine. "Everything you know and love burning. Chaos and carnage. The end of all you seek. The rise of The Devil."

"What?" Roxy gasped, reaching for him, but I snatched her hand and yanked it back. I knew better than to touch a Seer when they were lost to a vision.

There was a strange smell in the air like sulphur and the iron tang of blood.

Gabriel gasped and tipped his head back, looking up at the glass dome above our heads.

We looked up too and my heart leapt as I watched the water writhing against the glass until a vision appeared within it.

Roxy's fingers tangled with mine and I grasped her tightly as a ripple of dark energy coated the room.

I watched as the vision showed my father, lifting something wrapped in a red cloth and holding it close to his chest as triumph blazed in his eyes. The stars screamed and cursed as he began to unravel it and I shook my head in a fierce denial as the object he held bent them to his will.

The heavens turned against everyone we cared about. I could only stare as they showed us Lance in prison, silent threats lurking all around him and growing more dangerous the longer he remained behind bars. Darcy fell into a well of sorrow and rage, lashing out against the world without a care for her own fate. The other Heirs and Xavier were swept up in the carnage as bad luck trailed them, keeping them from happiness and putting them in danger time and again.

Meanwhile, luck favoured my father. He wielded the Imperial Star and used it to achieve his plans as he cast my mother aside and rose to the throne with Clara at his side.

A shadow fell over the whole of Solaria as his power grew and grew and even though I knew the visions couldn't predict the movement of the Nymphs, I felt in my heart that it was their influence I was watching.

"Chaos, carnage, despair, *death,*" Gabriel's voice echoed off of the walls and an unbearable coldness slid into my veins. "Unless you find the Imperial Star first."

The vision faded and my gaze slid to Roxy's as she looked back at me with a fearful look in her eyes.

"Is he going to win?" she breathed, tugging her hand back out of mine like she was going to bolt, but I moved to block her escape.

"Wait," I begged, my voice cracking as I tried to get my head around what we'd just seen. "There has to be something we can do. Maybe if-"

"What if it's already too late, Darius?" she demanded. "If his power grows like that he'll kill me. He'll kill Darcy. I can't let that happen."

Gabriel panted as he shook off the effects of the vision. "He hasn't found it yet," he growled. "There's still time. Still things that could change this fate."

"What can we do?" Roxy asked, shifting forward like she wanted to comfort him from the horror of the vision he'd just been subjected to.

"I…" Gabriel concentrated for a moment, his eyes glazing before he huffed in frustration. "The exact answer is hidden from me. But I do know that he's on the right trail and if we don't come up with a way to draw his attention away from his search then we won't have the time to find it before him."

"How long until he finds it?" I demanded and Gabriel's gaze unfocused as he dove back into the swirling current of his visions to try and find our answer.

"Three weeks. *Unless* you manage to stall him," he replied finally. "There are six ways this can go and only two of them will stop him from finding it in that time frame. But the price of stalling him will be high."

"What?" Roxy demanded. "What is the price?"

Gabriel frowned as he hunted for the answer and when he finally gave it, my blood ran cold.

"A royal sacrifice," he announced. "Of the highest kind."

"It won't come to that," I growled, refusing to even consider it. No one would pay in blood and death to stop my father. He'd caused too much pain already.

"That's all I know," Gabriel said, dropping his head as he fought against the weakness brought on by the intensity of the vision.

"Then we'll find the star before him," I announced. "Three weeks is plenty of time to screw with his fate."

Roxy watched me with wide eyes as I got to my feet and strode from the room, leaving her to care for her brother.

It tore at me to abandon her after I'd just sworn to fight for her, but I had to figure out how to find that fucking Imperial Star before my father did. Because as much as I'd been raised to hate and fear the blood of the royals, I knew now that the real monster in this kingdom had always been much closer to home.

And I refused to let him hurt Roxy or her sister while I still drew breath.

DARCY

CHAPTER FORTY FIVE

I trudged back to Aer Tower in my filthy Pitball uniform, my mood somewhere between misery and despair. It was the last day of term and we'd lost the final Pitball game of the season, meaning Neversky Academy had won the tournament.

The past three months in training had been abysmal. Professor Prestos had taken over coaching, but between her busy social life and the Elemental Combat classes she'd taken over from Orion too, she was finding it hard to cope. It made me realise how much of his time he'd given to this school, how he'd actually been more dedicated than half the staff here. Our training had fallen apart without him, and with me and Darius constantly distracted, it hadn't helped in our final match. We'd only been two points down, but it was still a sore loss for the school. Especially when they hadn't lost out on winning the tournament cup in years.

I didn't even remain at the stadium to get changed, I was heading back to my room for the longest shower in the history of Fae kind then I'd pack for tomorrow. Tory and I would be heading to the Palace of Souls for the summer. We'd passed our exams with flying colours, but even that wasn't enough to soothe the eternal, crushing ache in my heart over Orion.

My friends had said it would get easier, but if anything it was getting worse. A bitter reality was setting into me now and part of me just wanted to curl into a ball and hide away for the summer. But I couldn't do that. We had to try and find the Imperial Star before Lionel did. And with nothing to go on except a few ancient legends we'd dug up in the archives, I wasn't sure how we were going to pull it off.

Darius had Xavier spying on his family as much as possible and Gabriel was spending hours every day forecasting to try and get a glimpse of where the star was hidden. So far, they'd had little luck. But we wouldn't give up. Tomorrow, Tory and I were going to hunt through the library at the palace. Geraldine said there were whole tomes about the star in there, so the sooner we could start looking for more clues, the better.

I kicked off my shoes as I arrived at my room, locking the door and stripping off as I headed into the shower.

After a couple of hours, my bag was packed and I sat on my bed in some black shorts and a grey sports bra as I thumbed through a book about the ancient royals, the heat in the air growing stifling. I cast frost over the ceiling and cooled the air to shake off the summer warmth, listening to the laughter of students out in the halls as they readied for tonight's celebrations.

My Atlas pinged and I checked my messages, finding a couple from Tory after I'd missed dinner. She hounded me at every meal to make sure I was eating and I loved that she cared to make sure I didn't fade away. It had been a while since I'd skipped a meal, but tonight held a weight to it that I couldn't escape. It was the last day of our first year at Zodiac and I should have been celebrating with Orion. I should have been thanking him for everything he did to help me get here. Instead, we were thousands of miles apart and he was stuck underground in some miserable hellhole. I'd kept to my word and hadn't written to him, but even so, Darius had made no progress in encouraging him to agree to the appeal. Which made me truly fear he was never going to.

I spent the rest of the evening reading everything I could about the royals, but found no clues to the star's whereabouts. When I finally finished the book, it was gone midnight and my mind was on overdrive with worry. *We really have to find something tangible to go on soon or we're screwed.*

I moved to the window, cracking it open to let some air in and my gaze snagged on a light in The Wailing Wood. It was in the direction of King's Hollow, but it was too dark to tell exactly where it was coming from. I guessed the Heirs were still up partying.

My mind played tricks on me as shadows danced down on the grass below and I shivered as I moved away from the glass and dropped onto my bed.

I picked up my Atlas, scrolling through FaeBook posts as I tried to stop the quiet from dragging me back to the dark thoughts which were always hovering on the edges of my mind. A post about Orion made my stomach knot and I couldn't help but pause on it.

Marguerite Helebor:
Three reasons why I believe Professor Orion would never Dark Coerce a Vega into screwing him...
1. Er, why would he bother? The girl has blue hair and talks to ravens. Unless he's got a thing for freaks, there's no way he'd pick her of all students to risk his reputation on. #hehadbetteroptions
2. He wouldn't need to Coerce her to do shit. She was always drooling over him in class (according to a reliable source). I bet she begged to suck his

dick on a daily basis. #teacherspet #ibetshegotonherkneesforit
3. See number 1
Conclusion: Darcy Vega can perform Dark Coercion! Isn't it obvious?
She forced Professor Orion to screw her then made him take the
blame for it in court. We need to watch our backs everyone! Even
Professor Highspell agrees. #darkvegas #likefatherlikedaughter
#theressomethingnotrightaboutthem

I tossed my Atlas down beside me with a growl. *Now why did I torture myself by reading that?*

Marguerite only had a couple of brain cells, but she'd worked real hard at rubbing them together to come up with that vicious little post. It had fifty likes already and I couldn't believe people were actually lapping up her bullshit. It was bad enough that they swallowed Orion's story, now they were making up their own too.

I rolled onto my side with a huff, taking comfort in the fact that I at least wouldn't have to see her or any more of the bitch squad for the whole summer.

My Atlas pinged and I picked it up again, my heart beating out of tune at the sight of a group message from Gabriel to me and Tory.

Gabriel:
The love of my life just went into labour! I'm heading home. Wish me luck!
P.S.
I'll come to the palace soon and help you search for the Imperial Star. If I
see *anything in the meantime, I'll let you know.*

The biggest, most genuine smile I'd worn in ages spread across my face and i sat up in bed as I tapped out a reply, sending him a string of happy emojis at the end of it. I couldn't wait to meet my little niece or nephew. It was crazy to think we had a family, one that was actively growing too. After meeting Gabriel's family a few months back, I couldn't wait to have them over to the palace in the summer. Especially now there was going to be a whole new little life to meet. *Oooh and have cuddles with.* I shot Tory a quick message though she hadn't replied to Gabriel's yet so I guessed she was asleep.

Darcy:
Dibs on first cuddles!

My smile wouldn't go away and it was so good to actually feel *happy* for once. I gave up on trying to settle down and slid out of bed, kicking my sneakers on and heading out the door, not bothering to bring my Atlas as I didn't have any pockets. I'd go for a walk to expend this wild energy and try to calm my mind enough to get some sleep. Though I couldn't see it happening anytime soon. On top of this exciting news, I also had a pile of books to work through on my desk that might glean us some information about the Imperial Star. If I couldn't sleep then I could see a long night ahead of me searching through them. But right now, I just needed some air.

I soon stepped out onto the plain of grass beyond Aer Tower and headed across it into The Wailing Wood. I moved into the glowing orange light of one lamppost to the next, wondering if I should swing by The Orb to see if any of the A.S.S. were hanging out there. A lot of people had turned in for the night or headed home already. It was strange to think of this place sitting empty all summer and I was sure I was going to miss it.

The air was hot against my skin as I wound deeper into the forest, taking the long route that circled back around toward The Orb.

Footsteps padded somewhere along the path behind me and I turned to look back, finding no one there. I tried not to let that unsettle me, but found myself upping my pace when the footsteps sounded again then the leaves rustled somewhere above me.

It's just Fae in their Order forms.

But for some reason, it didn't feel like that. It felt like I was being watched….hunted.

I upped my pace and readied magic in my palms just in case and the footsteps sounded behind me once more.

I glanced back over my shoulder, casting fire into my palms and hunting the darkened path with my heart pounding harder against my chest. I'd travelled a fair distance from the last lamppost and this corner of the track was thickly shrouded in shadow.

Maybe I should fly out of here.

A bone curdling rattle started up right behind me and fear slashed through my heart as I swung around. Hands grabbed me and a scream tore from my lungs, echoing up into the night before magic pressed into my lungs and stopped the sound dead, trapping it in my chest and cutting off any chance of anyone knowing I was in trouble.

TORY

CHAPTER FORTY SIX ·

Igrowled at the world as my Atlas rang, drawing me from sleep and I tried to hide beneath my pillow in an attempt to ignore it.

Who the fuck is calling me now?

The moment the call ended, another one started up and a tingle of unease ran through me as I wondered who the hell would call me so insistently in the middle of the night.

I shoved the pillow off and reached for my Atlas, squinting at the screen and frowning in confusion as I spotted Diego's name on the caller ID.

"If you seriously think I'd be up for a midnight booty call with you, dude, you are abso-fucking-lutely mistaken," I snarled as I answered.

"Tory! Thank fuck, I've been trying to get hold of you. My mother just added another memory to the soul web. And it's bad. *Really* bad," his panicked tone made my heart leap and dread raced through me as I wondered whether Lionel had found the star. Were we already fucked? Gabriel had said we had three weeks to fuck up his plans and I'd wanted to believe we had all of that time to beat him to the Imperial Star, but maybe I'd been fucking deluded to trust in that.

"Just spit it out," I snapped as I pushed out of my bed and looked out of my window at the pitch black sky coated in a blanket of stars.

"Lionel took Darcy."

I fell still, every inch of blood in my skin freezing over as a wave of cold so intense it blinded me as it raced through my body. My ears were ringing, my heart pounding and my grip on my Atlas tightening like it was a lifeline, the only thing stopping my bones from turning to jelly and me collapsing into a heap of nothing on the floor.

"Where are they?" I demanded.

"I'm not totally sure. But I *think* they're at the Orions' house. I've only been there once but I think I recognised the room they were in," his shaky reply came and the fear in his voice was enough to banish mine.

True Fae didn't let fear stop them. My sister needed me and that was all that mattered. Terror would consume me if I let it. But I wouldn't let it. I hardened the walls around my emotions, locked down the paralysing fear deep inside my heart where Lionel Acrux couldn't touch it and sprung into motion.

"Tell me everything," I demanded as I ran to my closet and ripped it open, dragging on a pair of black yoga pants beneath Darius's Pitball jersey before he'd even gotten a word out.

"They have her in a huge dining hall with a roaring fire in the grate. Lionel and Clara are there. Darcy's tied to a chair and they're torturing her for information about the item they're looking for. They know you've been searching for it too-"

"Where are you?" I snapped as I kicked on my sneakers and pushed my door open.

"I've just left Aer Tower, I was going to come and break down your door if you didn't answer and-"

"Go back in and go to her room," I commanded. "See if there's anything there to confirm where they've taken her."

"What are you doing?" he demanded.

"Getting reinforcements. I'll come to you when I'm done." I cut the call and pounded my way up the stairs to Darius's room on the top floor.

I hammered my fist against his door and when he didn't answer right away, I tried the handle. The door was locked but magical locks had been on our Cardinal Magic exam and we'd gone above and beyond in our studies to master them.

I had to force myself to concentrate as my fear for Darcy distracted me, but on the third attempt, I managed to find the weak point in the lock he'd cast and forced my power into it, breaking the spell apart and shoving the door open in the same breath.

The scent of smoke and cedar washed over me as I stepped into the dark space, but one look at the freshly made bed let me know he wasn't here.

Fuck!

I dialled his number as I kicked his door closed behind me, but he didn't answer, his electronic voicemail bitch giving me the *please leave a message* bullshit. I did it because I needed his help and I didn't have time to call again.

"Darius, I...need you." *Good thing that doesn't sound utterly pathetic.* But for Darcy, I'd happily swallow my pride. "Lionel has taken Darcy. He's got her at the Orions' house and they're torturing her for information on our search for the Imperial Star. If you get this..." I huffed out a breath and forced my own insecurities and pride deep down into an icy pit of nothingness. "Please just come. I can't lose her. I just, *can't.*"

I cut the call, ran into his bathroom and destroyed the panel beneath the Jacuzzi bath with a blast of fire magic before grabbing a pouch of stardust from his hidden stash.

I ripped his Pitball jersey off and dropped it on the floor so that I was just wearing the crop top I had on beneath it and I could coax my wings from my flaming skin. I shoved Darius's window open and spread my wings as I dove out into the night, racing across the sky towards Aer Tower.

I flew faster than I'd ever flown before, a sharp pain twisting my heart with the certainty that my other half was in trouble. Fuck knew how long they'd already had her. What they'd done to her. Or what they were doing right now. The panic I was fighting to contain was breaking free of the dam.

I could cope with anything in this world but this. Not her. If anything happened to Darcy then all the light in the world would be stolen from me.

She was the light to my dark, the joy to my pain. I loved her more than life itself and there was no life to be had at all if I didn't have her by my side.

I made it to her window and ripped it open, causing Diego to shriek in fright as I leapt inside. Her room was a mess but it often was these days. She alternated between cleaning it like a woman possessed and living like some kind of wild bear with a hoard. I guessed sometimes she didn't care about it enough to tidy it now that Orion was gone and others she cleaned frantically just to have something to achieve which didn't involve him. My heart twisted to think of the pain she'd been in since his arrest. And now that motherfucking Dragon bastard had his claws in her too.

But I'd die before I'd let him take her from me.

"Is there anything here?" I asked as Diego recovered from his shock.

"Her Atlas," he pointed out. "And her door was unlocked."

"Show me the memory," I demanded, holding my hand out to him and he took it instantly.

I gasped as he dragged me down into the shadows at his side and a white cloud appeared out of the darkness, his shared memories appearing before me from the haze.

I was looking through the eyes of a woman as she walked down a long corridor in a gothic looking house, her high heels clipping along the wooden floorboards.

She approached a door but before it could open, a piercing scream cut through the air and pain tore through my chest as I recognised Darcy's voice.

The woman pushed the door open as the scream faded and the fear in me turned to agony which ripped me in two as I spotted Darcy tied to a chair in the centre of the room.

Lionel stood before her, his arms folded as he asked her a question and his voice filled with a vivid kind of excitement.

"Tell me where it's hidden," he growled.

"Fuck you," Darcy hissed, spitting blood from her lips as Clara cackled with glee.

"Again, Daddy?" she asked eagerly.

Lionel nodded firmly and she reached out to place her hands on either side of Darcy's temples as thick shadows poured from her palms.

Darcy screamed so loud it cut through me, tearing my soul to shreds and making my vision blur as I was filled with rage and the desperate need to help her.

I hardly even noticed as Diego dragged us back to reality and the shadow world faded.

"You're sure that's the Orions' house?" I demanded as I blinked back tears and locked Diego in my gaze.

"Yes," he breathed.

"I've never been there before. So you're going to have to take me."

"How?" he gasped, his eyes widening with fear.

"I've got stardust and I can get us off campus to use it."

I didn't wait for his reply before throwing a net of air magic around him and leaping back out of the window as I yanked him after me. I flew for the gap in the magical boundary surrounding campus as fast as I could, dragging Diego along with me as he screamed from within the bubble of air magic I was using to transport him. But I didn't have time to waste waiting for him to walk there, so I couldn't bring myself to care.

I dropped out of the sky beside the barrier, placing Diego down on his feet beside me as he panted fearfully.

"Come on," I commanded as I led the way through the gap in the defences to the outside world.

I dialled Darius again one last time, but my Atlas died before the second ring sounded. I cursed it and yanked the stardust from my pocket instead, handing it to Diego.

"I've never used stardust before," he breathed and the terror in his eyes looked almost set to consume him.

"It's easy. Just toss it over us and focus on the place we need to go," I replied.

"Okay…" Diego took a pinch of stardust from the pouch, released a shaky breath and then tossed it over our heads.

The stars twisted and whirled all around us as we were swept up into their embrace and I could only hope that we'd get there before it was too late.

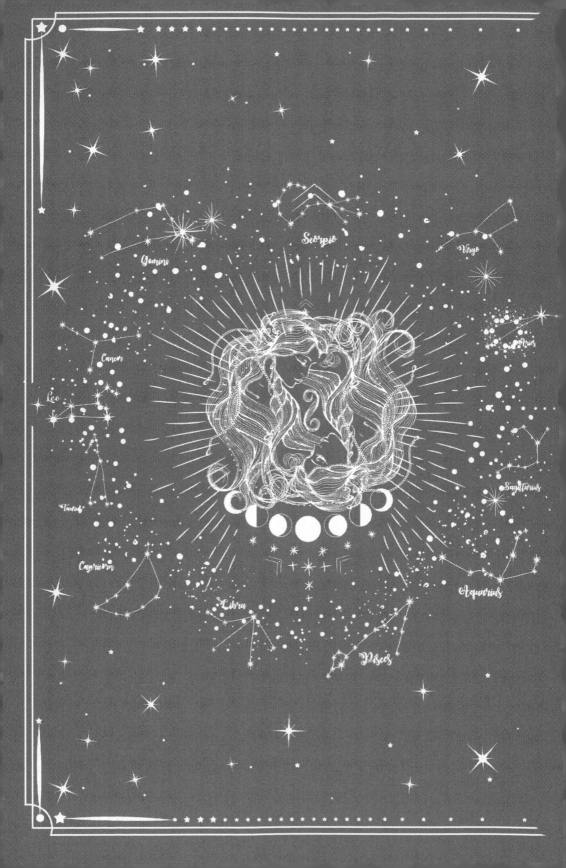

DARCY

CHAPTER FORTY SEVEN

I was trapped in a net, writhing against my binds as my captor cast powerful magic to keep me in place. Fear sliced into my veins as I cast fire in my palms, trying to burn my way free.

"Let me go!" I screamed just as I was dumped on a hard floor and my back impacted with it.

The vines uncoiled suddenly and I gazed up at the Heirs in the centre of the lounge in King's Hollow. Seth, Caleb and Max all waved their fingers at me which had been cast in an illusion to look like Nymph probes, laughing their asses of.

Relief flooded me, but anger quickly rose in its place.

"That's not funny," I growled, getting to my feet and extinguishing the fire in my palms, though I had a good mind to burn their asses in revenge.

Darius was in the corner of the room, shaking his head at them as he sipped on a beer.

"I told them it was stupid," he said.

"It was fucking hilarious." Seth fell down onto the couch, howling a laugh.

"You screamed like a Pegasus had rammed its horn up your ass." Caleb fell down beside him, grinning from ear to ear.

"Well you'd know." I planted my hands on my hips, raising my brows at him and the Vampire frowned for a second before falling apart again. Seth nuzzled in against him as they lost their shit and Max approached me, offering me a bottle of something called Rainbow Juice.

"Have a drink with us, little Vega," he said, conjuring a glass out of ice and pouring the liquid into it. It somehow stayed multi-coloured, glimmering enticingly.

"What is that stuff?" I took the cup, sniffing it and a heavenly sweetness filled my nose.

"It makes you giddy," Max said, his eyes brightening. "And you definitely look like you need a laugh."

"Where's Roxy?" Darius asked as he dropped into an armchair and hooked his Atlas off of a charging dock, switching it on.

"She's not attached to my hip at all times," I teased. "She went to bed." I took a sip of the juice and realised I'd actually just willingly drunk something an Heir had given me. *Holy shit, when did I start trusting Max Rigel?*

Seth and Caleb's laughter seemed to be wearing off just as a rush of energy poured into my limbs and a laugh exploded from my lips. Max immediately brushed his hand over my arm, trying to drink in the feeling and I didn't bother to put my barriers up as he fed on my happiness.

"Well that makes a change," Max said, a crease in his brow. "Any time I've gotten a reading on you these past few months, all I've felt is sad."

"So sad," I agreed with a wild laugh, placing the Rainbow Juice down on the coffee table as more laughter racked through me.

"Hey, let's prank someone else, what about that hat boy?" Caleb suggested excitedly, bouncing in his seat and Seth started yipping like a puppy beside him. The two of them were weirdly cute sometimes.

"His name's Diego," I said, still laughing. "Ohmagod his hat is so weird." I clutched my belly as another wave of mirth took hold of me and Max offered me the bottle again. I waved my hand to decline as tears rolled down my cheeks. "His – hat – is – knitted – to -his – abuela's – soul," I choked out and Seth howled with laughter, jumping up and grabbing the Rainbow Juice from Max before he could drink any.

Caleb shot forward, snatching it from him and downing a mouthful while Seth shoved him in the chest as he tried to get it back.

"Fuck," Darius gasped and we all rounded on him, my mirth finally subsiding as the dark expression on his face drove a dagger into my heart. He held his Atlas to his ear, clearly listening to something and Caleb suddenly planted the bottle down, shooting forward as he heard it too.

"What's going on?" I asked, worry burning a hole right through me.

"She's in trouble," Caleb burst out laughing then slammed a hand to his mouth as he tried to swallow back the effects of the juice.

"What do you mean she's in trouble? Who is?"

Darius stood suddenly, heat emanating off of his skin. "Roxy thinks my father has kidnapped you."

"What?" I gasped. "Why - *how*?"

"I don't know. But she's gone to the Orions' house to find you. I tried calling back but the line is dead."

Panic raced through my limbs and froze me solid for a full second.

"Fuck – no – have to help her." Caleb clutched his stomach as he laughed, waving a hand at me in apology. "It's not funny – can't stop."

Darius slammed a hand to his back and magic flared out from it in a wave of green. Caleb choked for a moment then drew in a breath as he was healed of the effects of the Rainbow Juice.

"Thanks," he rasped, his expression turning deadly serious in an instant.

I turned towards the window, and unleashing my wings from my back as fear blinded me.

"Darius, I need stardust," I begged, terror making Phoenix fire flood through my veins. I needed to get to her. Right now. "We have to go after her!" I yelled, but I realised I didn't need to as Caleb rushed to my side in a blur and the other Heirs moved into action.

"Meet at the perimeter," Darius barked, marching to a chest at the side of the room and grabbing a bulging backpack out of it before tossing it to Max as he and Seth ran for the door. Caleb shoved the window open and dove out of it without a word, his brow taut with worry.

"Everyone's coming?" I breathed in surprise as I climbed onto the window ledge.

"Of course they are," Darius growled firmly and my heart squeezed at that.

I leapt from the window, unleashing my wings and soaring over The Wailing Wood with my pulse drumming against my temples.

I'm coming, Tor. Hold on.

Seth's howl came from below and I spotted him in his huge white Wolf form carrying Max on his back as they raced beneath the trees. I beat my wings and a roar overhead made me flinch as Darius's golden Dragon form swept overhead. The wind rushed over me, dragging me on and I outpaced him once more, sailing over Earth Territory and landing close to the gap Orion had left in the fence.

Panic chewed me up from the inside, but I had to keep a level head.

What does Lionel want with her? Why would she think I'm there?

Caleb stood waiting for us, combing his fingers anxiously through his hair and Darius landed with a heavy thump beside him.

As I put my wings away, the thundering of heavy paws tore along the ground behind us and I turned as Seth and Max arrived. Seth shifted the same moment Darius did and Max tossed them clothes from the pack he was carrying like they'd done this routine a thousand times before. The moment they were dressed, Max took a pouch of stardust from the bag and we headed through the gap in the fence without a word needing to pass between us.

Seth's hands brushed over my arms as he followed me through, a whine leaving his throat. "She'll be okay. We'll get her back."

I nodded, steeling myself as Max moved through the fence and Darius grabbed the pouch from him.

"Stay together," Darius ordered as he took a pinch of the dust into his hand and we all crowded closer. "My father is not to be underestimated."

"What if this is a trap?" I breathed, my chest compressing, the terror for my sister making it hard to draw in air.

"Then we'll be as ready as we can be," Caleb said grimly. "Together, we're a force to be reckoned with."

I nodded, taking comfort in the fact that they were all blindly charging into battle with me. At least, that's what this felt like. As if a whole war was waiting beyond the stardust Darius was about to throw.

He tossed it into the air and I readied magic in my palms, unsure what to expect, but I'd face anything to get my sister back.

TORY

CHAPTER FORTY EIGHT

We crept across the grounds of the Orion Manor, tucked within a concealment spell which I'd managed to construct to help hide us in the shadows. It wasn't good enough to hold up against direct scrutiny but on the balmy summer night, it was more than enough to conceal us in the dark garden.

Diego was keeping so close to me that he kept bumping against my back and I was half tempted to tell him to just wait outside. He'd been doing a lot better in class, but he was nowhere near the strongest group in our Elemental Combat lessons and anyone we came across here would easily outmatch him.

They'd outmatch me too technically if we were talking skill, but if it came to it, I wasn't going to go for subtle. One of the first lessons I'd learned in our combat class was that might outweighed skill a lot of the time. Lionel and Clara were obviously powerful enough that that wouldn't help me much, but if Diego's family or any other Fae were here, I was willing to bet I could pack a strong enough punch to win out against them.

The building was mostly in darkness but to the east of the house, light shone through the curtains covering some of the lower windows.

My instincts told me that that was where they must be, but I wasn't going to head straight into it.

"I need you to cause a distraction," I hissed at Diego. I had a silencing bubble covering us but it didn't feel right to speak at a normal level.

"Like what?" he asked, his eyes widening fearfully.

"I'll start a fire and once I'm around the far side of the house, you use your air magic to coax the flames into action until they're big enough to draw attention, then just run for it. Daddy Acrux and his shadow bitch will come running, I'll grab Darcy and then we'll fly the fuck out of here. We should split the stardust so you can use your portion to escape back to the academy as soon as the fire has taken root."

"What if it goes wrong and you get caught?" he hissed anxiously.

"Then you still need to get back to the academy and you need to find Darius and get him to come save my ass." My gut twisted at the idea of dragging Darius into this. If he turned up and showed his hand in trying to help us against his father, I wasn't sure what Lionel might do to him in retaliation. I was also pretty damn surprised that I knew for a fact that he would come anyway. A hell of a lot had happened this year between us but I had to admit that right now, when it came down to the shit hitting the fan, I knew he'd be by my side if he could. Which meant I trusted him. And there weren't many more surprising things than that.

"Are you sure?" Diego asked, catching my hand to stop me from leaving.

"My sister is in there, Diego," I growled. "Even death itself couldn't stop me from going to help her."

"Okay," he agreed and before I knew what was happening, he'd thrown his arms around me. "Good luck," he breathed.

"You too." I accepted the bag of stardust from him once he'd taken his portion and turned my attention to creating a small blaze at the far corner of the house.

Diego took control of stoking the flames with his air magic and I slipped away from him as I skirted the huge building.

Half way along the wall, I found an open window and snuck in, dropping down into an empty bathtub as I paused to listen for sounds within the building.

All was quiet and my pulse was steady as I crept towards the door in the dark. I'd done more than my fair share of thieving to be confident in how to move through a house undetected. House burglaries hadn't really been my thing, but people often forgot that the simplest way to steal a bike was to steal the keys. And if people were dumb enough to leave their keys hanging on a hook by the door while they left their windows open, then they really were asking for me to come in and take them.

I inched the door open and slipped out into the corridor just as Darcy screamed from somewhere within the house.

I heard that sound like a punch to the heart and I started running towards it without hesitation.

My silencing bubble concealed my footsteps as I sped along the empty hallway but as I drew closer to the source of the screams, I forced myself to slow.

I wanted to leap into that room and kill every fucker in there who had dared to lay a hand on my sister, but I had to force myself to be smart. I had to wait for Diego's distraction to draw them out.

Light spilled beneath a door at the end of the corridor and my heart leapt at the sound of Lionel's voice coming from with in it.

"Tell us now, or you'll only suffer more," he snarled and my blood ran cold at his icy tone.

There was the sound of something breaking and then a curse. The scent of smoke filled the hallway and a chalky taste coated my tongue as I ducked beneath a curving staircase and allowed my concealment spell to hide me.

I shivered as the fear in me took the opportunity to raise its head and I tried to call on the comfort of my Phoenix fire to banish it. But instead of the warming calm of the flames, all I felt from the beast beneath my flesh was a sense of drowsiness as I tried to call on my Order.

The door burst open before me and I cringed back into the shadows as a blur of motion shot away from me towards the source of the fire at the far end of the house. A moment later, Lionel strode from the room too, the door swinging over behind him as his boots banged against the floorboards and he followed the Vampire, who I had to hope had been Clara, towards the source of the smoke.

I forced myself to remain still as I waited for him to move out of sight at the end of the corridor then lurched forward.

I dropped the concealment and silencing spells around me and threw a solid shield of air up instead before conjuring a blade of ice into my hand and running straight towards the room where they were holding my sister.

I just had to get in there, grab her and get out of this house. Once we were outside we could set our wings loose and fly. Even Clara couldn't catch us in the clouds. And though Lionel might chase us in his Dragon form, I'd out flown a Dragon before and the moment we were beyond the perimeter of this house we would use the stardust in my pocket to return to the academy. Easy.

I shoved the door open and ran forward several steps before falling still as I stared around at the empty dining room in confusion. There was a huge mahogany table to the right of the room and a fire in the hearth at the far end. A long window looked back out over the grounds of the estate and the curtains were wide. Fires burned in sconces around the room, casting the space in warm light but there was absolutely no sign of Darcy, or anyone else for that matter.

"I should have just counted on your stupidity sooner," Lionel's voice came from behind me and I whipped around as I tightened my hold on the shield that surrounded me.

"Where's my sister?" I snarled as his lips pulled into a deadly grin and he stepped away from where he'd been standing behind the door. My brain tried to comprehend how that was possible – I'd just watched him walk away down the corridor outside.

"Oh that's right, they don't teach you how to detect an illusion in your freshman year do they? Pity you don't have parents to assure you're as far ahead of the class as *my* Heir," Lionel mocked, flicking his fingers so that the sound of Darcy's screams filled the air and a chill raced down my spine.

"She's not here?" I breathed, relief spilling through me as I realised this was a trap. I was a stupid, idiotic bitch for walking into it, but I didn't even care in that moment. Because that meant Darcy was still safe.

"I suppose you believed I walked off down the corridor after Clara too?" he taunted as he took a step closer to me and my grip tightened on the ice blade in my hand.

There was a hunger in his eyes as his gaze skimmed over me which made my skin crawl.

He was wearing a white shirt with the buttons undone to reveal his muscular chest where I was surprised to see almost as much ink as Darius had. But his tattoos weren't filled with beauty and power like his son's. They were all made up of runes which seemed to writhe against his flesh like they were constructed out of the shadows themselves and the more my gaze lingered on them, the more I was sure that was true.

I backed up slowly as he closed in on me, happy to play the part of prey to this hunter if it got me closer to an exit.

"Is Diego working for you?" I growled, anger flaring through me at the thought of him betraying us. The perfect double agent, gaining our trust by admitting he'd been sent to spy on us and then playing us for fucking fools when we chose to believe he'd had a change of heart.

"Oh it was better than that. The Polaris boy is a pathetic specimen who really did fall for your charms. But he didn't account for my dear Clara. Her hold on the shadows lets her look through the eyes of anyone connected to the Polaris family soul web. We knew he'd changed sides, but we left him in place, using him to monitor you whether he wanted to or not."

"So why give him up now?" I asked, backing up again and hoping he wouldn't catch on to my ploy of moving closer to the window.

"Because I have need of a Vega. And my Seer predicted your sister leaving her room so that you wouldn't be able to locate her. And how you would believe the worst so easily. All it took was a few minutes of Drusilla watching an illusion of your dear sister being tortured to create the memory for the web. She delivered it to her spineless son and you came charging in like a warrior to rescue Gwendalina when you were really just a sacrificial lamb racing to the butcher's chopping block."

I swallowed thickly as I took in the depths of this plan. The way the stars had let things fall into line for him to allow all of this to come to pass. Why did they favour him and curse us? Were they seriously that keen for the entire kingdom to fall to ruin at the hands of this madman?

"What do you want me for?" I asked, lifting my chin as I looked into his cold eyes.

His blonde hair was swept away from his callous face and I was glad that there was so little of his looks in Darius.

"I am searching for something," he said slowly, wetting his lips as he took another step towards me. "Something which is bound to royal blood."

I kept my face blank, not wanting him to read anything into our own attempts to find the Imperial Star from the look on my face. Not that we'd had much luck yet, but with Gabriel's visions to help guide us, we were making some progress towards figuring out where it was.

"But I found out something troubling about it," he went on as if we were having a pleasant conversation over cream tea or something. "It turns out I need royal blood to wield it. And then I figured, *you* have more than enough blood to spare."

"You're not having a drop of my blood," I snarled.

I tried to urge my Phoenix to my flesh to help give me strength, but it still felt like it was sleeping and my heart fluttered uselessly as I tried to figure out what that meant.

Lionel watched me eagerly like he was waiting for me to make my move and I realised I really needed to do it.

"Come along now, *Princess,* let's not waste time."

I flicked my fingers at him and a fireball exploded in the space between us, blinding him for a moment as I turned and ran for the window.

A second fireball smashed the glass ahead of me and I leapt up onto the ledge, but I slammed into a solid wall of air magic before I could make it outside.

I cursed as I fell back onto my ass, tightening the shield I'd constructed around me as I threw the ice blade in my hand at him.

Lionel's gaze lit with glee as he melted it easily and he threw an explosion of fire magic ramming into my shield with enough force to make my breath catch.

"Why don't you hit me with some Phoenix fire?" he taunted as I conjured vines to erupt from the floorboards at his feet and tangle around his body.

I tried to reach for my Phoenix again as Lionel was forced to give his attention to fighting off the vines and my heart fluttered in panic as I failed to draw it from my skin.

"What have you done to me?" I snarled, throwing more magic into the vines and chasing it with ice to lock them in place around his legs.

"I didn't want you using your Order gifts to run away before you've offered up your services, so we filled the house with Order Suppressant. You won't be able to call on your beloved Phoenix for hours – at least not unless you take a shot of the antidote like Clara and I did." Lionel smirked at me as he revealed the full extent of this trap and I cursed myself for being such a headstrong idiot and walking straight into it.

I gaped at him in horror and Lionel took the opportunity to destroy my vines and ice with a powerful flood of fire magic before sending it flying my way.

I braced for it, building my own fire all around me as the heat of the flames only stoked my power and I drew all of his fire under my control too, absorbing the blast before throwing it back at him tenfold.

I snarled at him as he fought to shield himself and followed my attack up with a torrent of water which I froze all around the surface of his shield, growing it thicker and thicker to contain him as I raced for the smashed window again.

I swore in frustration as I found my way still blocked by his air shield and turned my attention to the wall instead as the sound of cracking ice filled the room.

I gathered power into my hands and launched fire and air at the wall with everything I had. Bricks and mortar exploded out from the side of the house and I tightened my grip on my shield as more of it came raining down on me.

I ran for the cavernous hole I'd punched into the wall of the house but Lionel threw whips of blazing fire after me.

They curled around my air shield, wrapping around it tightly and yanking me to a halt as I fought to keep the shield intact.

I gasped as my feet started sliding backward across the hardwood floor as Lionel used the whips to drag me back towards him.

I gritted my teeth and pushed more power into my shield, focusing on the sides of it where the whips were constricting.

Air magic slammed into the top of my shield with such force that it stole my breath and with my focus on holding the sides, his magic punched through mine.

I screamed as I was snared in a cage of air and yanked off of my feet.

My back collided with the mahogany dining table and pain splintered through my spine as cords of air magic twisted around me to hold me down.

I fought against them with everything I had but as my arms were pinned in place, it became more and more difficult to bend my power to my will.

Lionel moved to stand by my feet and I cursed him as I thrashed against the binds, managing to tear a leg free and kicking him square in the nose.

A tremendous snarl tore from his lips as blood spilled over his face and a flash of triumph filled me as I fought like a Tom cat to free myself from the rest of his magic.

Lionel grabbed my leg, his fingers digging into the calf with enough force to make me cry out as he pinned it to the table again.

But I wasn't going to give up. I fucking refused to bow to the whims of this psychopath and I was more than willing to bleed for my freedom if that was what it took to claim it.

The shadows licked keenly beneath my skin and I slid into their hold as easily as breathing, coating my flesh in darkness which hungered for blood.

Shadows coiled from my body, reaching for him eagerly and wrapping around his wrists as he fought to restrain me.

I urged them on as they pressed beneath his skin, heading for his heart, his soul, his power.

Lionel grunted as my shadows invaded him and a twisted smile captured my lips as I felt their hunger infecting me. The more I chased what they wanted, the tighter their grip on me grew and the sweeter their call sounded.

To my surprise, Lionel wasn't trying to fight me, instead his eyes lit with glee as I dipped further and further into the dark.

"That's it," he breathed, his grip on my leg loosening until he was caressing me instead of restraining me. "Embrace it."

His words sounded like a bell ringing in my ears as my entire body tingled with the pleasure the shadows were delivering to me. They ached for me to push even further into them, calling my name like the sweetest song. But as I drew closer to the oblivion they offered, the memory of my sister's voice called me back.

With a snarl of defiance, I pulled away from the dark, my back arching against the table as I tugged at the cords of magic restraining my wrists and I forced the shadows back beneath my flesh.

Lionel's lips curled back in a sneer and his magic quickly twisted around my free leg as he tied it down too.

Air magic tightened around my hands as they were pressed flat to the table, and he cast a tight shield around them, locking them still so that I couldn't cast any magic.

"What the fuck do you want?" I shouted at him as he reached up to heal the damage I'd done to his face.

"I need a Vega who is willing to bow to me," he purred as he moved around the table, his eyes lighting as he looked down at me, pinned beneath him like a butterfly on a board just waiting for the end.

"I'd sooner die," I snarled.

Lionel tutted like I was nothing more than an inconvenience to him. "It always amazes me how many Fae throw those words about like they're nothing. Yes, death can be a simple release, but what if it's not an easy affair? What if I stand here and cut you apart piece by piece until you agree to my terms? Any time you come close to death, I can just heal you and start again. How long do you think you will resist me then?"

He moved to look down into my eyes and I spat right in his face.

The psycho barely even flinched, but his gaze darkened hungrily as he reached out to brush my hair away from my face.

"All you have to do to make me stop, is give yourself to the shadows," he breathed as he moved around the table, his fingers trailing down my body from my neck all the way to my ankle and drawing a shudder of repulsion from my skin before he stopped by my feet. "Once you surrender to the power of the darkness, you will willingly follow the Shadow Princess and do my bidding when required."

"Never," I growled and the corner of his lips twitched in amusement.

I fought to contain my fear as he pulled my sneaker off and dragged his thumb up the sole of my foot.

"What are you doing?" I asked, my muscles bunching as he slid a knife from his belt.

"You need to know exactly who it is you belong to," Lionel breathed, his expression lighting hungrily. "And I have a little theory that with your Order form locked down, you'll no longer be immune to Dragon fire. How many times do you think I will have to burn my name into your flesh before the message sinks in?"

His grip on my foot tightened suddenly and I bucked against the table in panic as he placed the knife on the table and raised a finger, holding it close the sole of my foot so that I could feel the molten heat of his magic.

"Wait," I gasped but he didn't miss a beat as he pressed his finger to my flesh and began to brand the letter A into my foot.

The pain was blinding, every nerve in my body lighting up like it was on fire as I bucked against my restraints and his magic held me down. I'd never felt the pain of fire before and it was unlike anything I'd ever known. The burn that tore through me burrowed right through my flesh and set me alight with agony as he traced his finger over my skin.

I bit my tongue against the scream I wanted to release, tasting blood as I fought against it with everything I had and my heart pounded so hard I feared it would burst.

Lionel finally finished branding the X into my foot which completed his surname and I fell still against the table, panting as a tear slipped from the corner of my eye. But he wasn't done there.

"The only problem I have with burns," he said slowly as he lifted the knife from the table and pressed it to my skin. "Is that I don't get to see you bleed."

A scream lodged in my throat as the knife bit into my flesh and he drew a line of agony beneath his name, spilling the blood he was so eager to see.

I almost blacked out and when he drew the bloody knife away, I fell back against the table once more with my chest heaving as I fought to regain control of my thoughts.

The smile he gave me was one of pure glee as he moved to my side and slid his fingers across my stomach in a gentle caress which was somehow even worse than the kiss of the blade.

"You *will* scream for me, Roxanya," he promised as he lifted the knife and brushed it across my ribs, painting my flesh with my own blood. "It's only a matter of time."

My muscles clenched as he lifted the blade once more and my eyes rolled back in my head as the pain of his torture began all over again.

I clamped my eyes shut and I thought of my sister, focusing on the fact that she wasn't here and was safe away from this monster. That knowledge gave me strength as the pain ripped into me and the shadows begged for me to slip into them to escape it.

But I wouldn't. I refused. No matter what he did to me, I wouldn't become his puppet.

So I gritted my teeth against the agony of him carving into my body and branding me with his fire again and fought with all my strength not to scream.

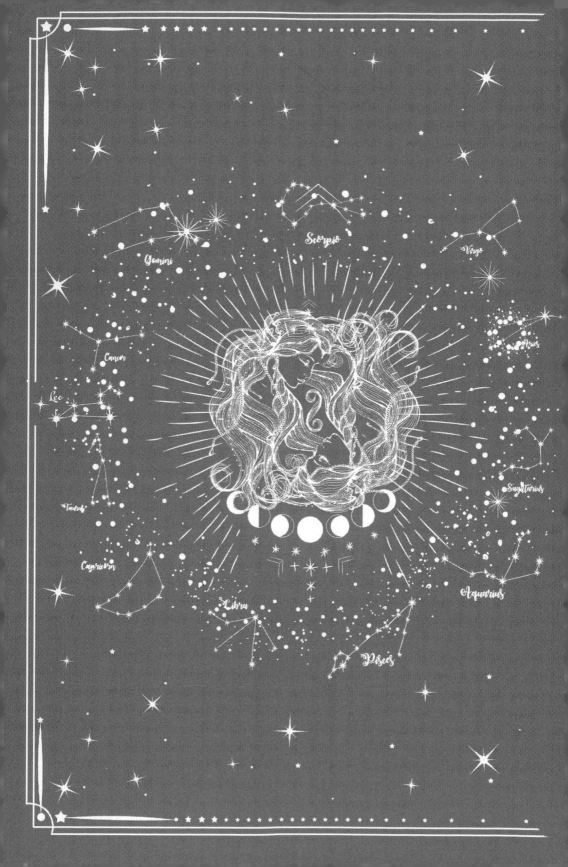

DARCY

CHAPTER FORTY NINE

We ran through the thick woodland at the edge of the property, racing toward the house somewhere ahead. None of us dared cast a Faelight in case we drew attention to ourselves.

In my heart, I was sure Tory was close. I could practically feel her presence calling to me as I raced over the uneven dusty ground, the scent of pine filling my nose. Rage tangled with hate inside me at knowing Lionel had her. And the images of what he might be doing to her made me almost drown in a sea of fury inside me. If he'd hurt my sister, I was going to kill him. I'd bring every ounce of my Phoenix fire down on his head and burn him out of this world forever.

The hoot of an owl sent a bolt of adrenaline through me as we weaved between the trees, sprinting along within a silencing bubble in the dark wood, growing ever closer to Tory.

"Wait," Caleb hissed from up ahead, pressing his back to a tree and we slowed before him as he turned his ear towards the house. We'd all decided to stay together, figuring we were stronger as a team. And if there was danger ahead, better to face it in a group than alone.

"What is it?" Darius growled impatiently, flexing his fingers as if his magic was aching to be set loose.

"I can hear crackling."

"Fire," Seth growled, sniffing the air and the scent of smoke reached me too.

"Yes and…there's movement out here, back the way we came. Beyond the perimeter," Caleb said, shutting his eyes as he focused. "It's far off, but it's headed this way."

"What is it?" I asked, glancing toward the house anxiously. I didn't to linger here a moment longer, but if Caleb was concerned, I had to wait.

"Footsteps," he breathed. "A lot of them. They're heavy too…."

"Nymphs," Max growled and my heart lurched.

"We need to move before we're surrounded then," Darius snarled and Caleb nodded, but caught his arm before he could run ahead.

"Think with your head not your heart," he warned, then looked to me. "Both of you. We can't storm in there unprepared."

Darius pulled out of his grip. "I know what I'm doing. We're wasting time here."

He ran on and anxiety danced through me as I raced after him, my pulse pounding solidly against the base of my throat. With the four Heirs here, we were strong enough to save Tory, I just knew it.

I caught sight of the house through the trees, embers glimmering by one end as smoke spiralled up towards the star spangled sky like the fire had just been put out. It was a clear night, though there was no moon out to offer us much light. But that just meant we remained well hidden from our enemies. And Lionel may have lured Tory here, but he didn't expect us to show up and tear his plans to shit. We had the advantage, we just had to keep a hold of it.

Darius reached the edge of the trees and I hurried to his side as he paused beside a large pine, seeming to wield the darkness around us with an illusion to keep us concealed. I sensed the Heirs gathering close behind us and tension prickled up my spine.

"We should split up now," Seth suggested. "Once we locate Tory, we can get inside without Lionel knowing we're all here."

"We can keep coming at him in a wave," Max agreed.

"Isn't it safer to stick together?" Caleb growled.

Tory's scream pierced the air, making my heart burst with fear and I took off running towards the house without a second thought. Darius tore along at my side, outpacing me as he sprinted toward the back door, his arms powering back and forth beside him.

The shadows suddenly reared up inside me, the pull of them overwhelmingly strong as they crashed against my thoughts and made my vision blur.

What's happening?!

My legs locked tight and I slammed to the ground, my voice clamped deep down inside my chest, unable to break free to shout out to Darius.

Caleb was at my side in a blur, pulling me into his arms and racing back into the trees as I convulsed, agony cutting deep into my soul.

He laid me down between the three of them, cursing as he pressed healing light into my flesh, his eyes wild with panic.

"What's wrong with her?" Seth asked in alarm.

"Fuck, I don't know," Max hissed.

"Darius ran on," Caleb hissed. "He's almost at the house."

They continued to try and heal me, but I couldn't be healed of this and my lips were locked tight, stopping me from telling them. The shadows were ripping at my chest, burrowing into every inch of my body and taking root. Pain blinded me as they clawed at my head and made my insides churn and ache.

"Hang in there, Darcy," Seth whimpered, clutching my hand as he offered more healing light.

Max pressed a palm to my forehead and I felt him try to pull at my emotions and sense what was happening. But he couldn't get into the fortress of my body as the shadows locked me in place on the ground. I would have screamed if my body had allowed it, but it didn't feel like it belonged to me anymore. Like I was trapped in a cell, tortured within my own flesh.

"I can help her," Clara's voice reached my ears, filling me with a dread so keen that it set my blood alight. But all I could do was lay there, hunting the darkness between the trees as I searched for her. The Heirs got to their feet, forming a protective wall in front of me as Clara's laughter rang out within the woods. "Did you come all this way to see little old me, boys?"

"Show yourself!" Max barked, ice encasing his palms as he prepared to fight.

Caleb was braced to move, his eye flitting back and forth as he hunted the darkness for her, a predator ready to pounce.

Ice dripped into my veins as the shadows pulled at me like puppet strings, drawing me to my feet, my vision shrouded in a black fog that slowly cleared away until my gaze was fixed on the backs of the Heirs' heads.

My hands raised of their own accord and I tried to call out in warning as I was forced to bend to Clara's will, her grip on the shadows that plagued me absolute.

Smoke swirled in my palms and I battled with all my might as I tried to make a single sound to warn them, but it was no use.

"Let's play a game," Clara sang. "First one to die wins!"

DARIUS

CHAPTER FIFTY

I ran towards Lance's childhood home like the demons of hell were chasing me. There was a fissure tearing through my chest, ripping me apart and peeling away all the layers of my flesh until there wasn't anything left in me but the monster my father had worked so tirelessly for me to become.

But he hadn't counted on the beast he'd trained turning on him. Hadn't counted on the wrath I'd rain down on him for touching one of the only good things in my life.

I'd been training to take him down for years and all he'd done was force my hand. This ended tonight.

Roxy's screams echoed out over the grounds and I felt the agony of them like a dagger to my heart.

I was going to fucking kill him. Enough was *enough*.

The others had fallen behind, but I couldn't slow down to find out why. Roxy needed me. Whatever the fuck was happening in that house, it was bad. And the chain which bound my heart to hers couldn't let her suffer for a single moment longer.

I half ripped the back door off of its hinges as I burst into the house and I tore inside where the scent of smoke from a recently doused fire caught in my throat.

But as I ran on, I realised that wasn't the only thing I was inhaling. My Dragon slipped from my grasp as it was locked in chains of steel beneath my flesh and I snarled loud enough to make my chest rumble as I realised the place had been filled with Order Suppressant to stop Roxy from using her Phoenix against the madman who'd sired me.

It didn't matter. I didn't need to rip him apart with teeth and claws, I'd happily tear him limb from limb with my bare hands.

Roxy screamed again just as I made it into the hallway and light from the dining hall drew my gaze to it as the sound of her agony broke something in me.

I threw the door open and cast water in the same breath, directing it at my father as I found him standing over Roxy where she was pinned to the dining table by cords of twisting air magic.

A roar burst from my lips as he fought to shield himself and I spotted the blood coating her skin, the words burned into her flesh countless times. Acrux. His name. *My* name. Decorating her perfect skin in red.

Father was yelling something at me, but I couldn't hear it. I couldn't grasp anything aside from the girl I loved pinned down on that table like a slab of meat for him to toy with.

He'd done countless things like that to me over the years. He'd beaten my brother into submission too. But not her. I wouldn't let him touch her ever again.

I charged across the room with my fists coated in ice, slamming into his shield with the force of a charging Minotaur.

Father's lips drew back in a savage snarl as he fought to maintain his magic, but nothing could match the rage in me as I threw my fists against it again and again.

His shield cracked and he stole the air from my lungs as he tried to stop me. I didn't even flinch as I threw every last bit of my magic into my next punch.

Father's shield shattered and my fist collided with his face, breaking his concentration so that air returned to my lungs once more.

I knocked him to the ground beneath me and he growled with the full ferocity of his Dragon as he fought back with fists coated in fire, slamming them into my sides and burning the flesh from my bones.

Roxy was calling my name and the rough edge her voice had gained from screaming was enough to break what little restraint I had left.

Father managed to throw me off of him but I hit back instantly, a wave of pure fire crashing into him before he could get a new shield in place, hot enough to boil him alive.

I ignored the pain of my own wounds as I clenched my fist and daggers of ice shot towards him, slicing into his flesh as he bellowed in fury.

He shoved himself to his feet and ran at me, but I cast ice on the floor before him, throwing my fist into his gut as he slipped and smiling savagely as I felt his ribs snap.

He wrapped his arms around me and took me down with a cry of rage. *"Stay down!"* he bellowed in my face, his voice laced with Dark Coercion as he slammed a fist into my jaw. *"And watch me break the girl who broke your heart."*

I fell still as he pushed himself upright, stalking away from me as the new brand on my arm flared with heat and the Phoenix flame Roxy had gifted me swept through my limbs and hunted down those commands. Her power burned away his dark magic like it was nothing and as he raised the knife above her again, my gaze locked with hers.

She was looking at me like my pain hurt her more than her own and the rage in me grew to new heights at the thought of what he'd done to her.

Father stood with his back to me as he focused on his work, raising the blade to cut into her flesh once more.

I was up in a heartbeat, my muscles bunching with power as magic coiled in my limbs with deadly intent.

"You should really stop underestimating me, Father," I snarled and he whipped around towards me, eyes wild in confusion as his dark magic failed to hold me.

"How?" he gasped, but I didn't bother to give him an answer.

I hit him with so much power that he was launched across the room before slamming into the wall in the midst of an inferno.

I stalked after him as I willed the flames to devour him and he fought with all he had to try and put them out.

When he launched himself from the fire and collided with me again, I was ready for it. We hit the floor in a tangle of fists and fury, each of us determined to beat the other into submission and paint the walls red with our victory. But for the first time ever, I could feel the cracks in his defences, I was gaining the upper hand. This beast in me had the scent of his blood now and it wouldn't relent until its bloodlust was sated.

Today was the last day Lionel Acrux would hurt someone I loved.

I'd been born to rule.

And I was going to claim my place in blood.

DARCY

CHAPTER FIFTY ONE ·

Shadows exploded from my palms, crashing into the shield Seth was casting around the three Heirs, but the force of the blow sent them tumbling to the ground. Clara gave me my voice back just in time to let me scream.

The three of them were on their feet again in seconds, turning towards me and backing up as they took in the sight of my raised hands and the shadows which were swirling ominously between my fingers.

"I can't stop it," I gasped, my heart drumming to a powerful heat. "Get away from me."

"Fuck," Seth spat, securing his shield around them.

"Come out and face us yourself, you coward!" Caleb roared into the trees just as another wave of power exploded from me.

The three of them were knocked apart, crashing into the undergrowth and my body turned sharply towards Max, striding forward as my palms raised. Shadows blasted from my hands and terror bound me as I begged him to move. His body dissolved to nothing and I realised it was an illusion he'd left there, making my heart squeeze with relief as I spotted him darting between the trees ahead of me.

Clara pressed her will into me once more and suddenly I was running towards Seth, blasting the shadows at him so he was forced to stand his ground and shield with all his might. Tendrils of darkness wrapped around his bubble of safety, squeezing and squeezing like a python around a jar. He roared as he threw all of his effort into maintaining it and I feared what would happen if I got past his defences.

"Stop it!" I screamed at Clara as her laughter rang out from somewhere in the canopy above us.

Caleb moved in a blur, climbing the tree at speed as he hunted her down and disappeared amongst the branches.

"Can't catch me!" Clara sang, her voice carrying away from us, but her grip on me never faltered.

The shadows wrapped tighter and tighter around Seth's shield and I felt it beginning to buckle, the magic barely holding under the intensity of the Fifth Element.

A weight collided with me and I hit the ground beneath the full weight of Max as he grabbed my wrists and bound my hands in ice, locking them above my head.

"It's alright, I won't let her have you," he growled, his eyes shining with that promise and giving me an inch of hope to hold onto.

"Tie her down," Seth demanded as he ran to my side.

"Hurry," I begged as shadows built in my palms, bubbling against the ice as they struggled to break through.

"Shit." Max shifted back onto his knees, holding out his hands and casting my hands in more and more ice.

A blur behind him made my heart jolt in terror. "Watch out!"

Clara slashed a knife across Max's back and he roared as he fell off of me, blood oozing through his white shirt. Seth cast a net of vines to try and catch her, but she was gone in a flash with Caleb racing after her. She was throwing everything she could into his way, blasting the forest apart and making the trees around us groan as their trunks nearly snapped under the force of her power.

Seth dove forward to heal Max and the ice started splintering and cracking around my fingers.

"*Seth*," I begged, my heart hammering. "Get away from here."

The ice exploded from my palms and I was forced to launch myself at them, latching two ropes of shadow around their throats and making them choke.

Seth threw out a palm and wind blasted into me, sending me flying away before he caught me on a cushion of air, saving me from the impact of the hard earth. The air continued to press me down, but he was half focused on healing Max and as another wave of shadows coiled from my body, his magic gave way.

I was forced to my feet, racing toward them and Clara sped by again, placing an ice cold dagger in my hand. Horror consumed me as her voice called back to me. "Let's carve up some Heirs, Darcy!" she laughed again like we were having fun in some game.

I gritted my teeth as she made my grip tighten around the blade and I strode towards Max and Seth as they hurriedly got up, raising their hands to fight me off.

"Don't hold back," I begged, my heart pounding to a terrifying beat as tension lined their features. "You have to stop me."

CALEB

CHAPTER FIFTY TWO

I shot away from Darcy as she threw shadows at Seth and Max and they yelled out at her to stop. I kept my focus on my target, carving a trail through the trees and circling back to the bitch responsible for this.

I bared my fangs as I shot towards Clara Orion, her shadowy eyes darting my way as I came for her, and a smile twisting her lips as if my arrival had made her damn day.

"Come catch me, little Vampire," she called, shooting away from me as she circled the others, trying to put them between us.

I snarled at her as Darcy cast a whip of shadows and Seth was forced to shield at the last moment, his grunt of effort giving away just how strong the strike had been. Max threw his power up to block Darcy too and she begged them to run as more shadows curled around her arms.

Clara continued to circle them, laughing like a little girl, trying to keep them between us so that I couldn't get my hands on her. I growled in frustration, throwing my influence into the ground at her feet to slow her as she tried to shoot away from me again.

She stumbled into the pit, vines snaring her for just long enough to make my speed count.

By the time she was ripping her way free of them, I was on her.

I threw my weight into her as we slammed down into the pit I'd created and my hands locked around her throat as the dirt rose up around us, burying her beneath me.

Clara laughed manically as I squeezed harder, my palms burning with heat as I wielded my fire magic against her too.

Shadows licked along her arms as she reached out and wrapped her fingers around my wrists and I gasped as the icy power of them sent pain raking through my body.

I released her in an instant, shooting back up onto the bank of the pit as I urged my earth magic to bury her beneath the ground, piling more and more power into the attack as she fought to dig her way free.

I snarled as I tightened my grip on my power, choking her with earth and making the ground squeeze and squeeze, until-

Clara burst from the dirt, cackling wildly as she rode on a wave of shadows and leapt straight for me with her fangs bared.

I twisted aside, throwing fire into her face, but the flames were swallowed by the shadows as she directed them to protect her.

"You've grown into such a big boy, Caleb," she giggled as she waited for my next move and I ignored her entirely. That thing wasn't the girl I used to play with when I came over to Darius's house as a kid. Whatever the fuck she was, it wasn't Fae anymore.

I shot around the pit, but a tendril of her dark magic caught my ankle and flipped me off of my feet before I could escape it.

My chin slammed into the ground and I tasted blood as my fangs cut into my tongue.

Clara was on me before I could do any more than roll over.

A cape of black shadows writhed around her flesh as she straddled my hips, the shadows looming all around as she directed them towards me. Her ice cold hands pressed to my chest and I gasped as the darkness she owned bled into me, hunting for my heart with deadly precision.

Everywhere the shadows touched came alive with agony and made my skull echo with the memories of all the worst things I'd ever done.

"You look tasty, Caleb," Clara moaned, licking her fangs as her gaze roamed over my throat.

I waited for her to lunge and caught her jaw in my hand with a flash of movement. My skin burned with fire magic and she howled in pain as I twisted her jaw with my enhanced strength until I heard it snap.

My other fist slammed into her side in the same movement and I gasped in relief as she was thrown off of me, taking her foul shadows with her.

I leapt to my feet with another snarl as I coated my arms in fire and caused the ground to tremble beneath her as she clambered upright again.

The shadows rose up all around her until she looked like nothing more than a blot of darkness beneath the trees. I'd learned my lesson. Those shadows weren't getting close to me again and as she ran at me, I darted aside, throwing a torrent of flames at her and burning her dark magic back.

She howled with frustration as the ground bucked and collapsed beneath her and I chanced a look towards Seth and Max to find that Clara's distraction was giving them an advantage.

Darcy was shouting at them to run as she was forced to hound after them with the shadows, but without Clara's full attention guiding her, her attacks were sloppy.

That was all the encouragement I needed. I bared my fangs at Clara as

I cast spears of wood into my hands and launched them at her one after the other.

She had to jump one and the next was consumed by the shadows, but I didn't slow as I just cast more and more of them into existence.

If I wanted to save the others, I needed to release Darcy from Clara's hold over her. And there was one sure way to do the job.

Clara Orion needed to die. And this time, she wouldn't be coming back from it.

DARCY

CHAPTER FIFTY THREE

Seth launched Max over my head with a blast of air. He landed behind me, locking his muscular arm around my shoulders as he tried to restrain me. My arm reached backwards over my head and I cast shadows around his face, suffocating him as he tried to get hold of the knife in my other hand. He cast a blade of ice into his palm and cut into my hand to try and make me drop the blade. I gasped as blood flowed, but my fingers wouldn't unlatch from it even though I willed them to with all my might.

"Stop – don't hurt her!" Seth demanded as he raced forward.

My free hand twisted towards Seth and smoke hurtled at him like a demon. He shielded against it and Max started to choke as the shadows wrapped around him and wrenched him off of me.

He froze my legs just as I was about to step forward, letting the ice travel further and further up my body to keep me in place.

"Run!" I insisted, but they shared a look that said they weren't going to abandon me here just as Clara ran by again with Caleb hot on her heels. Shadows blasted out behind her as he threw spears of wood at her back with a frightening strength, but she dissolved them again and again.

Ice clamped my arms to my sides and the knife slipped from my grip, the blade driving into the soft soil by my feet.

Relief made my breathing even out, but it only lasted a single moment as a rattling, sucking sound reached me from the trees.

Every part of me rippled with terror as heavy footfalls thumped this way and a beastly form stepped out of the darkness, the Nymph towering above us with its probed fingers outstretched and the sound of its rattle carving deep into my soul. Its gnarled, tree-like body loomed over me, its red eyes locked on me as it approached.

Seth and Max ran forward, shoulder to shoulder in front of me and I despised that I couldn't help, that I was bound by Clara's will, by the shadows. They ate into my essence, trying to make me fall into their hungry call.

Give in, Darcy, Clara's voice whispered in my head. *Come into the dark. You can be free here.*

Seth dove forward, bursting into his white Werewolf form and leaping for the throat of the Nymph with a savage snarl. Navy scales crawled across Max's bare arms and up the back of his neck as his Siren form took over and the rattle in the air tried to douse his magic.

The ice around me began to give and my lungs laboured as I tried to hold back against the force which had me in its grip. But it was no use and the ice shattered around me as the shadows found their way free once more.

They poured from me, winding around Max just as the Nymph knocked Seth into a tree with a nasty cracking sound and my heart clenched in terror.

The Nymph closed in on Max as I was forced to hold him still for the monster, hating that I wasn't able to break free of Clara's command, that I couldn't stop this creature of darkness. I called for my Phoenix and it rose its head, but the shadows kept pushing it down, deeper and deeper.

"Stop!" I screamed as the Nymph reached towards Max's heart with the sharpened probes of its hand, the Heir struggling uselessly against the shadows.

He roared in rage and pain as the beast's probes sliced into his chest and I screamed and begged for help, turning my gaze to the stars as they glittered unforgivingly down at us.

Another Nymph charged out of the trees, crashing into the one about to kill Max and sending it tumbling to the ground. The two of them started fighting, ripping up the dirt and knocking a tree over in the process, making the earth shudder beneath me.

Seth pounced on me out of nowhere and the shadows binding Max released him as his heavy paws crushed me to the ground. He bounded away a second later, diving at the Nymphs and tearing into their limbs as they fought. I'd never seen Nymphs act like that, but I guessed the prize of an Heir's magic was worth more than your average Fae.

Max hurriedly got up, backing away from them as he regained hold of his magic. I was forced back to my feet too, my hands raised once more but this time, Max didn't try to restrain me, he ran.

TORY

CHAPTER FIFTY FOUR

I thrashed against the table as the sickly warm trickle of blood slid over my skin from countless wounds and I cursed at Lionel as colourfully as I could manage while my body trembled from the pain.

Darius was fighting with a brutal savagery that made my heart pound and ache in equal measures. He was utterly fearless, entirely focused on ending the man before him as his father fought to keep him back. He threw everything he had into attacking, barely giving any time to defending himself aside from blocking the worst of his father's strikes.

Lionel was furious, the Dragon in him plain to see and with each blow he struck against his son, I grew more and more afraid that he'd kill him.

Darius roared with all the power of his Dragon as he threw a torrent of flames arcing across the room at Lionel who shielded with air before they could eviscerate him.

Darius ran at him again, but as the smoke cleared, Lionel stepped forward to meet him with shadows coiling around his body and a manic gleam in his eyes.

His gaze slid to me where I remained bound to the table by his magical chains and I cried out as he threw a blast of the dark magic straight for me.

Darius leapt into its path, taking the hit to the chest with no chance of shielding against it so that he was knocked back against the table.

"Darius!" I gasped, yanking on my bonds as I ached to help him and he grunted as he fought to heal himself from the damage the shadows had caused.

He twisted away from his father, throwing shards of ice his way to occupy him as he glanced down at me with pain in his eyes.

He reached for the magical chain which bound my ankle in place, but I shook my head fiercely.

"Finish him first," I snapped, not wanting him to waste a moment of time trying to free me in case it cost him this fight.

Lionel threw more shadows our way and Darius snarled as they burrowed into him, his hands writhing with darkness for a moment before he banished the shadows in favour of flames again.

I gritted my teeth against the agony of my wounds as I fought to break apart the air magic which immobilised my hands. The longer Lionel fought his son, the more I could feel his hold on the magic containing me slipping and the moment it cracked, I'd be ready.

Lionel threw shadows out from his body and I gasped as all of the light in the room was suddenly blotted out. A deep, pounding rhythm started up in my chest as the shadows within me rose up to the surface of my skin unbidden, aching to join with his and wreak havoc on the world.

I moaned, on the edge of ecstasy as they called to me, promising me freedom from the pain of my flesh and offering me all the power I could ever want and more.

But I didn't want power. I never had. Not like that. What I craved was love. Family. The kinds of things you couldn't just take and had to *earn*.

With a cry of effort, I drew on all of the strength in me and used it to force the shadows back. The dark energy in me had latched on to the shadows Lionel was commanding and as I banished mine, I stole his from him too, locking them down again and revealing the room once more.

Darius didn't miss a beat, charging forward with a bellow of rage and his fists coated in gloves of ice as he tackled Lionel to the ground and started pounding on him with a terrifying ferocity as he roared in his face.

My heart thrashed frantically as I watched this wild creature who'd offered me his love after all the shit we'd put each other through taking down the man who'd ruined him.

Darius beat him with a brutality that wouldn't be sated by anything less than death. Blood coated his hands, his arms, and even speckled his face, but he wouldn't relent as Lionel struggled beneath him. His features were set in a determined mask of rage and everything about him spoke of violence and danger which sent a shiver running right through me.

There was no doubt in my mind that the rage which had driven him to this was fuelled by his feelings for me. And knowing that he would risk it all for me made the pain in my body fade away as I watched him.

Darius was savage, brutal, vicious, broken and *mine*. And in that moment, I had no desire for the darkness in him to ever let up. I wanted him. Every damaged, depraved, dirty piece of his soul was made to fit with all the twisted, ruined parts of my own. And if the stars didn't like it then I'd happily climb up into the sky and tear them all down for him.

Right after I watched him kill his father.

SETH

CHAPTER FIFTY FIVE

Iraced around the Nymphs, howling as two more joined the fight. They couldn't touch my magic in my Wolf form, but that meant I had to rely on teeth and claws alone.

Max stood back as he shot ice blades at each one of the beasts, but Darcy was closing in on him from behind as Clara wielded her like a weapon.

I turned away from the Nymph I'd been charging down, racing towards Max instead as he was forced to shield himself from Darcy once more.

I barked to let him know I was coming and as shadows poured from her in waves, I leapt forward and he snatched hold of my fur in a move we'd practised a thousand times, his leg swinging over my back as I tore away into the trees.

"Fucking hell," Max growled, one hand fisting in my fur, his breaths coming heavily as I curved back towards the fight, my mind daggering towards Caleb as I hunted for him and Clara.

They had to tire soon, they'd been fighting with the full force of their Orders for too long. Surely it couldn't go on. One of them had to give in, I just prayed it was Clara.

I trusted that Caleb could bring that bitch to her knees, but I couldn't ignore the pinch of fear I had over him facing her alone. But with her speed, we couldn't easily help. So we had to focus on the Nymphs.

Max sat upright as I raced for a Nymph who was hunting us amongst the trees. He blasted ice at the beast and froze every inch of it solid, making it stumble blindly toward us.

I leapt off of the ground, my jaws outstretched, a snarl in my throat as my teeth clamped down on its head. I bit down with all my might, crunching through ice and bone until it died in my jaws, crashing to the ground beneath me.

I howled as it burst into ash and its blood ran hot and thick down my jaw, a tang of vile bitterness in my mouth.

"Seth – move!" Darcy yelled and I wheeled around just in time to avoid a tendril of shadow shooting towards us from her palms.

Max cast an ice shield and attached it to his arm, using it to deflect the shadows she sent after us.

I yelped as one caught my back leg and tumbled towards the ground, sending him flying from my back with fear rushing up my spine.

Max slammed into a tree and I rolled toward him, unable to stop from the speed I'd been running, my huge weight crushing him beneath me. He grunted in pain and I sprang onto my paws with a whine of concern, licking his face to check he was alright.

"Get out of here, idiot," he snarled, but I wasn't going anywhere.

He wheezed as he healed broken ribs and I turned my head to face Darcy as she ran toward us, a Nymph at her back with its blood red eyes set on me and Max.

"Both of you have to run!" Darcy begged, the pain in her eyes clear as she was forced to fight us once more. But I wasn't going to budge an inch until Max was healed.

His fingers tangled in my fur just as a plume of shadow raced toward us from her outstretched hands and I sprinted away as Max hauled himself onto my back.

A shadow collided with a tree ahead of us and I yelped as it started to fall, ducking my head as I put on a burst of speed to try and make it under before it fell.

I glanced over my shoulder as a Nymph chased after us and I skidded beneath the tree just before it crashed to the earth, the huge trunk taking the monstrous creature to the ground with a sickening crunch.

I turned back to face the fallen Nymph, kicking up dust on the ground and Max slammed a spear of ice into its skull with a violent blow. The Nymph shattered into dust with an echoing screech and I dashed away into the wood, turning my ears left and right as I hunted for Caleb.

Where are you Cal? Show me you're alright.

A whoosh of air sounded before a Vampire collided with me at full speed, knocking Max from my back and taking his place instead. I kept running for several beats as Clara's fingernails dug into my flesh, unable to slow down fast enough.

"Yah!" she cried excitedly, her knees driving into my shoulder blades so she could hold on.

I threw myself to the ground, rolling hard and slamming the weight of my head back against her face, making her scream in pain. I leapt back upright in a flash and she shot toward me, her fist slamming into my jaw. I snapped at her in retaliation, lunging and biting, but she moved at the speed of light, evading me as she threw punches that were almost hard enough to break bones.

"Silly puppy," she taunted, pausing just long enough for me to lunge and sink my teeth into her arm.

I didn't let go, digging my paws into the earth and tugging on her like a dog fighting for a bone. And this was a bone I was going to rip right from her fucking arm socket.

She screamed in pain, casting a huge blast of shadows at me that threw me away from her as I was forced to let go.

I landed heavily on the ground with pain splintering through me, my paw brushing something soft as I pushed myself upright. I spotted Max's bag there and shifted fast, yanking out some sweatpants and tugging them on before tearing off into the trees. I needed to buy myself a few moments to heal, padding as silently as a wolf cub into the darkness as I fixed the aching wounds across my body.

"Come out, come out little wolf," Clara sang then she yelped, the sound of someone hitting her reaching me. "Ah, Caleb Altair – play nice!"

"Fuck you, shadow whore," he spat and I circled back to help him, adrenaline surging into my blood as I crept behind a tree out of sight and slowly let a vine snake across the ground towards Clara. They were fighting in a blur I could barely register, but they weren't running for once. And when Vampires weren't running, they could be caught by sneaky Wolves.

With a flick of my wrist, the vine shot out at the perfect moment, latching around Clara's ankle and uprooting her so she faceplanted the ground. Caleb didn't waste a second of the advantage, a spear of wood expanding in his grip, raising it higher to build momentum for the blow.

A huge, rough hand suddenly latched around me from behind and I yelled in rage as I was thrown towards Caleb and the Nymph lurched down to press its probes directly against my heart, its rattle working to seize my magic in my chest. *Oh fuck!*

"Stop," Clara snarled at Caleb. "Or the Wolf is dead."

Terror took hold of me and I saw my death shining way too clearly in front of my eyes. Cal snarled, looking to me with his fangs bared and fear in his gaze.

"Stab her, Cal!" I demanded, but he tossed the spear aside, stepping back with his gaze fixed firmly on me.

Clara sprang to her feet, taking a bow. "Finish them!" she cried then shot away into the trees.

The probes sliced into my chest and I raised my hands with a cry of anger and pain, summoning the little magic I could reach to fight back. Before my power could escape my body, Caleb leapt onto the Nymph's back, biting straight into its bark-like throat and tearing at it with a barbarity that had my heart pounding.

The Nymph stumbled away from me with a wild shriek as Caleb ripped its throat out like an animal. I got to my feet and ran forward to help, casting a spear into my hand and ramming it into the Nymph's chest with a grunt of effort. It tumbled away into ash and Caleb hit the ground in front of me, pale and shaken, his mouth smeared with blood.

I reached out to wipe the vile black substance away from his lips and his eyes drilled into mine for two endless heartbeats.

"Help!" Max cried and we both turned and ran.

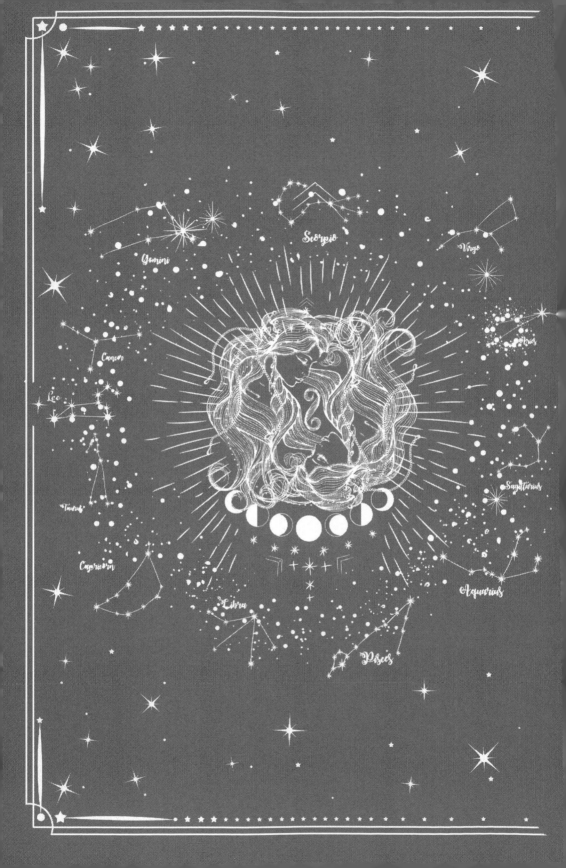

DARCY

CHAPTER FIFTY SIX

I had Max cornered against a tree, wrapped in lashes of shadow as Clara forced me to bind him there. I gritted my teeth, digging down inside me for my Phoenix as I tried to drag it to the surface of my skin.

Please, please come to me.

Fire seemed to burn in my periphery for a moment, the shadows casing their grip before they swelled up even more fiercely, sending a bite of pain deep under my flesh.

"Enough!" I screamed and Clara turned me away from Max, leaving him bound there and my breathing evened out.

Come into the darkness, what will it take pretty girl? Didn't losing my brother hurt you enough? I know you love him. All that heartbreak will disappear if you just give in to the shadows, Clara's voice filled my head and I tried to block it out as the shadows snaked through my chest, feeding on the dark emotions twisting inside me. *I love him too.*

"You don't love him, you hurt him – you're not his sister, you're a monster! I'd rather suffer forever over him than give myself to you!" I yelled, trying to find her amongst the trees, but her laughter seemed to come from everywhere around me.

I was forced to stop walking and my head tilted down, showing me the blade that was half buried in the ground.

"No," I growled, fire blooming in my veins as she tried to make me stoop down to retrieve it. I managed to fight back, my breaths coming raggedly as a blinding pain started up in my skull. But I held off from picking it up.

Just a little longer.

I have to stop this.

The shadows scraped along the inside of my body, no longer lulling and soothing like they usually were. They were a sharp weapon Clara was using against me. But I'd rather face her wrath than let her use me against the Heirs. I couldn't hurt them.

Her voice filled my head once more and I wanted to claw it out and banish it forever. *Just go into the shadows, let them take you away. I'll look after you, Darcy.*

"Go to hell!" I shouted but the darkness twisted inside me, drowning my resilience once more and making me crouch down to pick up the knife. The hilt was icily cold against my palm and I fought harder, fear ripping at my soul as she turned me to face Max, walking me toward him with a fierce intention.

"Stop it!" I screamed. "Don't hurt him."

Caleb shot towards me in a blur and my heart soared as I waited for him to take me down, but Clara intercepted him in a tremendous collision, sending them rolling away from me and snarling as they fought each other in the dirt.

Shadows crawled beneath my skin and made me step toward Max again, closer and closer as he struggled against his binds.

"You've got to get free," I begged of Max, my hand lifting, poised to strike as I came within a foot of him, the blade held up to his throat.

"I can't," Max growled, straining harder as he tried to get his hands free from the shadows that bound him. True fear flickered in his eyes and I blinked back tears, my hand beginning to shake.

"*Max,*" I groaned.

I willed my Phoenix to come to my aid, drawing on its power as I tried to heave it out of the darkness. And slowly, it started to rise, my veins humming with energy as the slightest spark lit under my skin. But it was too late, my arm slashing forward about to strike when hands twisted me around to face the other way.

The knife sliced across my attacker's throat and every piece of me screamed as I found myself looking into Seth's eyes, his grip on me loosening as blood poured down from the gaping wound.

"No!" I yelled, my voice raw as he staggered backwards, still clutching my arm and dragging me down with him to the ground.

Max was shouting, but I couldn't hear anything clearly apart from a violent ringing in my ears.

A clawing terror gripped me and the shadows rose up to claim me whole.

Seth clutched onto me, struggling to draw air against the blood. My hand was still locked around the knife and tears started pouring from my eyes at what I'd done.

"No, no, no," I begged, falling deeper and deeper into the darkness.

It wrapped around me like a current of cool water, trying to ease my racing heart and the fear that was raking at my core. But then my eyes met Seth's and I pulled away from it, a fierce heat building in me at what Clara had made me do.

"Just hold on," I choked out, my arms locked to my sides, stopping me from helping him. Seeing him like that, bloody and dying beneath me broke something inside me.

Fire caught in the deepest regions of my belly then burst through me in a shower of raging sparks, tearing through my being as pure agony fuelled me, giving me the strength to fight back.

My Phoenix reared her head and the fire burned brighter, hotter, my head falling back so I was forced to look up at the stars, the entire heavens seeming to ignite above me.

I gasped down a lungful of air as the fire chased out the cloying darkness in my body, hunting down every blackened, corrupted part of it and burning it to nothing. My wings burst from my back in a storm of fiery light and the last of the shadows were banished. Gone.

I was free and I didn't know how it was possible, but it was. And Clara no longer had control of me.

I frantically pressed my hands to Seth's throat, desperate to stem the flow of blood and try to heal what I knew I wasn't capable of healing. My magic attempted to hook onto his, failing again and again until I finally managed to latch onto it like we'd been taught in class. But I could instantly feel the extent of this wound and no matter how much energy I poured towards it, I couldn't fix it. I wasn't trained for this. I didn't know how to heal it. And that caused me the most desperate type of pain.

"Help!" I screamed, my voice hoarse and laced with hopelessness.

A horrible whine parted Seth's lips as he reached up to brush his bloody fingers across my cheek. "Together," he mouthed but I didn't know what he meant by that as tears rushed down my face, his hand falling back to the ground with a finality that hurt me.

Max was suddenly at my side, dropping to his knees and wrapping his hands over Seth's throat.

"Heal him," I begged, knowing I wasn't gifted enough to do it. But I could lend Max power.

"Clara," Max hissed in warning and my head snapped up as she caught hold of Caleb by the throat, slamming him against a tree.

I rose to my feet, my legs shaking as I raised my bloodstained hands and unleashed my Phoenix fire, sending it billowing toward her with the force of a hurricane, my teeth clenched as I aimed to destroy this bitch who had brought nothing but hell into our lives since her return.

Fury bubbled under my flesh and I let it fuel the dangerous fire pouring from my veins, showing her no mercy.

Clara shrieked in pain as my fire penetrated the shadows she was using to shield herself with, fleeing off into the darkness and Caleb slumped to his knees. His eyes locked onto Seth on the ground and his face became stricken with terror as he shot forward to join us.

I raised my hands and cast a circle of raging fire around us to keep Clara away before dropping to my knees and offering my wrist to Caleb.

"Bite me, take anything you need. All of it," I demanded.

He didn't hesitate, his fangs slicing into my wrist and his hands joined Max's over Seth's throat.

Max rested his free hand on my arm, looking to me with a grave intensity. "Let me feed on your emotions."

I nodded, forcing my barriers down so he had access to the frantic grief inside me and he winced as he drained it from me, fuelling his magic reserves.

The green healing light shone brighter between them and my heart pounded wildly as the jagged wound began to knit over. But if he was already gone, if it was too late-

A shadow dropped from the trees above us and Clara landed in the circle of flames, her body illuminated by the red and blue fire of my Order. Caleb yanked his fangs free of me and I rose to my feet to put myself between her and the Heirs, raising my hands and snarling at her as I hungered for her death.

I blasted the immense power from my body, but she shot sideways, giggling as she evaded it.

"I guess Seth won the game," she taunted as I roared my hate at her, casting a whip of Phoenix fire into my palm and slashing it through the air.

This time, she wasn't fast enough and it seared across her back, making her scream in pain. "You bitch!"

She raced at me and I cast a shield of fire in front of me as she tried to get close, making her cry out as she collided with it. She darted towards the Heirs instead, reaching down towards them and I hurriedly cast another ring of fire around them, extinguishing the outer ring to try and guide her away. She hissed as she was forced back by the flames, but waved something at me with a look of triumph and I realised she'd gotten hold of the blade.

"You're a monster," I cursed. "And I'll kill you for what you've done."

"What have I done?" she asked innocently, batting her lashes as she stepped sideways and I mimicked her, moving the opposite way to keep her in my sights.

"You hurt people. I don't know who you are, but you're not Clara Orion. You're just a hollow thing full of shadow and death," I spat.

"So which would you rather I give you, Darcy Vega? Shadow or death?" She flexed her fingers and I prepared to shield.

A Nymph stormed out from the trees behind her, slicing its probes into the back of her neck and lifting its arm so she was suspended off the ground, her legs kicking and wheeling as she screamed.

My heart beat wildly in shock as I ran forward, aiming my hands at her, unsure what the hell that creature was doing, but I was sure as shit going to take advantage of it. Fire scored from my palms, but Clara twisted her hand through the air and the Nymph dropped her in an instant as she took control of it, the fireball spearing up towards the sky instead.

She hit the ground on her knees, clutching the back of her neck with a snarl. I gathered all of my energy once more and released it with a yell of exertion, but she shot out of the way with her Vampire speed, making me curse in fury.

I tried to follow the racing blur of her through the trees, but I couldn't spot her and my gaze turned to the Nymph before me instead as I held my palms higher. Something stayed my hand before attacking it. It had helped me. Or that was how it seemed. But why?

The Nymph took a step away from me, bowing its head submissively and my heart trembled in my chest as I stared at it, fire swarming around my hands as I tried to figure out what it was doing.

Clara suddenly leapt onto its shoulders from behind, reaching over and slamming the knife into its chest again and again, making it release a horrible wailing sound. The Nymph fell to the ground beneath her as she struck at it like a psycho, stabbing and making my heart judder in alarm.

"You dare attack your princess?" she snarled, as the creature shuddered beneath her.

I released a tunnel of Phoenix fire with a shout of defiance and she leapt off of the Nymph, darting aside with a laugh.

"Bad girl," she chastised, lifting her hands to fight me and I planted my feet, ready to finish her.

Her head snapped up and she suddenly clutched her throat like she was in agony. "Daddy, no! I'm coming!"

I released my fire as fast as I could, my wings beating enough to lift me off of the ground as I poured an inferno from my body, determined to end her. She raced away and the fire scorched a path after her, turning the ground black. But she was too damn fast as she disappeared in the direction of the house and my shoulders sagged as I failed once more.

I turned to the Heirs, dousing the flames around them and finding Max and Caleb still working to revive Seth. Terror gripped my heart all over again.

He can't die. I couldn't bear it if he died.

I was about to go to them when a guttural cough caught my ear and I turned back to where the Nymph had fallen.

My heart ceased to beat as I spotted a boy there, caked in mud and blood. A boy with raven hair and pale skin. A boy who couldn't possibly be lying in the place of that Nymph.

"Diego?" I gasped, racing forward, confusion and fear strangling me as I fell down beside him and took in the gaping wounds that covered his chest.

I rested my hands over his skin as he blinked up at me, his cheeks splattered red and his eyes full of apology.

"I'm so s-sorry, Darcy," he rasped.

"I don't understand," I sobbed, trying to knit the wounds over, but they were so deep and I couldn't find his magic to hook onto. "Max!" I screamed, but Diego clutched my arm, shaking his head as panic took over me.

He can't be here. Why is he here??

"Fae magic can't heal me," he whispered and the reality of what he was wrapped around my throat like a vice.

"How can you….how are you here?" Tears ran down my cheeks as I desperately continued to try and heal him, but I could see it was no use. My magic couldn't latch onto his, it wasn't like with other Fae, but how could I accept this truth even though I'd seen it with my own eyes? What did it mean? *Please don't die.*

"I'm not your enemy," he swore and I could see the need in his eyes for me to believe that. I nodded, my tears splashing against his cheeks as I found his hand and clutched onto it tightly, not knowing what else to do. "I've done bad things," he whispered, his breathing growing shallower. "You'll see… you need to…take my hat." He coughed and blood speckled his lips which I quickly wiped away, hating that I couldn't do more for him.

"Just hold on," I begged of him, tears blurring my vision and pain wrapping around my heart. "There must be something I can do."

He shook his head slightly, acceptance settling over his expression. "I just wanted to be useful. Did I do okay? Was I good friend?" he asked, a tear rolling free of his eye.

"You're the best friend, Diego," I promised and a smile pulled up the corner of his mouth ever-so-slightly.

"You always felt like…home," he said on a guttural breath, then he fell horribly still, his eyes fixed on the stars above as they reflected in their glassy surface.

"*No*," I groaned, falling forward as grief took hold of me and I wrapped him in my arms, wishing I could have done more. Wishing I could make this right.

Don't die. You can't die.

His body suddenly turned to ash and a choked noise of pain escaped me as his remains danced away on the breeze, lost, gone forever. My friend. A boy I'd never see again.

A hand fell on my shoulder and I turned to find Seth there, his lips parted in shock, his throat smeared with blood, but somehow healed at last. I threw myself into his arms as relief crashed through me at finding him alive, unsure when exactly I'd gone from not only forgiving him, but to actually caring about him so deeply. My body shuddered as the weight of knowing he was okay tangled with the suffocating grief of losing Diego.

"I'm sorry," I sobbed as he held me.

"It's not your fault," he swore, clutching me tighter.

"I'm so glad you're okay," I said breathlessly and he nuzzled into my head.

"You too," he whispered against my cheek as more tears escaped me.

I knew I couldn't stay there in the safety of his arms any longer.

I had to get to Tory. I had to fight. I had to destroy the bitch who'd done this.

"Let's end this, babe," Seth growled in my ear and I nodded against his chest.

I got to my feet, forcing my tears away and burying my grief as I looked to the other Heirs, a powerful bond seeming to tie us together now. There was only one enemy that mattered, and it was time we defeated him. Together.

DARIUS

CHAPTER FIFTY SEVEN

My grip tightened around my father's throat and I snarled down at him as the strength in his muscles began to fall slack beneath me. His eyes were wide with horror as he looked up into the eyes of the monster he'd created and realised he'd built me in his image too thoroughly.

He'd spent his life chasing after power with an insatiable thirst and had trained me in the art of doing the same. But in his arrogance, he'd forgotten one vital thing. The Fae standing between me and my power, was *him*.

His boots scrambled against the floorboards and even the heat beneath his palms began to fade as death closed in on him and I was filled with lightness at the thought of it. Life without his shadow casting darkness over everything good I'd ever had. Xavier could be free. Mother too. Roxy and her sister would be safe. I'd have the power to get Lance out of prison. I'd have the power to do any fucking thing I pleased.

And I was more than willing to buy that power with his blood.

I growled as I squeezed the life from him. For Xavier. Lance. Mother. Roxy. And *me*.

"Daddy!" Clara's horrified shriek came a moment before she collided with me, using the full strength of her Order to knock me off of my father before I could finish the job.

"No!" I roared as Roxy screamed for me to watch out.

I leapt to my feet, casting a blade of ice into my palm as I ran towards him to finish what I'd started. Before I could move more than one step, Clara sped into my path, raising a hand as she smirked at me and I jolted to a halt as the shadows inside me spread beneath my flesh and took control of my limbs.

"Uh, uh, uh, naughty boy," Clara said, waggling a finger at me like I was a child as I fought against her hold on the shadows inside me with everything I owned. The blade of ice fell from my hand where it began to melt into a puddle of nothing on the floor along with all of my hopes and dreams.

Father rolled over with a snarl of rage, pushing himself to his knees as he raised a hand to his throat to heal the damage I'd done to him.

"What happened to fighting like Fae, you fucking coward!" I bellowed as I struggled against Clara's magic.

I'd been so close, so fucking close to ending him, destroying his legacy of terror and claiming my life back from him.

"You should know by now, Darius," Father hissed as he continued to heal himself. "That winning is about using whatever advantages you have. And my Guardian is an advantage you just can't match."

"Poor Daddy," Clara cooed as she dropped down before him where he knelt, tears watering in her eyes as she cupped his cheeks in her hands. "I wasn't here when you needed me. I'm a bad, bad, girl..."

Father ignored her as she shifted closer to him and started licking the blood from his cheek.

"I offered you the world, boy," he snarled at me. "And what did you choose? A girl who threatens everything you've ever known. Whose father was a savage who nearly destroyed our kingdom. Who broke your heart as easily as breathing."

"The world means nothing to me without her," I spat at him, my gaze slipping to Roxy where she watched me from the table, her wide eyes flashing with fear for me.

"Is that so?" Father stood so suddenly that he knocked Clara onto her ass and she huffed as she scrambled up behind him.

"What are we going to do, my king?" she whispered excitedly as they crossed the room towards Roxy and my heart thundered with panic.

"Don't," I breathed, unable to hide the terror in my voice as my father reached out to touch her cheek where he'd burned an X into her skin.

I could hardly bear to look at what he'd done to her. The guilt I felt over a member of my family being responsible for so much of her pain and suffering ate me alive from the inside out.

Roxy only gritted her jaw and waited, refusing to let so much as a single word pass her lips in protest for whatever he was planning.

"What would it take for you to kill this girl, Darius?" Father asked me in a dangerous voice.

"Nothing," I replied instantly. "I'd die first."

Triumph flashed in Father's eyes at my words and my pulse thundered in panic as I tried to figure out why. What possible reason could he have for being pleased over my feelings for a girl who could ruin everything for him?

He shifted his hand over Roxy's cheek and she fought a flinch as he traced the bloody cuts on her face with his forefinger. My eyes widened in confusion as green light lit beneath his palm and slowly, every cut and burn on her body healed over until she was left whole again, panting on the table while tugging at the flaming ropes which bound her.

"I hope you're not expecting me to thank you," she hissed, jerking her face away from him as he looked down at her like she was something he wanted to devour.

"Just let her go," I begged. I'd never begged that man for anything in my life, but for her I'd do it. I didn't care. No price was too high, no sacrifice too great. "I'll do whatever you want, be whoever you want. I'll marry Mildred, follow your commands, work every day to be the Heir you wanted. Just leave her alone."

"That you will," Father growled.

He stepped around the table, reaching out to grasp Roxy's hand in his own, smiling in a way that made panic tumble through me.

Roxy's gaze met mine and she bit into her bottom lip as fear flickered in her gaze.

"Roxanya Vega," Father growled, looking down at her as a dark smile pulled at his lips. "You will guard my life at the detriment of your own life. Nothing will ever be more important to you than that-"

"No," I gasped as the words from my past echoed over me. The words he'd spoken when he forced Lance to abandon the life he'd worked so hard for and stolen everything from him. "*Please*. Don't do this to her!" I fought against Clara's hold on me with everything I had, panic blinding me as Roxy looked between me and my father fearfully.

"Adiuro te usque in sempiternum," he continued, his eyes blazing with power as he cast the ancient magic and Clara clapped excitedly as a chain of power bound Roxy's hand to his. "Adiuro custodiet te milhi in filium."

Roxy gasped as the power of his magic drove into her body, invading her, changing her, binding her to the man who was forcing it upon her.

A roar burst from my lips as I fought the shadows with all I had, but their hold on me was complete and Clara's wild smile only grew as I tried to break their control.

"Adiuro te usque ad mortem!" Father cried and the strength of his magic made the walls tremble as it echoed around the room.

Roxy screamed as the magic burned into her and Father fell forward, bracing himself over her as he struggled against the burn of the bond as it was instated too.

My heart shattered for her as I watched the spell run its course, my limbs trembling as I was forced to bear witness to this travesty.

Roxy's grip on my father's hand tightened as her back arched against the table. I swear I could feel my soul breaking apart and withering inside me as I watched him steal her life from her.

The wave of magic faded between them and Father released her hand, smiling darkly as he looked down at the new Gemini brand on the crook of his arm beside the Cancer symbol he already held for Clara.

I could hardly bear to look at the Aries mark on Roxy's skin, but she was staring at it with a look of such horrified disgust on her face that it was clear she'd already realised what he'd done.

My Father stepped away from her, his eyes flashing with triumph as he looked directly at me.

"You will *never* beat me, Darius," he said in a low voice. "But every time you try, I'll make her pay the price."

Clara suddenly released me from the shadows and I roared as I launched myself at my father, a storm of fire building between my hands before I fired it at him with every drop of magic I had left to me.

My magic crashed against an air shield like a wave breaking against a cliff.

I dove through the smoke, but before I could get my hands on him, a soft body slammed into me instead.

I gasped as Roxy used her air magic to knock my legs out from under me, catching her waist and bringing her down with me as I fell back.

Her eyes filled with tears as she straddled me, pressing a dagger made of ice to my throat, the blade pressing down firmly enough to draw a bead of blood from my skin.

"I can't let you hurt him, Darius," she breathed and the horror she felt at the idea of that was clear as her gaze flared with rage and despair, and every plan I'd ever had for my father's demise came crashing down around us. "I'm his Guardian now. You'd have to kill me first."

TORY

CHAPTER FIFTY EIGHT

Darius was looking at me like the whole world had just imploded and I was about to be ripped right out of his arms.

He stood suddenly, lifting me off of his lap and planting me on my feet as he shoved me behind him and bared his teeth at his father and Clara.

"Name your price. Anything you want to undo this," he snarled, one hand staying clamped around my wrist like he thought if he could just keep hold of me then none of this was really happening.

Clara burst into laughter, clapping her hands like this was all some game.

"Don't you see, Darius?" she asked. "This is perfect. Now we're all just one big, happy family. We can get back to loving each other and making sure we keep Daddy happy. Maybe he'll even let you share her sometimes?"

Darius's grip on me tightened and he growled, rolling his shoulders back like he was aching to end this fight while not knowing how to go about it now.

There was no way for him to do it without having to get through me. When he'd attacked Lionel, I hadn't even been aware of myself moving before I'd leapt in front of him and even the thought of Darius attacking him now was filling my head with thoughts of how I'd immobilise him. But that was so fucked up because the thing I wanted most in this world was Lionel dead... didn't I?

"Tell me your price," Darius demanded furiously and Lionel's lips lifted into a smile that made a shiver of fear race down my spine.

"This isn't a negotiation, *boy*," he said. "She belongs with me now."

"You'll keep your fucking hands off of her," Darius growled and I reached out to wrap my fingers around his arm, touching the mark of the

Phoenix Kiss I'd given him as he continued to hold my other wrist.

"I don't believe in fate," I hissed. "Or destiny, or gods, deities, demons or even fucking lizard assholes choosing my life for me. So you can bind me to you or curse me or capture me but I will *never* be yours or anyone else's unless *I* choose it."

"Oh I think you'll choose it," Lionel purred and the deep rumble of his voice was kind of…soothing. *What the fuck?* "The Guardian bond does more than make you protect me. It will make you crave me too."

"It will make you love him like you should," Clara put in, bouncing on the balls of her feet.

"Never," I swore.

"What's your price?!" Darius shouted and I could feel him trembling where we held each other, the tremors in his skin making me shiver too. It was rage and fear and something much worse because the terrified look in his eyes said that he didn't really believe this could be undone. He'd lived it. He knew.

"Come with me, Roxanya," Lionel commanded, jerking his chin like the pompous ass he was.

My fucking foot shifted as some unrecognisable part of me ached to do just that. To go to him, make sure he was alright, reach out and touch him and-

What the fuck has he done to me??

The door burst open and we whirled around as Darcy, Caleb, Seth and Max practically fell inside.

My heart leapt to see them all here, their ferocious expressions and determined postures telling me in no uncertain terms that they'd come for me.

In all my life I'd only ever had one person who I could trust with that kind of loyalty. And to see her surrounded by boys who I had thought of as my enemies until recently set something blazing in my soul which I hadn't even known I'd been aching for.

"You're outnumbered," Darcy snarled, her eyes locking on Lionel as flames coated her fists. "So just let my sister leave."

"I think you're forgetting how Fae fight, Gwendalina," Lionel laughed. "But if you think you can take me on alone then feel free to try. Otherwise I'll be taking the two of you with me."

Darcy raised her hands and threw the flames she was holding at him with a shout of anger.

Fear sped through me and I leapt forward with a cry of panic, flinging my arms up as I tore out of Darius's grip and I tossed a shield up to protect Lionel. The fireball hit me in the chest as I failed to protect myself and Darcy cried out as I was knocked to the ground by the blast.

Lionel hadn't even flinched, his lips twitching with amusement like he was having the time of his fucking life. Clara had thrown a river of shadows between us and the others to protect him too and we were effectively cut off from them as it continued to writhe in the centre of the room.

"You shouldn't have done that," Clara hissed behind me as Darcy gaped at me in confusion.

"What's going on, Tor?" she asked, her gaze flicking between all of us as pain tightened my chest like it was being squeezed in a vice.

Before I could reply, the shadows in me flared to life and my limbs were flooded with dark energy as I got to my feet and moved to stand before Lionel and Clara. Adrenaline flooded my veins as I tried to figure out what the fuck was happening to me and Darius moved to my side, controlled by the shadows too.

"Shall we kill them?" Clara asked in a sugary voice.

"I need the twins," Lionel said firmly.

"Not that one," Clara said with a disappointed sigh, pointing at Darcy. "The shadows have left her."

My lips parted as I tried to figure out if that could be true and the look Darcy was giving me said it was.

"Then I suppose we don't need any of them," Lionel agreed slowly. "And wiping out the Heirs to the other Council seats will only make my ascension smoother..."

Clara giggled excitedly and I could feel the shadows growing within me as they moved to coat my body and flared to life in my palms.

I raised my hands without wanting to and Darius did the same at my side. Shadows burst from us so suddenly that they stole my breath, the raw power of them tearing through me like a hurricane and slamming across the room with more energy than I'd ever felt.

Darcy, Seth and Max all threw up their most powerful air shields to protect the four of them and when the shadows collided with them, there was a resounding boom which knocked all four of them off of their feet.

A shriek drew my attention to the hole in the wall and I gasped as I spotted movement outside, almost thinking the trees themselves were shifting before I realise what it was. Across the grounds, highlighted by starlight, a whole host of Nymphs were coming this way.

"Holy fuck," Caleb breathed as he looked out too and the others all gazed on in terror.

Neither Lionel nor Clara seemed concerned in the least and that might have been the most terrifying part of it all.

My hands lifted again as Clara laughed with glee and fear consumed me as I looked at Darcy, scrambling upright as she tried to prepare for the next attack.

"You can fight it Tory - you can break free too!" she yelled and I fought with everything I had to do just that, but with my Phoenix still sleeping deep within me thanks to the Order Suppressant gas, I didn't even know where to begin.

Power was building in my hands again, even more potent than the last time and Darius was cursing beside me as he tried to fight the shadows back too. But it was no good, they were only intensifying and any moment now I'd be forced to unleash them on Darcy and my friends-

"Wait," I gasped desperately, wondering if there was even the slightest chance that I could bargain with a mad man. "You want me, don't you? You want me to give in to the shadows and give you my blood? I'll do it. All of it. Whatever you want. Just let my sister go. Let them all go."

"Tory no!" Darcy shouted and Seth grabbed her as she tried to lunge towards me despite the river of shadows dividing us.

"Over my dead body," Darius snarled furiously beside me, but he couldn't move any more than I could.

My hands were shaking as the shadows coiled around them, but I was far more terrified of what they were about to do to Darcy and the Heirs than anything that might happen to me.

Footsteps sounded behind me and I shuddered as Lionel's hand slid over my shoulder, though I couldn't tell if it was in repulsion or pleasure and that was almost the most terrifying thing about this bond I now had with him.

"Say goodbye to your sister," he breathed, his lips brushing against my ear and making me shiver again.

"And Darius," I choked out. "All of them. Leave all of them here. Then I'll do whatever you want."

"If you're going with him, I'm coming too," Darius snarled.

"He'll come running back to the manor to find you either way," Lionel scoffed, but I ignored him.

"Do we have a deal?" I demanded.

There was a pause where only the sound of the host of Nymphs drawing ever closer to the house reached us and the fear of their arrival made my entire body feel numb.

"The moment you give yourself to the shadows, the three of us will leave," Lionel agreed, eyeing me hungrily. "Tick tock."

Clara released her hold on my shadows and I staggered forward as Darius was still frozen in her grasp.

Darcy started screaming at me, begging me to reconsider, swearing to fight and win but with the Nymphs coming, I knew that there wasn't any choice to be made. Lionel and Clara weren't going to let me leave and there was no more time for fighting. She had to get out of here before that army arrived or I'd lose her and even the thought of that had me falling apart.

Only the wall of shadow Clara had constructed between us was keeping her away from me and I knew I'd be doing the same in her position. But it was the only way.

I turned to Darius with my chest heaving and tears swimming in my eyes as he glared at me like I was ripping his heart out by doing this. But I didn't have a choice. I'd do anything for the love of my sister. And I'd do anything to protect him too.

"I need you to get Darcy out of here," I demanded. "If you meant all the things you said to me, if you feel any of it at all, you'll make sure she's safe."

"Don't do this," he begged and my heart twisted with agony as I felt the pain I was causing him by giving in to his father.

I leaned forward, closing the distance between us and the brush of his lips against mine was an agony unlike anything I'd ever known, because I knew what it was. What it had to be. It was goodbye.

"*Please*," I breathed, refusing to open my eyes as I pulled back and the warmth of him was lost to me.

"*Roxy*," he growled, and the raw agony of that one word was enough to drown me.

"Now," Lionel snapped and I forced myself to turn away from Darius as my heart broke for him all over again.

My gaze locked on Darcy's as I let the shadows in because I was weak. I couldn't face this darkness on my own. I wasn't sure what I even had if I didn't have her.

Tears flowed down her cheeks as Seth held her back and she watched as I sank into the darkness.

I couldn't count the amount of times I'd been tempted by the promise of oblivion the shadows offered me in the past few months, but she'd always been the reason I'd fought them off. It was a cruel twist of fate that she was now the reason I was giving in to them too.

But as the agony of that truth washed over me, the shadows rose up to claim it. To claim all the pain and heartache and sorrow in me and whisk it away like none of it had ever mattered at all.

The shadows swept up and over me like a tide which rushed through my veins in the most elating way. They ran beneath my flesh, lighting me up with a pleasure so intense that I forgot everything else in favour of serving them. They were ecstasy, rapture, bliss and euphoria and they set me free of all of my demons. There was no more pain or heartache, sorrow or despair. Just the darkest parts of me which hungered for corruption and thrived in sin. I let them have me with a smile on my face and a moan escaping my lips as I finally invited the darkness in.

It was a relief to give in at last. No more pain or regret or anguish.

Just power.

And I was more than ready to claim my share of that.

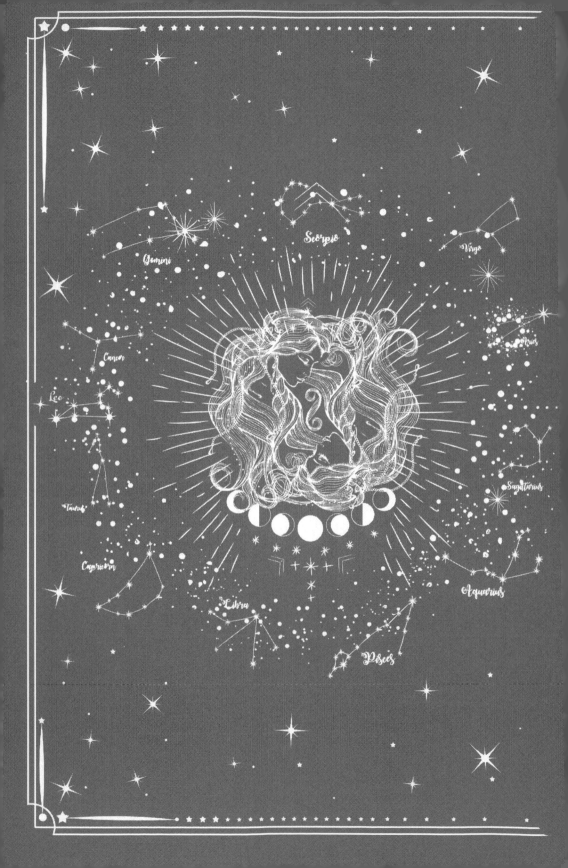

DARCY

CHAPTER FIFTY NINE

Before I could do anything to save my sister, Lionel transformed into his enormous green Dragon form, tearing down the ceiling and grabbing Tory and Clara in his claws.

I screamed as the world literally came crashing down around us and didn't have the strength to shield, my heart pounding a desperate, broken tune as I tried to run after my sister.

Darius ran to me amongst the falling roof and it took me a moment to realise that Max and Seth were shielding us as the whole house collapsed.

The walls crumbled around us and my heart crumbled along with them as Lionel stole my sister away and seemed to steal all hope along with her. We were buried beneath a ton of rubble and darkness descended as we were trapped in a bubble of a safety.

I turned my hands to the roof, looking to the Heirs. "Open the top of the shield, I'll blast through the rubble," I demanded and they did as I said, trusting me as they opened the shield enough to let my air magic blast a hole in the debris. I didn't waste a second, casting air beneath me to propel myself out onto the broken roof and Darius was thrown after me by one of the others.

"Darcy." he growled, but I ignored him, getting to my feet and racing up the shattered pieces of the roof as I searched the sky, agony spilling through me at the loss of Tory to the shadows and Lionel's clutches.

Please come back. I can't bear to be without you.

Darius stayed beside me as I scrambled up the bricks and mortar and the Heirs hurried close behind us as we made it onto the top of the rubble. Nymphs were clawing their way up the debris towards us, but I didn't care. I kept my gaze on the sky as I finally spotted Lionel in the distance, his dark green form nearly camouflaged against the night sky.

I gritted my teeth as I tried to force my wings from my body, fighting against the Order Suppressant even though it was futile. But I had to get Tory back. I couldn't just abandon her to this fate.

Darius caught my arm with a growl. "We have to get back to the academy, I promised to protect you."

"Screw you, let me go," I snarled as Max, Seth and Caleb formed a triangle around us, blasting magic at the Nymphs to keep them back.

"I've broken the wards around the house so we can stardust the fuck out of here," Max called.

Darius took a pouch of stardust from his pocket and I tried to snatch it from his grip, desperate to go after her, but he held it out of reach.

"Take us to Acrux Manor," I demanded, clawing at his arm and nearly drawing blood. My heart had been obliterated, a full half of it torn out and taken when she'd sacrificed herself for us, giving me no choice. But I refused to accept it.

"We can't fight him like this. We have to regroup. And I promised to keep you safe so I'm taking you back to Zodiac," Darius snarled, dragging me against him as tears burned heated trails down my cheeks.

"It's not your choice to make!" I screamed, shoving him in the chest as he struggled to hold onto me and try to open the pouch of stardust at the same time.

"We have to fucking go," Caleb barked, wheeling around and snatching the stardust from him.

"No!" I yelled, trying to pull free as he tossed a handful into the air and we were yanked into a galaxy of stars, my heart shattering, feeling as fragmented as the universe spreading out around me in splinters of light. But the pieces of my heart didn't glow, they were dark and jagged and full of pain.

My feet hit the ground and Darius yanked me into his chest, his arms crushing me in a fierce embrace as we landed beyond the fence ringing campus. And I finally gave in, falling apart in his arms.

"We can head to the Hollow, we'll make a plan," Seth whimpered, running his hand over my back as my tears flowed free. For my sister, for Diego. For everything I'd lost.

I ached for Orion with every part of my being, needing to crawl into his arms and seek the comfort of his words. He would have known what to do. He would have found a way to fix this. But he was gone. He'd cut me from his life and now Tory was gone too and I didn't think I could handle the loss of them both. It was too much to bear.

"I can't just leave her with him," I hissed, trying to pull myself together as a frantic energy crashed through my limbs. I stepped out of Darius's arms, wiping my tears away as I willed my heart to turn to iron, needing to focus. To fight.

"We won't," Darius agreed fiercely. "I'll tear the world down for her, but we can't win tonight."

I hated to accept those words, but I knew he wouldn't say them unless it was absolutely true. We were all tired, weakened and we had no idea what Lionel's next move would be.

But I had to rescue her. I *would* rescue her. If it cost me every broken piece of my soul to do it.

"This isn't over," I growled as the Heirs gathered around me in a circle. I looked between them, finding resilience in their eyes, their nods promising me they would fight for her too. I met Darius's dark-ringed gaze last and his head dipped.

I caught his chin, yanking it up so he looked me in the eye. "You don't give up on her."

"Never," he vowed with a dark growl that promised bloodshed. "But I fear my father is going to take the throne, Darcy. And there's nothing we can do to stop him now he has her."

I swallowed the sharp lump slicing into my throat as I clenched my jaw. "Then we make an oath. Right here. That we'll find the Imperial Star before he does. It's the only chance we have against him."

I held out my hand, wondering if they'd really do this, but they all moved forward without hesitation, laying their hands over mine.

"I vow on the stars that we'll find the Imperial Star before Lionel does," I breathed. "No matter what it takes."

They all spoke in unison, a clap of magic binding all five of us together in a star-bound promise that echoed through the universe. "No matter what it takes."

TORY

CHAPTER SIXTY

Strong hands gripped my upper arms and shook me until I blinked the shadows from my eyes.

I was standing on the roof of a tall tower on top of Acrux Manor with the warm wind tugging at my hair and the stars shining brightly above me.

"Are you ready to get to work, Roxanya?" Lionel purred as he looked into my eyes and I sighed as I glanced back at him. Something about him just made me feel like I belonged.

"What work?" I asked, a frown tugging at my brow as the shadows slipped around me, kissing my skin and whispering sweet nothings in my ears. They were hungry…so hungry.

"Do you want to please me?" Lionel asked, his hand moving to grasp my chin as he forced me to hold his gaze.

His eyes were dark green like his Dragon and captured all of my attention as I gazed into their depths and hunted within them for his shadows, wondering if they'd rise for me too. He'd put on a pair of grey slacks, a white button down and brown loafers which I guessed he'd kept here for his return.

"Yes," I breathed as my heart beat harder. I did want to please him. I wanted that more than…*anything*.

"Good girl." He shoved my face out of his grip, knocking me back a step as he turned and headed inside with Clara skipping forward to take his hand in hers.

My lip curled back as I watched them descending a curving staircase and I was left to follow behind.

Down we went. Down and down and down. Until all the summer

warmth was stolen and we entered a corridor well below the Manor where it was just as cold as the empty space inside my heart.

Lionel led the way through a long stone corridor, lighting sconces as we went with his fire magic.

Clara kept hold of his hand, swinging it back and forth and my gaze narrowed on the point of contact between them as the shadows swirled within me.

"Why?" I snapped, when I couldn't take it any longer.

"Because I'm the favourite," Clara hissed, shooting a glare over her shoulder which made me snarl.

Lionel tsked as he moved to open a heavy wooden door and I followed them inside. He pulled Clara aside so that I could look at the huge stone chamber. There was a chair in the centre of it with thick leather straps on the arms and legs. A row of hooks and knives and other torture devices hung along the wall to the left and a tank of cold water lay to the right.

"Do you want to be the favourite, Roxanya?" Lionel purred as he released Clara's hand and took a step towards me.

The shadows shifted within me, aching to feel that with an urgency I couldn't comprehend. "Yes," I breathed, taking a seat on the chair and waiting as he strapped me in.

"Then tell me who you love." He walked away from me as I frowned at the question, the shadows wild and seething beneath my skin.

I closed my eyes as I tried to answer, searching the deep chasm of nothing within me until I caught a glimmer of something which I'd lost.

"A girl with blue hair," I breathed as the echoes of memories stirred within my heart. "And a man with a dark soul."

Something slammed into my gut and the electric slice of pain that crashed through my body shattered me into a million pieces as agony ruled my flesh and the shadows reared up hungrily to feast on it.

I moaned in pleasure as the torture lingered in my body and my vision blacked out as the shadows veiled my eyes for a moment.

I sagged forward in the chair, panting and heaving as my heart raced and the bliss in my limbs threatened to ruin me as I bathed in the pure power of the shadows. It was so much pain and so much pleasure. I didn't know if I was screaming in agony or ecstasy.

"Wrong answer, Roxanya," Lionel growled as he moved to stand before me, my gaze landing on his expensive loafers as I tried to catch my breath. "Who do you love?"

I tipped my head back slowly, my gaze moving over every inch of him until I finally met his eyes and the bottomless depths that were waiting for me within them.

The Aries brand on my arm burned with the need to be closer to him and I whimpered as the shadows let me feel that ache for a moment before burying it again. But it was enough to give me my answer.

"You," I breathed as I stared up at him and the darkness in his eyes blossomed like the shadows in my soul. "Only you."

ALSO BY

CAROLINE PECKHAM

&

SUSANNE VALENTI

Brutal Boys of Everlake Prep
(Complete Reverse Harem Bully Romance Contemporary Series)
Kings of Quarantine
Kings of Lockdown
Kings of Anarchy
Queen of Quarantine
**

Dead Men Walking
(Reverse Harem Dark Romance Contemporary Series)
The Death Club
Society of Psychos
**

The Harlequin Crew
(Reverse Harem Mafia Romance Contemporary Series)
Sinners Playground
Dead Man's Isle
Carnival Hill
Paradise Lagoon

Harlequinn Crew Novellas
Devil's Pass
**

Dark Empire
(Dark Mafia Contemporary Standalones)
Beautiful Carnage
Beautiful Savage
**

The Ruthless Boys of the Zodiac
(Reverse Harem Paranormal Romance Series - Set in the world of Solaria)
Dark Fae
Savage Fae
Vicious Fae
Broken Fae
Warrior Fae

Zodiac Academy
(M/F Bully Romance Series- Set in the world of Solaria, five years after Dark Fae)
The Awakening
Ruthless Fae
The Reckoning
Shadow Princess
Cursed Fates
Fated Thrones
Heartless Sky
The Awakening - As told by the Boys

Zodiac Academy Novellas
Origins of an Academy Bully
The Big A.S.S. Party

Darkmore Penitentiary
(Reverse Harem Paranormal Romance Series - Set in the world of Solaria, ten years after Dark Fae)
Caged Wolf
Alpha Wolf
Feral Wolf
**

The Age of Vampires
(Complete M/F Paranormal Romance/Dystopian Series)
Eternal Reign
Eternal Shade
Eternal Curse
Eternal Vow
Eternal Night
Eternal Love
**

Cage of Lies
(M/F Dystopian Series)
Rebel Rising
**

Tainted Earth
(M/F Dystopian Series)
Afflicted
Altered
Adapted
Advanced
**

The Vampire Games
(Complete M/F Paranormal Romance Trilogy)
V Games
V Games: Fresh From The Grave
V Games: Dead Before Dawn
*

The Vampire Games: Season Two
(Complete M/F Paranormal Romance Trilogy)
Wolf Games
Wolf Games: Island of Shade
Wolf Games: Severed Fates
*

The Vampire Games: Season Three
Hunter Trials
*

The Vampire Games Novellas
A Game of Vampires
**

The Rise of Issac
(Complete YA Fantasy Series)
Creeping Shadow
Bleeding Snow
Turning Tide
Weeping Sky
Failing Light